# The Scout;
## or, The Black Riders of Congaree

*Available from the Simms Initiatives and the
University of South Carolina Press*

The Army Correspondence of Colonel John Laurens, ed.
As Good as a Comedy and Paddy McGann
Beauchampe
Border Beagles
Carl Werner, 2 vols.
The Cassique of Kiawah
Castle Dismal
Charlemont
The Charleston Book, ed.
Confession
Count Julian
The Damsel of Darien, 2 vols.
Dramas: Norman Maurice, Michael Bonham, and Benedict Arnold
Egeria
Eutaw
The Forayers
The Geography of South Carolina
The Golden Christmas
Guy Rivers
Helen Halsey
Historical and Political Poems (*which includes* Monody, The Vision of Cortes, The Tri-Color, Donna Florida, and Charleston and Her Satirists)
The History of South Carolina
Joscelyn
Katharine Walton
The Letters of William Gilmore Simms, Vol. 1
The Letters of William Gilmore Simms, Vol. 2
The Letters of William Gilmore Simms, Vol. 3
The Letters of William Gilmore Simms, Vol. 4
The Letters of William Gilmore Simms, Vol. 5
The Letters of William Gilmore Simms, Vol. 6 (exp. ed.)
The Life of Captain John Smith
The Life of the Chevalier Bayard
The Life of Francis Marion
The Lily and the Totem
Marie de Berniere
Martin Faber and Other Tales, 2 vols.
Mellichampe
The Partisan
Pelayo, 2 vols.
Poems, Descriptive, Dramatic, Legendary, and Contemplative, 2 vols.
The Remains of Maynard Davis Richardson
Richard Hurdis
Sack and Destruction of the City of Columbia
The Scout
Selections from the Letters and Speeches of the Hon. James H. Hammond, ed.
Simms's Poems Areytos
Social and Political Prose: Slavery in America/Father Abbot
South Carolina in the Revolutionary War
Southward Ho!
Stories and Tales
A Supplement to the Plays of William Shakespeare
Vasconselos
Views and Reviews in American Literature, History and Fiction, 2 vols.
Voltmeier
War Poetry of the South
The Wigwam and the Cabin
Woodcraft
The Yemassee

# The Scout;
## or, The Black Riders of Congaree

―⚯―

## William Gilmore Simms

*Critical Introduction and
Biographical Overview by David Moltke-Hansen
and Explanatory Notes by Edwin T. Arnold*

The University of South Carolina Press

New material © 2014 University of South Carolina

Cloth original published by Redfield, 1854
Paperback published by the University of South Carolina Press
Columbia, South Carolina 29208

www.sc.edu/uscpress

Manufactured in the United States of America

23 22 21 20 19 18 17 16 15 14
10 9 8 7 6 5 4 3 2 1

ISBN 978-1-61117-022-1 (pbk)

Published in cooperation with the Simms Initiatives, a project of the University of South Carolina Libraries with the generous support of the Watson-Brown Foundation. Thanks are also due to the Institute for Southern Studies at the University of South Carolina for permission to reprint the end notes.

# William Gilmore Simms: A Biographical Overview

*David Moltke-Hansen*

**Introduction**

*Harper's Weekly* put it succinctly in its July 2, 1870, issue: "In the death of Mr. Simms, on the 11th of June, at Charleston, the country has lost one more of its time-honored band of authors, and the South the most consistent and devoted of her literary sons" (qtd. In Butterworth and Kibler 125–26). Indeed no mid-nineteenth-century writer and editor did more than William Gilmore Simms to frame white southern self-identity and nationalism, shape southern historical consciousness, or foster the South's participation and recognition in the broader American literary culture. No southern writer enjoyed more contemporary esteem and attention, at least after Edgar Allan Poe moved north. Among American romancers (or writers of prose epics), only New Yorker James Fenimore Cooper was as successful by the 1840s. In those same years, Simms was the South's most influential editor of cultural journals. He also was the region's most prolific cultural journalist and poet, publishing an average of one book review and one poem per week for forty-five years.

Before his death Simms saw his national reputation fall along with the Confederacy he had vigorously supported and with the slave regime that many in the North had come to despise. Nevertheless reprints of most of the twenty titles in the selected edition of his works, first published between 1853 and 1860, appeared up until World War I. Thereafter only *The Yemassee*, an early romance about an Indian war in South Carolina, continued in print. The tide began to turn in the 1950s, when five volumes of Simms's letters appeared and a growing number of his works were issued in new editions. Publication in 1992 of the first literary biography, by John C. Guilds, and establishment of the William Gilmore Simms Society and the *Simms Review* the next year at once reflected and fostered this revived interest. Yet not until the 2011 launch of the digital Simms edition of the South Caroliniana Library of the University of South Carolina did scholars of southern, American, and nineteenth-century culture have the prospect of ready access to all of Simms's separately published works. With the University of South Carolina Press's cooperation, readers also will have access to sixty works in paperback editions by the end of 2014. Simms himself never saw nearly so many of his works in print at one time.

Clearly the decline in the critical standing of, and historical attention to, Simms and his oeuvre in the century after his death has reversed in the years since. The last three decades of the twentieth century saw more published on Simms than the previous hundred years (Butterworth and Kibler 126–200; MLA International). The last decade of the twentieth and first decade of the twenty-first centuries saw more dissertations and theses on him (forty-one) than had appeared in all the years before. This is not to say that Simms is yet given the attention directed to some of his contemporaries. For the first decade of the twenty-first century, the Modern Language Association International Bibliography lists roughly four times as many scholarly publications on James Fenimore Cooper, more than ten times as many on Nathaniel Hawthorne, and sixteen times as many on Edgar Allan Poe. Not surprisingly, therefore, Simms is not yet included in most anthologies of American literature, although he is a subject or a source in an expanding and ever more diverse body of scholarship.

To prepare to read Simms, it is important to see his writings in multiple contexts. He rarely wrote about himself outside of his more personal poems and his letters (some fifteen hundred of the many thousands of which survive). Yet he systematically drew on his background, personal experience, and relationships in his work. He also shaped that work through a progressively developed poetics and philosophy of life, history, and art. He did so in the context of his very broad reading of both contemporary and earlier Western literature and in the midst of multiple professional engagements and responsibilities. The richness and variety of these writings and involvements make Simms a key figure for future understanding of the literary culture, issues, and networks in mid-nineteenth-century America.

## Background

Simms's family history reflected the dynamics that fueled the spread southward and westward of the populations, plantation economy, and society of the South Atlantic states. Simms's ancestry also reflected the Scots-Irish and English roots of what became identified as southern culture by the 1830s, a generation after the end of most immigration to the region. Two of Simms's grandparents, William and Elisabeth Sims, were Scots-Irish and migrated to South Carolina from Ulster. One, John Singleton, was an American-born son of putatively English immigrants, who had come to South Carolina from Virginia. The fourth, Jane Miller, was daughter of two Scots-Irish and Irish descended people—John Miller, of North and then South Carolina, and Jane Ross. Ross's family also migrated to South Carolina from western Virginia, where members lived cheek by jowl with other Scots-Irish families, who migrated to the Carolinas (White, *Ross*). Simms's father and Uncle James migrated in 1808 from Charleston to Tennessee, then to Mississippi. This was after the bankruptcy of the elder William's business and the deaths of his wife and their other two sons. Following the last of these losses, the elder Simms's hair turned white in a week. To his anguished eyes, Charleston appeared "a place of tombs" (qtd. in Guilds 6, 12).

For the son, however, Charleston was home—so much so that he refused to leave his maternal grandmother and move to Mississippi when his uncle came to get him in 1816. Then the fifth largest and by far the wealthiest city, as well as one of the greatest ports, in America, Charleston was at the peak of its influence (Moltke-Hansen, "Expansion" 25-31; Rogers). Cotton culture on the sea islands to the south, begun in 1790, and rice culture in impounded lowcountry tidal marshes meant that the port was filled not only with sailors of many lands and languages, but also with enslaved people of many African and Creole cultures and speech ways (slaves continued to be imported legally in large numbers until 1808). This street life made vivid the transnational nature of plantation agriculture and the fact that the developing region's dramatically expanding borders "were not just geographic; they also were human, historical, and intellectual" (Moltke-Hansen, "Southern" 19).

Even more important for the future author, the expanding region's borders and nature were taking imaginative shape. The West of the senior William Gilmore Simms and the first Creek War in which he fought, the Revolutionary War of the young Simms's maternal grandfather, the backcountry of many related Scots-Irish settlers, all these became grist for a lonely, energetic boy, who spent as much time with books as he could (Simms, *Letters* 1:161). The possibilities of such settings, incidents, and characters were not confined to history alone. Simms reported that he "used to glow and shiver in turn over 'The Pilgrim's Progress,'" while "Moses' adventures in 'The Vicar of Wakefield' threw [him] into paroxysms of laughter" (Hayne 261-62). Sir Walter Scott's Border and medieval romances and James Fenimore Cooper's Leatherstocking tales also deeply colored his imagination (Simms, *Views* 1:248, and Moltke-Hansen, "Southern" 6-15). As affecting were the ghost stories and Revolutionary War tales of his grandmother and the verses sent, and tales told, by his father.

These diverse tales became reasons to explore—in books, but also on the ground. As a boy, Simms ranged through the city and along the banks of the Ashley River, which fed into Charleston Harbor. He did so in search of scenes of colonial and Revolutionary battles and incidents (*Letters* 1:lxii). He first heard his uncle's and father's many Irish and frontier stories when they visited in Charleston in 1816 and 1818, respectively. He heard more on his trips to Mississippi during the winter of 1824 through the spring of 1825 and again in 1826. The first trip took him through Georgia and Alabama, where he saw elements of the Creek and Cherokee nations. At the time, Simms later reported, he was a boy "cumbered with fragmentary materials of thought, . . . choked by the tangled vines of erroneous speculation, and haunted by passions, which, like so many wolves, lurked, in ready waiting, for their unsuspecting prey" (*Social* 6). When he first got to Mississippi, traveling partly by stage, partly by riverboat, and partly by horse, Simms learned that his father had just come back from "a trip of three hundred miles into the heart of the Indian country" (Trent 15). Later father and son "rode together on horseback to various settlements on the frontier of Alabama and Mississippi" (Guilds 10–11, 17–18). Simms recalled as well "having traveled 150 miles beyond the Mississippi" (Shillingsburg, "Literary Grist" 120). The next year he returned to the Southwest by ship. "During this [second] trip he carried a 'note book.'" There he jotted episodes, encounters, stories heard, characters seen, and descriptions of the landscapes unfolding around him. He also wrote "at least sixteen poems" (Kibler, "First"; Shillingsburg, "Literary Grist" 123).

Simms took a third western trip five years later, writing letters back to the newspaper that by then he was editing (*Letters* 1:10–38). Together these three trips provided materials for his writings over more than forty years. "The first . . . produced mainly short fiction; the second inspired much poetry; . . . the first and third . . . yielded three novels written in the 1830s" (Shillingsburg, "Literary Grist" 119). This was, in part, because of the trips' timing. Sixteen years after the first trip, Simms told students at the University of Alabama that in the interval their world had changed from a howling wilderness into a place of growing civilization (Simms, *Social* 5–6). Had he not gone when he did, he would have been too late to see the frontier. Later travels took him many other places and also provided much grist for his writing. Never again, however, did he experience the frontier firsthand. Furthermore, on these later trips Simms was a practiced professional writer, no longer that boy haunted by passions.

**Personal Life**

After the ten-year-old boy's momentous refusal to leave Charleston, his grandmother sent Simms for two years to the grammar school taught on the campus and by the faculty of the nearly moribund College of Charleston. By then he already was "versifying the events of the war [of 1812]," just concluded, publishing "doggerel" in the local papers, and learning to read in several languages (*Letters* 1:285). His trip west a decade later helped him decide to pursue both literature and a career in law, but back in Charleston—this despite his father's urging that he stay in Mississippi. Upon his return home, he began to read law and also launched a literary weekly, the *Album*, which ran for a year. He became engaged as well to Anna Malcolm Giles, daughter of a grocer and former state coroner.

A year later the young couple married. This was six months before Simms was admitted to the South Carolina bar, on his twenty-first birthday, not long before he was appointed as a city magistrate. Although living up the Ashley River in the more healthful, less expensive village of Summerville, Simms kept a law office in the city. Shortly after using his maternal inheritance to buy the *City Gazette* at the end of 1829 and moving down to Charleston Neck, just north of the city limits where he had lived as a boy, Simms lost both his father and his maternal grandmother. He also found himself attacked because of his Unionist stance in the Nullification crisis resulting from South Carolina's rejection of a federal tariff. Then, in early 1832, Simms's wife died. Soon after, he took his four-year-old daughter back to Summerville to live and determined to sell his newspaper and leave the state for a literary life in the North.

Fueling his ambition was the correspondence Simms had begun several years earlier with an accountant whom he had published in his *City Gazette* but not yet met—Scots immigrant James Lawson. At the time Lawson, seven years Simms's senior, edited a New York City newspaper and, in addition to writing plays and poetry, was a friend (and, later, informal literary agent) to a wide circle (McHaney, "An Early"). Simms's trip north in the summer of 1832 saw the two begin a lifelong friendship, cemented as they squired ladies about and interacted with Lawson's literary circle. In subsequent years Simms multiplied the number of his friendships, in both the North and the South, making them in some measure a replacement for the family that he had lost. Lawson remained the closest of his northern friends, while James Henry Hammond, a future governor and U.S. senator, became his closest friend in South Carolina.

Late in 1833, after his Summerville house burned, Simms wrote Lawson to say that he was enamored of "a certain fair one" (*Letters* 1:73). Seventeen-year-old Chevillette Eliza Roach was the daughter of "a literary-minded aristocrat of English descent" with two plantations on the banks of the Edisto River in Barnwell District (later County) (Guilds 70). The courtship was protracted, as Simms felt it necessary first to clear debts that friends had bought up on his behalf. He also was determined "to marry no woman" before he was "perfectly independent of her resources, and her friends" (*Letters* 1:78). Therefore he did not propose until the spring of 1836. The nuptials took place seven months later, and as a result, Simms came to call the four thousand acres of Woodlands Plantation, with its seventy slaves, home. It was twenty years, however, before he took over management of the plantation and, then, only in the wake of his father-in-law's final sickness and death. Five years after that, he lost his wife, the mother of fourteen of his fifteen children. Nine of the children Chevillette bore him had already died, devastating Simms repeatedly. Five were still living (three sons and two daughters), as was Simms's daughter by his first marriage, who helped raise the youngest of her siblings. Those remaining children—even Gilly, who fought in the Confederate army—all outlived their father. Gilly and a brother-in-law ran Woodlands after the war, when Simms, though dying of cancer, was earning what he could by writing again for publications in the North and editing one or another South Carolina newspaper.

**Career**

The trip north in 1832 did not result in Simms moving there. Except during the Civil War, however, he returned almost every year. This was because the contacts he made, and the exposure to literary culture that he enjoyed, helped him define his future as an author. Earlier he had written fiction and criticism as well as journalism, filling the pages of several short-lived cultural journals and his newspaper, but between the ages of nine and twenty-six Simms had focused his literary efforts primarily on poetry. Beginning with his first book of verse in 1825, he had published five small volumes in Charleston. A couple had received positive notice in New York, and in the fall of 1832, J. & J. Harper issued the sixth anonymously from there, *Atalantis: A Story of the Sea*. Coming back the following summer, Simms had in hand for the Harpers a gothic novella, *Martin Faber*, and after his return south, he also would send the manuscript of his first two-volume border romance, *Guy Rivers: A Tale of Georgia*.

The reception of these and the romances and short stories that followed quickly made Simms one of the nation's most successful fictionists. He continued to issue poetry as well—roughly a collection every three years over the thirty-seven years that he worked as a professional author. But this output was dwarfed by the fiction—on average a title every year (counting several serialized works but not counting the many revised editions). Then there were the two dozen separately published orations, histories, and biographies as well as edited collections of documents and dramas and a geography of South Carolina. Add to these the revised editions and the further printings and issues of his own works and it appears that Simms saw a title coming off the presses at the rate of one every three months or so. Making that figure all the more astounding is the fact that, during more than a dozen of those years (the early-to-mid 1840s, the late 1840s-to-early 1850s, and the mid-to-late 1860s), he also was editing a cultural journal or newspaper. Furthermore he contributed reams of reviews and poems, hundreds of op-ed pieces and columns, and dozens of short stories and public addresses, which were never collected and published in volume form.

His career mapped an arc. It ascended meteorically in the 1830s and peaked in the early-to-mid 1840s, before beginning to descend. One reason was the popularity of the historical fiction that Simms began to write. When he left behind the law, his first newspaper, and the Nullification controversy, as well as his sadness, historical fiction was all the rage. Sir Walter Scott had fueled the craze, beginning with the publication of his first Border romance in 1814. He died in September 1832. Seventeen years Simms's senior, James Fenimore Cooper, the closest America had to a Scott at the time, was at the peak of his reputation and success, having started publishing his romances in 1820. Thus the way had been prepared for a writer of Simms's historical imagination and preoccupations. Within five years of his first trip north, moreover, Lawson's (and now his) circle became loosely affiliated with a nationalistic and Democratic group, self-styled Young America, this after Young Italy and similar ethnic, nationalist, European, cultural and political movements (Moltke-Hansen, "Southern"). Edgar Allan Poe and other members gave Simms's first fictions positive, if not uncritical, attention.

By the end of the 1830s, paradoxically, Simms, like Cooper, found his success attracting unauthorized editions of his works because Britain and America did not have an international copyright agreement. Further, in the wake of the panic of 1837, Americans bought fewer books. Simms's response was to diversify his portfolio. He turned to biography and history, including his hugely successful *Life of Francis Marion* (1844). He also returned to the editor's chair, overseeing one and then another cultural journal. These were unlike the ones he had edited in the 1820s: they included contributions by numerous authors, not just those from Charleston, but from the region and also the North. The ambition motivating the journals was to connect and promote Charleston intellectually. Consequently the journals more closely resembled metropolitan quarterly reviews in their offerings.

The mid-1840s saw Simms involved in politics, even serving a term in the South Carolina legislature. By the middle of the Mexican-American War in 1847, he had concluded that the South needed to become an independent nation. Thereafter, although he maintained ties with many in the Young America circle, he no longer promoted his writings as fostering Americanism in literature (*Views*). Instead he increasingly emphasized the ways in which his three romance series—the colonial, the Revolutionary, and the border—were making tangible and meaningful the origins and development of the future southern nation and the sad but inevitable consequences for Native Americans (Watson, *From Nationalism*; compare Nakamura).

Sectional politics colored more and more of Simms's perceptions, speeches, and private communications. The rising tide of abolitionism had him aghast. It also fed his growing sense that his position in American letters was slipping. He returned to editing, and his poetry, which was more often explicitly about the South, became increasingly patriotic in tone. Although his first biographer, William Peterfield Trent, insisted that Simms's declining standing reflected the change in literary fashion from historical romances to realistic novels, Simms in fact wrote more and more as a social realist in the 1850s (Wimsatt, "Realism").

The Civil War consumed Simms. As he wrote Lawson, "Literature, especially poetry, is effectually overwhelmed by the drums, & the cavalry, and the shouting" (*Letters* 4:369–70). He did manage to editorialize often and to rework and finish things long on his desk, including poems, a novel, and a dramatic treatment of Benedict Arnold, the northern traitor in the Revolutionary War. Then, in the wake of the Confederacy's loss and the failure of his vision for the South, he found himself recording the loss in a new newspaper, dealing with the trauma in his poetry, and becoming more existential and psychological in his fictional treatments. Simms's old New York friends tried to help. He did edit and see through publication a volume of Confederate war poetry. Yet it is a measure of his reduced stature that the several new romances he published appeared only in serial form. In part this may have been because he was in a sense competing with himself. Publishers were beginning to reprint volumes out of the selected edition of his writings. Many of Simms's works were available in book form, just not new works.

**Associations**

As the *Letters* testify, Simms had complex, overlapping networks of friends and colleagues. As a boy and young man, he received the friendship, patronage, and commendation of a variety of well-placed people in Charleston, including Charles Rivers Carroll. It was Carroll with whom he read law, to whom he dedicated his first romance, and after whom he named a son. Both men were Unionists during the Nullification controversy. So were Hugh Swinton Legare (later U.S. attorney general) and the considerably older William Drayton, as well as lawyer and editor Richard Yeadon and Greenville, South Carolina, newspaper editor Benjamin Franklin Perry. Also considerably older was James Wright Simmons, who had joined with Simms to launch the *Southern Literary Gazette* in 1828, when Simms was twenty-two. Through him Simms had direct contact with such British literary figures as Leigh Hunt and Byron (Kibler, *Poetry* 15).

The next group of influential friends and collaborators that Simms acquired were members of the Lawson circle and included such figures as Edwin

Forrest, the Shakespearean actor, and Evert Duyckinck, who published several of Simms's volumes in Wiley and Putnam's series Library of American Books, which he edited. Among the many others were poets and editors William Cullen Bryant and Fitz-Greene Halleck. Simms also made nonliterary friends in New York and Philadelphia, such as John Jacob Bockee and William Hawkins Ferris, the cashier at the U.S. Treasury office in New York who, after the war, helped Simms, Henry Timrod (poet laureate of the Confederacy), and others.

As a Barnwell planter, Simms met a widening circle of South Carolina's leaders and literati. For instance his acquaintance with James Henry Hammond began in the late 1830s and deepened into a friendship in the early 1840s. It was in the early 1840s, too, when he again was editing cultural journals, that Simms became friends with many southern writers. He regarded several of them, including Virginians George Frederick Holmes, Edmund Ruffin, and Nathaniel Beverley Tucker as members, together with Hammond and himself, in a "sacred circle." Uniting the circle were members' devotion to the South and a shared sense of the marginal status and critical importance of the life of the mind in a largely rural and unintellectual region (Faust, *Sacred*). Others of Simms's wide connections in the region did not interact as much with each other, but Simms long corresponded with Maryland novelist and lawyer John Pendleton Kennedy, Irish-born Georgia poet Richard Henry Wilde, Alabama lawyer and writer Alexander Beaufort Meek, and Louisiana historian and assistant attorney general Charles Gayarré, among others. By the 1850s, when Simms once more returned to editing a cultural journal, many of the writers whom he recruited were members of a younger generation. Poets Paul Hamilton Hayne and Henry Timrod were two. Often they and a half dozen others of Simms's and their generations met in John Russell's Charleston Book Shop and adjourned to dinner at Simms's Smith Street home, "dubbed 'The Wigwam'" (*Letters* 1:cxxxvi). Shortly before his death fifteen or so years later, Simms wrote Hayne, "I am rapidly passing from the stage, where you young men are to succeed me" (*Letters* 5:287).

**Thought**

The welter of Simms's works disguises unities and dynamics of the thought underlying them. From early on Simms was convinced that art ennobles or transforms, as well as gives voice to individuals and societies; therefore it must be cultivated assiduously. Without the potential for high artistic attainment, he insisted, societies are not ready for the independence and regard of free peoples. This is where Simms the historian joined Simms the poet. Societies develop, he argued (using the stadialism of the Scottish historical school), from imitation through self-assertion to achievement and also from savagery through strife to settled agricultural communities and, ultimately, to a hierarchical civilization supporting a rich artistic life. It was the job of the artist to help envision the goal, inspire the pursuit, and inform the process. That process was at once progressive and dialectical. Order, without dynamism, stifled development, as did the obverse—the dominance by ungoverned impulses or uncontrolled license. This was true in the individual, but also in societies as a whole. War was necessary for civilization, but its success was measured in the securities of the home, the center of cultural production and reproduction.

Whether in the public or in the domestic arena, "the true governor, as [Thomas] Carlyle call[ed] him—the king man—" guided rather than impeded the forces of change and progress (Simms, "Guizot's" 122). There were few such men with the capacity to lead. The same was true of nations. Neither all people nor all peoples were equal in either capacity or attainment. That was why Native Americans were overrun and Africans had been enslaved by European peoples in the New World. Indeed, Simms argued, "slavery in all ages has been found the greatest and most admirable agent of Civilization," giving education and examples to less evolved peoples (*Letters* 3:174). The degree to which a people had evolved mattered. That was why, he held, Americans had won independence from the most powerful empire in the world. They had done so through their Revolution, led by an elite that felt correctly its time had come (Simms, "Ellet's" 328). By mid-1847 that also was Simms's judgment for the South: the region had evolved enough to become independent (*Letters* 2:332). The hope inspired and then failed him and the people he sought to lead.

While not all men could rise to the highest rank, they all had the same responsibility at home. There the father was patriarch, protector, and head, while the mother was nurturer, moral instructor, and heart. There, too, children's characters and minds were formed by age twelve ("Ellet's"). Children's upbringing was critical to citizenship, and it was through her sons and the support of her husband, father, and brothers that a woman shaped the public sphere. The culture and character instilled in the child expressed and informed not just the household, but the larger society—the people.

"The history of peoples and their embodiments in institutions, states, and artistic productions—these were the great subjects" in Simms's view (Moltke-Hansen, "Southern" 120). Yet "poets were the only class of philosophers who had recognized" this until his own day, when at last "we now read human histories. We now ask after the affections as well as the ceremonies of society" ("Ellet's" 319-20). Peoples or races—that is, ethnic groups—were not unchanging any more than were their politics and their cultures. They either advanced or were overrun by history. Further, new peoples emerged, and old identities were submerged. The Spanish conquistadors were the creation of centuries of conflict with the Moors: their motivation was the glory of conquest, not the routine of trade or the plow. On the other hand, the English settlements in North America reflected the impulse to transform the wilderness into verdant farms and build society (*Views* 64, 178–85; *Social* 8). The same impulse drove Americans westward in Simms's own day and gave Americans their Manifest Destiny.

To explore these facts of the South's settlement and its place in international conflicts, Simms wrote all together, between 1833 and 1863, two romances set in eighth-century Spain, two set during the Spanish exploration and conquest of the Americas and two during the later English colonization of South Carolina, seven set during the American Revolution, and—depending on how one counts—perhaps eight set on the borders of the nineteenth-century South. After the war he published one more Revolutionary romance and two more that, like it, were set beyond the boundaries of civilization. He also left two unfinished romances, also set beyond society's normal reach. These late works, however, no longer had as their framing justification the cultivation of the South's future and civilization.

White southerners had their independence foreclosed by the war. In his last works, therefore, Simms found himself exploring the psychological, philosophical, and historical impulses that led to the Confederacy's demise and what, in the aftermath, it meant to be a good man and to build for the future, however impoverished. On the first score, he argued that the impulse to idealism behind abolitionism ignored historical realities, becoming inhuman in its consequences. On the latter score, he affirmed responsibility for one's dependents and the virtues of stoicism, as well as a continued commitment to the beauty and truth of art and the impulses to the cultivated life and fields. Therefore, in the face of the burning of his Woodlands home and library in February 1865—during Sherman's march and in the midst of desperate circumstances—he insisted that home, or the ideals and past characterizing its potential, still was at the center of true civilization, but only if elevated by art (*Sense* 8, 17). It was wrong to measure civilization by the getting, spending, and mad dashing, or material progress and utilitarianism, characteristic of both a capitalistic North and also many southerners. These traits he often had attacked even before the war, insisting that "the work of the Imagination, which is the Genius of a race, is only begun when its material progress is supposed to be complete" (*Poetry* 12).

### Writings

Simms expressed many of his ideas most personally in letters and most cogently in essays, speeches, and occasional introductions to his books. But he illustrated them most fully in his fiction and poetry. By the time he arrived in New

York in 1832, he had formed many of the core ideals and beliefs that would shape his work. His application of them, however, modified his understanding over time. Growing as a writer and growing in knowledge and experience, he also grew as a thinker.

In his hierarchy of values, poetry came first. It was a prophetic calling as well as evocative of the deeply felt (or, sometimes, the fleeting) and thus testimony to the perdurance and transcendence of the beautiful and the human spirit. Yet, as Simms often ruefully reflected, prose spoke to many more people. That was a principal reason why he turned to writing prose epics or romances. He gave his most concerted consideration of poetry's value and roles in three lectures in Charleston in 1854. Over the prior three years he had given portions of them in Augusta, Georgia, Washington, D.C., and Richmond and Petersburg, Virginia. Entitled *Poetry and the Practical*, they did not see print until 1996, as Simms never found the time to expand them as he wanted. On the other hand, his last address on the same themes, *The Sense of the Beautiful*, was issued soon after he delivered it, also in Charleston.

Many of his important reviews have not yet been gathered, but Simms collected some in 1845–46, and *Views and Reviews in American Literature, History and Fiction* came out in 1846 and 1847 in two "series." Beginning with a consideration of "Americanism" in literature, the first series explored the themes and periods of American history for treatment by the novelist. Simms argued there, and in forewords to several of his romances, that fiction rendered the past more truthfully, interestingly, and tellingly than histories and biographies could because fiction—like poetry—required imagination to look beyond what is not known or expressed. The second series examined additional American writers and what distinguished them, for instance, in their humor.

Despite their early success, Simms's romances, novellas, and stories provoked mixed reviews. Poe eventually concluded that Simms had become "the best novelist which this country has, on the whole, produced" but also insisted that "he should never have written 'The Partisan,' nor 'The Yemassee.'" This was in a review of *Confession*. That novel, like the gothic *Martin Faber*, demonstrated, Poe contended, that Simms's "genius [did] not lie in the outward so much as in the inner world." Yet he nevertheless wrote of Simms's short-story collection *The Wigwam and the Cabin* that "in invention, in vigor, in movement, in the power of exciting interest, and in the artistical management of his themes, he has surpassed, we think, any of his countrymen." Other critics, especially in the genteel and Whiggish Knickerbocker circle, joined Poe in condemning what they considered to be the excessively graphic and vulgar qualities of many characters and scenes, and Simms's prolixity and sententiousness, in his romances (Butterworth and Kibler 64, 50).

The violent realism and earthiness of the romances did not result in realistic novels. Although Simms received early praise for his characterizations (particularly of women), he used the romance formula, with its stereotypic heroes and heroines, predictable themes, and conventional polarities. People were on quests or had lost their way or were fighting long odds or were carrying forward the banner of (and modeling) civilization or were mired in the slough of despond or were resisting all the claims of civilized society and behavior or were pursuing love interests. Deceitfulness, selfishness, and greed opposed honor, high-mindedness, and honesty against the backdrop of the South's development from the earliest days of Spanish exploration to the westward movement in Simms's own youth.

It was only gradually that Simms married the psychological acuity of some of his portraits of the interior struggles of his gothic characters and fiction to the historical romance. Helping him think through how to do so were the biographies he wrote in the mid-1840s, but also the incidents on which he focused particular fictions, such as the murder in *Beauchampe; or, The Kentucky Tragedy* (1842). However incomplete the blending of realism and romanticism or of stereotypical and socially individuated renderings through the 1840s, by the 1850s Simms fundamentally had made the transition to social realism in such works as *Woodcraft* and *The Cassique of Kiawah*. Indeed some scholars have considered *Woodcraft* the first realistic novel in America (Bakker; Wimsatt, "Realism").

In some sense disguising the transition is the fact that Simms also increasingly wrote as a humorist and, in so doing, often rendered his late narratives fabulistically, when not writing social comedy or stories of manners. This dimension of Simms's work was largely hidden, however, until the 1974 publication of *Stories and Tales*, volume 5 in the Centennial Simms edition. There, for the first time, readers had access in print to "Bald-Head Bill Bauldy." There, too, for the first time one could read together that story, "Legend of the Hunter's Camp," and "How Sharp Snaffles Got His Capital and Wife," which was published posthumously in *Harper's Magazine* in October 1870. These and other stories and tales made it clear that Simms was a fecund contributor to southern and American humor.

Humor let Simms take up issues that he could not otherwise address in print and still expect to be well received. He did so both during and after the war. The war also pushed Simms past the emerging fashion of social realism. Having destroyed the familiar, the preoccupation of much realistic fiction, the war made the liminal central (Shillingsburg, "Cub"). While his romances and tales had often explored life on the edge or in extreme circumstances, whether in war or on the frontier or on the verge of madness or in fanciful realms, it had done so against a backdrop of, and with the goal of affirming, social norms and development. In the war's wake that goal seemed absurd. Mythologized memories of a healthy past might nurture a sense of the beautiful but could not help one deal with the present. Thus Simms's conclusion, in a March 1869 letter to Paul Hamilton Hayne: "Let us bury the Past lest it buries us!" (*Letters* 5:214). Fifteen months later he lay dead in the 13 Society Street, Charleston, home of his oldest daughter, with the shell holes in the walls of the bedroom he had shared with several children.

**Posthumous Reputation**

The twenty years after Simms's death saw him often respectfully treated, first in obituaries, later in memoirs and columns, and also in literary dictionaries and encyclopedias. Yet Charles Richardson's 1887 *American Literature: 1607–1885* proved a harbinger of a shift: Simms, Richardson observed, was "more respected than read," having "won considerable note because he was so sectional" and then having "lost it because he was not sectional enough," although he showed "silly contempt for his Northern betters" (qtd. in Butterworth and Kibler 130). Five years later Trent's biography of Simms appeared. It was the first full-length, scholarly treatment. Its central thesis was that Simms's environment frustrated his abilities: the South was inimical to art and the life of the mind, and Charleston high society's hauteur marginalized Simms despite his talent and character. Trent's second thesis was that Simms's commitment to the romance and his romanticism meant that his works had become largely unreadable in an age of literary realism. Although Vernon Parrington and later scholars recognized Simms's impulses to realism, the two theses long shaped Simms criticism and, indeed, also helped frame study of antebellum southern literature and intellectual life (Parrington 119–30).

A Virginian born in 1862, Trent was a progressive who wanted a New South radically different from the old. He saw his pioneering study of Simms as an opportunity to criticize what the Civil War had made untenable. From his perspective the Old South was not the expanding and rapidly developing environment, with a deep history, that Simms portrayed, but a place where slavery stultified and stunted the growth and progress displayed by the North. Southern—especially South Carolinian—writers occasionally challenged Trent's agenda and conclusions, but those critiques had little impact. Not until after publication of the Simms letters in the 1950s did scholars begin to consider the author in the historical and contemporary contexts that he had rendered in his poetry and fiction. And not until after the centennial of his death did a growing number of scholars, having concluded that southern intellectual history was not an oxymoron, begin to study in detail the culture in which Simms participated and to which he contributed so voluminously and variously.

Some of these scholars also have had agendas: they have wanted to see Simms included in the American literary canon, for instance, or they have wanted to defend the heritage that in their view Trent, and so many others, inappropriately belittled or ignorantly dismissed. More fruitfully, other scholars have begun to reframe the understanding of nineteenth-century American intellectual life by stripping away preconceptions that characterized earlier evaluations of Simms and his contemporaries. They are closely examining the historical record and transatlantic and other contemporary contexts and developments in the process. Although the pursuit of canonical status in a post-canonical age seems quixotic at this point, the explosion of the canon is leading to more varied fare being offered and may, therefore, mean that Simms, once his work is widely available, will be more often anthologized as well as studied. Defensiveness about Simms and the antebellum South may warm the hearts of like-minded people, just as critics of the Old South have been encouraged by shared presuppositions and disdain. Yet dueling cultural ideologies do not advance comity and may only reinforce mutual incomprehensions. Continued, deep research in original sources and the theoretical reframing that Atlantic history, the history of the book, and other perspectives offer — these approaches promise most for further study of Simms, his works, and his world.

**Works Cited**

For amplified readings by and on Simms and on his world, go to http://simms.library.sc.edu/bibliography.php.

Bakker, Jan. "Simms on the Literary Frontier; or, So Long Miss Ravenel and Hello Captain Porgy: *Woodcraft* Is the First 'Realistic' Novel in America." In *William Gilmore Simms and the American Frontier*, edited by John Caldwell Guilds and Caroline Collins, 64–78. Athens: University of Georgia Press, 1997.

Butterworth, Keen, and James E. Kibler Jr. *William Gilmore Simms: A Definitive Guide*. Boston: G. K. Hall, 1980.

Faust, Drew Gilpin. *A Sacred Circle: The Dilemma of the Intellectual in the Old South, 1840–1860*. Baltimore: Johns Hopkins University Press, 1977.

Guilds, John C. *Simms: A Literary Life*. Fayetteville: University of Arkansas Press, 1992.

Hayne, Paul Hamilton. "Ante-Bellum Charleston." *Southern Bivouac* 1 (October 1885): 257–68.

Kibler, James E. "The First Simms Letters: 'Letters from the West' (1826)." *Southern Literary Journal* 19 (Spring 1987): 81–91.

———. *The Poetry of William Gilmore Simms: An Introduction and Bibliography*. Columbia: Southern Studies Program, University of South Carolina, 1979.

McHaney, Thomas L. "An Early 19th-Century Literary Agent: James Lawson of New York." *Publications of the Bibliographical Society of America* 64 (Spring 1970): 177–92.

Moltke-Hansen, David. "The Expansion of Intellectual Life: A Prospectus." In *Intellectual Life in Antebellum Charleston*, edited by Michael O'Brien and David Moltke-Hansen, 3–44. Knoxville: University of Tennessee Press, 1986.

———. "Southern Literary Horizons in Young America: Imaginative Development of a Regional Geography." *Studies in the Literary Imagination* 42, no. 1 (2009): 1–31.

Nakamura, Masahiro. *Visions of Order in William Gilmore Simms: Southern Conservatism and the Other American Romance*. Columbia: University of South Carolina Press, 2009.

Parrington, Vernon L. *The Romantic Revolution in America, 1800–1860*. Vol. 2 of *Main Currents in American Thought*. New York: Harcourt, Brace and Company, 1927.

Rogers, George C., Jr. *Charleston in the Age of the Pinckneys*. Columbia: University South Carolina Press, 1980.

Shillingsburg, Miriam J. "The Cub of the Panther: A New Frontier." In *William Gilmore Simms and the American Frontier*, edited by John Caldwell Guilds and Caroline Collins, 221–36. Athens: University of Georgia Press, 1997.

———. "Literary Grist: Simms's Trips to Mississippi." *Southern Quarterly* 41, no. 2 (2003): 119-34.

Simms, William Gilmore. *Atalantis: A Story of the Sea: In Three Parts*. New York: J. & J. Harper, 1832.

———. *Beauchampe; or, The Kentucky Tragedy*. 2 vols. Philadelphia: Lea and Blanchard, 1842.

———. *The Cassique of Kiawah: A Colonial Romance*. New York: Redfield, 1859.

———. *Confession; or, The Blind Heart. A Domestic Story*. 2 vols. Philadelphia: Lea and Blanchard, 1841.

———. "Ellet's 'Women of the Revolution.'" *Southern Quarterly Review*, n.s. 1 (July 1850): 314-54.

———. "Guizot's Democracy in France." *Southern Quarterly Review* 15, no.29 (1849): 114-65.

———. *Guy Rivers: A Tale of Georgia*. 2 vols. New York: Harper & Brothers, 1834.

———. *The Letters of William Gilmore Simms*. Edited by Mary C. Simms Oliphant, Alfred Taylor Odell, and T. C. Duncan. 6 vols. Columbia: University of South Carolina Press, 1952-82.

———. *The Life of Francis Marion*. New York: Henry G. Langley, 1844.

———. *Martin Faber, the Story of a Criminal; and Other Tales*. 2 vols. New York: Harper & Brothers, 1837.

———. *Poetry and the Practical*. Edited by James E. Kibler. Fayetteville: University of Arkansas Press, 1996.

———. *The Sense of the Beautiful: An Address . . . before the Charleston County Agricultural and Horticultural Association, May 3, 1870*. Charleston: Charleston County Agricultural and Horticultural Association, 1870.

———. *The Social Principle: The Source of National Permanence. An Oration, Delivered before the Erosophic Society of the University of Alabama . . . December 13, 1842.* Tuscaloosa: Erosophic Society, University of Alabama, 1843.

———. *Stories and Tales.* Vol. 5 of *The Writings of William Gilmore Simms.* Centennial edition; introductions, explanatory notes, and texts established by John Caldwell Guilds. Columbia: University of South Carolina Press, 1974.

———. *Views and Reviews in American Literature, History and Fiction.* 2 vols. New York: Wiley and Putnam, 1845 (1846).

———. *The Wigwam and the Cabin.* 2 vols. New York: Wiley and Putnam, 1845–46.

———. *Woodcraft, or Hawks about the Dovecote: A Story of the South, at the Close of the Revolution.* New York: Redfield, 1854.

Trent, William Peterfield. *William Gilmore Simms.* Boston: Houghton, Mifflin, 1892.

Wakelyn, Jon L. *The Politics of a Literary Man: William Gilmore Simms.* Westport, Conn.: Greenwood Press, 1973.

Watson, Charles S. *From Nationalism to Secessionism: The Changing Fiction of William Gilmore Simms.* Westport, Conn.: Greenwood Press, 1993.

White, William B., Jr. *The Ross-Chesnut-Sutton Family of South Carolina.* Franklin, N.C.: Privately printed, 2002.

Wimsatt, Mary Ann. "Realism and Romance in Simms's Midcentury Fiction." *Southern Literary Journal* 12, no. 2 (1980): 29–48.

# Critical Introduction

THE REVOLUTIONARY ROMANCES

*David Moltke-Hansen*

William Gilmore Simms, preeminent mid-nineteenth-century southern author, wrote eight novels set during the American Revolution and its immediate aftermath. This introduction provides an overview. Although it covers all eight works, one volume—*Woodcraft*—has a separate introduction in this edition from the University of South Carolina Press and the William Gilmore Simms Initiatives. This is because it is the single work that has attracted the most attention from twentieth- and twenty-first-century critics.

From the outset the American Revolution compelled attention from writers and artists. Yet fictionists were slow to follow advocates like Thomas Paine, poets like Philip Freneau, and painters like Jonathan Trumbull. When novelists finally did, Simms proved the most prolific. His contributions remained unrivalled in their extent long after his death. It was only in the wake of World War I, when the Revolution's sesquicentennial approached, that other novelists began to treat more or less as fully as had Simms the subject of the War for Independence. Notably, in most of eight historical novels with characters from his native Maine, Kenneth Roberts turned to the subject, or the years just before and after, again and again. Van Wyck Mason did the same in the six volumes of his "American Revolution" series.

Still later writers followed suit as the war's bicentennial approached. Often this was in multi-generational family chronicles that included the Revolution but ranged much earlier or later. Among the most popular are Inglis Fletcher's "Carolina Chronicles" (12 vols.), John Jakes' "Kent Family Chronicles" (8 vols.), and Elswyth Thane's "Williamsburg" series (7 vols.). Several recent series with a more military focus treat just the Revolution. They include Edward Cline's "Sparrowhawk" (6 vols.), James Nelson's "Revolution at Sea Saga" (5 vols.), and Adam Rutledge's "Patriots" (6 vols.).

Simms paved the way for all these series, though not many authors have known their debt. At one level, his accomplishment was to give narrative form and force to the complicated ebb and flow of the Revolution in his native South Carolina. By doing so over a third of a century, starting just after the conclusion of the war's semi-centennial, he also helped claim the Revolution for

America's imaginative life. Before considering his individual titles, their publication and reception, and their later, critical standing, it is important to understand what motivated him. Then one can assess the series as a whole and ask its value to twenty-first-century readers.

**The Revolution's Changing Significance, 1815-45**

To a remarkable degree, the Revolution framed Simms's boyhood. The future author was nine years old when America's so-called second revolution, the War of 1812, finished. During the conflict, his immigrant father fought under General Andrew Jackson in the Red Stick or First Creek War. That conflict led the budding poet to effuse in verse. Inspired as well by his Charleston, S. C. grandmother's tales of his mother's family in the Revolution, the young Simms was in the habit of scouting old war sites in the surrounding countryside (Simms, *The Partisan* [1835] vii-viii; Guilds, *Simms* 7, 11).

This enthusiasm was further stoked by the fact that the American Revolution was gaining literary purchase. First came the hagiographies, memoirs, and historical accounts of the founders, together with reams of verse and documentary compilations. Then the story tellers started. Washington Irving's *The Sketchbook of Geoffrey Crayon, Gent.* appeared in 1820 and contained "The Legend of Sleepy Hollow" and "Rip Van Winkle," tales set immediately before and after the war. James Fenimore Cooper's *The Spy* came out in 1821 and his *The Pilot: A Tale of the Sea* two years later. Both these novels had Revolutionary settings—in the one case upstate New York (Irving's setting as well) and in the other the English coast and seas. It was in this latter environment that American naval hero John Paul Jones preyed on British shipping with storied success. Inspired by *the Spy* and by work editing a two-volume history of the Revolution, Mainer John Neal penned *Seventy-Six; or, Love and Battle* in just under a month in 1822.

At the time the sixteen-year old Simms thought of himself as a poet, not a fictionist. Despite his subsequent work as a journalist during the early 1830s, he did not shift his primary literary production from poetry to prose until after his 1832 trip to New York to launch a national literary career (Kibler, *The Poetry*; Brennan). He published his first gothic novella, *Martin Faber*, the next year. Then, over the course of two years, he wrote three romances. These commenced the three series that occupied him much of the rest of his life. He began the Border series in 1834 with *Guy Rivers: A Tale of Georgia*, set during the gold rush that started in 1828 in the northern corner of the state. The series ultimately treated the westering edge of southern settlement, from Georgia to Texas, as well as the southern backwoods, from the mountains of North Carolina to the swamps of Florida, in Simms's own life time.

The other series quickly followed. Simms started the Colonial in 1835 with *The Yemassee. A Romance of Carolina*, about a 1715-16 conflict between Native Americans and British colonists and their African slaves. The wider series broadly treated the periods of European exploration and colonization in the Americas from the 16th through the early 18th centuries. The third series, the Revolutionary, focused on that war in South Carolina. Simms delivered *The Partisan: A Tale of the Revolution* to Harper & Brothers, his publishers, just six months after the publication of John Pendleton Kennedy's Revolutionary novel *Horseshoe Robinson: A Tale of the Tory Ascendency*, set as well in the backcountry of South Carolina (Kennedy viii).

Simms subsequently wrote poetry, short stories, and novellas, as well as biographies and essays, in each of the subject areas of his series. Yet the majority of his output in all three was in long-form fiction—what he called romances. In making the move from poetry to romance, he followed the example of Sir Walter Scott. Scott died just as Simms's sixth volume of verse and first New York-published book, the 1832 dramatic poem *Atalantis*, was coming off the press to national critical acclaim. It was nearly 40 years earlier that the Scottish author began collecting and publishing the ballads of his country. Then, in 1814, he started his prolific and successful career as a novelist or romancer.

Scott judged fiction more accessible to broad readerships than poetry, and it was important to him to influence as many as possible. This was especially so in light of his goal of fostering a shared sense of British nationality among the Scots and the English—people of fraught histories, diverse origins, and deep antipathies. To this end, he examined not only the interactions of these ethnicities, which he did in *his* Border romances, set on the English-Scottish border. He also treated the earlier conflicts of Highlanders and Lowlanders in Scotland and of Anglo-Saxons and Normans in England. He did this to help people understand how Scottish and English identities had arisen out of the clashes and mixing of earlier ethnicities (Simms, *Views and Reviews. First Series* 40-41; Moltke-Hansen, "Southern Literary Horizons" 6-13).

The reason for such fictional narratives, Scott contended, was that ballads and other traditional lays do not have the same sweep as, for instance, *The Iliad*. A people's rise, conflicts, and conquests, myths, heroes, and villains, he concluded, need to be set and narrated on a large scale. Ancient bards did this formerly in epics chanted across generations. In a later and literate age, however, the surest way to provide people with a sense of their stirring past and mythic memories was in print. In type, prose carried the individual reader more effectively than poetry. The latter was supremely an oral and aural art.

Consequently, Scott, with others, developed the romance to tell epic stories in prose (Lukacs). It was different from the novel in both its purpose and its subject. As Simms put it in his "Advertisement" to *The Yemassee*, "the domestic novel [of Fielding and Richardson] ..., confined to the felicitous narrative of common and daily occurring events, is altogether a different sort of composition." Its standards are not "those of the epic," but the romance's are. That is why, Simms also insisted, "the modern romance is a poem in every sense of the word" (vi).

Though deploying Scott's formula, Simms was not a copycat (Holman, *The Roots* 50-60). His subjects were American (*The Yemassee* [1835] vii). As Scott wrote of the ethnogenesis of the Scots, the English, and the British, Simms treated Americans' emergence as a people out of their diverse origins and historical experiences. He and Scott shared a genre, because it was the necessary and appropriate form for the subject matter and purposes of each. In time, Simms would have an elaborate understanding of what that meant. Yet, despite his clarity about the genre, he did not start with a grand plan to fictionalize Americans' rise and spread westward. His initial intention for the Revolutionary series was just a trilogy "devoted to the illustration of the war of the Revolution in South Carolina" (Simms, *The Partisan* [1854] v).

While feeling his way toward a larger vision, Simms alternated among his three series. In the subset of his American-focused review essays and lectures, gathered in *Views and Reviews in American Literature, History and Fiction* and issued in 1846-47, he laid out his rationale for the three. The case he made was one trumpeted by his friends in the informal association of nationalist, Democratic writers centered in New York—the Young America circle (Widmer). Although adumbrated already in his 1835 preface to *The Yemassee* and elaborated over the next months in both his first two Revolutionary romances, *The Partisan* and *Mellichampe*, the argument he advanced was in a sense his *ex post facto* justification of his practice. He claimed that he was writing what the Alabama poet and politician Alexander B. Meek came to call, in an 1844 oration, *Americanism in Literature* (*Views and Reviews. First Series* 1-19).

Anticipating Meek, Simms lectured in 1842 on "The Epochs and Events of American History, as Suited to the Purposes of Art in Fiction." He explained that he saw American history divided into four epochs—that of initial European exploration and conquest in the three-quarters of a century or so after Columbus made landfall in the new world; the subsequent two centuries of British colonial settlement and continuing conflict with Native Americans and rival European powers; the two decades that saw the British American move from remonstrance to Revolution and independence; and the subsequent western expansion, self-development, and Manifest Destiny of the new nation and people (*Views and Reviews. First Series* 20-101). In treating each of these epochs in romances, Simms published at least two dozen long-form fictions — a third of them in the Revolutionary series.

While all three series shared common purposes, Simms had particular reasons to treat the Revolution as and when he did. A supporter of his father's old commander, President Andrew Jackson, and the Union during the bitter campaign of the early 1830s to have South Carolina unilaterally nullify federal tariffs, he was keen to assert the Palmetto State's role in the making of the American nation. The political passions of the nullification episode reminded him, too, that "the excesses of patriotism, when attaining power, have been but too frequently productive of a tyranny more dangerous in its exercise, and more lasting in its effects, than the despotism which it was invoked to overthrow" (*Mellichampe* [1836] v; Wakelyn 19-50). His early Revolutionary romances also "suggested clews [sic] to the historian ... and laid bare to other workers ... the veins of tradition which everywhere enrich" South Carolina. True, his "friends denounced [his] waste of time," but the result was that the Palmetto State had "furnished more materials for the use of art and fiction ... than half the states in the Union" (Simms, *Katherine Walton* [1854] 3).

These early Revolutionary romances reflected as well a commitment to realism. This was despite their conventional, romantic, chief protagonists. Indeed, many criticized Simms for the vulgarity and violence of his secondary characters. He answered the charge with a rhetorical question that reflected his dedication to historical verisimilitude: "Does the story profess to belong to a country and to a period of history which are alike known — and does it misrepresent either?" The implied answer to the first part of the question was "yes" and, to the second part, "no." Clearly, as he insisted, he had no desire "to make a fairy tale ... in which none but the colors of the rose and rainbow shall predominate" (*Mellichampe* [1836] ix).

Rather, Simms's "object usually [was] to adhere, as closely as possible, to the features and the attributes of real life." Further, it seemed to him obvious "that vulgarity and crime must always preponderate ... in the great majority during a period of war." Because, "to paint morally, the historic novelist must paint truly," Simms concluded that the fact that "the low characters predominate" should not surprise his readers (*Mellichampe* [1836] x-xii). The need to reiterate the point against a persistent strain in the criticism of his work may have been behind his observation in the historical overview with which he began his third Revolutionary romance, *The Kinsman: or The Black Riders of Congaree*: "That atrocious and reckless warfare between the whigs and the tories, which had deluged the fair plains of Carolina with native blood, was now at its height" (17). The romance that started there was his last in the series for almost a decade.

**Southern Honor and the American Revolution**

When Simms returned to writing Revolutionary romances in 1849, he still had these earlier motives and judgments. Yet, in the interval, his rationales for writing had shifted. He had developed new intellectual and political priorities. He addressed these initially in review essays penned between 1845 and 1852. He published three of the essays as *South-Carolina in the Revolutionary War: Being a Reply to Certain Misrepresentations and Mistakes of Recent Writers, in Relation to the Course and Conduct of This State* (1853) (Moltke-Hansen, "Why History Mattered"; Simms, *Letters* 6: 328 n. 8). There he argued that novelists, editors, biographers, and historians were mischaracterizing the course and conduct of the Revolution and of the Revolutionaries in the South—especially South Carolina. Even such an eminent southern writer as John Pendleton Kennedy had made material errors in his *Horse-Shoe Robinson*. These were not justified by the demands of his story or the faulty memory of the real Horse-Shoe Robinson. The consequence of such mistakes was to make the patriots appear less, and the British more, effective than they were (Simms, *South Carolina in the Revolutionary War* 60-72).

Even more galling was the critique of the patriots for excesses against the loyalists. Simms early acknowledged both the fact and, in particular instances, the unfortunate consequences. Yet he vehemently resisted reading those instances as normative (*Mellichampe* [1836] iv-v; Moltke-Hansen, "Why History Mattered"). Many loyalists earned the vigor of the actions against them. Many patriots were sorely provoked. The civil warfare between para-military forces of both sides inevitably produced violent interactions. To take the viewpoint of "the Descendants of the loyalists," as did Ann Pamela Cunningham, granddaughter of an up country South Carolina tory colonel, was to use "about the worst authorities ... on the subject of the Revolution"; for those descendants were seeking to assuage their "mortification" and to meet the need "to make out a case" for their own families (*Letters* 6: 330; Moltke-Hansen, "Why History Mattered").

Simms argued the point so strongly because it was part of a larger debate about the role of the South in the Revolution. Northern editors and writers contended increasingly that it took northern troops to drive the British army from Georgia and South Carolina to Yorktown and surrender. This was because the South's population was divided in the conflict and, indeed, often resisted the patriot forces. To the contrary, Simms insisted, local partisans in South Carolina repeatedly saved the American army. Moreover, they did this while also fighting "all the tories who infested [the state], though these were mostly *refugees from all the States south of New York*, who had taken refuge in

[British] Florida, & who followed in the wake of the British when they penetrated Geo. & S. C." (*Letters* 6: 330).

Simms contended that the South's leadership largely supported the Revolution but that the many recent Scottish and German immigrants tended to loyalism. Unlike the Irish and Scots-Irish, who often hated the English and also unlike the descendants of Huguenot immigrants, they owed too much to the British Crown ("Ellet's"). Further, at least in South Carolina, they made up "nearly half of [the colony's] population" and "had not been in the country 10 years" (*Letters* 6: 330). At the time, by contrast, New England was overwhelmingly settled by descendants of people who had arrived before the English Civil War over a century and a quarter before. The populations of the two regions therefore were very different in their make ups.

New Englanders, according to Simms, mostly were local patriots, not active on behalf of the larger cause of American independence. Consequently, South Carolina "sent, in proportion, more troops into the war than any other colony" (*Letters* 6: 330). Moreover, had it not been for southern leaders such as George Washington, the light of liberty would have been snuffed out. "You assailed my country ... unjustly," Simms wrote New England historian Lorenzo Sabine. He then lamented Sabine's "abuse of partial facts; and the evident purpose which it betrayed, rather to goad, sting, wound & disparage, than to be historically just & true" (*Letters* 6: 328-29).

These points mattered not only because of the importance of historical accuracy. They had political ramifications. Charles Sumner of Massachusetts used the introduction to the 1847 edition of Sabine's *The American Loyalists, or Biographical Sketches of Adherents to the British Crown in the War of the Revolution* in his attack in a speech in the United States Senate on South Carolina and one of its senators, Andrew Butler. He characterized the Palmetto State as stained by "its imbecility from Slavery, confessed through the Revolution," and then "made the state out to be unpatriotic and un-American, not only in 1856 but at least as far back as the Revolutionary War," three quarters of a century and more before (Shillingsburg, "Simms's Failed Lecture Tour" 185). That attack, Simms maintained, was what provoked the notorious "cudgelling" [sic] of Sumner on the Senate floor by Congressman Preston Brooks, Butler's South Carolina relation. Sabine "also misled Mr. [Daniel] Webster, who fell into a good deal of spoken blundering, in [his address to the New England Society of] Charleston, touching the vast number of New Englanders who perished in our battles" (*Letters* 6: 331).

Simms intended his fall 1856 lecture tour of the North, just months after Brooks used his gutta percha cane on Sumner, to set the record straight and to maintain the honor of South Carolina's role in the Revolution. Not surprisingly, given those intentions, the tour was a disaster and had to be cut short. His references to "Sumner's attack on S.C. as that of a deliberate & wanton malignant" antagonized his audiences (Shillingsburg, "Simms's Failed Lecture Tour" 191). The newspapers replied in kind, claiming that Simms was "seeking to do, in the historical field, what Brooks had done in the physical" (194). The next year Simms lectured on his northern reception for a southern audience. Northerners, he insisted, were morally incapable of listening to southern viewpoints, because the "politico-social relations of the two great sections" were "in absolute and direct antagonism" (188; Hagstette, "Private vs. Public" 52-58).

These intellectual and political conclusions were not the only developments that shaped Simms's return to his Revolutionary romance series. He formed new aesthetic goals as well. Although an early advocate of realism in fiction, he did not begin as a literary realist. Instead he regarded everyday life as being in the scope of the novelist; he was rather an epic writer of romances. Then it occurred to him that he could fuse these approaches, creatively using the tensions and differences between them (Ackerman 165).

Simms's fourth Revolutionary romance, *Katherine Walton*, reflected the change. Its purpose was "the delineation of the social world of Charleston, during the Revolutionary period" (*Katherine Walton* [1854] 3). Simms still considered the work a romance but used its social realism to attack aristocratic prejudice in the manner of William Makepeace Thackeray (Watson, *From Nationalism* 92-93). According to Mary Ann Wimsatt, "the Loyalists, who controlled government, churches, and clubs, continued the city's glittering amusements—a fact that made [the city] ripe for treatment in the novel of manners vein" (*The Major Fiction* 179). Consequently, "for the first time in the Revolutionary War series, ... Simms [made] social hostilities rather than military maneuvers the backbone of a book" (179-80).

Because *Katherine Walton* was the first novel serialized in *Godey's Lady's Book*, the most widely circulated American cultural journal of the day, it presumably had more readers than any other of Simms's Revolutionary romances. Yet many scholars consider Simms's next his best. *The Sword and the Distaff; or, "Fair, Fat and Forty," A Story of the South, at the Close of the Revolution* appeared in serial form, too, but in Charleston. Publication started in February 1852. The book came out that fall—also in Charleston—before the conclusion of the serialization and its Philadelphia publication from the same plates the next year. Subsequently it became known by the title of its revised, 1854, Redfield edition: *Woodcraft; or, Hawks about the Dovecote. A Story of the South at the Close of the Revolution* (Bakker).

In its serial form, Simms's work overlapped with the last segments of the serialization of Harriet Beecher Stowe's famous abolitionist novel *Uncle Tom's*

*Cabin*, which ran for 40 weeks between 5 June 1851 and 4 March 1852. Simms contended shortly afterwards that his romance was the best answer to Stowe's work (*Letters* 3: 222). He did not mean that he wrote to reply to Stowe, as many others in fact eventually did. After all, he initially published for a largely southern audience—the only time he did so in his Revolutionary series. Moreover, he could not have been writing in reply because of the near simultaneity of the publications of his and Stowe's works.

Rather, scholars understand Simms to have meant either of two things. One is that the social world and relations conveyed in his domestic romance gave a radically more accurate and positive picture of slavery and the plantation South than did Stowe's sentimental domestic novel. Both works were critical of failings of the institution, but to different ends (Watson, "Simms's Answer"). Social order wins in the one, and moral order loses in the other. The second reading of Simms's assertion is that his melding of sentimental domestic fiction with the romance was radically more effective than Stowe's appropriation of the romance structure for her work. In making this case, Zeno Ackerman argues that Simms and Stowe both dealt with responses to the disruption of the plantation idyll—by war in one case, by progressive, capitalist alienation in the other case (165). Whatever Simms meant, it aggrieved him that Stowe's book sold hugely, while his did not, published as it initially was in a small circulation journal and then in a North becoming more and more abolitionist in sentiment.

As James Kibler argues in his introduction to *Woodcraft*, Simms did not believe that the success of South Carolina plantation society was guaranteed. Rather, it had to be achieved again and again (xxviii-xxxi). To survive it also had to be protected from hostile influences. Yet historically the social order did carry forward. Once carved out of the wilderness and later restored after the disruptions and devastation of the Revolution, plantations remained the epitome of patriarchal order, and, under the guiding hand of plantation mistresses, the big house served as their moral centers. This ideal, Simms understood, was not always the reality, but it was, he maintained, the cultural, social, and ethical norm.

Modern critics argue that Simms's patriarchal plantation purveyed a fantasy. Like other slave owners, Simms deceived himself about the bonds between slaves and masters. Most slaves did not happily think of themselves as members of their masters' families, black and white. Neither did they believe they owned their masters as much as their masters owned them. Nor did slaves all love their owners or, as happened repeatedly in Simms's romances, reject the chance of freedom (Genovese and Fox-Genovese; Foley; King 140; Shelton 77). At the same time as scholars criticize, however, they praise the verisimilitude of the details of Simms's renderings—not just in *Woodcraft*, but in all the Revolutionary romances.

Simms scoured the written record available to him in manuscript as well as print, conducted oral history interviews, sought out informants about incidents and places he did not know, and weighed the relative merits of his evidence. He began as a boy, musing about the stories implicit "in "the local tradition, which, unconsciously, [his] mind began to throw together, and to combine in form." As he explained in the revised and expanded introduction to the 1854 edition of *The Partisan*, "even where the written history has not been found, tradition and the local chronicles, preserved as family records, have furnished adequate authorities." He concluded: "a sober desire for history—the unwritten, the unconsidered, but veracious history—has been with me, in this labour, a sort of principle" (vii-ix).

Even when he originally wrote *The Partisan*, Simms understood, as he rephrased the point in 1854, that "History ... is quite too apt to overlook the best essentials of society—such as constitute the moving impulses of men to action—in order to dilate on great events,—scenes in which men are merely massed, while a single favourite overtops all the rest, the Hero rising to the Myth, and absorbing within himself all the consideration which a more veracious and philosophical mode of writing would distribute over states and communities, and the humblest walks of life." Although in his romance "the persons of the Drama, many of them, are names of the nation, familiar to our daily reading," the focus of *The Partisan* was not on them, but on "the little nucleus of the Partisan squad ... first formed in the recesses of the swamp" (*The Partisan* xi).

That preoccupation let Simms show "how the personal wrong ... goaded the indifferent into patriotism ... [and] the submissive into rebellion" (*The Partisan* [1835] ix, viii). In doing so, he was explaining why things happened as and when they did. His purpose, as he observed in his 1835 introduction, was to "give a story of events, rather than of persons"(x). Events moved men and moved history forward. The treatment of events gave one the opportunity to explore history's unfolding and the consequences (Holman, *The Roots* 35). The why of history, nevertheless, was different than the what.

### Literary Realism, Sectionalism, and the Postbellum Turn

Simms's sense of the "what" of history shifted between the early 1840s and the '50s. The fundamental question in *Woodcraft* is not about the motivations and actions of the Revolution, which is finished, but about the restoration of a moral order and economy in the face of the war's social dislocations. Those disruptions challenged the character of both individuals and the community. In the process of shifting to this focus, Simms turned the historical romance into a novel of social realism and manners or a domestic romance (Dale). Indeed, Jan Bakker argues that *Woodcraft* is "the First 'Realistic' Novel in America" (64-78). That may slight *Katherine Walton* (Wimsatt, "Realism and Romance"). In any event, the post-*Woodcraft* Revolutionary novels, although set in war-time, carried forward this social critical emphasis. Conservative, low country aristocrats continued to be objects of attack, as were the unworthy low-born, twisted by greed and hate.

Individuals of these castes at opposite ends of the social spectrum were too often tories. "Unable to lead themselves," according to Simms, they "threw themselves, as so many dead weights, about the car of *movement* [sic]; and it is no reproach to those who did lead, that they were passed over, or flung off, by the wheels" ("*Civil Warfare*" 260-61). "The language he used to describe the tyranny of the tories in 1780 was the same as he used to describe the tyranny of the nullifiers ... and [also] the tyranny of Northern interests in the 1850s" (Moltke-Hansen, "Ordered Progress" 138). Tory forces and their partisan opposition figure centrally in the last two of his antebellum Revolutionary romances, published in 1855-56. There they play key roles in the run up to, and the ultimate outcome of, the Battle of Eutaw Springs. This engagement is the event around which *The Forayers; or The Raid of the Dog-Days* and *Eutaw: A Sequel to The Forayers, or the Raid of the Dog-Days. A Tale of the Revolution* revolve.

The critique of the failures of leadership and allegiance in these romances grew out of deep frustration. Starting in the mid-'40s, Simms first ramped up this criticism in other writings. Like the tory elite, too many of the antebellum South's leading citizens were temporizing about the region's political future. Increasing Simms's sense of urgency was his apprehension about capitalism's growing and coercive influence. It infected not just politics, but also cultural life and other spheres. Avarice and the new, socially destructive methods of wealth's generation were undermining political resolve and corrupting arts'— and thought's—producers, productions, and consumers as well as social relations. His Revolutionary romances of the '50s all show this process. In doing so, they reflect what Amy Kaplan argues literary realism is: a "strategy for imagining and managing the threats of social change" (ix).

The disease of capitalism, Simms believed, had been at work longer and had infected more people and more of life in the industrializing and urbanizing North and Britain of his day than in his region. Yet, as his Colonial and Revolutionary romances show, the South was not immune. Moreover, capitalism progressively compromised the social, cultural, and political health of the region as the nineteenth century advanced (Minguera; Pearce). At least slavery, he contended, isolated the South from some of the worst consequences of the disease (Ackerman 165).

This belief was in part why Simms proposed the extension of the South's slave regime over countries on the Caribbean littoral. That goal, in Simms's view, was southerners' manifest destiny. Besides, Mexicans and others needed to be disciplined and civilized by the institution (*Self-Development* 22-23). This aggrandizing vision was part of Simms's design to protect southern rights against an overweening North. The South would do so by augmenting its influence and political power ("The Southern Convention"). Simms's ambitions became greater still: establishment of the sovereignty and nationhood of the southern people. Only in this way, he eventually concluded, could the extension and preservation of his people's way of life and independence be assured. In his eyes as well, these were fundamentally the same motivations and objectives as those which animated America's Revolutionary founders.

The study of the Revolution, then, revealed the way forward, not just the heroics and necessities of an earlier age. History was about the future—until, that is, the Civil War created a chasm between the slave regime and its aftermath. In the process, the war turned the burgeoning South of Simms's Border Romance series, westward expansion, and Manifest Destiny into the Old South of beguiling and fading memories, timeless tradition, and social order. It also proved that the reasoning undergirding Simms's antebellum historical thought was wrong. The South was not destined for independence; white southerners would not become their own nation, and slavery was not the future of a Caribbean basin dominated by them (Moltke-Hansen, "When History Failed" 27-30).

Yet even after Confederate defeat Simms continued the fight against capitalism. Shortly before his death in 1870, he told the ladies of the Charleston Horticultural Society that they must be resolute in their efforts to stem capitalism's corrupting and debasing influence. They needed to do this to preserve the South's distinction, culture, and values. The remembered patriarchal order of the antebellum plantation, centered on the big house run by the plantation mistress, might be no more; nonetheless it offered a model to inform his auditors' sense of a healthy society. At the same time, the sacrifices of the Civil War in defense of the southern way of life required the continuing commitment to that life (*The Sense of the Beautiful*; Georgini; John Miller). Sadly, in Simms's view, what that defense could not do was free the South from Yankeedom.

The last of his Revolutionary romances, *Joscelyn*, serially published in 1867, reflected the shift in historical perspective and reality with which Simms had to deal after defeat. The chief protagonist, Stephen Joscelyn, is unlike earlier leading men of the series: he is a cripple, physically and psychologically. He is driven to fight against his demons as well as for the patriot cause. War is an inner tumult as much as an outward conflict. The notorious tory Thomas Browne, based on a historical figure, in effect loses himself and the last battle of the story in his parallel struggle. Joscelyn, though, finally affirms his manhood, his honor, and his sanity. His concluding victory is as much personal as military or political.

War's fortunes are uncertain, but a man can be responsible for himself. In the end, the inference seems to be, character is achieved (or lost), not simply a birthright and an example, as it was for Simms's early romance heroes. One's conduct is all one can control in the face of chaotic military and political conflict and social upheaval. Indeed, character is the fundamental measure of success and the chief bulwark against disorder and dissolution. Simms went on to suggest to the ladies of the Horticultural Society that, by this measure, the conquering Yankees had failed. This was because of how they behaved not only in the winning, but also in the aftermath of victory (*The Sense of the Beautiful*; Georgini; John Miller). Morally and aesthetically, therefore, victory should still go to the South.

Joscelyn's story revealed Simms shifting from a social to a psychological understanding of war and literary realism. The move shaped all three of his last published romances, including two in the Border series—*Voltmeier, or The Mountain Men* and *The Cub of the Panther; A Mountain Legend*, both serially issued in 1869. The move reflected as well Simms's preoccupation with states of mind back to his early days as a writer of gothic tales (Hagstette, "Screams from the South"). Unlike his late romances, however, those tales did not—could not—use the intellectual and aesthetic tools of the psychological realism just beginning to emerge in literature at mid-century. Furthermore, even among his last long fictions only *Joscelyn* and the unpublished and incomplete pirate romance "The Brothers of the Coast" deal with the impact of war on the individual or use war as a metaphor, as well as an occasion, for the inner conflicts and moral dilemmas of their protagonists (Meriwether). Some scholars even consider *Joscelyn* a proto-existentialist work (Moltke-Hansen, "When History Failed" 29-30).

**The Eight Revolutionary Romances**

*Joscelyn* is the last written but the first in its chronological setting, treating as it does the Revolution's beginnings in the backcountry along the Georgia-South Carolina border in 1775. Before going back to the beginning, Simms thought of *The Partisan* as his opening, as well as his first, work in the series. He explained the relations of his earlier Revolutionary romances in the "Historical Summary" with which he introduced *The Forayers*. "The 'Partisan'," he observed there, closed with the melancholy defeat of the first southern continental army under [General Horatio] Gates, at Camden. "Mellichampe" illustrated the interval between this event and the arrival of [General Nathanael] Greene, with the rude material for the organization of a second army; and was more particularly intended to do honor to the resolute and hardy patriotism of the scattered bands of patriots, who still maintained a predatory warfare against the foe among the swamps and thickets, rather keeping alive the spirit of the country, than operating decisively for its rescue. "The Scout," originally published under the name of "The Kinsmen," occupied a third period, when the wary policy of Greene began to make itself felt, in the gradual isolation and overthrow of the detached posts and fortresses which the enemy had established with the view to overawe the people in the leading precincts of the state; while "Katherine Walton," closing the career of certain parties, introduced to the reader by the "Partisan," and making complete the trilogy begun in that work, was designed to show the fluctuations of the contest, the spirit with which it was carried on, and to embody certain events of great individual interest, connected with the fortunes of persons not less distinguished by their individual worth of character, and their influence upon the general history, than by the romantic circumstances growing out of their career.

This narrative brought down the record to a period, when, for the first time, the British were made to understand that the conflict was doubtful; that their conquests were insecure, and that, so far from extending their arms over the interior, it became a question with them whether they should be able to maintain their hold upon the strong places of which they had so long held possession. ... To maintain themselves in Charleston and Savannah, the necessity was pressing that they should contract their powers and concentrate their forces. Reinforcements from Europe were hardly to be expected. The British empire was in a state of exhaustion, and the army of the invader was now half made up of the provincial loyalists (4-5).

At that point Simms resumed the historical narrative in *The Forayers* and its sequel, *Eutaw*. In doing so, he continued to "seek to illustrate the social condition of the country, under the influence of those strifes and trials which give vivacity to ordinary circumstances, and mark with deeper hues, and stronger colors, and sterner tones, the otherwise common progress of human hopes and fears, passions and necessities" (5). *Woodcraft* followed chronologically, although appearing right after *Katherine Walton* and, so, before *The Forayers*. Together, the seven antebellum Revolutionary romances treat the period "from the fall of the city of Charleston, in 1780," to the months after "the provisional articles of peace, between the King of Great Britain, and the revolted colonies of America, were signed at Paris, on the 13th November, 1782" (*The Partisan* [1854] vii; *Woodcraft* 5). At his death, Simms had plans for at least one additional romance for the series, presumably to help fill in the four-plus year gap between the action of *Joscelyn* and that of *The Partisan* (*Letters* 4: 625-26).

It only became possible to read all eight of the works in the series in book form during the bicentennial of the Revolution. Until the University of South Carolina Press issued *Joscelyn* in the Centennial Simms edition in 1975, that work had been available just in serial form. The next year, for the bicentennial, the Southern Studies Program of the University issued all eight romances. For the first time, they also were available with annotations explaining historical and literary references. It is with the permission of the program's successor, the Institute for Southern Studies, that those annotations and texts are made available here.

To recap, drawing on the introduction to the bicentennial edition, the eight novels of Simms's Revolutionary series first appeared in the following order:

*The Partisan: A Tale of the Revolution.* 2 volumes. (1835) New York: Harper & Brothers. Revised edition, entitled *The Partisan: A Romance of the Revolution*, New York: Redfield, 1854. Simms began this first novel in his Revolutionary War series early in 1835. He had a dozen chapters finished by June, and the book was published in November. He revised it extensively for publication, in January 1854, in the Redfield selected edition of his works. It deals with the 1780 Battle of Camden and its aftermath, especially the guerilla warfare by partisan forces under Francis Marion and other militia commanders. Like most of the other titles in the series, it was many times reprinted, first by Redfield and later by other publishers, but without further revision or correction by the author.

*Mellichampe: A Legend of the Santee.* 2 volumes. (1836) New York: Harper & Brothers. Revised edition, New York: Redfield, 1854. Simms's second novel of the Revolution was begun soon after publication of *The Partisan* and was issued apparently in October the next year. Revised for publication in March 1854 in the Redfield edition, it was many times reprinted but, as in the case of other volume in the series, without further revision or correction by the author. The story follows the fictional band of Francis Marion's partisans in their conflicts with loyalist and British forces in the wake of the Battle of Camden.

*The Kinsmen; or the Black Riders of Congaree: A Tale.* 2 volumes. (1841) Philadelphia: Lea and Blanchard. Revised edition, entitled *The Scout; or The Black*

*Riders of Congaree*, New York: Redfield, 1854. Simms began writing his third novel of the Revolution early in 1840, and it was published in February 1841. Revised extensively for inclusion in September 1854 in the Redfield edition of his works, with its new title, the novel was many times reprinted in that form. It opens shortly after the Battle of Hobkirk's Hill, or the second Battle of Camden, in May 1781. The action ends with the British departure from the Star Fort at Ninety-Six, S. C. the following month. A good brother is a partisan leader and chief protagonist; a bad brother is secretly the tory head of the Black Riders and a rival in love. Allied with the partisan leader is Supple Jack Bannister, the "authentic voice of the liberty-loving frontiersman," a recurrent figure in all three of Simms's romance series and also the Scout of the retitled and revised version of the novel (5).

*Katherine Walton; or, the Rebel of Dorchester: An Historical Romance of the Revolution in Carolina.* (1850-51) A shorter version was the first novel to appear serially in *Godey's Lady's Book* (February-December 1850), under the title "Katherine Walton; or, the Rebel's Daughter: A Tale of the Revolution." The initial book publication was by A. Hart in Philadelphia in 1851. The revised edition, entitled *Katherine Walton; or, The Rebel of Dorchester*, was included in the Redfield edition in 1854 and many times reprinted in that form. Although the work had been planned much earlier, the actual writing of this fourth novel of the Revolution apparently was not begun until the fall of 1849. Set in Charleston, the novel examines the social world there under British occupation and, because of this setting, has more unity of action and scene than other novels in the series. Simms called it the "most *symmetrical & truthful* of all my Revolutionary novels" (*Letters* 6: 120).

*The Sword and the Distaff; or, "Fair, Fat and Forty," A Story of the South, at the Close of the Revolution.* (1852) Charleston: Walker, Richards & Co. Retitled issue, entitled *Woodcraft; or, Hawks about the Dovecote: A Story of the South at the Close of the Revolution*, New York: Redfield, 1854. First published serially in semi-monthly supplements to the *Southern Literary Gazette* (February-November, 1852) and reprinted often from the Redfield edition, this fifth of the Revolutionary novels is set during the chaotic close and aftermath of the war, beginning with the British evacuation of Charleston in December 1782 and moving to Glen-Eberley plantation on the Ashepoo River south of the city, where the plantation community is striving to reestablish relative civil order and comity. Because the plates of the serialized version were used for the first Charleston printing of the book, that was called the second edition. Lippincott, Grambo of Philadelphia reissued the work from the same plates and with the same title in 1853. The Redfield edition was stereotyped by C. C. Savage of New York with modest emendations.

*The Forayers; or, The Raid of the Dog-Days.* (1855) New York: Redfield. This novel covers the British retreat from Ninety-Six and the lead up to the Battle of Eutaw Springs. Simms started the composition in November 1854, while finalizing the revisions for the Redfield edition of *Guy Rivers*. In February 1855, he claimed to be half finished. The novel appeared nine months later. In the interval, Simms staged his play *Michael Bonham*, gave an oration "On the Choice of a Profession" at the College of Charleston, revised *Border Beagles*, *Confession*, and *Beauchampe* for the Redfield edition of his selected works, and read proof on *Guy Rivers*. Like the other romances in the Redfield edition, *The Forayers* was reprinted many times.

*Eutaw: A Sequel to The Forayers, or the Dog-Days. A Tale of the Revolution.* (1856) New York: Redfield. This sequel completes the story of the British withdrawal from their outpost at Ninety-Six, including the Battle of Eutaw Springs, the last major engagement of the Carolina theatre, and that battle's aftermath. First reprinted by Redfield in 1858, the novel saw many subsequent reprintings.

*Joscelyn: A Tale of the Revolution.* (1867) Columbia, S. C.: University of South Carolina Press, 1975. First published serially in *The Old Guard* (January-December 1867), a copperhead (northern Democratic) journal. The serial publication stopped with several installments still to come. Consequently this last of the Revolutionary romances is not quite complete. Simms conceived the work as early as March 1858, when he was making plans to visit Augusta, Ga. to familiarize himself with the setting (*Letters* 4: 41, 72, 82). Afraid of how he would treat the tories in their history, the local media reacted negatively, and Simms determined not to return (83-4). Nevertheless, he intended to resume work on the book in 1860, before family issues, health, financial problems, and the secession crisis intervened. By October 1866 he had written 120 pages. The serialization of the work over the next year meant he was writing to deadline just ahead of the printers.

**Critical Reception and Subsequent Reappraisal**

The initial receptions of these eight novels reflected more than changing standards and tastes or the increase in sectional animosities. In the mid-1830s, when Simms began producing long fiction, the historical romance was a widely approved genre. By 1850, after Simms returned to romance writing, it was still popular among readers but becoming passé among the *literati*. In the English-speaking world Dickens was supplanting Scott as the dominant writer, while the novel was supplanting the romance, and literary realism was transforming Romanticism. Simms responded to these changes, incorporating social and then psychological realism in his fiction and appreciatively reading Dickens (Moltke-Hansen, "A Revolutionary Critic"). Nevertheless, his continued adherence to the romance form made him appear increasingly as a member of an older literary generation (Holman, *The Roots* 75-86; Wimsatt, *The Major Fiction* 8-9).

The diminishment of Simms's currency is shown by the fact that, after 1860, the only new works he published in book form were three collections that he edited: one of Confederate poetry, one of his friend James Henry Hammond's speeches and writings, and one an edition of the Revolutionary War letters of Col. John Laurens of South Carolina. He also produced a couple of pamphlets: an account of the *Sack and Destruction of the City of Columbia, S.C.*, in 1865, issued by his own press, and his final address, *The Sense of the Beautiful*, which was locally published as well. His last romances appeared just in periodicals despite his efforts to see them issued in book form. Neither did he have success with the ideas for other books that he floated to his publishers (Moltke-Hansen, "When History Failed" 14-19).

In effect, the Civil War ended Simms's career as an American author. The fact that the selected Redfield edition of his writings, including the first seven of his Revolutionary romances, continued to be reprinted emphasized all the more that Simms was an antebellum figure. He was regarded as a representative of the Old South, not the New. His world and slavery were in the past in the eyes of most postbellum publishers and readers. Yet, while true so far as it goes, this narrative is too simple.

After all, it was Simms's 1850 romance *Katherine Walton* that had the widest readership of all the works in the Revolutionary series. Furthermore, Simms always got mixed reviews even from his admirers, such as Edgar Allan Poe. Too, his sometime enemies, such as those in the *Knickerbocker* circle, did not review him in exclusively negative terms (Moltke-Hansen, Introduction, *Views and Reviews*). Indeed, the *Knickerbocker* praised *The Partisan* shortly after its 1835 publication, saying, "of all of the efforts of the author, we esteem this, in many respects, the best" (6 [Dec. 1835], 577). Yet it was just over a year later that Poe, in the *Southern Literary Messenger*, excoriated its "blunders," "bad taste," and "shockingly bad" English (2 [Jan. 1837], 117-21).

The next romance, *Mellichampe*, had the *Knickerbocker* thinking that Simms would "soon be at the front rank of American writers" (8 [Dec. 1836], 735-37). Upon publication of the third in the series, *The Kinsmen*, five years later, Poe concluded in *Graham's* that, "since the publication of the Pathfinder [by James

Fenimore Cooper], we have seen nothing equal to" this newest work by Simms (18 [Mar. 1841] 143). In the interval, however, Simms had a falling out with the editor of the *Knickerbocker*, and that journal was becoming increasingly — though not consistently — dismissive (Butterworth and Kibler 39-54). In turn, Simms was becoming more vociferous about nationalism in literature.

The dyspeptic conclusion of the *Knickerbocker* in 1842 was that Simms's nationalism was a "device to secure an extrinsic and undue consideration for flimsy novels" (20 [Aug. 1842]), 199-200). Yet Poe's judgment in the *Broadway Journal* three years later was that Simms was "the best novelist which this country has, upon the whole, produced" (2 [4 Oct. 1845], 190-91). As if this were not confusing enough, Charleston poet, editor, and young Simms protégé Paul Hamilton Hayne maintained, in his 1854 Charleston *Weekly News* reviews of the new Redfield edition of the early Revolutionary romances, first that *The Partisan* was "the nearest perfection," then, months later, that *Mellichampe* was (47 [4 Feb. 1854], 2; n. s. 4 [6 Apr. 1854], 2). Fifteen years after Simms's death, however, Hayne called *Eutaw* the best ("Antebellum Charleston" 257-68).

Also approving of *Eutaw*, *Godey's* nevertheless was rueful at the time of the romance's publication nearly thirty years before. This was because Simms's "commemoration of events" of the Revolution did not evoke "pleasant recollection" among the British (53 [July 1856], 84). His choice of subject did him honor, then, but hurt his trans-Atlantic sales and standing. Writing in 1856 as well, Simms's friend James Henry Hammond, U. S. Senator from South Carolina, went so far as to urge Simms to "cease to write novels." In his view his literary friend could not "better these last" — *The Forayers* and *Eutaw* (*Letters* 3: 425 n).

On balance, the later Revolutionary romances were esteemed more and read less than the first four. This was despite the perception of both contemporary critics and subsequent scholars that the 1850s saw Simms at the height of his power as a fictionist (Guilds, *Simms* 191-233). His youthful enthusiasm was tempered and to some extent disciplined by experience. Shaping his works as well, as David Newton observes, was the fact that by then "Simms had spent more than a decade [as an editor and contributor] on a succession of failed Southern literary journals." Consequently, he was deeply frustrated "over the lack of an intellectually engaged readership in the South" (Afterword 496-97). This led him, Newton argues, to focus in his later Revolutionary romances "on acts of reading — both literal and imaginative" (497).

By reading, Simms did not mean only the consumption of and response to literature or print. Woodcraft was a form of reading, and society and the political realm required reading every bit as much as the forest and books. Yet the need for and value of reading ran deeper. "The novels interrogate a culture," Newton continues, "where education possesses a marginal value at best, where economic, political, and material priorities overshadow the importance of a morally and spiritually informed imagination" (Afterword 497-98). That imagination was necessary for the creation of a country and advance of a people. "The reader's ability to recognize the signs and traces, both natural and human, thus become essential in making appropriate moral and imaginative judgments and in understanding the social and human complexities that are presented" (500). As the motto on the crest that Simms designed for himself read, *"video volans"* — I see soaring.

The revolution advocated in these later romances is much deeper, therefore, than the pursuit of independence by bold and desperate bands of partisans. It is the achievement of self-worth, cultural independence, and moral and spiritual progress. The fruits of the political and military revolution were the civilization that Simms was helping to create and the character and community that he was helping to inspire, shape, and preserve. The artist made fully meaningful the promise of America's founding. Nationalism was not just the formation and perpetuation of a polity, but the expression and the achievement of a rising people and culture. That is why Simms insisted on nationalism in literature. It also is why the suppression of his new nation through the Confederacy's defeat meant the necessary re-imagination of both self-worth and cultural independence — the work he sought to advance in the last of his Revolutionary romances, *Joscelyn*.

The generally high regard accorded the later Revolutionary romances at the time of their publication did not carry forward after the Civil War. To judge by the number of reprints of the Redfield edition, Simms's works continued to sell for almost half a century. Yet, enthralled by modernism, postbellum critics were increasingly derogatory of Simms's historical romances. An early case in point is Simms's first academic biographer, William Peterfield Trent. His 1892 assessment was that, in contrast to Edgar Allan Poe, whom he later championed, Simms was too enmeshed in his slave society and in the romance tradition to write successfully according to modernism's aesthetic criteria (Trent, *William Gilmore Simms*; Trent *et al.*, *Edgar Allan Poe*). Although in some respects admiring, Vernon Parrington later also judged Simms as "essentially a failed realist," at once constrained and compromised by his literary and social environment (Parrington 2: 119-30; Wimsatt, *The Major Fiction* 8).

It was not until after World War II that Hugh Holman suggested that Simms's literary substance might be "of minor importance in terms of [its] intrinsic value today" but "of major importance in terms of the degree to which [Simms] embodied the attitudes and formalized the assumptions of a region" (Holman, "Status" 181). Holman subsequently called attention to the ways that the first seven Revolutionary romances explored the civil war of the early

1780s. What fascinated him was how Simms portrayed the war as a class conflict. Of the 98 characters, 30 were upper class—seven of them tories. Of the 21 poor whites, 18 were tories. Of the 25 middle class representatives, seven also were. Of the dozen slaves, only one was (*The Roots* 35-47).

What Holman did not do in his essay, but others have done, is consider the impact of Simms's own times on his historical portrayals. It mattered that Simms was writing after the Palmetto State first was riven by the nullification controversy and then as it moved toward Civil War (Higham; Taylor; Wakelyn; Watson). While acknowledging the point, other scholars have contended that such readings have missed critical literary dimensions. After all, these later writers have insisted, Simms self-consciously used literary forms to literary ends. Moreover, his standing among his contemporaries put him at the forefront of American literature up through the so-called American renaissance of the early 1850s (Guilds, *Simms* 191-233; Wimsatt, *The Major Fiction* 156-210).

Yet the only work in the Revolutionary series to receive substantial literary analysis from these recent critics is *Woodcraft*. Generally it is read alone rather than in tandem with other romances. There are three principal exceptions. Some scholars compare or assume differences between northern and southern romances (Simpson; Nakamura; Taylor). Some look for themes uniting Simms's different romance series or consider tropes, such as that of the hero, common to Simms and other antebellum southern writers (Grammer; Kolodny; Kreyling, *Figures* 30-51; Nakamura). Finally, there are those who ask how the changing politics of Simms's day shaped his writing (Higham; Kreyling, *Inventing* 93-104; Taylor; Wakelyn; Watson).

Despite these inquiries, many aspects of Simms's Revolutionary series have not been substantially considered. No effort has gone into comparison of more recent Revolutionary series with it. No one has juxtaposed Simms's historical romances with those of nineteenth-century European romantic nationalists. Indeed, American critics who have treated Simms have shown little awareness, beyond Sir Walter Scott, of the trans-Atlantic national romantic tradition. Instead they have privileged a different romantic strain, embodied in the romantic genius at odds with or critical of society (Rubin). The one book-length study of Simms's historical thought focuses on the non-fiction (Busick). Shrewd and deeply learned readings of historicism and historical thought in antebellum southern culture do not dwell on the theoretical and practical concomitants of Simms's historicist preoccupations and pursuits (O'Brien 2:591-682; Fox-Genovese and Genovese 125-248).

The scholarly neglect is even greater for Simms's Revolutionary fictions than for his Border and Colonial romances. This is despite the relatively high regard given several of the Revolutionary works. One reason is that Simms's treatment of Native Americans has claimed much of the attention given to him since the 1835 publication of *The Yemassee*, the only one of his works always to have remained in print (Guilds and Hudson; Frye; Moltke-Hansen, Introduction, *The Yemassee*). The frontier themes, characters, language, and humor of the Border romances in turn fit into the study of the realism of Mark Twain and those in the southern and frontier humor tradition who influenced, or were influenced by, him (Parks; Wimsatt, "The Evolution"; Wimsatt, "Simms and Southwest Humor"). Too, these topics have shaped treatments of and courses in American exceptionalism, Manifest Destiny, and their literary refractions (Guilds and Collins).

Yet these same issues and elements occur in the Revolutionary romances. That fact, however, has not claimed attention except, in passing, from Mary Ann Wimsatt and John C. Guilds (Wimsatt, *The Major Fiction* 57-84, 156-95; Guilds, *Simms*). Rather than accept the point, Masahiro Nakamura argues that, on the one hand, the Revolutionary romances are about the construction of an ordered society, based on the plantation. On the other hand, the Border romances are about the challenge of the frontier and disorder to that society (*Visions of Order*). The counter argument is that Simms insistently explored the relationship of order to those conditions and developments that both threatened to undermine and made necessary social and cultural progress (Moltke-Hansen, "Ordered Progress").

**Future Study**

These debates may serve as background to the future study of the Revolutionary series. Yet those investigations will engage issues that earlier treatments did not: the relationship of colonialism to post-colonialism; the impact of the Revolution on gender, race, and class relations; the antebellum constructions and perceptions of these relationships and their rationales. Behind these sorts of questions are others about the purposes and original standing of such literature as Simms wrote and about the purposes of reading such works more than a century and a half after their production.

Holman did not emphasize part of the fascination of Simms's portrait of Revolutionary South Carolina society: that picture reveals a world dramatically at odds with the received view of the plantation South. Contrary to the stereotype, that world is not old, even though the environs of Charleston may be. Many of the characters there are recent arrivals rather than exemplars of ancient traditions. They also are multi-cultural. Class and other divisions fissure the society, as well as destabilize conventional understandings of it. Some elite men are afraid to lead or incapable of leadership. When failed by men, women sometimes take matters into their own hands. Greed is a prime motivator and especially destructive of poor whites. So is willful ignorance. The frontier is close at hand, as is violence. America's birth pangs are dreadful. And yet liberty is won, and social order in the end is advanced, if only provisionally.

How did these awarenesses frame the thinking, by Simms and others, of developments in their own day? How and why did these white southerners decide that America's fragility could become the South's strength? In the end, the Revolutionary romances are about much more than their subject matter or the series' place in either Simms's *oeuvre* or the (former) American canon. Read with Simms's 16-plus other long fictions, they reflect a more insistent and influential epic vision of the American South than that of any other author. None of the twentieth- and twenty-first-century Revolutionary War series, even those set in the South, has had a comparable impact, although many of these later titles have sold much more than any of Simms's ever did.

The epic vision and ambition that came to shape Simms's work had historical consequences. More than a century later, Faulkner implicitly critiqued it in his Yoknapatawpha series, turning his southern vision into an anti-epic. The writing of the historical Revolution as an epic conflict meant that Simms and many of his readers came to see war as an instrument of progress, at least up until the Civil War (Moltke-Hansen, "When History Failed" 5-10). Given Simms's complex understanding of the Revolution's divisions, course, and consequences, this was not simply the result of jingoistic pride. Compelling all the same, his epic reading and orientation made the Civil War in effect a reprise and a continuation of the Revolution (Watson, "Simms and the American Revolution").

This belief helped shape and color Simms's enthusiasm for secession and the conflict that followed. During that conflict he continued his research and writing on the Revolution, completing his drama on Benedict Arnold as a meditation on the requirements of citizenship and patriotism (Moltke-Hansen, "When History Failed" 10-14). This commitment to literature as a patriotic act and evocation had earlier, and has had later, American advocates. It fueled Confederate literature, as recent scholarship has shown (Bernath; Hutchison 18-98). It also was especially strong in parts of the Europe of Simms's day and later, a point that has long engaged students of nationalism (Moltke-Hansen, "Identity Politics").

In a post-modern and multi-cultural era, it is difficult to recover the intensity of the nationalist impulse in cultural production. Focusing on the epoch of America's political emergence, Simms's Revolutionary romances provide an opportunity to assess the impulse in his time and place. More, they invite consideration of the roles of history and art in framing identity. Because Simms privileged nationalism, he made it a political weapon. In his hierarchy of values, nationalism trumped racial, ethnic, and class interests that challenged its success. Simms confronted these conflicts by showing elements of them—for instance, the clashes between tories and patriots—while denying others—for instance, the African American impulse to freedom.

Simms used nationalism as well to perpetuate patriarchal authority and gendered roles, while critiquing those men who failed their responsibility in these roles (Simms, "Ellet's"). Treating history providentially, furthermore, he eventually made American liberty a basis to argue for southern independence. In doing so, he pointed to the path he believed the region's leaders should take in that pursuit. The complex negotiation of these multiple priorities and goals through his Revolutionary romances make those works rich sites for the recovery and critique of a long lost but once regnant artistic and political ambition. Simms did more to frame and to promote that ambition than did any other southern man of letters.

**Works Cited**

Ackerman, Zeno. *Messing with Romance: American Poetics and Antebellum Southern Fiction*. Frankfurt: Peter Lang, 2012.

Bakker, Jan. "Simms on the Literary Frontier; or, So Long Miss Ravenel and Hello Captain Porgy: *Woodcraft* Is the First 'Realistic' Novel in America." *William Gilmore Simms and the American Frontier*. Ed. John C. Guilds and Carolina Collins. Athens.: U of Georgia P, 1988. 64-78.

Bernath, Michael T. *Confederate Minds: The Struggle for Intellectual Independence in the Civil War South*. Chapel Hill: U of North Carolina P, 2010.

Brennan, Matthew C. *The Poet's Holy Craft: William Gilmore Simms and Romantic verse Traditions*. Columbia: U of South Carolina P, 2010.

Busick, Sean R. *A Sober Desire for History: William Gilmore Simms as Historian*. Columbia: U of South Carolina P, 2005.

Butterworth, Keen, and James E. Kibler. *William Gilmore Simms: A Reference Guide*. Boston: G. K. Hall & Co., 1980.

Dale, Corinne. "William Gilmore Simms's Porgy as a Domestic Hero," *Southern Literary Journal* 13.1 (1980): 55-71.

"Editor's Table." *Knickerbocker* 20 (Aug. 1842): 199-200.

Foley, Ehren. "Isaac Nimmons and the Burning of Woodlands: Power, Paternalism, and the Performance of Manhood in William Gilmore Simms's Civil War South." *William Gilmore Simms's Unfinished Civil War: Consequences for a Southern Man of Letters*. Ed. David Moltke-Hansen. Columbia: U of South Carolina P, 2013. 89-111.

Fox-Genovese, Elizabeth, and Eugene Genovese. *The Mind of the Master Class: History and Faith in the Southern Slaveholders' Worldview*. Cambridge and New York: Cambridge UP, 2005.

Frye, Steven. "Simms's *The Yemassee*, American Progressivism and the Dialogue of History." *Southern Quarterly* 35.3 (1997): 83-89.

Genovese, Eugene, and Elizabeth Fox-Genovese. *Fatal Self-Deception: Slaveholding Paternalism in the Old South*. Cambridge and New York: Cambridge UP, 2011.

Georgini, Sara. "The Angel and the Animal." *William Gilmore Simms's Unfinished Civil War: Consequences for a Southern Man of Letters*. Columbia: U of South Carolina P, 2013. 212-23.

Grammer, John M. *Pastoral and Politics in the Old South*. Baton Rouge: Louisiana State UP, 1996.

Greenspan, Ezra. "Evert Duyckinck and the History of Wiley and Putnam's Library of American Books, 1845-1847." *American Literature* 64.4 (1992): 677-93.

Guilds, John C. *Simms: A Literary Life*. Fayetteville: U of Arkansas P, 1992.

——— and Caroline Collins, eds. *William Gilmore Simms and the American Frontier*. Athens: U of Georgia P, 1997.

——— and Charles Hudson, eds. *An Early and Strong Sympathy: The Indian Writings of William Gilmore Simms*. Columbia: U of South Carolina P, 2003.

Hagstette, Todd. "Private vs. Public Honor in Wartime South Carolina: William Gilmore Simms in Lecture, Letter, and History." *William Gilmore Simms's Unfinished Civil War: Consequences for a Southern Man of Letters*. Ed. David Moltke-Hansen. Columbia: U of South Carolina P, 2013. 48-67.

———. "Screams from the South: The Southern Psycho-gothic Novels of William Gilmore Simms." MA thesis. College of Charleston, 1998.

Hayne, Paul Hamilton. "Ante-Bellum Charleston." *Southern Bivouac* 1 (Oct. 1885): 257-68.

———. Rev. of *Mellichampe*. By William Gilmore Simms. Charleston *Weekly News* n.s. 4 (6 Apr. 1854): 2.

———. Rev. of *The Partisan*. By William Gilmore Simms. Charleston *Weekly News* n.s. 3 (7 Jan. 1854): 2.

Higham, John. "The Changing Loyalties of William Gilmore Simms." *Journal of Southern History* 9.2 (1943): 210-23

Holman, C. Hugh. *The Roots of Southern Writing: Essays on the Literature of the American South*. Athens: U of Georgia P, 1972.

———. "The Status of Simms." *American Quarterly* 10 (Summer 1958): 181-85.

Holt, Keri. "Reading Regionalism across the War: Simms and the Literary Imagination of Post-Bellum Literary Magazines." *William Gilmore Simms's Unfinished Civil War: Consequences for a Southern Man of Letters*. Ed. David Moltke-Hansen. Columbia: U of South Carolina P, 2013. 159-82.

Hutchison, Coleman. *Apples & Ashes: Literature, Nationalism, and the Confederate States of America*. Athens: U of Georgia P, 2012.

Justus, James. *Fetching the Old Southwest: Humorous Writing from Longstreet to Twain*. Columbia: U of Missouri P, 2004.

Kaplan, Amy. *Social Construction of American Realism*. Chicago: U of Chicago P, 1988.

Kennedy, John Pendleton. *Horse Shoe Robinson; A Tale of the Tory Ascendency*. 2 vols. Philadelphia: Carey, Lea and Blanchard, 1835.

Kibler, James Everett. Introduction. *Woodcraft; or, Hawks about the Dovecote*. By William Gilmore Simms. Columbia: U of South Carolina P, 2012. xxiii-xxxvi.

———. *The Poetry of William Gilmore Simms: An Introduction and Bibliography*. Columbia: Southern Studies Program, 1979.

King, Vincent. "'Foolish Talk 'Bout Freedom': Simms's Vision of America in *The Yemassee*." *Studies in the Novel* 35.2 (2003): 139-48.

Kolodny, Annette. "The Unchanging Landscape: The Pastoral Impulse in Simms's Revolutionary Romances." *Southern Literary Journal* 5 (Fall 1972): 46-67.

Kreyling, Michael. *Figures of the Hero in Southern Narrative*. Baton Rouge: Louisiana State UP, 1987.

———. *Inventing Southern Literature*. Jackson: UP of Mississippi, 1998.

"Literary Notices." *Godey's* 53 (July 1856): 84.

Lukacs, Georg. *The Historical Novel*. Trans. Hannah Mitchell and Stanley Mitchell. London: Merlin P, 1962. Trans. of *Der historische Roman*, 1937.

Meriwether, Nicholas G. "An Unfinished Reconstruction: Simms's 'The Brothers of the Coast.'" *William Gilmore Simms's Unfinished Civil War: Consequences for a Southern Man of Letters*. Ed. David Moltke-Hansen. Columbia: U of South Carolina P, 2013. 185-201.

Miller, John D. "The Sense of Things to Come: Redefining Gender and Promoting the Lost Cause in *The Sense of the Beautiful*." *William Gilmore Simms's Unfinished Civil War: Consequences for a Southern Man of Letters*. Ed. David Moltke-Hansen. Columbia: U of South Carolina P, 2013. 224-38.

Miller, Perry. *The Raven and the Whale: The War of Words and Wits in the Era of Poe and Melville*. New York: Harcourt, Brace and Co., 1956.

Minguera, Corey Don. "'Cash Is Conqueror': The Critique of Capitalism in Simms's 'The Western Emigrants' and 'Sonnet—The Age of Gold.'" *Simms Review* 17.1-2 (2009): 87-96.

Moltke-Hansen, David. "A Critical Revolution and a Revolutionary Critic." *William Gilmore Simms's Selected Reviews on Literature and Civilization*. Ed. James Everett Kibler and David Moltke-Hansen. Columbia: U of South Carolina P, 2014: forthcoming.

———. "Identity Politics and the Civil War: The Transformation of South Carolina's Public History, 1862-2012." *Historically Speaking* 14.1 (2013): forthcoming.

———. Introduction. *Views and Reviews in American Literature, History and Fiction. First and Second Series*. By William Gilmore Simms. Columbia: U of South Carolina P, 2013. Forthcoming.

———. Introduction. *The Yemassee: A Romance of Carolina*. 1854. Columbia: U of South Carolina P, 2013.

———. "Ordered Progress: The Historical Philosophy of William Gilmore Simms." *"Long Years of Neglect": The Work and Reputation of William Gilmore Simms*. Ed. John Caldwell Guilds. Fayetteville: U of Arkansas P, 1988. 126-47.

———. "Southern Literary Horizons in Young America: Imaginative Development of a Regional Geography." *Studies in the Literary Imagination* 42.1 (2009): 1-31.

———. "When History Failed: William Gilmore Simms's Artistic Negotiation of the Civil War's Consequences." *William Gilmore Simms's Unfinished Civil War: Consequences for a Southern Man of Letters*. Columbia: U of South Carolina P, 2013. 3-31.

———. "Why History Mattered: The Background of Ann Pamela Cunningham's Interest in the Preservation of Mount Vernon," *Furman Studies* n. s. 26 (Dec. 1980): 34-42.

Nakamura, Masahiro. *Visions of Order in William Gilmore Simms: Southern Conservatism and the Other American Romance*. Columbia: U of South Carolina P, 2009.

Newton, David W. Afterword. *Eutaw: A Sequel to* The Forayers, or The Raid of the Dog Days. By William Gilmore Simms. Ed. David W. Newton. Fayetteville: U of Arkansas P, 2007. 495-511.

O'Brien, Michael. *Conjectures of Order: Intellectual Life and the American South, 1810-1860*. 2 vols. Chapel Hill: U North Carolina P, 2004.

Parks, Edd Winfield. "The Three Streams of Southern Humor." *Georgia Review* 9 (Summer 1955): 147-59.

Parrington, Vernon L. *Main Currents in American Thought*. 3 vols. New York: Harcourt, Brace and Co., 1927-30. [The chapter on Simms, "William Gilmore Simms: Charleston Romancer," appears in Vol. 2: 119-30.]

Pearce, Colin D. "All Aboard! 'The Philosophy of the Omnibus' and the Problem of Progress in William Gilmore Simms." *Simms Review* 18.1-2 (2010): 71-91.

Poe, Edgar Allan. Rev. of *The Kinsmen*. By William Gilmore Simms. *Graham's* 18 (Mar. 1841): 143

———. Rev. of *The Partisan*. By William Gilmore Simms. *Southern Literary Messenger* 2 (Jan. 1836): 117-21.

———. Rev. of *The Wigwam and the Cabin*. By William Gilmore Simms. *Broadway Journal* 2 (4 Oct. 1845): 190-91.

Rev. *Mellichampe*. By William Gilmore Simms. *Knickerbocker* 8 (Dec. 1836): 735-37.

Rev. *The Partisan*. By William Gilmore Simms. *Knickerbocker* 6 (Dec. 1835): 577.

Rubin, Louis D. *The Edge of the Swamp: A Study of Literature and Society of the Old South*. Baton Rouge: Louisiana State UP, 1989.

Shelton, Austin J. "African Realistic Commentary on Culture Hierarchy and Racistic Sentimentalism in *The Yemassee*." *Phylon* 25.1 (1964): 72-8.

Simms, William Gilmore. "The Civil Warfare in the Carolinas and Georgia, during the Revolution." *Southern Literary Messenger* 12.5-7 (1846): 257-65, 321-36, 385-400.

———. "Ellet's 'Women of the Revolution.'" In *William Gilmore Simms's Selected Reviews on Literature and Civilization*. Ed. James Everett Kibler and David Moltke-Hansen. Columbia: U of South Carolina P, 2014: forthcoming.

———. *Eutaw: A Sequel to* The Forayers, or The Raid of the Dog-Days. A Tale of the Revolution. 1856. Columbia: U of South Carolina P, 2013.

———. *The Forayers: or The Raid of the Dog-Days*, 1855. Columbia: U of South Carolina P, 2013.

———. *Joscelyn. A Tale of the Revolution*. Columbia: U of South Carolina P, 2013.

———. *Katherine Walton: or The Rebel of Dorchester*. Rev. ed. 1854. Columbia: U of South Carolina P, 2013.

———. *The Kinsmen: or The Black Riders of Congaree. A Tale.* 2 vols. Philadelphia: Lea and Blanchard, 1841.

———. *The Letters of William Gilmore Simms.* 6 vols. Ed. Mary C. Simms Oliphant *et al.* Columbia: U of South Carolina P, 1952-2012.

———. *Mellichampe. A Legend of the Santee.* 2 vols. New York: Harper & Brothers, 1836.

———. *Mellichampe: A Legend of the Santee.* Rev. ed. 1854. Columbia: U of South Carolina P, 2013.

———. *The Partisan: A Tale of the Revolution.* 2 vols. New York: Harper and Brothers, 1835.

———. *The Partisan: A Romance of the Revolution.* Rev. ed. 1854. Columbia: U of South Carolina P, 2013.

———. *The Scout: or The Black Riders of Congaree.* Rev. ed. of *The Kinsmen.* 1854. Columbia: U of South Carolina P, 2013.

———. *The Sense of the Beautiful. An Address.* Charleston: Charleston County Agricultural and Horticultural Association, 1870.

———. *Self-Development. An Oration Delivered before the Literary Societies of Oglethorpe University; Georgia; November 10, 1847.* Milledgeville.: Thalian Society, 1847.

———. *South-Carolina in the Revolutionary War: Being a Reply to Certain Misrepresentations and Mistakes of Recent Writers, in Relation to the Course and Conduct of This State.* Charleston: Walker and Evans, 1853.

———. "The Southern Convention." *William Gilmore Simms's Selected Reviews on Literature and Civilization.* Ed. James Everett Kibler and David Moltke-Hansen. Columbia: U of South Carolina P, 2014: forthcoming.

———. *The Sword and the Distaff; or, "Fair, Fat and Forty," A Story of the South at the Close of the Revolution.* Charleston: Walker, Richards, and Co., 1852.

———. *Views and Reviews in American Literature, History and Fiction. First and Second Series.* 1845 [1846-47]. Columbia: U of South Carolina P, 2013.

———. *Woodcraft: or, Hawks about the Dovecote. A Story of the South at the Close of the Revolution.* 1854. Columbia: U of South Carolina P, 2012.

———. *The Yemassee: A Romance of Carolina.* 2 vols. New York: Harper & Brothers, 1835.

Simpson, Lewis P. *The Dispossessed Garden: Pastoral and History in Southern Literature.* Athens.: U of Georgia P., 1975.

Smith, Steven D. "Imagining the Swamp Fox: William Gilmore Simms and the National Memory of Francis Marion." *William Gilmore Simms's Unfinished Civil War: Consequences for a Southern Man of Letters.* Ed. David Moltke-Hansen. Columbia: U of South Carolina P, 2013. 32-47.

Stafford, John. *The Literary Criticism of "Young America": A Study in the Relationship of Politics and Literature, 1837-1850.* Berkeley and Los Angeles: U of California P, 1952.

Taylor, William R. *Cavalier and Yankee: The Old South and American National Character.* Cambridge: Harvard UP, 1961.

Trent, William P. *William Gilmore Simms.* Boston: Houghton Mifflin, 1892.

Wakelyn, Jon L. *The Politics of a Literary Man: William Gilmore Simms.* Westport., CT: Greenwood P, 1973.

Watson, Charles S. *From Nationalism to Secessionism: The Changing Fiction of William Gilmore Simms.* Westport, CT: Greenwood P, 1993.

——. "Simms and the American Revolution." *Mississippi Quarterly* 29 (1976): 76-89.

——. "Simms's Answer to *Uncle Tom's Cabin*: Criticism of the South in *Woodcraft*." *Southern Literary Journal* 9.1 (1976): 78-90.

Widmer, Edward L. *Young America: The Flowering of Democracy in New York City.* New York: Oxford UP, 1999.

Wimsatt, Mary Ann. "The Evolution of Simms's Backwoods Humor." In *"Long Years of Neglect": The Work and Reputation of William Gilmore Simms.* Ed. John C. Guilds. Fayetteville: U of Arkansas P, 1988. 148-65.

——. *The Major Fiction of William Gilmore Simms.* Baton Rouge: Louisiana State UP, 1989.

——. "Realism and Romance in Simms's Midcentury Fiction." *Southern Literary Journal* 12.2 (1980): 29-48.

——. "Simms and Southwest Humor." *Studies in American Humor* 3 (Nov. 1979): 118-30.

# THE SCOUT

OR

## THE BLACK RIDERS OF CONGAREE

By W. GILMORE SIMMS, Esq.

AUTHOR OF "THE PARTISAN," "MELLICHAMPE," "KATHARINE WALTON,"
"WOODCRAFT," "THE YEMASSEE," "GUY RIVERS," ETC.

"Failing I know the penalty of failure
Is present infamy and death. . . . . . pause not;
I would have shown no mercy, and I seek none."
MARINO FALIERO.

NEW AND REVISED EDITION.

REDFIELD
110 AND 112 NASSAU STREET, NEW YORK.
1854.

TO

## COLONEL WILLIAM DRAYTON,

OF SOUTH CAROLINA,

I INSCRIBE THIS ROMANCE OF THE REVOLUTION IN OUR
NATIVE STATE.

THE AUTHOR.

# THE SCOUT.

## CHAPTER I.

HISTORICAL SUMMARY.—THE SWAMP RETREAT.

AT the period when our story opens, the colonies of North America united in resistance to the mother-country, had closed the fifth year of their war of independence. The scene of conflict was by this time almost wholly transferred from the northern to the southern colonies. The former were permitted to repose from the struggle; in their security almost ceasing to recognise the necessity of arms; while the latter, as if to compensate for their respite, in the beginning of the conflict, were subjected to the worst aspects and usages of war. The south, wholly abandoned to its fate by the colonies north of the Potomac, was unequal to the struggle single-handed. Their efforts at defence, however earnestly made, were for a time, apparently made in vain. Inexperienced in regular warfare, with officers as indiscreet and rash as brave, they were everywhere exposed to surprise and consequently to defeat. They lacked money, rather than men, experience and training, rather than courage, concentration and unity, rather than strength. The two frontier colonies, South Carolina and Georgia—most feeble and most exposed, as lying upon the borders of Florida, which adhered to the crown, and which had proved a realm of refuge to all the loyalists when driven out from the other colonies—were supposed by the British commanders to be entirely recovered to the sway of their master. They suffered, in consequence, the usual fortune of the vanquished. But the very suffering proved that they lived, and the struggle for freedom was continued. Her battles,

"Once begun,
Bequeathed from bleeding sire to son,
Though often lost,"

were never considered by her friends in Carolina to be utterly hopeless. Still, they had frequent reason to despair. Gates, the successful commander at Saratoga, upon whose great renown and feeble army the hopes of the south, for a season, appeared wholly to depend, had suffered a terrible defeat at Camden—his militia scattered to the four winds of Heaven—his regulars almost annihilated in a conflict with thrice their number, which, for fierce encounter and determined resolution, has never been surpassed; while he, himself, a fugitive, covered with shame and disappointment, vainly hung out his tattered banner in the wilds of North Carolina—a colony sunk into an apathy which as effectually paralysed her exertions, as did the presence of superior power paralyse those of her more suffering sisters. Conscious of indiscretion and a most fatal presumption —the punishment of which had been as sudden as it was severe —the defeated general suffered far less from apprehension of his foes, than of his country. He had madly risked her strength, at a perilous moment, in a pitched battle, for which he had made no preparation—in which he had shown neither resolution nor ability. The laurels of his old renown withered in an instant— his reputation was stained with doubt, if not with dishonor. He stood, anxious and desponding, awaiting, with whatever moral strength he could command, the summons to that tribunal of his peers, upon which depended all the remaining honors of his venerable head.

General Greene succeeded to the command of the miserable remnant of the southern army. Cool, prudent, and circumspect, rather than brilliant, as a soldier, this gentleman was, perhaps, one of the best that could be chosen for directing the efforts of a people whose impulses but too frequently impaired their conduct—who were too eager to be wary, and who suffered perpetually from the rash and headstrong courage of their native leaders and their own indifference to the usual duties which belong to a vigilant and cautious command. The enterprise which moved Greene to reconduct the continentals and the southern militia, back to South Carolina, then wholly in the possession of the British, has been described as singularly bold and audacious. But how he could have achieved the deliverance of the country, without pressing into it, we do not see. To enter the disputed province, to seek, find, and fight his enemy, was the very business for which he had been despatched, and the only question is as to the conduct which he should display, in contrast with that of Gates. His true merit lay in the prudence with which he prosecuted an enterprise, which the latter had sacrificed by conceit and improvidence. The genius of Greene was eminently cautious, and his progress in South Carolina was unmarked by any rashness of movement, or extravagance of design. He was very soon made conscious that, with the mere fragments of an army — and such an army! — naked men, undrilled militia, few in number, disheartened by defeat, unprovided with arms — he could hope for nothing but disaster, unless through the exercise of that ever-watchful thought, and rigorous prudence, by which, almost wholly, the great captain is distinguished. His wariness formed an essential part of his resolution, and quite as much as his valor, contributed to effect his object. If he did not always beat, he at length succeeded in finally baffling his opponents. He avoided the conflict which the more presumptuous Gates had too rashly invited. To baffle the invader, he well knew, was the best policy by which to conquer him. The fatigue of forced marches and frequent alarms to the soldier, in an unknown and hostile country, is more discouraging than the actual fight with a superior foe. Every hour of delay added to the army of Greene while it diminished that of the British. The militia recovered breath and courage, and once more rallied around the continental standard. Small but select bodies of troops came to her aid from the neighboring states. North Carolina began to arouse and shake herself free from her slumbers. Her yeomen began to feel the shame of previous flight and inaction. Virginia, though scarcely so active as her own safety and sense of duty should have made her, was not altogether indifferent to the earnest entreaties for assistance of the general of the south; and from Maryland and Delaware came a band, few but fearless, and surpassed by none of all the troops that were ever raised in America. The tried and tough natives of the mountains and the swamps emerged once more from their hiding-places under their ancient leaders; more resolute in the cause of liberty, and more vigorous in their labors for its attainment, from the shame and the sorrow which followed their previous and frequent disappointments.

The countenance of the British commander became troubled as he surveyed the gathering aspects of evil in that horizon, from which he fondly fancied that he had banished every cloud. His troops were summoned to arms and to renewed activity; and Greene was no longer in a condition to elude the arms of his adversary. Nor did he now so much desire it. The accessions of force which his army had received, and which drew upon him the regards of Lord Cornwallis, had necessarily encouraged the American general, and inspirited his purposes. His policy, though still properly cautious, lost something of its seeming timidity; and he boldly penetrated, in the face of the foe, into the state which he came to deliver. A series of small and indecisive, but brilliant adventures, which followed the dispersion of his light troops over the country, contributed equally to enliven the hopes of the commander and the courage of his men. The battle of King's Mountain had been fought by the brave mountaineers of Virginia, and the two Carolinas, in which the British force under Ferguson—their ablest partisan commander in the south—was utterly annihilated. Tarleton, hitherto invincible, was beaten by Morgan at the Cowpens, with a vastly inferior army; while Marion, smiting the tories, hip and thigh, in the swamps below, and Sumter, in a succession of brilliant and rapid actions, in the middle country, had paralyzed the activity and impaired seriously the strength of those smaller parties of the British, which were employed to overawe the inhabitants and secure the conquests which had been already made. In an inconceivably short space of time, the aspect of things in South Carolina underwent a change. The panic which followed the defeat of Gates, had worn off. Disaffection so effectually showed itself in every section of the state, that the British power was found active and operative only in those portions where they held strong garrisons. Greene, however, while these events were passing, was kept sufficiently employed by the able captains who opposed him. Brought to action at Guilford, he was forced, rather than beaten, from the field; and a few days enabled him to turn upon his pursuer, and to dog his flight from the state which he could not keep, to that in which he became a captive.

But, in leaving Carolina, Cornwallis left the interests of his master in the custody of no inferior representative. Lord Rawdon, afterward the earl of Moira, succeeded him in the command. He was unquestionably one of the ablest general officers of the British army; and through a protracted trial of strength with his opponent, he sustained the duties of his trust with equal skill, vigilance, and valor. The descent of Greene into South Carolina, brought him into that same neighborhood which had proved so fatal to Gates. His appearance was followed by the sharp action of Hobkirk's Hill, in which Rawdon displayed many of those essential qualities of conduct which entitle him to the name of an able soldier. The field remained with the British, but it yielded them none but barren fruits. It gave them the triumph, but not the success. The victory was only not with Greene. It must have been, but for a misapprehension of his orders, on the part of one of his best officers, having command of a favorite regiment.

Our story opens at this period. The battle of Hobkirk's Hill was productive of effects upon both of the contending parties, which brought about an equal crisis in their fortunes. The losses of the two armies on that occasion, were nearly the same. But, in the case of Rawdon, the country offered but few resources against any external pressure; and immediate and utter ruin must have followed his defeat. He had exhausted the means, ravaged the fields, trampled upon the feelings, and mocked the entreaties of the surrounding inhabitants. Despair had taught them a spirit of defiance, and the appearance of an American army which was able to maintain its ground even after defeat, encouraged them to give to that feeling its proper utterance.

Conwallis had long before complained to the British ministry that he was "surrounded by timid friends and inveterate foes;" and the diminution of British strength and courage, which necessarily followed the flight of that commander into Virginia, together with the defeats sustained at Cowpens and King's Mountain, naturally enough increased the timidity of the one, and the inveteracy of the other party. That atrocious and reckless warfare between the whigs and tories, which had deluged the fair plains of Carolina with native blood, was now at its height. The parties, in the language of General Greene, pursued each other like wild beasts. Pity seemed utterly banished from their bosoms. Neither sex nor age was secure. Murder lurked upon the threshold, and conflagration lighted up, with the blazing fires of ruin, the still, dark hours of midnight. The reckless brutality of the invader furnished a sufficient example and provocation to these atrocities; and the experience of ages has shown that hate never yet takes a form so hellish, as when it displays itself in the strifes of kindred.

It does not need that we should inquire, at this late day, what were the causes that led to this division among a people, in that hour so unseasonably chosen for civil strife—the hour of foreign invasion. It is sufficient for our present purpose that the fact, however lamentable, is equally unquestionable and well known. Our narrative seeks to illustrate some of the events which grew out of, and characterized, this warfare. We shall be compelled to display, along with its virtues of courage, patriotism, and endurance, some of its crimes and horrors! Yet vainly, as unwisely, would we desire to depict, in human language, its measureless atrocities. The heart would sicken, the mind revolt with loathing, at those hideous details, in which the actors seem to have studiously set themselves free from all the restraints of humanity. To burn and slay were not the simple performances of this reckless period and ravaged country. To burn in wantonness, and to murder in cold blood, and by the cruellest tortures, were the familiar achievements of the time;—and the criminal was too frequently found to exult over his evil deeds, with the sanguinary enthusiasm of the Mohawk warrior, even though the avenging retribution stood beside him with warning finger and uplifted knife. The face of the country was overrun by outlaws. Detached bands of ruffians, formed upon the frontiers of Georgia, and in the wilds of Florida—refugees from all the colonies—availed themselves of the absence of civil authority, to effect a lodgment in the swamps, the forests, and the mountains. These, mounted on fleet horses, traversed the state with the wind; now here, now there; one moment operating on the Savannah, the next on the Peedee; sometimes descending within sight of the smokes of the metropolis; and anon, building their own fires on the lofty summits of the Apalachian ridge.

Harassed by the predatory inroads of these outlawed squadrons, stung by their insults, and maddened by their enormities, the more civil and suffering inhabitants gathered in little bands for their overthrow; and South Carolina, at the period of our narrative, presented the terrible spectacle of an entire people in arms, and hourly engaging in the most sanguinary conflicts. The district of country called "Ninety-Six," in the neighborhood of which our story will partly lie, is estimated to have had within its borders, at the close of the Revolution, no less than fifteen hundred widows and orphans, made so during its progress. Despair seems to have blinded the one party as effectually to the atrocity of their deeds, as that drunkenness of heart, which follows upon long-continued success, had made insensible the other;—and as that hour is said to be the darkest which more immediately precedes the dawn, so was that the bloodiest in the fortunes of Carolina which ushered in the bright day of her deliverance. We now proceed with our narrative.

The dusky shadows of evening were approaching fast. Clouds, black with storm, that threatened momently to discharge their torrents, depended gloomily above the bosom of the Wateree. A deathlike stillness overhung the scene. The very breezes that had swayed the tops of the tall cypresses, and sported capriciously with the purple berries of the green vines that decorated them, had at length folded themselves up to slumber on the dark surface of the sluggish swamps below. No voice of bird or beast, no word of man, denoted, in that ghost-like region, the presence of any form of life. Nothing in its aspects, certainly, could persuade the casual wayfarer to suspect that a single human heart beat within those wild and dark recesses. Gloomy, and dense, and dim, at all seasons, the very tribute of the spring in this—the generous gifts of flowers and fruitage—only served to increase the depth of its shadow in the rank exuberance of its vegetable life. The vines, and shrubs, and briers, massed themselves together in an almost solid wall upon its edge, and forbade to penetrate; and even where, through temporary vistas, the eye obtained a passage beyond this formidable barrier, the dismal lakes which it encountered—still and black—filled with the decayed trunks of past centuries, and surmounted by towering ranks of trees yet in the vigor of their growth, defied the examination of the curious, and seemed to rebuke, with frowning and threatening shadows, even the presumption of a search.

But, in the perilous times of our history, these seeming discouragements served the kindly purposes of security and shelter. The swamps of Carolina furnished a place of refuge to the patriot and fugitive, when the dwelling and the temple yielded none. The more dense the wall of briers upon the edge of the swamp, the more dismal the avenues within, the more acceptable to those who, preferring Liberty over all things, could there build her altars and tend her sacred fires, without being betrayed by their smokes. The scene to which our eyes have been addressed, still and deathlike as it appears, is full of life—of hearts that beat with hope, and spirits that burn with animation; and sudden, even as we gaze, the sluggish waters of the lake are rippling into tiny waves that betray the onward motion of some unwonted burden. In the moment of its deepest silence, a rustling is heard among the green vines and crowding foliage. A gentle strife takes place between the broken waters and the rude trunks of the cypresses; and the prow of an Indian canoe shoots suddenly through the tangled masses, and approaches the silent shore. There is no word—no voice. A single person stands upright in the centre of the little vessel and guides it in its forward progress through the still lagune. Yet no dip of oar, no stroke of paddle betrays his efforts, and impairs the solemn silence of the scene. His canoe speeds along as noiselessly and with as little effort, as did that fairy bark of Phædria sung by Spenser, which carried Sir Guyon over the Idle lake to the Enchanted island: —

> "Withouten oare or pilot it to guide,
> Or winged canvass with the wind to fly."

The navigator of our little canoe is indebted for her progress to no magical "pin," such as impelled the vessel of Phædria and obeyed the least touch of that laughing enchantress. Still, the instrument which he employed, if less magical in its origin, was quite as simple in its use. It called for almost as little exertion of his arm. His wand of power was an ordinary cane, nearly twenty feet in length, the vigorous growth of the swamp around him, to the slender extremity of which, a hook, or finger, was fastened, formed out of the forked branches of some stubborn hickory; one prong being tightly bound to the reed, by deer-sinews, while the other was left free, to take hold of the overhanging limbs of trees, or the waving folds of wandering vines or shrubs, impelling the bark forward in any direction, according to the will of the navigator. It was thus that our new acquaintance brought his "dugout" forward to the shore from the secret recesses of the Wateree swamp. Its yellow waters parted, without a murmur, before his prow, at the slightest touch of this simple agent; and the obedient fabric which it impelled with a corresponding flexibility, yielding itself readily, shot from side to side, through the sinuous avenues of the swamp, as if endued with a consciousness and impulse of its own; pressing along in silence and in shadow; now darting freely forward where the stream widened into little lakelets; now buried in masses of the thicket, so dense and low, that the steersman was compelled to sink upon his knees in order to pass beneath the green umbrageous arches.

In such a progress the scene was not without its romance. Picturesque as was this mode of journeying, it had its concomitants by which it was rendered yet more so. The instrument which impelled the vessel, drew down to the hand of the steersman the massy vines of the thousand varieties of wild grape with which the middle country of Carolina is literally covered.

These fling themselves with the wind in which they swing and sport, arching themselves from tree to tree, and interlacing their green tresses until the earth below becomes a stranger to the sun. Their blue clusters droop to the hand, and hang around the brows of the fainting and feeble partisan, returning from the conflict. He forgets the cruelties of his fellow man, in solacing himself with the grateful tributes which are yielded him by the bounteous nature. Their fruits relieve his hunger and quench his thirst—their green leaves refresh his eye—their shadows protect him from the burning sunbeams, and conceal him from the pursuit of the foe.

Dark, wild, and unlovely as the entrance of the swamp might seem, still, to the musing heart and contemplative spirit it had its aspects of beauty, if not of brightness; and, regarded through the moral medium as a place of refuge to the virtuous and the good, when lovelier spots afforded none, it rises at once before the mind, into an object of sacred and serene delight. Its mysterious outlets, its Druid-like nooks, its little islands of repose, its solemn groves, and their adorning parasites, which clamber up and cling to its slender columns a hundred feet in air, flinging abroad their tendrils, laden with flaunting blossoms and purple berries—all combined to present a picture of strange but harmonious combination, to which the youthful steersman who guides our little bark is evidently not insensible. He pauses at moments in favorite spots, and his large blue eye seems to dilate as, looking upward, he catches some bright, but far and foreign glimpses of the heavens, through the ragged openings in the umbrageous forest. While he thus gazes upward, seemingly forgetful of the present in the remote, we may observe him at our leisure.

His was a countenance to invite and reward examination. Were the features of the face sure indices always of the individual character—which we do not believe—those of the person now before us would not misbeseem those of a great landscape painter. Could we suppose that the season and region of which we write were favorable to such employments, we might well suspect him of being a travelling artist. The calm, yet deep contemplative eye; the upward, outward look; the wandering mood; the air of revery; the delicate mouth; the arching brow;—these, and other characteristics which are indefinable, would seem to indicate in the proprietor a large taste for the picturesque. Yet was there a something still about the stranger that declared, quite as strongly, for a stern decision of temper, a direct aim, an energetic will, and a prompt and rapid execution of his purposes. It would not, indeed, be altogether safe to say, that, when he paused in his progress through the swamp, it was not because of some more serious purpose than belonged to a desire to contemplate the picturesque in its aspects. A just caution, the result of that severe experience which the Carolinians had suffered in the beginning of their conflict with the mother-country, may have prompted him to wait, and watch, and listen, long before he approached the land. His movements were all marked by the vigilance of one who was fully conscious of the near neighborhood of danger. Before his vessel could emerge from the covert, and when a single moment would have thrust her against the shore, he grasped with his hook a swinging vine which he had already left behind him, and arrested her motion. His boat swung lightly upon her centre, and remained stationary for a brief instant, while, drawing from his vest a small whistle, made of the common reed, he uttered a clear, merry note, which went, waking up a hundred echoes, through the still recesses of the swamp. His whistle, thrice repeated, brought him as many faint responses from the foot of the hills to which he was approaching. As if assured by these replies, our steersman threw up his cane once more, grappled with a bough beyond him, gave a single pull, and the bark shot forward. A mass of vines and overhanging branches, almost reaching to the water, lay between him and the spot of shore to which his prow was directed. As he neared this barrier, he threw himself flat in his boat, and she passed under it like an arrow, rushing up, in the next moment, upon the gravelly shore. He leaped instantly upon the bank, drew the canoe forward to the shelter of a clump of bushes growing down to the water, and fastened her securely, and out of sight. Another whistle from the wooded hills above now seemed to indicate the route which he should take; and, promptly following where it led, he was soon joined by one who appeared to have been calmly expecting his appearance. A description of the two thus meeting, with such a clew to their objects as may seem proper to be given at this early period in our progress, may well be reserved for another chapter.

## CHAPTER II.

### THE FRIENDS—A CONFERENCE.

THE stranger, as he leaped upon the solid earth, appeared of a noble and commanding presence. In shape he was symmetrically and vigorously made. Tall, erect, and muscular, his person was that of one who had been long accustomed to hardy and active exercises. In his movements there was a confident ease—the result equally of a fearless spirit and a noble form—which tallied well with a certain military exactness of carriage; commending his well-finished limbs to the eye, while conveying to the mind of the observer an impression, not less favorable, of the noble and firm character of their proprietor. Nor were the features of his countenance wanting in anything which was needful to support this impression. His face was full, but not fleshy; the skin of a clear red and white, which the summer sun had simply darkened into manliness. His eye, of a lively and intelligent blue, might have denoted a rather preponderating playfulness of temper, but for the sterner expression of his mouth, the lines of which were more angular than round, the lips being too thin for softness, and, when compressed, indicating a severe directness of purpose, which the gentler expression of his other features failed entirely to qualify. He had a lofty forehead, broad, intellectual and contemplative. His hair, which was of a dark brown, was long, and, like his beard, had been suffered to remain untrimmed, possibly as much in compliance with the laws of necessity as of taste. We have already intimated that the stranger was youthful. He had probably beheld some twenty-five or thirty summers, though it may be that premature toils and trials had anticipated the work of time, and made him seem somewhat older than he really was. He had, in the *tout ensemble* of his face, the appearance of one who had just arrived at the equal maturity of mind and body.

His dress was simple, and characterized by as little pretension as could possibly be found in one who was not only young, but evidently in the military. In its material and make it corresponded with that of the ordinary woodmen of the country. His pantaloons consisted of a dark blue homespun, the legs being wrapped in leggings of a somewhat coarser texture and darker hue. From these the original dye had been obliterated in blotches, here and there; or so obscured by stains from the yellow waters of the swamp, with which the wearer had been so recently familiar, that it would require a very discriminating eye to determine at a glance of what color they originally were. A hunting-shirt of a deeper blue than that of his under clothes, and perhaps of better material, which reached midway between his hips and knees, completed the essential parts of his costume. This portion of the dress was evidently made with some regard to the shape, and, possibly, the tastes of the wearer; a matter not so certainly clear in the case of the pantaloons. It fitted closely, without a wrinkle, and displayed the symmetry and muscle of his form to the greatest possible advantage. It had been ornamented, it would seem, in better days, with a deep fringe of a color somewhat more showy than that of the garment; but of this only a few occasional traces now remained, to testify, much more effectually, to the trials through which it had passed, than its own former brightness and integrity. The little cape which surmounted the coat, and fell back upon the shoulders, had fared rather more fortunately than the rest of the garment, and formed no unseemly finish to the general fitness of the costume; particularly as the wearer, with a better taste than prevailed then, or has prevailed since, had freed his neck from all the buckram restraints of gorget, cravat, or stock —bandages which fetter the movements of the head, without increasing its dignity or comfort. Enough of the broad sunburned bosom was revealed by the open shirt in front, to display that classic superiority of air of which modern fashions almost wholly deprive the noblest aspect. Upon his head, without shading his brow, rested a cap of otter-skin, rude and ample in its make, the work, most probably, of some favorite slave. A small yellow crescent, serving the purpose of a button, looped up one of the sides in the centre, and might, on occasion, have sustained a feather. Plain moccasins of buckskin, the original yellow of which had been entirely lost in the more doubtful colors acquired in the swamp, completed the externals of his dress. It may be added that he wore no visible armor; but once, as he stooped to fasten his skiff beside the shore, the butt of a heavy pistol might have been seen protruding from beneath the thick folds of his hunting-shirt. From the unnatural fullness of the opposite breast, it would not be rash to conjecture that this weapon of war was not without its fellow.

The stranger ascended from the banks and made his way toward the foot of the heights, that, skirting the northern edges of the Wateree, conduct the eye of the spectator to the lofty summits of the Santee hills beyond. Here he was joined by the person, whose answering signal he had heard, and, who had evidently been for some time expecting him. This was a man of middle size, stout, well-made, coarse in feature, strong of limb, active of movement, apparently without the refining influences of society and education, and evidently from the lower orders of the people. Let not this phrase, however, be understood to signify anything base or unbecoming. Though a poor man, or new acquaintance was not the work of one of nature's journeymen, fashioned when the "master hand" was weary. With head and feet equally bare, he carried the one with a virtuous erectness that could not be well misunderstood; while the other were set down with the freedom and fearlessness of a man conscious that he walked the soil of his native land in the full performance of the equal duties of the patriot and warrior. In this hand he grasped a rifle of immoderate length, the fractured stock of which, lashed together with buckskin thongs, bore tokens of hard usage in more respects than one.

The unquestionable poverty of this man's condition—which, indeed, was that of the whole American army—did not seem to have any effect upon his deportment or to give him any uneasiness. He seemed not to know that his garments suffered from any peculiar deficiencies; and never did the language of a light heart declare itself with so little reservation from a blue eye and a good-natured physiognomy. The slight cloud of anxiety which hung at moments above his brow, and which gathered there in consequence of cares of no ordinary kind, could not long, at any time, withstand the buoyant action of the cheerful spirit within. This constantly shone out from his face, and spoke aloud in the clear, ringing tones of his manly and not unmusical accents. Drawing nigh to our first acquaintance, he grasped his hand with the joyous look in a warm manner of one who felt, in the meeting with his comrade, something of a sentiment far stronger than that which governs the ordinary friendships among men. Nor was the manner of his comrade less decided, though, perhaps, more quiet and subdued. The behavior of the twain was that of an intimacy unbroken from boyhood, and made mutually confident by the exercise of trusts which had been kept equally sacred by both the parties.

"Well, Clarence, I'am glad you've come. I've been waiting for you a'most two hours. And how goes it in the swamp—and did you git the letters?"

"I did: all's well with us—pretty much as when you left. But how with you, Jack? What news do you bring? Is the coast clear—have the light troops gone in?"

"Well, I reckon I may say yes. Greene's drawed off from Camden sence the brush at Hobkirk's, and there's no telling jest now which way he's going. As for Marion, you know its never easy to say where to look for him. Lee's gone down on the s'arch somewhere below, and we're all to be up and busy at short notice. I hear tell of great things to do. Our gin'ral, Sumter, is in motion, and picking up stragglers along the Catawba. I reckon he'll soon be down, and then gallop's the word. Something too I hear of Colonel Tom Taylor at Granby, and—"

"Enough, enough, Jack; but you say nothing of Butler and his men? Are they out of the way—are they off? If you know nothing about him—"

"Well, I reckon they're at Granby by this time. They've

given up the hunt as a bad job. I saw Joe Clinch, one of his troop, only two days ago, and gin him a sort of hint that the chap they were after was more like to be found above the Congaree than in these parts. 'For what's to save him,' I said to Joe, 'down here in this neighborhood, where we're all true blue, and he a firehot tory?' That was a good reason for Clinch and all his troop, I reckon. They tuk it for one, and by peep of dawn, they were streaking it along the river road. They've got to 'Ninety-Six,' by this time, and even if they ha'n't, it's all the same to us. They're out of your way."

"But you did wrong, John Bannister, in saying that Edward Conway was a tory. He himself denies it."

"Well, Clarence, that's true, but I don't see that his denying it makes much difference. It's natural enough that a man should say he's no tory when he's in a whig camp. The vartue of a whole skin depends upon it. There's a chance of broken bones if he says otherwise, which Ned Conway ain't a going to resk."

"At least, for my sake, John Bannister, give Edward Conway the benefit of your doubts," replied the other, with an expression of grave displeasure on his countenance. "We do not know that he is a tory, and the best of men have been the victims of unjust suspicion. I must repeat that you did wrong, if you loved me, in calling him by such a name."

"Ah, Clarence, he's your hafe-brother, and that's the reason you ain't willing to believe anything agin him; but I'm dub'ous I said nothing worse than the truth when I told Clinch he was a tory. I'm sure the proofs agin him would have hung up many a tall chap like himself."

"No more, Jack Bannister—no more," said the other, gloomily. "It is enough that he is my brother. I am not willing to examine his demerits. I know, and acknowledge to you, that many things in his conduct look suspicious; still I prefer to believe his word—his solemn oath—against all idle reports—reports, which are half the time slanders, and which have destroyed, I verily believe, many lives and characters as worthy as our own. You know that I have no reason to love Edward Conway. We have never been friends, and I have no partialities in his favor. Still, he is the son of my father, and I am bound to defend him while I remain unconvinced of his treachery. I am only afraid that I am too willing to believe what is said in his prejudice. But this I will not believe so long as I can help it. He solemnly assures me he has never joined the tories. He would scarcely swear to a falsehood."

"Well, that's the same question, Clarence, only in another language. The man that would act a lie, wouldn't stop very long to swear to one. Now, if Edward Conway didn't jine the tories, who did he jine? He didn't jine us, did he? Did he swear to that, Clarence?"

"No! no! Would to God he could!"

"Well, then, what is it that he does say? I'm a-thinking that it's good doctrine to believe, in times like these, that the man that ain't with us is agin us. Let him show what he did with himself sence the fall of Charleston. He warn't there. You don't see his name on the list of prisoners—you don't hear of his parole, and you know he's never been exchanged. It mought be that he went in the British regiments to the West Indies, where they carried a smart chance of our people, that wouldn't ha' got any worse character by taking to the swamps as we did. Does he say that he went there?"

"He does not—he declines giving any account of himself; but still denies, most solemnly, that he ever joined the tories."

"I'm mightly afeard, Clarence—now, don't be angry at what I'm a-going to say—but I'm mightly afeard Edward Conway ain't telling you the truth. I wouldn't let him go free—I'd hold him as a sort of prisoner and keep watch upon him. You've saved him when he didn't desarve to be saved by anybody, and least of all by you;—and you have a sort of nateral right to do with him jest as you think proper and reasonable. I'm for your keeping him, like any other prisoner, and counting him in at the next exchange. He'll go for somebody that'll pull trigger for his country."

"Impossible! How can you give me such counsel? No, no, Jack, let him be all that you think him, the tory and the traitor, still he comes from my father's loins, and though another mother gave us suck, yet I feel that I should defend him as a brother, though he may not be altogether one. He shall suffer no harm at hands of mine."

"Well, I'm sure I don't say he ought. To keep him under a strong thumb and forefinger—to keep him, as I may say, out of mischief and out of danger till the time of exchange comes round, won't be to do him any harm. It's only one way of feeding a mouth that, mought be, couldn't feed itself so well in these tough times; and taking a little Jamaica from other mouths that mought like it jest as well, and desarve it a great deal better."

"What, Jack, do you begrudge Edward Conway the pitiful fare which we can give him in the swamp? You are strangely altered, Jack, toward him. You were once his playmate in boyhood as well as mine."

"Yes, Clarence, and 'twas then, so far back as them same days of our boyhood—and they were mighty sweet days, too, I tell you—that I found him out, and l'arned to mistrust him. God knows, Clarence, and you ought to know too, that Jack Bannister would like, if he could, all the flesh and blood in this world that was ever a kin to your'n. I tried mighty hard to love Ned Conway as I loved you, but it was like fighting agin natur'. I tried my best, but couldn't make it out with all my trying; and when I caught him in that business of the dock-tailed horse—"

"Do not remind me of these matters, now, Jack; I'm afraid I remember them too well already."

"You're only too good for him, Clarence. I somehow almost think he ain't naterally even a half-brother of your'n any how. You don't look like him; neither eye, nor mouth, nor nose, nor chin, nor hair, nor forehead—all's different as ef you ha'd come from any two families that lived at opposite eends of the river, and never seed one another. But, as you say, I won't 'mind you of any matters that you don't want to hear about. Them days is over with me, and with him; and so I'll shut up on that subject. As for begrudging him the bread and bacon, and the drop of Jamaica, sich as we git in the swamp yonder—well, I won't say nothing, because, you see, I can't somehow think you meant to say what you did. All that I do say, Clarence, is, that I wish I had enough to give him that would persuade him to show clean hands to his friends and blood-kin, and come out for his country, like every man that has a man's love for the airth that raised him."

"I know you mean him no wrong, Jack, and me no pain, when you advise me thus; but my word is pledged to Edward Conway, and I will keep it, though I perish."

"And don't I tell you to keep it, Clarence? You promised to save him from Butler's men, that was a-hunting him; and what better way than to keep him close from sight; for, if he once gits a-going agin, and they find his tracks, it won't be your boldness or my quickness that'll git him into the swamp so easily. If Butler's men hadn't been up-countrymen, that didn't onderstand swamp edication, no how, he wouldn't have had such a quiet time of it where we put him. Well, you've done what you promised, and what, I reckon, every man was bound to do by his blood-kin. You've saved him from his inemies; but there's no need you should give him your best nag that he may gallop full-speed into their pastures. Now, that's what you're a-thinking to do. And why should you? If he ain't a tory, and hasn't been one, why shouldn't he be a whig? Why shouldn't he do what he ought to ha' done five years ago—jine Sumter's men, or Marion's men, or Pickins' men, or any men that's up for the country—and run his bullets with a tory's name to each? I don't think Ned Conway a coward, no how, and when he won't come out for his country, at a pushing time like this, I can't help considering him a mighty suspicious friend."

"Enough, Jack; the more you speak, and I think, of this matter, the more unhappy it makes me," replied the other. "If I dared to think, I should probably come to more serious conclusions than yourself on the subject of my brother's conduct; which, I confess is altogether inscrutable. I have only one course before me, and that is to set him free, even as he desires, and let him choose his own route hence forward. I have not spared argument to persuade him to our ranks, and he holds out some hopes to me, that when he has finished certain private business he will do so."

"Private business! Lord ha' mercy upon us! How can a

body talk of private business, when throat-cutting is so public? —When there's a sort of Injin bounty for sculps, and it takes more than a man's two hands to keep his own skin and teeth from going off, where they are worth their weight in gold? Private business! Look you, Clarence, did you think to ask him when he had last seen Miss Flora Middleton?

"No, I did not," returned the other, abruptly, and with some impatience in his manner. "Why should I ask him that? I had no reason to suppose that he had any particular reason for seeing her at this, or at any other time."

"Now, Clarence, you needn't be telling me that, when I know so much better. I know that if he hasn't a reason for seeing her, he's always had a mighty strong wish that way; and as for your own feelin's, Lord bless you, Clarence, it's no fault of your'n, if every second man in the regiment don't know the soft place in the colonel's heart by this time, and can't put his finger on it whenever he pleases. If you love Flora Middleton there's no harm in it; and if Edward Conway loves her too—"

He paused, and looked at his companion with the air of one who is doubtful of the effect of that which he has already said.

"Well! What then?" demanded the other.

"Why, only, there's no harm, perhaps, in that either."

"Ay, but there is, John Bannister, and you know it;" cried the other, almost fiercely. "Edward Conway knew that I loved Flora Middleton long before he had ever seen her."

"Very true; but that's no good reason why he shouldn't love her when he did see her, Clarence."

"But it is good reason why he should not seek her with his love."

"I reckon, Clarence, he don't much stand upon such a reason. There's nothing brotherly in love matters, Clarence; and even if there was, Ned Conway is about the last person to make much count of it."

"He does—he shall! Nay, on this point I have his assurance. He tells me that he has not sought her—he has not seen her for months."

"And did Edward Conway really tell you so, Clarence?"

"He did—it was almost his last assurance when I left him."

"Then he told you a most despisable and abominable lie. He has seen her within the last three weeks."

"Ha! how know you?"

"From little Joe, the blacksmith, that was down by Watson's before it was taken from the British. Little Joe went with him to Brier Park, and saw him and Miss Flora in the piazza together."

The young man clutched the butt of the pistol in his bosom with a convulsive grasp, but soon relaxed it. He struck his forehead, the next moment, with his open palm, then strode away from his companion, as if to conceal the emotion which he could not so easily overcome.

"Well," he exclaimed, returning, "I had a strange fear—I know not why—that there was something insincere in his assurance. He made it voluntarily—we had not named her—and even as he spoke, there was a something in his face which troubled me, and made me doubtful of his truth. But he will go too far—he will try the force of blood beyond its patience."

"There's nothing, Clarence, in the shape of licking that sich a person don't desarve. I followed out more of his crooks than one, years ago, when there was no war; and he had all the tricks of a tory even then."

"That he should basely lie to me, and at such a moment! When I had risked life to save him!—When!—but let me not grow foolish. Enough, that I know him and suspect him. He shall find that I know him. He shall see that he can not again cheat me with loving language and a Judas kiss."

"Ah, Clarence, but you can cheat yourself. He knows how quick you are to believe; and when he puts on them sweet looks, and talks so many smooth words, and makes b'lieve he's all humility, and how sorry he is for what he's done, and how willing he is to do better—and all he wants is a little time—as if ever a man wanted time to get honest in! Look you, Clarence, you're my colonel, and what's more, I'm your friend—you know I love you, Clarence, better than one man ever loved another, and jest as well as Jonathan ever loved David, as we read in the good book; but, with all my love for you, Clarence, d—n my splinters, if you let Ned Conway cheat you any longer with his sweet words and sugar promises, I'll cut loose from you with a jerk that'll tear every j'int out of the socket. I won't be the friend of no man that lets himself be cheated. As for hating Ned Conway, as you sometimes say I do, there, I say, you're clean mistaken. I don't hate him—I mistrust him. I've tried mighty hard to love him, but he wouldn't let me. You know how much I've done to save him from Butler's men; but I saved him on your account, not because I think he desarves to be saved. I'm dub'ous that he is a tory, and a rank tory too, if the truth was known, jest as they charge it upon him. I'm dub'ous he'll jine the British as soon as he can git a chance; and I'm more than dub'ous, that, if you don't git before him to your mother's plantation, and run the niggers into the swamp out of his reach, he'll not leave you the hair of one—he'll have 'em off to Charleston by some of his fellows, and then to the West Injies, before you can say Jack Robinson, or what's a'most as easy, Jack Bannister. There's another person I think you ought to see about, and that's Miss Flora. Either you love her, or you don't love her. Now, if you love her, up and at her, at once, with all your teeth sot, as if you had said it with an oath; for though I know this ain't no time to be a-wiving and a-courting, yet, when the varmints is a-prowling about the poultry-yard, it's no more than sense to look after the speckled pullet. Take a fool's wisdom for once, and have an eye to both eends of the road. Go over to the plantation, and when you're thar', you can steal a chance to cross over to Middleton's. It's my notion you'll find Ned Conway at one place or t'other."

"I'll think of it," said Conway, in subdued tones; "meantime, do you take the canoe back to the island and bring him out. The horses are in readiness?"

"Yes, behind the hill. I'll bring him out if you say so, Clarence; but it's not too late to think better of it. He's safe, for all parties, where he is."

"No, no, Jack; I've promised him. I'll keep my promise. Let him go. I fear that he has deceived me. I fear that he will still deceive me. Still I will save him from his enemies, and suppress my own suspicions. It will be only the worse for him if he does me wrong hereafter."

"Clarence, if he turns out to be a tory, what'll our men say to hear you harbored him?"

"Say!—perhaps, that I am no better."

"No, no! they can't say *that*—they sha'n't say it, when Jack Bannister is nigh enough to hear, and to send his hammer into the long jaws that talk sich foolishness; but they'll think it mighty strange, Clarence."

"Hardly, Jack, when they recollect that he is my father's son."

"Ah, Lord, there's mighty few of us got brothers in these times in Carolina. A man's best brother now-a-days is the thing he fights with. His best friend is his rifle. You may call his jack-knife a first-cousin, and his two pistols his eldest sons; and even then, there's no telling which of them all is going to fail him first, or whether any one among 'em will stick by him till the scratch is over. Edward Conway, to my thinking, Clarence, was never a brother of your'n, if 'brother' has any meaning of 'friend' in it."

"Enough, enough, Jack. Leave me now, and bring him forth. I will do what I promised, whatever may be my doubts. I will guide him on his way, and with this night's work acquit myself of all obligations to him. When we next meet, it shall be on such terms as shall for ever clear up the shadows that stand between us. Away, now!—it will be dark in two hours, and we have little time to waste. The storm which threatens us will be favorable to his flight."

## CHAPTER III.

### THE RETROSPECT—THE FUGITIVE.

THE dialogue between the two friends, which has just been given, will convey to the mind of the reader some idea of the situation of the parties. We have not aimed to describe the manner of this dialogue, preferring infinitely that the interlocutors should speak entirely for themselves. It may be stated in this place, however, that, throughout the interview, the sturdy counsellor, whose honest character and warm friendship constituted his perfect claim to speak unreservedly to his superior, betrayed a dogged determination not to be satisfied with the disposition which the latter had resolved to make of one whom he was pleased to consider in some sort a prisoner. On the other hand, the younger of the two, whom we have known by the name of Clarence Conway, and who held a colonel's command over one of those roving bodies of whig militia, which were to be found at this period in every district of the state—though resolute to release his brother from the honorable custody in which circumstances had placed him—still seemed to regret the necessity by which he was prompted to this proceeding. There were various feelings contending for mastery in his bosom. While he did not believe in the charges of political treachery by which his half-brother was stigmatized, he was yet anything but satisfied that his purposes were politically honest or honorable. Equally dubious with his companion on the subject of Edward Conway's principles, he was yet not prepared to believe in the imputation which had been cast upon his performances. He suspected him, not of fighting for the enemy, but of the meaner and less daring employment, of speculating in the necessities of the country; and, in some way or other, of craftily availing himself of its miseries and wants, to realize that wealth, the passion for which constituted, he well knew, a leading and greedy appetite in the character of his kinsman.

Clarence Conway was the youngest son of a gentlemen who came from the West Indies, bringing with him an only child — then an infant — the fruit of a first marriage with a lady of Barbadoes, who died in bringing it into the world. The graceful form, pleasing manners, and varied intelligence of this gentleman, gained him the favor of a young lady of the Congaree, who became his wife. One son, our hero, was born to this union; and his eyes had scarcely opened upon the light, when his father fell a victim to fever, which he caught in consequence of some rash exposure among the swamps of the low country. The infant, Clarence, became the favorite of his grandparents, by whom he was finally adopted. He thus became the heir of possessions of a vastness and value infinitely beyond those which, by the laws of primogeniture, necessarily accrued to his half-brother.

The anxiety of Edward Conway to be the actual possessor of his rights, became so obvious to all eyes, that Mrs. Conway yielded him early possession, soon after her husband's death, and retired to one of the plantations which had descended from her father to her son. Edward Conway did not long retain the estate left him by his father. He was sagacious or fortunate enough to sell it, and realize its value in money, before the strifes of the Revolution became inevitable. With the conquest of Carolina by the British, he almost disappeared from sight; but not until himself and half-brother had already come into conflict on grounds which did not involve any reference to the politics of the country. This collision between them was of such a nature — already hinted at in the previous chapter — as to bring into active exercise the anger of the one, and the dissimulation of the other. To Clarence Conway, therefore, the unfrequent appearance of Edward afforded but little discontent. The late return of the latter, under circumstances of suspicion — under imputations of political treachery, and accusations of crime — now bewildered the more frank and passionate youth, who lamented nothing half so much as to be compelled to call him kinsman. He knew the wilfulness of heart which characterized him, and dreaded lest he should abuse, in a respect purely personal, the freedom which he was about to confer upon him. His own ability to follow, and to watch the object of his suspicions, was very limited at this period. His movements were governed by his military position, by prudence, and certain other relations of a more private nature, which shall be considered as we proceed.

With no such restraints as these, and once more safe from the dangers which had compelled him to seek shelter at the hands of his brother in the swamp, the future conduct of Edward Conway filled the mind of Clarence with many apprehensions; the more strongly felt, since his falsehood, in a particular respect, had been revealed by his companion. There was, as the latter had phrased it, a weak or tender spot in the bosom of Clarence Conway, which led him to apprehend everything of evil, should Edward prove false to certain pledges which he had voluntarily made, and proceed to a dishonorable use of his liberty. But it was a point of honor with him not to recede from his own pledges; nor to forbear, because of a revival of old suspicions, the performances to which they had bound him. Yet, in the brief hour that followed the departure of Jack Bannister, how much would his young commander have given, could he have taken his counsel — could he have kept, as a prisoner, that person whose passions he well knew, and whose dissimulation he feared. He thus nearly argued himself into the conviction — not a difficult one at that period — that it was his public duty to arrest and arraign, as a criminal to his country, the person against whom the proofs were so strikingly presumptive.

As he reflected upon this subject, it seemed to astonish even himself, the degree of criminality which he was now willing to attach to his kinsman's conduct. How was it that he had become so generally suspected? How easy, if he were able, to prove his fidelity? Why was he absent from the field? Where had he been? Though proof was wanting to show that he had been active in the British cause, yet none was necessary to show that he had been wholly inactive for the American. More than once, in the interval which followed from the first futile attempts to the final and successful invasion of the state, by the enemy, had Clarence sought him, to stimulate his patriotism, and urge him to the field. All their conferences were devoted to this object;

the youth sometimes assuming a language in the controversy, which nothing but the purity of his patriotism and his own obvious disinterestedness, could have justified from the lips of a younger brother.

But his exhortations fell upon unheeding ears—his arguments in barren places. There were no fruits. Edward Conway contrived with no small degree of art to conceal his real sentiments, at a time when the great body of the people were only too glad to declare themselves, either on one side or the other. Subsequently, when the metropolis had fallen, the same adroitness was exercised to enable him to escape from the consequences of committal to either. How this was done—by what evasions, or in what manner—Clarence Conway was at a loss to understand.

As the war proceeded, and the invasion of the colony became general, the active events of the conflict, the disorders of the country, the necessity of rapid flight, from point to point, of all persons needing concealment, served to prevent the frequent meeting of the kinsmen;—and circumstances, to which we have already adverted, not to speak of the equivocal political position of the elder brother, contributed to take from such meetings what little gratification they might have possessed for either party. Whenever they did meet, the efforts of Clarence were invariably made, not to find out the mode of life which the other pursued, but simply to assure himself that it was right and honorable. To this one object all his counsels were addressed; but he was still compelled to be content with a general but vague assurance from the other, that it was so. Still there was one charge which Edward Conway could not escape. This was the omission of that duty to his country, which, in a season of invasion, can not be withheld without dishonoring either the manhood or the fidelity of the citizen. Clarence was not willing to ascribe to treachery this inaction; yet he could not, whenever he gave any thought to the subject, attribute it to any other cause. He knew that Edward was no phlegmatic; he knew that he was possessed of courage—nor courage merely; he knew that a large portion of audacity and impulse entered into his character. That he was active in some cause, and con-

2*

stantly engaged in some business, Edward Conway did not himself seek to deny. What that business was, however, neither the prayers nor the exhortations of Clarence and his friends could persuade him to declare; while the discovery of a circumstance, by the latter, which led him to apprehend the interference of the former in another field than that of war, contributed still farther to estrange them from each other. Enough now has been said to render the future narrative easy of comprehension.

While, with vexing and bitter thoughts, Clarence Conway awaited the progress of his companion, with the fugitive whom he had given into his charge, Supple Jack (for that was the *nom de guerre* conferred by his comrades upon the worthy woodman, in compliment to certain qualities of muscle which made his feats sometimes remarkable) penetrated into the recesses of the swamp, with a degree of diligence which by no means betokened his own disposition of mind in regard to the particular business upon which he went. But Supple Jack was superior to all that sullenness which goes frowardly to the task, because it happens to disapprove it. As a friend, he counselled without fear; as a soldier, he obeyed without reluctance.

He soon reached the little island on the edge of the Wateree river, where Clarence Conway had concealed his kinsman from the hot hunt which had pursued him to the neighborhood. So suddenly and silently did he send his canoe forward, that her prow struck the roots of the tree, at whose base the fugitive reclined, before he was conscious of her approach.

The latter started hastily to his feet, and the suspicious mood of Supple Jack was by no means lessened, when he beheld him thrust into his bosom a paper upon which he had evidently been writing.

To the passing spectator Edward Conway might have seemed to resemble his half-brother. They were not unlike in general respects—in height, in muscle, and in size. The air of Clarence may have been more lofty; but that of Edward was equally firm. But the close observer would have concurred with the woodman, that they were, as kinsman, utterly unlike in almost every other respect. The aspect of Clarence Conway was bright and open, like that of an unclouded sky; that of Edward was dark, reserved and lowering. There was usually a shyness and a suspiciousness of manner in his glance and movement; and, while he spoke, the sentences were prolonged, as if to permit as much premeditation as possible between every syllable. His smile had in it a something sinister, which failed to invite or soothe the spectator. It was not the unforced expression of a mind at ease — of good-humor — of a heart showing its clear depths to the glances of the sun. It was rather the insidious lure of the enchanter, who aims to dazzle and beguile.

As such only did our woodman seem to understand it. The strained and excessive cordiality of Edward Conway, as he bounded up at his approach — the hearty offer of the hand — met with little answering warmth on the part of the former. His eye encountered the glance of the fugitive without fear, but with a cold reserve; his hand was quickly withdrawn from the close clutch which grasped it; and the words with which he acknowledged and answered the other's salutation were as few as possible, and such only, as were unavoidable. The fugitive saw the suspicion, and felt the coldness with which he was encountered. Without seeming offended, he made it the subject of immediate remark.

"Ha, Jack, how is this? Friends — old friends — should not meet after such a fashion. Wherefore are you so cold? Do you forget me? Have you forgotten that we were boys together, Jack — playmates for so many happy years?"

"No, no! I hain't forgotten anything, Edward Conway, that a plain man ought to remember;" replied the woodman, taking literally the reproach of his companion. "But we ain't boys and playmates any longer, Edward Conway. We are men now, and these are no times for play of any sort; and there's a precious few among us that know with whom we can play safely, nowadays, without finding our fingers in the wolf's mouth."

"True enough, Jack; but what's true of other people needn't be true of us. Times change; but they shouldn't change friends. We are the same, I trust, that we have ever been to one another,"

This was said with an eager insinuating manner, and the hand of Conway was a second time extended to take that of the other. But, without regarding the movement, Supple Jack replied with a blunt resoluteness of demeanor, which would most effectually have rebuffed any less flexible spirit:—

"I reckon we a'n't, Edward Conway, and it's of no use to beat about the bush to find out what to say. Times change and we change, and it's onnatural to expect to keep the same face in all weathers. I know there's a mighty great change in me, and I'm thinking there's the same sort of change going on in a'most everybody. I used to be a quiet peaceable sort of person, that wouldn't hurt a kitten; and now I'm wolfish more than once a week, and mighty apt to do mischief when I feel so. I used to believe that whatever a pair of smooth lips said to me was true, and now I suspicions every smooth speaker I meet, as if he wor no better than a snake in the grass. 'Tain't in my natur to keep the same face and feelin's, always, any more than the weather, and I tell you plainly I'm quite another sort of person from the boy that used to play with you, and Clarence Conway, long time ago."

"Ah, Jack, but you hav'n't changed to him—you are the same friend to Clarence Conway as ever."

"Yes, bless God for all his marcies, that made me love the boy when he was a boy, and kept the same heart in me after he came to be a man. I a'n't ashamed to say that I love Clarence the same as ever, since he never once, in all my dealings with him, boy and man, ever gin me reason to distrust him. He's mighty like an oak in two ways—he's got the heart of one, and there's no more bend in him than in an oak."

The cheek of the fugitive was flushed as he listened to this simple and earnest language. He was indiscreet enough to press the matter farther.

"But why should you distrust me, Jack Bannister? You have known me quite as long as you have known Clarence, we have played as much together—"

"Ay!" exclaimed the other abruptly, and with a startling energy. "But we hav'n't fou't together, and bled together, and slept together, and starved together, Edward Conway. You hav'n't been so ready as Clarence to come out for your country. Now, I've starved in his company, and run, and fou't, and been with him in all sorts of danger, and he's never been the first to run, and he's always been the last to feel afraid, and to show that he was hungry. For nine months we had but one blanket between us, and that was half burnt up from sleeping too close to the ashes one cold night last Christmas. It's sich things that made us friends from the beginning, and it's sich things that keep us friends till now. You don't seem altogether to remember, that you and me war never friends, Edward Conway, even when we war playmates; and the reason was I always mistrusted you. Don't think I mean to hurt your feelings by telling you the truth. You're a sort of prisoner, you see, and it would be mighty ongenteel for me to say anything that mought give offence, and I ax pardon if I does; but as I tell you, I mistrusted you from the beginning, and I can't help telling you that I mistrust you to the eend. You ha'n't got the sort o' ways I like, and when that's the case, it's no use to strain one's natur' to make a liking between feelings that don't seem to fit. Besides, you hev' a bad standing in the country. These men of Butler's swear agin you by another name, and it looks mighty suspicious when we come to consider that none of the whigs have anything to say in your behalf."

"One thing is certain, John Bannister," replied the fugitive composedly; "you at least preserve your ancient bluntness. You speak out your mind as plainly as ever."

"I reckon its always best," was the answer.

"Perhaps so, though you do me injustice, and your suspicions are ungenerous. It is unfortunate for me that, for some little time longer I must submit to be distrusted. The time will come, however, and I hope very soon, when you will cease to regard me with doubt or suspicion."

"Well, I jine my hope to your'n in that matter; but, till that time comes round, Edward Conway, I mought as well say to you that we are *not* friends, and I don't think it 'ill make us any nearer even if you war to prove that you're no tory. For why —I know that you're no friend to Clarence, for all he's done for you."

"Ha, Bannister—how—what know you?"

"Enough to make me say what I'm saying. Now, you hear me, jest once, for the first and last time that I may ever have a chance of letting you see my mind. I know enough to know that you've been a-working agin Clarence, and I suspicions you ha'n't done working agin him. Now, this is to let you onderstand that Jack Bannister has nara an eye in his head that don't watch for his friend and agin his enemy: and I tell you all in good natur', and without meaning any malice, that, whatever harm you do to him, that same harm I'll double and treble upon you, though I wait and watch, out in the worst weather, and walk on bloody stumps, to do it. I suspicions you, Edward Conway, and I give you fair warning, I'll be at your heels, like a dog that never barks to let the world know which way he's running."

"A fair warning enough, Bannister," replied the fugitive with recovered composure, and a moderate show of dignity. "To resent your language, at this time, would be almost as foolish as to endeavor to prove that your suspicions of me are groundless. I shall not feel myself less manly or less innocent by forbearing to do either."

"Well, that's jest as you think proper, Edward Conway; I must ax your pardon agin for saying rough things to a man that's a sort of prisoner, but I'm thinking it's always the cleanest play to speak the truth when you're forced to it. You've been talking at me ever sence the time I helped Clarence to git you into the swamp, as if I had been some old friend of your'n; and it went agin me to stand quiet and hear you all the time, and not set you right on that matter. Now, as the thing's done, with your leave we'll say no more about it. My orders from the colonel war to carry you out of the swamp; so you'll make ready as soon as you can, for there's precious little of daylight left for a mighty dark sort of navigation.

"And where is he—where do you take me?" demanded the fugitive.

"Well, it's not in my orders to let you know any more than I've told you: only I may say you don't go out exactly where you came in."

## THE RETROSPECT — THE FUGITIVE. 39

"Enough, sir. I presume that my brother's commands will insure me a safe guidance ? I am ready to go with you."

This was said with that air of resentment which amply proved to the woodman that his blunt freedoms had been sensibly felt. He smiled only at the distrust which the words of the fugitive seemed to betray, and the haughtiness of his manner appeared rather to awaken in the honest scout something of a pleasurable emotion.

"Well," he muttered half aloud as he prepared to throw the boat off from her fastenings; "well, it's not onreasonable that he should be angry. I don't know but I should like him the better if he would throw off his coat and back all his sly doings at the muzzle of the pistol. But I have no patience with anything that looks like a sneak. It's bad enough to be dodging with an enemy, but to dodge when a friend's looking arter you, is a sort of sport I consider mighty onbecoming in a white man. It's nigger natur', and don't shame a black skin, but — well, you're ready, Mr. Edward? Jest take your seat in the bottom, and keep stiddy. It's a ticklish sort of navigation we've got before us , and our dug-out a'n't much more heavier than a good-sized calabash. She'll swim if we're stiddy, but if you dodge about we'll spile our leggins, and mought be, have to swim for it. Stiddy, so. Are you right, sir?"

"Steady — all right!" was the calm, low response of the fugitive, as the canoe darted through the lagune.

## CHAPTER IV.

#### THE KINSMEN.

THE boat, under the adroit management of Supple Jack, soon reached the shore where Clarence Conway awaited them. Standing side by side, there was little obvious difference between the persons of the kinsmen. They were both equally tall, strongly made and symmetrical—each had the same general cast of countenance—the hair was not unlike; the complexion of Edward was darker than that of Clarence. The difference between them, physically, if not so obvious, was yet singularly marked and substantial. There was that in the expression of their several faces, which, to the nice physiognomical critic, did not inaptly illustrate the vital differences in the two characters as they will be found to display themselves in the progress of this narrative. The forehead and chin of the former were much smaller than those of the younger. The cheek-bones were higher; the lips, which in Clarence Conway were usually compressed, giving an air of decision to his mouth which approached severity, were, in the case of Edward, parted into smiles, which were only too readily and too easily evoked, not, sometimes, to awaken doubts of their sincerity in the mind of the spectator. Some well-defined lines about the upper lip and corners of the mouth, which signified cares and anxieties, tended still more to make doubtful the prompt smile of the wearer. The difference of five years—for that period of time lay between their several ages—had added a few wrinkles to the cheeks and brow of the elder, which nowhere appeared upon the face of the younger. A conscience free from reproach, had probably saved him from tokens which are quite as frequently the proofs of an ill-ordered life as of age and suffering. Some other leading differences between the two might be traced out by a close observer, and not the least prominent of these exhibited itself at the moment of their present meeting, in the over-acted kindness and extreme courtesy of the fugitive kinsman. His sweet soft tones of conciliation, his studied gentleness of accent, and the extreme humility of his gesture—all appeared in large contrast with the simple, unaffected demeanor of the younger. The feelings of Clarence were all too earnest for mannerism of any sort; and, motioning Jack Bannister aside, he met his half-brother with an air full of direct purpose, and a keenly-awakened consciousness of the dark doubts renewed in his mind upon that mystery which rose up like a wall between them.

It was difficult to say, while Edward Conway was approaching him, whether sorrow or anger predominated in his countenance. But the face of the fugitive beamed with smiles, and his hand was extended. The hand remained untaken, however, and the eye of the elder brother shrunk from the encounter with the searching glance of Clarence. A slight suffusion passed over his cheek, and there was a tremor in his voice as he spoke, which might be natural to the resentment which he must have felt, but which he showed no other disposition to declare.

"So cold to me, Clarence? What now should awaken your displeasure? You have behaved nobly in this business—do not send me from you in anger!"

"I have behaved only as a brother, Edward Conway. Would that you could feel like one! You have again deceived me!" was the stern, accusing answer.

"Deceived you!" was the reply, and the eye of the speaker wandered from the strong glance of his kinsman, and his lips whitened as he spoke; "how, Clarence—how have I deceived you?"

"But this day you assured me, on your honor, that you had not sought Flora Middleton since my last conference with you on the subject. I now know that you have been at Brier Park within the last three weeks."

The practised cunning of the worldling came to the relief of the accused, and Edward Conway availed himself of one of those petty evasions to which none but the mean spirit is ever willing to resort.

"Very true, Clarence; but I did not *seek* Flora in going there.

I happened to be in the neighborhood at nightfall, and saw no good reason for avoiding a good supper and a comfortable bed, which I knew the hospitalities of Brier Park would always afford me. I *did go* there—that is true—saw Flora and all the family—but it is nevertheless equally true, that in going there I did not *seek* her."

"But you withheld the fact of your being there, Edward Conway, and left the impression on my mind that you had not seen her."

"I did not seek to convey such an impression, Clarence; I simply spoke to the point, and spoke with literal exactitude."

"You have a legal proficiency in language," was the sarcastic comment. "But for this I should probably have heard the whole truth. What good reason was there why you should be so partial in your revelations? Why did you not tell me all?"

"To answer you frankly, Clarence," replied the other, with the air of a man unbuttoning his bosom to the examination of the world—"I found you jealous and suspicious on this subject —in just the mood to convert the least important circumstance into a cause of doubt and dissatisfaction; and, therefore, I withheld from you a fact which, however innocent in itself, and unworthy of consideration, I was yet well aware, in your mood of mind, would assume an importance and character which justly it could not merit. Besides, Clarence, there were so many subjects of far more interest to *my* mind, of which we had no speech, that I did not care to dwell upon the matter longer than was necessary. You forget, Clarence, that I had not seen you for months before this meeting."

The suspicions of the younger were in no respect disarmed or lessened by this explanation. Edward Conway had somewhat overshot his mark when he spoke so slightingly of a subject to which Clarence attached so high an importance. The latter could not believe in the indifference which the other expressed in reference to one so dear to himself as Flora Middleton; and, in due degree as he felt the probability that so much merit as he esteemed that maiden to possess, could not fail to awaken the tender passion in all who beheld her, so was he now inclined to consider the declaration of his kinsman as an hypocrisy equally gross and shallow. He resolved, internally, that he should neither deceive his judgment nor disarm his watchfulness; that, while he himself forbore reproaches of every sort, which, indeed, at that moment, would have seemed ungenerous and ungracious, he would endeavor to maintain a *surveillance* over his rival's movements, which would at least defeat such of his machinations as might otherwise tend to beguile from himself the affections of the beloved object. The closing words of Edward Conway suggested a natural change of the subject, of which Clarence quickly availed himself.

"You remind me, Edward Conway, that, though we have spoken of various and interesting subjects, you have not yet given me the information which I sought, on any. The one most important to both of us, Edward Conway—to our father's family, to the name we bear, and the position we should equally sustain, as well to the past as to the future, in the eye of our country—is that of your present public course. On that subject you have told me nothing. Of your position in this conflict I know nothing; and what little reaches my ears from the lips of others, is painfully unfavorable. Nay, more, Edward Conway, I am constrained to think, and I say it in bitterness and sadness, that what you have said, in reply to my frequent and earnest inquiries on this point, has seemed to me intended rather to evade than to answer my demands. I can not divest myself of the conviction that you have spoken on this subject with as careful a suppression of the whole truth, as this morning when you gave me the assurance with regard to Flora Middleton."

A heavy cloud darkened, though for a moment only, the face of the elder Conway.

"There are some very strong prejudices against me in your mind, Clarence, or it would not be difficult for you to understand how I might very naturally have secrets which should not be revealed, and yet be engaged in no practices which would either hurt my own, or the honor of my family."

"This I do not deny, Edward, however suspicious it may seem that such secrets should be withheld from an only brother, whose faith you have never yet found reason to suspect; whose prudence you have never found occasion to distrust. But I do not ask for any of your secrets. I should scorn myself for ever did I feel a single desire to know that which you have any good reason to withhold from me. It is only that I may defend you from injustice—from slander—from the suspicions of the true and the worthy—that I would be fortified by a just knowledge of your objects and pursuits. Surely, there can be no good reason to withhold this knowledge, if what you do is sanctioned by propriety and the cause for which we are all in arms."

"It is sanctioned by the cause for which we are in arms," replied the other, hastily. "Have I not assured you that I am no traitor—that my fidelity to my country is not less pure and perfect than your own? The slanderer will defame and the credulous will believe, let us labor as we may. I take no heed of these—I waste no thought on such profitless matters; and you, Clarence, will save yourself much pain, and me much annoying conjecture, if you will resolve to scorn their consideration with myself, and cast them from your mind. Give them no concern. Believe me to be strangely and awkwardly placed; but not criminal—not wilfully and perversely bent on evil. Is not this enough? What more shall I say? Would you have me—your elder brother—bearing the same name with yourself—declare to you, in words, that I am not the black-hearted, bloodthirsty, reckless monster, which these wide-mouthed creatures, these blind mouths and bitter enemies, proclaim me?"

"But why are these men of Butler *your* enemies? They are not the enemies of your country."

"I know not that," said the other hastily.

"Your doubt does them, gross injustice," replied Clarence Conway, with increased earnestness; "they are known men—tried and true—and whatever may be their excesses and violence, these are owing entirely to the monstrous provocation they have received. How can it be, Edward, that you have roused these men to such a degree of hostility against yourself? They bear to you no ordinary hate—they speak of you in no ordinary language of denunciation—"

"My dear Clarence," said the other, "you seem to forget all the while, that they never spoke of me at all—certainly not by name. They know me not—they have most assuredly confounded me with another. Even if I were indeed the person whom they hate, to answer your questions would be no easy matter. As well might I undertake to show why there are crime and injustice in the world, as why there are slander and suspicion. These are plants that will grow, like joint-grass, in every soil, weed and work at them as you may."

"It is nevertheless exceedingly strange, Edward," was the musing answer of the still unsatisfied Clarence; "it is strange how any set of men should make such a mistake."

"The strangest thing of all is, that my own brother should think it so. Why should you?"

"Should I not?

"Wherefore?—You can not believe that I am, indeed, what they allege me to be—the chief of the Black Riders—that dreaded monster—half-man, half-dragon—who slays the men, swallows the children, and flies off with the damsels. Ha! ha! ha! Really, Clarence, I am afraid you are as credulous now at twenty-five as you were at five."

"It is not *that* I believe, Edward Conway. If I did, the name of my father, which you bear, had not saved your life. But, why, again, are you suspected? Suspicion follows no actions that are not doubtful—it dogs no footsteps which are straightforward—it haunts no character, the course of which has been direct and unequivocal? My unhappiness is that you have made yourself liable to be confounded with the criminal, because you have not been seen with the innocent. You are not with us, and the natural presumption is that you are with our enemies."

"I should not care much for the idle gabble of these country geese, Clarence, but that you should echo their slanders—that you should join in the hiss!"

This was spoken with the air of mortified pride, such as might be supposed the natural emotion of every honorable spirit, assailed by the doubts of friend or kinsman.

"I do not—all I demand of you is that confidence which would enable me to silence it."

"As well attempt to silence the storm. The attempt would

be idle; and, if made, where should we begin? What suspicion must I first dissipate? Whose poisonous breath must I first encounter? This story of the Black Riders, for example — do you really believe, Clarence, in the alleged existence of this banditti?"

"I do! — I can not believe otherwise."

"Impossible! I doubt it wholly. These dastardly fellows of Butler have fancied half the terrors they describe. Their fears have magnified their foes, and I make no question they have slandered as civil a set of enemies as ever had a professional sanction for throat-cutting. Really, Clarence, the very extravagance of these stories should save you from belief; and I must say, if you do believe, that a little more of the brotherly love which you profess, should keep you from supposing me to be the savage monster of whom they give such horrid traits in the chief of this Black banditti. My very appearance — in our youth, Clarence, considered not very much unlike your own — should save me from these suspicions. See! — my skin is rather fair than dark; and as for the mass of hair which is said to decorate the chin, and the black shock which surrounds the face of the formidable outlaw — none who looks at my visage will fancy that Esau could ever claim me for his kinsman. My vanity, indeed, is quite as much touched as my honor, Clarence, that my smooth visage should suffer such cruel mirepresentation."

And as the speaker concluded this rhapsody, his eye suddenly wandered from that of the person he addressed, and rested upon the belt which encircled his own body — a belt of plain black leather, secured by an ordinary iron buckle, painted of the same color, and freshly varnished. An uneasy upward glance, at this moment, encountered that of his kinsman, whose eyes had evidently followed his own, to the examination of the same object. In this single glance and instant, it seemed that the moral chasm which had always existed between their souls, had yawned wider and spread farther than before. There was a mutual instinct where there was no mutual sympathy. The disquiet of the one, and the doubts of the other, were reawakened; and though neither spoke, yet both understood the sudden difficulties of further speech between them. Another voice, at this moment, broke the silence, which it did not however relieve of any of that painful pressure which the interview possessed over both the interested parties. The impatience of the worthy woodman had brought him sufficiently nigh to hear some of the last words of the elder kinsman.

"Well," said he, bluntly, "if long talking can make any case cl'ar, then it's pretty sartin, Edward Conway, that they've mightily belied you. What you say is very true about skin, and face, and complexion, and all that. Naterally, you ha'n't no great deal of beard, and your shock, as it stands, wouldn't be a sarcumstance alongside of the colonel's or my own. But I've hearn of contrivances to help natur in sich a matter. I've hearn of livin' men, and livin' women too, that dressed themselves up in the sculps of dead persons, and made a mighty pretty figger of hair for themselves, when, naterally they had none. Now, they do say, that the Black Riders does the same thing. Nobody that I've ever hearn speak of them, ever said that the sculps was nateral that they had on; and the beards, too, would come and go, jist according to the company they want to keep. It's only a matter of ten days ago—the time you may remember, by a mighty ugly run you had of it from these same boys of Butler—that I was a-going over the same ground, when, what should I happen to see in the broad track but one of these same changeable sculps—the sculp for the head and the sculp for the chin, and another sculp that don't look altogether so nateral, that must ha' gone somewhere about the mouth, though it must ha' been mighty onpleasant, a-tickling of the nostrils; for you see, if I knows anything of human natur, or beast natur, this sculp come, at first, from the upper side of a five year old fox-squirrel, one of the rankest in all the Santee country. I knew by the feel somewhat, and a little more by the smell. Now, Mr. Edward Conway, if you'll jist look at these here fixin's, you won't find it so hard to believe that a fair-skinned man mout wear a black sculp and a mighty dark complexion onderneath, if so be the notion takes him. Seein's believing. I used to think, before we went out, that it was all an ole woman's story, but as sure as a gun, I found these sarcumstances, jist as you see 'em, on the broad path down to the Wateree; and I reckon that's a strong sarcumstance, by itself, to make me think they was made for something, and for somebody to wear. But that's only my notion. I reckon it's easy enough, in sich times as these, for every man to find a different way of thinking when he likes to."

The articles described by the woodman were drawn from his bosom as he spoke, and displayed before the kinsmen. The keen eyes of Clarence, now doubly sharpened by suspicion, seemed disposed to pierce into the very soul of Edward Conway. He, however, withstood the analysis with all the calm fortitude of a martyr. He examined the several articles with the manner of one to whom they were entirely new and strange; and when he had done, quietly remarked to the deliberate woodman, that he had certainly produced sufficient evidence to satisfy him, if indeed he were not satisfied before, "that a man, disposed to adopt a plan of concealment and disguise, could readily find, or make, the materials to do so."

"But this, Clarence," said he, turning to his kinsman, "this has nothing to do with what I was saying of myself. It does not impair the assurance which I made you—"

Clarence Conway, who had been closely examining the articles, without heeding his brother, demanded of the woodman why he had not shown them to him before.

"Well, colonel, you see I didn't find them ontil the second day after the chase, when you sent me up, to scout along the hills."

"Enough!—Bring up the horses."

"Both?" asked the woodman, with some anxiety.

"Yes! I will ride a little way with my brother."

The horses were brought in a few moments from the mouth of a gorge which ran between the hills at the foot of which they stood. The promptness of the woodman's movements prevented much conversation, meanwhile, between the kinsmen; nor did either of them appear to desire it. The soul of Clarence was full of a new source of disquiet and dread; while the apprehensions of Edward Conway, if entirely of another sort, were yet too active to permit of his very ready speech. As the kinsmen were preparing to mount, Supple Jack interposed, and drew his superior aside.

"Well, that's the matter now?" demanded Clarence impatiently. "Speak quickly, Jack—the storm is at hand—the rain is already falling."

"Yes, and that's another reason for your taking to the swamp ag'in. In three hours the hills will tell a story of every step that your horse is taking."

"Well, what of that?"

"Why, matter enough, if the tories are on the look out for us, which I'm dub'ous is pretty much the case. I didn't altogether like the signs I fell in with on the last scout, and if so be that Edward Conway is one of these Black Riders, then it's good reason to believe they'll be looking after him in the place where they lost him."

"Pshaw, no more of this," said the other angrily.

"Well, Clarence, you may 'pshaw' it to me as much as you please, only I'm mighty sartain, in your secret heart, you don't 'pshaw' it to yourself. It's a strange business enough, and it's not onreasonable in me to think so—seeing what I have seen, and knowing what I know. Now that Butler's boys are gone upward, these fellows will swarm thick as grasshoppers in all this country; and it's my notion, if you will go, that you should keep a sharp eye in your head, and let your dogs bark at the first wink of danger. I'm dub'ous you're running a mighty great risk on this side of the Wateree. There's no telling where Marion is jist at this time; and there's a rumor that Watson's on the road to jine Rawdon. Some say that Rawdon's going to leave Camden, and call in his people from Ninety-Six and Augusta; and if so, this is the very pairt of the country where there's the best chance of meeting him and all of them. I wouldn't ride far, Clarence; and I'd ride fast; and I'd git back as soon as horseflesh could bring me. Sorrel is in full blood now, and he'll show the cleanest heels in the country, at the civillest axing of the spur."

"You are getting as timid, Jack, as you are suspicious," said the youth kindly, and with an effort at composure, which was not successful. "Age is coming upon you, and I fear, before the campaign is over, you'll be expecting to be counted among the non-combatants. Don't apprehend for me, Jack; I will return before midnight. Keep up your scout, and get a stouter heart at work—you couldn't have a better one."

"That's to say, Clarry, that I'm a durn'd good-natered fool for my pains. I onderstands you—"

The rest was lost to the ears of Clarence Conway, in the rush of his own and the steed of his companion.

The worthy scout, however, continued the speech even after the departure of all hearers.

"But, fool or not, I'll look after you, as many a fool before has looked after a wiser man, and been in time to save him when he couldn't save himself. As for you, Ned Conway," he continued in brief soliloquy, and with a lifted finger, "you may draw your skairts over the eyes of Clarence, but it'll take thicker skairts than yourn to blind Jack Bannister. You couldn't do it altogether when we war boys together, and I'm a thinking— it'll be a mighty onbecoming thing to me, now that I'm a man, if I should let you be any more successful. Well, here we stand. The thing's to be done; the game's to be played out; and the stakes, Ned Conway, must be my head agin yourn. The game's a fair one enough, and the head desarves to lose it, that can't keep its place on the shoulders where God put it."

With this conclusive philosophy, the scout tightened his belt about his waist, threw up his rifle, the flint and priming of which he carefully examined, then, disappeared for a brief space among the stunted bushes that grew beside the swamp thicket. He emerged soon after, leading a stouf Cherokee pony, which had been contentedly ruminating among the cane-tops. Mounting this animal, which was active and sure-footed, he set off in a smart canter upon the track pursued by his late companions, just as the rainstorm, which had been for some time threatening, began to discharge the hoarded torrents of several weeks upon the parched and thirsting earth.

## CHAPTER V.

### THE BLACK RIDERS OF CONGAREE.

WHILE the kinsmen were about to leave the banks of the Wateree, for the Santee hills beyond, there were other parties among those hills, but a few miles distant, preparing to move down, on the same road, toward the Wateree. The eye of the skulking woodman may have seen, toward nightfall, a motley and strange group of horsemen, some sixty or seventy in number, winding slowly down the narrow gorges, with a degree of cautious watchfulness, sufficient to make them objects of suspicion, even if the times were not of themselves enough to render all things so. The unwonted costume of these horsemen was equally strange and calculated to inspire apprehension. They were dressed in complete black — each carried broadsword and pistols, and all the usual equipments of the well-mounted dragoon. The belt around the waist, the cap which hung loosely upon the brow; the gloves, the sash — all were distinguished by the same gloomy aspect. Their horses alone, various in size and color, impaired the effect of this otherwise general uniformity. Silently they kept upon their way, like the shadows of some devoted band of the olden time, destined to reappear, and to reoccupy, at certain periods of the night, the scenes in which they fought and suffered. Their dark, bronzed visages, at a nearer approach, in nowise served to diminish the general severity of their appearance. Huge, bushy beards, hung from every chin, in masses almost weighty enough to rival the dense forests which are worn, as a matter of taste, at the present day, in the same region, by a more pacific people. The mustache ran luxuriant above the mouth, greatly cherished, it would seem, if not cultivated; for no attempt appeared to be made by the wearer, to trim and curl the pampered growth, after the fashion of Russians and Mussulmans. The imperial tuft below, like that which decorates so appropriately the throat of the turkey, seemed designed, in the case of each of our sable riders, to emulate in length and dimensions, if not in fitness, that of the same pretentious bird. Some of these decorations were, doubtlessly, like those which became the spoil of our worthy woodman in a previous chapter, of artificial origin; but an equal number were due to the bounteous indulgence of Dame Nature herself. Of the troop in question, and their aspects, something more might be said. They had evidently, most of them, seen service in the "imminent deadly breach." Ugly scars were conspicuous on sundry faces, in spite of the extensive foliage of beard, which strove vainly to conceal them; and the practised ease of their horsemanship, the veteran coolness which marked their deliberate and watchful movements, sufficiently declared the habitual and well-appointed soldier.

Still, there was not so much of that air of military subordination among them which denotes the regular service. They were not what we call regulars—men reduced to the conditions of masses, and obeying, in mass, a single controlling will. They seemed to be men, to whom something of discipline was relaxed in consideration of other more valuable qualities of valor and forward enterprise, for which they might be esteemed. Though duly observant not to do anything which might yield advantage to an enemy, prowling in the neighborhood, still, this caution was not so much the result of respect for their leader, as the natural consequence of their own experience, and the individual conviction of each of what was due to the general safety. They were not altogether silent as they rode, and when they addressed their superiors, there was none of that nice and blind deference upon which military etiquette, among all well-ordered bodies of men, so imperatively insists. The quip and crack were freely indulged in—the ribald jest was freely spoken; and, if the ribald song remained unsung, it was simply because of a becoming apprehension that its melodies might reach other ears than their own.

Their leader, if he might be so considered, to whom they turned for the small amount of guidance which they seemed to need, was scarcely one of the most attractive among their number. He was a short, thick set, dark-looking person, whose stern and inflexible features were never lightened unless by gleams of anger and ferocity. He rode at their head, heard in silence the most that was said by those immediately about him, and if he gave any reply, it was uttered usually in a cold, conclusive monosyllable. His dark eye was turned as frequently upward to the lowering skies as along the path he travelled. Sometimes he looked back upon his troop—and occasionally halted at the foot of the hill till the last of his band had appeared in sight above. His disposition to taciturnity was not offensive to those to whom he permitted a free use of that speech in which he did not himself indulge; and, without heeding his phlegm, his free companions went on without any other restraint than arose from their own sense of what was due to caution in an enemy's country.

Beside the leader, at moments, rode one who seemed to be something of a favorite with him, and who did not scruple, at all times to challenge the attention of his superior. He was one—perhaps the very youngest of the party—whose quick, active movements, keen eyes, and glib utterance, declared him to belong to the class of subtler spirits who delight to manage the more direct, plodding, and less ready of their race. It is not improbable that he possessed some such influence over the person whom we have briefly described, of which the latter was himself totally unconscious. Nothing in the deportment of the former would have challenged a suspicion of this sort. Though he spoke freely and familiarly, yet his manner, if anything, was much more respectful than that generally of his companions. This man was evidently a close observer, as even his most careless remarks fully proved; and the glances of disquiet which the leader cast about him, at moments, as he rode, did not escape his notice. Upon these he did not directly comment. His policy, of course, did not suffer him so greatly to blunder as to assume that a lieutenant, or captain, of dragoons could be disquieted by any thing. When he spoke, therefore, even when his purpose was counsel or suggestion, he was careful that his language should not indicate his real purpose. We take up the dialogue between the parties at a moment, when, pausing at the bottom of one hill, and about to commence the ascent of another, the leader of the squad cast a long thoughtful glance skyward, and dubiously, but unconsciously, shook his head at the survey.

"We are like to have the storm on our backs, lieutenant, before we can get to a place of shelter; and I'm thinking if we don't look out for quarters before it comes down in real earnest, there'll be small chance of our finding our way afterward. The night will be here in two hours and a mighty dark one it will be, I'm thinking."

The lieutenant again looked forward, and upward, and around him, and a slight grunt, which was half a sigh, seemed to acknowledge the truth of the other's observations.

"I doubt," continued the first speaker, "if our drive to-day will be any more lucky than before. I'm afraid it's all over with the captain."

Another grunt in the affirmative; and the subordinate proceeded with something more of confidence.

"But there's no need that we should keep up the hunt in such a storm as is coming on. Indeed, there's but little chance of finding anybody abroad but ourselves in such weather. I'm thinking, lieutenant, that it wouldn't be a bad notion to turn our heads and canter off to old Muggs's at once."

"Old Muggs! why how far d'ye think he's off?"

"Not three miles, as I reckon. We've gone about seven from Cantey's, he's only eight to the right, and if we take a short cut that lies somewhere in this quarter—I reckon I can find it soon—we'll be there in a short half hour."

"Well! you're right—we'll ride to Muggs's. There's no use keeping up this cursed hunt and no fun in it."

"Yes, and I reckon we can soon make up our minds to get another captain."

A smirk of the lips, which accompanied this sentence, was intended to convey no unpleasant signification to the ears of his superior.

"How, Darcy—how is it—have you sounded them? What do they say now?" demanded the latter with sudden earnestness.

"Well, lieutenant, I reckon we can manage it pretty much as we please. That's my notion."

"You think so? Some of them have a strange liking for Morton."

"Yes, but not many, and they can be cured of that."

'Enough, then, till we get to Muggs's. Then we can talk it over. But beware of what you say to *him*. Muggs is no friend of mine, you know."

"Nor is he likely to be, so long as he wears that scar on his face in token that your hand is as heavy as your temper is passionate. He remembers that blow!"

"It isn't that, altogether," replied the other; "but the truth is, that we English are no favorites here, even among the most loyal of this people. There's a leaning to their own folks, that always gets them the preference when we oppose them; and old Muggs has never been slow to show us that he has no love to spare for any king's man across the water. I only wonder, knowing their dislikes as I do, that there's a single loyalist in the colony. These fellows that ride behind us, merciless as they have ever shown themselves in a conflict with the rebels, yet there's not one of them who, in a pitched battle between one of us and one of them, wouldn't be more apt to halloo for him than for us. Nothing, indeed, has secured them to the king's side but the foolish violence of the rebels, which wouldn't suffer the thing to work its own way; and began tarring and feathering and flogging at the beginning of the squabble. Had they left it to time, there wouldn't have been one old Muggs from Cape Fear to St. Catharine's. We shouldn't have had such a troop as that which follows us now; nor would I, this day, be hunting, as lieutenant of dragoons, after a leader, who—"

"Whom we shall not find in a hurry, and whom we no longer need," said the subordinate, concluding the sentence which the other had partly suppressed.

"Policy! policy!" exclaimed the lieutenant. "That was Rawdon's pretext for refusing me the commission, and conferring it upon Morton. He belonged to some great family on the Congaree, and must have it therefore; but, now, he can scarcely refuse it, if it be as we suspect. If Morton be laid by the heels, even as a prisoner, he is dead to us. The rebels will never suffer him to live if they have taken him."

"No, indeed," replied the other; "he hasn't the first chance. And that they *have* taken him, there is little doubt on my mind."

"Nor on mine. What follows if the men agree?"

"What should follow? The friends of Morton can say nothing. The command naturally falls into your hands without a word said."

"I'm not so sure of that, either. There's some of them that don't care much about Morton, yet don't like me."

"Perhaps! But, what of that? The number's not many, and we can put them down, if it comes to any open opposition. But we'll see to that this very night, when we get to Muggs's."

"For Muggs's, then, with all the speed we may. Take the lead, yourself, Darcy, and see after this short cut. You know the country better than I. We must use spur, if we would escape the storm. These drops are growing bigger, and falling faster, every moment. Go ahead, while I hurry the fellows forward at a canter; and even that will barely enable us to save our distance."

"It matters little for the wetting, lieutenant, when we remember what's to follow it. Promotion that comes by water is not by any means the worse for the wetting. The shine gets dim upon the epaulettes; but they are epaulettes, all the same. There's the profit, lieutenant—the profit!"

"Ay, the profit! Yes, that will reconcile us to worse weather than this; but—"

The sentence was left unfinished, while the subordinate rode ahead and out of hearing. The lieutenant signalled his men, as they slowly wound down the hill, to quicken pace; and while he watched their movements, his secret thoughts had vented in a low soliloquy.

"True! the event will reconcile us to the weather. The prize is precious. Power is always precious. But here the prize is something more than power; it is safety—it is freedom. If Morton is laid by the heels for ever, I am safe. I escape my danger—my terror—the presence which I hate and fear! I do not deceive myself, though I may blind these. Edward

Morton was one in whose presence I shrunk to less than my full proportions. That single act—that act of shame and baseness—made me his slave. He, alone, knows the guilt and the meanness of that wretched moment of my life. God! what would I not give to have that memory obliterated in him who did, and him who beheld, the deed of that moment. I feel my heart tremble at his approach—my muscles wither beneath his glance; and I, who fear not the foe, and shrink not from the danger, and whom men call brave—brave to desperation—I dare not lift my eyes to the encounter with those of another having limbs and a person neither stronger nor nobler than my own. He down, and his lips for ever closed, and I am free. I can then breathe in confidence, and look around me without dreading the glances of another eye. But, even should he live—should he have escaped this danger—why should I continue to draw my breath in fear, when a single stroke may make my safety certain—may rid me of every doubt—every apprehension? It must be so. Edward Morton, it is sworn. In your life my shame lives, and while your lips have power of speech, I am no moment safe from dishonor. Your doom is written, surely and soon, if it be not already executed."

These words were only so many indistinct mutterings, inaudible to those who followed him. He commanded them to approach, quickened their speed, and the whole troop, following his example, set off on a smart canter in the track which Darcy had taken. Meanwhile, the storm, which before had only threatened, began to pour down its torrents, and ere they reached the promised shelter at Muggs's—a rude cabin of pine logs, to which all direct approach was impossible, and which none but an initiate could have found, so closely was it buried among the dense groves that skirted the river swamp, and may have formed a portion of its primitive domain. Here the party came to a full halt, but the object at which they aimed appeared to be less their own than their horses and equipments. These were conducted into yet deeper recesses, where, in close woods and shrubbery, in which art had slightly assisted nature, they were so bestowed as to suffer only slightly from the storm. The greater portion of the troop took shelter in the cabin of

3*

Muggs, while a small squad still kept in motion around the neighborhood, heedless of the weather, and quite as watchful from long habit, as if totally unconscious of any annoyances.

The establishment of Muggs was one, in fact, belonging to the party. The host himself was a retired trooper, whom a wound in the right arm had so disabled that amputation became necessary. Useless to the troop in actual conflict, he was yet not without his uses in the position which he held, and the new duties he had undertaken. He was a blunt, fearless old soldier, a native of the neighborhood, who, being maimed, was tolerated by the whigs as no longer capable of harm; and suffered to remain in a region in which it was thought, even if disposed to do mischief, his opportunities were too few to make his doings of very serious importance. He sold strong liquors, also — did not villanously dilute his beverages — and, as he made no distinction between his customers, and provided whigs and tories at the same prices, there was no good reason to expel him from his present position by way of punishing him for a course of conduct in which so heavy a penalty seemed already to have been attached. He was prudent enough — though he did not withhold his opinions — to express them without warmth or venom; and, as it was well known to the patriots that he had never been a savage or blood-thirsty enemy, there was a very general disposition among them to grant him every indulgence. Perhaps, however, all these reasons would have been unavailing in his behalf, at the sanguinary period of which we write, but for the excellence of his liquors, and the certainty of his supply. His relations with the British enabled him always to provide himself at Charleston, and every public convoy replenished his private stores. It should be also understood that none of the whigs, at any moment, suspected the worthy landlord of a previous or present connection with a band so odious as that of the Black Riders. The appearance of these desperadoes was only a signal to Muggs to take additional precautions. As we have already stated, a portion of the band was sent out to patrol the surrounding country; and the number thus despatched, on the present occasion, was, by the earnest entreaty of the host, made twice as large as the lieutenant thought there was any occasion for. But the former insisted, with characteristic **stubbornness,** and with a degree of sullenness in his manner which was foreign to his usual custom.

"I'm not over-pleased to see you here at all, this time, lieutenant, though I reckon you've a good reason enough for coming. There's a sharp stir among the rebels all along the Wateree, and down on the Santee, there's no telling you how far. As for the Congarees, it's a-swarm thar', in spite of all Bill Cunningham can do, and he's twice as spry as ever. Here, only two days ago, has been that creeping critter, Supple Jack; that come in, as I may say, over my shoulder, like the old Satan himself. At first I did think it was the old Satan, till he laughed at my scare, and then I know'd him by his laugh. Now, it's not so easy to cheat Supple Jack, and he knows all about your last coming. He's willing to befriend me, though he gin me fair warning, last time he was here, that I was suspicioned for loving you too well. Now, split my cedars, men, I've got mighty little reason to love you—you know that—and I'm thinking, for your sake and mine both, the sooner you draw spur for the mountains, the smoother will be the skin you keep. I don't want to see the ugly face of one of you for a month of Sundays."

"Why, Muggs—old Muggs—getting scared in the very beginning of the season! How's this?—what's come over you?" was the demand of half a dozen.

"I've reason to be scared, when I know that hemp's growing for every man that's keeping bad company. Such rapscallions as you, if you come too often, would break up the best 'mug' in the country."

The landlord's pun was innocent enough, and seemed an old one. It awakened no more smile on his lips than upon those of his guests. It was spoken in serious earnest. He continued to belabor them with half playful abuse, mingled with not a few well-intended reproaches, while providing, with true landlord consideration, for their several demands. The Jamaica rum was put in frequent requisition—a choice supply of lemons was produced from a box beneath the floor, and the band was soon broken up into little groups that huddled about, each after its own fashion, in the several corners of the wigwam. The rain meanwhile beat upon, and, in some places, through the roof—the rush of the wind, the weight of the torrent, and the general darkness of the scene, led naturally to a considerable relaxation even of that small degree of discipline which usually existed among the troop. Deep draughts were swallowed; loud talking ensued, frequent oaths, and occasionally a sharp dispute, qualified by an equally sharp snatch of a song from an opposite quarter, proved all parties to be at ease, and each busy to his own satisfaction.

The lieutenant of the troop, whom we have just seen acting in command, was perhaps the least satisfied of any of the party. Not that he had less in possession, but that he had more in hope. He suffered the jibe and the song to pass; the oath roused him not, nor did he seem to hear the thousand and one petty disputes that gave excitement to the scene. He seemed disposed—and this may have been a part of his policy—to release his men from all the restraints, few though they were, which belonged to his command. But his policy was incomplete. It was not enough that he should confer licentious privileges upon his followers—to secure their sympathies, he should have made himself one of them. He should have given himself a portion of that license which he had accorded to them. But he was too much of the Englishman for that. He could not divest himself of that haughty bearing which was so habitual in the carriage of the Englishman in all his dealings with the provincial, and which, we suspect, was, though undeclared, one of the most active influences to provoke the high-spirited people of the south to that violent severing of their connection with the mother-country, which was scarcely so necessary in their case as in that of the northern colonies.

Our lieutenant—whose name was Stockton—it is true, made sundry, but not very successful efforts, to blend himself with his comrades. He shared their draughts, he sometimes yielded his ears where the dialogue seemed earnest—sometimes he spoke, and his words were sufficiently indulgent; but he lacked utterly that ease of carriage, that simplicity of manner, which alone could prove that his condescension was not the result of effort, and against the desires of his mind. His agent, Darcy, was more supple as he was more subtle. He was not deficient in those arts which, among the ignorant, will always secure the low. He drank with them, as if he could not well have drunk without them—threw himself among their ranks, as if he could not have disposed his limbs easily anywhere else; and did for his superior what the latter could never have done for himself. He operated sufficiently on the minds of several to secure a faction in his favor, and thus strengthened, he availed himself of the moment when the Jamaica had proved some portion of its potency, to broach openly the subject which had hitherto been only discussed in private.

Of the entreaties, the arguments, or the promises made by Ensign Darcy to persuade the troop into his way of thinking, we shall say nothing. It will be sufficient for our purpose that we show the condition of things at this particular juncture. Considerable progress had now been made with the subject. It had, in fact, become the one subject of discussion. The person whom it more immediately concerned, had, prudently, if not modestly, withdrawn himself from the apartment, though in doing so, he necessarily exposed himself to some encounter with the pitiless storm. The various groups had mingled themselves into one. The different smaller topics which before excited them, had given way before the magnitude of this, and each trooper began to feel his increased importance as his voice seemed necessary in the creation of so great a personage as his captain.

So far, Darcy had no reason to be dissatisfied with his performances. Assisted by the Jamaica, his arguments had sunk deep into their souls. One after another had become a convert to his views, and he was just about to flatter himself with the conviction that he should soon be rejoiced by the unanimous shout which should declare the nomination of their new captain, when another party, who before had said not a single word, now joined in the discussion after a manner of his own. This was no less important a personage than Muggs, the landlord.

"Counting sculps before you take 'em! I wonder where the dickens you was brought up, Ensign Darcy. Here now you're for making a new cappin, afore you know what's come of the old. You reckon Ned Morton's dead, do you? I reckon he's alive and kicking. I don't *say* so, mind me. I wouldn't swear sich a thing on Scripture book, but I'm so nigh sure of it, that I'd be willing to swear never agin to touch a drop of the stuff if so be he is not alive."

"But, Muggs — if he's alive, where is he?"

"Gog's wounds! that's easier asked than answered; but if we go to count for dead every chap that's missing, I'd have to go in mourning mighty often for the whole troop of you, my chickens. It's more reasonable that he's alive jist because we don't hear of him. We'd ha' hearn of him soon enough if the rebels had a got him. We'd ha' seen his hide upon a drumhead, and his own head upon a stump, and there wouldn't ha' been a dark corner on the Wateree that wouldn't ha' been ringing with the uproar about it. I tell you, my lads, that day that sees the death of Ned Morton, won't be a quiet day in these parts. There'll be more of a storm in these woods than is galloping through 'em now. If you don't cry that day, the rebels will; and let them lose what they may in the skrimmage, they'll have a gain when they flatten him on his back!"

"Ah, Muggs!" exclaimed Darcy, "I'm afraid you let your wishes blind you to the truth. I suppose you don't know that we got the captain's horse, and he all bloody?"

"Don't I know, and don't I think, for that very reason too, that he's safe and sound, and will soon be among you. You found his horse, but not him. The horse was bloody. Well! If the blood had been his, and vital blood, don't you think you'd ha' found the rider as well as the horse? But, perhaps, you didn't stay long enough for the hunt. Folks say you all rode well enough that day. But if the cappin was mortal hurt and you didn't find him, are you sure the rebels did? I'm a thinking, not, by no manner of means. For, if they'd ha' got him, what a hello-balloo we should have had. No, to my thinking, the cappin lost the horse a-purpose when he found he couldn't lose the rebels. The whole troop of Butler was upon him, swearing death agin him at every jump. Be sure now, Ned Morton left the critter to answer for him, and tuk to the swamp like a brown bear in September. I can't feel as if he was dead; and, if he was, Ensign Darcy, I, for one, wouldn't help in making a cappin out of any but one that comes out of the airth. I'm for country born, if any."

"Well, Muggs, what objection do you find to the lieutenant?"

"He's not country born, I tell you."

"But he's a good officer—there's not a better in the country than Lieutenant Stockton."

"That mout be, and then, agin, it moutn't. I'm a-thinking Ben Williams is about as good a man as you could choose for your cappin, if so be that Ned Morton's slipped his wind for sartin. I don't see Ben here to-night—at this present—but look at him when he comes in, and you'll say that's the man to be a cappin. He's a dragoon, now, among a thousand, and then, agin, he's country born."

"But, Muggs, I don't see that your argument goes for much. An American born is a king's man, and a British born is the same, and it's natural, when they're fighting on the same side, that a British born should have command just the same as the American."

"I don't see that it's natural, and I don't believe it. There's a mighty difference between 'em to my thinking. As for your king's men and British men, I'm one that wishes you had let us alone to fight it out among ourselves, rebel and loyal, jist as we stand. It was a sort of family quarrel, and would ha' been soon over, if you hadn't dipped a long spoon into our dish. They'd ha' licked us or we'd ha' licked them, and which ever way it went, we'd all ha' been quiet long afore this. But here you come, with your Irishmen, and your Yagers, your Scotchmen and your Jarmans, and you've made the matter worse without helping yourselves. For, where are you? As you whar? No, by the powers! You say Rawdon's licked Greene. It's well enough to say so. But where's Greene and where's Rawdon? If you ain't hearn, I can tell you."

"Well?" from half a dozen. "Let's hear! The news! The news!"

"Well! It's not well—not well for you, at least; and the sooner you're gone from these parts the better. Rawdon that licked Greene is about to run from Greene that he licked. I have it from Scrub Heriot—little Scrub, you know—that they've had secret council in Camden, and all's in a mist thar—the people half scared to death, for they say that they can't get bacon or beans, and Rawdon's going to vackyate, and sw'ars, if he has to do so, he'll make Camden sich a blaze that it'll light his way all down to Charlestown. I'm a-looking out for the burst every night. That's not all. Thar's as fresh a gathering of the rebels along the Santee and Pedee under Marion, as if every fellow you had ever killed had got his sculp back agin, and was jest as ready to kick as ever. Well, Tom Taylor's brushing like a little breeze about Granby, and who but Sumter rides the road now from Ninety-Six to Augusta? Who but he? Cunningham darsn't show his teeth along the track for fear they'll be drawed through the back of his head. Well, if this is enough to make you feel scarey, ain't it enough to make Ned Morton keep close and hold in his breath till he find a clean country before him. Don't you think of making a new cappin till you're sartin what's come of the old; and if it's all over with him, then I say look out for another man among you that comes out of the natteral airth. Ben Williams for me, lads, before any other."

"Hurrah for Ben Williams!" was the maudlin cry of half a dozen. The lieutenant at this moment reappeared. His glance was frowningly fixed upon the landlord, in a way to convince Muggs that he had not remained uninformed as to the particular course which the latter had taken. But it was clearly not his policy to show his anger in any more decided manner, and the cudgels were taken up for him by Darcy, who, during the various long speeches of the landlord had contrived to maintain a running fire among the men. He plied punch and persuasion—strong argument and strong drink—with equal industry; and the generous tendencies of the party began everywhere to overflow. He felt his increasing strength, and proceeded to carry the attack into the enemy's country.

"The truth is, Muggs, you have a grudge at the lieutenant ever since you had that brush together. You can't so readily forget that ugly mark on your muzzle."

"Look you, Ensign Darcy, there's something in what you

say that a leetle turns upon my stomach; for you see it's not the truth. I have no more grudge agin Lieutenant Stockton than I have agin you. As for the mark you speak of, I do say, it did him no great credit to make such a mark on a one-armed man; though I'd ha' paid him off with a side-wipe that would ha' made him 'spectful enough to the one I had left, if so be that Ben Williams hadn't put in to save him. That was the only onfriendly thing that Ben ever done to me to my knowing. No! I han't no grudges, thank God for all his blessings, but that's no reason why I shouldn't say what I do say, that Cappin Ned Morton's the man for my money; and, though I can't have much to say in the business, seeing I ain't no longer of the troop, yet if 'twas the last word I had to retickilate, I'd cry it for him. Here's to Ned Morton, boys, living or dead."

"And here's to Lieutenant Stockton, boys, and may he soon be captain of the Black Riders."

"Hurrah for Stockton! Hurrah!" was the now almost unanimous cry, and Stockton, advancing, was about to speak, when the faint sounds of a whistle broke upon the night, imparting a drearier accent to the melancholy soughing of the wind without. The note, again repeated, brought every trooper to his feet. The cups were set down hastily — swords buckled on — caps donned, and pistols examined.

"To horse!" was the command of Stockton, and his cool promptitude, shown on this occasion, was perhaps quite enough to justify the choice which the troop had been about to make of a new captain. "To horse!" he cried, leading the way to the entrance, but ere he reached it, the door was thrown wide, and the ambitious lieutenant recoiled in consternation, as he encountered, in the face of the new-comer, the stern visage of that very man, supposed to be dead, whom he equally feared and hated, and whose post he was so well disposed to fill. The chief of the Black Riders stood suddenly among his followers, and the shouts for the new commander were almost forgotten in those which welcomed the old. But let us retrace our steps for a few moments, and bring our readers once more within hearing of the kinsmen.

## CHAPTER VI

#### FIRST FRUITS OF FREEDOM.

It is not important to our narrative, in returning to the place and period when and where we left the rival kinsmen, that we should repeat the arguments which the younger employed in order to persuade the other to a more open and manly course of conduct in his political career. These arguments could be of one character only. The style in which they were urged, however, became somewhat different, after the final interview which they had in the presence of the sturdy woodman. The display which Supple Jack had made of the disguises which he had found upon the very road over which Edward Conway had fled, and about the very time when he had taken shelter in the swamp from the pursuit of Butler's men, would, to any mind not absolutely anxious not to believe, have been conclusive of his guilt. Edward Conway felt it to be so in his own case, and readily concluded that Clarence would esteem it so. The few reflections, therefore, which time permitted him to make, were neither pleasant nor satisfactory; and when he galloped off with his younger brother, he had half a doubt whether the latter did not meditate his sudden execution, as soon as they should be fairly concealed from the sight of the woodman. He knew enough of the character of Clarence to know that he would as soon destroy his own brother for treachery — nay, sooner — than an open enemy; and the silence which he maintained, the stern, rigid expression of his features, and the reckless speed at which he seemed resolved to ride, contributed in no small degree to increase the apprehensions of the guilty man. For a brief space that ready wit and prompt subterfuge, which had enabled him hitherto to play a various and very complicated game in life, with singular adroitness and success, seemed about to fail.

He felt his elasticity lessening fast—his confidence in himself declining; his brain was heavy, his tongue flattened and thick.

Besides, he was weaponless. There was no chance of success in any conflict, unless from his enemy's generosity; and upon that, in those days, the partisan who fought on either side made but few calculations. A club, the rudest mace, the roughest limb of the lithe hickory, became an object of desire to the mind of the conscious traitor at this moment. But he did not truly understand the nature of that mind and those principles, to which his own bore so little likeness. He little knew how strong and active were those doubts—the children of his wish—which were working in the bosom of Clarence Conway in his behalf.

At length the latter drew up his steed, and exhibited a disposition to stop. The rain, which by this time had become an incessant stream, had hitherto been almost unfelt by both the parties. The anxiety and sorrow of the one, and the apprehensions of the other, had rendered them equally insensible to the storm without.

"Edward Conway," said the younger, "let us alight here. Here we must separate; and here I would speak to you, perhaps for the last time, as my father's son."

Somewhat reassured, Edward Conway followed the example of his kinsman, and the two alighted among a group of hills, on the eastern side of which they found a partial protection from the storm, which was blowing from the west. But little did either need, at that moment, of shelter from its violence. Brief preparation sufficed to fasten their steeds beneath a close clump of foliage, and then followed the parting words of the younger, which had been so solemnly prefaced.

"Now, Edward Conway, my pledges to you are all fulfilled—my duties, too. I have done even more than was required at my hands by any of the ties of blood. I have been to you a brother, and you are now free."

"You do not repent of it, Clarence?"

"Of that, it is fitting that I say nothing rashly. Time will show. But I need not say to you, Edward Conway, that the discovery of these disguises, under circumstances such as Jack Bannister detailed before you, has revived, in all their force, my old suspicions. God knows how much I have striven to set my soul against these suspicions. God only knows how much I would give could I be sure that they were groundless. I dare not for my father's sake believe them—I dare not for my own. And this dread to believe, Edward Conway, is, I fear, the only thing that has saved, and still saves you, from my blow. But for this, kinsman or no kinsman, your blood had been as freely shed by these hands, as if its sluices were drawn from the least known and basest puddle in existence."

"I am at your mercy, Clarence Conway. I have no weapons. My arms are folded. I have already spoken when I should have been silent. I will say no more—nothing, certainly, to prevent your blow. Strike, if you will: if I can not convince you that I am true, I can at least show you that I am fearless."

The wily kinsman knew well the easy mode to disarm his brother—to puzzle his judgment, if not to subdue his suspicions.

"I have no such purpose!" exclaimed Clarence, chokingly. "Would to heaven you would give me no occasion to advert to the possibility that I ever should have. But hear me, Edward Conway, ere we part. Do not deceive yourself—do not fancy that I am deceived by this show of boldness. It did not need that you should assure me of your fearlessness. That I well knew. It is not your courage, but your candor, of which I am doubtful. The display of the one quality does not persuade me any the more of your possession of the other. We are now to part. You are free from this moment. You are also safe. Our men are no longer on the Wateree;—a few hours' good riding will bring you, most probably, within challenge of Watson's sentinels. If you are the foe to your country, which they declare you, he is your friend. That you do not seek safety in our ranks, I need no proof. But, ere we part, let me repeat my warnings. Believe me, Edward Conway, dear to me as my father's son, spare me, if you have it in your heart, the pain of being your foe. Spare me the necessity of strife with you. If it be that you are a loyalist, let us not meet. I implore it as the last favor which I shall ever ask at your hands; and I implore it with a full heart. You know that we have not always been friends. You know that there are circumstances, not involving our principles, on which we have already quarrelled, and which are of a nature but too well calculated to bring into activity the wildest anger and the deadliest hate. But, however much we have been at strife—however I may have fancied that you have done me wrong—still, believe me, when I tell you that I have ever, in my cooler moments, striven to think of, and to serve you kindly. Henceforward our meeting must be on other terms. The cloud which hangs about your course—the suspicion which stains your character in the minds of others—have at last affected mine. We meet, hereafter, only as friends or foes. Your course must then be decided—your principles declared—your purpose known; and then, Edward Conway, if it be as men declare, and as I dare not yet believe, that you are that traitor to your country—that you do lead that savage banditti which has left the print of their horses' hoofs, wherever they have trodden, in blood—then must our meeting be one of blood only; and then, as surely as I shall feel all the shame of such a connection in my soul, shall I seek, by a strife without remorse, to atone equally to my father and to my country for the crime and folly of his son. Fondly do I implore you, Edward Conway, to spare me this trial. Let our parting at this moment be final, unless we are to meet on terms more satisfactory to both."

The elder of the kinsmen, at this appeal, displayed more emotion, real or affected, than he had shown at any time during the interview. He strode to and fro among the tall trees, with hands clasped behind, eyes cast down upon the earth, and brows contracted. A single quiver might have been seen at moments among the muscles of his mouth. Neither of them seemed to heed the increasing weight of the tempest. Its roar was unheard—its torrents fell without notice around and upon them. The reply of Edward Conway was at length spoken. He approached his brother. He had subdued his emotions, whatever might have been their source. His words were few—his utterance composed and calm. He extended his hand to Clarence as he spoke.

"Let us part, Clarence. It does not become me to make further assurances. To reply, as I should, to what you have said, might be, probably, to increase the width and depth of that chasm which seems to lie between us. I can not say that I am satisfied with your tone, your temper, the position which you assume, and the right which you claim to direct, and warn, and counsel!—and when you threaten!—But enough! Let us part before anything be said which shall make you forget anything which you should remember, or me that I owe my life to your assistance. What is said is said—let it be forgotten. Let us part."

"Ay, let us part: but let it not be forgotten, Edward Conway?"

"True, true! Let it not be forgotten. It shall not be forgotten. It can not be. It would not be easy for me, Clarence, to forget anything which has taken place in the last ten days of my life."

There was a latent signification in what was said by the speaker to arouse new suspicions in the mind of the younger of the kinsmen. He saw, or fancied that he saw, a gleam of ferocity shine out from the eyes of his brother, and his own inflammable temper was about to flare up anew.

"Do you threaten, Edward Conway? Am I to understand you as speaking the language of defiance?"

"Understand me, Clarence, as speaking nothing which should not become a man and your brother."

The reply was equivocal. That it was so, was reason sufficient why Clarence Conway should hesitate to urge a matter which might only terminate in bringing their quarrel to a crisis.

"The sooner we separate the better," was his only answer. "Here, Edward Conway, is one of my pistols. You shall not say I sent you forth without weapons to defend you, into a forest field possibly, with foes. The horse which you ride is a favorite. You have lost yours. Keep him till you are provided. You can always find an opportunity to return him when you are prepared to do so; and should you not, it will make no difference. Farewell: God be with you—but remember!—remember!"

The youth grasped the now reluctant hand of the elder Conway; wrung it with a soldier's grasp—a pressure in which mingled feelings, all warm, all conflicting, had equal utterance;—then, springing upon his steed, he dashed rapidly into the forest and in a few moments was hidden from sight in its thickest mazes.

"Remember. Yes, Clarence Conway, I will remember. Can I ever forget! Can I ever forget the arrogance which presumes to counsel, to warn, and to threaten—to pry into my privacy—to examine my deeds—to denounce them with shame and threaten them with vengeance. I will remember—to requite! It shall not be always thus. The game will be in my hands ere many days, and I will play it as no gamester, with all upon the cast, ever yet played the game of life before. Without pause or pity—resolved and reckless—I will speed on to the prosecution of my purposes, until my triumph is complete! I must beware, must I?—I must account for my incomings and outgoings? And why, forsooth? Because I am *your* father's son. For the same reason do you beware! I were no son of my father if I did not resent this insolence."

He had extricated his horse from the cover which concealed him while he was giving utterance to this soliloquy. The noble animal neighed and whinnied after his late companion. The plaintive appeal of the beast seemed to irritate his rider, whose passions, subjected to a restraint which he had found no less necessary than painful, were now seeking that vent which they had been denied for an unusual season; and under their influence he struck the animal over the nostril with the heavy hand of that hate which he fain would have bestowed upon his master.

"Remember!" he muttered, as he leaped upon the saddle. "I need no entreaty to this end, Clarence Conway. I must be a patriot at your bidding, and choose my side at your suggestion; and forbear the woman of my heart in obedience to the same royal authority. We shall see!—We shall see!"

And, as he spoke, the sheeted tempest driving in his face the while—he shook his threatening hand in the direction which his brother had taken. Turning his horse's head upon an opposite course, he then proceeded, though at a less rapid rate, to find that shelter, which he now, for the first time, began to consider necessary.

It may have been ten minutes after their separation, when he heard a sound at a little distance which aroused his flagging attention.

"That whistle," said he to himself, "is very like our own. It may be! They should be here, if my safety were of any importance, and if that reptile Stockton would suffer them. That fellow is a spy upon me, sworn doubly to my destruction, if he can find the means. But let me find him tripping, and a shot gives him prompt dismissal. Again!—it is!—they are here—the scouts are around me, and doubtlessly the whole troop is at Muggs's this moment. *There*, he could do me no harm. Muggs is sworn my friend against all enemies, and he is true as any enemy.—Again, the signal! They shall have an echo."

Speaking thus he replied in a sound similar to that which he heard, and an immediate response, almost at his elbow, satisfied him of the truth of his first impression. He drew up his steed, repeated the whistle, and was now answered by the swift tread of approaching horses. In a few moments, one, and then another—appeared in sight, and the captain of the Black Riders of Congaree once more found himself surrounded by his men.

Their clamors, as soon as he was recognised, attested his popularity among his troop.

"Ha, Irby!—Ha, Burnet! Is it you?—and you, Gibbs—you Fisher: I rejoice to see you. Your hands, my good fellows. There! There! You are well—all well."

The confused questions and congratulations, all together, of the troopers, while they gave every pleasure to their chieftain, as convincing him of their fidelity, rendered unnecessary any attempt at answer or explanation. Nor did Edward Conway allow himself time for this. His words, though friendly enough, were few; and devoted, seemingly, to the simple business of the troop. Captain Morton—for such was the name by which only he was known to them—with the quickness of a governing instinct, derived from a few brief comprehensive questions, all that he desired to know in regard to their interests and position. He ascertained where the main body would be found, and what had taken place during his absence; and proceeded instantly to the reassumption of his command over them.

"Enough of this, my good fellows. I will see to all this at Muggs's. We have no time now for unnecessary matter. You have work on hand. Burnet, do you take with you Gibbs, Irby, and Fisher. Push your horses down for the Wateree by the first road running left of where we now stand. Do you know the route? It leads by the clay diggings of the old Dutchman — the brick-burner — what's his name?"

"I know it, sir——"

"Enough, then. Take that road — put the steel into your nags, but send them forward. If you are diligent you will overtake one of our worst enemies — a friend of Butler — a rebel — no less than Colonel Conway. Pursue and catch him. You can not fail to overtake him if you try for it. Take him prisoner — alive, if you can. I particularly wish that you should have him alive; but, remember, take him at every hazard. Living or dead, he must be ours."

The dragoon lingered for further orders.

"If you succeed in taking him, bring him on to Muggs's. Give the signal before you reach his cabin, that there may be no surprise — no mistake. Something depends on your observance of this caution; so, you will remember. Away, now, and ride for life."

Their obedience was sufficiently prompt. In an instant they were on their way, pursuing the track which Clarence had taken for the Wateree.

"Now!" exclaimed the outlaw-chief, with exultation — "now there is some chance for vengeance. If they succeed in taking him alive, I will practise upon him to his utter blindness — I will do him no harm, unless a close lodging-house will do him harm. If they kill him — well, it is only one of those chances of war which he voluntarily incurs: it is only the lower cast of the die. Yet, I trust it may not be so. I am not yet prepared for that. He is my father's son. He has stood beside me in danger. He deserves that I should spare him. But, even for all this he may not be spared, if he is to triumph over me — to sway me with his arrogance — to achieve all victories in love as in war. In love! — God, what a strange nature is this of mine! How feeble am I when I think of her! And of her I can not help but think; her beauty, her pride of soul—ay, even her arrogance, I can think of with temper and with love. But his—no, no! He has spoken too keenly to my soul; and when he forbids that I should seek and see *her*, he forfeits every claim. Let them slay him, if they please: it can only come to this at last."

And, with these words, striking with his open palm upon the neck of his horse, he drove him forward to Muggs's. His entrance we have already seen, and the wonder it excited: the wonder in all, the consternation in one. The troopers, with one voice, cried out for their ancient captain; and Stockton, confounded and defeated, could only hoarsely mingle his congratulations with the rest, in accents more faltering, and, as the outlaw captain well apprehended, with far less sincerity.

## CHAPTER VII.

### CAPTIVITY — FINESSE.

Edward Morton bestowed upon his second officer but a single glance, beneath which his eye fell and his soul became troubled. That glance was one of equal scorn and suspicion. It led the treacherous subordinate, with the natural tendency of a guilty conscience, to apprehend that all his machinations had been discovered; that some creature of his trust had proved treacherous; and that he stood in the presence of one who had come with the full purpose of vengeance and of punishment.

But, though secure as yet, in this respect, Lieutenant Stockton was not equally so in others, scarcely of less consequence. He had neglected, even if he had not betrayed, his trust. He had kept aloof from the place of danger, when his aid was required, and left his captain to all those risks—one of which has been already intimated to the reader—which naturally followed a duty of great and peculiar exposure, to which the latter had devoted himself. Even when his risk had been taken, and the dangers incurred, Stockton had either forborne that search after his superior, or had so pursued it as to render his efforts almost ineffectual.

But he had undertaken the toils of villany in vain, and without reaping any of its pleasant fruits. The return of his superior, as it were from the grave, left him utterly discomfited. His rewards were as far off as ever from his hopes; and, to his fears, his punishments were at hand.

His apprehensions were not wholly without foundation. So soon as the chief of the Black Riders could relieve himself from the oppressive congratulations which encountered his safe restoration to his troop, he turned upon the lieutenant, and, with an indignation more just than prudent, declared his disapprobation of his conduct.

"I know not, Lieutenant Stockton, how you propose to satisfy Lord Rawdon for your failure to bring your men to Dukes's, as I ordered you; but I shall certainly report to him your neglect in such language as shall speak my own opinion of it, however it may influence his. The consequences of your misconduct are scarcely to be computed. You involved me individually in an unnecessary risk of life, and lost a happy opportunity of striking one of the best blows in the cause of his majesty which has been stricken this campaign. The whole troop of the rebel Butler was in our hands; they must have been annihilated but for your neglect—a neglect, too, which is wholly unaccountable, as I myself had prescribed every step in your progress, and waited for your coming with every confidence in the result."

"I did not know, sir, that there was any prospect of doing anything below here, and I heard of a convoy on the road to General Greene——"

"Even that will not answer, Lieutenant Stockton. You were under orders for one duty, and presumed too greatly on your own judgment when you took the liberty of making a different disposition of the troop left to your guidance. You little dream, sir, how nigh you were to ruin. But a single hour saved you from falling in with all Sumter's command, and putting an end for ever to your short-lived authority. And yet, sir, you are ambitious of sole command. You have your emissaries among the troop urging your fitness to lead them; as if such proofs were ever necessary to those who truly deserve them. Your emissaries, sir, little know our men. It is enough for them to know that you left your leader in the hands of his enemies, at a time when all his risks were incurred for their safety and your own."

"I have no emissaries, sir, for any such purpose," replied the subordinate, sulkily; his temper evidently rising from the unpleasant exposure which was making before those who had only recently been so well tutored in his superior capacities. "You do me injustice, sir—you have a prejudice against me. For—"

"Prejudice, and against *you!*" was the scornful interruption of the chief. "No more, sir; I will not hear you farther. You shall have the privilege of being heard by those against whom you can urge no such imputations. Your defence shall be made before a court martial. Yield up your sword, sir, to Mr. Barton."

The eye of the lieutenant, at this mortifying moment, caught that of the maimed veteran Muggs; and the exulting satisfaction which was expressed by the latter was too much for his firmness. He drew the sword, but instead of tendering the hilt to the junior officer who had been commanded to receive it, confronted him with the point, exclaiming desperately—

"My life first! I will not be disgraced before the men!"

"Your life, then!" was the fierce exclamation of Morton, spoken with instant promptness, as he hurled the pistol with which Clarence Conway had provided him, full in the face of the insubordinate. At that same moment, the scarcely less rapid movement of Muggs, enabled him to grasp the offender about the body with his single arm.

The blow of the pistol took effect, and the lieutenant would have been as completely prostrated, as he was stunned by it, had it not been for the supporting grasp of the landlord, which kept him from instantly falling. The blood streamed from his mouth and nostrils. Half conscious only, he strove to advance, and his sword was partially uplifted as if to maintain with violence the desperate position which he had taken; but, by this time, a dozen ready hands were about him. The weapon was wrested from his hold, and the wounded man thrust down upon the floor of the hovel, where he was held by the heavy knee of more than one of the dragoons, while others were found equally prompt to bind his arms.

They were all willing to second the proceedings, however fearful, of a chief whose determination of character they well knew, and against whom they also felt they had themselves somewhat offended, in the ready acquiescence which most of them had given to the persuasive arguments and entreaties of Darcy. This latter person had now no reverence to display for the man in whose cause he had been only too officious. He was one of those moral vanes which obey the wind of circumstances, and acquire that flexibility of habit, which, after a little while, leaves it impossible to make them fix anywhere. He did not, it is true, join in the clamor against his late ally; but he kept sufficiently aloof from any display of sympathy. His own selfish fears counselled him to forbearance, and he was not ambitious of the crown of martyrdom in the cause of any principle so purely abstract as that of friendship. To him, the chief of the Black Riders gave but a single look, which sufficiently informed him that his character was known and his conduct more than suspected. The look of his superior had yet another meaning, and that was one of unmitigated contempt.

Unlike the lieutenant, Darcy was sufficiently prudent, however, not to display by glance, word, or action, the anger which he felt. He wisely subdued the resentment in his heart, preferring to leave to time the work of retribution. But he did not, any more than Stockton, forego his desire for ultimate revenge. He was one of those who could wait, and whose patience, like that of the long unsatisfied creditor, served only to increase, by the usual interest process, the gross amount of satisfaction which must finally ensue. It was not now for the first time that he was compelled to experience the scorn of their mutual superior. It may be stated, in this place, that the alliance between Stockton and himself was quite as much the result of their equal sense of injury, at the hands of Morton, as because of any real sympathy between the parties.

"Take this man hence," was the command of Morton, turning once more his eyes upon the prostrate Stockton. "Take him hence, Sergeant Fisher—see him well bestowed—have his wants attended to, but see, above all things, that he escape not. He has gone too far in his folly to be trusted much longer with himself, till we are done with him entirely. This, I trust, will soon be the case."

This order gave such a degree of satisfaction to the landlord, Muggs, that he found it impossible to conceal his delight. A roar of pleasure burst from his lips.

"Ho! ho! ho!—I thought it would be so.—I knew it must come to this. I thought it a blasted bad sign from the beginning, when he was so willing to believe the cappin was turned into small meat, and the choppings not to be come at. There's more of them sort of hawks in these parts, cappin, if 'twas worth any white man's while to look after them."

The last sentence was spoken with particular reference to Ensign Darcy, and the eyes of the stout landlord were fixed upon that person with an expression of equal triumph and threatening; but neither Darcy nor Morton thought it advisable to perceive the occult signification of his glance. The occupations of the latter, meanwhile, did not cease with the act of summary authority which we have witnessed. He called up to him an individual from his troop whose form and features somewhat resembled his own—whose general intelligence might easily be conjectured from his features, and whose promptness seemed to justify the special notice of his captain. This person he addressed as Ben Williams—a person whom the landlord, Muggs, had designated, in a previous chapter, as the most fitting to succeed their missing leader in the event of his loss. That Morton himself entertained some such opinion, the course of events will show.

"Williams," he said, after the removal of Stockton had been effected—"there is a game to play in which you must be chief actor. It is necessary that you should take my place, and seem for a while to be the leader of the Black Riders. The motive for this will be explained to you in time. Nay, more, it is necessary that I should seem your prisoner. You will probably soon have a prisoner in fact, in whose sight I would also occupy the same situation. Do with me then as one.—Hark!—That is even now the signal!—They will soon be here. Muggs, bar the entrance for a while, until everything is ready. Now, Williams, be quick; pass your lines about my arms and bind me securely. Let one or more of your men watch me with pistols cocked, and show, all of you, the appearance of persons who have just made an important capture. I will tell you more hereafter."

The subordinate was too well accustomed to operations of the kind suggested, to offer any unnecessary scruple, or to need more precise directions. The outlaw was bound accordingly; placed, as he desired, upon a bulk that stood in a corner of the wigwam, while two black-faced troopers kept watch beside him. The signal was repeated from without; the parties, from the sound, being evidently close at hand. The chief of the outlaws whispered in the ear of his subordinate such farther instructions as were essential to his object.

"Keep me in this situation, in connection with the prisoner—should he be brought—for the space of an hour. Let us be left alone for that space of time. Let us then be separated, while you come to me in private. We shall then be better able to determine for the future."

The hurried preparations being completed, the chief, now seemingly a closely-watched and strongly-guarded prisoner, gave orders to throw open the entrance, and, in the meantime, subdued his features to the expression of a well-grounded dissatisfaction with a situation equally unapprehended and painful.

The capture of Clarence Conway was not such an easy matter. It will be remembered that, when he separated from his brother, under the influence of feelings of a most exciting nature, he had given his horse a free spur, and dashed forward at full speed to regain his place of safety in the swamp. The rapidity of his start, had he continued at the same pace, would have secured him against pursuit. But, as his blood cooled, and his reflective mood assumed the ascendency, his speed was necessarily lessened; and, by the time that his treacherous kinsman was enabled to send the troopers in pursuit, his horse was suffered quietly to pick his way forward, in a gait most suited to his own sense of comfort.

The consequence was inevitable. The pursuers gained rapidly upon him, and owing to the noise occasioned by the rain pattering heavily upon the leaves about him, he did not hear the sound of their horses' feet, until escape became difficult. At the moment when he became conscious of the pursuit, he was taught to perceive how small were his chances of escape from it. Suddenly, he beheld a strange horseman, on each side of him, while two others were pressing earnestly forward in the rear. None of them could have been fifty yards from him at the moment when he was first taught his danger. The keenness of the chase, the sable costume which the pursuers wore, left him in no doubt of their character as enemies; and with just enough of the sense of danger to make him act decisively, the fearless partisan drew forth his pistol, cocked it without making any unnecessary display, and, at the same time, drove the rowel into the flanks of his steed.

A keen eye sent forward upon the path which he was pursuing, enabled him to see that it was too closely covered with woods to allow him to continue much farther his present rate of flight, and with characteristic boldness, he resolved to turn his course to the right, where the path was less covered with undergrowth, and on which his encounter would be with a single enemy only. The conflict with him, he sanguinely trusted, might be ended before the others could come up.

The action, with such a temperament as that of Clarence Conway, was simultaneous with the thought; and a few moments brought him upon the one opponent, while his sudden change of direction, served, for a brief space, to throw the others out.

The trooper, whom he thus singled out for the struggle, was a man of coolness and courage, but one scarcely so strong of limb, or so well exercised in conflict, as the partisan. He readily comprehended the purpose of the latter, and his own resolution was taken to avoid the fight, if he could, and yet maintain his relative position, during the pursuit, with the enemy he chased. To dash aside from the track, yet to push forward at the same time, was his design; at all events, to keep out of pistol-shot himself, for a while at least, yet be able, at any moment, to bring his opponent within range of his own weapon. Such a policy, by delaying the flight of the latter, until the whole party should come up, would render the capture inevitable.

But he was not suffered to pursue this game at his own pleasure. The moment he swerved from the track, Conway dashed after him with increased earnestness, taking particular care to keep himself, meanwhile, between the individual and his friends. In this way he seemed to drive the other before him, and, as his own speed was necessarily increased under these circumstances, the man thus isolated became anxious about his position, and desirous to return. In a mutual struggle of this sort, the event depended upon the comparative ability of the two horses, and the adroitness, as horsemen, of the several riders. In both respects the advantage was with Conway; and he might have controlled every movement of his enemy, but for the proximity of those who were now pressing on behind him.

The moment became one of increasing anxiety. They were approaching rapidly nigher, and the disparity of force in their favor was too considerable to leave him a single hope of a successful issue should he be forced to an encounter with the whole of them. The wits of the partisan were all put into activity. He soon saw that he must drive the individual before him entirely out of his path, or be forced to stand at bay against an attack in which defence was hopeless. His resolve was instantaneous; and, reasonably calculating against the probability of any pistol-shot from either taking effect while under rapid flight, and through the misty rain then driving into their mutual faces, he resolved to run down his enemy by the sheer physical powers of his horse, in defiance of the latter's weapon and without seeking to use his own. He braced himself up for this exertion, and timed his movement fortunately, at a moment when, a dense thicket presenting itself immediately in the way of the man before him, rendered necessary a change in the direction of his flight.

His reckless and sudden plunge forward discomposed the enemy, who found the partisan on his haunches at a time when to turn his steed became equally necessary and difficult. To wheel aside from the thicket was the instinctive movement of the horse himself, who naturally inclined to the more open path; but, just under these circumstances, in his agitation, the trooper endeavored to incline his bridle hand to the opposite side, in order that he might employ his weapon. The conflict between his steed's instinct and his own, rendered his aim ineffectual. His pistol was emptied, but in vain; and the rush of Conway's horse immediately followed. The shock of conflict with the more powerful animal, precipitated the trooper, horse and man, to the earth, and the buoyant partisan went over him with the rapidity of a wind-current.

A joyous shout attested his consciousness of safety—the outpourings of a spirit to which rapid action was always a delight, and strife itself nothing more than the exercise of faculties which seemed to have been expressly adapted for all its issues of agility and strength. Secure of safety, Conway now dashed onward without any apprehension, and exulting in the fullest sense of safety; but, in a moment after, he had shared the fortune of him he had just overthrown. A sudden descent of one of the Wateree hills was immediately before him, and in the increasing dimness of the twilight, and under the rapidity of his flight, he did not observe that its declivity of yellow clay had been freshly washed into a gulley. His horse plunged forward upon the deceptive and miry surface, and lost his footing. A series of ineffectual plunges which he made to recover himself, only brought the poor beast headlong to the base of the hill, where he lay half stunned and shivering. His girth had broken in the violent muscular efforts which he made to arrest his fall, and his rider, in spite of every exertion of skill and strength, was thrown forward, and fell, though with little injury, upon the yellow clay below. He had barely time to recover his feet, but not his horse, when the pursuers were upon him. Resistance, under existing circumstances, would have been worse than useless; and with feelings of mortification, much better imagined than described, he yielded himself, with the best possible grace, to the hands of his captors.

## CHAPTER VIII.

### ROUGH USAGE AMONG THE RIDERS.

Nothing could exceed the surprise of Clarence Conway, when, conducted by his captors into the house of Muggs, he beheld the condition of his kinsman. His ardent and unsuspicious nature at once reproached him with those doubts which he had entertained of the fidelity of the latter. He now wondered at himself for the ready credence which he had been disposed to yield, on grounds so slight and unsatisfactory as they then appeared to be, to the imputations against one so near to him by blood; and with the natural rapidity of the generous nature, he forgot, in his regrets for his own supposed errors, those of which his brother had, as he well knew, most certainly been guilty. He forgot that it was not less a reproach against Edward Conway — even if he was misrepresented as friendly to the cause of the invader — that he had forborne to show that he was friendly to that of his country; and, in that moment of generous forgetfulness, even the suspicious conduct of the fugitive, in relation to his own affair of heart, passed from his memory.

"Can it be! — Is it you, Edward Conway, that I find in this predicament?" were his first words when — the speaker being equally secured — they were left alone together.

"You see me," was the reply. "My ill reputation with the one side does not, it appears, commend me to any favor with the other."

"And these men?" said Clarence, inquiringly.

"Are, it would seem, no other persons than your famous Black Riders. I have had a taste of their discipline already, and shall probably enjoy something more before they are done with me. It appears that they have discovered that I am as rabid a rebel as, by Butler's men, I was deemed a tory. They charge me with some small crimes — such as killing king's men and burning their houses, stabbing women and roasting children —to all of which charges I have pleaded not guilty, though with very little chance of being believed. I can not complain, however, that they should be as incredulous in my behalf as my own father's son."

"Do not reproach me, Edward. Do me no injustice. You can not deny that circumstances were against you, so strong as almost to justify belief in the mind of your father himself. If any man ever struggled against conviction, I was that man."

"Clarence Conway, you perhaps deceive yourself with that notion. But the truth is, your jealousy on the subject of Flora Middleton has made you only too ready to believe anything against me. But I will not reproach *you*. Nay, I have resolved, believe what you may, hereafter to say nothing in my defence or justification. I have done something too much of this already for my own sense of self-respect. Time must do the rest—I will do no more."

The generous nature of Clarence deeply felt these expressions. His wily kinsman well understood that nature, and deliberately practised upon it. He listened to the explanations and assurances of the former with the doggedness of one who feels that he has an advantage, and shows himself resolute to keep it. Still he was too much of a proficient in the knowledge of human nature to overact the character. He spoke but few words. He seldom looked at his brother while he spoke, and an occasional half-suppressed sigh betokened the pains of a spirit conscious of the keenest wrong, yet too proud even to receive the atonement which reminds him of it. An expression of sorrow and sadness, but not unkindness, prevailed over his features. His words, if they did not betoken despondency, yet conveyed a feeling almost of indifference to whatever might betide him. The language of his look seemed to say—

"Suspected by my best friends, my father's son among them, it matters little what may now befall me. Let the enemy do his worst. I care not for these bonds—I care for nothing that he can do."

Nothing, to the noble heart, is so afflicting as the consciousness of having done injustice; and to witness the suffering of another, in consequence of our injustice, is one of the most excruciating of human miseries to a nature of this order. Such was the pang at this moment in the bosom of Clarence Conway. He renewed his efforts to soothe and to appease the resentments of his kinsman, with all the solicitude of truth.

"Believe me, Edward, I could not well think otherwise than I have thought, or do other than I have done. You surely can not deny that you placed yourself in a false position. It would have been wonderful, indeed, if your course had not incurred suspicion."

"True friendship seldom suspects, and is the last to yield to the current, when its course bears against the breast it loves. But let us say no more on this subject, Clarence. It has always been a painful one to me; and just now, passing, as I may say, from one sort of bondage to another, it is particularly so. It is, perhaps, unnecessary, situated as we are, that we should any longer refer to it. The doubts of the past may be as nothing to the dangers of the future. If this banditti be as you have described them, we shall have little time allowed us to discuss the past; and, for the future!——"

He paused.

"And yet, believe me, Edward, it makes me far happier to see you in these bonds, subjected to all the dangers which they imply, than to suffer from the accursed suspicion that you were the leader of this banditti."

"I thank you—indeed I thank you very much—for nothing! It may surprise you to hear me say that your situation yields me no pleasure. Your sources of happiness and congratulation strike me as being very peculiar."

"Edward Conway, why will you misunderstand me?"

"Do I?"

"Surely. What have I said to make you speak so bitterly?"

"Nothing, perhaps;—but just now, Clarence, my thoughts and feelings are rather bitter than sweet, and may be supposed likely to impart something of their taste to what I say. But I begged that we might forbear the subject—all subjects—at this time; for the very reason that I feared something might be spoken by one or both which would make us think more unkindly of each other than before—which would increase the gulf between us."

"I think not unkindly of you, Edward. I regret what I have spoken unkindly, though under circumstances which, I still insist, might justify the worst suspicion in the mind of the best of friends. There is no gulf between us now, Edward Conway."

"Ay, but there is; an impassable one for both—a barrier which we have built up with mutual industry, and which must stand between us for ever. Know you Flora Middleton? Ha! Do you understand me now, Clarence Conway? I see you do —you are silent."

Clarence was, indeed, silent. Painful was the conviction that made him so. He felt the truth of what his brother had spoken. He felt that there *was* a gulf between them; and he felt also that the look and manner of his kinsman, while he spoke the name, together with the tone of voice in which it was spoken, had most unaccountably, and most immeasurably, enlarged that gulf. What could be the meaning of this? What was that mysterious antipathy of soul which could comprehend so instantly the instinct hate and bitterness in that of another? Clarence felt at this moment that, though his suspicions of Edward Conway, as the chief of the Black Riders, were all dissipated by the position in which he found him, yet he loved him still less than before. The tie of blood was weakened yet more than ever, and its secret currents were boiling up in either breast, with suppressed but increasing hostility.

The pause was long and painful which ensued between them. At length Clarence broke the silence. His manner was subdued, but the soul within him was strengthened. The course of his kinsman had not continued to its close as judicious as it seemed at the beginning. It had been a wiser policy had he forborne even the intimation of reproach—had he assumed an aspect of greater kindness and love toward his companion in misfortune, and striven, by a studious display of cheerfulness, to prove to his brother that he was only apprehensive lest the situation in which the latter had found him might tend too much to his own self-reproach.

Such would have been the course of a generous foe. Such should have been the course of one toward a generous friend. Forbearance, at such a moment, would have been the very best proof of the presence of a real kindness. But it was in this very particular that the mind of Edward Conway was weak. He was too selfish a man to know what magnanimity is. He did not sufficiently comprehend the nature of the man he addressed; and, though the situation in which the latter found him had its effect, yet the policy, which he subsequently pursued, most effectually defeated many of the moral advantages which must have resulted to him, in the mind of his brother, from a more liberal train of conduct.

The reference to Flora Middleton placed Clarence on his guard. It reminded him that there were more grounds of difference between himself and kinsman than he had been just before prepared to remember. It reminded him that Edward Conway had been guilty of a mean evasion, very like a falsehood, in speaking of this lady; and this remembrance revived all his former personal distrusts, however hushed now might be all such as were purely political. Edward Conway discovered that he had made a false move in the game the moment that his brother resumed his speech. He was sagacious enough to perceive his error, though he vainly then might have striven to repair it. Clarence, meanwhile, proceeded as follows, with a grave severity of manner, which proved that, on one subject at least, he could neither be abused nor trifled with.

"You have named Flora Middleton, Edward Conway. With me that name is sacred. I owe it to my own feelings, as well as to her worth, that it should not be spoken with irreverence. What purpose do you propose by naming her to me, at this moment, and with such a suggestion?"

The outlaw assumed a bolder tone and a higher position than he took when the same subject was discussed between them in the swamp. There was an air of defiance in his manner, as he replied, which aroused all the gall in his brother's bosom.

"Am I to tell you now, for the first time, Clarence Conway, that I love Flora Middleton?"

"Ha!—Is it so?—Well!"

"It is even so! I love Flora Middleton—as I long have loved her."

"You are bold, Edward Conway! Am I to understand from this that you propose to urge your claims?"

"One does not usually entertain such feelings without some hope to gratify them; and I claim to possess all the ordinary desires and expectations of humanity."

"Be it so, then, Edward Conway," replied Clarence, with a strong effort at composure. "But," he added, "if I mistake not, there was an understanding between us on this subject. You—"

"Ay, ay, to pacify you—to avoid strife with my father's son, Clarence Conway, I made some foolish promise to subdue my own feelings out of respect to yours—some weak and unmanly concessions!"

"Well! Have you now resolved otherwise?"

"Why, the truth is, Clarence, it is something ridiculous for either of us to be talking of our future purposes, while in such a predicament as this. Perhaps we had better be at our prayers, preparing for the worst. If half be true that is said of these Black Riders, a short shrift and a sure cord are the most probable of their gifts. We need not quarrel about a woman on the edge of the grave."

"Were death sure, and at hand, Edward Conway, my principles should be equally certain, and expressed without fear. Am I to understand that you have resolved to disregard my superior claims, and to pursue Flora Middleton with your attentions?"

"Your superior claims, Clarence," replied the other, "consist simply, if I understand the matter rightly, in your having seen the lady before myself, and by so many months only having the start of me in our mutual admiration of her charms. I have not learned that she has given you to suppose that she regards you with more favor than she does myself."

A warm flush passed over the before pale features of Clarence Conway. His lip was agitated, and its quivering only suppressed by a strong effort.

"Enough, sir!" he exclaimed—"we understand each other."

There **was** probably some little mockery in the mood of Edward Conway as he urged the matter to a further point.

"But let me *know*, Clarence. Something of my own course will certainly depend—that is, if I am ever again free from the clutches of these——" The sentence was left unfinished by the speaker, as if through an apprehension that he might have more auditors than the one he addressed. He renewed the sentence, cautiously omitting the offensive member:—

"Something of my course, Clarence, will surely depend on my knowledge of your claims. If they are superior to mine, or to those of a thousand others—if she has given you to understand that she has a preference——"

The flush increased upon the cheek of the younger kinsman as he replied—

"Let me do her justice, sir. It is with some sense of shame that I speak again of her in a discussion such as this. Miss Middleton has given me no claim—she has shown me no preference—such as I could build upon for an instant. But, my claim was on *you*, Edward Conway. You were carried by me to her dwelling. She was made known to you by me; and, before this was done, I had declared to you my own deep interest in her. You saw into the secret and sacred plans of my heart—you heard from my own lips the extent of my affection for her; and—but I can speak no more of this without anger, and anger here is impotence. Take your course, Edward Conway, and assert your desires as you may. Henceforward I understand you, and on this subject beg to be silent."

Edward Conway was not unwilling that further discussion of this subject should cease. He had effected the object which he aimed at when he broached it; and tacitly it was felt by both parties, that words were no longer satisfactory, as weapons, in such an argument as theirs. The silence was unbroken by either, and the two fettered captives sat apart, their eyes no longer meeting.

The hour had elapsed which, by the previous instructions of the outlaw chief, had been accorded to the interview between himself and kinsman. The object of his *finesse* had, as he believed, been fully answered; and, at this stage of the interview,

Williams his counterfeit presentment made his appearance, with all due terrors of authority, clad in sable, savage in hair and beard, with a brow clothed in gloomy and stern purposes, and as if prepared to pronounce the doom which the fearful reputation of the Black Riders might well have counselled the innocent prisoner to expect. But something further of the farce remained to be played out, and Clarence Conway was the curious witness to a long examination to which his fellow-prisoner was subjected, the object of which seemed to be to establish the fact that Edward Conway was himself a most inveterate rebel. A part of this examination may be given.

"You do not deny that your name is Conway?"

"I do not," was the reply.

"Colonel Conway, of Sumter's Brigade?"

"*I* am Colonel Conway, of Sumter's Brigade," said Clarence, interposing.

"Time enough to answer for yourself when you are asked! —that story won't go down with us, my good fellow," sternly exclaimed the acting chief of the banditti. "Shumway," he exclaimed, turning to a subordinate, "why the d—l were these d—d rebels put together? They have been cooking up a story between them, and hanging now will hardly get the truth out of either! We'll see what Muggs can tell us. He should know this fellow Conway."

"Muggs has gone to bed, sir."

"Wake him up and turn him out, at the invitation of a rope's end. I'm suspicious that Muggs is half a rebel himself, he's lived so long in this rascally neighborhood, and must be looked after."

Shumway disappeared, and the examination proceeded.

"Do you still deny that you are Colonel Conway, of Sumter's brigade? Beware now of your answer—we have other rebels to confront you with."

The question was still addressed to the elder of the kinsmen. His reply was made with grave composure. "I do. My name is Conway, as I declared to you before; but I am not of Sumter's brigade, nor of any brigade. I am not a colonel, and never hope to be made one."

"Indeed! but you hope to get off with that d—d pack of lies, do you, in spite of all the evidence against you? But you are mistaken. I wouldn't give a continental copper for the safety of your skin, colonel."

"If the commission of Governor Rutledge of South Carolina will be any evidence to show who is, and who is not, Colonel Conway, of Sumter's brigade," was the second interruption of Clarence, "that commission will be found in my pocket."

"And what will that prove, you d—d rebel, but that it has been slipped from one to the other as you each wanted it. Your shifting commissions are well known make-shifts among you, and we know too well their value to put much faith in them. But can you guess, my good fellow," turning to Clarence, "you, who are so anxious to prove yourself a colonel — can you guess what it will cost you to establish the fact? Do you know that a swinging bough will be your first halting-place, and your first bow shall be made to a halter?"

"If you think to terrify me by such threats, you are mistaken in your man," replied Clarence, with features which amply denoted the wholesale scorn within his bosom; "and if you dare to carry your threats into execution, you as little know the men of Sumter's brigade, the meanest of whom would promptly peril his own life to exact fearful and bloody retribution for the deed. I am Colonel Conway, and, dog of a tory, I defy you. Do your worst. I know you dare do nothing of the sort you threaten. I defy and spit upon you."

The face of the outlaw blackened:—Clarence rose to his feet.

"Ha! think you so? We shall see. Shumway, Frink, Gasson!—you three are enough to saddle this fiery rebel to his last horse. Noose him, you slow moving scoundrels, to the nearest sapling, and let him grow wiser in the wind. To your work, villains—away!"

The hands of more than one of the ruffians were already on the shoulders of the partisan. Though shocked at the seeming certainty of a deed which he had not been willing to believe they would venture to execute, he yet preserved the fearless aspect which he had heretofore shown. His lips still uttered the language of defiance. He made no concessions, he asked for no delay—he simply denounced against them the vengeance of his command, and that of his reckless commander, whose fiery energy of soul and rapidity of execution they well knew.

His language tended still farther to exasperate the person who acted in the capacity of the outlaw chief. Furiously, as if to second the subordinates in the awful duty in which they seemed to him to linger, he grasped the throat of Clarence Conway with his own hands, and proceeded to drag him forward. He did not see the significant gesture of head, glance of eye, and impatient movement of Edward Conway, while he thundered out his commands and curses. The latter could not, while seeking to preserve the new character in which he had placed himself, take any more decided means to make his wishes understood; and it was with feelings of apprehension and annoyance, new even to himself, that he beheld the prompt savage, to whom he had intrusted the temporary command, about to perform a deed which a secret and mysterious something in his soul would not permit him to authorize or behold, however much he might have been willing to reap its pleasant fruits when done.

There was evidently no faltering in the fearful purpose of his representative. Everything was serious. He was too familiar with such deeds to make him at all heedful of consequences; and the proud bearing of the youth; the unmitigated scorn in his looks and language; the hateful words which he had used, and the threats which he had denounced; while they exasperated all around, almost maddened the ruffian in command, to whom such defiance was new, and with whom the taking of life was a circumstance equally familiar and indifferent.

"*Three* minutes for prayer is all the grace I give him!" he cried, hoarsely, as he helped the subordinates to drag the destined victim toward the door.

These were the last words he was allowed to utter. He himself was not allowed a single minute. The speech was scarcely spoken, when he fell prostrate on his face, stricken in the mouth by a rifle-bullet, which entered through an aperture in the wall opposite. His blood and brains bespattered the breast of Clarence Conway, whom his falling body also bore to the floor of the apartment.

A wild shout from without followed the shot, and rose, strong and piercing, above all the clamor within. In that shout Clarence could not doubt that he heard the manly voice of the faithful Jack Bannister, and the deed spoke for itself. It could have been the deed of a friend only.

## CHAPTER IX.

### A CRISIS.

THE sensation produced on all the parties by this sudden stroke of retribution was indescribable. The fate of Clarence Conway was suspended for a while. The executioners stood aghast. They relaxed their hold upon the prisoner; all their powers being seemingly paralyzed in amazement and alarm. Tacitly, every eye, with the instinct of an ancient habit, was turned upon Edward Conway. He, too, had partaken, to a large degree, of the excitement of the scene. The old habits of command reobtained their ascendency. He forgot, for the instant, the novel position in which he stood; the assumed character which he played, and all the grave mummery of his bondage and disguise. Starting to his feet, when the first feeling of surprise had passed, he shouted aloud in the language of authority.

"Away, knaves, and follow. Why do you gape and loiter? Pursue the assassin. Let him not escape you! Away!"

He was obeyed by all the troopers present. They rushed headlong from the dwelling with a sanguinary shout. The two brothers, still bound, were left alone together. The paroxysm of passion in the one was over. He was recalled to a consciousness of the wily game he had been playing the moment that he started to his feet and issued his commands. The pressure of the tight cords upon his arms, when he would have extended them to his men, brought back all his memories. In an instant he felt his error, and apprehended the consequences. His eye naturally turned in search of his kinsman, who stood erect, a surprised but calm spectator.

He had witnessed the action, had seen the excitement, and heard the language of Edward Conway; but these did not seem to him too extravagant for the temper of one easily moved, who was yet innocent of any improper connection with the criminals. The circumstances which had taken place were sufficiently exciting to account for these ebullitions, without awakening any suspicions of the truth. It is true that the fierce command, so familiarly addressed to the robbers by their prisoner, did seem strange enough to the unsuspecting Clarence; but even this was natural enough. Nor was it less so that they should so readily obey orders coming from any lips which, to them, conveyed so correctly the instructions to their duty. Besides, the clamor, the uproar, the confusion and hubbub of the scene, not to speak of those conflicting emotions under which Clarence Conway suffered at a moment so full, seemingly, of the last peril to himself, served to distract his senses and impair the just powers of judgment in his mind. He felt that Edward Conway had acted unexpectedly — had shown a singular activity which did not seem exactly called for, and was scarce due to those in whose behalf it was displayed; but, making due allowance for the different effects of fright and excitement upon different temperaments, he did not regard his conduct as strange or unnatural, however unnecessary it might seem, and, perhaps, impolitic. It was the first thought in this mind that Edward Conway, in his great agitation, did not seem to recollect that the assassination which had taken place was probably the only event which could then have saved his life.

These reflections did not occur to the mind of the latter. Conscious of equal guilt and indiscretion, the apprehensions of Edward Conway were all awakened for his secret. The lowering and suspicious glance which he watched in the eye of his kinsman, and which had its origin in a portion of the previous conference between them, he was at once ready to ascribe to the discovery, by the latter, of his own criminal connection with the outlaws. In his anxiety, he was not aware that he had not said enough to declare his true character — that he had only used the language which any citizen might employ without censure, on beholding the performance, by another, of any sudden and atrocious outrage.

So impressed was he with the conviction that he had betrayed the whole truth by his imprudence, that the resolution in his mind was partly formed to declare himself boldly and bid defiance to all consequences. What had he now to fear? was his natural reflection. Why should he strive longer to keep terms with one with whom he must inevitably break in the end? Clarence Conway was his rival, was his enemy, and was in his power. He had already felt the humiliation resulting from the unbecoming equivocal positions in which he stood to him. He had bowed to him, when he felt how much more grateful would be the mood to battle with him. He had displayed the smile of conciliation, when, in his heart, he felt all the bitterness of dislike and hate. Why should he longer seek to maintain appearances with one from whom he now had seemingly nothing to fear? Why not, at once, by a bold avowal of his course, justify, in the language of defiance, the hostile position in which he stood equally to his country and his kinsman?

Such a course would amply account for the past; and, in those arguments by which the loyalists of that day found a sanction for their adherence to the mother-country, he might well claim all the rights of position due to one, whatever may be his errors of judgment, who draws his sword in behalf of his principles.

Such were some of the arguments drawn from the seeming necessity of the case, which rapidly passed through the mind of Edward Conway as he watched the play of mingled surprise and disquiet in the features of his kinsman. But they were not conclusive. They were still combated by the last lingering sentiments of humanity and blood. Clarence Conway was still his kinsman, and more than that, he owed him a life.

"Besides," was the language of his second thoughts, "his myrmidons even now may be around us. Let us first see the result of this pursuit."

New apprehensions arose from this last reflection. That the followers of Clarence Conway were not far off was the very natural reflection of every mind, after the sudden and fearful death of him who had been the chosen representative of their chief. That the shot which slew Williams was meant for the chief of the Black Riders, was his own reflection; and it counselled continued prudence for the present. The game which he proposed in the prosecuting his purposes equally with Flora Middleton and his brother, was best promoted by his present forbearance—by his still continuing, at least while in the presence of Clarence Conway, to preserve his doubtful position as a prisoner.

He sank back, accordingly, upon the bulk from which he had arisen in the first moment of the alarm. His efforts were addressed to the task of composing his features, and assuming the subdued aspect of one who stands in equal doubt and apprehension of his fate. Some moments of anxiety elapsed, in which neither of the kinsmen spoke. Clarence, in the meantime, had also resumed his seat. He no longer looked toward his companion. His heart was filled with apprehension, in which his own fate had no concern. He trembled now for the life of the faithful woodman—for he did not doubt that it was he—who had tracked his footsteps, and so promptly interfered at the hazard of his own life, to exact that of his enemy. The senses of the youth were sharpened to an intense keenness. He could hear the distant clamors of the hunt without. The shouts and shrieks of rage, breaking, as they rose, far above the rush of the winds and the monotonous patterings of the rain. He was roused from an attention at once painful and unavoidable by the accents of his kinsman.

"Clarence!" said the latter, "this is a terrible affair—the murder of this man!"

"Scarcely so terrible to me;" was the cold reply—"it prolonged my life—the wretch would have murdered me, and I look upon his corse without horror or regret!"

"Impossible! His purpose was only to intimidate—he would never have dared the commission of such a crime."

"You are yet to learn the deeds of the Black Riders; you know not how much such outlawed wretches will dare in the very desperation of their hearts."

"That was a dreadful deed, however;—so swift, so sudden,

I confess it almost unmanned me. I felt desperate with terror I know not what I said."

"So I thought," replied Clarence, "for you actually shouted to the wretches to pursue the murderer, and he, too, that noble fellow, Jack Bannister. He has stood between me and death before. You also, Edward Conway, owe him a life."

"Do you think it was he, Clarence?"

"I have no doubt of it. I am sure of his halloo."

"If they catch him!—"

"God forbid that they should!"

"If they should not, we shall probably pay for his boldness. They will wreak their fury on our heads, if they be the bloody wretches that you describe them."

"I am prepared for the worst. I am their prisoner, but I fear nothing. I, at least, Edward Conway, am somewhat protected by the rights and usages of war; but you—"

"Much good did these rights promise you a few minutes past," said the other, sarcastically, "unless my conjecture be the right one. According to your notion, precious little respect would these men have had for the usages of war. Their own usages, by your own showing, have long since legitimated hanging and burning, and such small practices."

"I should not have perished unavenged. Nay, you see already how closely the avenger follows upon the footsteps of the criminal. For every drop of my blood shed unlawfully, there would be a fearful drain from the heart of every prisoner in the hands of Sumter."

"That, methinks, were a sorry satisfaction. To me, I confess, it would afford very little pleasure to be told, while I am swinging, that some one or more of my enemies will share my fate in order that the balance-sheet between the two armies may be struck to their mutual satisfaction. My manes would, on the other side of Styx, derive small comfort from beholding the ghost of my foe following close behind me, with a neck having a like ugly twist with my own, which he admits having received on my account."

"The jest is a bald one that's born under the gallows," replied Clarence, gravely, with a whig proverb.

"Ay, but I am not there yet," replied the other; "and, with God's blessing, I hope that the tree and day are equally far distant which shall witness such an unhappy suspension of my limbs and labors."

"If I stand in such peril," replied Clarence Conway, "holding as I do a commission from the state authorities, I can not understand how it can be that you should escape, having, unhappily, no such sanction, and being so much more in danger from their suspicion. I sincerely trust that you will escape, Edward Conway; but you see the perilous circumstances in which you are placed by your unhappy neglect of the proper duties to your country and yourself."

"I am afraid, Clarence, that your commission will hardly prevail upon them to make any difference in their treatment of us."

"And yet, I wish to Heaven Edward Conway, that both of my father's sons were equally well provided."

"Do you really wish it, Clarence?"

"From my soul I do," was the reply. "Gladly now, could I do so, would I place my commission in your hands."

"Indeed! would you do this, Clarence Conway? Are you serious?" demanded the elder kinsman, with looks of considerable interest and surprise.

"Serious! Do you know me so little as to make such an inquiry! Would I trifle at such a moment with any man?—Could I trifle so with a kinsman? No! Bound as we both are, the desire is idle enough; but, could it be done, Edward Conway, freely would I place the parchment in your hands with all the privileges which belong to it."

"And you——"

"Would take my risk—would defy them to the last—and rely upon their fears of that justice which would certainly follow any attempt upon my life while I remain their prisoner."

The chief of the Black Riders rose from the bulk on which he had been seated, and twice, thrice, he paced the apartment without speaking. Deep shadows passed over his countenance, and low muttering sounds, which were not words, escaped at moments through his closed teeth. He seemed to be struggling with some new emotion, which baffled his control and judgment equally. At length he stopped short in front of his kinsman. He had succeeded in composing his features, which were now mantled with a smile.

"Clarence," he exclaimed, "you are a very generous fellow. You always were, even in your boyhood. Your proffer to me loses nothing of its liberality because it would be injurious rather than beneficial to me. Your intention is everything. But, I can not accept your gift—it would be to me the shirt of Nessus. It would be my death, and if you take my counsel you will say nothing of it. Better by far had you left it in the swamp. Have you forgotten that I am here, under these very bonds, charged with no worse offence than that of being Colonel Clarence Conway. If I could be secure from this imputation, perhaps I would escape with no worse evil than the scars they have given me."

"True, true! These after matters had driven the other from my thought. I recollect—I had even given my testimony on that head.—If it will serve you, I will again repeat the truth, though they hew me down the next instant."

"Say nothing rashly, Clarence. You are as excessively bold as you are generous—every way an extravagant man. Suppress your commission, if you can, for I'm doubtful if it can do you any good with these people, and it may do you serious harm. They make little heed, I fear, of law and parchment. But hark! The shouting becomes nearer and louder. They are returning; they have taken the assassin!"

"God forbid!" was the involuntary ejaculation of Clarence, while a cold shudder passed over his frame at the apprehension. "God forbid! Besides, Edward Conway, he is no assassin."

"Still generous, if not wise!" was the remark of his companion, who added: "Perhaps, Clarence, our only hope of safety depends upon their having their victim."

"I love life; life is precious to me," said the other; "but it would be a bitterness and a loathing could I feel it were to be purchased by the sacrifice of that worthy fellow."

"We shall soon see. Here they come. Our trial is at hand."

No more words were permitted to either speaker. The uproar of conflicting voices without, the questioning and counselling, the cries and clamors, effectually stunned and silenced the two within. Then came a rush. The door was thrown open, and in poured the troop, in a state of fury, vexation, and disappointment.

They had failed to track the assassin. The darkness of the night, the prevalence of the storm, and the absence of every trace of his footsteps — which the rain obliterated as soon as it was set down — served to baffle their efforts and defeat their aim. They returned in a more savage mood of fury than before. They were now madmen. The appetite for blood, provoked by the pursuit, had been increased by the delay. Ben Williams, the man who was slain, was a favorite among the troop. They were prepared to avenge him, and, in doing this, to carry out the cruel penalty which he was about to inflict on the prisoner in the moment when he was shot down. Led on by one of the party by whom Clarence had been originally made prisoner, they rushed upon him.

"Out with him at once!" was the cry of the infuriate wretches. "To the tree — to the tree!"

"A rope, Muggs!" was the demand of one among them; and sharp knives flashed about the eyes of the young partisan in fearful proximity.

"What would you do, boys?" demanded Muggs, interposing. He alone knew the tie which existed between the prisoner and his commander. He also knew, in part at least, the objects for which the latter had put on his disguise.

"Let the prisoner alone to-night, and give him a fair trial in the morning."

"Who talks of fair trial in the morning? Look at Ben Williams lying at your foot. You're treading in his blood, and you talking of fair trial to his murderer."

"But this man ain't his murderer!"

"Same thing — same thing — wa'n't it on his account that he was shot? Away with him to the tree. Away with him!"

"Haul him along, fellows! Here, let me lay hand on his collar," cried a huge dragoon from behind. "Give's a hold on him and you'll soon see him out."

A dozen hands grappled with the youth. A dozen more contended that they might do so likewise.

"Scoundrels, give me but room and I will follow you," cried Clarence with a scorn as lofty as he would have shown in a station of the utmost security, and with tones as firm as he ever uttered at the head of his regiment.

"If nothing but my blood can satisfy you for that which is shed, take it. You shall not see me shrink from any violence which your ruffian hands may inflict. Know that I despise and defy you to the last."

"Gag him — stop his mouth. Shall the rebel flout us on our own ground?"

"Bring him forward. The blood of Ben Williams cries out to us;—why do you stand with open mouths there? Shove him ahead."

Amid such cries as these, coupled with the most shocking oaths and imprecations, they dragged forward the youth slowly, for their own numbers and conflicting violence prevented co-operation. They dragged him on until, at length, he stood in the blood, and just above the body, of the murdered man. He did not struggle, but he shrunk back naturally, with some horror, when he felt the clammy substance sticking to his feet. He readily conjectured whence it came — from what sacred sources of human life; — and, though a fearless soldier — one who, in the heat of battle, had often shed the blood of his enemy — yet the nature within him recoiled at the conviction that he stood in a puddle, which, but a little time before, had beat and bounded, all animation, and strength, and passion, in the bosom of a living man.

His shuddering recoil was mistaken by the crowd for resistance, and one ruffian, more brutal than the rest, renewing his grasp with one hand upon the collar of the youth, with the other struck him in the face.

The blow, that last indignity and violence to which the man submits, roused the swelling tides in the bosom of the youth beyond their wonted bounds. With an effort which seemed rather an emotion of the soul than a physical endeavor, he put forth his whole strength, and the cords snapped asunder which had confined his arms, and with the rapidity of lightning he retorted the blow with such sufficient interest as prostrated the assailant at his feet.

"Now, scoundrels, if you must have blood, use your knives— for no rope shall profane my neck while I have soul to defy and power to resist you. Dogs, bloodhounds that you are, I scorn, I spit upon you. Bring forth your best man—your chief, if you have one to take the place of this carcass at my feet, that I may revile, and defy, and spit upon him also."

A moment's pause ensued. The noble air of the man whom they environed—the prodigious strength which he had shown in snapping asunder the strong cords which had secured his limbs, commanded their admiration. Courage and strength will always produce this effect, in the minds of savage men. They beheld him with a momentary pause of wonder; but shame, to be thus baffled by a single man, lent them new audacity. They rushed upon him.

Without weapons of any kind, for he had been disarmed when first made a captive, they had no occasion to resort to that degree of violence in overcoming him, to which he evidently aimed to provoke them. It was his obvious desire to goad them on to the use of weapons which would take life, and thus effectually defeat their purpose of consigning him to the gallows;—that degrading form of death from which the gentle mind shrinks with a revulsion which the fear of the sudden stroke or the swift shot, could never occasion. Hence the abusive and strong language which he employed—language otherwise unfamiliar to his lips.

His desire might still have been gratified. Several of the more violent among the young men of the party were rushing on him with uplifted hands, in which the glittering blade was flashing and conspicuous. But the scornful demand of Clarence, with which he concluded his contumelious speech, brought a new party into the field.

This was no other than his kinsman. He had been a looker-on for some moments—not long—for the whole scene took far less time for performance than it now takes for narration. He had watched its progress with new and rather strange emotions. At one moment, the selfish desires of his heart grew predominant. He thought of Flora Middleton, and he sank back and closed his eyes upon the objects around him, saying, in his secret heart—

"Let them go on—let him perish—why should I preserve from destruction the only obstacle to my desires?"

At the next moment, a better spirit prevailed within him. He remembered the services of Clarence to himself.—He owed to him his life; and, but now, had not the generous youth tendered him for his extrication and sole use that document, which he fancied would be all-powerful in securing his own safety. The image of their mutual father came, also, to goad the unworthy son to a sense of his duty; and when he heard the fierce, proud accents of the youth—when he heard him call for "their best man, their chief, that he might defy and spit upon him," he started to his feet.

There was but a moment left him for performance if his purpose was to save. The knives of the infuriate mob were already flourishing above their victim, and in their eyes might be seen that fanatical expression of fury which is almost beyond human power to arrest. A keen, quick, meaning glance, he gave to the landlord, Muggs; whose eyes had all the while been anxiously watchful of his leader. At the sign the latter made his way behind him, and, unobserved, with a single stroke of his knife, separated the cord which bound his arms. In another instant his voice rose superior to all their clamors.

"Hold, on your lives!" he exclaimed, leaping in among the assailants. "Back, instantly, fellows, or you will make an enemy of me! Let the prisoner alone!"

"Gad, I'm so glad!" exclaimed Muggs, while the big drops of perspiration poured down his forehead. "I thought, cappin, you couldn't stand by, and see them make a finish of it."

## CHAPTER X.

#### SHADOWS OF COMING EVENTS.

"HOLD, comrades, you have done enough. Leave the prisoner to me! Colonel Conway, you demanded to look upon the chief of the Black Riders. He is before you. He answers, at last, to your defiance."

And with these words, with a form rising into dignity and height, in becoming correspondence, as it were, with the novel boldness of his attitude, Edward Conway stood erect and confronted his kinsman. In the bosom of the latter a thousand feelings were at conflict. Vexation at the gross imposition which had been practised upon him — scorn at the baseness of the various forms of subterfuge which the other had employed in his serpent-like progress; but, more than all, the keen anguish which followed a discovery so humiliating, in the bosom of one so sensible to the purity of the family name and honor — all combined to confound equally his feelings and his judgment. But his reply was not the less prompt for all this.

"And him, thus known, I doubly scorn, defy and spit upon!"

He had not time for more. Other passions were in exercise beside his own; and Edward Conway was taught to know, by what ensued, if the truth were unknown to him before, that it is always a far less difficult task to provoke, than to quiet, frenzy — to stimulate, than to subdue, the ferocity of human passions, when at the flood. A fool may set the wisest by the ears, but it is not the wisest always who can restore them to their former condition of sanity and repose. The congratulations of Muggs, the landlord, which, by the way, spoke something in his behalf, promised for a while to be without sufficient reason.

The captain of the Black Riders met with unexpected resistance among his troop. The murdered man had been a favorite, and they were not apt to be scrupulous about avenging the death of such among their comrades as were. Even at a time when a moderate degree of reason prevailed among them, it was not easy to subdue them to placability and forbearance in regard to a prisoner; the very name of whom, according to their usual practice, was synonymous with victim. How much less so, at this juncture, when, with their blood roused to tiger rage, they had been suffered to proceed to the very verge of indulgence, before any effort, worthy of the name, on the part of an acknowledged superior, had been made to arrest them!

Edward Morton felt his error, in delaying his interposition so long. If his purpose had been to save, his effort should have been sooner made, and then it might have been effected without the more serious risk which now threatened himself, in the probable diminution of his authority. He estimated his power too highly, and flattered himself that he could at any moment interpose with effect. He made no allowance for that momentum of blood, which, in the man aroused by passion and goaded to fury, resists even the desires of the mind accustomed to control it; even as the wild beast, after he has lashed himself into rage, forgets the keeper by whom he is fed and disciplined, and rends him with the rest.

Edward Morton stood erect and frowning among those whom he was accustomed to command—and their obedience was withheld! His orders were received with murmurs by some—with sullenness by all. They still maintained their position—their hands and weapons uplifted—their eyes glaring with savage determination;—now fixed on their threatened victim, and now on their commander; and without much difference in their expression when surveying either.

"Do ye murmur—are ye mutinous? Ha! will ye have me strike, men, that ye fall not back? Is it you, Barton, and you, Fisher.—You, of all, that stand up in resistance to my will! Ensign Darcy, it will best become you to give me your prompt obedience. I have not forgotten your connection with Lieutenant Stockton. Fall back, sir—do not provoke me to anger: do not any of you provoke me too far!"

The man addressed as Barton—a huge fellow who made himself conspicuous by his clamors from the first—replied in a style which revealed to Morton the full difficulties of his position.

"Look you, Captain Morton, I'm one that is always for obedience when the thing's reasonable; but here's a case where it's unreasonable quite. We ain't used to see one of us shot down without so much as drawing blood for it. Ben Williams was my friend; and, for that matter, he was a friend with every fellow of the troop. I, for one, can't stand looking at his blood, right afore me, and see his enemy standing t'other side, without so much as a scratch. As for the obedience, Captain, why there's time enough for that when we've done hanging the rebel."

"It must be now, Mr. Barton. Muggs, that pistol! Stand by me with your weapon. Men, I make you one appeal! I am your captain! All who are still willing that I should be so, will follow Muggs. Muggs—behind me. March! By the God of Heaven, Mr. Barton, this moment tries our strength. You or I must yield. There is but a straw between us. There is but a moment of time for either! Lower your weapon, sir, or one of us, in another instant, lies with Ben Williams."

The huge horseman's pistol which Muggs handed to his leader at his requisition, had been already cocked by the landlord. It was lifted while Morton was speaking—deliberately lifted—and the broad muzzle was made to rest full against the face of the refractory subordinate. The instant was full of doubt and peril, and Clarence Conway forgot for the time his own danger in the contemplation of the issue.

But the courage of the moral man prevailed over the instinct of blood. Edward Morton saw that he was about to triumph. The eye of the fierce mutineer sunk beneath his own, though its angry fires were by no means quenched. It still gleamed with defiance and rage, but no longer with resolution. The fellow looked round upon his comrades. They had shrunk back—they were no longer at his side; and no small number had followed the landlord and were now ranged on the side of their captain. Of those who had not taken this decided movement, he saw the irresoluteness, and his own purpose was necessarily strengthened. It is this dependence upon sympathy and association which constitutes one of the essential differences between the vulgar and the educated mind. Brutal and bold as he was, Barton was not willing to left alone. The chief of the Black Riders saw that the trial was fairly over—the strife had passed. The evil spirit was laid for the present, and there was no longer anything to fear.

"Enough!" he exclaimed, lowering his weapon, and acting with a better policy than had altogether governed his previous movements.

"Enough! You know me, Barton, and I think I know you. You are a good fellow at certain seasons, but you have your blasts and your hurricanes, and do not always know when to leave off the uproar. You will grow wiser, I trust; but, meanwhile, you must make some effort to keep your passions in order. This rough treatment of your friends, as if they were foes, won't answer. Beware. You have your warning."

"Yes," growled the ruffian, doggedly, still unwilling altogether to submit; "but when our friends stand up for our foes, and take sides against us, I think its reasonable enough to think there's not much difference between 'em, as you say. I'm done, but I think it's mighty hard now-a-days that we can't hang a rebel and a spy, without being in danger of swallowing a bullet ourselves. And then, too, poor Ben Williams! Is he to lie there in his blood, and nothing to be done to his enemy?

"I say not that, Mr. Barton. The prisoner shall have a trial; and if you find him guilty of connection with the man who shot Williams, you may then do as you please. I have no disposition to deprive you of your victim; but know from me, that, while I command you, you shall obey me—ay, without asking the why and wherefore! I should be a sorry captain—nay, you would be a sorry troop—if I suffered your insubordination for an instant. Away, now, and make the circuit—all of you but Shumway and Irby. See to your powder, that it be kept dry; and let your horses be in readiness for a start at dawn. This country is to hot for you already; and with such management as you have had in my absence, it would become seven times hotter. Away."

They disappeared, all but the two who were excepted by name. To these he delivered the prisoner.

"Shumway, do you and Irby take charge of the rebel Lodge him in the block, and let him be safely kept till I relieve you. Your lives shall answer for his safety. Spare none who seek to thwart you. Were he the best man in the troop, who approached you suspiciously, shoot him down like a dog."

In silence the two led Clarence Conway out of the house. He followed them in equal silence. He looked once toward his kinsman, but Edward Morton was not yet prepared to meet his glance. His head was averted, as the former was followed by his guards to the entrance. Clarence was conducted to an outhouse—a simple but close block-house, of squared logs—small, and of little use as a prison, except as it was secluded from the highway. Its value, as a place of safekeeping, consisted simply in its obscurity. Into this he was thrust headlong, and the door fastened from without upon him. There let us leave him for a while, to meditate upon the strange and sorrowful scene which he had witnessed, and of which he had been a part.

His reflections were not of a nature to permit him to pay much attention to the accommodations which were afforded him. He found himself in utter darkness, and the inability to employ his eyes led necessarily to the greater exercise of his thoughts. He threw himself upon the floor of his dungeon, which was covered with pine-straw, and brooded over the prospects of that life which had just passed through an ordeal so narrow. Let us now return to his kinsman.

Edward Morton had now resumed all the duties of his station as chief of the Black Riders. In this capacity, and just at this this time, his tasks, as the reader will readily imagine, were neither few in number nor easy of performance. It required no small amount of firmness, forethought, and adroitness, to keep in subjection, and govern to advantage, such unruly spirits. But the skill of their captain was not inconsiderable, and such were the very spirits whom he could most successfully command. The coarser desires of the mind, and the wilder passions of the man, he could better comprehend than any other. With these he was at home. But with these his capacity was at an end. Beyond these, and with finer spirits, he was usually at fault.

To be the successful leader of ruffians is perhaps a small

merit. It requires cunning, rather than wisdom, to be able simply to discover the passion which it seeks to use; and this was the chief secret of Edward Morton. He knew how to make hate, and jealousy, and lust, and fear, subservient to his purposes, already roused into action. It is doubtful, even, whether he possessed the cold-blooded talent of Iago, to awaken them from their slumbers, breathe into them the breath of life, and send them forward, commissioned like so many furies, for the destruction of their wretched victim. A sample has been given already of the sort of trial which awaited him in the control of his comrades.

But there were other difficulties which tasked his powers to the utmost. The difficulties which environed the whole British army were such as necessarily troubled, in a far greater degree, its subordinate commands. The duties of these were more constant, more arduous, and liable to more various risk and exposure. The unwonted successes of the American arms had awakened all the slumbering patriotism of the people; while the excesses of which such parties as that which Morton commanded had been guilty, in the hey-day of their reckless career, had roused passions in the bosom of their foes, which, if better justified, were equally violent, and far less likely, once awakened, to relapse into slumber. Revenge was busy with all her train in search of Morton himself, and the gloomily-caparisoned troop which he led. It was her array from which he so narrowly escaped when he received the timely succor of his kinsman in the swamp. A hundred small bodies like his own had suddenly started into existence and activity around him, some of which had almost specially devoted themselves to the destruction of his troop. The wrongs of lust, and murder, and spoliation, were about to be redressed; and by night, as by day, was he required to keep his troop in motion, if for no other object than his own safety; though, by this necessity, he was compelled to traverse a country which had been devastated by the wanton hands of those whom he commanded. On the same track, and because of the same provocation, were scattered hundreds of enemies, as active in pursuit and search as he was in evasion. He well knew the fate which awaited him if caught, and involuntarily shuddered as he thought of it: death in its most painful form; torture fashioned by the most capricious exercise of ingenuity; scorn, ignominy, and contumely, the most bitter and degrading, which stops not even at the gallows, and, as far as it may, stamps the sign of infamy upon the grave.

These were, in part, the subject of the gloomy meditations of the outlawed chief when left alone in the wigwam of Muggs, the landlord. True, he was not without his resources—his disguises—his genius! He had been so far wonderfully favored by fortune, and his hope was an active, inherent principle in his organization. But the resources of genius avail not always, and even the sanguine temperament of Edward Morton was disposed to reserve, while listening to the promises of fortune. He knew the characteristic caprices in which she was accustomed to indulge. He was no blind believer in her books. He was too selfish a man to trust her implicitly; though, hitherto, she had fulfilled every promise that she had ever made.

The signs of a change were now becoming visible to his senses. He had his doubts and misgivings; he was not without audacity—he could dare with the boldest; but his daring had usually been shown at periods, when to dare was to be cautious. He meditated, even now, to distrust the smiles of fortune in season—to leave the field of adventure while it was still possible and safe to do so.

His meditations were interrupted at this moment, and, perhaps, assisted, by no less a person than Muggs, the landlord. He made his appearance, after a brief visit to an inner shanty—a place of peculiar privity—the sanctum sanctorum—in which the landlord wisely put away from sight such stores as he wished to preserve from that maelstrom, the common maw. The landlord was one of the few who knew the secret history of the two Conways; and, though he knew not all, he knew enough to form a tolerably just idea of the feelings with which the elder regarded the younger kinsman. He could form a notion, also, of the sentiments by which they were requited. In Muggs, Edward Morton had reason to believe that he had a sure friend—one before whom he might safely venture to unbosom some of his reserves. Still, he was especially careful to show not all, nor the most important—none, in fact, the revelation of which could possibly be productive of any very serious injury or inconvenience. He, perhaps, did little more than stimulate the communicative disposition of "mine host," who, like most persons of his craft, was garrulous by profession, and fancied that he never ministered perfectly to the palates of his guests, unless when he accompanied the service by a free exercise of his own tongue.

"Well, cappin, the game of fox and goose is finished now, I reckon. There's no chance to play possum with your brother any longer. It's lion and tiger now, if anything."

"I suppose so," replied the other, with something of a sigh. The landlord continued:—

"The question now, I reckon—now, that you've got him in your clutches—is what you're to do with him. To my thinking, it's jest the sort of question that bothered the man when he shook hands with the black bear round the tree. It was a starve to hold on and a squeeze to let go, and danger to the mortal ribs whichever way he took it."

"You have described the difficulty, Muggs," said the other, musingly—"what to do with him is the question."

"There's no keeping him here, that's cl'ar."

"No. That's impossible!"

"His friends, I reckon, are nigh enough to get him out of the logbox, and it's cl'ar they know where to find him. That shot that tumbled poor Williams was mighty nigh and mighty sudden, and was sent by a bold fellow. I'm onsatisfied but there was more than one."

"No—but one," said Morton—"but one!"

"Well, cappin, how do you count? There wa'n't no track to show a body where to look for him. The wash made the airth smooth again in five shakes after the foot left the print."

"It's guesswork with me only, Muggs."

"And who do you guess 'twas, cappin?"

"Supple Jack!"

"Well, I reckon you're on the right trail. It's reasonable enough. I didn't once think of him. But it's cl'ar enough to everybody that knows the man, that Supple Jack's jist the lad to take any risk for a person he loves so well. But, you don't think he come alone? I'm dub'ous the whole troop ain't mighty fur off."

"But him, Muggs! He probably came alone. We left him, only an hour before I came, on the edge of the Wateree—a few miles above this. He and Clarence gave me shelter in the swamp when I was chased by Butler's men, and when that skulking scoundrel, Stockton, left me to perish. Clarence rode on with me, and left Supple Jack to return to the swamp, where they have a first rate hiding-place. I suspect he did not return, but followed us. But of this we may speak hereafter. The question is, what to do with the prisoner—this bear whom I have by the paws, and whom it is equally dangerous to keep and to let go."

"Well, that's what I call a tight truth; but it's a sort of satisfaction, cappin, that you've still got the tree a-tween you; and so you may stop a while to consider. Now I ain't altogether the person to say what's what, and how it's to be done; but if so be I can say anything to make your mind easy, cappin, you know I'm ready."

"Do so, Muggs: let me hear you," was the reply of the outlaw, with the musing manner of one who listens with his ears only, and is content to hear everything, if not challenged to find an answer.

"Well, cappin, I'm thinking jest now we're beset all round with troubles; and there's no telling which is biggest, closest, and ugliest—they're all big, and close, and ugly. As for hiding Clarence Conway here, now, or for a day more, that's onpossible. It's cl'ar he's got his friends on the track, one, mout be, a hundred; and they can soon muster enough to work him out of the timbers, if it's only by gnawing through with their teeth. Well, how are you to do then? Send him under guard to Camden? Why, it's a chance if all your troop can carry themselves there, without losing their best buttons by the way. It's a long road, and the rebels watch it as close as hawks do the farmyard in chicken season. That, now, is about the worst sign for the king's side that I've seed for a long spell of summers. It shows pretty cl'ar that we ain't so strong as we was a-thinking. The wonder is, where these troopers come from; and the worst wonder is, where they get their boldness. Once on a time, when Tarleton first begun to ride among us, it was more like a driving of deer than a fighting of men; but it seems to me that the rebels have got to be the drivers, and o' late days they scamper us mightily. I see these things better than you, cappin, and, perhaps, better than the rebels themselves; for I ain't in the thick. I'm jest like one that's a-standing on a high hill and looking down at the fighting when it's a-going on below. I tell you, cappin, the game's going agin the king's people. They're a-losing ground — these men's getting fewer and fewer every day, and jest so fast do I hear of a new gathering among the whigs. I tell you agin, cappin, you're beset with troubles."

"I know it, Muggs. Your account of the case is an accurate one. We are in a bad way."

"By jingo, you may say so, cappin. You are, as I may say in a mighty bad way — a sort of conflusteration, that it puzzles my old head more than I can tell rightly, to onbefluster. Then, as for the prisoner —"

"Ay, *that*, Muggs. Speak to *that*. What of him? — let me hear your advice about the prisoner. How is he to be disposed off?"

"Well now, cappin — there's a-many ways for doing that, but which is the right and proper one — and when it's done, will it sarve the purpose? I'm afeard not — I'm not knowing to any way how to fix it so as to please you. It's pretty sartain he's your enemy in war and your enemy in peace; and if all things that's said be true, about him and Miss Flora, it don't seem to me that you'd ha' been any worse off — if so be your father had never given you this brother for a companion."

The outlaw chief looked up for the first time during the interview, and his eye, full of significance, encountered that of the landlord.

"Ay, Muggs, the gift was a fatal one to me. Better for me — far better — had he never seen the light; or, seeing it, that some friendly foe had closed it from his eyes, while he — while we were both — in a state of innocence."

"Gad, captain, I was thinking at one time to-night that black

Barton would have done you a service like that; and I was a-thinking jest then, that you wa'n't unwilling. You kept so long quiet, that I was afeard you'd have forgotten the blood-kin, and let the boys had the game their own way."

"You were afraid of it, were you?" said Morton, his brow darkening as he spoke.

"Ay, that I was, mightly. When I thought of the temptations, you know;—Miss Flora and her property—and then the fine estates he got by his mother's side and all that was like to fall to you, if once he was out of the way—I begun to trimble —for I thought you couldn't stand the temptation. 'He's only to keep quiet now and say nothing, and see what he'll get for only looking on.' That was the thought that troubled me. I was afeard, as I tell you, that you'd forget blood-kin, and everything, when you come to consider the temptations."

The outlaw rose and strode the floor impatiently.

"No, no, Muggs; you had little cause to fear. He had just saved my life—sheltered me from my enemies—nay, would have yielded me his own commission as a protection, which he supposed would be effectual for his own or my safety. No, no! I could not suffer it. Yet, as you say, great, indeed, would have been the gain—great was the temptation."

"True, cappin, but what's the gain that a man gits by bloodying his hands agin natur'? Now, it's not onreasonable or onnatural, when you have tumbled an open enemy in a fair scratch, to see after his consarns, and empty his fob and pockets. But I don't think any good could come with the gain that's spotted with the blood of one's own brother—"

"He's but a half-brother, Muggs," said Morton, hastily. "Different mothers, you recollect."

"Well, I don't see that there's a much difference, cappin. He's a full brother by your father's side."

"Yes, yes!—but Muggs, had he been slain by Barton and the rest, the deed would have been none of mine. It was a chance of war, and he's a soldier."

"Well, cappin, I'm not so certain about that. There's a difference I know, but—"

"It matters not! He lives? He is spared, Muggs—spared,

perhaps, for the destruction of his preserver. I have saved his life; but he knows my secret. That secret!—That fatal secret! Would to God!—"

He broke off the exclamation abruptly, while he struck his head with his open palm.

"My brain is sadly addled, Muggs. Give me something—something which will settle it and compose my nerves. You are happy, old fellow—you are happy, and—safe! The rebels have forgiven you—have they not?"

"Well, we have forgiven each other, cappin, and I have found them better fellows nigh, than they war at a distance;" replied the landlord, while he concocted for the outlaw a strong draught of punch, the favorite beverage of the time and country.

"If I ain't happy, cappin, it's nobody's fault but my own. I only wish you were as safe, with all your gettings, as I think myself with mine; and you mought be, cappin;—you mought."

A look of much significance concluded the sentence.

"How—what would you say, Muggs?" demanded the outlaw, with some increase of anxiety in his manner.

The reply of the landlord was whispered in his ears.

"Would to heaven I could!—but how?—How, Muggs, is this to be done?"

The answer was again whispered.

"No, no!" replied the other, with a heavy shake of the head. "I would not, and I dare not. They have stood by me without fear or faithlessness, and I will not now desert them. But enough of this for the present. Get me your lantern, while I seek this brother of mine in private. There must be some more last words between us."

## CHAPTER XI.

### THE TRUE ISSUE.

PRECEDED by the landlord Muggs, who carried a dark lantern, Morton took his way to the secluded block-house in which his kinsman was a prisoner. The only entrance to this rude fabric was closely watched by the two persons to whom Clarence was given in charge. These found shelter beneath a couple of gigantic oaks which stood a little distance apart from one another, yet sufficiently nigh to the block-house to enable the persons in their shadow, while themselves perfectly concealed, to note the approach of any intruder. Dismissing them to the tavern, the chief of the Black Riders assigned to Muggs the duty of the watch, and having given him all necessary instructions, he entered the prison, the door of which was carefully fastened behind him by the obedient landlord.

The lantern which he bore, and which he set down in one corner of the apartment, enabled Clarence to distinguish his brother at a glance; but the youth neither stirred nor spoke as he beheld him. His mind, in the brief interval which had elapsed after their violent separation in the tavern, had been busily engaged in arriving at that stage of stern resignation, which left him comparatively indifferent to any evils which might then occur. Unable to form any judgment upon the course of his brother's future conduct, he was not prepared to say how far he might be willing to go—and how soon—in permitting to his sanguinary troop the indulgence of their bloody will. Wisely, then, he had steeled his mind against the worst, resolved, if he had suffer death in an obscurity so little desired by the youthful and ambitious heart, to meet its bitter edge with as calm a countenance as he should like to display, under a similar trial, in the presence of a thousand spectators.

Edward Morton had evidently made great efforts to work his

mind up to a similar feeling of stern indifference; but he had not been so successful, although, at the moment, untroubled by any of those apprehensions which were sufficiently natural to the situation of his brother. His face might have been seen to vary in color and expression as his eye turned upon the spot where Clarence was sitting. The moral strength was wanting in his case which sustained the latter. The consciousness of guilt enfeebled, in some degree, a spirit, whose intense selfishness alone — were he unpossessed of any other more decisive characteristics — must have been the source of no small amount of firmness and courage. As if ashamed, however, of his feebleness, and determined to brave the virtue which he still felt himself compelled to respect, he opened the conference by a remark, the tone and tenor of which were intended to seem exulting and triumphant.

"So, Colonel Conway, you find your wisdom has been at fault. You little fancied that you were half so intimate with that fierce bandit — that renowned chieftain — of whom report speaks so loudly. It does not need that I should introduce you formally to the captain of the Black Riders of Congaree."

The youth looked up, and fixed his eye steadily on that of the speaker. Severe, indeed, but full of a manly sorrow, was the expression of that glance.

"Edward Conway," he replied, after a brief delay, "you do not deceive me by that tone — nay, you do not deceive yourself. Your heart, instead of exultation, feels at this moment nothing but shame. Your eye gazes not steadily on mine. Your spirit is not that of a fearless man. You shrink, Edward Conway, in spite of your assumed boldness, with all the cowardice of a guilty soul."

"Cowardice! — do you charge *me* with cowardice?"

"Ay, what else than cowardice has made you descend to the subterfuge and the trick — to the base disguise and the baser falsehood? These, too, to your brother, even at the moment when he was risking his own life to rescue that which you have dishonored for ever."

"I will prove to you, in due season, that I am no coward, Clarence Conway," replied the other, in hoarse and nearly undistinguishable accents; "you, at least, are seeking to convince me that you are none, in thus bearding the lion in his den."

"The lion! Shame not that noble beast by any such comparison. The fox will better suit your purpose and performance."

With a strong effort the outlaw kept down his temper, while he replied—

"I will not suffer you to provoke me, Clarence Conway. I have sought you for a single object, and that I will perform. After that—that over—and the provocation shall be met and welcomed. Now!——"

The other fiercely interrupted him, as he exclaimed—

"Now be it, if you will! Free my hands—cut asunder these degrading bonds which you have fixed upon the arms whose last offices were employed in freeing yours, and in your defence—and here, in this dungeon, breast to breast, let us carry out that strife to its fit completion, which your evil passion, your cupidity or hate, have so dishonestly begun. I know not, Edward Conway, what perversity of heart has brought you to this wretched condition—to the desertion of your friends—your country—the just standards of humanity—the noble exactions of truth. You have allied yourself to the worst of ruffians, in the worst of practices, without even the apology of that worst of causes which the ordinary tory pleads in his defence. You can not say that your loyalty to the king prompts you to the side you have taken, for I myself have heard you declare against him a thousand times; unless, indeed, I am to understand that even ere we left the hearth and burial-place of our father, you had begun that career of falsehood in which you have shown yourself so proficient. But I seek not for the causes of your present state; for the wrongs and the dishonor done me. If you be not utterly destitute of manhood, cut these bonds, and let the issue for life and death between us determine which is right."

"There! You have your wish, Clarence Conway." And, as he spoke, he separated the cords with his hunting-knife, and the partisan extended his limbs in all the delightful consciousness of recovered freedom.

"You are so far free, Clarence Conway!—your limbs are unbound, but you are unarmed. I restore you the weapon with which you this day provided me. It would now be easy for you to take the life of him whom you so bitterly denounce. I have no weapon to defend myself; my bosom is without defence."

"What mean you? Think you that I would rush on you unarmed—that I seek unfair advantage?"

"No, Clarence; for your own sake and safety, I would not fight you now."

"Why for my safety?" demanded the partisan.

"For the best of reasons. Were you to succeed in taking my life, it would avail you nothing, and your own would be forfeit. You could not escape from this place, and fifty weapons would be ready to avenge my death."

"Why, then, this mockery—this cutting loose my bonds—this providing me with weapons?" demanded Clarence.

"You shall see. You know not yet my desire. Hear me. My purpose is to acquit myself wholly of the debt I owe you, so that, when we do meet, there shall be nothing to enfeeble either of our arms, or diminish their proper execution. Once to-night I have saved you, even at the peril of my own life, from the fury of my followers. I have already severed your bonds. I have restored your weapon, and before the dawn of another day, the fleet limbs of your own charger shall secure your freedom. This done, Clarence Conway, I shall feel myself acquitted of all those burdensome obligations which, hitherto, have made me suppress the natural feelings of my heart—the objects of my mind—the purposes of interest, ambition, love—all of which depend upon your life. So long as you live, I live not—so long as you breathe, my breath is drawn with doubt, difficulty, and in danger. Your life has been in my hands, but I could not take it while I was indebted to you for my own. By to-morrow's dawn I shall be acquitted of the debt—I shall have given you life for life, and liberty for liberty. After that, when we next meet, my gifts shall be scorn for scorn and blow for blow. You have my purpose."

Clarence Conway heard him with patience, but with mixed feelings. He was about to reply in a similar spirit, but a nobler sentiment arose in his bosom with the momentary pause which he allowed himself for thought. He kept down the gushing blood which was about to pour itself forth in defiance from his laboring breast, and spoke as follows—

"I will not say, Edward Conway, what I might safely declare of my own indifference to your threats. Nay, were I to obey the impulses which are now striving within me for utterance, I should rather declare how happy it would make me were the hour of that struggle arrived. But there are reasons that speak loudly against the wish. For your sake, for our father's sake, Edward Conway, I would pray that we might never meet again."

"Pshaw! these are whining follies!—the cant of the girl or. the puritan. They do not impose on *me*. Your father's sake and mine, indeed! Say nothing for yourself—for your own sake—oh, no! no! you have no considerations of self—none! Philanthropic, patriotic gentleman!"

The keen eye of Clarence flashed angrily as he listened to this sneer. He bit his lip to restrain his emotion, and once more replied, but it was no longer in the language of forbearance.

"I am not unwilling to say, for *my* sake also, Edward Conway. Even to you I need not add, that no mean sentiment of fear governs me in the expression. Fear I have of no man. Fear of you, Edward Conway—you, in your present degraded attitude and base condition—the leagued with ruffians and common stabbers—a traitor and a liar!—Fear of *you* I could not have! Nor do you need that I should tell you this. You feel it in your secret soul. You know that I never feared you in boyhood, and can not fear you now. My frequent experience of your powers and my own, makes me as careless of your threats, as that natural courage, which belongs to my blood and mind, makes me insensible to the threats of others. Go to—you can not bully me. I scorn—I utterly despise you."

"Enough, enough, Colonel Conway. We understand each other," cried the outlaw, almost convulsed with his emotions. "We are quits from this hour. Henceforward I fling the ties of blood to the winds. As I do not feel them, I will not affect them. I acknowledge them no more. I am not your father's son—not your brother. I forswear, and from this moment I shall for ever deny the connection. I have no share in the base puddle which fills your veins. Know me, henceforth, for a nobler spirit. I glory in the name which scares your puny squadrons. I am the chief of the Black Riders of Congaree—that fell banditti which makes your women shiver and your warriors fly—upon whom you invoke and threaten vengeance equally in vain. I care not to be distinguished by any other name or connection. You, I shall only know as one to whom I am pledged for battle, and whom I am sworn to destroy. You know not, forsooth, what has driven me to this position! I will tell you here, once for all; and the answer, I trust, will conclude your doubts for ever. Hate for *you*—for *you* only! I hated you from your cradle, with an instinct which boyhood hourly strengthened, and manhood rendered invincible. I shall always hate you; and if I have temporized heretofore, and forborne the declaration of the truth, it was only the more effectually to serve and promote purposes which were necessary to that hate. That time, and the necessity of forbearance, are at an end. I can speak, and speak freely, the full feeling of my soul. Accident has revealed to you what, perhaps, I should have wished for a while longer to withhold; but that known, it is now my pride to have no further concealments. I repeat, therefore, that I loathe you from my soul, Clarence Conway; and when I have fairly acquitted myself of the debt I owe you, by sending you to your swamp in safety, I shall then seek, by every effort, to overcome and destroy you. Do you hear me?—am I at last understood?"

"I hear you," replied Clarence Conway, with a tone calm, composed even; and with looks unmoved, and even sternly contemptuous. "I hear you. Your violence does not alarm me, Edward Conway. I look upon you as a madman. As for your threats—pshaw, man! You almost move me to deal in clamors like your own. Let us vapor here no longer. I accept your terms. Give me my freedom, and set all your ruffians on the track. I make no promise—I utter no threat—but if I fail to take sweet revenge for the brutal outrages to which I have this night been subjected by you and your myrmidons, then may Heaven fail me in my dying hour!"

"We are pledged, Clarence Conway," said the outlaw; "before daylight I will conduct you from this place. Your horse shall be restored to you. You shall be free. I then know you no more—I fling from me the name of kinsman."

"Not more heartily than I. Black Rider, bandit, outlaw, or ruffian! I shall welcome you to the combat by any name sooner than that which my father has made sacred in my ears."

Morton bestowed a single glance on the speaker, in which all the hellish hate spoke out which had so long been suppressed, yet working in his bosom. The latter met the glance with one more cool and steady, if far less full of malignity.

"Be it, then, as he wills it!" he exclaimed, when the outlaw had retired; "he shall find no foolish tenderness hereafter in my heart, working for his salvation! If we must meet—if he will force it upon me—then God have mercy upon us both, for *I* will have none! It is his own seeking. Let him abide it! And yet, would to God that this necessity might pass me by! Some other arm—some other weapon than mine—may do me justice, and acquit me of this cruel duty!"

Long and earnest that night was the prayer of Clarence, that he might be spared from that strife which, so far, threatened to be inevitable. Yet he made not this prayer because of any affection—which, under the circumstances, must have been equally misplaced and unnatural—which he bore his kinsman. They had never loved. The feelings of brotherhood had been unfelt by either. Their moods had been warring from the first —it does not need that we should inquire why. The sweet dependencies of mutual appeal and confidence were unknown to, and unexercised by, either; and, so far as their sympathies were interested, Clarence, like the other, would have felt no more scruple at encountering Edward Conway in battle, than in meeting any indifferent person, who was equally his own and the foe of his country.

But there was something shocking to the social sense, in such a conflict, which prompted the prayers of the youth that it might be averted; and this prayer, it may be added, was only made when the excitement which their conference had induced, was partly over. His prayer was one of reflection and the mind. His blood took no part in the entreaty. At moments, when feeling, moved by memory, obtained the ascendency—even while he strove in prayer—the boon which he implored was forgotten; and, rising from his knees, he thought of nothing but the sharp strife and the vengeance which it promised. Perhaps, indeed, this mood prevailed even after the supplication was ended. It mingled in with the feelings which followed it, and whenever they became excited, the revulsion ceased entirely, which a more deliberate thought of the subject necessarily occasioned. The passion of the gladiator was still warm, even after the prayer was ended of the Christian man.

## CHAPTER XII.

### THINGS IN EMBRYO.

EDWARD MORTON kept his promise. Before the dawn of the following day he released his kinsman from prison. He had previously sent his followers out of the way—all save the landlord, Muggs—who could scarcely be counted one of them—and some two or three more upon whom he thought he could rely. He was not without sufficient motive for this caution.— He had his apprehensions of that unruly and insubordinate spirit which they had already shown, and which, baffled of its expected victim, he reasonably believed might once more display itself in defiance. A strange idea of honor prompted him at all hazards to set free the person, the destruction of whom would have been to him a source of the greatest satisfaction. Contradictions of this sort are not uncommon among minds which have been subject to conflicting influences. It was not a principle, but pride, that moved him to this magnanimity. Even Edward Conway, boasting of his connection with the most atrocious ruffians, would have felt a sense of shame to have acted otherwise.

The noble animal which Clarence rode was restored to him at his departure. Morton, also mounted, accompanied him, in silence, for a mile beyond the secluded spot which the robbers had chosen for their temporary refuge. He then spoke at parting.

"Colonel Conway, your path is free, and you are also! Before you lies the road to the Wateree, with which you are sufficiently acquainted. Here we separate. I have fulfilled my pledges. When next we meet I shall remind you of yours. Till then, farewell."

He did not wait for an answer, but striking his rowel fiercely into the flanks of his horse, he galloped rapidly back to the place which he had left. The eye of Clarence followed him with an expression of stern defiance, not unmingled with sadness, while he replied :—

"I will not fail thee, be that meeting when it may. Sad as the necessity is, I will not shrink from it. I, too, have my wrongs to avenge, Edward Conway. I, too, acknowledge that instinct of hate from the beginning, which will make a labor of love of this work of vengeance. I have striven, but fruitlessly, for its suppression;—now let it have its way. The hand of fate is in it. We have never loved each other. We have both equally doubted, distrusted, disliked—and these instincts have strengthened with our strength, grown with our growth, and their fruits are here! Shall I, alone, regret them? Shall they revolt my feelings only? No! I have certainly no fear—I shall endeavor to free myself from all compunction! Let the strife come when it may, be sure I shall be last to say, 'Hold off —are we not brethren?' You fling away the ties of blood, do you? Know from me, Edward Conway, that in flinging away these ties, you fling from you your only security. They have often protected you from my anger before—they shall protect you no longer."

And slowly, and solemnly, while the youth spoke, did he wave his open palm toward the path taken by his brother. But he wasted no more time in soliloquy. Prudence prompted him, without delay, to avail himself of the freedom which had been given him. He knew not what pursuers might be upon his path. He was not satisfied that his kinsman would still be true, without evasion, to the assurances which he had given in a mood of unwonted magnanimity. He plied his spurs freely, therefore, and his steed acknowledged the governing impulse. Another moment found him pressing toward the swamp.

But he had scarcely commenced his progress, when a well-known voice reached his ears, in a friendly summons to stop; while on one hand, emerging from the forest, came riding out his faithful friend and adherent, Jack Bannister.

"Ah, true and trusty, Jack. Ever watchful. Ever mindful of your friend—worth a thousand friends—I might well have looked to see you as nigh to me in danger as possible. I owe you much, Jack—very much. It was you, then, as I thought, whose rifle——"

"Worked that chap's buttonhole," was the answer of the woodman, with a chuckle, as shaking aloft the long ungainly but unerring instrument, with one hand, he grasped with the other the extended hand of his superior.

"I couldn't stand to see the fellow handle you roughly, Clarence. It made the gall bile up within me; and though I knowed that 'twould bring the whole pack out upon me, and was mighty dub'ous that it would make the matter worse for you; yet I couldn't work it out no other way. I thought you was gone for good and all, and that made me sort of desp'rate. I didn't pretty much know what I was a-doing, and, it mought be, that Polly Longlips" (here he patted the rifle affectionately) "went off herself, for I don't think I sighted her. If I had, Clarence, I don't think the drop would ha' been on the button of him that tumbled. I'm a thinking 'twould ha' drawn blood that was a mighty sight more nigh to your'n, if there was any good reason that your father had for giving Edward Conway the name he goes by. I suppose, Clarence, you're pretty nigh certain now that he's no ra'al, proper kin of your'n, for you to be keeping him out of harm's way, and getting into it yourself on account of him.

"And yet, he saved me from those ruffians, Jack."

"Dog's meat! Clarence, and what of that? Wa'n't it him that got you into their gripe; and wouldn't he ha' been worse than any sarpent that ever carried p'ison at the root of his upper jaw, if he hadn't ha' saved you, after what you'd done for him jest afore? Don't talk to me of his saving you, Clarence—don't say anything more in his favor, or I'll stuff my ears with moss and pine gum whenever you open your lips to speak. You've stood by him long enough, and done all that natur' called for, and more than was nateral. Half the men I know, if they had ever been saved by any brother, as you've been saved by him, would ha' sunk a tooth into his heart that wouldn't ha' worked its way out in one winter, no how. But you've done with him now, I reckon; and if you ain't, I'm done with you. There'll be no use for us to travel together, if you ain't ready to use your knife agen Edward Conway the same as agin any other tory."

"Be satisfied, Jack. I'm sworn to it—nay, pledged to him by oath—when we next meet to make our battle final. It was on this condition that he set me free."

"Well, he's not so mean a skunk after all, if he's ready to fight it out. I didn't think he was bold enough for that. But it's all the better. I only hope that when the time comes, I'll be the one to see fair play. I'll stand beside you, and if he flattens you—which, God knows, I don't think it's in one of his inches to do—why, he'll only have to flatten another. It's cl'ar to you now, Clarence, that you knows all about him."

"Yes! He is the leader of the Black Riders. He declared it with his own lips."

"When he couldn't help it no longer. Why, Clarence, he 'twas, that sent them fellows a'ter you that tuk you. I didn't see it, but I knows it jest the same as if I did. But, though you know that he's a tory and a Black Rider, there's a thousand villanies he's been doing, ever since we played together, that you know nothing about; and I'm 'minded of one in preticular that happened when you was at college in England, by the coming of old Jake Clarkson!—You 'member Jake Clarkson, that planted a short mile from your father's place, don't you?—he had a small patch of farm, and did boating along the river, like myself."

"Yes, very well—I remember him."

"Well, him I mean. Old Jake had a daughter—I reckon you don't much remember her, Mary Clarkson—as spry and sweet a gal as ever man set eyes on. I had a liking for the gal

—I own it, Clarence—and if so be things hadn't turned out as they did, I mought ha' married her. But it's a God's blessing I didn't; for you see Edward Conway got the better of her, and 'fore Jake know'd anything about it, poor Mary was a-carrying a bundle she had no law to carry. When they pushed the gal about it, she confessed 'twas Edward Conway's doings; and she told a long gal's story how Edward had promised to marry her, and swore it on Holy Book, and all that sort of thing, which was pretty much out of reason and nater—not for him to speak it, but for her to be such a child as to believe it. But no matter. The stir was mighty great about it. Old Jake carried a rifle more than three months for Edward Conway, and he took that time to make his first trip to Florida; where, I'm thinking, bad as he was before, he larn'd to be a great deal worse. It was there that he picked up all his tory notions from having too much dealing with John Stuart, the Indian agent, who, you know, is jist as bad an inimy of our liberties as ever come out of the old country. Well, but the worst is yet to tell. Poor Mary couldn't stand the desartion of Edward Conway and the diskivery of her sitiation. Beside, old Jake was too rough for the poor child, who, you know, Clarence, was a'most to be pitied; for it's mighty few women in this world that can say no when they're axed for favors by a man they have a liking for. Old Jake was mighty cross; and Molly, his wife, who, by nature, was a she-tiger, she made her tongue wag night and day about the sad doing of the poor gal, 'till her heart was worn down in her bosom, and she didn't dare to look up, and trimbled whenever anybody came nigh to her, and got so wretched and scary at last, that she went off one night, nobody knows whar, and left no tracks. Well, there was another stir. We were all turned out on the sarch, and it was my misfortune, Clarence, to be the first to find out what had become of her. Dickens! it makes my eyes water to this day!"

"And where did you find her, Jack?"

"Didn't find her, Clarence; but found out the miserable end she made of herself. We found her bonnet and shawl on the banks of the river, but her body we couldn't git! The rocks at the bottom of the Congaree know all about it, I reckon."

"I have now a faint recollection of this story, Bannister. I must have heard it while in England, or soon after my return."

" 'Twas a bad business, Clarence; and I didn't feel the smallest part of it. I didn't know till I come across the gal's bonnet how great a liking I had for her. I reckon I cried like a baby over it. From that day I mistrusted Edward Conway worse than p'ison. There was a-many things, long before that, that made me suspicion him; but after that, Clarence, I always felt, when I was near him, as if I saw a great snake, a viper, or a mockasin, and looked all round for a chunk to mash its head with."

"And what of her old father, Jack?"

"Why, he's come up to join your troop. I was so full of thinking 'bout other matters yesterday, when I saw you, that I quite forgot to tell you. He's been fighting below with Marion's men, but he wanted to look at the old range, and so he broke off to go under Sumter;—but the true story is, I'm thinking, that he's hearn how Edward Conway is up here somewhar, a-fighting, and he comes to empty that rifle at his head. He'll say his prayers over the bullet that he uses at him, and I reckon will make a chop in it, so that he may know, when his inimy is tumbled, if the shot that does the business was the one that had a commission for it."

"And Clarkson is now with us? In the swamp?"

"I left him at the 'Big Crossings.' But, Clarence, don't you say nothing to him about this business. It's a sore thing with him still, though the matter is so long gone by. But everything helps to keep it alive in his heart. His old woman's gone to her long home; and though she had a rough tongue and a long one, yet he was usen to her; and, when he lost little Mary, and then her, and the tories burnt his house, it sort-a cut him up, root and branch, and made him fretful and vexatious. But he'll fight, Clarence, like old blazes—there's no mistake in him."

"I will be careful, Jack; but a truce to this. We have but little time for old histories; and such melancholy ones as these may well be forgotten. We have enough before us sufficiently sad to demand all our attention and awaken our griefs. To business now, Jack. We have idled long enough."

"Ready, colonel. Say the word."

"Take the back track, and see after these Black Riders. We are fairly pledged now to encounter them—to beat them—to make the cross in blood on the breast of the very best of them."

"Edward Conway at the head of them!"

"Edward Conway no longer, John Bannister. He himself disclaims the name with scorn. Let him have the name, with the doom, which is due to the chief of the banditti which he leads. That name has saved him too long already. I rejoice that he now disclaims it, with all its securities. After him, John Bannister. If you have skill as a scout, use it now. After what has passed between us, he will be on my heels very shortly. He may be, even now, with all his band. I must be prepared for him, and must distrust him. It is therefore of vast importance that all his movements should be known. To your discretion I leave it. Away. Find me in the swamp to-morrow at the Little Crossings. We must leave it for the Congaree in three days more. Away. Let your horse use his heels."

A brief grasp of the hand, and a kind word, terminated the interview between the youthful partisan and his trusty follower. The latter dashed abruptly into the woods bordering the swamp, while the former, taking an upper route, pursued the windings of the river, till he reached the point he aimed at. We will not follow the course of either for the present, but return to the house of Muggs, and observe, somewhat further, the proceedings of the outlawed captain.

There, everything had the appearance of a rapid movement. The troopers, covered by a thick wood, were preparing to ride. Horses, ready caparisoned, were fastened beneath the trees, while their riders, singly or in groups, were seeking in various ways to while away the brief interval of time accorded them in the delay of their chief officer.

He, meanwhile, in the wigwam of Muggs, seemed oppressed by deliberations which baffled for the time his habitual activity. He sat upon the same bulk which he had occupied while a prisoner the night before, and appeared willing to surrender himself to that fit of abstraction which the landlord—though he watched it with manifest uneasiness—did not seem bold enough to interrupt. At length the door of the apartment opened, and the presence of a third person put an end to the meditations of the one and the forbearance of the other party.

The intruder was a youth, apparently not more than seventeen years of age. Such would have been the impression on any mind, occasioned by his timid bearing and slender figure; indeed, he would have been called undersized for seventeen. But there was that in his pale, well-defined features, which spoke for a greater maturity of thought, if not of time, than belongs to this early period in life. The lines of his cheeks and mouth were full of intelligence—that intelligence which results from early anxieties and the pressure of serious necessities. The frank, free, heedless indifference of the future, which shines out in the countenance of boyhood, seemed utterly obliterated from his face. The brow was already touched with wrinkles, that appeared strangely at variance with the short, closely cropped black hair, the ends of which were apparent beneath the slouched cap of fur he wore. The features were pensive, rather pretty, indeed, but awfully pale. Though they expressed great intelligence and the presence of an active thought, yet this did not seem to have produced its usual result in conferring confidence. The look of the youth was downcast, and when his large dark eyes ventured to meet those of the speaker, they seemed to cower and to shrink within themselves; and this desire appeared to give them an unsteady, dancing motion, which became painful to the beholder, as it seemed to indicate apprehension, if not fright, in the proprietor. His voice faltered too when he spoke, and was only made intelligible by his evident effort at deliberateness.

Like that of the rest of the troop, the costume of the youth was black. A belt of black leather encircled his waist, in which pistols and a knife were ostentatiously stuck. Yet how should one so timid be expected to use them? Trembling in the presence of a friend, what firmness could he possess in the encounter with a foe? Where was the nerve, the strength, for the deadly issues of battle? It seemed, indeed, a mockery of fate—a cruelty—to send forth so feeble a frame and so fearful a spirit, while the thunder and the threatening storm were in the sky. But no such scruples appeared to afflict the chief; nor did he seem to recognise the expression of timidity in the boy's features and manner of approach. Perhaps, he ascribed his emotions to the natural effect of his own stern manner, which was rather increased than softened as he listened to the assurance which the boy made that all was ready for a movement.

"You have lingered, boy!"

"Barton and the ensign were not with the rest, sir, and I had to look for them!"

"So!—plotting again, were they? But they shall find their match yet! Fools! Blind and deaf fools, that will not content themselves with being knaves to their own profit, but press on perversely as knaves, to their utter ruin. But go, boy—see that your own horse is ready; and hark ye, do not be following too closely at my heels. I have told you repeatedly, keep the rear when we are advancing, the front only when we are retreating. Remember."

The boy bowed respectfully, and left the room.

"And now, Muggs, you are bursting to speak. I know why, wherefore, and on what subject. Now, do you know that I have but to reveal to the troop the suggestion you made to me last night, to have them tear you and your house to pieces? Do you forget that desertion is death, according to your own pledges?"

"I am no longer one of the troop," replied the landlord hastily.

"Ay, that may be in one sense, but is scarcely so in any other. You are only so far released from your oath that no one expects you to do *active* duty. But, let them hear you speak, even of yourself, as last night you spoke to me, of *my* policy, and they will soon convince you that they hold you as fairly bound to them *now*, as you were when all your limbs were perfect. They will only release you by tearing what remains asunder."

"Well, but cappin, suppose they would, as you say. There's no reason why they should know the advice I give to you; and there's no reason why you shouldn't take that advice. We're besot, as I said before, with dangers. There's Greene with his army, a-gaining ground every day. There's Sumter, and Marion, and Pickens, and Maham, and——"

"Pshaw, Muggs! what a d——d catalogue is this; and what matters it all? Be it as you say—do I not know? Did I not know, at the beginning, of all these dangers? They do not terrify me now, any more than then! These armies that you speak of are mere skeletons."

"They give mighty hard knocks for skilitons. There's that affair at Hobkirk's——"

"Well, did not Rawdon keep the field?"

"Not over-long, cappin, and now——"

"Look you, Muggs, one word for all. I am sworn to the troop. I will keep my oath. They shall find no faltering in me. Living or dead, I stand by them to the last; and I give you these few words of counsel, if you would be safe. I will keep secret what you have said to me, for, I believe, you meant me kindly; but let me hear no more of the same sort of counsel. Another word to the same effect, and I deliver you over to the tender mercies of those with whom the shortest prayer is a span too long for an offender whose rope is ready and whose tree is near."

These words were just spoken as the boy reappeared at the door and informed the chief that the troop was in motion. The latter rose and prepared to follow. He shook hands with the landlord at parting, contenting himself with saying the single word, "Remember!"—in a tone of sufficient warning—in reply to the other's farewell. In this, Edward Morton displayed another sample of the practised hypocrisy of his character. His first mental soliloquy after leaving the landlord, was framed in such language as the following—

"I like your counsel, Master Muggs, but shall be no such fool as to put myself in your power by showing you that I like it. I were indeed a sodden ass, just at this moment, when half of my troop suspect me of treachery, to suffer you to hear, from my own lips, that I actually look with favor upon your counsel. Yet the old fool reasons rightly. This is no region for me now. It will not be much longer. The British power is passing away rapidly. Rawdon will not sustain himself much longer. Cornwallis felt that, and hence his pretended invasion of Virginia. Invasion, indeed!—a cover only to conceal his own flight. But what care I for him or them? My own game is of sufficient importance, and that is well nigh up. I deceived myself when I fancied that the rebels could not sustain themselves through the campaign; and if I wait to see the hunt up, I shall have a plentiful harvest from my own folly. No, no! I must get out of the scrape as well as I can, and with all possible speed. But no landlords for confidants. A wise man needs none of any kind. They are for your weak, dependent, adhesive people; folks who believe in friendships and loves, and that sort of thing. Loves! Have I, then, none—no loves? Ay, there are a thousand in that one. If I can win *her*, whether by fair word or fearless deed, well! It will not then be hard to break from these scoundrels. But, here they are!"

Such was the train of Edward Morton's thoughts as he left the landlord. Followed by the boy of whom we have already spoken, he cantered forth to the wood where the troop had formed, and surveyed them with a keen, searching, soldierly eye.

Morton was not without military ambition, and certainly possessed, like his brother, a considerable share of military talent. His glance expressed pleasure at the trim, excellent dress and aspect of his troop. Beyond this, and those common purposes of selfishness which had prompted the evil deeds, as well of men as leader, he had no sympathies with them. Even as he looked and smiled upon their array, the thought rapidly passed through his mind—

"Could I run their heads into the swamp now, and withdraw my own, it were no bad finish to a doubtful game. It must be tried; but I must use them something further. They can do good service yet, and no man should throw away his tools till his work is ended."

Brief time was given to the examination. Then followed the instructions to his subordinates, which do not require that we should repeat them. The details that concern our narrative will develop themselves in proper order, and in due season. But we may mention, that the chief of the outlaws made his arrangements with some reference to the rumors of disaffection among his men which had reached his ears. He took care to separate the suspected officers, in such a way as to deprive them, for the present, of all chance of communion; then, taking the advance, he led the troop forward, and was soon found pursuing the track lately taken by Clarence Conway.

## CHAPTER XIII.

### NEW PRINCIPLES DISCUSSED BY OLD LAWS.

THE last words of the chief of the Black Riders, as he left the presence of the landlord, had put that worthy into a most unenviable frame of mind. He had counselled Morton for his own benefit—he himself had no selfish considerations. He flattered himself that the relation in which he stood to the parties between which the country was divided, not to speak of his mutilated condition, would secure him from danger, no matter which of them should finally obtain the ascendency. That he should be still held responsible to his late comrades, though he no longer engaged in their pursuits and no longer shared their spoils, was a medium equally new and disquieting through which he was required to regard the subject. The stern threat with which Morton concluded, left him in little doubt of the uncertain tenure of that security which he calculated to find among his old friends; and, at the same time, awakened in his heart some new and rather bitter feelings in reference to the speaker. Hitherto, from old affinities, and because of some one of those nameless moral attachments which incline us favorably to individuals to whom we otherwise owe nothing, he had been as well disposed toward Edward Morton as he could be toward any individual not absolutely bound to him by blood or interest. He had seen enough to like in him, to make him solicitous of his successes, and to lead him in repeated instances, as in that which incurred the late rebuke, to volunteer his suggestions, and to take some pains in acquiring information which sometimes proved of essential benefit to the outlaw. It was partly in consequence of this interest, that he acquired that knowledge of the private concerns of Morton which prompted the latter, naturally enough, to confer with him, with tolerable freedom, on a number of topics strictly personal to himself, and of which the troop knew nothing. Conscious of no other motive than the good of the outlaw; and not dreaming of that profounder cunning of the latter, which could resolve him to adopt the counsel which he yet seemed to spurn with loathing, the landlord, reasonably enough, felt indignant at the language with which he had been addressed; and his indignation was not lessened by the disquieting doubts of his own safety which the threats of Morton had suggested. It was just at the moment when his conclusions were most unfavorable to the outlaw, that the door of his wigwam was quietly thrown open, and he beheld, with some surprise, the unexpected face of our worthy scout, Jack Bannister, peering in upon him. The latter needed no invitation to enter.

"Well, Isaac Muggs," said he, as he closed and bolted the door behind him, "you're without your company at last. I was a'most afear'd, for your sake in pretic'lar, that them bloody sculpers was a-going to take up lodging with you for good and all. I waited a pretty smart chance to see you cl'ar of them, and I only wish I was sartin, Muggs, that you was as glad as myself when they concluded to make a start of it."

"Ahem!—To be sure I was, friend Supple," replied the other with an extra show of satisfaction in his countenance which did not altogether conceal the evident hesitation of his first utterance.—"To be sure I was; they'd ha' drunk me out of house and home if they had stopped much longer. A kag of lemons a'most—more than two kags of sugar, best Havana—and there's no measuring the Jamaica, wasted upon them long swallows. Ef I a'n't glad of their going, Jack, I have a most onnateral way of thinking on sich matters."

The keen eyes of Supple Jack never once turned from the countenance of the landlord, as he detailed the evils of consumption among his guests; and when the latter had finished, he coolly replied:—

"I'm afear'd, Isaac Muggs, you ain't showing clean hands above the table. That's a sort of talking that don't blind my eyes, even ef it stops my ears. Don't I know it would be mighty onnateral if you wa'n't glad enough to sell your kags of lemons, and your kags of sugar, and your gallons of rum, pretic'larly when, in place of them, you can count me twenty times their valley in British gould? No, Muggs, that sort o' talking won't do for me. Take the cross out of your tongue and be pretic'lar in what you say, for I'm going to s'arch you mighty close this time, I tell you."

"Well but, Supple, you wouldn't have me take nothing from them that drinks and eats up my substance?"

"Who talks any sich foolishness but yourself, Muggs?—I don't. I'm for your taking all you can get out of the inimy; for it's two ways of distressing 'em, to sell 'em strong drink and take their gould for it. The man that drinks punch is always the worse for it; and it don't better his business to make him pay for it in guineas. That's not my meaning, Muggs. I'm on another track, and I'll show you both eends of it before I'm done."

"Why, Supple, you talks and looks at me suspiciously," said the landlord, unable to withstand the keen, inquiring glances of the scout, and almost as little able to conceal his apprehensions lest some serious discovery had been made to his detriment.

"Look you, Isaac Muggs, do you see that peep-hole there in the wall?—oh, thar! jest one side of the window—the peep-hole in the logs."

"Yes, I see it," said the landlord, whose busy fingers were already engaged in thrusting a wadding of dry moss into the discovered aperture.

"Well, it's too late to poke at it now, Muggs," said the other. "The harm's done a'ready, and I'll let you know the worst of it. Through that peep-hole, last night, I saw what was a-going on here among you; and through that peep-hole, it was this same Polly Longlips"—tapping his rifle as he spoke—"that went off of her own liking, and tumbled one big fellow; and was mighty vexatious, now, when she found herself onable to tumble another."

"Yes, yes—Polly Longlips was always a famous talker," murmured the landlord flatteringly, and moving to take in his remaining hand the object of his eulogium. But Supple Jack evidently recoiled at so doubtful a liberty in such dangerous times, and drew the instrument more completely within the control of his own arm.

"She's a good critter, Muggs, but is sort o' bashful among strangers; and when she puts up her mouth, it ain't to be kissed or to kiss, I tell you. She's not like other gals in that pretic'lar. Now, don't think I mistrust you, Muggs, for 'twould be mighty timorsome was I to be afeard of anything you could do with a rifle like her, having but one arm to go upon. It's only a jealous way I have, that makes me like to keep my Polly out of the arms of any other man. It's nateral enough, you know, to a person that loves his gal."

"Oh yes, very nateral, Supple; but somehow, it seems to me as if you did suspicion me, Supple—it does, I declar'."

"To be sure I do," replied the other, promptly. "I suspicious you've been making a little bit of a fool of yourself; and I've come to show you which eend of the road will bring you up. You know, Muggs, that I know all about you—from A to izzard. I can read you like a book. I reckon you'll allow that I have larn'd *that* lesson, if I never larn'd any other."

"Well, Supple, I reckon I may say you know me pretty much as well as any other person."

"Better—better, Muggs!—I know you from the jump; and I know what none of our boys know, that you did once ride with these Black—"

"Yes, Supple, but—" and the landlord jumped up and looked out of the door, and peered, with all his eyes, as far as possible into the surrounding wood. The scout, meanwhile, with imperturbable composure, retained the seat which he had originally taken.

"Don't you be scarey," said he, when the other had returned, "I've sarcumvented your whole establishment—looked in at both of your blocks, and all of your cypress hollows, not to speak of a small ride I took after your friends—"

"No friends of mine, Supple, no more than any other people

that pay for what they git," exclaimed the apprehensive landlord.

"That's the very p'int I'm driving at, Muggs. You know well enough that if our boys had a guess that you ever rode with that 'ere troop, it wouldn't be your stump of an arm that'd save you from the swinging limb."

"But I never did hide that I fou't on the British side, Supple!" said the other.

"In the West Indies, Isaac Muggs. That's the story you told about your hurts, and all that. If you was to tell them, or if I was to tell them, any other story now, that had the least smell of the truth in it, your shop would be shut up for ever in this life, and — who knows? — maybe never opened in the next. Well, now, I'm come here this blessed day to convart you to rebellion. Through that very peep-hole, last night, I heard you, with my own ears, talking jest as free as the rankest tory in all the Wateree country."

"Oh, Lord, Supple, wa'n't that nateral enough, when the house wor full of tories?"

"'Twa'n't nateral to an honest man at any time," replied the other indignantly; "and let me tell you, Muggs, the house wa'n't full — only Ned Conway was here, with his slippery tongue that's a wheedling you, like a blasted blind booby, Muggs, to your own destruction. That same fellow will put your neck in the noose yet, and laugh when you're going up."

A prediction so confidently spoken, and which tallied so admirably with the savage threat uttered by the outlaw at his late departure, drove the blood from the cheeks of the landlord, and made him heedless of the harsh language in which the scout had expressed himself. His apology was thus expressed:—

"But 'twas pretty much the same thing, Supple — he was their cappin, you know."

"Cappin! And what does he care about them, and what do they care about him, if they can get their eends sarved without each other? It wouldn't be a toss of a copper, the love that's atween them. He'll let them hang, and they'll hang him, as soon as it's worth while for either to do so. Don't I know, Muggs? Don't I know that they're conniving strong agin him even now, and don't I calkilate that as soon as the Congaree country gits too hot to hold Rawdon, this Ned Conway will be the first to kill a colt to 'scape a halter? He'll ride a horse to death to get to Charleston, and when there, he'll sink a ship to git to the West Indies. He knows his game, and he'll so work it, Isaac Muggs, as to leave your neck in the collar without waiting to hear the crack."

"You're clean mistaken, Supple, for 'twas only this morning that I cautioned the captain 'bout his men, and I gin him my counsel to take the back track and find his way to the seaboard; but he swore he'd never desart the troop, and he spoke mighty cross to me about it, and even threatened, if I talked of it another time to him, to set the troopers on me."

"More knave he, and more fool you for your pains," said the other irreverently; "but this only makes me the more sartin that he means to finish a bad game by throwing up his hand. He's made his Jack, and he don't stop to count. But look you, Isaac Muggs, all this tells agin you. Here, you're so thick, hand and glove, with the chief of the Black Riders, that you're advising him what to do; and by your own words, he makes out that you're still liable to the laws of the troop. Eh? what do you say to that?"

"But that's only what *he said*, Supple, and it's what was a-worrying me when you come in."

"Look you, Muggs, it ought to worry you! I'm mighty serious in this business. I'm going to be mighty strick with you. I was the one that spoke for you among our boys, and 'twas only because I showed them that I had sort o' convarted you from your evil ways, that they agreed to let you stay here in quiet on the Wateree. Well, I thought I *had* convarted you. You remember that long summer day last August, when Polly Longlips gin a bowel-complaint to Macleod, the Scotch officer. You was with him in the boat, and helped to put him across the Wateree. Well, when we was a-burying him—for he died like a gentleman bred—I had a call to ax you sartin questions, and we had a long argyment about our liberties, and George the Third, and what business Parlyment had to block up Boston harbor, and put stamps on our tea before they let us drink it.

Do you remember all them matters and specifications, Isaac Muggs?"

"Well, Supple, I can't but say I do. We did have quite a long argyment when the lieutenant was a dying, and jest after the burial."

"No, 'twas all the while we was a-laying in the trench; for I recollect saying to you, when you was a pitying him all the time, that, ef I was sorry for the poor man's death, I wasn't sorry that I killed him, and I would shoot the very next one that come along, jest the same; for it made the gall bile up in me to see a man that I had never said a hard word to in all my life, come here, over the water, a matter, maybe, of a thousand miles, to force me, at the p'int of the bagnet, to drink stamped tea. I never did drink the tea, no how. For my own drinking, I wouldn't give one cup of coffee, well biled, for all the tea that was ever growed or planted. But, 'twas the freedom of the thing that I was argying for, and 'twas on the same argyment that I was willing to fight. Now that was the time, and them was the specifications which made us argyfy, and it was only then, when I thought I had convarted you from your evil ways, that I tuk on me to answer for your good conduct to our boys. I spoke to the colonel for you, jest the same as ef I had know'd you for a hundred years. It's true I did know you, and the mother that bore you, and a mighty good sort of woman she was; but it was only after that argyment that I felt a call to speak in your behalf. Now, Isaac Muggs, I ain't conscience-free about that business. I've had my suspicions a long time that I spoke a leetle too much in your favor; and what I heard last night—and what I seed—makes me dub'ous that you've been a sort o' snake in the grass. I doubt your convarsion, Isaac Muggs; but before I tell you my mind about the business, I'd jest like to hear from your own lips what you think about our argyment, and what you remember, and what you believe."

The landlord looked utterly bewildered. It was evident that he had never devoted much time to metaphysics; and the confusion and disorder of the few words which he employed in answer, and the utter consternation of his looks, amply assured the inflexible scout that the labor of conversion must be entirely gone over again.

"I see, Isaac Muggs, that you're in a mighty bad fix, and it's a question with me whether I ought raly to give you a helping hand to git out of it. Ef I thought you wanted to git at the truth—"

"Well, Supple, as God's my judge, I sartinly do."

"I'd go over the argyment agin for your sake, but—'

"I'd thank you mightily, Supple."

"But 'twon't do to go on forgetting, Muggs. The thing is to be onderstood, and if it's once onderstoood, it's to be believed; and when you say you believe, there's no dodging after that. There's no saying you're a tory with tories, and a whig with whigs, jest as it seems needful. The time's come for every tub to stand on its own bottom, and them that don't must have a turn—inside out! Now, there's no axing you to fight for us, Muggs—that's out of natur'—and I'm thinking we have more men now than we can feed; but we want the truth in your soul, and we want you to stick to it. Ef you're ready for that, and raly willing, I'll put it to you in plain argyments that you can't miss, onless you want to miss 'em; and you'll never dodge from 'em, if you have only half a good-sized man's soul in you to go upon. You've only to say now, whether you'd like to know—"

The landlord cut short the speaker by declaring his anxiety to be re-enlightened, and Supple Jack rose to his task with all the calm deliberation of a practised lecturer. Coiling up a huge quid of tobacco in one jaw, to prevent its interfering with the argument, he went to the door.

"I'll jest go out for a bit and hitch 'Mossfoot,'"—the name conferred upon his pony, as every good hunter has a tender diminutive for the horse he rides and the gun he shoots—"I'll only go and hitch 'Mossfoot' deeper in the swamp, and out of harm's way for a spell, and then be back. It's a three minutes' business only."

He was not long gone, but, during that time, rapid transitions of thought and purpose were passing through the mind of the veteran landlord. Circumstances had already prepared him to recognise the force of many of the scout's arguments. The very counsel he had given to Edward Morton originated in a conviction that the British cause was going down—that the whigs were gaining ground upon the tories with every day's movement, and that it would be impossible for the latter much longer to maintain themselves. The policy of the publican usually goes with that of the rising party. He is not generally a bad political thermometer, and Muggs was a really good one. Besides, he had been stung by the contemptuous rejection of his counsel by the chief whom he was conscious of having served unselfishly, and alarmed by the threats which had followed his uncalled-for counsel.

The necessity of confirming his friends among the successful rebels grew singularly obvious to his intellect, if it had not been so before, in the brief absence of the scout; and when he returned, the rapidly quickening intelligence of the worthy landlord made the eyes of the former brighten with the satisfaction which a teacher must naturally feel at the wonderful progress and ready recognition of his doctrines.

These, it will not be necessary for us entirely, or even in part, to follow. The worthy woodman has already given us a sufficient sample of the sort of philosophy in which he dealt; and farther argument on the tyranny of forcing "stamped tea" down the people's throats, "will they, nill they," may surely be dispensed with. But, flattering as his success appeared to be at first, Supple Jack was soon annoyed by some doubts and difficulties which his convert suggested in the progress of the argument. Like too many of his neighbors, Isaac Muggs was largely endowed with the combative quality of self-esteem. This, as the discussion advanced, was goaded into exercise; and his fears and his policy were equally forgotten in the desire of present triumph. A specimen of the manner in which their deliberations warmed into controversy may be passingly afforded.

"It's agin natur' and reason, and a man's own seven senses," said Supple Jack, "to reckon on any man's right to make laws for another, when he don't live in the same country with him. I say, King George, living in England, never had a right to make John Bannister, living on the Congaree, pay him taxes for tea or anything."

"But it's all the same country, England and America, Jack Bannister."

"Jimini!—if that's the how, what makes you give 'em different names, I want to know?"

"Oh, that was only because it happened so," said the landlord, doubtfully.

"Well, it so happens that I won't pay George the Third any more taxes. That's the word for all; and it's good reason why I shouldn't pay him, when, for all his trying, he can't make me. Here he's sent his rigiments—rigiment after rigiment—and the queen sent her rigiment, and the prince of Wales his rigiment —I reckon we didn't tear the prince's rigiment all to flinders at Hanging Rock!—Well, then, there was the Royal Scotch and the Royal Irish, and the Dutch Hessians;—I suppose they didn't call them royal, 'cause they couldn't ax in English for what they wanted:—well, what was the good of it?—all these rigiments together, couldn't make poor Jack Bannister, a Congaree boatmen, drink stamped tea or pay taxes. The rigiments, all I've named, and a hundred more, are gone like last autumn's dry leaves; and the only fighting that's a-going on now, worth to speak of, is American born 'gainst American born. Wateree facing Wateree—Congaree facing Congaree—Santee facing Santee—and cutting each other's throats to fill the pockets of one of the ugliest old men—for a white man—that ever I looked on. It spiles the face of a guinea where they put his face. Look you, Isaac Muggs, I would ha' gathered you, as Holy Book says it, even as a hen gathers up her chickens. I'd ha' taken you 'twixt my legs in time of danger, and seed you safe through—but you wouldn't! I've tried to drive reason into your head, but it's no use; you can't see what's right, and where to look for it. You answer everything I say with your eyes sot, and a cross-buttock. Now, what's to be done? I'm waiting on you to answer."

"Swounds, Supple, but you're grown a mighty hasty man o' late," replied the landlord, beginning to be sensible of the imprudence of indulging his vanity at a moment so perilous to his fortune. "I'm sure I've tried my best to see the right and the reason. I've hearn what you had to say——"

"Only to git some d—d crooked answer ready, that had jist as much to do with the matter as my great grand-daughter has. You hearn me, but it wa'n't to see if the truth was in me; it was only to see if you couldn't say something after me that would swallow up my saying. I don't see how you're ever to get wisdom, with such an understanding, unless it's licked into you by main force of tooth and timber."

"I could ha' fou't you once, John Bannister, though you are named Supple Jack," replied the landlord with an air of indignant reproach, which, in his own self-absorption, escaped the notice of the scout.

"It's no bad notion *that*," he continued, without heeding the language of the landlord. "Many's the time, boy and man, I have fou't with a fellow when we couldn't find out the right of it, any way; and, as sure as a gun, if I wan't right I was sartain to be licked. Besides, Isaac Muggs, it usen to be an old law, when they couldn't get at the truth any other way, to make a battle, and cry on God's mercy to help the cause that was right. By Jimini, I don't see no other way for us. I've given you all the reason I know on this subject — all that I can onderstand, I mean — for to confess a truth, there's a-many reasons for our liberties that I hear spoken, and I not able to make out the sense of one of them. But all that I know I've told you, and there's more than enough to make me sartin of the side I take. Now, as you ain't satisfied with any of my reasons, I don't see how we're to finish the business onless we go back to the oldtime law, and strip to the buff for a fight. You used to brag of yourself, and you know what I am, so there's no use to ax about size and weight. If you speak agreeable to your conscience, and want nothing better than the truth, then, I don't see but a rigilar fight will give it to us; for, as I told you afore, I never yet did fight on the wrong side, that I didn't come up ondermost."

The scout, in the earnestness with which he entertained and expressed his own views and wishes, did not suffer himself to perceive some of the obstacles which lay in the way of a transaction such as he so deliberately and seriously proposed. He was equally inaccessible to the several attempts of his companion to lessen his regards for a project, to which the deficiency of a limb, on the part of one of the disputants, seemed to suggest a most conclusive objection. When, at length, he came to a pause, the landlord repeated his former reproachful reminiscence of a period when the challenge of the scout would not have gone unanswered by defiance.

"But now!" and he lifted the stump of his remaining arm, in melancholy answer.

"It's well for you to talk big, John Bannister; I know you're a strong man, and a spry. You wa'n't called Supple Jack for nothing. But there was a time when Isaac Muggs wouldn't ha' stopped to measure inches with you in a fair up and down, hip and hip, hug together. I could ha' thrown you once, I'm certain. But what's the chance now with my one arm, in a hug with a man that's got two? It's true, and I believe it, that God gives strength in a good cause; but it's quite onreasonable for me to hope for any help, seeing as how I can't help myself, no how. I couldn't even come to the grip, however much I wanted to."

"Sure enough, Muggs, and I didn't think of that, at all. It was so natural to think that a man that let his tongue wag so free as your'n had two arms at least to back it. I'm mighty sorry, Muggs, that you ain't, for it's a great disapp'intment."

This was spoken with all the chagrin of a man who was discomfited in his very last hope of triumph.

"Well, you see I ain't," said the other, sulkily; "so there's no more to be said about it."

"Yes; but you ain't come to a right mind yit. It's cl'ar to me, Isaac Muggs, that one thing or t'other must be done. You must cut loose from the Black Riders, or cut loose from us. You knows the resk of the one, and I can pretty much tell you what's the resk of the other. Now, there's a notion hits me, and it's one that comes nateral enough to a man that's fou't, in his time, in a hundred different ways. One of them ways, when I had to deal with a fellow that was so cl'ar behind me in strength that he couldn't match me as we stood, was to tie a hand behind my back, or a leg to a pine sapling, and make myself, as it wor, a lame man till the fight was over. Now, look you, Muggs, if it's the truth your really after, I don't care much if I try that old-fashion way with you. I'm willing to buckle my right arm to my back."

"Swounds, Supple, how you talk! Come, take a drink."

"I'll drink when the time comes, Isaac Muggs, and when it's needful; but jest now, when it's the truth I'm after, I don't suffer no divarsions. I stick as close to it, I tell you, as I does to my inimy. I don't stop to drink or rest till it's a-lying fair before me. Now, it's needful for your sake, Muggs, that you come to a right sense of the reason in this business. It's needful that you give up Black Riders, tories, British, Ned Conway, ugly faces, and the old sarpent. My conscience is mightily troubled becaise I stood for you, and it's needful that you come to a right onderstanding afore I leave you. I've sworn it, Isaac Muggs, by Polly Longlips, as we rode along together, and Mossfoot pricked up his ears as if he onderstood it all, and was a witness for us both. Now, you know what an oath by Polly Longlips means, Isaac. It means death to the inimy—sartin death, at any reasonable distance. I don't want your life, man;—by the hokey, I don't;—and that's why I want to put the reason in you, so that you might say to me at once that you're done with these black varmints, for ever. They can do you no good—they can't help you much longer; and the time's a-coming, Isaac Muggs, when the whigs will sweep this country, along the Wateree, and the Congaree, and Santee, with a broom of fire, and wo to the skunk, when that time comes, that can't get clear of the brush—wo to the 'coon that's caught sticking in his hollow! There's no reason you shouldn't onderstand the liberty-cause, and there's every reason why you should. But as you can't onderstand my argyment——"

"Well, but Supple, you're always in such a hurry!—"

"No hurry—never hurried a man in argyment in all my life; but when he's so tarnal slow to onderstand—"

"That's it, Supple, I'm a slow man; but I begin to see the sense of what you say."

"Well, that's something like, Muggs; but a good gripe about

the ribs, a small tug upon the hips, pretic'larly if we ax the blessing of Providence upon the argyment, will be about as good a way as any to help your onderstanding to a quicker motion. It'll put your slow pace into a smart canter."

"Psho, Supple! you're not serious in thinking that there's anything in that?"

"Ain't I, then? By gum, you don't know me, Isaac Muggs, if you think as you say. Now, what's to hender the truth from coming out in a fair tug between us? Here we stand, both tall men, most like in height and breadth, nigh alike in strength by most people's count; about the same age, and pretty much the same experience. We've had our tugs and tears, both of us, in every way; though, to be sure, you got the worst of it, so far as we count the arm; but as I tie up mine, there's no difference. Now I say, here we stand on the banks of the Wateree. Nobody sees us but the great God of all, that sees everything in nater'. He's here, the Bible says — he's here, and thar, and everywhar, and He sees everything everywhar. You believe all that, don't you, Isaac Muggs? for ef you don't believe that, why, there's no use in talking at all. There's an eend of the question."

The landlord, though looking no little mystified, muttered assent; and this strange teacher of a new, or, rather, reviver of an old faith, proceeded with accustomed volubility:—

"Well, then, here, as we are, we call upon God, and tell him how we stand. Though, to be sure, as he knows all, the telling wouldn't be such a needcessity. But, never mind—we tell him. I say to him, Here's Isaac Muggs—it ain't easy for him to onderstand this argyment, and unless he onderstands, it's a matter of life and death to him;—you recollect, Muggs, about the oath I tuk on Polly Longlips. He wants to larn, and it's needful to make a sign which'll come home to his onderstanding more cl'arly than argyment by man's word of mouth. Now then we pray—and you must kneel to it beforehand, Muggs. I'll go aside under one tree, and do you take another; and we'll make a hearty prayer after the proper sign. If the Lord says I'm right, why you'll know it mighty soon by the sprawl I'll give you; but if I'm wrong, the tumble will be the other way, and I'll make the confession, though it'll be a mighty bitter needcessity, I tell you. But I ain't afeard. I'm sartin that my argyment for our rights is a true argyment, and I'll say my prayers with that sort of sartinty, that it would do your heart good if you could only feel about the same time."

"If I thought you was serious, Jack Bannister; but I'm jub'ous about it."

"Don't be jub'ous. I'm ser'ous as a sarpent. I b'lieve in God—I b'lieve he'll justify the truth, whenever we axes him in airnest for it! My old mother—God rest her bones and bless her sperrit!—she's told me of more than twenty people that's tried a wrestle for the truth. There was one man in partic'lar that she knows in Georgia : his name was Bostick. He used to be a drummer in General Oglethorpe's Highland regiment. Well, another man, a sodger in the same regiment, made an accusation agin Bostick for stealing a watch-coat, and the sarcumstances went mighty strong agin Bostick. But he stood it out; and though he never shot a rifle in his life before, he staked the truth and his honesty on a shot; and, by the hokey, though, as I tell you, he never lifted rifle to his sight before, he put the bullet clean through the mouth and jaw of the sodger, and cut off a small slice of his tongue, which was, perhaps, as good a judgment agin a man for false swearing as a rifle-shot could make. Well, 'twa'n't a month after that when they found it was an Ingin that had stole the coat, and so Bostick was shown to be an honest man, by God's blessing, in every way."

There was something so conclusive on the subject in this, and one or two similar anecdotes, which Supple Jack told, and which, having heard them from true believers in his youth, had led to his own adoption of the experiment, that the landlord, Muggs, offered no further doubts or objections. The earnestness of his companion became contagious, and, with far less enthusiasm of character, he was probably not unwilling—in order to the proper adoption of a feeling which was growing momently in favor in his eyes—to resort to the wager of battle as an easy mode of making a more formal declaration in behalf of the dominant faction of the state. The novelty of the suggestion had its recommendation also; and but few words more were wasted, before the two went forth to a pleasant and shady grass-plot, which lay some two hundred yards further in the hollow of the wood, in order that the test so solemnly recommended, on such high authority, should be fairly made in the presence of that High Judge only, whose arbitrament, without intending any irreverence, was so earnestly invoked by the simple woodman of Congaree.

## CHAPTER XIV.

### THE TRIAL FOR THE TRUTH.

No change could have been suddenly greater than that which was produced upon the countenance and conduct of John Bannister, when he found himself successful in bringing the landlord to the desired issue. His seriousness was all discarded,—his intense earnestness of air and tone, and a manner even playful and sportive, succeeded to that which had been so stern and sombre. He congratulated Muggs and himself, equally, on the strong probability, so near at hand, of arriving at the truth by a process so direct, and proceeded to make his arrangements for the conflict with all the buoyancy of a boy traversing the playground with "leap-frog" and "hop o' my thumb."

The landlord did not betray the same degree of eagerness, but he was not backward. He might have had his doubts about the issue, for Supple Jack had a fame in those days which spread far and wide along the three contiguous rivers. Wherever a pole-boat had made its way, there had the name of Jack Bannister found repeated echoes. But Muggs was a fearless man, and he had, besides, a very tolerable degree of self-assurance, which led him to form his own expectations and hopes of success. If he had any scruples at all, they arose rather from his doubt, whether the proposed test of truth would be a fair one—a doubt which seemed very fairly overcome in his mind, as indeed it should be in that of the reader, if full justice is done to the final argument which the scout addressed to his adversary on this subject.

"There never was a quarrel and a fight yet that didn't come out of a wish to l'arn or to teach the truth. What's King George a-fighting us for this very moment? Why, to make us b'lieve in him. If he licks us, why we'll believe in him; and if we licks him, 'gad, I'm thinking he'll have to b'lieve in us. Aint that cl'ar, Muggs? So, let's fall to—if I licks you, I reckon you'll know where to look for the truth for ever after; for I'll measure your back on it, and your breast under it, and you'll feel it in all your bones."

The ground was chosen—a pleasant area beneath a shadowing grove of oaks, covered with a soft greenward, which seemed to lessen, in the minds of the combatants, the dangers of discomfiture. But when the parties began to strip for the conflict, a little difficulty suggested itself which had not before disturbed the thoughts of either. How was the superfluous arm of Supple Jack to be tied up? Muggs could evidently perform no such friendly office; but a brief pause given to their operations enabled the scout to arrange it easily. A running noose was made in the rope, into which he thrust the unnecessary member, then gave the end of the line to his opponent, who contrived to draw it around his body, and bind the arm securely to his side—an operation easily understood by all schoolboys who have ever been compelled to exercise their wits in securing a balance of power, in a like way, among ambitious rivals.

As they stood, front to front opposed, the broad chest, square shoulders, voluminous muscle, and manly compass of the two, naturally secured their mutual admiration. Supple Jack could not refrain from expressing his satisfaction.

"It's a pleasure, Isaac Muggs, to have a turn with a man of your make. I ha'n't seen a finer buzzum for a fight this many a day. I think, ef anything, you're a splinter or two fuller across the breast than me;—it may be fat, and ef so, it's the worse for you; but ef it's the solid grain and gristle, then it's only the worse for me. It makes me saddish enough when I look on sich a buzzum as yourn, to think that youre cut off one half in a fair allowance of arm. But I don't think that'll work agin you in this.'bout, for, you see, you're used to doing without it, and making up in a double use of t'other; and I'm beginning a'ready to feel as if I warn't of no use at all in the best part of my body. Let's feel o' your heft, old fellow."

A mutual lift being taken, they prepared to take hold for the grand trial; and Supple Jack soon discovered, as he had suspected, that the customary disuse of the arm gave to his opponent an advantage in this sort of conflict, which, taken in connection with his naturally strong build of frame, rendered the task before him equally serious and doubtful. But, with a shake of the head as he made this acknowledgment, he laid his chin on the shoulder of the landlord, grasped him vigorously about the body; and Muggs, having secured a similar grasp, gave him the word, and they both swung round, under a mutual impulse, which, had there been any curious spectator at hand, would have left him very doubtful, for a long time, as to the distinct proprietorship of the several legs which so rapidly chased each other in the air.

An amateur in such matters—a professional lover of the "fancy"—would make a ravishing picture of this conflict. The alternations of seeming success—the hopes, the fears, the occasional elevations of the one party, and the depressions of the other—the horizontal tendency of this or that head and shoulder—the yielding of this frame and the staggering of that leg, might, under the pencil of a master, be made to awaken as many sensibilities in the spectator as did ever the adroit rogueries of the modern Jack Sheppard. But these details must be left to artists of their own—to the Cruikshankses!—or that more popular, if less worthy fraternity, the "Quiz," "Phiz," "Biz," "Tiz," &c., tribe of artists in Bow-street tastes and experiences, who do the visage of a rascal *con amore*, and contrive always that vice shall find its representation in ugliness. We have neither the tastes nor the talents which are needful to such artist, and shall not even attempt, by mere word-painting, to supply our deficiencies. Enough to say, that our combatants struggled with rare effort and no small share of dexterity as well as muscle. Muggs was no chicken, as Supple Jack was pleased to assure him; and the latter admitted that he himself was a tough colt, not easy to be put upon four legs, when his natural rights demanded only two. The conflict was protracted till both parties were covered with perspiration. The turf, forming a ring of twenty feet round or more, was beaten smooth, and still the affair was undecided. Neither had yet received a fall. But Supple Jack, for reasons of his own, began to feel that the argument was about to be settled in favor of right principles.

"Your breath's coming *re*ther quick now, Isaac Muggs—I'm thinking you'll soon be convarted! But it's a mighty strong devil you had in you, and I'm afeard he'll make my ribs ache for a week. I'll sprawl him, though, I warrant you.

"Don't be too sartin, Jack," gasped the other.

"Don't!—Why, love you, Muggs, you couldn't say that short speech over again for the life of you."

"Couldn't eh!"

"No, not for King George's axing."

"Think so, eh?"

"Know so, man. Now, look to it. I'll only ax three tugs more. There—there's one."

"Nothing done, Jack."

"Two—three! and where are you now?" cried the exulting scout, as he deprived his opponent of grasp and footing at the same moment, and whirled him, dizzy and staggering, heels up and head to the earth.

But he was not suffered to reach it by that operation only. His course was accelerated by other hands; and three men, rushing with whoop and halloo from the copse near which the struggle had been carried on, grappled with the fallen landlord, and plied him with a succession of blows, the least of which was unnecessary for his overthrow.

It seemed that Supple Jack recognised these intruders almost in the moment of their appearance; but so sudden was their onset, and so great their clamor, that his fierce cry to arrest them was unheard, and he could only make his wishes known by adopting the summary process of knocking two of them down, by successive blows from the only fist which was left free for exercise.

"How now! Who ax'd you to put your dirty fingers into my dish, Olin Massey? or you, Bob Jones? or you, Payton Burns? This is your bravery, is it, to beat a man after I've down'd him, eh?"

"But we didn't know that 'twas over, Seargeant. We thought you was a-wanting help," replied the fellow who was called Massey — it would seem in mockery only. He was a little, dried-up, withered atomy — a jaundiced "sand-lapper," or "clay-eater," from the Wassamasaw country — whose insignificant size and mean appearance did very inadequate justice to his resolute, fierce, and implacable character.

"And if I was a-wanting help, was you the man to give me any? Go 'long, Olin Massey — you're a very young chap to be here. What makes you here, I want to know?"

"Why, didn't you send us on the scout, jist here, in this very place?" said the puny but pugnacious person addressed, with a fierceness of tone and gesture, and a fire in his eye, which the feebleness of his form did not in the least seem to warrant.

"Yes, to be sure; but why didn't you come? I've been here a matter of two hours by the sun; and as you didn't come, I reckoned you had taken track after some tory varmints, and had gone deeper into the swamp. You've dodged some tories, eh?"

"No, ha'n't seen a soul."

"Then, by the hokey, Olin Massey, you've been squat on a log, playing old sledge for pennies!"

The scouting party looked down in silence. The little man from Wassamasaw felt his anger subside within him.

"Corporal Massey, give me them painted darlings out of your pockets, before they're the death of you. By old natur, betwixt cards and rum, I've lost more of my men than by Cunningham's bullets or Tarleton's broadswords. Give me them cards, Olin Massey, and make your respects to my good natur, that I don't blow you to the colonel."

The offender obeyed. He drew from his pocket, in silence, a pack of the dirtiest cards that ever were thumbed over a pine log, and delivered them to his superior with the air of a schoolboy from whom the master had cruelly taken, "at one fell swoop," top, marbles, and ball.

"There," said Supple Jack, as he thrust them into his pocket—" I'll put them up safely, boys, and you shall have 'em ag'in, for a whole night—after our next brush with the tories. Go you now and git your nags in readiness, while I see to Muggs. I'll jine you directly at the red clay."

When they had disappeared, he turned to the landlord, who had meanwhile risen, though rather slowly, from the earth, and now stood a silent spectator of the interview.

"Now, Muggs, I reckon we'll have to try the tug over agin. These blind boys of mine put in jest a moment too soon. They helped to flatten you, I'm thinking; and so, if you ain't quite satisfied which way the truth is, it's easy to go it over agin."

The offer was more liberal than Muggs expected or desired. He was already sufficiently convinced.

"No, no, Supple; you're too much for me!"

"It's the truth that's too much for you, Muggs—not me! I reckon you're satisfied now which way the truth is. You've got a right onderstanding in this business."

The landlord made some admissions, the amount of which, taken without circumlocution, was, that he had been whipped in a fair fight; and, according to all the laws of war, as well as common sense, that he was now at the disposal of the victor. His acknowledgments were sufficiently satisfactory.

"We've prayed for it, Muggs, and jest as we prayed we got it. You're rubbing your legs and your sides, but what's a bruise and a pain in the side, or even a broken rib, when we've got the truth? After that, a hurt of the body is a small matter; and then a man don't much fear any sort of danger. Let me know that I'm in the right way, and that justice is on my side, and I don't see the danger, though it stands in the shape of the biggest gun-muzzle that ever bellowed from the walls of Charlestown in the great siege. Now, Muggs, since you say now that you onderstand the argyment I set you, and that you agree to have your liberties the same as the rest of us, I'll jist open your eyes to a little of the resk you've been a-running for the last few days. Look—read this here letter, and see if you can recollect the writing."

The blood left the cheeks of the landlord the instant that the scout handed him the letter.

"Where did you find it, Supple?" he gasped, apprehensively.

"Find it! I first found the sculp of the chap that carried it," was the cool reply. "But you answer to the writing, don't you—it's your'n?"

"Well, I reckon you know it, Supple, without my saying so."

'Reckon I do, Muggs—it's pretty well known in these parts; and s'pose any of our boys but me had got hold of it! Where would you be, I wonder?—swinging on one of the oak limbs before your own door; dangling a good pair of legs of no sort of use to yourself or anybody else. But I'm your friend, Muggs; a better friend to you than you've been to yourself. I come and argy the matter with you, and reason with you to your onderstanding, and make a convarsion of you without trying to frighten you into it. Now that you see the error of your ways, I show you their danger also. This letter is tory all over, but there's one thing in it that made me have marcy upon you—it's here, jist in the middle, where you beg that bloody tory, Ned Conway, to have marcy on his brother. Anybody that speaks friendly, or kind, of Clarence Conway, I'll help him if I can. Now, Muggs, I'll go with you to your house, and there I'll burn this letter in your own sight, so that it'll never rise up in judgment agin you. But you must make a clean breast of it. You must tell me all you know, that I may be sure you feel the truth according to the lesson, which, with the helping of God, I've been able to give you."

The landlord felt himself at the mercy of the scout; but the generous treatment which he had received from the worthy fellow—treatment so unwonted at that period of wanton bloodshed and fierce cruelty—inclined him favorably to the cause, the arguments for which had been produced by so liberal a disputant. His own policy, to which we have already adverted more than once, suggested far better; and, if the landlord relented at all in his revelations, it was with the feeling—natural, perhaps, to every mind, however lowly—which makes it revolt at the idea of becoming treacherous, even to the party which it has joined for purposes of treachery. The information which the scout obtained, and which was valuable to the partisans, he drew from the relator by piecemeal. Every item of knowledge was drawn from him by its own leading question, and yielded with broken utterance, and the half-vacant look of one who is only in part conscious, as he is only in part willing.

"Pretty well, Muggs, though you don't come out like a man who felt the argyment at the bottom of his onderstanding. There's something more now. In this bit of writing there's a line or two about one Peter Flagg, who, it seems, carried forty-one niggers to town last January, and was to ship 'em to the West Injies. Now, can you tell if he did ship them niggers?"

"I can't exactly now, Supple—it's onbeknown to me."

"But how come you to write about this man and them niggers?"

"Why, you see, Peter Flagg was here looking after the captain."

"Ah!—he was here, was he?"

"Yes; he jined the captain just before Butler's men gin him that chase."

"He's with Ned Conway then, is he?"

"No, I reckon not. He didn't stay with the captain but half a day."

"Ah! ha!—and where did he go then?"

"Somewhere across the river."

"Below, I'm thinking."

"Yes, he took the lower route; I reckon he went toward the Santee."

"Isaac Muggs, don't you know that the business of Pete Flagg is to ship stolen niggers to the West Injy islands?"

"Well, Supple, I believe it is, though I don't know."

"That's enough about Pete. Now, Muggs, when did you see Watson Gray last? You know the man I mean. He comes from the Congaree near Granby. He's the one that watches Brier Park for Ned Conway, and brings him in every report about the fine bird that keeps there. You know what bird I mean, don't you?"

"Miss Flora, I reckon."

"A very good reckon. Well! you know Gray?"

"Yes—he's a great scout—the best, after you, I'm thinking, on the Congaree."

"Before me, Muggs," said the scout, with a sober shake of the head. "He's before me, or I'd ha' trapped him many's the long day ago. He's the only outlyer that's beyond my heft, that I acknowledge on the river: but he's a skunk—a bad chap about the heart. His bosom's full of black places. He loves to do ugly things, and to make a brag of 'em afterward, and that's a bad character for a good scout. But that's neither here nor thar. I only want you now to think up, and tell me when he was here last."

"Well!—"

"Ah, don't stop to 'well' about it," cried the other impatiently—"speak out like a bold man that's jest got the truth. Wa'n't Watson Gray here some three days ago—before the troop came down—and didn't he leave a message by word of mouth with you? Answer me that, Muggs, like a good whig as you ought to be."

"It's true as turpentine, Supple; but, Lord love you, how did you come to guess it?"

"No matter that!—up now, and tell me what that same message was."

"That's a puzzler, I reckon, for I didn't onderstand it all myself. There was five sticks and two bits of paper—on one was a long string of multiplication and 'rithmetic—figures and all that!—on the other was a sort of drawing that looked most like a gal on horseback."

"Eh!—The gal on horseback was nateral enough. Perhaps I can make out that; but the bits of stick and 'rithmetic is all gibberish. Wa'n't there nothing that you had to say by word of mouth to Ned Conway?"

"Yes, to be sure. He left word as how the whigs was getting thicker and thicker—how Sumter and Lee marked all the road from Granby down to Orangeburg with their horse-tracks, and never afeard; and how Greene was a-pushing across toward Ninety-Six, where he was guine to 'siege Cruger."

"Old news, Muggs, and I reckon you've kept back the best

for the last. What did he have to say 'bout Miss Flora? Speak up to that!"

"Not a word. I don't think he said anything more, onless it was something about boats being a-plenty, and no danger of horse-tracks on the river."

"There's a meaning in that; and I must spell it out," said the scout; "but now, Muggs, another question or two. Who was the man that Ned Conway sent away prisoner jest before day?"

"Lord, Supple, you sees everything!" ejaculated the landlord. Pressed by the wily scout, he related, with tolerable correctness, all the particulars of the affray the night before between the captain of the Black Riders and his subordinate; and threw such an additional light upon the causes of quarrel between them as suggested to the scout a few new measures of policy.

"Well, Muggs," said he, at the close, "I'll tell you something in return for all you've told me. My boys caught that same Stockton and trapped his guard in one hour after they took the road; and I'm glad to find, by putting side by side what they confessed and what you tell me, that you've stuck to the truth like a gentleman and a whig. They didn't tell me about the lieutenant's wanting to be cappin, but that's detarmined me to parole the fellow that he may carry on his mischief in the troop. I'm going to leave you now, Muggs; but you'll see an old man coming here to look after a horse about midday. Give him a drink, and say to him, that you don't know nothing about the horse, but there's a hound on track after something, that went barking above, three hours before. That'll sarve his purpose and mine too: and now, God bless you, old boy, and, remember, I'm your friend, and I can do you better sarvice now than any two Black Riders of the gang. As I've convarted you, I'll stand by you, and I'll never be so far off in the swamp that I can't hear your grunting, and come out to your help. So, good-by, and no more forgitting of that argyment."

"And where are you going now, Supple?"

"Psho, boy, that's telling. Was I to let you know that, Watson Gray might worm it out from under your tongue, without taking a wrastle for it. I'll tell you when I come back."

And with a good-humored chuckle the scout disappeared, leaving the landlord to meditate, at his leisure, upon the value of those arguments which had made him in one day resign a faith which had been cherished as long — as it had proved profitable. Muggs had no hope that the new faith would prove equally so; but if it secured to him the goodly gains of the past, he was satisfied. Like many of the tories at this period, he received a sudden illumination, which showed him in one moment the errors for which he had been fighting five years. Let not this surprise our readers. In the closing battles of the Revolution in South Carolina, many were the tories, converted to the patriot cause, who, at the eleventh hour, displayed the most conspicuous bravery fighting on the popular side. And this must not be suffered to lower them in our opinion. The revolutionary war, in South Carolina, did not so much divide the people, because of the tendencies to loyalty, or liberty, on either hand, as because of social and other influences — personal and sectional feuds — natural enough to a new country, in which one third of the people were of foreign birth.

## CHAPTER XV.

### GLIMPSES OF PASSION AND ITS FRUITS.

SUPPLE JACK soon joined his commander, bringing with him, undiminished by use or travel, all the various budgets of intelligence which he had collected in his scout. He had dismissed the insubordinate lieutenant of the Black Riders on parole; not without suffering him to hear, as a familiar *on dit* along the river, that Captain Morton was about to sacrifice the troop at the first opportunity, and fly with all his booty from the country.

"I've know'd," said he to himself, after Stockton took his departure, " I've know'd a smaller spark than that set off a whole barrel of gunpowder."

To his colonel, having delivered all the intelligence which he had gained of the movements as well of the public as private enemy, he proceeded, as usual, to give such counsel as the nature of his revelations seemed to suggest. This may be summed up in brief, without fatiguing the reader with the detailed conversation which ensued between them in their examination of the subject.

"From what I see, colonel, Ned Conway is gone below. It's true he did seem to take the upper route, but Massey can't find the track after he gits to Fisher's Slue" (diminutive for sluice). "There, I reckon, he chopped right round, crossed the slue, I'm thinking, and dashed below. Well, what's he gone below for, and what's Pete Flagg gone for across to the Santee?—Pete, that does nothing but ship niggers for the British officers. They all see that they're got to go, and they're for making hay while the sun is still a-shining. Now, I'm thinking that Ned Conway is after your mother's niggers. He'll steal 'em and ship 'em by Pete Flagg to the West Indies, and be the first to follow, the moment that Rawdon gits licked by Greene. It's cl'ar to me that you ought to go below and see about the business."

The arguments of the woodman were plausible enough, and Clarence Conway felt them in their fullest force. But he had his doubts about the course alleged to be taken by his kinsman, and a feeling equally selfish, perhaps, but more noble intrinsically, made him fancy that his chief interest lay above. He was not insensible to his mother's and his own probable loss, should the design of Edward Conway really be such as Bannister suggested, but a greater stake, in his estimation, lay in the person of the fair Flora Middleton; and he could not bring himself to believe, valuing her charms as he did himself, that his kinsman would forego such game for the more mercenary objects involved in the other adventure.

The tenor of the late interview between himself and the chief of the Black Riders, had forced his mind to brood with serious anxiety on the probable fortunes of this lady; and his own hopes and fears becoming equally active at the same time, the exulting threats and bold assumptions of Edward Conway—so very different from the sly humility of his usual deportment—awakened all his apprehensions. He resolved to go forward to the upper Congaree, upon the pleasant banks of which stood the princely domains of the Middleton family; persuaded, as he was, that the rival with whom he contended for so great a treasure, equally wily and dishonorable, had in contemplation some new villany, which, if not seasonably met, would result in equal loss to himself and misery to the maiden of his heart.

Yet he did not resolve thus, without certain misgivings and self-reproaches. His mother was quite as dear to him as ever mother was to the favorite son of her affections. He knew the danger in which her property stood, and was not heedless of the alarm which she would experience, in her declining years and doubtful health, at the inroad of any marauding foe. The arguments of a stronger passion, however, prevailed above these apprehensions, and he contented himself with a determination to make the best of his way below, as soon as he had assured himself of the safety and repose of everything above. Perhaps, too, he had a farther object in this contemplated visit to Flora Middleton. The counsel of Bannister on a previous occasion, which urged upon him to bring his doubts to conviction on the subject of the course which her feelings might be disposed to take, found a corresponding eagerness in his own heart to arrive at a knowledge, always so desirable to a lover, and which he seeks in fear and trembling as well as in hope.

"I will but see her," was his unuttered determination, "I will but see her, and see that she is safe, and hear at once her final answer. These doubts are too painful for endurance! Better to hear the worst at once, than live always in apprehension of it."

Leaving the youthful partisan to pursue his own course, let us now turn for a while to that of Edward Morton, and the gloomy and fierce banditti which he commanded. He has already crossed the Wateree, traversed the country between that river and the Congaree; and after various small adventures, such as might be supposed likely to occur in such a progress, but which do not demand from us any more special notice, we find him on the banks of the latter stream, in the immediate neighborhood of the spot where it receives into its embrace the twin though warring waters of the Saluda and the Broad—a spot, subsequently, better distinguished as the chosen site of one of the loveliest towns of the state—the seat of its capital, and of a degree of refinement, worth, courtesy, and taste, which are not often equalled in any region, and are certainly surpassed in none.

Columbia, however, at the period of our story, was not in existence; and the meeting of its tributary waters, their striving war, incessant rivalry, and the continual clamors of their strife, formed the chief distinction of the spot; and conferred upon it no small degree of picturesque vitality and loveliness. A few miles below, on the opposite side of the stream, stood then the flourishing town of Granby—a place of considerable magnitude and real importance to the wants of the contiguous country, but now fallen into decay and utterly deserted. A garrisoned town of the British, it had just before this period been surrendered by Colonel Maxwell to the combined American force under Sumter and Lee—an event which counselled the chief of the Black Riders to an increased degree of caution as he approached a neighborhood so likely to be swarming with enemies.

Here we may as well communicate to the reader such portions of the current history of the time, as had not yet entirely reached this wily marauder. While he was pursuing his personal and petty objects of plunder on the Wateree, Lord Rawdon had fled from Camden, which he left in flames; Sumter had taken Orangeburg; Fort Motte had surrendered to Marion; the British had been compelled to evacuate their post at Nelson's ferry; and the only fortified place of which they now kept possession in the interior was that of Ninety-Six; a station of vast importance to their interests in the back country, and which, accordingly, they resolved to defend to the last extremity.

But though ignorant of some of the events here brought together, Edward Morton was by no means ignorant of the difficulties which were accumulating around the fortunes of the British, and which, he naturally enough concluded, must result in these, and even worse disasters. Of the fall of Granby he was aware; of the audacity and number of the American parties, his scouts hourly informed him, even if his own frequent and narrow escapes had failed to awaken him to a sense of the prevailing dangers. But, governed by an intense selfishness, he had every desire to seek, in increased caution, for the promotion of those interests and objects, without which his patriotism might possibly have been less prudent, and of the proper kind. He had neither wish nor motive to go forward rashly; and, accordingly, we find him advancing to the Saluda, with the slow, wary footsteps of one who looks to behold his enemy starting forth, without summons of trumpet, from the bosom of every brake along the route.

It was noon when his troop reached the high banks of the river, the murmur of whose falls, like the distant mutterings of ocean upon some island-beach, were heard, pleasantly soothing, in the sweet stillness of a forest noon. A respite was given to the employments of the troop. Scouts were sent out, videttes stationed, and the rest surrendered themselves to repose, each after his own fashion: some to slumber, some to play, while others, like their captain, wandered off to the river banks, to angle or to meditate, as their various moods might incline.

Morton went apart from the rest, and found a sort of hiding-place upon a rock immediately overhanging the river, where, surrounded by an umbrageous forest-growth, he threw his person at length, and yielded himself up to those brooding cares which he felt were multiplying folds about his mind, in the intangling grasp of which it worked slowly and without its usual ease and elasticity.

The meditations are inevitably mournful with a spirit such as his. Guilt is a thing of isolation always, even when most surrounded by its associates and operations. Its very insecurity tends to its isolation as completely as its selfishness. Edward Morton felt all this. He had been toiling, and not in vain, for a mercenary object. His spoils had been considerable. He had hoarded up a secret treasure in another country, secure from the vicissitudes which threatened every fortune in that where he had won it; but he himself was insecure. Treachery, he began to believe, and not a moment too soon, was busy all around him. He had kept down fear, and doubt, and distrust, by a life of continual action; but it was in moments of repose like this, that he himself found none. It was then that his fears grew busy — that he began to distrust his fate, and to apprehend that all that future, which he fondly fancied to pass in serenity of fortune, if not of mind and feeling, would yet be clouded and compassed with denial. His eye, stretching away on either hand, beheld the two chafing rivers rushing downward to that embrace which they seem at once to desire and to avoid. A slight barrier of land and shrubbery interposes to prevent their too sudden meeting. Little islands throw themselves between, as if striving to thwart the fury of their wild collision, but in vain! The impetuous waters force their way against every obstruction; and wild and angry, indeed, as if endued with moral energies and a human feeling of hate, is their first encounter — their recoil — their return to the conflict, in foam and roar, and commotion, until exhaustion terminates the strife, and they at length repose together in the broad valleys of the Congaree below.

The turbulence of the scene alone interested the dark-bosomed spectator whose fortunes we contemplate. He saw neither its sublime nor its gentle features — its fair groves — its sweet islands of rock and tufted vegetation, upon which the warring waters, as if mutually struggling to do honor to their benevolent interposition, fling ever their flashing, and transparent wreaths of whitish foam. His moody thought was busy in likening the prospect to that turbulence, the result of wild purposes and wicked desires, which filled his own bosom. A thousand impediments, like the numerous rocks and islands that rose to obstruct the passage of the streams which he surveyed, lay in his course, baffling his aim, driving him from his path, resisting his desires, and scattering inefficiently all his powers. Even as the waters which he beheld, complaining in the fruitless conflict with the rude masses from which they momently recoiled, so did he, unconsciously, break into speech, as the difficulties in his own future progress grew more and more obvious to his reflections.

"There must soon be an end to this. That old fool was right. I should be a fool to wait to see it. Once, twice, thrice, already, have I escaped, when death seemed certain. Let me not provoke Fortune — let me not task her too far. It will be impossible to baffle these bloodhounds much longer! Their scent is too keen, their numbers too great, and the spoil too encouraging. Besides, I have done enough. I have proved my loyalty. Loyalty indeed!—a profitable pretext!—and there will be no difficulty now in convincing Rawdon that I ought not to be the last to linger here in waiting for the end. That end —what shall it be?—A hard fight—a bloody field—a sharp pain and quiet! Quiet!—that were something, too, which might almost reconcile one to linger. Could I be secure of that, at the risk of a small pain only; but it may be worse. Captivity were something worse than death. In their hands, alive, and no Spanish tortures would equal mine. No! no! I must not encounter that danger. I must keep in reserve one weapon at least, consecrated to the one purpose. This—this! must secure me against captivity!"

He drew from his bosom, as he spoke these words, a small poniard of curious manufacture, which he contemplated with an eye of deliberate study; as if the exquisite Moorish workmanship of the handle, and the rich and variegated enamel of the blade, served to promote the train of gloomy speculation into which he had fallen. A rustling of the leaves—the slight step of a foot immediately behind him—caused him to start to his feet;—but he resumed his place with an air of vexation, as he beheld in the intruder, the person of the boy whom we have seen once before in close attendance upon him.

"How now!" he exclaimed impatiently; "can I have no moment to myself—why will you thus persist in following me?"

"I have no one else to follow," was the meek reply—the tones falling, as it were, in echo from a weak and withered heart.

"I have no one else to follow, and—and—"

The lips faltered into silence.

"Speak out—and what?—"

"You once said to me that I should go with none but you— oh, Edward Conway, spurn me not—drive me not away with those harsh looks and cruel accents;—let me linger beside you —though, if you please it, still out of your sight; for I am desolate—oh! so desolate, when you leave me!—you, to whom alone, of all the world, I may have some right to look for protection and for life."

The sex of the speaker stood revealed—in the heaving breast—the wo-begone countenance—the heart-broken despondency of look and gesture—the tear-swollen and down-looking eye. She threw herself before him as she spoke, her face buried in her hands and prone upon the ground. Her sobs succeeded her speech, and in fact silenced it.

"No more of this, Mary Clarkson, you disturb and vex me. Rise. I have seen, for some days past, that you had some new tribulation—some new burden of wo to deliver;—out with it now—say what you have to say;—and, look you, no whinings! Life is too seriously full of real evils, dangers, and difficulties, to suffer me to bear with these imaginary afflictions."

"Oh, God, Edward Conway, it is not imaginary with me. It is real—it is to be seen—to be felt. I am dying with it. It is in my pale cheek—my burning brain, in which there is a constant fever. Oh, look not upon me thus—thus angrily—for, in truth I am dying. I feel it! I know that I can not live very long;—and yet, I am so afraid to die. It is this fear, Edward Conway, that makes me intrude upon you now."

"And what shall I do, and what shall I say to lessen your fears of death? And why should I do it—why, yet more, should you desire it? Death is, or ought to be, a very good thing for one who professes to be so very miserable in life as yourself. You heard me as you approached?—if you did, you must have heard my resolution to seek death, from my own weapon, under certain circumstances. Now, it is my notion that whenever life becomes troublesome, sooner than grumble at it hourly, I should make use of some small instrument like this. A finger prick only—no greater pain—will suffice, and put an end to life and pain in the same instant."

"Would it could! would it could!" exclaimed the unfortunate victim of that perfidy which now laughed her miseries to scorn.

"Why, so it can! Do you doubt? I tell you, that there is no more pain, Mary, in driving this dagger into your heart—into its most tender and vital places—than there would be, burying it in your finger. Death will follow, and there's the end of it."

"Not the end, not the end—if it were, Edward Conway, how gladly would I implore from your hand the blessing of that lasting peace which would follow from its blow. It is the hereafter—the awful hereafter—which I fear to meet."

"Pshaw! a whip of the hangman—a bugbear of the priests, for cowards and women! I'll warrant you, if you are willing to try the experiment, perfect security from all pain hereafter!"

And the heartless wretch extended toward her the hand which contained the glittering weapon. She shuddered and turned away—giving him, as she did so, such a look as, even he, callous as he was, shrunk to behold. A glance of reproach, more keen, deep, and touching, than any word of complaint which her lips had ever ventured to utter.

"Alas! Edward Conway, has it really come to this! To you I have yielded everything—virtue, peace of mind—the love of father, and of mother, and of friends—all that's most dear—all that the heart deems most desirable—and you offer me, in return, for these—death, death!—the sharp, sudden poniard— the cold, cold grave! If you offer it, Edward Conway—strike! —the death is welcome! Even the fear of it is forgotten. Strike, set me free;—I will vex you no longer with my presence."

"Why, what a peevish fool you are, Mary Clarkson! though, to be sure, you are not very different from the rest. There's no pleasing any of you, do as we may. You first come to me to clamor about your distaste of life, and by your perpetual grumblings you seek to make it as distasteful to me as to yourself. Well, I tell you—this is *my* remedy—this sudden, sharp dagger! Whenever I shall come to regard life as a thing of so much misery as you do, I shall end it; and I also add, in the benevolence of my heart—'here is my medicament—I share it with you!' —and lo! what an uproar—what a howling. Look you, Mary, you must trouble me no longer in this manner. I am, just now, in the worst possible mood to bear with the best friend under the sun."

"Oh, Edward Conway, and this too!—this, after your promise! Do you remember your promise to me, by the poplar spring, that hour of my shame?—that awful hour! Oh! what was that promise, Edward Conway? Speak, Edward Conway! Repeat that promise, and confess I was not all guilty. No, no! I was only all credulous! You beguiled me with a promise— with an oath—a solemn oath before Heaven—did you not?— that I should be your wife. Till then, at least, I was not guilty!"

"Did I really make such a promise to you—eh?" he asked with a scornful affectation of indifference.

"Surely, you will not deny that you did?" she exclaimed, with an earnestness which was full of amazement.

"Well, I scarcely remember. But it matters not much, Mary Clarkson. You were a fool for believing. How could you suppose that I would marry you? Ha! Is it so customary for pride and poverty to unite on the Congaree that you should believe? Is it customary for the eldest son of one of the wealthiest families to wed with the child of one of the poorest? Why, you should have known by the promise itself that I was amusing myself with your credulity—that my only object was to beguile you—to win you on my own terms—not to wear you! I simply stooped for conquest, Mary Clarkson, and you were willing to believe any lie for the same object. It was your vanity that beguiled you, Mary Clarkson, and not my words. You wished to be a fine lady, and you are——"

"Oh, do not stop. Speak it all out. Give to my folly and my sin their true name. I can bear to hear it now without shrinking, for my own thoughts have already spoken to my heart the foul and fearful truth. I am, indeed, loathsome to myself, and would not care to live but that I fear to die. 'Tis not the love of life that makes me turn in fear from the dagger which you offer. This, Edward Morton—'tis this which brings me to you now. I do not seek you for guidance or for counsel —no, no!—no such folly moves me now. I come to you for protection—for safety—for security from sudden death—from the judge—from the avenger! *He* is pursuing us—I have seen him!"—and, as she spoke these almost incoherent words, her eye looked wildly among the thick woods around, with a glance full of apprehension, as if the danger she spoke of was in reality at hand. Surprise was clearly expressed in the features of her callous paramour.

"He! Of whom speak you, child? Who is it you fear?"— and his glance followed the wild direction of her eyes.

"My father!—Jacob Clarkson! He is in search of me—of you! And oh! Edward Conway, I know him so well, that I tell you it will not be your high connections and aristocratic birth that will save you on the Congaree from a poor man's rifle, though these may make it a trifling thing for you to ruin a poor man's child. He is even now in search of us—I have seen him! I have seen the object of his whole soul in his eye, as I have seen it a hundred times before. He will kill you—he will kill us both, Edward Conway, but he will have revenge!"

"Pshaw, girl! You are very foolish. How can your father find us out? How approach us? The thought is folly. As an individual he can only approach us by coming into the line of our sentinels; these disarm him, and he then might look upon us, in each other's arms, without being able to do us any injury."

"Do not speak so, Edward, for God's sake!—in each other's arms no longer—no more!"—and a sort of shivering horror passed over her frame as she spoke these words.

"As you please!" muttered the outlaw, with an air and smile of scornful indifference. The girl proceeded—

"But, even without weapons, the sight of my father—the look of his eyes upon mine—would kill me—would be worse than any sort of death! Oh, God! let me never see him more! Let him never see me—the child that has lost him, lost herself, and is bringing his gray hairs in sorrow to the grave."

"Mary Clarkson, who do you think to cheat with all this hypocrisy of sentiment? Don't I know that all those fine words and phrases are picked out of books. This talk is too customary to be true."

"They may be!—they were books, Edward Conway, which you brought me, and which I loved to read for your sake. Alas! I did not follow their lessons."

"Enough of this stuff, and now to the common sense of this business. You have seen your father, you say; where?"

8

"On the Wateree; the day before you came back from your brother in the swamp!"

"Brother me no brothers!" exclaimed the outlaw fiercely; "and look you, girl, have I not told you a thousand times that I wish not to be called Conway. Call me Morton, Cunningham, John Stuart, or the devil—or any of the hundred names by which my enemies distinguish me and denominate my deeds; but call me not by the name of Conway. I, too, have something filial in my nature; and if you wish not to see the father you have offended, perhaps it is for the same reason that I would not hear the name of mine. Let that dutiful reason content you—it may be that I have others; but these we will forbear for the present. What of Jacob Clarkson, when you saw him? Where was he?—how employed?—and where were *you*, and who with you?"

"Oh, God! I was fearfully nigh to him, and he saw me!—He fixed his keen, cold, deathly eye upon me, and I thought I should have sunk under it. I thought he knew me; but how could he in such a guise as this, and looking, as I do, pale withered, and broken down with sin and suffering."

"Pshaw! Where was all this?"

"At Isaac's tavern. There was none there beside myself and Isaac. He came in and asked for a calabash of water. He would drink nothing, though Muggs kindly offered him, but he would not. He looked at me only for an instant; but it seemed to me, in that instant, that he looked through and through my soul. He said nothing to me, and hardly anything to Isaac—though he asked him several questions; and when he drank the water, and rested for a little while, he went away. But, while he stayed, I thought I should have died. I could have buried myself in the earth to escape his sight; and yet how I longed to throw myself at his feet, and beg for mercy! Could I have done that, I think I should have been happy. I should have been willing then to die. But I dared not. He hadn't a human look—he didn't seem to feel;—and I feared that he might kill me without hearkening to my prayer."

"Muggs should have told me of this," said the other, musingly.

"He must have forgot it, on account of the uproar and great confusion afterward."

"That is no good reason for a cool fellow like him. I must see into it. It was a strange omission."

"But what will you do, Edward—where shall we fly?"

"Fly! where should we fly—and why? Because of your father? Have I not already told you that he can not approach us to do harm; and, as for discovering us, have you not seen that he looked upon his own child without knowing her; and I'm sure he can never recollect me as the man who once helped him to provide for the only undutiful child he had."

"Spare me! Be not so *cruel* in your words, Edward, for, of a truth, though I may escape the vengeance of my father, I feel certain that I have not long—not very long—to live."

"Nor I, Mary; so, while life lasts, let us be up and doing!" was the cold-blooded reply, as, starting to his feet, as if with the desire to avoid further conference on an annoying subject, he prepared to leave the spot where it had taken place.

Her lips moved, but she spoke not. Her hands were clasped, but the entreaty which they expressed was lost equally upon his eyes and heart; and if she meant to pray to him for a further hearing, her desire was unexpressed in any stronger form. By him it remained unnoticed. Was it unnoticed by the overlooking and observant God!—for, to him, when the other had gone from sight and hearing, were her prayers then offered, with, seemingly, all the sincerity of a broken and a contrite spirit.

## CHAPTER XVI.

A GLIMPSE OF BRIER PARK: THE OATH OF THE BLACK RIDERS.

By evening of the same day, the scouts made their appearance, and their reports were such as to determine the captain of the Black Riders to cross the Congaree and pursue his objects, whatever they might be, along its southern banks. Sufficient time for rest had been allotted to his troop. He believed they had employed it as assigned; little dreaming how busy some of them had been, in the concoction of schemes, which, if in character not unlike his own, were scarcely such as were congenial with his authority or his desires. But these are matters for the future.

Though resolved on crossing the river, yet, as the chosen ferry lay several miles below, it became necessary to sound to horse; and, about dusk, the troop was again put in motion, and continued on their route till midnight.

They had compassed but a moderate distance in this space of time, moving as they did with great precaution; slowly of course, as was necessary while traversing a country supposed to be in the full possession of an enemy, and over roads, which, in those days, were neither very distinct, nor fairly open, nor in the best condition. They reached the ferry, but halted for the remainder of the night without making any effort to cross.

At the dawn of day, Mary Clarkson, still seemingly a boy, was one of the first, stealing along the bank of the river, to remark the exquisite beauty of the prospect which on every side opened upon her eye. The encampment of the Black Riders had been made along the river bluff, but sufficiently removed from its edge to yield the requisite degree of woodland shelter. The spot chosen for the purpose was a ridge unusually elevated for that portion of the stream, which is commonly skirted by an alluvial bottom of the richest swamp undergrowth. This, on either hand, lay below, while the river, winding upon its way in the foreground, was as meek and placid as if it never knew obstacle or interruption.

Yet, but a few miles above, how constant had been its strife with the rocks—how unceasing its warring clamors. But a few of these obstructions, and these were obstructions in appearance only, occurred immediately at the point before us; and these, borne down by the violence of the conflict carried on above, might seem rather the trophies of its own triumph, which the river brought away with it in its downward progress—serving rather to overcome the monotony of its surface, and increase the picturesque of its prospect, than as offering any new obstacle, or as provoking to any farther strife. Its waters broke with a gentle violence on their rugged tops, and passed over and around them with a slight murmur, which was quite as clearly a murmur of merriment as one of annoyance.

Around, the foliage grew still in primitive simplicity. There, the long-leafed pine, itself the evidence of a forest undishonored by the axe, reared its lofty brow, soaring and stooping, a giant surveying his domain. About him, not inferior in pride and majesty, though perhaps inferior in height, were a numerous growth of oaks, of all the varieties common to the region;—tributary, as beauty still must ever be to strength, were the rich and various hues of the bay, the poplar, the dogwood, and the red bud of the sassafras—all growing and blooming in a profligate luxuriance, unappreciated and unemployed, as if the tastes of the Deity, quite as active as his benevolence, found their own sufficient exercise in the contemplation of such a treasure, though man himself were never to be created for its future enjoyment.

But beyond lay a prospect in which art, though co-operating with nature to the same end, had proved herself a dangerous rival. Stretching across the stream, the eye took in, at a glance, the territory of one of those proud baronial privileges of Carolina—the seat of one of her short-lived nobility—broad fields, smooth-shaven lawns, green meadows melting away into the embrace of the brown woods—fair gardens—moss-covered and solemn groves; and in the midst of all, and over all—standing upon the crown of a gently sloping hill, one of those stern, strong, frowning fabrics of the olden time, which our ancestors devised to answer the threefold purposes of the dwelling, the chapel, and the castle for defence.

There, when the courage of the frontier-men first broke ground, and took possession, among the wild and warlike hunters of the Santee, the Congaree, and the Saluda, did the gallant General Middleton plant his towers, amidst a region of great perils, but of great natural beauty. With fearless soul, he united an exquisite taste, and for its indulgence he was not unwilling to encounter the perils of the remote wilderness to which he went. Perhaps, too, the picturesque of the scenery was heightened to his mind by the dangers which were supposed to environ it; and the forest whose frowning shades discouraged most others, did not lose any of its attractions in his sight, because it sometimes tasked him to defend his possessions by the strong arm and the ready weapon. The bear disputed with him the possession of the honey-tree; and the red man, starting up, at evening, from the thicket, not unfrequently roused him with his fearful halloo, to betake himself to those defences, which made his habitation a fortress no less than a dwelling.

But these, which are difficulties to the slothful, and terrors to the timid, gave a zest to adventure, which sweetens enterprise in the estimation of the brave; and it did not lessen the value of Brier Park to its first proprietor because he was sometimes driven to stand a siege from the red men of the Congaree.

But the red men disappeared, and with them the daring adventurer who planted his stakes, among the first, in the bosom of their wild possessions. He, too, followed them at the appointed season; and his proud old domains fell into the hands of gentler proprietors. Under the countenance of her venerable grandmother, Flora Middleton—truly a rose in the wilderness—blossomed almost alone; at a time when the region in which the barony stood, was covered with worse savages than even the Congarees had been in the days of their greatest license.

But the besom of war—which swept the country as with flame and sword—had paused in its ravages at this venerated threshold. With whig and tory alike, the name of old General Middleton, the patriarch of the Congaree country, was held equally sacred;—and the lovely granddaughter who inherited his wealth, though celebrated equally as a belle and a rebel, was suffered to hold her estates and opinions without paying those heavy penalties which, in those days, the possession of either was very likely to incur.

Some trifling exceptions to this general condition of indulgence might occasionally take place. Sometimes a marauding party trespassed upon the hen-roost, or made a bolder foray into the cattle-yard and storehouses; but these petty depredations sunk out of sight in comparison with the general state of insecurity and robbery which prevailed everywhere else.

The more serious annoyances to which the inhabitants of Brier Park were subject, arose from the involuntary hospitality which they were compelled to exercise toward the enemies of their country. Flora Middleton had been forced to receive with courtesy the "amiable" Cornwallis, and the brutal Ferguson; and to listen with complacency to words of softened courtesy and compliment from lips which had just before commanded to the halter a score of her countrymen, innocent of all offence, except that of defending, with the spirit of manhood and filial love, the soil which gave them birth. The equally sanguinary and even more stern Rawdon—the savage Tarleton, and the fierce and malignant Cunningham, had also been her uninvited guests, to whom she had done the honors of the house with the grace and spirit natural to her name and education, but never at the expense of her patriotism.

"My fair foe, Flora," was the phrase with which—with unaccustomed urbanity of temper, Lord Cornwallis was wont to acknowledge, but never to resent, in any other way—the boldness of her spoken sentiments. These she declared with equal modesty and firmness, whenever their expression became necessary; and, keen as might be her sarcasm, it bore with it its own antidote, in the quiet, subdued, ladylike tone in which it was uttered, and the courteous manner which accompanied it. Grace and beauty may violate many laws with impunity, and praise, not punishment, will still follow the offender.

Such was the happy fortune of Flora Middleton—one of those youthful beauties of Carolina, whose wit, whose sentiment, pride and patriotism, acknowledged equally by friend and foe, exercised a wondrous influence over the events of the war, which is yet to be put on record in a becoming manner.

The poor outcast, Mary Clarkson—a beauty, also, at one time, in her rustic sphere, and one whose sensibilities had been unhappily heightened by the very arts employed by her seducer to effect her ruin—gazed, with a mournful sentiment of satisfaction, at the sweet and picturesque beauty of the scene. Already was she beginning to lose herself in that dreamy languor of thought which hope itself suggests to the unhappy as a means to escape from wo, when she found her reckless betrayer suddenly standing by her side.

"Ha, Mary, you are on the look-out, I see—you have a taste, I know. What think you of the plantations opposite? See how beautifully the lawn slopes up from the river to the foot of the old castle, a glimpse of whose gloomy, frowning visage, meets your eye through that noble grove of water oaks that link their arms across the passage and conceal two thirds—no less—of the huge fabric to which they lead. There now, to the right, what a splendid field of corn—what an ocean of green leaves. On the left do you see a clump of oaks and sycamores—there, to itself, away—a close, dense clump, on a little hillock, itself a sort of emerald in the clearing around it. There stands the vault—the tomb of the Middleton family. Old Middleton himself sleeps there, if he can be said to sleep at all; for they tell strange stories of his nightly rambles after wolves and copper-skins. You may see a small gray spot, like a chink of light, peeping out of the grove—that is the tomb. It is a huge, square apartment—I have been in it more than once—partly beneath and partly above the ground. It has hid many more living than it will ever hold dead men. I owe it thanks for more than one concealment myself."

"You?"

"Yes! I have had a very comfortable night's rest in it, all things considered; and the probability is not small that we shall take our sleep in it to-night. How like you the prospect?"

The girl shuddered. He did not care for any other answer, but proceeded.

"In that old cage of Middleton there is a bird of sweetest

song, whom I would set free. Do you guess what I mean, Mary?"

The girl confessed her ignorance.

"You are dull, Mary, but you shall grow wiser before long. Enough for the present. We must set the troop in motion. A short mile below and we find our crossing place, and then— hark you, Mary, you must keep a good look-out to-night. If there was mischief yesterday, it is not yet cured. There is more to-day. I shall expect you to watch to-night, while I *prey*."

He chuckled at the passing attempt at a sort of wit, in which, to do him justice, he did not often indulge, and the point of which his companion did not perceive; then continued—

"Perhaps it should be 'prowl' rather than watch. Though, to prowl well requires the best of watching. You must do both. You *prowl* while I *prey*—do you understand?"

He had given a new form to his phrase, by which he made his humor obvious; and, satisfied with this, he proceeded more seriously—

"Give up your dumps, girl. It will not be the worse for you that things turn out to please me. These rascals must be watched, and I can now trust none to watch them but yourself."

At this confession, her reproachful eyes were turned full and keenly upon him. He had betrayed the trust of the only being in whom he could place his own. What a commentary on his crime, on his cruel indifference to the victim of it! He saw in her eyes the meaning which her lips did not declare.

"Yes, it is even so," he said; "and women were made for this, and they must expect it. Born to be dependants, it is enough that we employ you; and if your expectations were fewer and humbler, your chance for happiness would be far greater. Content yourself now with the conviction that you have a share in my favor, and all will go well with you. The regards of a man are not to be contracted to the frail and unsatisfying compass of one girl's heart; unless, indeed, as you all seem to fancy, that love is the sole business of a long life. Love is very well for boys and girls, but it furnishes neither the food nor the exercise for manhood. If you expect it, you live in vain. Your food must be the memories of your former luxuries. Let it satisfy you, Mary, that I loved you once."

"Never, Edward—you never loved me; not even when my confidence in your love lost me the love of all other persons. This knowledge I have learned by knowing how I have myself loved, and by comparing my feelings with the signs of love in you. In learning to know how little I have been loved, I made the discovery of your utter incapacity to love."

"And why, pray you?" he demanded, with some pique; but the girl did not answer. He saw her reluctance, and framed another question.

"And why, then, after this discovery, do you still love me, and cling to me, and complain of me?"

"Alas! I know not why I love you. That, indeed, is beyond me to learn. I have sought to know—I have tried to think—I have asked, but in vain, of my own mind and heart. I cling to you because I can cling nowhere else; and you have yourself said that a woman is a dependant—she must cling somewhere! The vine clings to the tree though it knows that all its heart is rotten. As for complaint, God knows I do not come to make it—I do not wish, but I can not help it. I weep and moan from weakness only, I believe, and I shall soon be done moaning."

"Enough—I see which way you tend now. You are foolish, Mary Clarkson, and war with your own peace. Can you never be reconciled to what is inevitable—what you can no longer avoid? Make the best of your condition—what is done can't be amended; and the sooner you show me that you can yield yourself to your fate with some grace, the more certain and soon will be the grace bestowed in turn. You are useful to me, Mary; and as women are useful to men—grown men, mark me—so do they value them. When I say 'useful,' remember the word is a comprehensive one. You may be useful in love, in the promotion of fortune, revenge, ambition, hope, enterprise—a thousand things and objects, in which exercise will elevate equally your character and condition. Enough, now. You must show your usefulness to-night. I go on a business of peril, and I must go alone. But I will take you with me a part of the way, and out of sight of the encampment. To the encampment you must return, however, and with such precaution as to keep unseen. I need not counsel you any further—your talents clearly lie that way. Love is a sorry business—a sort of sickness—perhaps the natural complaint of overgrown babies of both sexes, who should be dosed with caudle and put to bed as soon after as possible. Do you hear, child? Do you understand?"

Thus substantially ended this conference—the singular terms of which, and the relation between the parties, can only be understood by remembering that sad condition of dependence in which the unhappy girl stood to her betrayer. She was hopeless of any change of fortune—she knew not where to turn—she now had no other objects to which she might presume to cling. She remembered the humbler love of John Bannister with a sigh—the roof and the affections of her father with a thrill, which carried a cold horror through all her veins. A natural instinct turned her to the only one upon whom she had any claim—a claim still indisputable, though it might be scorned or denied by him; and, without being satisfied of the truth of his arguments, she was willing, as he required, to be useful, that she might not be forgotten.

While the troop was preparing to cross the river, it was joined, to the surprise of everybody and the chagrin of its commander, by the refractory lieutenant, Stockton.

He related the events which occurred to him somewhat differently from the truth. According to his version of the story, the guard to whom he had been intrusted was attacked by a superior force, beaten, and probably slain—he himself seasonably escaping to tell the story. It was fancied by himself and friends that his narrow escape and voluntary return to his duty would lessen his offence in the eye of the chief, and probably relieve him from all the consequences threatened in his recent arrest.

But the latter was too jealous of the disaffection prevailing among his men, and too confident in the beneficial influence of sternness among inferiors, to relax the measure of a hair in the exercise of his authority. He at once committed the traitor a close prisoner, to the care of two of his most trusty adherents; and resolutely rejected the applications offered in his behalf by some of the temporizers—a class of persons of whom the Black Riders, like every other human community, had a fair proportion.

The river was crossed a few miles below the Middleton Barony. A deep thicket in the forest, and on the edge of the river swamp, was chosen for their bivouac; and there, closely concealed from casual observation, the chief of the Black Riders, with his dark banditti, awaited till the approach of night, in a condition of becoming quiet. He then prepared to go forth, alone, on his expedition to the barony; and it was with some surprise, though without suspicion of the cause, that Mary Clarkson perceived, on his setting out, that he had discarded all his customary disguises, and had really been paying some little unusual attention to the arts of the toilet. The black and savage beard and whiskers, as worn by the troopers generally—a massive specimen of which had fallen into the hands of Supple Jack on a previous occasion—had disappeared from his face; his sable uniform had given place to a well-fitting suit of becoming blue; and, of the costume of the troop, nothing remained but the dark belt which encircled his waist.

Mary Clarkson was not naturally a suspicious person, nor of a jealous temper; and the first observation which noticed these changes occasioned not even a surmise in relation to their object. She obeyed his intimation to follow him as he prepared to take his departure; and, availing herself of the momentary diversion of such of the band as were about her at the moment, she stole away and joined him at a little distance from the camp, where she received his instructions as to the game which he required her to play.

The quiet in which Morton had left his followers did not long continue after his departure. The insubordinates availed themselves of his absence to try their strength in a bolder measure than they had before attempted; and a body of them, rising tumultuously, rushed upon the guard to whom Stockton had been given in charge, and, overawing all opposition by their superior numbers, forcibly rescued him from his bonds.

Ensign Darcy was the leader of this party. He had found it no difficulty to unite them in a measure which they boldly assumed to be an act of justice, levelled at a species of tyranny to which they ought never to submit. Disaffection had spread much further among his troop than Edward Morton imagined. Disasters had made them forgetful of ancient ties, as well as previous successes. Recently, their spoils had been few and inconsiderable, their toils constant and severe, and their dangers great. This state of things inclined them all, in a greater or less degree, to be dissatisfied; and nothing is so easy to vulgar minds, as to ascribe to the power which governs, all the evils which afflict them.

The leaders of the meeting availed themselves of this natural tendency with considerable art. The more ignorant and unthinking were taught to believe that their chief had mismanaged in a dozen instances, where a different course of conduct would have burthened them with spoils. He had operated on the Wateree and Santee, when the Congaree and the Saluda offered the best field for the exercise of their peculiar practices.

That "frail masquer," to whom the cold-blooded Morton had given in charge the whole espionage which he now kept upon his troop, came upon their place of secret consultation at a moment auspicious enough for the objects of her watch. They had assembled—that is, such of the band (and this involved a majority) as were disposed to rebel against their present leader— in a little green dell, beside a rivulet which passed from the highlands of the forest into the swamp. Here they had kindled a small fire, enough to give light to their deliberations; had lighted their pipes, and, from their canteens, were seasoning their deliberations with the requisite degree and kind of spirit. With that carelessness of all precautions which is apt to follow any decisive departure from the usual restraints of authority, they had neglected to place sentries around their place of conference, who might report the approach of any hostile footstep; or, if these had been placed at the beginning, they had been beguiled by the temptations of the debate and the drink to leave their stations, and take their seats along with their comrades.

Mary Clarkson was thus enabled to steal within easy hearing of all their deliberations. Stockton, with exemplary forbearance and a reserve that was meant to be dignified, did not take much part in the proceedings. Ensign Darcy, however, was faithful to his old professions, and was the principal speaker. He it was who could best declare what, in particular, had been the omissions of the chief; and by what mistakes he had led the troop from point to point, giving them no rest, little food, and harassing them with constant dangers and alarms.

The extent of his information surprised the faithful listener, and informed her also of some matters which she certainly did not expect to hear.

Darcy was supported chiefly by the huge fellow already known by the name of Barton—the same person who had led the insubordinates in Muggs' cabin, when Edward Morton, at the last moment, sprang up to the rescue of his kinsman. This ruffian, whose violence then had offered opposition to his leader, and could only be suppressed by the show of an equal violence on the part of the latter, had never been entirely satisfied with himself since that occasion. He was one of those humble-minded persons of whom the world is so full, who are always asking what their neighbors think of them; and being a sort of braggart and bully, he was annoyed by a consciousness of having lost some portion of the esteem of his comrades by the comparatively easy submission which he then rendered to his leader. This idea haunted him, and he burned for some opportunity to restore himself in their wonted regards. Darcy discovered this, and worked upon the fool's frailty to such a degree, that he was persuaded to take the lead in the work of mutiny, and to address his specious arguments to those doubtful persons of the gang whom the fox-like properties of the ensign would never have suffered him directly to approach. Their modes of convincing the rest were easy enough, since their arguments were plausible, if not true, and there was some foundation for many of the objections urged against their present commander.

"Here, for example," said Darcy; "here he comes to play the lover at Middleton place. He dodges about the young woman when it suits him; and either we follow him here, and hang about to keep the rebels from his skirts, or he leaves us where we neither hear nor see anything of him for weeks.

Meanwhile, we can do nothing—we dare not move without him; and if we do any creditable thing, what's the consequence? Lieutenant Stockton there can tell you. He's knocked over like a bullock, and arrested—is attacked by the rebels, makes a narrow escape, comes back like a good soldier, and is put under arrest again, as if no punishment was enough for showing the spirit of a man."

"Ah, yes, that wa'n't right of the captain;" said one of the fellows, with a conclusive shake of the head.

"Yes, and all that jist after the lieutenant had been busy for five days, through storm and rain, looking after him only," was the addition of another.

"It's a God's truth, for sartin, the captain's a mighty changed man now-a-days," said a third.

"He ain't the same person, that's a cl'ar," was the conviction of a fourth; and so on through the tale.

"And who's going to stand it?" cried the fellow Barton, in a voice of thunder, shivering the pipe in his hand by a stroke upon the earth that startled more than one of the doubtful.

"I'll tell you what, men—there's no use to beat about the bush when the thing can be made plain to every men's onderstanding. Here it is. We're in a mighty bad fix at present, any how; and the chance is a great deal worse, so long as we stand here. Here, the whigs are quite too thick for us to deal with. It's either, we must go up to the mountains or get down toward the seaboard. I'm told there's good picking any way. But here we've mighty nigh cleaned out the crib;—there's precious little left. What's to keep us here, I can't see; but it's easy to see what keeps Captain Morton here. He's after this gal of Middleton's; and he'll stay, and peep, and dodge, and come and go, until he gits his own neck in the halter, and may-be our'n too. Now, if you're of my mind, we'll leave him to his gal and all he can get by her, and take horse this very night, and find our way along the Saludah, up to Ninety-Six. That's my notion; and, as a beginning, I'm willing to say, for the first, let Harry Stockton be our captain from the jump."

"Softly, softly, Barton," said the more wily Darcy; "that can hardly be, unless you mean to put the garrison of Ninety-

Six at defiance also. You'll find it no easy matter to show a king's commission for the lieutenant; and it'll be something worse if Ned Morton faces you just at the moment when Balfour, or Rawdon, or Stuart, or Cruger, has you under examination. No, no! There's no way of doing the thing, unless you can show them that Ned Morton's a dead man or a traitor. Now, then, which shall it be?"

"Both!" roared Barton. "I'm for the dead man first. We can go in a body and see for ourselves that he's done up for this world, and we can go in the same body to Cruger at Ninety-Six and show that we want a captain, and can't find a better man than Harry Stockton."

"But he ain't dead," said one of the more simple of the tribe.

"Who says he ain't?" growled the ruffian Barton—"when I say he is? He's dead—dead as a door nail; and we'll prove it before we go to Cruger. Do you suppose I'm going with a lie in my mouth? We must make true what we mean to say."

"You're right, Barton," quietly continued Darcy; "but perhaps 'twould be well, men, to let you know some things more. Now, you must know that Middleton place has been let alone, almost the only house, since the beginning of the war. Old Middleton was a mighty great favorite among the people of all these parts when he was living; and Lord Cornwallis hearing that, he gave orders not to do any harm to it or the people living there. Well, as they were women only, and had neither father, brother, nor son, engaged in the war, there was no provocation to molest them; and so things stand there as quietly as they did in 'seventy-five.' In that house, men, there's more good old stamped plate than you'll find in half the country. I reckon you may get barrels of it, yet not have room for all. Well, there's the jewels of the women. It's a guess of mine only, but I reckon a safe one, when I say that I have no doubt you'll find jewels of Flora Middleton enough to help every man of us to the West Indies, and for six months after. Now, it's a question whether we let the captain carry off this girl with all her jewels, or whether we come in for a share. It's my notion it's that he's aiming at. He don't care a fig what becomes of us if he can carry off this plunder, and this is the secret of all his doings. I know he's half mad after the girl, and will have her, though he takes her with his claws. I move that we have a hand in the business. It's but to steal up to Brier Park, get round the place, sound a rebel alarm, and give him a shot while he's running. After that, the work's easy. We can then pass off upon the women as a rebel troop, and empty the closets at our leisure."

The temptations of this counsel were exceeding great. It was received without a dissenting voice, though there were sundry doubts, yet to be satisfied, among the more prudent or the more timid.

"But the boy—that strange boy, Henry. He's with him. What's to be done with him?"

Mary Clarkson had been a breathless listener during the whole of this conference. Her emotions were new and indescribable. Heretofore, strange to say, she had never entertained the idea, for a single instant, of Edward Morton loving another woman. She had never, during the marauding life of danger which he pursued, beheld him in any situation which might awaken her female fears. Now, the unreserved communication and bold assertion of Darcy, awakened a novel emotion of pain within her heart, and a new train of reflection in her mind.

"This, then," she mused to herself, as she recollected the conversation that morning with her seducer—"this, then, is the bird that he spoke of—the sweet singing-bird in that gloomy castle, which he determined to release. Strange that I had no fear, no thought of this! But he can not love her—No! no! he has no such nature. It is not possible for him to feel as I have felt."

She strove to listen again, but she heard little more. Her mind had formed a vague impression of his danger, but it was associated with images equally vague in form, but far more impressive in shadow, of the fair woman whose beauty and whose wealth were like supposed to be potential over the rugged chief of that fierce banditti. She began to think, for the first time, that there was some reason in the complainings of the troop;

but their suggestion to murder the criminal, revived in all its force, if not her old passion, at least her habitual feeling of dependence upon him. The idea of losing for ever the one who, of all the world, she could now seek, was one calculated to awaken all her most oppressive fears; and, with a strong effort at composure, she now bent all her attention to ascertain what were the precise means by which the outlaws proposed to effect their objects. The farther details of Darcy enlightened her on this head, and she was about to rise from her lowly position and hiding-place, and steal away to Brier Place, in order to awaken Morton to his danger, when the inquiry touching her own fate commanded her attention.

"What of the boy, Henry—what shall be done with him? I'm thinking he's the one that reports everything to the captain. What shall we do with him?"

"Cut his throat, to be sure. He is no use to any of us; and if we silence the captain, we must do for him also. I recken they're together now."

"The getting rid of the boy is a small matter," said Darcy; "let's settle about the principal first, and the rest is easily managed. We must set about this affair seriously—there must be no traitors. We must swear by knife, bullet, tree, and halter—the old oath!—there must be blood on it! Whose blood shall it be?"

"Mine!" exclaimed Barton, as he thrust forth his brawny arm to the stroke, and drew up the sleeve. Mary Clarkson was still too much of a woman to wait and witness the horrid ceremonial by which they bound themselves to one another; but she could hear the smooth, silvery voice of Darcy, while she stole away on noiseless feet, as he severally administered the oath, upon the gashed arm of the confederate, to each of the conspirators.

"Swear!"

And the single response of the first ruffian, as he pledged himself, struck terror to her heart and gave fleetness to her footsteps.

"By knife, cord, tree, and bullet, I swear to be true to you, my brothers, in this business;—if I fail or betray you, then let knife, cord, tree, or bullet, do its work!—I swear!"

The terrible sounds pursued her as she fled; but even then she forgot not what she had heard before, of that "sweet singing bird, in that gloomy cage," to both of which she was now approaching with an equal sentiment of curiosity and terror.

## CHAPTER XVII.

### SOME LOVE PASSAGES AT BRIER PARK.

MEANWHILE, the chief of the Black Riders pursued his noiseless way to the scene of his projected operations. Familiar with the neighborhood, it was not a difficult matter for him to make his progress with sufficient readiness through the gloomy forests. The route had been often trodden by him before — often, indeed, when the fair Flora Middleton little dreamed of the proximity of her dangerous lover — often, when not a star in the sky smiled in encouragement upon his purposes.

The stars were smiling now — the night was without a cloud, unless it were a few of those light, fleecy, transparent robes, which the rising moon seems to fling out from her person, and which float about her pathway in tributary beauty; and she, herself, the maiden queen, making her stately progress through her worshipping dominions, rose with serene aspect and pure splendor, shooting her silver arrows on every side into the thicket, which they sprinkled, as they flew, with sweet, transparent droppings, of a glimmering and kindred beauty with her own. The winds were whisht or sleeping. The sacred stillness of the sabbath prevailed in the air and over the earth, save when some nightbird flapped a drowsy wing among the branches which overhung its nest, or, with sudden scream, shrunk from the slanting shafts of light now fast falling through the forests.

Were these tender aspects propitious to the purposes of the outlaw? Were those smiles of loveliness for him only? No! While he pursued the darker passages of the woods, studiously concealing his person from the light, other and nobler spirits were abroad enjoying it. Love, of another sort than his, was no less busy; and, attended by whatever success, with a spirit far more worthy of the gentler influences which prevailed equally above the path of both.

The outlaw reached the grounds of the ancient barony. He had almost followed the course of the river, and he now stood upon its banks. His path lay through an old field, now abandoned, which was partly overgrown by the lob-lolly, or short-leafed pine. The absence of undergrowth made his progress easy. He soon found himself beside the solemn grove which had grown up, from immemorial time, in hallowed security around the vaulted mansion in which slept the remains of the venerable casique of Congaree—for such was old Middleton's title of nobility. He penetrated the sacred enclosure, and, as he had frequently done before, examined the entrance of the tomb, which he found as easy as usual.

The dead in the wilderness need no locks or bolts for their security. There are no resurrectionists there to annoy them. Edward Conway looked about the vault, but there he did not long remain. Pressing forward, he approached the park and grounds lying more immediately about the mansion. Here, a new occasion for caution presented itself. He found soldiers on duty—sentinels put at proper distances; and, fastened to the swinging limbs of half a dozen trees, as many dragoon horses.

He changed his course and proceeded on another route, with the hope to approach the dwelling without observation; but here again the path was guarded. The watch seemed a strict one. The sentinels were regular, and their responses so timed, as to leave him no prospect of passing through the intervals of their rounds. Yet, even if this had been allowed him, what good could be effected by it? He could not hope, himself unseen, to approach the person he sought. Yet he lingered and watched, in the eager hope to see by whom she was attended. What guest did she entertain?

To know this, his curiosity became intense. He would probably have risked something to have attained this knowledge;

but, under the close watch which environed the habitation, his endeavor promised to be utterly hopeless.

This conviction, after a while, drove him back to the tomb, with curses on his lips and fury in his heart. He was not one of those men who had known much, or had learned to endure any disappointment; and his anger and anxiety grew almost to fever when, after successive and frequent attempts to find an open passage to the house, he was compelled to give up the prospect in despair.

The guests seemed in no hurry to withdraw; the lights in the dwelling were bright and numerous. He fancied, more than once, as he continued his survey, that he could hear the tones of Flora's harpsichord, as the winds brought the sounds in the required direction. The twin instincts of hate and jealousy informed him who was the guest of the maiden. Who could it be but Clarence Conway—that kinsman who seemed born to be his bane—to whom he ascribed the loss of property and position; beneath whose superior virtue his spirit quailed, and to a baseless jealousy of whom might, in truth, be ascribed much of the unhappy and dishonorable practices which, so far, he had almost fruitlessly pursued. His was the jealousy rather of hate than love. Perhaps, such a passion as the latter, according to the opinion of Mary Clarkson, could not fill the bosom of one so utterly selfish as Edward Morton. But he had his desires; and the denial of his object—which, to himself, he dignified with the name of love—was quite enough to provoke his wrath to frenzy.

"All, all, has he robbed me of!" he muttered through his closed teeth.—"The love of parents, the regards of friends, the attachment of inferiors, the wealth of kindred, and the love of woman. He stole from me the smiles of my father—the playmate from my side; the rude woodman, whose blind but faithful attachment was that of the hound, abandoned me to cling to him; and now!—but I am not sure of this! *He* is not sure! Flora Middleton has said nothing *yet* to justify his presumption, and I have sown some bitter seeds of doubt in *her* soul, which— if she be like the rest of her sex, and if that devil, or saint, that serves him, do not root up by some miraculous interposition—

will yet bring forth a far different fruit from any which he now hopes to taste. Let her but be shy and haughty—let him but show himself sensitive and indignant—and all will be done. This meeting will prove nothing; and time gained now is, to me, everything. In another week, and I ask no further help from fortune. If I win her not by fair word, I win her by bold deeds; and then I brush the clay of the Congaree for ever from my feet! The waves of the sea shall separate me for ever from the doubts and the dangers, numerous and troublesome, which are increasing around me. This silly girl, too, whom no scorn can drive from my side—I shall then, and then only, be fairly rid of her!"

He threw himself on the stone coping which surrounded the vault, and surrendered himself up to the bitter meditations which a reference to the past life necessarily awakens in every guilty bosom. These we care not to pursue; but, with the reader's permission, will proceed—without heeding those obstructions which drove the chief of the Black Riders to his lurking-place in the vault—to the mansion of the lovely woman whose fortunes, though we have not yet beheld her person, should already have awakened some interest in our regards.

The instinct of hate in the bosom of Edward Morton had informed him rightly. The guest of Flora Middleton was his hated kinsman. He had reached the barony that very evening, and had met with that reception, from the inmates of Brier Park, which they were accustomed to show to the gentlemen of all parties in that time of suspicion and cautious policy. The grandmother was kind and good-natured as ever; but Clarence saw, in Flora Middleton, or fancied that he saw, an air of haughty indifference, which her eyes sometimes exchanged for one of a yet more decided feeling. Could it be anger that flashed at moments from beneath the long dark eyelashes of that high-browed beauty? Was it indignation that gave that curl to her rich and rosy lips; and made her tones, always sweet as a final strain of music, now sharp, sudden, and sometimes harsh?

The eyes of Clarence looked more than once the inquiry which he knew not how to make in any other way; but only once did the dark-blue orbs of Flora encounter his for a prolonged moment; and then he thought that their expression was again changed to one of sorrow. After that, she resolutely evaded his glance; and the time, for an hour after his arrival, was passed by him in a state of doubtful solicitude; and by Flora, as he could not help thinking, under a feeling of restraint and excessive circumspection, which was new to both of them, and painful in the last degree to him. All the freedoms of their old intercourse had given way to cold, stiff formalities; and, in place of "Flora" from his lips, and "Clarence" from hers, the forms of address became as rigid and ceremonious between them as the most punctilious disciplinarian of manners, in the most tenacious school of the puritans, could insist upon.

Flora Middleton was rather remarkable than beautiful. She was a noble specimen of the Anglo-Norman woman. Glowing with health, but softened by grace; warmed by love, yet not obtrusive in her earnestness. Of a temper quick, energetic, and decisive; yet too proud to deal in the language of either anger or complaint; too delicate in her own sensibilities to outrage, by heedlessness or haste, the feelings of others. Living at a time, and in a region, where life was full of serious purposes and continual trials, she was superior to those small tastes and petty employments which disparage, too frequently, the understandings of her sex, and diminish, unhappily, its acknowledged importance to man and to society. Her thoughts were neither too nice for, nor superior to, the business and the events of the time. She belonged to that wonderful race of Carolina women, above all praise, who could minister, with equal propriety and success, at those altars for which their fathers, and husbands, and brothers fought—who could tend the wounded, nurse the sick, cheer the dispirited, arm the warrior for the field—nay, sometimes lift spear and sword in sudden emergency, and make desperate battle, in compliance with the requisitions of the soul, nerved by tenderness, and love, and serious duty, to the most masculine exertions—utterly forgetful of those effeminacies of the sex, which are partly due to organization and partly to the arbitrary and, too frequently, injurious laws of society.

In such circumstances as characterized the time of which we write, women as well as men became superior to affectations of every kind. The ordinary occupations of life were too grave to admit of them. The mind threw off its petty humors with disdain, and where it did not, the disdain of all other minds was sure to attend it. Flora never knew affections—she was no fine lady—had no humors—no vegetable life; but went on vigorously enjoying time in the only way, by properly employing it. She had her tastes, and might be considered by some persons as rather fastidious in them; but this fastidiousness was nothing more than method. Her love of order was one of her domestic virtues. But, though singularly methodical for her sex, she had no humdrum notions; and, in society, would have been the last to be suspected of being very regular in any of her habits. Her animation was remarkable. Her playful humor—which took no exceptions to simple unrestraint—found no fault with the small follies of one's neighbor; yet never trespassed beyond the legitimate bounds of amusement.

That she showed none of this animation—this humor—on the present occasion, was one of the chief sources of Clarence Conway's disquietude. Restraint was so remarkable in the case of one whose frank, voluntary spirit was always ready with its music, that he conjured up the most contradictory notions to account for it.

"Are you sick?" he asked; "do you feel unwell?" was one of his inquiries, as his disquiet took a new form of apprehension.

"Sick—no! What makes you fancy such a thing, Colonel Conway? Do I look so?"

"No; but you seem dull—not in spirits—something must have happened—"

"Perhaps something has happened, Cousin Clarence." This was the first phrase of kindness which reminded Clarence of old times. He fancied she began to soften. "Cousin Clarence" was one of the familiar forms of address which had been adopted by the maiden some years previously, when, mere children, they first grew intimate together.

"But I am not sick," she continued, "and still less ought you to consider me dull. Such an opinion, Clarence, would annoy many a fair damsel of my acquaintance."

She was evidently thawing.

"But on that head, Flora, you are too secure to suffer it to annoy you."

"Perhaps I am: but you have certainly lost the knack of saying fine things. The swamps have impaired your politeness. That last phrase has not bettered your speech, since I am at liberty to take it as either a reproach or a compliment."

Clarence felt that the game was growing encouraging.

"Can there be a doubt which? As a compliment, surely. But let me have occasion for another, the meaning of which shall be less liable to misconstruction. Let me lead you to the harpsichord."

"Excuse me — not to-night, Clarence;" and her present reply was made with recovered rigidity of manner.

"If not to-night, Flora, I know not when I shall hear you again — perhaps not for months — perhaps, never! I go to Ninety-Six to-morrow."

Her manner softened as she replied:—

"Ah! do you, Clarence? — and there, at present, lies the whole brunt of the war. I should like to play for you, Clarence, but I can not. You must be content with music of drum and trumpet for a while."

"Why, Flora — you never refused me before?"

"True — but ——"

"But what! — only one piece, Flora."

"Do not ask me again. I can not — I *will* not play for you to-night; nay, do not interrupt me, Clarence: my harpsichord *is* in tune, and I am *not* seeking for apologies. I tell you I *will not* play for you to-night, and perhaps I will never play for you again."

The young colonel of cavalry was astounded.

"Flora — Flora Middleton!" was his involuntary exclamation. The venerable grandmother echoed it, though her tones were those of exhortation, not of surprise.

"Flora — Flora, my child — what would you do?" she continued with rebuking voice and warning finger.

"Nay, mother," said the maiden assuringly — "let me have my own way in this. I like frankness, and if Clarence be what he has always seemed — and we always believed him — he will

9

like it too. I am a country-girl, and may be permitted a little of the simplicity—you call it bluntness, perhaps—which is natural to one."

"Flora, what can be the meaning of this?" demanded the lover with unaffected earnestness and astonishment. "In what have I offended you? For there is some such meaning in your words."

The maiden looked to her grandmother, but did not answer; and Conway, though now greatly excited, could readily perceive that she labored under feelings which evidently tried her confidence in herself, and tested all her strength. A deep suffusion overspread her cheek, the meaning of which, under other circumstances, he might have construed favorably to his suit. Meanwhile, the old lady nodded her head with a look of mixed meaning, which one, better read in the movements of her mind, might have found to signify, "Go through with what you have begun, since you have already gone so far. You can not halt now."

So, indeed, did it seem to be understood by the maiden; for she instantly recovered herself and continued:—

"Give me your arm, Clarence, and I will explain all. I am afraid I have overtasked myself; but the orphan, Clarence Conway, must assert her own rights and character, though it may somewhat impair, in the estimation of the stronger sex, her pretensions to feminine delicacy."

"You speak in mysteries, Flora," was the answer of the lover: "surely the orphan has no wrong to fear at my hands; and what rights of Flora Middleton are there, disputed or denied by me, which it becomes her to assert with so much solemnity, and at such a fearful risk?"

"Come with me, and you shall know all."

She took his arm, and, motioning her head expressively to her grandmother, led the way to the spacious portico, half-embowered by gadding vines—already wanton with a thousand flowers of the budding season—which formed the high and imposing entrance to the ancient dwelling. The spot was one well chosen for the secrets of young lovers—a home of buds, and blossoms, and the hallowing moonlight—quiet above in the sky, quiet on the earth; a scene such as prompts the mind to dream that there may be griefs and strifes at a distance—rumors of war and bloodshed in barbarian lands, and of tempests that will never trouble ours. Clarence paused as they emerged into the sweet natural shadows of the spot.

"How have I dreamed of these scenes, Flora—this spot—these flowers, and these only! My heart has scarcely forgotten the situation of a single bud or leaf. All appears now as I fancy it nightly in our long rides and longer watches in the swamp."

She answered with a sigh:—

"Can war permit of this romance, Clarence? Can it be possible that he who thinks of blood, and battle, and the near neighborhood of the foe, has yet a thought to spare to ladies' bowers, vines, blossoms, and such woman-fancies as make up the pleasures of her listless moods, and furnish, in these times, her only, and perhaps her best society."

"I think of them as tributary to her only, Flora. Perhaps I should not have thought of these, but that you were also in my thoughts."

"No more, Clarence; and you remind me of the explanation which I have to make, and to demand. Bear with me for a moment; it calls for all my resolution."

She seated herself upon a bench beneath the vines, and motioned him to a place beside her. After a brief delay—a tribute to the weaknese of her sex—she began as follows:—

"Clarence Conway, before I saw you to-night, I had resolved henceforward to regard and treat you as the most indifferent stranger that ever challenged the hospitality of my father's dwelling. But I have not been able to keep my resolution. Your coming to-night reminds me so much of old times, when I had every reason to respect—why should I not say it?—to *like* you, Clarence, that I feel unwilling to put you off as a stranger, without making such explanations as will justify me in this course. Briefly, then, Clarence Conway, some things have reached my ears, as if spoken by you, and of me—such things as a vain young man might be supposed likely to say of any young woman who has suffered him to think that she had thoughts for nothing beside himself I will not tell you, Clarence, that I believed all this. I could not dare—I did not wish to believe it; but, I thought it not impossible that you had spoken of me, perhaps too familiarly, without contemplating the injury you might do me and—do yourself. Now, if you knew anything of a maiden's heart, Clarence Conway—nay, if you knew anything of mine—you would readily imagine what I must have felt on hearing these things. The burning blushes on my cheeks now, painfully as I feel them, were as nothing to the galling sting of the moment when I heard this story."

"But you did not believe it, Flora!"

"Believe it? no! not all—at least—"

"None! none!" repeated the youth, with stern emphasis, as he laid his hand upon her arm, and looked her in the face with such an expression as falsehood never yet could assume.

"That I should speak this of you, and that you should believe it, Flora Middleton, are things which I should have fancied equally impossible. Need I say that it is all false—thoroughly false; that your name has never passed my lips but with feelings of the profoundest reverence; that—but I blush too, at the seeming necessity of saying all this, and saying it to you: I thought—I could have hoped, Flora Middleton, that you, at least, knew me better than to doubt me for a moment, or to listen with credulous ear to such a miserable slander. The necessity of this explanation, next to the sorrow of having given pain to you, is the keenest pang which you could make me suffer."

"Be not angry, Clarence," she said gently—"remember what society exacts of my sex—remember how much of our position depends upon the breath of man;—our tyrant too often—always our sole judge while we dwell upon the earth. His whisper of power over us, is our death;—the death of our pride—of that exclusiveness of which he, himself, is perhaps, the most jealous being; and whether the tale of his abuse of this power, be true or not—think how it must wound and humble—how it must disturb the faith, with the judgment, of the poor woman, who feels that she is always, to some degree, at the mercy of the irresponsible despot whom she must fear, even when she can not honor. I mention this to excuse the promptness of my resentment. I tell you, Clarence Conway, that a woman of my frank nature, is compelled to be resentful, if she would subdue the slanderer to silence. Slander is of such mushroom growth, yet spreads over so large a surface, that it is needful at once to check the first surmises, and doubts, and insinuations with which it begins its fungous, but poisonous existence. My feeling on this subject—my keen jealousy of my own position—a jealousy the more natural, as, from the frankness of my disposition, I am frequently liable to be misunderstood, has possibly led me to do you injustice. Even when this reached my ears, I did not believe it altogether. I thought it not improbable, however, that you had spoken of me among your friends, and——"

"Forgive me that I interrupt you, Flora. I feel too much pain at what you say—too much annoyance—to suffer you to go on. Let me finish my assurances. I shall employ but few words, and they shall be final, or—nothing! I have no friends to whom I should ever speak a falsehood of any kind—none to whom I would ever utter, with unbecoming familiarity, the name of Flora Middleton. If I have spoken of you in the hearing of others, it has been very seldom; only, perhaps, when it seemed needful for me to do so—perhaps never more than once; and then never in disparagement of that modesty which is the noblest characteristic of your sex. But!——"

He paused! He was reminded at this moment of the late conference which he had with Edward Conway. In that conference he had certainly asserted a superior right, over his kinsman, to approach Flora Middleton with love. This assertion, however, only contemplated the relative position of the brothers, one to the other; and was accompanied by an express disclaimer, on the part of Clarence, of any influence over the maiden herself; but the recollection of this circumstance increased the difficulties in the way of an explantation, unless by the adoption of a single and very simple—but a very direct course—which is always apt to be regarded as one of great peril by all youthful lovers. Clarence Conway was one of those men who know only the Alexandrine method of getting through the knots of the moral Gordius.

"I *have* spoken of you, Flora—nay, I have spoken of you,

and in reference to the most delicate subject in the history of a woman's heart. Thus far I make my confession, and will forbear with your permission saying more—saying what I mean to say—until I have craved of you the name of him who has thus ventured to defame me:"

"I can not tell you, Clarence."

"Can not, Flora?—Can not!—"

"*Will not*, is what I should say, perhaps; but I have used those words once already, to-night, when I felt that they must give you pain; and I would have forborne their use a second time. I can, certainly, tell you from whom I heard these things, but I will not."

"And why not, Flora? Would you screen the slanderer?"

"Yes!—For a very simple reason;—I would not have you fight him, Clarence.——"

"Enough, Flora, that I know the man. None could be so base but the person whom you know as Edward Conway, but whom I know——"

He paused—he could not make the revelation.

"Ha! Tell me, Clarence—what know you of Edward Conway, except that he is your near kinsman?"

"That which makes me blush to believe that he is my father's son. But my knowledge is such, Flora, that I will not tell it you. It differs from yours in this respect, that, unhappily, it is true—all true—terribly true! Know, then, that, to him—to Edward Conway—long ago, did I declare, what I once already presumed to declare to you—that I loved you—"

"Let me not hear you, Clarence," said the maiden timidly, rising as she spoke. But, he took her hand, and with a gentle pressure restored her to her seat beside him.

"I must. It is now necessary for my exculpation. Before he saw you, he knew that I loved you, and was the faithless *confidante* of my unsuspecting affections. He betrayed them. He sought you thenceforward with love himself. Words of anger—blows, almost—followed between us; and though we did not actually reach that issue, yet suspicion, and jealousy, and hate, are now the terms on which we stand to each other. He poured this cursed falsehood into your ears, I have reason to think, but ten days ago. Within the same space of time I have saved his life. To him, only, have I spoken of you in terms liable to misrepresentation. I did not speak of having claims upon you, Flora, but upon him;—I charged him with treachery to *my* trust, though I did not then dream that he had been the doubly-dyed traitor that I have since found him."

"Let us return to the parlor, Clarence."

"No, Flora," said the youth, with mild and mournful accents. "No, Flora Middleton, let our understanding be final. To-morrow I go to Ninety-Six, and God knows what fate awaits me there. You, perhaps, can assist in determining it, by the response which you make to-night. I wrote you by John Bannister, Flora—I know that you received that letter—yet you sent me no answer."

"Let me confess, also, Clarence:—But three days before I received your letter, I was told of this."

"Ha! Has the reptile been so long at his web?" exclaimed the youth—"But I will crush him in it yet."

"Beware! Oh! Clarence Conway, beware of what you say. Beware rash vows and rash performances. Do you forget that the man of whom you speak is your brother—the son of your father?"

"Why should I remember that which he has himself forgotten;—nay, which he repudiates with bitterest curses, and which the black deeds of his wretched life—of which, as yet, you know nothing—have repudiated more effectually than all. But I would not speak of him now, Flora. I would, if possible, exclude all bitterness from my thought—as in speaking to you, I would exclude it from my lips. Hear me, Flora. You know the service I am sent upon. You can imagine some of its dangers. The employment now before me is particularly so. The strife along the Saluda is one of no ordinary character. It is a strife between brothers, all of whom have learned to hate as I do, and to seek to destroy with an appetite of far greater anxiety. The terms between whig and tory, now, are death only. No quarter is demanded—none is given."

"I know! I know! Say no more of this horrible condition of things. I know it all."

"The final issue is at hand, and victory is almost in our grasp. The fury of the tories increases with their despair. They feel that they must fly the country, and they are accordingly drenching it with blood. I speak to you, therefore, with the solemnity of one who may never see you more. But if we do meet again, Flora, dear Flora—if I survive this bloody campaign—may I hope that then—these doubts all dispersed, these slanders disproven—you will look on me with favor; you will smile—you will be mine; mine only—all mine!"

The tremors of the soft white hand which he grasped within his own assured the lover of the emotion in her breast. Her bosom heaved for an instant, but she was spared the necessity of making that answer, which, whether it be "no" or "yes," is equally difficult for any young damsel's utterance. A sharp, sudden signal whistle was sounded from without at this moment; —once—twice—thrice;—a bustle was heard among the few dragoons who had been stationed by the prudent commander about the premises; and, a moment after, the subdued tones of the faithful Supple Jack apprized his captain that danger was at hand.

"Speak!—speak to me, Flora, ere I leave you—ere I leave you, perhaps, for ever! Speak to me!—tell me that I have not prayed for your love and devoted myself in vain. Send me not forth, doubtful or hopeless. If it be——"

Sweet, indeed, to his heart, were the tremulous beatings which he distinctly heard of hers. They said all that her lips refused to say. Yet never was heart more ready to respond in the affirmative—never were lips more willing to declare themselves. One reflection alone determined her not to do so. It was a feeling of feminine delicacy that prompted her, for the time, to withhold the confession of feminine weakness.

"What!"—such was the reflection as it passed through her mind—"bring him to these shades to hear such a confession! Impossible! What will he think of me? No! no!—not to-night. Not *here*, at least!"

She was still silent, but her agitation evidently increased; yet not more than that of her lover. The summons of the faithful scout was again repeated. The circumstances admitted of no delay.

"Oh, speak to me, dearest Flora. Surely you can not need any new knowledge of what I am, or of the love that I bear you. Surely, you can not still give faith to these wretched slanders of my wretched brother!"

"No! no!" she eagerly answered. "I believe you to be true, Clarence, and as honorable as you are faithful. But in respect to what you plead, Clarence, I can not answer now—not *here*, at least. Let me leave you now!"

"Not yet, Flora! But one word."

"Not *here*, Clarence—not *here!*" with energy.

"Tell me that I may hope!"

'I can tell you nothing now, Clarence—not a word *here*."

Her lips were inflexible; but if ever hand yet spoke the meaning of its kindred heart, then did the soft, shrinking hand which he grasped nervously in his own, declare the meaning of hers. It said "hope on—love on!" as plainly as maiden finger ever said it yet; and this was all—and, perhaps, enough, as a first answer to a young beginner—which she then vouchsafed him, as she glided into the apartment. In the next moment the faithful Supple Jack, clearing, at a single bound, the height from the terrace to the upper balcony, in which the interview had taken place, breathed into the half oblivious senses of his commander the hurried words—

"The British and tories are upon us, Clarence! We have not a moment to lose!"

## CHAPTER XVIII.

### A CONFERENCE IN THE TOMB.

THESE words at once awoke the young soldier to activity. Clarence Conway was not the man to become subdued by "Amaryllis in the shade," nor meshed, fly-like, in the "tangles of any Næera's hair." A new mood possessed him with the communication of his faithful scout, who, by the way, also performed the duties of his lieutenant.

"Get your men instantly to horse, Jack Bannister, and send them forward on the back track to the river," was the prompt command of the superior.

"Done a'ready, colonel," was the respectful answer.

"Good;—and, now, for your report."

The examination which followed was brief, rapid, and comprehensive. Though fond of long speeches usually, Jack Bannister was yet the model of a man of business. He could confine himself, when needful, to the very letter.

"From whence came the enemy?—above or below?"

"Below, sir."

"What force do your scouts report to you?"

"Large!—I reckon it's Rawdon's whole strength; but the advance only is at hand."

"Rawdon, ha! He goes then to the relief of 'Ninety Six.' I trust he goes too late. But *our* business is scarce with him. What cavalry has he? Did you learn *that?*"

"It's mighty small, I'm thinking; but we can't hear for sartin. It's had a monstrous bad cutting up, you know, at Orangeburg, and don't count more, I reckon, than sixty men, all told. That's the whole force of Coffin, I know."

"We must manage that, then! It's the only mode in which we can annoy Rawdon and baffle his objects. Between 'Brier

Park' and 'Ninety-Six' we should surely pick up all of his flock —and *must?* Are the scouts in? All?"

"All but Finley—I'm jub'ous he's cut off below. They've caught him napping, I reckon."

"If so, he has paid before this, the penalty of his nap. We must be careful not to incur like penalties. We have nothing to do but to draw off quietly from Brier Park, taking the back track by the river, and plant ourselves in waiting a few miles above. There are a dozen places along the road where we can bring them into a neat ambush, which will enable us to empty their saddles. What do the lower scouts say of their order of march?"

"Precious little! They had to run for it—Coffin's cavalry scouring pretty considerably ahead. But they keep up a mighty quick step. It's a forced march, and his cavalry is a mile or more in advance."

"They march without beat of drum?"

"Or blast of bugle;—so quiet you can hardly hear the clatter of a sabre. Nothing but the heavy tread of their feet."

"Enough. As you have sent the troop forward, let your scouts file off quietly after them. Keep close along the river, and let them all be in saddle when I reach them at the end of the causey. Rawdon will probably make the 'Barony' his place of rest to-night. He must have marched forty miles since last midnight. Pity we had not known of this! That fellow, Finley—he was a sharp fellow, too—but no matter! Go you now, Bannister. Have my horse in readiness by the old vault; and let your scouts, in filing off, dismount and lead their horses, that there may be no unnecessary clatter of hoofs. Away, now—I will but say farewell to Mrs. Middleton and Flora."

"Tell 'em good-by for me, too, colonel, if you please; for they've always been mighty genteel in the way they've behaved to me, and I like to be civil."

Clarence promised him, and the excellent fellow disappeared, glad to serve the person whom he most affectionately loved. Clarence then proceeded to the apartment in which the ladies were sitting, and suffering under the natural excitement produced by the intelligence, always so startling in those days, of the approach of a British army. Brief words at parting were allowed to the lovers; and whether Mrs. Middleton conjectured, or had been told by Flora, of what had taken place between them, the old lady was civil enough to leave the couple together without the restraint of her maternal presence. Preliminaries, at such moments, among sensible people, are usually dispensed with.

"You will not answer me, Flora?"

"Spare me Clarence—not now."

"Not now! Think, dearest Flora, of the circumstances under which I leave you: the force that drives me from your presence! Remember the danger that follows my footsteps, and the dangers which I am bound to seek. I may never again behold you—may lose, in the skirmish of the dawn, the hope, the fear, the thousand dreams and anxieties which now possess and alternately afflict and delight my heart. Let me not go forth trembling with this doubt. But one word—one only—which shall fill my bosom with new spirit, strength and courage. Speak, dearest Flora—but a single word!"

"Ah, Clarence, urge me not! What I should say might have a very different effect upon you; might subdue your spirit, disarm your strength; make your heart to waver in its courage; might——"

"Enough! enough! I ask for no other answer!" he exclaimed, with bright eyes and a bounding spirit. "Nothing *could* do that but the fear of losing a treasure suddenly won, and so precious, over all things, in my sight. But I trust that this sweet conviction, dear Flora, will have no such effect upon my spirit. If, before, I fought only for my country, I now fight for love and country; and the double cause should occasion double courage! Farewell—farewell! God be with you, and his angels watch over you, as fondly, as faithfully, and with more ability to serve you, than your own Clarence. Farewell, farewell!"

Hastily seizing her hand, he carried it to his lips with a fervent pressure; then, elastic with new emotions of delight, that made him heedless and thoughtless of the danger, he hurried downward into the court-yard below. The area lay in utter silence. The scouts had gone, the sentinels withdrawn; and, with a single glance up to the apartment where he had left the lady of his love, the youthful partisan took his way after his lieutenant. Let us only follow him so far as to look after other agents in our narrative, who lie upon his route, and whom we may no longer leave unnoticed.

Long and wearisome, indeed, had been the hour of anxious watch which the chief of the Black Riders had maintained over the barony, in his gloomy hiding-place. Twenty times, in that period, had he emerged from the tomb, and advanced toward the dwelling of the living. But his course was bounded by the military restraints which the timely prudence of Conway, and the watchfulness of Bannister, had set around the mansion. Vainly, from the cover of this or that friendly tree, did his eyes strain to pierce the misty intervals, and penetrate the apartment whose gay lights and occasional shadows were all that were distinguishable. Disappointed each time, he returned to his place of concealment, with increasing chagrin; plunging, in sheer desperation, down into its awful and dark recesses, which to him presented no aspects of either awe or darkness.

At length, however, the sound of a movement near the mansion awakened in him a hope that his tedious watch would shortly end. Slight though the noises were, under the cautious management of Bannister, the calling in of the sentries, and their withdrawal, necessarily reached his ears, and prepared him for the movement of the troop which followed. Each trooper leading his steed with shortened rein, they deployed slowly beside the tomb, little dreaming whom it harbored; and the outlaw was compelled, during their progress, to observe the most singular quiet.

The vaulted habitations of the dead were no unfrequent hiding-places in those days for the living, and, to a trooper, trained in the swamp warfare, to convert every situation of obscurity and darkness into a place of retreat or ambush, the slightest circumstance or movement on his part, he well knew, would result in their sudden search of his gloomy house of refuge. Through a chink in the decaying floor of the vault, he watched their progress; and when they had gone from sight, swallowed up in the deep blank of the forest along the margin of the river, he once more ascended to the light.

His path now promised to be free. He knew the troop to be one of his brother's regiment—a small though famous squadron —"The Congaree Blues"—proverbial for bold riding, happy horsemanship, and all of that characteristic daring which everywhere marked the southern cavalry throughout the war. The uniform he readily distinguished, though not the persons. He fancied that his brother was among them; and, hearing no further sound, with that impatience which was natural to his desires, and which was necessarily increased by the restraints to which they had been subjected, he prepared to go boldly forward to the mansion.

But the coast was not yet clear. He had advanced a few paces only, when he heard the faint, but mellow tones of a distant bugle, rising and falling in sweet harmony with the light zephyrs which bore them to his ears. These sounds now furnished him with the true reason for his brother's flight, and this was of a sort which should not have troubled him. The enemies of his kinsman, according to his profession, were not unlikely to be his friends; yet the business upon which the heart of Edward Morton was set, and the position in which he then stood, were such as to make the presence of a British force almost as little desirable to him as had been that of his brother. His present objects admitted of no friendships. Thoroughly selfish, they could only be prosecuted at the expense of the cause in which he was engaged, and at the sacrifice of that band with which, for life and death, his own life—if his oath to them were of any value—was solemnly and indissolubly connected.

Bitterly, therefore, and with renewed vexation, did he listen to the sweet but startling tones of that sudden trumpet. Cursing the course of events which, so far, that night, seemed destined to baffle his purposes, he stood for a few moments, in doubt, upon the spot where the sounds first struck his ears; hesitating whether to go forward boldly, or at once return to his place of safety.

To adopt the former course, was, in his present undisguised condition, to declare to Flora Middleton the fact, which he had hitherto studiously concealed from her knowledge, of his connection with the British cause. Such a revelation, he well knew, would, in the mind of one so religiously devoted to the whig party as was that maiden, operate most unfavorably against his personal pretensions, on the success of which, he still flattered himself, he might, in some degree, rely.

While he doubted and deliberated on his course, he was startled by other sounds, which warned him of the necessity of a prompt determination. The heavy footsteps of a man, whose tread was measured like that of a soldier, were heard approaching through the grove that extended from the dwelling in the direction of the tomb; and the outlaw moved hurriedly back to the shelter he had left.

He was scarcely rapid enough in his movements. The person approaching was no other than Clarence Conway. He had just parted, as we have seen, with Flora Middleton. Her last words were still sounding in his ears like some sweet, melancholy music, which the language of one heart delivers, in love, for the consolation of another. The last pressure of her hand seemed still to make itself felt from his own, upward, to his heart, with a sensation which carried a thrill of joy to its deepest recesses. With the bugle of the enemy sounding on the track behind him, he had then no thought, no feeling for the enemy—and, certainly, no fear. Foes, at that moment, if not forgotten, awakened no emotion in his bosom which a smile of indifference upon his lips did not sufficiently express.

From musings, the dreamy languor of which may be readily imagined, he was awakened by the sudden glimpse he had caught of his kinsman's person. The mere human outline was all that he beheld, and this for an instant only. At first, he was disposed to fancy that it was one of his own dragoons, all of whom had gone forward in that direction, and one of whom might have been left in the hurry of his comrades, or possibly detached on some special service.

But the retreat of the outlaw had been too precipitate—too like a flight—not to awaken instantly the suspicions of the partisan. To challenge the fugitive by the usual summons was probably to alarm his own enemies, and was a measure not to be thought of. To hurry in pursuit was the only mode of ascertaining his object, and this mode was put in execution as promptly as resolved upon.

The partisan rushed forward, but the object of his pursuit was no longer to be seen. The old field, on one hand, was bare and desolate—the park, on the left, did not attract the youth's attention. Obviously, the melancholy grove which led to and environed the ancient vault, was that to which the footsteps of the fugitive would most naturally incline. Into the deep shadows of this he pressed forward, until he stood beside the tomb. Then, and not till then, did he speak, challenging the fugitive to "stand" whom he could no longer see.

The summons was heard the moment after the outlaw had buried himself in his place of concealment. The tones of his brother's voice arrested the outlaw. That voice awakened all his rage and hate, while reminding him of his gage of battle; and when he remembered that Clarence Conway had but that instant left the presence of the woman whom he sought, and whom he had not been permitted to see—when he remembered that he was his hated rival, and when he thought that his lips might even then be warm with the fresh kisses of hers—the feelings in his heart were no longer governable! Uniting with that gnawing impatience, which had grown almost to a fever, and was a frenzy, under his late constraint, they determined him against all hazards; and, darting from the vault, he answered the summons of his foe with a hiss of scorn and defiance.

"Stand thou!—Clarence Conway—wretch and rebel! We are met on equal terms at last."

"Ay," cried the other, nowise startled at the sudden apparition; "well met!" and as the outlaw sprang forward from the tomb with uplifted dagger, Clarence met him with his own.

A moment's collision only had ensued, when the latter struck his weapon into the mouth of his enemy, with a blow so forceful as to precipitate him back into the cavern which he had just left. Clarence sprang into the tomb after him, and there, in the deep darkness of the scene, among the mouldering coffins and dry bones of the dead, the brothers grappled in deadly desperation.

Death, and the présence of its awful trophies, had no terrors for either. The living passions of the heart were triumphant over their threatening shadows, and the struggle was renewed between the two with a degree of hate and fury that found increase rather than diminution from the solemn and dark associations by which they were encompassed. But few words were spoken, and those only in the breathing intervals which their struggles left them. The language of the outlaw was that of vituperation and hate; that of Conway, an indignation natural to feelings which revolted at the brutal and sanguinary rage of his enemy, tempered, at the same time, with equal scorn and resolution.

In Clarence Conway, the chief of the Black Riders saw only the imbodied form of all the evil influences which he had felt or fancied from his boyhood; the long-engendered envy and malice of twenty years finding, at length, its unqualified expression. In his eyes, he was the hateful rival who had beguiled from him, with equal facility, the regards of parents, the attachments of friends, the smiles of fortune, and the love of woman.

Clarence, on the other hand, no longer saw the kinsman of his youth — the son of the same father — in the person of the outlaw; or, if he remembered the ties of blood at all, it was only to warm his hostility the more against one who had so commonly outraged, and so cruelly dishonored them! It was as the betrayer of his country, and the associate of the most savage outlaws that ever arrayed themselves against her peace and liberty, that he struck, and struck with fatal design to destroy and extirpate! Nor need it be denied that these motives were stimulated by the conviction that he himself fought for life, with a personal foe who had threatened him with all the haunting dangers of an enduring and bloody enmity — a hatred born without cause, and nourished without restraint — warmed by bad passions, mean rivalry, and a suspicious selfishness, which no labor of love could render reasonable, and which could only finally cease in the death of one or both of the combatants. The incoherent language, the broken words, and fiendish threatenings of the outlaw, left nothing on this subject to conjecture; and while the two writhed together in their narrow apartment, the otherwise horrible stillness of their strife might be thought relieved and rendered human by the bursts of passion and invective which fell the while from the lips of both. But these caused no interruption to the conflict. They fought only with daggers, though both were provided with sword and pistol. A mutual sense of the proximity of those whom neither wished to alarm, rendered them careful not to employ weapons which could draw a third party to the scene of strife. Besides, the dagger was the only weapon that might be employed in their limited area with any propriety. This weapon, deadly in the close struggle as it usually is, was rendered less effectual in the imperfect light of the place, and by the baffling readiness of their rival skill. They both felt that the struggle must be fatal, and did not, accordingly, suffer their rage to disarm their providence and caution. Still, several wounds had been given and received on either side. One of these had penetrated the right arm of the partisan, but the point of the dagger had been diverted, and the wound was one of the flesh only, not deep nor disabling. The outlaw had been less fortunate. That first blow, which he had received in the mouth at the entrance of the vault, had necessarily influenced the combat as first blows usually do; and, though not of serious hurt, for the point of the weapon found resistance against his clenched teeth, two of which were broken, still it seriously affected the relations of the parties. The one it encouraged, the other it provoked to increased anger, which impaired his coolness. A second and third wound in each of his arms had followed in the vault, and a moment came in which a fourth promised to be final.

Clarence had grappled closely with his kinsman, had borne him backward, and succeeded in prostrating him, face upward, upon the pile of coffins which rose in the centre of the tomb. Here, with his knee upon the breast of his enemy, one hand upon his throat, and the other bearing on high the already dripping steel, the stroke and the death seemed equally inevitable. So, indeed, the outlaw considered it; and the language of his lips at that moment of his greatest peril, spoke more decisively for his manhood than, perhaps, it had ever done before.

"Strike!" he cried; "I fear you not! The devil you have

served has served you faithfully in turn! I ask you not for mercy—I loathe you, Clarence Conway—I loathe and curse you to the last. Strike then, as I should have stricken you, had the chance fallen to my lot."

The weakness of a human and a social sentiment made the youth hesitate. He shivered as he thought upon the ties of blood—ties which *he* could never entirely forget, however much they might be scorned by his profligate brother. He was still his father's son—he would have spared—he wished to spare him.

While he hesitated, a new and desperate effort was made by the prostrate outlaw. Hope and fear united for a last and terrible struggle. He half rose—he grasped the arm with which Clarence held him, with demoniac strength, and flinging himself upward, with the exercise of all that muscle which he possessed in almost equal degree with his brother, he had nearly shaken himself free from the hold which the latter had taken upon him.

It was then that the dagger of Clarence descended!—then, when it became obvious that no indulgence could be given to his foe without danger to himself. But the blow, even then, was not final—not fatal. It touched no vital region. The desperate effort of the outlaw, though it failed in its object, effected another, which operated to his partial safety. The mouldering coffins upon which he was stretched yielded beneath his gigantic struggles, sank under the violence and pressure, and, ere the blow reached the heart of the threatened victim, came down, with a fearful crash, in fragments upon the damp floor of the vault. The dagger-point barely grazed the breast of the falling man; and Clarence, still grappling with his foe and grappled by him in turn, was dragged downward to the earth, and the two lay together for an instant, without strife, among the crushed and bleached bones of bygone generations. Both were breathless, but there was no mitigation of their fury. With some difficulty they scrambled to their feet, separated for a moment, but only, in the next, to renew their terrible embrace.

"Let there be an end to this!" said Morton, hoarsely. "Let us go forth into the moonlight; we can do nothing here, it seems."

"Ay, anywhere!" was the reply of the other; "but let it be quickly: I have not a moment to spare."

"A moment should suffice for either, and would have done so, had there been sufficient light for the business. So far, Clarence Conway, you have had the matter all to yourself. But there is a day for every dog, they tell us; and, though still there be no daylight, I trust that my day is at hand. Lead the way; I am ready. Let the dagger still be the weapon. It is a sure one, and makes but little clatter. Besides, it brings us so much the nigher to each other, which is brotherly, you know."

The sterner, perhaps the nobler, features of the outlaw stood out in bolder relief at the moment which he himself believed was one of the greatest danger. Morton was not deficient in animal courage. It was only less frequently apparent, because, like the Italian, he preferred the practice of a subtler agent. A fierce laugh concluded his attempt at playfulness. To this the heart of Clarence gave back no response. Though not less fearless than his brother — nay, though greatly excited by the strife — it yet had, to his mind, the aspect of a horror which he could not complacently behold. The few moments consumed in this brief dialogue had brought him back to those reflections which the provocation of the strife had almost wholly banished. But he suffered no mental or moral scruples, at such a moment, to impair his manhood.

"I too am ready," was his only answer as he left the vault. He was followed by the outlaw; and there, in another moment, they stood together on the green sward before the tomb, fiercely confronting each other with eyes of mortal hate — utterly unmoved by the pure and placid smiles of that maiden moon whose blessed light they were about to employ for the most unblessed purpose.

## CHAPTER XIX.

### THE COMBAT OF THE BROTHERS.

The ancient additaments for the groundwork of the grand or terrible, the wild or warlike, would have borne aspects not unlike their own. Ordinarily, the painter of the darker passions is very apt to accompany their explosion with a sympathetic action on the part of the natural world. The hero, just before committing the deed of blood, stalks upon the scene, surrounded by the gloomy shadows of the night; storm and thunder attend upon his footsteps, and the fiery eyes of the rebuking heaven glare along his path in flashes of impetuous lightning. A voice of warning is heard to mutter in the sky. The bloody dagger, the awful sign of the crime which is already acted in the mind of the criminal, hangs in the air above him, and marshals him the way that he must follow; while the ghosts of the past reappear, shaking their gory locks, to impede or to precipitate the ghost-like progress of the future. All things are made to act in harmony with that terrible passion which has already thrown over the heart of the possessor the uniform "brown horror" which distinguishes its own unvarying aspect. There is no blue in the transparent softness of the noonday sky; there is no living green in the fresh sward of the luxuriant earth; the songs of the one, and the mellow voices of the other, receive their savage or sad tones wholly from the desolate or depraved soul which speaks in the bosom of the fated actor. All forms and features, sights and sounds, are made to correspond with his prevailing passion; and the hues of sky and land become naturally incarnadined by the bloody mood which governs in his soul. The voices which he hears, whether of earth or sky, are only such as rise from the groaning victims, who start, perhaps, from the embrace of slumber, to sleep in that of death.

But, very different from these were the auxiliary aspects of that scene upon which the rival kinsmen were about to contend. Never was night more beautiful, more uniformly beautiful and tender, in any one of its thousand attributes and agents. The moon, almost at her full, was high above the forest tops, and hallowing its deep and dim recesses with innumerable streams of glory from her own celestial fountain. Few were the clouds that gathered about her path, and these, sharing in her gifts of beauty, became tributary to her lustrous progress. A gentle breeze, rising from the east, accompanied her march, and the tall pines swayed to and fro beneath its pressure, yielding a whispering music, like those faint utterances of a sweet complaint which are made by the curling billows of the sea, when they break and die away in a languid struggle with the shore. These breathings found fit fellowship in the gentle murmurs of the Congaree, as it rippled away on its sleepless path, at a little distance from the scene of strife. Lighted by the moon above, its winding form might be seen, in silvery glimpses, where the vistas of the woods had been opened by that tasteful art which had presided over the barony from its first settlement. Nothing was dark, nothing sad, stern, or terrible, but the human agents of the scene.

There they stood, frowning defiance upon each other, and looking grim and ghastly, in the pure, sweet atmosphere of light by which they were enveloped. The aspect of the outlaw was particularly terrible, in consequence of the wound which he had received in the mouth at the beginning of the conflict. The upper lip was divided by the stroke, the teeth shattered; and, smeared and clotted with blood, his face presented the appearance of one already stamped with all the features of the grave, and marked with an expression of hate and passion which increased its terrors. That of the partisan was stern, but unruffled — pale, but inflexible. His eyes were full of that fiery energy which, perhaps, distinguished equally the characters of the brothers. The lips were closely compressed, and resembled that sweet serenity, that resigned and noble melancholy, which peculiarly distinguishes the same feature in the instance of nearly every Indian warrior that we have ever seen. There was no faltering in his soul — he was as firm of purpose as his enemy; but there were other moods at work within him which the outlaw could not feel. Clarence Conway was not the person to entertain hate alone, to the exclusion of other and better feelings.

The outlaw unbuckled the sabre from his side, the sable belt, and threw them down, with the pistols which he carried, at the foot of the vault. He seemed resolute that there should be no possible obstruction to his movements in the struggle which was about to take place. Clarence Conway, on the other hand, took no such precaution. He calmly surveyed the movements of his opponent without changing muscle or positions. His eye glanced, however, with a momentary anxiety, to the clear blue vault, and the pale, pure presence looking down upon him from above, and turned involuntarily, though for a single instant only, to the distant dwelling of Flora Middleton. But this was not a moment to betray the weakness of the sentimentalist or lover. His enemy stood before him, and was ready. The outlaw had witnessed the direction of his foeman's eye, and the words of provocation gushed from him in increasing bitterness.

"Ay, look, Clarence Conway—look! It may be for the last time! For that matter we may both look; for I tell you, there shall be no child's play between us. Here, on this green turf, and under that smiling heaven, shall I be stretched in death, ere I yield up a single sentiment of that hate which makes it necessary that one of us should die for the peace and security of the other."

"And is it necessary, either for your peace or mine, that such should be the case?" demanded Clarence Conway.

"Ay! absolutely necessary. We can not breathe the same atmosphere. Come!"

Their arms were raised, their feet planted in opposition—their eyes fixed upon each other, and riveted in glassy, serpent-like watchfulness and calm.

"Are you ready?" was the question of the outlaw.

"Stay!" replied Clarence, while he continued to regard his enemy with a face of increased deliberation.

"Stay!—and why should we stay?" retorted the other. "Are you so soon quieted! Does your stomach revolt at the idea of a final struggle which shall end the strife between us?"

"It does!"

"Ha! Has it then come to that?" was the ironical speech of the outlaw; but Clarence interrupted him with a cool firmness of tone and look which disarmed the intended sarcasm.

"You may spare your irony, Edward Morton. That I fear you not, you should know. That I am your superior in strength you have long since discovered—that I am, at least, your match with any weapon known to either of us, you can not deny; and you know that I have no dread of death."

"To what does all this tend? It means everything or nothing. Grant what you have said, still it does not follow that you shall triumph over me. You may slay me, but I can grapple with you, Clarence Conway—I can rush upon your weapon, and, sacrificing myself, succeed in killing you! Ha! is not that undeniable also?"

"Perhaps so;" was the deliberate answer. "But even this does not influence me in what I mean to say. There is a consideration of far more weight which would make me avoid this conflict."

"Ah! it is that, eh? But you shall not avoid it! I am a desperate man, Clarence Conway, and such a man always has the life of his enemy at the point of his dagger!"

"Be it so; but hear me. For all your crimes, all your hate and hostility to me—all your treachery to your country—still I shall find no pleasure in being your executioner."

"Indeed! But be not too sure. It has not yet come to that!" cried the other. "There are two to play at this game, and I flatter myself that I shall turn the tables upon you this bout. We have some light now on the subject, and these pricks which you gave me in the dark, have rather warmed me for the conflict. They rather better my chances, by rousing me to the proper feeling of strife; as, to graze the bear with a bullet, is to make him more affectionate in his squeeze. So, look to it! our embrace will be a close one. Come on quickly. We can not too soon make a finish now."

"You deceive yourself, Edward Conway—fatally deceive

yourself if you have such a fancy;" replied Clarence solemnly. "If we encounter again I shall kill you. Nothing can save you. I feel it—I know it. I can not help but kill you."

"Insolent braggart! But, come on!"

"I have said nothing but the truth, and what I feel must be the result of this struggle. Hear me but an instant more, and judge. I shall find no pleasure in taking your life. I can not forget many things, and I am not desperate. However you may deride and despise the claims of blood and the opinions of society, it is impossible for me to do so. For this reason I would forego the indulgence of those passions, Edward Conway—"

"Not Conway—Morton, Cunningham!—anything but Conway!"

A smile of scorn passed over the lips of Clarence.

"I thank you for your correction," he said. "But this is a small matter. To return. My passions and enmities are scarcely less active than yours; but I would forego their enjoyment because of my greater responsibilities. I now make you an offer. Let us not fight; and you shall go free. I will facilitate your progress to Charleston—nay, insure it—and you will then be enabled, unencumbered by the villanous banditti to which you have been attached, to fly the country. I know that you have a large booty stored away in Jamaica—enough to give you competence for life. Let that suffice you. Leave the country while the chance is allowed you—while you may do so in safety. Three weeks hence, and Greene will traverse all this region!"

"Fool fancies!" exclaimed the other rudely. "Those are Rawdon's trumpets."

"You will not long hear them, except sounding the retreat. The war is well nigh over."

"Pshaw! this is mere folly. We came here to fight, I think. The sooner the better! Come on!"

"I would save you—spare you!"

"I shall not spare *you!* Your conceit is insufferable, and shall be whipped out of you, by heavens! this very night. Come on, then; I long to give or take my quittance. Your head is turned, I see, by that woman. Your Flora, my Flora

—the Flora of Congaree—you have been lipping, have you?—and you like the taste—sweet flavor!—"

"Ruffian—wretch?" cried Clarence, with a fury that seemed as little governable now as that of the outlaw, "you are doomed. I can not spare you now."

"I ask you not. Let the steel speak for both of us. Mine has been blushing at the time you have consumed in prating. Come on—come on! Strike as if your heart were in it, Clarence Conway, for, by God's death, I will have it in your heart, if hell has not grown deaf to human prayer. Good blade, to your work! It is some pleasure, Clarence Conway, to know that yours is tolerably pure blood—at least it will do no dishonor to my dagger."

The struggle followed instantaneously. The outlaw proceeded to act his declared intentions. His object seemed to be to get within the arm of his opponent—to close at all hazards, and sacrifice himself in the bloody determination to destroy his enemy.

But Clarence was no ordinary foe. His anger did not deprive him of his coolness, and his skill with the weapon was far beyond that of most men of his time. Still, it required all his watchfulness and circumspection—all his readiness of eye and arm—to baffle the purpose of the other. The blind fury of the outlaw, perhaps, served him quite as effectually as did his own resources. It made him fearless, but not fearful—full of purposes of dangers, but not dangerous—that is, comparatively speaking—for, so long as the partisan preserved his composure, and kept only on the defensive, his enemy did not find it so certainly true as he had affirmed, that a desperate man always carries the life of his enemy at the point of his dagger. He had tried this more than once, and had always been repelled, sometimes with hurts, which were not always slight, though, as yet, in no case dangerous.

His constant failure warned him of the folly of his own fury, and its utter ineffectiveness to achieve the object of his desires. He recovered himself, and adopted another policy. He renewed those coarse sneers and insinuations which had been always effectual in provoking Clarence, and which had closed their previous conference. He spoke of Flora Middleton, and in such language as was admirably calculated to throw a lover off his guard.

"You flatter yourself," he said, "that you have just made a conquest; but have you asked its value? I tell you, Clarence Conway, if ever woman spoke falsely, Flora Middleton spoke falsely to you when she consented to be yours. I know her; nay, man, when you charged me with having been to Brier Park, you knew but half the truth. Shall I tell you that she was then as indulgent to the chief of the Black Riders as she has been since to his more moral kinsman? Here, by this old vault, did he walk with her at evening; and you know what it is, or you should know, to wander among dim groves at sunset with a romantic damsel. The heart will yield then, if ever. It softens with the hour, and melts. Ha! are you touched—touched at last? Know, then, it was my turn to lip and to taste as cordially—"

"Liar! dog! reptile!" cried Clarence, striking at him furiously as he heard these words; "Know I not that you have striven to fill her pure ears with falsehoods almost as foul as those you would now thrust into mine?"

"You have it!" cried the other, with a yell of delight, as his lunge carried the point of his dagger into the breast of the partisan; fortunately a flesh-wound only, but one in dangerous proximity to the angry heart that was now boiling in its neighborhood. The youth felt his imprudence; but if he had not, there was a counselling friend at hand, who did not suffer him to go unreminded. This was Jack Bannister, who, in the shelter of a tree contiguous, to which he had crawled unseen, had been a spectator of the brief conflict, during the short time it had lasted, on the outside of the vault.

"Don't you let him fool you, Clarence; he's only trying to make you mad—that's his trick. But don't you mind him—he's a born liar, and if you stick as you should, he'll die with a lie in his mouth. Strike away, Clarence, as you can strike; and only forget that you ever had a father who was so foolish as to git a son of the wrong breed. Put it to him, and shut up your nater till it's all done. God ha' mercy 'pon me, but it seems so nateral for me now to want to put in and kill him!"

"Ha! you have brought your bullies upon me!" were the words of Morton, as the first accents of Bannister reached his ears. "But I fear them not!"—and he renewed the assault with increased determination; if that indeed were possible.

"Keep back—meddle not, John Bannister!" cried Clarence. "I need no assistance."

"I know it, Clarence; but, Lord love you! don't git into a foolish passion. Go to it as ef 'twas a common work you was a-doing—splitting rails, or digging ditches, or throwing up potato-hills. Jest you hit and stick as ef you was a-managing a dug-òut, or a raft, or some sich foolish consarn. For sich a foul-mouth as he to talk agin Miss Flora! Why, it's as foolish as a wolf to bark at the moonlight. But don't let me interrupt you. Go to it! I'm jest a-looking on to see the eend, and obsarve fair play; only make haste, Clarence; shut him up as soon as you can, for the bugle's a sounding from the head of the avenue, and there's little time to lose."

The warning was not to be disregarded, and Clarence Conway soon brought the strife to an issue. The resumption of his caution provoked the outlaw into a renewal of his rashness, and his dagger-hand was caught in the grasp of the partisan at the same moment when the weapon of the other sunk into his breast. Clarence relaxed his hold upon his victim the instant that the blow was delivered. He fancied that he had given him the *coup de grace* as he intended; and a strange, keen, sudden pang rushed like lightning through his own bosom.

The outlaw, meanwhile, felt himself about to fall. A faintness covered his frame; his sight was growing dark; and, with the last convulsive moment of reflection, he threw himself forward upon the breast of his enemy, whose dagger-point was now turned toward the ground. His left arm was tightly clasped about the form of Clarence; while his right, with all the remaining consciousness of his mind, and the concentrated, but fast failing vigor of his frame, addressed a blow at the heart of the latter, which it needed sufficient strength only to render fatal.

But the arm of the outlaw sank down in the effort ere the

dagger reached its mark. His hold upon his enemy was instantly relaxed, and he fell fainting at the feet of Clarence, ere the latter had sufficiently recovered from the horror which he felt, to be altogether conscious of the danger from which he had escaped. With every justification for the deed which necessity could bring, he yet felt how full of pain and sorrow, if not of crime, was the shedding of a brother's blood.

## CHAPTER XX.

### CAPRICES OF FORTUNE.

WE have omitted, in the proper place, to record certain events that happened, during the progress of the conflict, in order that nothing should retard the narrative of that event. But, ere it had reached its termination, and while its results were in some measure doubtful, a new party came upon the scene, who deserves our attention, and commanded that of the faithful woodman. A cry—a soft but piercing cry—unheard by either of the combatants, first drew the eyes of the former to the neighboring wood from which it issued; and, simultaneously, a slender form darted out of the cover, and hurried forward in the direction of the strife. Bannister immediately put himself in readiness to prevent any interference between the parties; and, when he saw the stranger pushing forward, and wielding a glittering weapon in his grasp, as he advanced, he rushed from his own concealment, and threw himself directly in the pathway of the intruder. The stranger recoiled for an instant, while Bannister commanded him to stand.

"Back!" said the latter, "back, my lad, till it's all over. It won't be long now, I warrant you. They'll soon finish it; but until they've done——"

He drew a pistol from his belt, which he cocked, presented, and thus closed the sentence. The stranger shrunk back at this sudden and sturdy interruption; but, recovering a moment after, appeared determined to press forward. The second warning of the scout was more imperative than the first.

"Stand back, I tell you!" cried the resolute woodman, "or by blazes, I'll send daylight and moonlight both through you with an ounce bullet. I ain't trifling with you, stranger; be sartin, I'm serious enough when I take pistol in hand. Back, I tell you, till the tug's over, and then you may see and be seen. Move another step and I'll flatten you."

"No, no, no!" was the incoherent response; "let me pass! I *will* pass!"

The sounds which assured the woodman of the determination of the stranger, were so faintly and breathlessly articulated, that, at any other time, Jack Bannister would have only laughed at the obstinate purpose which they declared; but the moment was too precious for his friend, and he was too earnest in securing fair play for all parties, not to regard their tenor rather than their tone.

"If you do, I'll shoot you, as sure as a gun!" was his answer.

"They will kill him!" murmured the stranger, in accents of utter despondency. He struck his head with his palm in a manner of the deepest wo; then, as if seized with a new impulse, waved a dagger in the air, and darted upon the woodman.

So sudden was the movement and unexpected, that Bannister never thought to shoot, but, clubbing his pistol, he dealt the assailant a blow upon the skull, which laid him prostrate. A faint cry escaped the lips of the youth in falling; and Bannister fancied that his own name formed a part of its burden. He was also surprised when he recollected that the enemy, though rushing on him with a dagger, had yet forborne to use it, although sufficient opportunity had been allowed him to do so, had such been his purpose, in the surprise occasioned by his first onslaught. But the moment was not one favorable to reflection. Clarence had now overcome his enemy, who was prostrate and insensible; and, faint himself, was bending over him in a fruitless effort to stanch the blood which issued from a deep wound on the side. Bannister approached him with the inquiry—

"God be thanked, Clarence, that you are uppermost. How is it with him? Is he dead?"

"I hope not. He breathes still. There is motion in his heart."

"I'm sorry for it, Clarence. I ain't sorry that you ha'n't killed him, for I'd rather you shouldn't do it; but I'm mighty sorry he's not dead. It'll be all the better for him if he is. 'Twould save a neck smooth to the last. But come, there's a great stir at the house. I can hear the voices."

"But we can not leave him here, Jack. Something must be done for him. Would to God I had never seen him, for I feel most wretched, now that it's all over."

"'Tain't a time to feel such feelings. You couldn't help it, Clarence. He would force it upon you. Didn't I hear him myself? But it's no use talking here. We must brush up and be doing. I've given a knock to a chap here, that's laid him out as quiet as you laid the other. A small chap he was. I might have stopped him, I'm thinking, with a lighter hand: but I hadn't time to think, he jumped so spry upon me."

"Who is he?" demanded Clarence.

"I don't know; a friend to Edward Conway, looking after him, I reckon. I'll see all about him directly, when once you're off. But you must trot at once. There's a mighty stir all about the house, and I'm thinking, more than once, that I've hearn a whoo-whoop-halloo, below thar in the direction of the flats. 'Twas a mighty suspicious sort of whoop for an owl to make, and I'm jub'ous 'twa'n't one that had a good schoolmaster. 'Twa'n't altogether nateral."

"What are we to do with him?" demanded Clarence, as he gazed with an aspect of complete bewilderment, now at the body of his kinsman, and now at the distant mansion.

"Do! I take it, it's jest the reasonable time to hearken to the words of scripter: 'Let the dead bury their dead;' and though I can't exactly see how they're to set about it, yet, when people's hard pushed as we are, it's very well to put upon holy book all such difficult matters as we can't lay straight by our own hands. I'm thinking, we'd best lay him quietly in the vault and leave him."

"But he's not dead, Bannister, and with care might recover."

"More's the pity. It's better for you and me, and himself

too, if he don't recover; and it seems to me very onnateral that you should take pains first to put him to death, and the next moment worry yourself to bring him to life again."

"I took no such pains, Bannister. I would not have struck him if I could have avoided the necessity, and I strove to avoid making his wounds fatal."

"I'm sorry for that agin. But this ain't no time for palavering. You'll soon have these dragoons of Coffin scouring the grounds of the barony, aud Rawdon's too good a soldier not to have his scouts out for three good miles round it. Them trumpets that we hear are talking some such language now; and we must ride pretty soon, or we'll be in a swamp, the waters rising, the dug-out gone, and a mighty thick harricane growing in the west."

"I can not think of leaving the body thus, Bannister."

"And you resk your own body and soul — or your own body, which is pretty much the soul of the 'Congaree Blues'—ef you stop to take care of him," replied the woodman.

"What are we to do?"

"Clarence, trust to me. Take your horse—you'll find him in that hollow—and get to the head of the troop before Coffin's hoofs tread upon its tail. I'll be mighty soon after you; but before I start, I'll give 'em a blast of my horn, and a scare from my puppy-dog here"—meaning his pistol—"which 'll be pretty sure to bring a dozen of 'em on my track. When they come here, they'll find the body of Edward Conway, and this lad that I flattened; and they can do for 'em all that's needful. I'm a hoping that this here person," pointing to the chief of the Black Riders, "is out of his misery for ever, and won't trouble the surgeont with much feeling of his hurts. As for the other lad, I don't think I could ha' hurt him much with the butt only, though I struck him mighty quick, and without axing how much or how little he could stand. Trust to me, Clarence, and go ahead."

Obviously, this was the only course to be pursued in order to reconcile the duties and desires which the partisan entertained. He took not a single further look at his enemy, whose grim and ghastly features, turned upward in the moonlight, presented an aspect far more fearful than any which the simple appearance of death could present; and, with a few words of parting direction to the woodman, he hurried away to the hollow where his horse had been concealed. In a few moments after, the sturdy Bannister rejoiced, as his ear caught the slow movement of his departing hoofs.

The bold fellow then — before putting his design in execution, of alarming the British at the mansion and bringing them down upon the spot — true to the business of the scout, stole forward in the direction of the dwelling, in order to ascertain what he could, as to the disposition and strength of the force which had come and was still advancing. A perfect knowledge of the place, its points of retreat and places of shelter, enabled him to reach a station where he saw quite as much as he desired. The cavalry, a small body of men, were evidently drawn up as a guard along the avenue, for the reception of the commander-in-chief; and while Bannister admired their array, and noted the stealthy caution which marked their movements, he was also enable to count their numbers with tolerable certainty.

"More than they told me," he muttered to himself; "but a good ambushment will make up the difference, by thinning them a little."

Having satisfied his curiosity, and perceiving that the main body of the British army was at hand, he contented himself with observing, with soldierly admiration, the fine appearance of the troops — a body consisting chiefly of the Irish regiments, then newly arrived from Europe — and the excellent order of their march; and then stole away, as quietly as he approached, to the place where he had left the wounded.

Returning with as stealthy a movement as at his departure, he was surprised to discover that the body of the stranger whom he had knocked down was no longer where he had left it. A considerable curiosity filled his bosom to discover who this person was. His conduct had been somewhat singular; and Bannister was almost sure, that when he inflicted the blow which had laid him prostrate, the stranger had uttered his own name in falling; and that, too, in tones which were neither strange nor those of an enemy. His first impression was that this person had feigned unconsciousness, but had taken advantage of his momentary absence to steal off into the contiguous woods. To seek him there under present circumstances, and with so little time as was allowed him, would be an idle attempt; and the woodman, with some disappointment, turned once more to the spot where the outlaw was lying.

To his surprise, he found a second person with him, whom a nearer glance discovered to be the very person whose absence he had regretted. The stranger was lying upon the body of Edward Morton, and seemingly as lifeless as himself: but he started up when he heard the footsteps of Bannister, and made a feeble attempt to rise from the ground, but fell forward with an expression of pain, and once more lay quiescent upon the body of the outlaw.

The scout drew nigh and addressed the youth with an accent of excessive kindness; for the milk of a gentle as well as a generous nature, flowing in his heart from the beginning, had not been altogether turned by the cruel necessities of the warfare in which he was engaged. But, though he spoke the kindest words of consolation and encouragement known to his vocabulary, and in the kindest tones, he received no answer. The youth lay in a condition of equal stillness with him whose body he seemed resolved to cover with his own.

Bannister readily conceived that he had swooned. He advanced accordingly, stooped down, and turned the face to the moonlight. It was a fair face and very pale, except where two livid streaks were drawn by the now clotted blood, which had escaped from beneath the black fur cap which he wore. This, upon examination, the scout found to be cut by the pistol-blow which he had given; and it was with a shivering sensation of horror, to him very unusual, that, when he pressed lightly with his finger upon the skull below, it felt soft and pulpy.

"Lord forgive me!" was the involuntary ejaculation of the woodman—"Lord forgive me, if I have hit the poor lad too hard a blow."

His annoyance increased as he beheld the slight and slender person of the youth.

"There was no needcessity to use the pistol, poor fellow. A fist blow would have been enough to have kept him quiet"—and, muttering thus at intervals, he proceeded to untie the strings which secured the cap to the head of the stranger. These were fastened below the chin; and, in his anxiety and haste, the woodman, whose fingers may readily be supposed to have been better fitted for any less delicate business, contrived to run the slip into a knot, which his hunting knife was finally employed to separate.

The cap was removed; and in pressing the hair back from the wound, he was surprised at its smooth, silk-like fineness and unusual length. This occasioned his increased surprise; and when, looking more closely, he saw in the fair light of the moon, the high narrow white forehead in connection with the other features of the face, a keen and painful conjecture passed through his mind, and with tremulous haste and a convulsive feeling of apprehension, he tore open the jacket of dismal sable which the unconscious person wore, and the whole mournful truth flashed upon his soul.

"God ha' mercy, it is a woman!—it is she—it is poor Mary. Mary—Mary Clarkson! Open your eyes, Mary, and look up. Don't be scared—it's a friend—it's me, Jack Bannister! Your old friend, your father's friend. God ha' mercy! She don't see, she don't hear—she can't speak. If I should ha' hit too hard! if I should ha' hit too hard."

The anxiety of the honest fellow as he addressed the unconscious victim of his own unmeditated blow would be indescribable. He sat down on the sward and took her head into his lap, and clasped her brows, and laid his ear to her heart to feel its beatings, and when, with returning consciousness, she murmured a few incoherent words, his delight was that of that one frantic.

He now laid her down tendency, and ran off to a little spring which trickled from the foot of the hill, with the position of which he was well acquainted. A gourd hung upon the slender bough of a tree that spread above the basin. This he hastily scooped full of water, and ran back to the unfortunate girl. She had somewhat recovered during his absence—sufficiently to know that some one was busy in the work of restoration and kindness.

"No, no," she muttered, "mind not me—go to him—him! Save him before they kill him."

"Him, indeed! No! Let him wait. He can afford to do it, for I reckon it's all over with him. But you, Mary, dear Mary: tell me, Mary, that you are not much hurt—tell me that you know me; it was I who hurt you; I—your old friend, John Bannister, Mary; but it's a God's truth, I didn't know you then. I'd ha' cut off my right arm first, Mary, before it should ever have given pain to you."

"Leave me, if you have mercy—I don't want your help; you can't help me—no! no! Go to him. He will bleed to death while you are talking."

"Don't tell me to leave you, Mary; and don't trouble yourself about him. He'll have all the help he needs—all he desarves; but you! look up, dear Mary, and tell me if you know me. I am still your friend, Mary—your father's friend."

The mention of her father seemed to increase her sufferings.

"No! no!—not that!"—she muttered bitterly; and writhing about with an effort that seemed to exhaust all her remaining strength, she turned her face upon the ground, where she lay insensible.

Never was mortal more miserable or more bewildered than our worthy scout. He now suffered from all the feelings, the doubt and indecision, which had beset his commander but a little while before. To remain was to risk being made a prisoner; yet to leave the poor victim of his own random blow, in her present condition, was as painful to his own sense of humanity as it was unendurable by that tender feeling which, as we have already intimated, possessed his heart in an earlier day for the frail victim of another's perfidy. This feeling her subsequent dishonor had not wholly obliterated; and he now gazed with a sort of stupid sorrow upon the motionless form before him, until his big, slow gathering tears fell thick upon her neck, which his arm partially sustained; while his fingers turned over the long silken hair, portions of which were matted with her blood, in a manner which betrayed something of a mental self-abandonment—a total forgetfulness of duty and prudence—on the part of one of the hardiest scouts in the whole Congaree country.

How long he might have lingered in this purposeless manner, had not an interruption, from without, awakened him to a more resolute, if a less humane course, may not be conjectured. In that moment the resources of the strong man were sensibly diminished. The hopes and loves of his early youth were busy at his heart. Memory was going over her tears and treasures, and wounds which had been scarred by time and trial were all suddenly reopened.

In this musing vein he half forgot the near neighborhood of his enemies, and the dangers which awaited him in the event of captivity. These were dangers, be it remembered, of no common kind. It was not then the mere prospect of restraint which threatened the rebel if taken prisoner. The sanguinary rage of party had to be pacified with blood; and it is strongly probable that the merciless executions of which the British commanders were so frequently guilty in the south, were sometimes prompted by a desire to conciliate the loyalists, of the same region, who had personal enmities to gratify, and personal revenges to wreak, which could be satisfied in scarcely any other way.

Of these dangers the sturdy woodman was made most unexpectedly conscious by hearing the tones and language of military command immediately behind him. A guard was evidently approaching, sentinels were about to be placed, and the sounds which startled him on one side were echoed and strangely answered by a sudden clamor of a most unmilitary character which rose, at nearly the same instant, from the swamps and flats which lay along the river a few hundred yards below.

Mary Clarkson could have explained the mystery of the latter noises, were she conscious enough to hear; but such was not the case. Her consciousness was momentary; and when obvious, betrayed itself in expressions which now denoted a wandering intellect.

A stern agony filled the heart of the scout as he rose to his feet, lifted her tenderly in his arms, and bore her toward the tomb, before the entrance of which he laid her gently down, in a spot which he knew would make her conspicuous to the eyes of the first person approaching. He had barely disengaged her from his arms, and was still bending over her with a last look, the expression of which, though unseen by any, spoke more effectually the anguish which he felt, than could ever have been conveyed by the rude and simple language of his lips, when he felt a hand upon his shoulder—a quick, firm grasp—followed by the sounds of a voice, which it soon appeared that he knew.

"Oh! ho! Caught at last, Supple Jack; Supple, the famous! Your limbs will scarcely help you now. You are my prisoner."

"Not so fast, Watson Gray—I know you!" replied the scout, as he started to his feet and made an effort to turn; but his enemy had grappled him from behind, had pinioned his arms by a grasp from limbs as full of muscle as his own, and was, in fact, fairly mounted upon his back.

"And *feel* me too, Jack Bannister, I think. There's no getting loose, my boy, and your only way is to keep quiet. There are twenty Hessians at my back to help me, and as many Irish."

"More than enough, Watson Gray, for a poor Congaree boatman. But you're rether vent'rous, I'm thinking, to begin the attack. You ought to ha' waited for a little more help, Watson Gray. You're rather a small build of a man, if my memory sarves me rightly—you ha'n't half of my heft, and can't surely think to manage me."

"I do, indeed!" was the answer. "If I'm light, you'll find me strong—strong enough to keep your arms fast till my wild Irish come up, and lay you backward."

"Well, that may be, Watson. But my arms ain't my legs, my lad. Keep *them*, if you can."

Thus speaking, greatly to the surprise of the assailant, he grasped the enclasping arms of the latter with his muscular fingers, held them with a hold as unyielding as their own, and rising erect, set off, at a smart canter down the hill in the direction of the river. This proceeding was one which had formed no part of Watson Gray's calculations; and he became suddenly and awkwardly aware that there was an unpleasant change in the relations of the parties.

"The boot's on t'other leg, I'm thinking, Watson Gray," chuckled our scout of Congaree. To this offensive suggestion the other had no answer, in words; but he employed all his breath and effort with the view to extricating himself from the biped whose shoulders he had so indiscreetly mounted. But the performance, and the desire, are notoriously very different things. In spite of all his struggles, Jack Bannister kept on his way down hill, and Watson Gray, perforce, kept in his uneasy place of elevation. He had not calculated *all* the resources of his great antagonist, and now cursed himself for his overweening confidence in his own.

"It's but nateral that you should kick and worry, at riding a nag that you ha'n't bitted, Watson Gray, but it's of no use; you're fairly mounted, and there's no getting off in a hurry," was the consoling language of the scout as he ran toward the wood with his captive. "I see that you never hearn of the danger of shaking hands with a black bear. The danger is that you can't let go when you want to. A black bear is so civil an animal, that he never likes to give up a good acquaintance, and he'll hold on, paw for paw with you, and rubbing noses when he can, though it's the roughest tree in the swamp that stands up between him and his friend. Your arms and shoulders, I reckon, are jist as good and strong as mine. But your body ain't got the weight, and I could carry you all day, on a pinch, and never feel the worse for it. You see how easy we go together!"

"D—n you, for a cunning devil," cried the embarrassed Gray, kicking and floundering curiously, but vainly striving to get loose.

"Don't you curse, Watson Gray;—it sort o' makes you feel heavier on my quarters."

"Let me down, Bannister, and you may go free, and to the devil where you came from."

"Well, you're too good. You'll let me go free?—I'm thinking that it's you that's my prisoner, my boy. I'll parole you as soon as I reach my critter."

"I'll shout to the Hessians to shoot you as you run," vociferated the other.

"Will you, then. You don't consider that your back will first feel the bullets. You're a cunning man, Watson Gray. I've always said you were about the best scout I know'd in the whole Congaree country, and it's a long time since we've been dodging after one another. I was a little jub'ous, I confess, that you were a better man than myself. I was: but you made a poor fist of this business — a poor pair of fists, I may say," concluded the woodman with a chuckle.

"So I did — a d—d poor business of it!" groaned the other. "I should have put my knife into your ribs, or had the scouts round you first."

"The knife's a bad business, Watson," was the reply of the other; — "a good scout, that's not onnatural, never uses it when less hurtful things will answer. But it's true you should ha' put your Hessians between me and the woods before you cried out 'you're my prisoner!' If ever a man jumps into detarmination at all, it's jist when he hears some such ugly words, on a sudden, in his ears; and when I felt you, riding so snugly on my back, I know'd I had you, and could ha' sworn it."

A desperate effort to effect his release, which Watson Gray made at this time, put a stop to the complacent speech of the other, and made him less indulgent.

"I'll cure your kicking, my lad," said he, as, backing himself against a pine-tree, he subjected his involuntary burden to a succession of the hardest thumps which he could inflict upon him, by driving his body with all its force against the incorrigible and knotty giant of the forests. The gasping of the captive, which ensued, sufficiently attested the success of this measure; and an attempt which Gray made, a moment or two after, to get the ear of Supple Jack within his teeth — which was answered by a butt that almost ruined his whole jaw — terminated the fruitless endeavors of the former to free himself from his awkward predicament.

Meanwhile, the stir and confusion were increasing behind the fugitives, and it was a wonder to both that they had not been pursued. The sounds, imperfectly heard by the woodman, seemed to be those of actual conflict; but he felt himself secure, and his thoughts reverted, over all, to the poor Mary Clarkson — the victim of the outlaw with whom she had been left, and, perhaps, his own victim. The poor fellow regarded himself with horror when he thought of the cruel blow his hand had inflicted.

But he had no time for these reflections; and the necessity of joining his commander, nerved him to new vigor in his progress. He had now reached the place where his horse was concealed. His first movement was to pitch his captive over his head; which he did very unexpectedly to the latter. In the next moment, his knee was upon his breast, and with pistol presented to his mouth, he made Watson Gray surrender his weapons. These consisted only of two hunting knives, and an ordinary pocket pistol. He then rifled his pockets of all which they contained, kept his papers, but generously restored his money.

"Now, Watson Gray, you're a Congaree man, like myself, and ef I've thumped you a little hard as we run, put it down to the needcessity of the case and not because I wanted to hurt you. I'll let you off now, on your parole, that you may go back and help Ned Conway. You've been his helper and adviser a mighty long time, and you've done for him a precious deal of ugly business. He'll need more help now, I'm thinking, than you can give him. There's a poor boy there—too—a young slender chap, that I hit with a'most too heavy a hand, I'm afeard, and if you can do anything for her——"

"Her!" said the other.

"Oh, yes—the truth-will out—she's a gal though in no gal's clothes. Perhaps you know her. You ought to—you know enough of Ned Conway's wickedness to know that. Take care of that gal, Watson Gray, and if physic can do her good, see that she gets it. I ax it of you as a favor. You're a stout fellow, Watson, and I've long tried to have a turn with you. I'm thinking you're a better scout than I am; but there's no discredit to you to say that you want my heft and timbers. In a close tug I'm your master; but I'm jub'ous you'd work through a swamp better than me. See to that gal, Watson, for the sake of that Congaree country. She's one of our own children, I may say, seeing we're both from the river;—and if there's any cost that you're at, in helping her, either for food or physic, let me know of it, and you shall have it paid back to you, ef I dig the gold out of some inemy's heart. Good by, now, Watson, and remember you must never take a bear by the paws till you've first made tarms with him about letting go."

## CHAPTER XXI.

#### PROGRESS AND SUSPENSE.

"Was ever poor devil caught so completely in his own trap before!" was the querulous exclamation of Watson Gray, as, with a painful effort, he rose from the ground where his adversary had so ungently stretched him out. "Egad, I'm sore all over; though I think there's no bone broken!" He rubbed his arms and thighs while he spoke, with an anxious earnestness which showed that he spoke in all sincerity, though still with some doubt whether his limbs preserved their integrity.

"Confound the scamp! I thought I had him sure. His arms fastened, his back turned!—who'd have thought of such a canter down hill with a strong man over his shoulders! Well, he certainly deserves the name of Supple Jack! He's earned it fairly by this bout, if he never did before. If ever fellow was strong and supple over all the men I ever knew, he's the man. But for those sleepy Hessians, I'd have had him; and I wonder what can keep them now. The dull, drowsy, beef-eyed Dutchmen—what the d—l are they after? What stir's that?"

A buzz of many voices in earnest controversy, in the direction of the vault, arrested the speaker in his soliloquy, and stimulated his apprehensions.

"By Jupiter! they're fighting among themselves! What an uproar! They're are loggerheads, surely—the Hessian boobies!"

The anxiety of the scout made him half forgetful of his bruises as he turned toward the spot from whence the clamor rose. There seemed sufficient cause to justify the apprehensions which he had expressed. The uproar which first startled him was followed by oaths, execrations, and finally the clash of arms. He hurried forward to the scene of the uproar, and arrived not a moment too soon to prevent bloodshed. It will be necessary that we should retrace our steps for a while in order to ascertain the causes of the present commotion.

It will be remembered that Mary Clarkson left the bivouac of the Black Riders at the very time when, going through the bloody ceremonial of pledging themselves to one another for the performance of a new crime, they led her to suppose that they would very shortly follow upon her footsteps. This, to a certain extent, was, indeed, the fact. They followed her, but not so soon as she expected; and she reached the miserable man for whom she had sacrificed the life of woman's life, in full time to have forewarned him of their approach and purpose, had this, under the circumstances, been either necessary or possible. We have already seen what those circumstances were; and the cruel insults which followed her unselfish devotion to a creature so little deserving the care of any heart. The chief of the outlaws had already fallen beneath the arm of his kinsman.

The Black Riders had still some arrangements to make—some stimulating liquors to quaff, and purposes to fulfil scarcely less stimulating—before they started for the work of treachery and murder. One of these arrangements was the elevation of Stockton to the chief command, as if Morton were already dead. Ensign Darcy, by a natural transition, and as a becoming reward for his good service, was promoted at the same time to the station which the other had so lately filled.

Morton had his friends among the banditti, who simply submitted to proceedings which they could not baffle, and openly dared not resist. They, however, held themselves in reserve, with a mental determination to defeat, if possible, the dark purposes of their companions before they could possibly carry them out to completion. But this determination was ineffective for the time, simply because it was individual in each man's bosom. They had had no opportunity allowed them for deliberation, and, being half suspected of lukewarmness, they were not suffered to get together unwatched and unobserved by the dominant faction.

Elated with his success, the arrogant Stockton fancied that the path of the future was fairly open before his steps, unembarrassed by all obstructions, and the smiles of good fortune beckoning him to the conquest. There was but one task before him necessary to render all things easy, and that a malignant sentiment of hate goaded him on to perform. The murder of Edward Morton—his personal enemy—the man who knew his secret baseness, and who scorned him in consequence—was yet to be executed; and this—when he thought of the past, its bitterness and contumely—of the future, its doubts and dangers—became a task of grateful personal performance. To this task, when all the ceremonials were over, of his own and confederate's elevation, he accordingly hurried.

His men were soon put in readiness, and Darcy, who had traversed the ground more than once before, took charge of the advance. Their plans were simple, but sufficient, had the circumstances continued throughout as they were at the beginning. They had meditated to advance upon, and to surround the mansion, in which they supposed their captain to be; then, raising the cry of " Sumter," create an alarm, in the confusion of which Morton was to be put to death.

It need not be said that the unexpected approach of a British army, under a forced march, and without any of the usual bruit attending on the progress of a large body of men, utterly baffled all their calculations; and when, following the path toward the tomb, which Morton had originally taken, Lieutenant Darcy arrived at the spot, he found it almost in complete possession of soldiery, consisting of the very Hessians—some twenty in number—on the assistance of whom Watson Gray had so confidently calculated when he made the rash attempt on the person of Jack Bannister.

The Hessian troops had never before been seen by the Black Riders, and Darcy immediately jumped to the conclusion that these were partisan troops of Lee's legion, which he knew had, a little time before, been seen in the neighborhood; and the conjecture was a natural one, not only that they might be there still, but that Morton might already have become their captive. The incautious movement of these soldiers suggested to Darcy, who was not without his ambition, the project of capturing the whole of them. They were evidently as careless of danger, as if they had never known what apprehension was; and finding them squatting around some object near the tomb, busy in low discussion, the next most natural conjecture, to one of his marauding habits, was, that they had already rifled the mansion, and were now sharing its plunder.

The cupidity of the habitual robber rendered his judgment easy of access to any suggestion which favored the mercenary passions of his heart; and, taking that for granted which was merely possible, and waiting for no further knowledge of the truth, Darcy stole back to Stockton, who was following with the main body, and readily filled his mind with the ideas which predominated in his own. But few questions were asked by the new captain. The information of Darcy seemed to cover all the ground; and they both were instantly ripe for action.

"There are not twenty—squat upon the turf—some of their arms lie beside them, and some upon the tomb; and the plunder, if one may judge from the interest they take in it, must be rather more than has blessed their eyes for many a day. We can surround them in a jiffy, without striking a blow."

"But Morton!—do you see nothing of him?" demanded Stockton anxiously.

"No! But if these fellows found him at the house, they've saved us some trouble. They've done for him already."

"Enough!—set on, and lead the way. Manage it, Darcy, to suit yourself; you alone know the path."

"Hark! a trumpet! I have heard that trumpet once before. It must be at the mansion."

"The more need for hurry. These fellows are a squad of Lee's or Sumter's, who have rifled the house before the main body came up. We must be in time to relieve them of their burden before they get help from the strongest. After that, we can push up for the house, and see what is to be done with the rest."

"Keep all still, then," said Darcy. "I'll undertake to surround these rascals, and relieve them of their plunder, without emptying a pistol. Let your horses be fastened here, and we'll go on foot the rest of the journey. Dismount—dismount; we have but a few hundred yards to go."

Such were the arrangements of the Black Riders; and yielding the management of the affair entirely to Darcy, Stockton followed with his band in silence. With the stealthy progress of the Indian, each individual passed to his appointed station, until the tomb, and all about it, was completely environed with a *cordon militaire,* from which nothing could escape. A signal whistle warned them to be in readiness, and a second commanded the movement.

The operation was fully successful. The Hessians were surrounded before sword could be drawn or yager lifted. Nothing could well exceed the astonishment of the mutual parties, the captors equally with the captive. The Hessians, with an army of two thousand men or more at hand, were confounded to find themselves, on a sudden, in custody of a force not twice their own number; while the amazement of the Black Riders was scarcely less, when they heard the clamors of the people they had made captive, in a language which they could not comprehend, and the harsh sounds of which seemed to them so shocking and unnatural. Their disappointment was something increased, also, to discover, that instead of the treasure of the house of Middleton—the family plate and ladies' jewels—the supposed plunder around which the Hessians had been squatting was neither more nor less than the body, seemingly dead, of the tender boy who usually attended upon their captain.

It was at this moment of confusion on both hands, and before anything could be understood or anything explained, that Watson Gray made his appearance, to the satisfaction of one at least of the parties.

"How now, Darcy? what's the matter here? What are you doing with these men? Let them go."

"Let them go, indeed! when we've just taken them. Let them rather go to the gallows."

"Gallows! why, who do you take these fellows for?"

"Lee's legion—or a part of it."

"Indeed? Had your courage ever carried you nigh enough to Lee's legion, you'd have found out your mistake. Why, man, what are you thinking of? These are his majesty's new levies, hired or bought from the prince of Hesse Cassel, at two and sixpence a-head, and d—d extravagant pay, too, for such heads as they've got. Let them go—they're Hessians!"

A gibberish, utterly beyond translation by any present, arose in echo from the captured foreigners, in full confirmation of this assurance. By this time Stockton made his appearance, and the face of Watson Gray might have been seen to indicate some surprise when he saw him. Gray knew the relation in which Stockton stood to his captain, and was instantly assured that the latter had never deputed to him the chief command in his absence. The circumstance looked suspicious; but Gray was too old a scout to suffer his suspicions to be seen, until he knew in what condition the game stood.

"Ah, Stockton!" he said, indifferently—"is that you? but where's Ben Williams? is he not in command?"

"No, I am," said Stockton—"I am for the present. We came to look after the captain."

"The captain?—why, where did he leave you?"

"In the swamp flats, some two miles below."

"And what brings you to look after him? Did he order it?"

"No," said Darcy, taking up the tale with an adroitness of which he knew that Stockton was no master—"no; but we heard trumpets, and as he stayed rather long, we were apprehensive about him. When we came, and saw these fellows here, with strange uniforms, we took 'em for Lee's legion, as we heard that Lee was dodging about this neighborhood."

"And you really have never seen Lee's uniforms, ensign?"

"No, never: we've been operating above, you know; and—"

"You have not found the captain, then?"

"Not yet, and what to do——"

"I'll tell you: look there and you'll find him. The sooner we attend to him the better."

He led the way to the body of Edward Morton as he spoke, stooped down with composure, but interest, and proceeded to examine it for the signs of life which it contained. The wily Darcy followed his example, and his conduct, in turn, suggested to Stockton that which it would be proper for him to pursue. Much time was not given to the examination, and still less in vain regrets and lamentations. The selfishness of man's nature soars triumphant above all other considerations, in a time of war; and life becomes as small a subject of consideration as any one of its own circumstances.

"Some ugly hurts here, I reckon," said Darcy; "we must get him to the house and to the hands of the surgeon, as soon as possible."

"Does he live?" asked Stockton in a whisper, over Darcy's shoulder.

"Ay, he lives!" was the answer made by Gray, in tones which were somewhat sharpened by asperity; "there's life enough to go upon, and, with good care, he'll be able shortly to be in the saddle. If we can stop the blood, there's nothing to be afraid of, I'm thinking."

This man boldly took the lead, as a man having his wits about him will be always apt to do, in seasons of sudden peril and great surprise. Even Stockton tacitly submitted to his guidance.

"Give way there, my good fellows, and let's see what we're about. Here, one of you take that door, there—the door of the vault—from its hinges, and we'll carry him to the house on that."

Watson Gray muttered through his closed teeth at the conclusion; and his hands were unconsciously pressed upon his hips as he spoke: "He'll have an easier ride than I had of it. My bones will talk of Jack Bannister for a month."

The door of the vault was soon brought forward, and the Black Riders, with careful hands, raised their captain upon it. Darcy and Stockton both busied themselves in this service. But, though performed with great caution, the motion recalled the wounded man to consciousness and pain, and two or three half-stifled moans escaped from his lips. He muttered a few words, also, which showed that he still fancied himself engaged in all the struggles of a protracted and doubtful strife.

When Gray had seen him fairly placed upon the frame, which was amply large, he thought of the poor girl whom the earnest solicitations of Supple Jack had commended to his care; and, with a degree of interest and tenderness which could scarcely have been expected from one habitually so rough, he himself assisted to place the slight form of the victim beside the body of her betrayer.

By this time, however, the friendly stupor which had first come to her relief, no longer possessed her faculties. She had recovered her consciousness, but under the burning pressure of fever, which filled her mind with all the fancies of delirium. She raved of a thousand things, incoherently, which perhaps none present could in any way comprehend, but the one individual who was engaged in conducting the operations. He, too, harsh as was his nature, callous and insensible—the creature of the cruel man whose profligate passions he served, and who had reduced her to the thing she was,—he, too, did not appear entirely unaffected by the wild agony which her ravings denoted and expressed. He walked beside her, as a dozen of the soldiers carried the litter toward the house; and few were the words, and those only such as seemed to be necessary, which he uttered during the mournful procession.

"You had better set your men in handsome order, Stockton. You will meet Lord Rawdon at the house, with all his suite, and a fine show of military. He likes to see handsome dressing and a good front, and he'll look to you for it while the captain's sick."

"A cursed chance, this," muttered Stockton, as he drew aside with Darcy to put in execution the suggestions of the scout. "Who'd have thought it? Rawdon here, and we know not a word about it!"

"It's devilish fortunate we did not rush on in the dark. That peep of mine was well thought on. But it makes very little difference, except the loss of the plunder. Morton's pretty well done for. No less than five wounds upon him—two in the jaw and three in the body."

"But how came it? who could have done it?" said Stockton.

"That matters less than all. Some friend, I take it, who knew what we wished most, and saved us the trouble of the performance."

"But how strange! and how stranger than all that we should have been deceived in that boy—that Henry!"

"Ay!—but let us hurry on, and show alacrity as well as

order. Of course we'll say nothing about the captaincy. You're still lieutenant only, and if Morton dies——"

"He must die!" said the other.

"Ay, he must. Rawdon will leave him a surgeon, and we will find a guard; and if he survives the one, there's but little chance of his getting off from the other. Eh! what think you?"

"It will do," was the significant answer of Stockton. They understood each other thoroughly, before they put their men in order. The thoughts of Watson Gray were not less busy, as he pursued his way alone with the wounded persons; nor were they more favorable to the conspirators, than was the determination of those friendly to their captain. He knew, better than any other man, the true history of the latter, and the sort of relation in which he stood to his troop. He was not ignorant, also, of the scorn which Morton felt for Stockton, and the hate, more deadly because secret, with which the other requited it. He could readily conceive, at the same time, that Stockton's interest would lie in the death of his captain; and, putting all these things together in his mind, he determined to keep his eyes open, and watchful of every movement of the parties.

"Rawdon will take them with him to Ninety-Six," he muttered, as he came to this conclusion.

"I will persuade him to do so, at least, and the chances are fair that they will get themselves knocked on the head before the siege is over. But, whether they do or not, we shall gain time; and if Morton's hurts are curable, we shall know it before they get back, and provide accordingly. But one thing must be cared for. Rawdon must not know Morton in the house of Flora Middleton. That would spoil all. I must speak with him before the body arrives. He must leave the matter to me."

Whatever may have been the tie that attached Watson Gray to the chief of the Black Riders, his course was evidently that of a true and shrewdly thinking friend. He had no sooner determined what was proper for him to do, than he hurried ahead of the procession, and made his appearance in the spacious hall of the mansion several minutes before it could possibly arrive. His lordship was in the parlor with the ladies, but Gray knew him to be a man of business, with whom business is always a sufficient plea for any interruption.

"Say to his lordship that Watson Gray would speak with him in private, on matters of some importance," he said to an officer in attendance, who knew the estimation in which the scout was held, and at once disappeared to do his bidding.

## CHAPTER XXII.

### A CONFERENCE WITH THE ENEMY.

LORD RAWDON appears in the history of the war in the southern colonies, to have been one of the sternest leaders of the time: as sanguinary in his temper as Earl Cornwallis, and without any of those impulses of a better temper which have secured for the latter, from one of the American captains, the doubtfully deserved epithet of the "amiable Cornwallis." Rawdon left himself open neither to the lurking irony nor the obvious flattery of such an epithet. His discipline was rigid to the last degree; his temper cold and inflexible; and he seems to have regarded the enemies whom he had the fortune to conquer, as something which, like the spoil he won, he might easily dispose of according to the mood which governed him at the moment, and not under the direction of any fixed principles or written laws. His cruelties, open and specious, are on record; but these do not concern us at this moment; and we must admit that the king of England had no representative in all the Revolution who was more constant to his duties or more resolute in their performance. Lord Rawdon had also the merit of being a gentleman; a hard, cold, inflexible soldier—too free to shed blood, and not politic enough to do so at the right time and in the right place; obdurate in his purpose and unpliant in his feelings—but still a gentleman: a qualification for his crimes of perhaps very small intrinsic value, but one which he possessed in common with very few, among the many with whom he co-operated during his career in the southern country.

Well acquainted with the character of the Middleton family, it had been, as we have already elsewhere intimated, the policy of this commander, as well as of him by whom he had been preceded, to treat the inmates of the barony with all indulgence. Their popularity with the surrounding country, which it was desirable to conciliate, was a sufficient reason for an indulgence which, in the reckless career of the invaders, they had not been disposed to extend to many; and the time was fast approaching when, in the declining power of their arms, their desperation led them to withdraw even this degree of favor, in the vain hope to coerce the patriotism which they found it impossible to persuade or seduce.

Already had the tone of British superiority been lowered. They could no longer maintain themselves in their strongholds; and, evacuating Camden under the accumulating pressure of the American forces, Rawdon was even now on his way to Ninety-Six, to protract the hour of its downfall. This was the last stronghold left them in the interior, and to delay, not to baffle its assailants, in the work of conquest, was now the only hope of the British commander. The political aspects of the time were all unfavorable to British ascendency; and the temper of his lordship underwent a corresponding change with his changing fortunes. This could be seen by the Middletons the moment when he announced himself their guest, with the air and manner of one who feels all the changes in his own fortunes, and readily divines the effect of such change upon his reluctant host. He looked, though he did not say:—

"I know that you receive me with reluctance—that my presence is hateful to you—nay, that you perceive and exult in my approaching overthrow—but I still have the power to compel your respect, and I may yet awaken your fears. You shall receive me, and seem glad to do so."

But the suspicious mood of Rawdon became quieted when, in the gentle and easy deportment of the ladies, he failed to behold the exulting expression of those sentiments which he fancied might fill their bosoms. They were superior to that vulgar sentiment of triumph which shows itself in the ill-disguised grin, or in the reserved and chilling demeanor. A quiet dignity and a gentle grace were apparent in the conduct of both, in receiving the British chief: and this, in the younger of the two ladies, was mingled with some little tremulousness — the result of her consciousness of what had just before taken place between herself and Clarence Conway — which Rawdon was not unwilling to ascribe to the agitation which his own presence must naturally produce upon a very youthful mind.

This notion pleased his self-complacency, and made the work of soothing more easy to the ladies; but they could still perceive that they had assumed, as enemies, in the recent successes of their countrymen, and increased importance in his eyes, which lessened his smiles, and probably increased their dangers;— and they were soon made to understand this difference in a more direct and decided manner.

Tea, at the time the bane of the country, though the blessing of the ladies, was the crowning dish of the evening repast; and this commodity, though employed simply in compliment to the Briton, gave Rawdon an opportunity to say something on the subject of their loyalty, as he sat down the rich bowl of gold-rimmed China, from which, in that day of a luxury far more ostentatious than ours, though of far less general ostentation, the precious beverage was drunk.

"I rejoice to see, ladies, that your patriotism — so I think you call this flinging away your king and country — takes counsel of good taste, and does not allow you to fling away your tea-bowls also. It would have been a serious trial of faith to your sex to have given up the celestial liquor for more than a season."

The old lady answered smartly, with no small portion of that spirit which then distinguished the dames of Carolina.

"I can not accept your compliment to our tastes, my lord, at the expense of our patriotism. You perceive that while your lordship drinks tea, we confine ourselves to such beverage only as our milch cattle yield us. Sometimes we regale ourselves on Indian tea, which is made of the Cussenca leaf; but this only when our milk fails us, which is no unfrequent event, since the Black Riders have found their way into our neighborhood."

"And their presence, madam, is only another evil consequence of your patriotism. But surely the whole burden of this complaint should not fall upon the Black Riders. There have been such 'Riders' as follow Lee and Sumter in this neighborhood lately; of whom report speaks not more favorably; and who probably love milch cattle quite as well as anybody else. Nay, my fair young mistress," addressing himself to Flora, "there is another Rider, black enough in my eyes, but, perhaps, anything but black in yours. Ha! you can guess who I mean by this description; and I will not name him for your sake;—but let me catch him!" and he raised a threatening finger, while a half smile rested upon his lips. Flora could not altogether suppress the blush which found its way to her cheeks, and was as little able to control the irony that rose at the same time to her lips.

"Ah, my lord, you are too severe upon our poor sex; but—"
She paused, and the color heightened upon her cheeks.
"But what?" he asked, seeing her hesitate.
"But what if he catches you, my lord?"
"Flora, Flora!" said the grandmother, with a look and voice of warning. A momentary gravity overspread the face of Rawdon, and his severe features, under the dark shade of his lowering brows, almost startled Flora with a sentiment of apprehension for her own imprudence; but the good sense and breeding of his lordship came to her relief as well as his own.

"Ah, my fair foe," he said with a smile of good nature, "still incorrigible—still dangerous. The tongues of your Carolina ladies inflict deeper wounds than the swords of your heroes."
"I would you could think so, my lord."
"Why, they do," he answered, "they do."
"Nay, my lord, I will not contradict you, and yet I am trying to persuade myself that you will think otherwise before you come back from 'Ninety-Six.'"
"And do you find the task of self-persuasion difficult? I should think not; and least, you *hope* I will come back?"
"Yes, my lord, I hope so—in safety; but with such opinions as will make you think better of our soldiers, and, in this reason, find a much farther journey necessary."
"What, to Charleston, eh? a forced march back?"

"To England, my lord; to England; at that distance there will be some chance of our being better friends, and we shall then resume our tea."

"But without the duties?" he said laughing.

"Not altogether, my lord. I, for one, feel all the disposition to be the dutiful friend—if you please the dutiful child—of England;—but not the subject, not the slave! Her victim, rather!"

"Ah, my fair Flora, we wish no sacrifice: none of *you*, at least. We shall drag no damsel to the altar, unless it be to one of her own choosing. But, in return for this sharp speech of yours, fair lady, suffer me to know when Colonel Conway was here last; how long since he has taken his departure, and where I may expect to find him?"

"He has been here, my lord, I frankly tell you, but when he left I will not say. You will find him——"

She hesitated as if in meditation, while her large brilliant eyes shone without a cloud upon her auditor, and her form seemed to dilate in more than feminine majesty as she rose to leave the room:—

"Stay, Miss Middleton," said his lordship, "you have not told me where I may expect to find Colonel Conway."

Her answer was immediate, with flashing eyes, and fearless accents.

"You may expect to find him, my lord, wherever an ambush can be laid; whenever a bold soldier may fancy that his sword can make an enemy feel; or a good blow can be struck for the liberties of his country."

"Humph!" exclaimed Rawdon, gravely, though without displeasure, as Flora left the room. "Your granddaughter, Mrs. Middleton, is quite as fierce a rebel as ever."

"She is young, my lord, and very enthusiastic, but though she speaks thus, I'm sure she is quite as unhappy at this war as any of us. We all wish it well over."

"That is saying everything for the right side. To wish it *well* over, madam, is simply to wish our king his own again. But now, that your daughter has withdrawn, let me remind you, Mrs. Middleton, of the royal favor to yourself and family——"

"To *me*, my lord;—to *my* family!" was the reply of the venerable lady, with some appearance of astonishment.

"Yes, madam, in the immunity you have so long enjoyed, when it has been well known to his majesty's commanders in the South, that your own and the sentiments of your granddaughter—your opinions and wishes—are all unfavorable to his authority."

"Am I to understand, my lord, that his majesty's officers are instructed to wage war against the opinions of the women as well as the swords of the men of Carolina?"

"No, madam, far from it; but those opinions sharpen those swords——"

"I am proud, my lord, to think, and hear you acknowledge that such is the case!"

"I had not thought, madam, to have hearkened to this language from your lips. The protection you have enjoyed—your immunities from the confiscation which has usually followed disloyalty—should, I think, have prompted a degree of gratitude for his majesty's government, which would have saved his representative from such an answer."

"You mistake, my lord, in some important particulars. My immunities are not due to his majesty's government. If they are to be spoken of as due anywhere, they must be ascribed to that sense of manliness in the soldiers of both sides in this bloody warfare, all of whom, it seems to me, would have blushed the color of your scarlet, my lord, at doing hurt to two lone women in the wilderness."

Rawdon did blush with vexation at the retort, as he answered it with a strong effort at gentlemanly composure.

"You have surely mistaken me, Mrs. Middleton. My purpose was simply to intimate that his majesty's officers have been at some pains, more than is customary in a country which has been so completely covered with contending armies, to preserve from detriment and hurt your possessions and interests."

"I confess, my lord, the amount of what you now say seems to me to differ little from what was said before. You have forborne to seize my own and my child's property, though we have been bold enough to think that you had no right to seize it; and for this you demand our gratitude. My lord, I understand, though you have not spoken, the real purpose which you feel unwilling to declare. I can very well comprehend the difficulties under which his majesty's arms labor at present. I know that their supplies are everywhere cut off; and that they look to what are called 'forced loans' to enable them to prosecute the war."

"You are well informed, I perceive, madam. Am I to understand that the rebel Sumter has been recently your guest?"

"Within ten days, my lord; and my opinions being such as they are, I placed in his hands, for the use of my country, the entire plate of the Middleton barony, and every jewel of value which belonged to myself and child. The few spoons which graced our board to-night, and the bowl in which our children have been baptized from immemorial time, are all that were kept back from the free gift which my feelings made to my friends. These, my lord——"

"Of these, madam, the cause of my king does not make it necessary that I should deprive you," replied Rawdon, with a graceful dignity which left nothing to be complained of. "Your plate would have been important to us, Mrs. Middleton; and you will do us the justice to believe that, knowing as we did its great intrinsic value, we did not make this requisition until the last hour, and then only in obedience to necessities which none but ourselves can comprehend. Believe me, madam, though I am somewhat disappointed, it is a pain spared me, which I would have felt, in depriving you of this family treasure. Nor can I complain, regarding your social attachments with respect, that you have yielded it to the hands of those who will make use of it against me. I must do as well as I can without it. Let me not lose your esteem, my dear madam, because of my proposition, which you will also do me the justice to believe was not less painful than unavoidable."

The message of Watson Gray was received at this moment, and the venerable old lady disappeared with a kind courtesy, leaving his lordship free to the interview with the scout.

"A brave-hearted old woman!" said his lordship, during the brief interval in which he remained alone. "She has given a monstrous subsidy to Greene, which will keep him on his legs a while, and perhaps trip ours; and yet I can not be angry with her. The stock is a good one; one would almost wish a mother or a daughter of such a noble heart and so fearless a temper. Ah, Gray, I've been looking for you. When did you get over from the Wateree?"

"I left there yesterday morning. I rode all night, and had to make more than two turns between the Hills and the Congaree, to get out of the way of Marion's men, who seem to me to be thicker than ever. Your lordship's for Ninety-Six?"

"Yes; can you tell me anything about it? These rascally horse of Lee and Conway have, I fear, cut off all my messengers to Cruger, as they certainly have cut off everything, in the shape of intelligence, from me."

"Ninety-Six is dreadful hard pressed, your lordship; that's all I know, and that was my knowledge three days ago."

"I fear I shall be too late," said Rawdon. "But you wished to see me on other business. What is it?"

"Does your lordship know that Colonel Conway, with all his troop, has been here within the last hour? Your coming scared him from his roost."

"Indeed, so lately!" said his lordship. "Then he can not even now be far. We must send Major Banks after him;"— and his lordship was about to summon a messenger.

"If I might venture to counsel your lordship, you will do nothing to-night. It will be only to send your detachment into an ambush. This is what Conway expects, and what he will prepare for."

"But we can not suffer him to lie or loiter about our encampment; we must brush him off at the risk of a sting."

"No, your lordship; but a double guard and extra videttes will serve all necessary purposes, and, with the dawn, Major Banks can be in motion. Now, however, Conway is in possession of his own ground, all of which he knows, while Major Banks will be moving to danger with a blind across his eyes."

"You are right; and what has Conway been doing here, and where is his brother—our desperado of the Congaree?"

"Here, also!—within a hundred yards of us."

"Ha! How is it I have not seen him, then?"

"You will see him shortly, my lord, and in bad condition. The brothers have met, single-handed; and they have brought the old grudge to a finish, I'm afraid. There has been a desperate fight between them, and the captain is very much hurt. It is somewhat doubtful if he ever gets over it."

"And the other—the rebel—has he escaped?—goes he scot free?"

"That I can't tell. I should think not, however; for, knowing how Ned Morton hates him, and how many good reasons he has for killing him, he would run all risks of his own life to make a finish of the other. His condition makes me think that the other must be hurt; but his hurts can not be serious, for he certainly got off."

"How heard you this, Gray?"

"From that rascally fellow, Bannister, otherwise called Supple Jack—the same who carried off Colonel Cruger's black charger from the Forks of Congaree. The colonel offered twenty guineas to take the scout alive, and I thought I had him at one time to-night. But I caught a Tartar. He gave me a strange trot, and such a shaking as I shall feel in all my bones for a month to come."

Here Gray gave a full description of the scene, at which his lordship's muscles relaxed infinitely; and he then proceeded to narrate those other details which led him to the subject of Morton's attendance. On this head it was necessary to exercise some adroitness. It was no part of Gray's policy to let Rawdon see that a provincial scout should presume to suspect the integrity of a royal officer, and he studiously forbore, in consequence, to declare those suspicions which he felt of Stockton.

"It is important that the connection of Captain Morton with the Black Riders should not be suspected while he lies here wounded. No guard could possibly save him from the rebels, should they be able to identify his person. Here, he is known as Edward Conway, the brother of one who is no small favorite with the ladies of the barony. This will save him from danger without, and secure him good attendance within. Miss Middleton, herself, will, I think, see to that, if on the score of his connections only. I will provide the guard for Captain Morton, and you can take with you his troop, which is under the command of Lieutenant Stockton, a brave man and a good officer. They are pretty strong, and the greatest daredevils under the sun. You'll get good service out of them, and will need them, too, my lord, if, as I suspect, you are somewhat short of cavalry."

"You think rightly, Gray; and your plans are good. I will leave a surgeon's assistant with Morton, which is all that I can do; but my own surgeon will see to his hurts before he goes."

"Your lordship will be so good as to remember that Captain Morton is no more than Mr. Conway here."

"Ay, ay; but what noise is that below?"

"The captain's body, I reckon. Will your lordship look at him?"

"Is he sensible—conscious?"

"I think not yet, my lord. He was in a swoon when I left him, in consequence of loss of blood."

"It will not need then. I will send Mr. Coppinger to examine his hurts, and as I am to know nothing about him, you must take your own course to get him domiciled among the ladies."

"That is easily done, your lordship," said Gray, retiring; "I have your lordship's permission to make the necessary arrangements." .

"You have; send me Lieutenant Farrington, who waits without," said Rawdon, as the other left the room.

It scarcely need be said that the wily Gray succeeded in all his present purposes. His opinions were esteemed to be sufficiently sound, by his lordship, to be followed implicitly. Lieutenant Stockton was relieved from the care of his captain, and ordered to place himself, with his whole troop, under the command of Major Banks, of the British cavalry; and the bare intimation of Edward Conway's situation, to the ladies of the barony, secured for the wounded man one of the most comfortable chambers in the mansion. Nor did Watson Gray neglect the forlorn and outcast damsel whom John Bannister had commended to his care. An adjoining apartment was readily procured for her in the same spacious dwelling, and the surgeon's aid was solicited for the poor victim as soon as it had been bestowed upon her betrayer. We leave Edward Conway in the same house with Flora Middleton — but as yet utterly unconscious of her presence and near neighborhood — while we pursue the route taken by his brother.

## CHAPTER XXIII.

### A MIDNIGHT ATTACK — A PRISONER.

CLARENCE CONWAY was not far distant from the British camp, and was soon found by John Bannister, after the latter had taken his leave of Watson Gray. The partisan had already reached his troop, and got it in partial readiness for immediate exercise. His force was little more than that of a captain's command, consisting of some eighty-five men all told; but, on occasion, his regiment might be made complete. Such fluctuations were constant in the American army; and were inevitably consequent to the miserable system then prevalent in regard to militia service. Marion's brigade has been known to range from eighty to eight hundred men; nor was this difference, in scarcely any case, the result of disaster. The volunteers came and went, according to circumstances of more or less necessity, and sometimes as it suited their inclinations.

There were always good reasons for this seeming laxity of discipline, as well because of the pressure of a far superior foe, as in the exhausted condition of the country of Carolina; where, for a space of nearly two years, few crops of any kind had been planted; and it became next to impossible to find food and forage for any large body of men and horse, for any considerable time together. The service was of a sort, also, to render small bodies of horse far more useful than grand armies; and where food was to be procured, and brought from a great distance, such detachments were of the very last importance. Conway's regiment, according to the necessities of the service, was in half a dozen hands; Sumter had a portion of it at this very moment on the Santee; Marion on the Pedee; while Greene exercised the remaining divisions as Conway, employed the small body in his immediate command—in cutting off supplies, intercepting messengers, overawing the disaffected, and hanging upon the skirts of the enemy while they marched, as in the case of Rawdon's army, at this very time, in a body too large for any more bold procedure.

Bannister found his leader well prepared for movement, and anxiously awaiting him. The former told his story in a few words, not entirely omitting the ludicrous passages which had taken place between himself and Gray. As the connection between this latter person and Edward Morton was very well known to Clarence, the mind of the latter was rendered rather more easy on the subject of his brother. He knew that Morton was of sufficient importance to the British army, to make his restoration the particular charge of Rawdon; but his satisfaction on this subject was somewhat qualified when he remembered that the patient would, necessarily, become an occupant of the same dwelling with Flora Middleton. His anxieties were such as are natural enough to the lover, who, in such cases, will always be apt to fancy and to fear a thousand evil influences. He had no doubts of the firmness and fidelity of Flora; but, knowing the evil connections of Morton, he dreaded lest the latter should find some means to abuse the hospitality which he well knew would be accorded him. These thoughts were troublesome enough to render activity desirable by way of relief; and after a brief space given to consultation with his favorite scout, and little private meditation, he determined to beat up the quarters of Rawdon before morning.

It was midnight when Bannister began to bestir himself and his comrades for this purpose. The troop had been suffered to snatch a few hours of repose on the edge of a little bay, that stretched itself nearly to the river bank on one hand, and to the main road of the country on the other; in such a position of security, and under such good watch, that no apprehension could be excited for their safety. A dense thicket covered their front; beyond, and lying between the thicket and the barony, was an open pine wood, the undergrowth being kept down by the destructive practice, still barbarously continued in the south, of firing the woods annually in the opening of the spring. This wood was traversed by the scouts of Conway, who saw the advanced videttes of the British, without suffering themselves to be seen, and gradually receded as the latter continued to approach; still, however, keeping a keen eye upon the stations which they severally assumed.

On the present occasion, following the suggestions of Watson Gray, Lord Rawdon had doubled his sentries, and increased the usual number of videttes. His post was well guarded, though nothing could have been more idle than the fear, that a force such as he commanded could be securely annoyed by any of the roving squads of horse which the Americans had dispersed about the country. But, at this time, the timidity of the British increased hourly in due degree with the increased audacity of the Americans. There was too much at stake to suffer any British commander to omit any of the usual safeguards of an army; and their plans and performances, from this period, show a degree of scrupulous caution, which at certain periods of strife—and this was one of them in their situation—may, with justice, be considered imbecility. To dash for a moment into the camp of the British, and carry off a group of captives, was one of the ordinary proofs of the novel confidence which the partisans had acquired of their own prowess, during the year in progress.

Conway, however, was not the man to do anything rashly at such a moment. If caution was necessary to the British, prudence was also a high virtue, at this particular juncture, with the Americans. Before he led his men forward, he determined to explore the British camp himself; and, having arranged with Bannister for a concerted espionage, the two went forward for this purpose, though on different routes. Conway pursued the way through the pine-forest in front, while Bannister took an opposite but parallel course along the high road, which he crossed for this purpose. They were absent about two hours, and, in the meantime, everything was quiet enough in the camps. At the end of this period they returned in safety; and a mutual report enabled them to determine upon the course which they were to take.

They had satisfied themselves of the true position of the British army, and discovered, that while the sentries were doubled on the path to which it was advancing, they had not conceived it necessary to place more than an ordinary watch on that which they had passed over during the day. By making a small circuit of a mile and a half along a negro footpath, which carried them through a swamp on the right, Conway found that he could get into the British rear, and probably use the sabre to advantage on the edge of the encampment. This was to be done with the main body of the troop, while a feint was to be made with the residue along the better guarded British line in front.

It was near two o'clock in the morning when the preparations of the partisans were completed; and John Bannister had already gathered together the division which had been assigned him, when his sleeve was plucked by a soldier whose person he could not distinguish in the shadows where they stood. This person called him aside for a moment, and Bannister then discovered him to be the father of poor Mary Clarkson. This man was a sullen, dark, solitary, but unsubdued spirit—who said nothing, felt nothing, asked for nothing, complained of nothing, and had but one desire in the world. John Bannister had missed sight of Clarkson for some time till now; and, perhaps, had rather avoided him since his return from the scene in which his unlucky arm inflicted the unintentional injury upon his unhappy daughter. He now shrunk to look upon the miserable old man; and when he spoke to him, it was with a feeling of compunctious sorrow, almost as great as he would have felt had he himself inflicted upon the unhappy father the vital injury which was due to Edward Morton only.

"You ha'n't spoke to me about going with you, Jack Bannister," said Clarkson, with some irritation in his tones; "but I'm going with you jest the same."

"No, Jake, you're to keep with Lieutenant Peyton's party, that's to make a feint here in front. He'll call you up, the moment we set off."

"I don't stay with him, Jack; I must keep with you or the colonel," said the man, doggedly.

"But why, Jake? why won't you stay?"

"You're going to strike at the camp, ain't you? You'll ride up to the barony, perhaps?"

"May be so—there's no tellin' yet."

"That's why I want to go with you or the colonel."

"Well now. Jake, I'd much rather you'd stay with the lieutenant."

"It's onpossible," said Clarkson, obstinately. "Look you, Jack Bannister, I don't take it as friendly, that you didn't tell tell me that Ned Conway was at the barony."

"How do you know? who told you?" demanded the woodman in some astonishment.

"Never you mind. I know that you saw him there; and what's more, I know that the colonel fou't with him, and 's hurt him mightily. But I know he's not got what's to finish him; and I'll go where there's any chance to do it."

"Lord, Jake, there's no chance. We'll not get nigher to the camp than the outposts, and if we can carry off a few outskairters, it's all we look for. Ned Conway is at the house, I reckon, snug in his bed, with more than a thousand men close round him. There's no chance for you to reach him."

"I reckon I can work through all of them, John Bannister, seeing what's my business. I must go with you or the colonel, no mistake."

Bannister knew his man—knew how idle was everything like expostulation; and though he also well knew that such a determination as Clarkson expressed was only likely to insure his being knocked on the head sooner than any of the rest, yet, as that was only a chance of war among military philosophers, he let him have his own way, and quietly enrolled him with the rest.

It would have been a study for the painter to have seen the savage old man reload his rifle, pick the touchhole, put in extra priming, and turn the bullet in his jaws, ere he wrapped it in the greasy fold of buckskin of which his patches were made.

"Poor old fellow!" muttered Bannister to himself as he beheld these operations. I'm thinking he says a prayer every time he chooses a bullet; I'm sure he does whenever he's grinding his knife."

It was with some reluctance that Clarkson was persuaded to gird a sabre at his side. The instrument was new to his hand, but he clutched it with sufficient familiarity when Bannister told him it was heavy and sharp enough to cleave a man through from his shoulder to his thigh.

All being now in readiness, Conway gave instructions to Lieutenant Peyton to make no movement on the front, until sufficient time had been allowed him for getting into the rear of the encampment; and then to give the alarm, and beat up the enemy's quarters, with all the clamor he could command. By two and two, he led his troops forward, each man on foot and guiding his steed with shortened rein, until they had passed the narrow open neck of high land on which the public road ran, and which separated the one bay, which he had lately occupied, from another to which he now bent his steps. A British vidette was stationed not more than a hundred yards from the point of passage, and great indeed were the anxieties of Clarence and of all, until the horses ceased to traverse the highland, and entered upon the mucky unresounding footing of the swamp.

But they escaped without notice. The British sentinel was in his drowsiest mood — drunk perhaps — and suffered the passage to be effected without alarm. The last two files were now entirely beyond his hearing, and Conway, throwing off the difficult restraint which his impatience felt as a curb and bit, gave orders to his followers to mount and follow him at as swift a pace as possible, through the negro trail which they now traversed. Then, a silence as awful as that of the grave descended upon the forest which he had left, and prevailed over the region for a space of nearly two hours more; when Lieutenant Peyton prepared to make the feint which was to divert the attention of the British camp from the point which was more certainly threatened. With twenty men, judiciously scattered along the front, so as to present an object of equal alarm to the whole line of the enemy's sentries, he slowly advanced, and having that advantage which arises from a perfect knowledge of his ground, his approach remained unseen and unsuspected until it was almost possible for his pistols to be emptied with some prospect of each bullet being made to tell upon its separate victim.

A silence almost equally great prevailed over that vast hive of human hearts which was then beating within the immediate precincts of the barony. Sleep had possessed the great body of its inmates. Exhaustion had done its work. The forced marches of Lord Rawdon, stimulated as they had been by the fear of losing the last and strongest outposts of his government, together with its brave and numerous garrison, had severely tested the strength and the spirit of his troops, and deep was the lethargy of all those to whom the privilege of sleep had been accorded. Nor were those to whom sleep had been expressly denied, in a condition of much more ability and consciousness. The sentinels, though strictly cautioned, had suffered themselves to be persuaded that there could be no danger in a region in which they well knew there was no enemy imbodied in sufficient force to make itself feared by their own; and if they had not formally yielded themselves up to sleep upon their places of watch, they at least made no serious effort to escape its grateful influences, and were no longer vigilant as they would have been in a time of danger. Throughout the avenue, and ranged along the grounds of the park which lay beside it, two thousand men, in groups, lay upon their arms, in happy slumber, uncovered to the serene sky of May; while, in the silvery glances of the soft moonlight, which glistened brightly from his steel cap and polished bayonet, the drowsy sentinel performed his weary round of watch; or, leaning in half consciousness only, against the massive trunk of some ancient oak, yielded himself, in momentary forgetfulness, to dream of the green island or the heathery highlands of his European home.

In the mansion where Lord Rawdon had taken up his abode, the same silence prevailed, but not the same degree of apathy. Busy and sad hearts, and suffering forms, were wakeful in its several chambers. Rawdon himself slept; but, in the apartment assigned to the chief of the Black Riders, Watson Gray was an anxious watcher. The surgeon had examined and dressed the wounds of the former, upon which he had as yet declined to give an opinion. Conway had lost much blood, and this, Gray very well knew, was rather favorable than otherwise to his condition. The patient lay, not sleeping, perhaps, but with his eyes closed and his senses seemingly unobservant. An occasional groan escaped him, as if unconsciously. Exhaustion, rather than repose, was signified by his quiescence.

In another part of the house lay his suffering victim. The mind of Mary Clarkson wandered in all the misdirected heat of delirium, the result equally of mental and physical pain. By her side sat Flora Middleton. The sex of the poor victim had been made known to the mistress of the mansion, through the medium of the servants, by the timely management of Watson Gray; but that wily associate of the outlaw chief, had not omitted the opportunity which it afforded him of turning the event to favorable account in behalf of the man he served so faithfully.

"It's a poor girl," he said to the servant to whom his information was intrusted, "that followed Colonel Conway from the Congaree, and when he and his brother fought by the vault, which they did about your young mistress, the poor girl jumped between them to save the colonel, and got her hurts that way. She is only dressed in boy's clothes that she mightn't be known among the troop."

The falsehood found its way to the ears for which it was intended; and the proud heart of Flora Middleton rose in indignation as she heard it.

"But the wretched woman is yet a woman, and she's suffering," was the humane sentiment with which she silenced the communicative negro. "She is a woman, whatever may be her vices, and I will see to her myself."

And when she beheld her, she could no longer scorn the frail victim of a misplaced affection and a reckless lust.

Emaciated and wan, the miserable girl sang and gibbered with all the unconcern of the confirmed maniac; and prated at intervals of the chidish follies which are usully the prime sources of pleasure to the child. She spoke of girlish wants and girlish pleasures, and ran on in a manner of inconsiderate merriment, which was of all things the most mournful and heart-sickening to contemplate. But she seemed neither to see nor hear. It was only when the surgeon pressed his hand upon the wounded skull that she lapsed away into utter silence, which was accompanied by a vacant stare upon the operator, so hideous in the deathlike imbecility which it expressed, as to make Flora shudder and turn away with a sickening horror that took from her all strength to serve or to assist. It was only when the surgeon had finished the operations which he deemed necessary, that she could resume strength to return to the chamber, and the patient then lay in a condition of stupor that secured her effectual silence for the time.

Not a word now escaped her lips; but a choking sob occasionally heaved her bosom as if with convulsion; and amply denoted the " perilous stuff" which lay thick and deadly about her heart. Flora Middleton sat beside her, with one female servant in attendance, when all the rest had retired. Her personal presence was not necessary, but she could not sleep on account of the troublesome and humiliating fancies which possessed her, on the subject of the story which she had heard in regard to Clarence Conway. That she should have surrendered her best affections to one who could thus abuse and degrade the warmest, if not the loftiest devotion of her sex, was, indeed, a subject of humiliating consideration to a spirit so proud as hers; and it was with a feeling of relief that the sudden sharp shot of the assault, and the wild ringing of the midnight trumpet, while it denoted the approach of unexpected conflict, disturbed the train of painful thought into which her mind had unavoidably fallen.

The tumult without was as wild and terrible as it had been sudden. A moment of the deepest midnight stillness had been succeeded by one of the fiercest uproar. Excited, rather than alarmed, she hurried from the chamber, and encountered at the head of the stairway the person of Lord Rawdon, who was joined a moment after by Watson Gray. His lordship saw her, and a smile, which was scarcely one of good nature, overspread his countenance as he remarked—

"Your rebel colonel is busy among us, Miss Middleton;—he is a bold fellow, but will pay for his rashness."

"I told your lordship that you would soon find him, but he is even more easy of access than I thought him," was the reply of the maiden, who, at the moment, had forgotten everything that she had ever heard to her lover's disadvantage, and now glowed with all the natural pride of one who joyed in the courage of her countryman.

"I trust that he will wait to receive my acknowledgments for his early attentions;" was the answer of his lordship, uttered through his closed teeth, as he hurried down the steps.

But the wish of his lordship was not gratified. The alarm was not of long continuance, though, in the brief space of time which it had occupied, it had been sharp in equal degree, and the surprise of the camp had been made with as much success as its audacity deserved. The sentries had been hewn down at their posts, one patrol entirely cut off, and a party of the assailants, penetrating to the head of the avenue, had cut in pieces a half score of Hessians before they had well started from their slumbers. The whole affair had been the work of a few moments only, and when the British were in condition to meet the invader, there was no enemy to be found. They had dissipated with the flexibility of the atmosphere, in the obscure haze of which they completely vanished from the eyes of the pursuing and vengeance-breathing soldiery.

In the lower hall of the mansion, Lord Rawdon received the report of the officers of the night, to whom, it may be supposed, his countenance was in no respect gracious. Naturally stern of temper, the annoyance was calculated to increase its severity, and add to the habitual harshness of his manner. He stood against the chimney-place, as the several officers in command made their appearance, and his keen eyes examined them with frowning expression from beneath the thick bushy brows, which were now contracted into one overhanging roof, and almost concealed the orbs in turn from the sight of those whom they surveyed. Sharp, indeed, was the examination which followed, and bitter, though brief, were the various comments which his lordship made on the several events of the evening as they were reported in his hearing.

"Majoribanks," said he, "you were in charge of the camp appointments for the night. You will make your full returns at morning of the officers on duty; and let them report to you the

## A MIDNIGHT ATTACK—A PRISONER.

names of the last relief. What is the report you make of the camp now? What is the killed, wounded, and missing?"

The portly, fine-looking, and truly noble officer whom he addressed, answered with equal ease and dignity.

"The returns are ready for your lordship now," placing the papers in his hands—"this, your lordship will perceive, is the list of officers and guards on duty; and here is a brief summary of the killed and wounded, which are found. It will need an inspection of the rolls of companies to ascertain the missing, and this can not be so well done till daylight."

"'Tis well, sir—you are prompt and ready. I wish your officers of the night had known their duty so well." And with this speech he bestowed upon the surrounding group a single glance of vexation and reproof.

"Humph!" he exclaimed as he read—"Can it be possible! So many slain outright; good fellows too—not apt to sleep upon their posts"—and he enumerated with his voice and finger—"Fergus, Childs, Spohrs, Dilworth, Moony, Wagner—fourteen slain and as many wounded! D—nation! These rascals must have been drunk, or there has been treachery!"

He crumpled the memorandum in his hands, and, utterly unable to control his indignation, flung it from him, and trampled it on the floor.

"By heavens, these beggarly rebels will learn to walk by noonday into our camps, and hew and havoc where they think proper. The British name will be a subject for their mockery; and, as for our valor!—for shame, for shame, gentlemen; what will be thought of this proceeding? what report shall I make of this conduct to our king?"

He strode, unanswered, to and fro, along the unoccupied portion of the hall; the officers, under his rebuke, looking with downcast eyes, that did not once venture to meet his glance.

"And what of the enemy, Majoribanks? Have they got off in utter safety? If I mistake not, I heard a full platoon from the grenadiers——"

"We have found but one dead body, your lordship."

"Indeed!—but one body. Oh! this is very rare success! They will fight us all night, and every night, on the same terms:" and his lordship laughed outright in very chagrin and bitterness.

"And one prisoner;"—continued Majoribanks.

"Ah:—one prisoner! Well, you hung him, did you?"

"No, your lordship: we did not hang him;" was the cold but respectful answer of Majoribanks. "We knew not that such a proceeding would be either proper or desirable."

Rawdon's eyes gleamed with a savage keenness of glance on the speaker, as he replied—

"Ha! you did not, eh? Well, let it be done instantly! I will answer for its propriety. Gray," he continued, turning to the scout, who stood at the entrance, "see to it. You shall be our provost for the occasion. Find out the nearest tree—not in sight of the dwelling, mark me—and let the rope be a good one. Let him be hung with due propriety."

Majoribanks turned away to conceal his emotion, while Gray replied—

"May it please your lordship, it might be advisable to examine the person before hanging him. He can probably give you some valuable intelligence—something, perhaps, about 'Ninety-Six.'"

"True, true!—it does please me. Bring him before us. I will examine him myself."

An officer disappeared, and a few moments only had elapsed, when, conducted by a file of soldiers, our old associate John Bannister was placed before the British commander.

## CHAPTER XXIV.

### A REPRIEVE FROM THE GALLOWS.

THE sturdy boatman of the Congaree was in no ways daunted when dragged into that imposing presence. On the contrary, his person seemed to have risen in elevation and acquired new erectness, in defiance of the cords which secured his arms, and in spite of an evident halt in his walk, the consequence of some injury which he had probably sustained in the melée which had just taken place. An easy but not offensive smile was upon his countenance as he entered, and though erect and manly, there was nothing insolent or ostentatious in his carriage. He bowed his head respectfully, first to his lordship and then to the surrounding officers, and having advanced almost to the centre of the room, paused in waiting and without a word. Rawdon surveyed his person with little interest, and was evidently annoyed by the coolness, deliberation, and conscious dignity of the woodman's bearing.

"Who are you, fellow?" he demanded.

"My name's John Bannister, your lordship. I'm a sort of scouting serjeant, when I'm in the woods, for Col. Conway's rigiment; but with my hands hitched behind me, jest now, I don't feel as if I was anybody."

"Your sense of insignificance is more likely to be increased than diminished, fellow! Speak up and tell us what you know. Your master! Where is he now?"

"Well, your lordship, if I've rightly larned my catechism, he's looking down upon us now, and listening to every word that's said."

"See to the doors and windows," exclaimed Rawdon hastily, as he put his hand upon his sword, while his flashing eyes turned to the windows of the apartment:—" who knows but we may have another visit from this audacious rebel. He has had every encouragement to come again."

A silent chuckle of the scout attested his satisfaction at the mistake into which he had led his captor, in consequence of his peculiar modes of speech and thinking.

"What does the fellow mean by this insolence? Speak, sirrah, ere I send you to the halbirds!"

"And if your lordship did, I reckon I should speak pretty much as I do now. Your lordship asked me where my master is; and as I know no master but God Almighty, I reckon I answered no more than rightly, when I said he was looking, jest this very moment, down upon our proceeding. By the catechis' I was always taught that he was pretty much here, thar, and every whar;—a sort of scout for the whole univarse, that don't want for any sleep, and never made a false count of the number sent out agin him——"

"Is the fellow mad?" demanded Rawdon, with impatience, interrupting the woodman, who seemed very well disposed to expatiate longer upon this copious subject. "Who knows anything of this fellow?"

"I do, your lordship," whispered Watson Gray, but in tones that reached the ears of Bannister. "He's the same person that I told you of to-night—he's the famous scout that Col. Cruger offered twenty guineas for, for stealing his horse."

The last words awakened all Bannister's indignation, which he expressed without heeding the presence in which he stood.

"Look you, Watson Gray," said he, "that's not so genteel, all things considerin'; and I'll look to you to answer it some day. The horse was a fair prize, taken from the enemy's quarters at the resk of my neck——"

"That risk is not over, scoundrel; and that you may be made justly sensible of it, let the provost take him hence to a tree. Let it be done at once. We shall save Cruger his twenty guineas."

Here Watson Gray again whispered in the ears of his lordship.

"Ah, true," said the latter: then, addressing Bannister, he asked in accents of unusual mildness:—

"Are you willing to save your life, my good fellow? Speak quickly, for we have little time to waste, and you have none to spare."

"Well, I reckon, your lordship, as I'm a good fellow, I oughtn't to be afeard either to live or to die; though, if the choice is given me, living's my preference at this present. I might have a different choice next week, or even to-morrow, for anything I know jest now."

"Too many words by half, sirrah. Hear me: you can save your life by proving yourself honest once in a way. Speak the truth to all the questions I ask you, and no prevarication."

"I'll try, your lordship," said the scout quietly, as he turned a huge quid of tobacco in his mouth and voided it behind him on the floor, with a coolness which did not lessen his lordship's indignation.

"How many men were with your colonel in this assault to-night?"

"Well, about thirty men, I reckon—which wa'n't more than half his force: t'other half played with the sentinels along the woods above."

"Thirty men! Was ever heard the like! Thirty men to beat up the quarters of a British general, and ride over a whole army of two thousand men!"

"There's more, I reckon, your lordship," said Gray, in a whisper, "Colonel Conway sometimes has a whole regiment, and I've seldom known him with less than a hundred."

"Hark ye, fellow, if you are found in a falsehood, that instant I send you to the gallows," exclaimed Rawdon, sternly, addressing the scout.

"And if your lordship believes a man that does his talking in a whisper, in preference to him that speaks out, it's likely you'll send all your prisoners thar. It's no use for *me* to tell you the truth, when there's a man behind you that's been known on the Congaree ever since I was knee-high to a splinter, to be a born liar. Ef he's let, in a whisper, to outtalk a man that does his talking outright, and like a man, aboveboard, then there's but little use in my opening my mouth at all. Ef you believe *him*, you can't believe *me*—though, to speak a truth that there's no denying, I ain't very willing to tell your lordship anything about the consarns of the troop. I'm jub'ous ef that ain't treasonable."

"You are very scrupulous all at once, my fine fellow—but, whether you are believed or not, we shall still hear what you have to say. Does the garrison at 'Ninety-Six' hold out?"

"I reckon not now. It did yesterday morning, but 'twas mighty hard pushed then; and as we caught all your messengers, and got all your letters to Colonel Cruger, I'm thinking he's given in, seeing there was no sort of chance of your lordship's coming.

"D—nation! I sent two messengers since Sunday."

"I reckon your lordship's count ain't altogether right; for I myself caught three. I choked one chap till he emptied his throat of a mighty small scrap of intelligence that he had curled up like a piece of honest pigtail in his jaws; and we physicked another before he surrendered the screw-bullet that he swallowed. The third one gin up his paper like a good fellow, j'ined our troop, and helped us powerful well in the little brush we made in the avenue to-night. He's a big fellow, a Dutchman by birth, that come out of the forks of Edisto. His name's a mighty hard one to spell, and I can't say that I altogether remember it; but he showed us five guineas that your lordship gin him to go to 'Ninety-Six,' and I reckon he'd ha' gone if we hadn't caught him. He fou't powerful well to-night, for I watched him."

John Bannister was evidently not the person from whom much intelligence could be extracted, though he was quite liberal in yielding that which it gave his lordship little pleasure to hear. Every word which he uttered seemed to be peculiarly chosen to mortify his captors. Not that the worthy scout had any such intention, for he well knew the danger to himself of any such proceeding; and, as we have said before, his manner, though loftier than usual, was unobtrusive, and certainly never intended anything like insolence. His free speech came from his frank nature, which poured forth the honest feelings of his mind without much restraint, and utterly regardless of the situation in which he stood. He was just sufficiently cautious to baffle his examiners on every subject, the truth of which might affect unfavorably the troop and the service in which it was engaged. Rawdon soon discerned the character of the person with whom he had to deal; and, provoked beyond patience by the annoying detail the scout had given of the capture of his three messengers, he thus summarily cut short the conference:

"You are a good scout, John Bannister, and your loss, I have no doubt, will be severely felt by your leader. Provost, take him to the end of the lane, give him three minutes for prayer, and then hang him to the tallest tree in front of the avenue. Let him hang till daylight, that the Irish regiments may see and take warning from the spectacle. It may cure a few of them of the disease of desertion, which is so apt to afflict so many. Go, my good Bannister, my provost will see to your remaining wants. I think your colonel will feel your loss very much."

"I'm jest now of the same opinion, your lordship," replied the scout, composedly; "but I'm not thinking he's so nigh losing me altogether. I don't think my neck in so much danger yet, because I reckon your lordship won't be so venturesome as to hang up a prisoner-of-war, taken in an honest scrimmage."

"Ah! that is *your* opinion. We differ! Take him hence, Provost, and do as I bid you. Let it be done at once. A short shrift saves many unpleasant reflections."

Such was the cool, stern decision of his lordship, to whose haughty mind the *sang froid* of Bannister was eminently insulting.

"I would jest like to let your lordship know before I leave you——" was the beginning of another speech of Bannister's, which the angry gesture of Rawdon did not suffer him to finish. The provost and his attendants seized on the prisoner, in obedience to the lifted finger of his lordship, and were about to hurry him, still speaking, from the apartment, when they were stopped at the door by the sudden entrance of Flora Middleton.

"Stay!" she exclaimed, addressing the officer—"stay, till I have spoken with his lordship."

Rawdon started back at beholding her, and could not refrain from expressing his surprise at her presence.

"At this time of the night, Miss Middleton, and here?"

"Very improper conduct, your lordship would intimate, for a young lady; but the circumstances must excuse the proceeding. I come to you, sir, in behalf of this poor man, who is your prisoner, and whom I understand you are about to execute, in violation of the laws of humanity, and, as I believe, the laws of war."

His lordship was evidently annoyed.

"You have chosen a very unnecessary labor, Miss Middleton, and pardon me if I think a very unbecoming one. I may be permitted, surely, to know what the laws of war require, and greatly regret that Miss Middleton can not believe me sufficiently well informed in regard to those of humanity."

"Pardon me, my lord, if, in my excited emotions, my words should happen to offend. I do not mean offence. I would not intrude upon a scene like this, and can not think that my interposition to save life, and to prevent murder, can properly be called an unbecoming interference."

"Murder!" muttered his lordship through his closed teeth, while — as if to prevent his frowns from addressing themselves to the fair intruder — he was compelled to avert his face.

"Yes, my lord, murder; for I know this man to be as worthy and honest a citizen as ever lived on the Congaree. He has always been my friend and the friend of the family. He has never avowed his loyalty to the king — never taken protection; but, from the first, has been in arms, under either Pickens or Sumter, in opposition to his majesty. The fate of war throws him into your hands——"

"And he must abide it, lady. He has been such a consistent rebel, according to your own showing, that he well deserves his fate. Provost, do your duty!"

"My lord, my lord, can it be that you will not grant my prayer — that you will not spare him?"

"It would give me pleasure to grant any application to one so fair and friendly, but——"

"Oh, deal not in this vain language at such a time, my lord. Do not this great wrong. Let not your military pride seduce you into an inhumanity which you will remember in after days with dread and sorrow. Already they charge you with blood wantonly shed at Camden—too much blood—the blood of the old and young—of the gray-headed man and the beardless boy alike. But, I believe it not, my lord—no! no! Turn not away from me in anger—I believe it not—I would not wish to believe it."

"Too much, too much!" murmured Majoribanks, as he regarded the fair speaker, and saw the dark spot turn to crimson on the brow of the stern and savage captain. He well perceived, whatever might have been his hopes of her pleading before, that her last allusion to the Camden massacres had spoiled the effect of all.

"Your entreaty is in vain, Miss Middleton. The man is doomed. He shall be an example to warn others against shooting down sentinels at midnight."

"No! no! Be not inflexible—spare him; on my knees, I implore you, my lord. I have known him long, and always worthily; he is my friend, and a noble-hearted creature. Send not such a fellow to the gallows; send the ruffian, the murderer, the spy, but not a worthy man like this."

"Rise, Miss Middleton; I should be sorry to see you kneel, without succeeding in your prayer, either to God or mortal."

"You grant it, then!" she exclaimed eagerly, as he raised her from the floor.

"Impossible! The man must die."

She recoiled from his hands, regarded him with a silent but searching expression of eye, then turned to the spot where John Bannister stood. The worthy scout no longer remained unmoved. Her interposition had softened the poor fellow, whom the threatening danger from his foes had only strengthened and made inflexible and firm. He now met her glance of bitterness and grief, while a smile mingled sweetly upon his face with the big tear which was swelling in his eye.

"God bless you, my dear miss Flora!—you're an angel, if ever there was one on such a place as airth; and I'm jest now thankful to God for putting me in this fix, ef it's only that I might know how airnestly and sweetly he could send his angel to plead in favor of a rough old Congaree boatman like me. But don't you be scared for they can't do me any hurt after all;

and if his lordship had only listened to me a leetle while longer at first, he'd ha' been able to have said the handsome thing, and consented to all you axed him. Look here, my lord, 'twon't do to hang me, unless you'd like to lose a better man in the bargain."

A look of inquiry was all that his lordship deigned the speaker, who, turning to the provost, begged him to take his grasp from his shoulder.

"I can't run, you see, ef I wanted to, and somehow I never could talk to my own liking, when I had the feel of an inemy's hand upon me."

"Speak up, fellow," said Majoribanks, who saw the increasing vexation of Rawdon, "and tell his lordship what you mean."

"Well, the long and short of the matter's this, your lordship. If you look at your roll, I reckon you'll find a handsome young cappin, or mou't-be a major, among your missing. I made him a prisoner myself, at the head of the avenue, on the very first charge to-night, and I know they've got him safe among my people; and his neck must be a sort of make-weight agin mine. I ain't of much 'count anyhow, but the 'Congaree Blues' has a sort of liking for me, and they can find any quantity of rope and tree when there's a need for it. If you hang me, they'll hang him, and your lordship can tell best whether he's worth looking after or not. It's a thing for calculation only."

"Is this the case? Is there any officer missing?" demanded Rawdon, with a tone of suppressed but bitter feeling.

"Two, your lordship," replied the lieutenant of the night—"Major Penfield and Captain Withers."

"They *should* hang! They deserve it!" exclaimed Rawdon; but an audible murmur from the bottom of the hall, warned him of the danger of trying experiments upon the temper of troops who had just effected a painful forced march, and had before them a continuation of the same, and even severer duties.

"Take the prisoner away, and let him be well guarded," said his lordship.

Flora Middleton, relieved by this order, gave but a single glance of satisfaction to the woodman, as she glided out of the apartment.

With the dawn of day the British army was under arms, and preparing to depart. Our heroine, who had enjoyed no rest during the night, and had felt no desire for it, under the numerous anxieties and painful feelings which filled her heart, took her station in the balcony, where she could witness all their movements. And no more imposing array had ever gratified her eyes. Lord Rawdon was then in command of the very élite of the British army. The hardy and well-tried provincial loyalists formed the nucleus of the efficient force of near three thousand men, which he commanded; and these, many of them well mounted, and employed as dragoons and riflemen at pleasure, were, in reality, the chief reliance of his government. The Hessians had been well thinned by the harassing warfare of two seasons, and were neither numerous nor daring; but nothing could exceed the splendid appearance of the principal force which he brought with him from Charleston, consisting of three full regiments, fresh from Ireland, with all the glow of European health upon their cheeks, full-framed, strong and active; martial in their carriage, bold in action, and quite as full of vivacity as courage.

Flora Middleton beheld them as they marched forward beneath her eyes, with mingling sentiments of pity and admiration. Poor fellows! They were destined to be terribly thinned and humbled by the sabre of the cavalry, the deadly aim of the rifle, and that more crushing enemy of all, the pestilential malaria of the southern swamps. How many of that glowing and numerous cavalcade were destined to leave their bones along the banks of the Wateree and Santee, in their long and arduous marchings and counter-marchings, and in the painful and perilous flight which followed to the Eutaws, and from the Eutaws to Charleston. On this flight, scarce two months after, fifty of these brave fellows dropped down, dead in the ranks, in a single day; the victims of fatigue, heat and a climate which mocked equally their muscle, their courage, and vivacity; and which not even the natives at that season could endure without peril. The brave and generous Majoribanks himself—the most honorable and valiant of enemies—little did Flora Middleton fancy, as he passed his sword-point to the earth in courteous salute, and smiled his farewell, while marching at the head of his battalion beneath the balcony, that he, too, was one of those who should find his grave along the highways of Carolina, immediately after the ablest of his achievements at Eutaw, where to him, in particular, was due the rescue of the British lion from the claws of the now triumphant eagle.

## CHAPTER XXV.

#### NINETY-SIX — A FLIGHT BY NIGHT.

CLARENCE CONWAY, with a single exception, had every reason to be satisfied with the result of his expedition. He had lost but one man slain; and but two were missing. One of these, as we have seen, was John Bannister; the other was the unhappy father of Mary Clarkson. The reader is already apprized of the situation of the former; of the latter neither party had any present knowledge. Conway was utterly ignorant, and very anxious about the fate of his trusty agent. The loss of John Bannister could not be compensated to him, by any successes, whether as a soldier or a man. He was incomparable as a scout; almost as much so in personal conflict; superior in judgment in most matters relating to partisan warfare; but, over all, he was the friend, the ever-faithful, the fond; having an affection for his leader like that of Jonathan of old, surpassing the love of woman.

Clarence Conway did full justice to this affection. He loitered and lingered long that night before leaving the field of conflict, in the hope to see the trusty fellow reappear; and slow indeed were his parting footsteps when, at the dawn of day, he set his little band in motion for the Saluda. This measure was now become one of stern necessity. He had done all that could be required of him, and much more than had been expected. It was not supposed that with a force so small as his he could possibly occasion any interruption or delay in the progress of an army such as that led by Rawdon; and he had most effectually performed those duties along the Congaree which had been done by Sumter and Marion on the waters of the Santee below. Every messenger between Rawdon and Ninety-Six had been cut off; and, while the urgent entreaties of Cruger, having command of the latter garrison, had failed in most cases to reach the ears of Rawdon, the despatches of the latter, promising assistance, and urging the former to hold out, had been invariably intercepted. Nor were the performances of the gallant young partisan limited to these small duties only. He had, in concert with Colonel Butler, a famous name among the whigs of Ninety-Six, given a terrible chastisement to the sanguinary tory, Cunningham, in which the troop of the latter was utterly annihilated, and their leader owed his escape only to the fleetness of an inimitable steed. But these events belong not to our story.

With a sad heart, but no diminution of enterprise or spirit, Colonel Conway took up the line of march for the Saluda, with the purpose of joining General Greene before Ninety-Six; or, in the event of that place being already in possession of the Americans, of extending his march toward the mountains, where General Pickens was about to operate against the Cherokee Indians.

But though compelled to this course by the pressure of the British army in his rear, his progress was not a flight. His little band was so compact, and so well acquainted with the face of the country, that he could move at leisure in front of the enemy, and avail himself of every opportunity for cutting off stragglers, defeating the operations of foraging parties, and baffling every purpose or movement of the British, which was not covered by a detachment superior to his own. Such was his purpose, and such, to a certain extent, were his performances.

But Conway was soon made sensible of the inefficiency of his force to contend even with the inferior cavalry of the enemy. These were only inferior in quality. In point of numbers they were vastly superior to the Americans. The measures which Rawdon had taken to mount the loyalists in his army, had, to the great surprise of the Americans, given him a superiority in this particular, which was equally injurious to their hopes and unexpected by their apprehensions. The march of the British, though urged forward with due diligence by their stern commander, was, at the same time, distinguished by such a degree of caution as effectually to discourage Conway in his attempts upon it. The onslaught of the previous night justified the prudence of this wary general. The audacity of the Americans was, at this period, everywhere felt and acknowledged, and by none more readily than Rawdon. His advanced guard was sent forward in treble force: his provincial riflemen skirted the woods on the roadside while his main army defiled between, and his cavalry scoured the neighboring thickets wherever it was possible for them to hide a foe. Conway was compelled to console himself with the profitless compliment which this vigilance paid to his spirit and address; and, after hovering for the best part of a day's march around the path of the advancing enemy, without an opportunity to inflict a blow, he reluctantly pressed forward with increased speed for Ninety-Six, to prepare General Greene for the coming of the new enemy. Our course is thither also.

The post of Ninety-Six was situated on the crown of a gentle but commanding eminence, and included within its limits the village of the same name. This name was that of the county, or district, of which it was the county-town. Its derivation is doubtful; but most probably it came from its being ninety-six miles from Prince George, at the period of its erection the frontier post of the colony. Its history is one of great local interest. Originally a mere stockade for the defence of the settlers against Indian incursion, it at length became the scene of the first conflicts in the southern country, and perhaps in the revolutionary war. It was here that, early in 1775, the fierce domestic strife first began between the whigs and tories of this region;—a region beautiful and rich by nature, and made valuable by art, which, before the war was ended, was turned into something worse than a howling wilderness. The old stockade remained at the beginning of the Revolution, and when the British overran the state, they garrisoned the place, and it became one of the most valuable of that cordon of posts which they established around and within it. Its protection and security were of the last importance to their interests. It enabled them to maintain a communication with the Cherokees and other Indians; and to keep in check the whig settlements on the west of it, while it protected those of the loyalists, north, south, and east. The most advanced post which they occupied, its position served to strengthen their influence in Camden and Augusta, and assisted them to overawe the population of Georgia and North Carolina. It was also, for a long period, the chief depôt of recruits; and drew, but too successfully, the disaffected youth of the neighborhood into the royal embrace.

The defences of this place had been greatly strengthened on the advance of the American army. Colonel Cruger, an American loyalist, who was intrusted with the command, was an officer of energy and talents, and proved himself equally adequate and faithful to the trust which was reposed in him. Calling in the aid of the neighboring slaves, he soon completed a ditch around his stockade, throwing the earth parapet height upon it, and securing it within, by culverts and traverses, to facilitate the communication in safety between his various points of defence. His ditch was further secured by an abattis; and, at convenient distances within the stockade, he erected strong block-houses of logs.

But the central and most important point in his position, lay in a work of considerable strength — which the curious in antiquarian research and history may see to this day in a state of comparative perfectness — called the "Star Battery." It stood on the southeast of the village which it effectually commanded, was in shape of a star, having sixteen salient and returning angles, and communicated by lines with the stockade. In this were served three pieces of artillery, which, for more ready transition to any point of danger, were worked on wheel carriages.

On the north side of the village arises a copious fountain, of several eyes, which flows through a valley. From this rivulet the garrison obtained its supplies of water. The county prison, lying contiguous to this valley and commanding it, was also fortified; as was another stockade fort, lying on the opposite side of the valley, of considerable strength, and having within it a couple of block-houses which assisted in covering the communication with the spring. A covert way led from the town to the rivulet; and the whole, including the village, was enclosed by lines of considerable extent and height. To defend his position, Cruger had a select force of six hundred men, many of them riflemen of the first quality, and not a few of them fighting, as they well knew, with halters about their necks.

Greene commenced the siege under very inauspicious circumstances, and with a force quite inadequate to his object. This siege formed one of the most animated and critical occurrences during the southern war, and had already lasted near a month, when Colonel Conway joined his little troop to the force of the commander-in-chief. The available army of Greene scarcely exceeded that of Cruger. He had no battering cannon; and there was no mode of succeeding against this "Star" redoubt, which was the chief point of defence, but in getting over or under it. Both modes were resolved upon. Regular approaches were made, and, on the completion of the first parallel, a mine was begun under cover of a battery erected on the enemy's right.

This work was prosecuted day and night. No interval was permitted. One party labored, while a second slept, and a third guarded both. The sallies of the besieged were constant and desperate; not a night passed without the loss of life on both sides; but the work of the Americans steadily advanced. The second parallel was at length completed, the enemy summoned to surrender, and a defiance returned to the demand. The third parallel was then begun, and its completion greatly facilitated by the invention of a temporary structure of logs, which, from the inventor's name, were called the "Maham towers." These were, in fact, nothing more than block-houses, constructed of heavy timbers, raised to a height superior to that of the beleaguered fort, and filled with riflemen. These sharp-shooters succeeded, in a little time, in driving the artillerists of the garrison from their guns. Hot shot were tried to destroy the towers, but the greenness of the wood, in June, rendered the effort unavailing. The artillery of the "Star" could no longer be used by daylight, and by night it was little to be dreaded.

The garrison was now greatly straitened. Their provisions were fast failing them; they could no longer venture for water to the rivulet. Women were employed for this purpose by daylight, and men in women's clothing; and by night they received their supplies with the help of naked negroes. Other means were found for conveyance. Burning arrows were shot into the fort, but Cruger promptly threw off the roofs of his houses. An attempt was made to destroy the abattis by fire, but drew down death on every one of the daring fellows who attempted it. Beside the "Maham towers," one of which was within thirty yards of the enemy's ditch, the besiegers had erected several batteries for cannon. One of these, twenty feet in height, and within one hundred and forty yards of the "Star," so completely commanded it, that it became necessary to give its parapet an increased elevation. Bags of sand were employed for this purpose. Through these, apertures were left for the use of small-arms; and the removal of the sand-bags by night, gave room for the use of the artillery. Bloody and deadly was the strife that ensued for ten days, between the combatants. During this period not a man could show himself, on either side, without receiving a shot. As the conflict approached its termination it seemed to acquire increased rancor; and an equal desperation, under different motives, appeared to govern both parties.

This could not be sustained long; and the fall of the garrison was at hand. Cruger still held out in the hope of succor, for which he had long implored his commander. He had sufficient reasons, apart from the natural courage which the good soldier may possess, for making him defend his post to the very last extremity. There were those within its walls to whom no indulgence would have been extended by its captors—men whose odious crimes and bloody deeds had long since forfeited the security even of those laws which are allowed to temper with mercy the brutalities of battle. But their apprehensions, and the resolution of Cruger, could not long supply the deficiencies under which the besieged were suffering. Only two days more were allotted them for the retention of a post which they had so gallantly defended. But these two days were of the last importance for good or evil to the two parties. In this period the American commander was apprized of the circumstances which rendered it necessary that the place should be carried by assault or the siege raised. The arrival of Conway announced the approach of Rawdon, and the same night furnished the same important intelligence to Cruger. But for this intelligence that very night must have witnessed the surrender of the post.

The circumspection and close watch which had been maintained so long and so well by the American general and his able subordinates, and which had kept the garrison in utter ignorance of the march of Rawdon from Charleston, was defeated at the last and most important moment from a quarter which had excited no suspicions. The circumstance has in it no small portion of romance. A young lady, said to be beautiful, and certainly bold—the daughter of one tried patriot and the sister of another—had formed in secret a matrimonial connection with a British officer, who was one of the besieged. Her residence was in the neighborhood, and she was countenanced, in visiting the camp with a flag, on some pretence of little moment. She was received with civility and dined at the general's table. Permitted the freedom of the encampment, she was probably distinguished by her lover from the redoubt, and contrived to convey by signs the desire which she entertained to make some communication to the besieged. The ardor of the lover and the soldier united to infuse a degree of audacity into his bosom, which prompted him to an act of daring equally bold and successful. He acknowledged her signal, darted from the redoubt, received her verbal communication, and returned in safety amidst a shower of bullets from the baffled and astonished sentinels. Such is the story told by tradition. It differs little from that which history relates, and in no substantial particular; what is obscure in the tale, but increases what is romantic. The *feu de joie* of the besieged and their loud huzzas apprized the American general of their new hopes; and too plainly assured him that his labor was taken in vain.

Colonel Conway was admitted that night to the tent of the general, where a council of war was to be held as to the course now to be pursued. Greene necessarily presided. Unmoved by disappointment, unembarrassed by the probable defeat of his hopes and purposes, this cheerful and brave soldier looked around him with a smile of good humor upon his military family while he solicited their several opinions. His fine manly face, bronzed by the fierce glances of the southern sun, and heightened by an eye of equal spirit and benevolence, wore none of that dark disquietude and sullen ferocity, the sure token of vindictive and bad feelings, which scowled in the whole visage of his able opponent, Rawdon. A slight obliquity of vision, the result of small-pox in his youth, did not impair the sweetness of his glance, though it was sufficiently obvious in the eye which it affected. Conway had seen him more than once before, but never to so much advantage as now, when a defeat so serious as that which threatened his hopes, and rendered necessary the measure of consultation then in hand. He looked for the signs of peevishness and vexation but he saw none. Something of anxiety may have clouded the brow of the commander but such an expression only serves to ennoble the countenance of the man whose pursuits are elevated and whose performances are worthy. Anxiety makes the human countenance only the more thoroughly and sacredly human. It is the sign of care, and thought, and labor, and hope — of all the moral attributes which betoken the mind at work, and most usually at its legitimate employments.

On the right hand of Greene sat one who divided between himself and the commander-in-chief the attention of the ardent young partisan. This was the celebrated polish patriot Kosciuzko. He had served throughout the siege as chief engineer, and, under his guidance, the several approaches had been made. His tall, erect, military form, pale, thin and melancholy features, light brown hair, already thinned above his lofty brow, together with the soft blue eye which lightened them up at moments with almost girlish animation, seemed to the mind of Conway inexpressibly touching. The fate and name of Kosciuzko were so intimately connected with those of his country, that the eye of the spectator beheld the miseries of Poland in the sad features of its melancholy exile. His words, few, and sweetened as it were by the imperfect English in which they were expressed, riveted the attention of all, and were considered with marked deference by the commander, to whom they were addressed.

There were many other brave men at that council-board, some of whom Clarence Conway now beheld for the first time, whose deeds and reputation had reached his ears, and whose persons he now examined with momently-growing interest.

There was Lee of the legion, whom Greene emphatically styled the eye and wing of his army; Campbell of the Virginians, who subsequently fell at the Eutaw, while bravely leading on his command; Kirkwood of the Delawares, happily designated as the continental Diomed, a soldier of delightful daring; Howard of the Marylanders; Rudolph of the legion, Armstrong, and Benson, and others, whose presence would enlighten any council-board, as their valor had done honor to every field in which they fought. Our hero had enough to do, after conveying to the council all his intelligence, to note and study the features of his associates—to weigh the words which they uttered—and to endeavor, for himself, to judge in what degree they severally deserved the high reputations which they bore. He was not disposed or prepared, perhaps, to offer any suggestions himself. He was better pleased to study and to listen.

The consultation was brief. The points to be discussed were few.

"You perceive, gentlemen," said Greene, opening the proceedings, "that our toils appear to have been all taken in vain. Apprized of Lord Rawdon's approach, the garrison will now hold out until the junction is effected, and for that we can not wait; we are in no condition to meet Lord Rawdon single-handed. Colonel Conway, whose exertions merit my warmest acknowledgments, represents his force as quite too formidable for anything that we can oppose to him. He brings with him three fresh regiments from Ireland, the remains of the regiment of Boze, near six hundred loyalists whom he has mounted as cavalry, besides Coffin's dragoons—in all, an army little short of three thousand men. To this we can oppose scarce eight hundred in camp and fit for duty; Marion and Sumter are too far, and too busy below, to leave me any hope of their co-operation before Rawdon comes within striking distance; and the presence of his lordship in such force will bring out Cunningham and Harrison, with all their loyalists, who will give sufficient employment for Pickens and Washington above. Retreat becomes absolutely necessary; but shall our labors here for the last month be thrown away? Shall we give up 'Ninety-Six' without a struggle? Shall we not make the effort to win the post, and behind its walls prepare for the reception of Rawdon?"

The unanimous opinion of the council tallied with the wishes of the commander. The assault was resolved upon. The necessary orders were given out that night, and the army was all in readiness on the morning of the 18th of June to make the final attempt. The forlorn hope was led, on the American left, against the 'Star' battery, by Lieutenants Seldon and Duval. Close behind them followed a party furnished with hooks fastened to staves, whose particular duty it was to pull down the sand-bags which the enemy had raised upon their parapet. Colonel Campbell next advanced to the assault at the head of the first Maryland and Virginian regiments. These all marched under cover of the approaches, until they came within a few yards of the enemy's ditch. Major Rudolph commanded the forlorn hope on the American right against the stockade, supported by the legion infantry, and Kirkwood's Delawares. The forts, the rifle-towers, and all the American works, were manned and prepared to sweep the enemy's parapet, previous to the advance of the storming party. Duval and Seldon were to clear the abattis and occupy the opposite curtain, then, driving off the enemy, were to open the way for the workmen. The sand-bags pulled down, Campbell was to make the attack, availing himself of their aid in clambering up the parapet. To Colonel Lee was left the assault upon the stockades, of which, when obtained, he was simply to keep possession and wait events.

A discharge of artillery at noon was the signal for the assault, which was followed by the prompt movement of the storming parties. An uninterrupted blaze of artillery and small-arms covered the advance of the forlorn hope; and, enveloped in its shadowing smokes, this gallant little band leaped the ditch and commenced the work of destruction.

But the besieged who had so bravely and for so long a time defended their ramparts, and whom the approach of Lord Rawdon had inspired with fresh confidence and courage, was prepared for their reception. They met the attack with equal coolness and determination. The assailants were encountered by bristling bayonets and levelled pikes, which lined the parapet, while a stream of fire, poured forth from intervals between the sand-bags, was productive of dreadful havoc among them. The form of the redoubt gave to the besieged complete command over the ditch, and subjected the besiegers to a cross-fire, which the gradual removal of the abattis only tended to increase.

For the details of this action, the reader will look to other histories. Enough if, in dealing with this (to us) purely episodical matter, we give the result. The attempt was desperate; but so was the hope. The Americans fought well, but on the most unfortunate terms of combat. This is not the place to criticise the transaction; but, some day, the military critic will find it instructive to review this, among other great actions of our Revolutionary war, and will be able to point out clearly the miserable mistakes, the result of equal ignorance and imbecility, by which the native valor of the people was continually set at naught. There were mistakes enough in this siege and assault of 'Ninety-Six,' to decide the latter before it was begun. Enough now, that the day was lost, almost as soon as begun. The hope of the assailants, small at the beginning, was very soon utterly dissipated; and mortified and pained, less at being baffled than at the loss of so many brave men, Greene gave the orders which discontinued the assault.

Yet, for near three quarters of an hour, did these brave fellows persist, notwithstanding the fall of two thirds of their number and both their leaders. This daring and enduring courage enabled them to occupy the curtain, and maintain, hand to hand, the conflict with the garrison. They yielded at length, rather than to the summons of their commander than to their own fear of danger. The greater part of their men were killed or wounded;

but the latter were brought off amid the hottest fire of the garrison.

The misfortunes of Greene did not end here. The British general was at hand, and, the dead being buried, the American commander struck his tents, and commenced the retreat which carried Clarence Conway still further from a region in which all his feelings and anxieties were now deeply and doubly interested. We will not attempt to pursue his flight, but, retracing our steps in a quarter to which he dare not turn, we will resume our march along with that of the British army, when they left the Middleton barony to advance upon Ninety-Six.

But, in going back to Brier Park, it is not our purpose at this time to trespass again upon its inmates. We shall simply join company with our ancient friend, John Bannister, and trace his progress, as a prisoner, in the train of his captors.

Watson Gray—having been intrusted by Lord Rawdon with the exclusive disposition of this business, in consequence of the suggestions which the latter had made him the night before—had very naturally assigned the custody of the scout to the Black Riders, of whom, under a roving commission, Gray ranked as an inferior officer. He had every reason for believing the charge to be a secure one. Bannister had long been an object of dislike and apprehension to this troop, as he had on several occasions discovered their most secret haunts, and beaten up their quarters. His skill in the woods was proverbial, and dreaded by all his enemies accordingly; and the recent display which he had made in the case of Gray himself, of that readiness of resource which had rendered him famous, was very well calculated to mortify the latter, and make him desirous of subjecting his own captor to all the annoyance likely to follow captivity.

Whatever may have been the motives by which he was governed in this proceeding, it was very evident that Supple Jack could not have been put into less indulgent custody. But circumstances baffle the wisest, in spite of all precautions; and events which are utterly beyond human foresight suddenly arise to confound all the calculations of the cunning. John Bannister found a friend among the Black Riders when he little expected one. When the army came to a halt that night, which was not till a tolerably late hour, their camp was made on the northern side of the Little Saluda, just within the line of the present district of Edgefield; a commanding spot was chosen for the bivouac, and every precaution taken to secure it from disturbance for the night.

The preparations for supper produced the customary stir and excitement for a while; but the supper itself was soon discussed. Excessive fatigue had lessened appetite, and sleep was alone desirable to the regiments, which had been pressed forward to the utmost of their marching powers, from the very first moment of their leaving Charleston. The intense heat of the climate, at that season, made this task an inappreciably severe one. The duties of the cavalry had been, if possible, still more severe than those of the infantry; compelled, as they constantly were, to make continual and large circuits through the country, around the line of march of the army, in order to defeat the perpetual ambuscades of the Americans, who, in small parties, hovered about the march, and made frequent dashes, which were almost as successful as frequent, whenever opportunity, or remissness of the enemy, seemed to invite adventure. For the first time, for a long period, the circumstances of the campaign seemed to promise impunity to the encampment; and, with a pleasant feeling of relief, the British troops prepared to make the most of their securities. Rest, repose, sleep—these were now the only objects of desire; and the several groups crouched about beneath the forest-trees, without much pause or choice, sinking down simply in the shade, upon the dry leaves, with cloak or blanket wrapped about them.

The Black Riders were stationed beside a grove which skirted one of the forks of the little Saluda, and were not the last to avail themselves of the general privilege of sleep. A few trees sufficed to cover their entire troop, and they clustered together in several small bodies, the horses of each group being fastened to swinging limbs of trees close to those which sheltered their riders, in order that they might be ready at hand in any sudden emergency.

In the centre of one of these squads lay John Bannister. He

was bound hand and foot; the bandages upon the latter members being only put on for sleeping purposes, to be withdrawn when the march was resumed. A few rods distant, paced a sturdy sentinel, to whom the double duty was entrusted of keeping equal watch upon the horses and the prisoner. With this exception, Bannister was almost the only person whose eyes were unsealed by slumber in the encampment of the dragoons. He was wakeful through anxiety and thought; for, though one of the most cheerful and elastic creatures breathing, he had too many subjects of serious apprehension, to suffer him to enjoy that repose which his body absolutely needed. There was yet another reason to keep him wakeful. He was very far from being resigned to his fate. He had no taste for the condition of the prisoner; and the moment that found him a captive found him meditating schemes for his own deliverance. His plans had reference to himself entirely. He was one of those self dependent people, who never care to look abroad for those resources which may be found within; and, closing his eyes where he lay, and affecting the sleep which he could not obtain, he wearied himself with the examination of a hundred different plans for escaping from his predicament.

While he lay in this position he heard some one approach and speak to the sentinel. A brief dialogue ensued between them, carried on in terms quite too low to be distinguished by him; but the tones of the stranger's voice seemed familiar to the ear of the listener. Bannister opened his eyes and discerned the two persons; but, in consequence of the umbrage of the trees between, he could only see their lower limbs; after a while one of them disappeared, and fancying that it was the stranger, and that the sentinel would again resume his duties, the prisoner again shut his eyes and tried to resume the train of meditation which the intrusion had disturbed. He had not long been thus engaged when he was startled by the low accents of some one speaking behind the trunk of the tree against which his head was leaned, and addressing him by name.

"Who speaks?" he demanded, in the same whispering tones in which he had been addressed.

"A friend."

"Who?"

"Muggs."

"What, Isaac?"

"The same."

"Ah, you varmint! after I convarted you, you'll still follow the British."

"Hush!" whispered the other, with some trepidation in his tones. "For God's sake, not so loud. Stockton and Darcy and two more are jest under the oaks to the left, and I'm jub'ous they're half awake now."

"But how come you here, Muggs?"

"Why, nateral enough. I hearn the army was on its march, and I reckoned there was guineas to be got by way in exchange for rum and sugar; so I hitched horse and wagon together, and turned sutler for the troop as I used to; and mighty glad are they to see me; and mighty glad I am to see you, Jack Bannister, and to try and give you a help out of your hitch."

"I'm jub'ous of you, Isaac Muggs. I'm afeard you ain't had a full couvarsion."

"Don't you be afeard. Trust to me."

"How? Trust to you for what? Will you loose me—git me a horse and a broadsword—hey? Can you do this for the good cause, Isaac, and prove your convarsion?"

"Don't talk, but turn on your side a leetle, so that I can feel where your hands are tied. Be quick—I hain't much time to spare. Ben Geiger, who is your sentry, is gone to my wagon to get a drink, and will be back pretty soon, and I'm keeping watch for him, and a mighty good watch I'll keep."

"There—cut, Muggs, and let me git up; but you must cut the legs loose too. They've hitched me under and over, as ef I was a whole team by myself."

"And so you are, John Bannister; but you mustn't git up when I cut you loose."

"Thunder! and why not, Muggs? What's the use of loosing foot and fingers, if one's not to use them?"

"Not jest yet; because that'll be getting Ben Geiger into a scrape, and me at the back of it. You must wait till he's changed for another sentry, and till I gives the signal. I'll whistle for you the old boat-horn tune that's carried you many a long night along the Congaree — you remember? Well, when you hear that you may know that the sentry's changed. Then watch the time, and when the t'other sentinel draws off toward the horses, you can crawl through them gum-bushes on all fours and git into the bay. As for the horse, I'm jub'ous there's no getting one easy. They'll make too much trampling. But I'll meet you on t'other side of the bay, and bring you a pistol, or sword, or whatever I can find."

"Well, well! You bring the sword and pistol. It'll be mighty hard, where there's so many, if I can't find the nag myself."

"Work your hands," said the landlord.

"They're free! they're free!" was the exulting response of the scout, almost too loudly expressed for prudence.

"Hush, for God's sake! and don't halloo until you're out of the bush. Take the knife now in your own hands, and cut loose your feet. But you must lie quiet, and let the ropes rest jest where they are. Make b'lieve you're asleep till you hear my whistle, and then crawl off as if you were all belly, and wriggle away as quiet as a blacksnake. I must leave you now. It's a'most time for Ben Geiger to get back."

The scout did not await a second suggestion to apply the keen edge of the hunter's knife, which the landlord furnished him, to the cords which fastened his feet. These he drew up repeatedly with the satisfaction of one who is pleased to exercise and enjoy the unexpected liberty which he receives; but the suggestions of the landlord, which were certainly those of common sense, warned him to limit these exercises, and restrain his impatient members, till the time should arrive for using them with advantage. He accordingly composed himself and them, in such a manner as to preserve the appearance of restraint; arranged the perfect portions of the ropes above his ankles, and tucked in the several ends between and below. Then, passing his hands behind him, as before, he lay on his back outstretched with all the commendable patience of a stoic philosopher awaiting the operations of that fate with which he holds it folly if not impertinence to interfere.

The landlord, meanwhile, had resumed the duties of the sentinel, and was pacing the measured ground with the regularity of a veteran, and the firm step of one who is conscious of no failure of duty. The scout's eyes naturally turned upon him with an expression of greatly increased regard.

"Well," said he, in a mental soliloquy, "I was half jub'ous I'd have to lick Muggs over agin, before he could be brought to a reasonable way of thinking. I was mightily afeard that he only had half an onderstanding of the truth when I gin him that hoist on the Wateree; but it's a God's providence that orders all things, in his blessed mercy, for the best, and lets one licking answer for a stout man's convarsion. I'm jub'ous, if Muggs hadn't ha' lost one arm in the wars, if he would have onderstood the liberties we're fighting for half so easily. Liberty's a difficult thing to be onderstood at first. It takes mighty hard knocks and a heap of thinking, to make it stand out cl'ar in the daylight; and then it's never half so cl'ar, or half so sweet, as when there's some danger that we're going to lose it for ever, for good and all. If ever I wanted to teach a friend of mine how to believe in the reason of liberty, I'd jis lock him up in a good strong jail for three months, or mou't be six, put on a hitch of ploughline on hands and legs, and then argy with him to show that God made a mighty great mistake when he gin a man a pair of feet and a pair of hands, when he might see for himself that he could sleep in the stumps at both ends and never feel the want of 'em. But there comes Ben Geiger, I suppose, and I must lie as if my legs were stumps only. Lord! I'll show 'em another sort of argyment as soon as Isaac gives that old Congaree whistle. It's only some twenty steps to the wood, and I reckon it can't be much more to the bay, for the airth looks as if it wanted to sink mighty sudden. These chaps round me snort very loud—that's a sign, I've always hearn, of sound sleeping. I don't much mind the resk of getting off to the bay; but I'm getting too fat about the ribs to walk a long way in this hot weather. Noise or no noise, I must pick out one of them nags for the journey. Let 'em snort. I don't much mind pistol-bullets when they fly by night at a running horseman. They're like them that shoot 'em. They make a great bellowing, but they can't see. Let 'em snort; but ef I work my own legs this night, it'll be to pick out the best nag in that gang, and use him by way of preference."

Time moved very slowly, in the estimation of the anxious scout. Ben Geiger, the sentry, had resumed his watch and walk. Muggs had disappeared, and solemn was the silence that once more prevailed over the encampment. Two full hours had elapsed since the limbs of Bannister had been unloosed, and still he waited for the signal which was to apprize him that the moment for their use was at hand. But it came out at last, the long wailing note, such as soothes the heart with sweet melancholy, untwisted from the core of the long rude wooden bugle of the Congaree boatman, as he winds his way upon the waters of that rapid rushing river. The drowsy relief-guard soon followed, and Ben Geiger disappeared to enjoy that luxury of sleep from which his successor was scarcely yet entirely free. He rubbed his eyes and yawned audibly while moving to and fro with unsteady step along the beaten limits of his round. His drowsy appearance gave increased encouragement to the woodsman. But even this was not necessary to impart confidence to so cool a temper, so cheerful a spirit, and so adroit a scout. The sentry had looked upon the prisoner and the horses in the presence of the guard when Geiger was relieved. Satisfied that all was safe, he had started upon his march; and, giving sufficient time to the guard to resume their own slumbers, Jack Bannister now prepared himself for his movement.

This event, which would have been of great importance, and perhaps of trying danger to most persons in his situation, was really of little consequence in his eyes. With the release of his hands and feet he regarded the great difficulty as fully at an end. The risk of pistol-shot, as we have seen from his soliloquy, he considered a very small one. Besides, it was a risk of the war in which he was engaged, and one which he had incurred a hundred times before. On foot, he well knew that he could surpass the best runner of the Indian tribes, and once in the thick bay which was contiguous, he could easily conceal himself beyond the apprehension of cavalry. If he had any anxiety at all, it was on the subject of choosing a horse from the cluster that were attached to the swinging limbs of the adjacent oaks. He felt that, with the opportunity before him, and with choice allowed, it was incumbent upon him to choose with reference to his reputation no less than to his escape. To choose an inferior brute, having the pick of the best, would have argued greatly against the understanding of the scout, and would have filled his soul with a bitter sense of mortification. But hear him, as he deliberates, and you will be satisfied that he is not the person to throw away a good chance, and disregard the value of a proper choice.

"There's a dark bay, I'm thinking, that, as well as I can make out in the moonlight, is about the best. The black is a monstrous stout animal, but too high and heavy for the sand roads. The gray is a little too showy for a scout that ought to love the shade better than the sunshine. I reckon I'll resk the bay. He ain't too heavy, and he ain't too low. He has legs enough for his body, and his body looks well on his legs. He'll *do*, and if I could only take the saddle from the black and clap it on the bay, I'd be a made horseman. It's a prime English saddle, and I reckon the holsters don't want for filling. It's mighty tempting, but——"

A favorable opportunity for making a movement now suggesting itself, his soliloquy was cut short. The scout had his eyes all around him. The sentinel's back was toward him, and he commenced his progress. To the citizen, uninformed in the artifices of Indian warfare, the mode of operations adopted and pursued by our scout, would have been one of curious contemplation and study. It is probable that such a person, though looking directly at the object, would have been slow to discern its movements, so sly, so unimposing, so shadowy as they were. With the flexibility of a snake the body of our scout seemed to slide away almost without the assistance of hands and feet. No obvious motion betrayed his progress, not the slightest rustling in the grass, nor the faintest crumpling of the withered leaf of the previous autumn. His escape was favored by the gray garments which he wore, which mixed readily with the misty shadows of the night and forest. Amid their curtaining umbrage it was now impossible for the sentinel to perceive him while pursuing his rounds; and, aware of this, he paused behind one of the trees on the edge of the encampment, and gently elevating his head, surveyed the path which he had traversed. He could still distinguish the sounds of sleep from several groups of his enemies. The moonlight was glinted back from more than one steel cap and morion, which betrayed the proximity of the Black Riders. There lay Stockton, and Darcy, and the rest of that fearful band whose pathway had been traced in blood along the Congaree and Saluda. More than one of the associates of the scout had fallen by their felon hands. Well might Jack Bannister grind his teeth together as he surveyed them. How easy, with their own broadswords, to make his way, even at little hazard to himself, over severed necks and shoulders spouting with their gore.

The feeling was natural to the man, but for an instant only. Bannister dismissed it with a shudder; and turning warily in another direction, he proceeded to put in execution his design of choosing the best horse from among the group, for the purpose of making his flight as agreeable to himself, and as costly to his enemies, as was possible. Circumstances seemed to favor him, but he never forewent his usual caution. He proceeded with sufficient gentleness, and produced no more disturbance among the animals than they habitually occasioned among themselves. His closer examination into their respective qualities confirmed the judgment which he had previously formed while watching them from a distance. The dark bay was the steed that promised best service, and he succeeded with little difficulty in detaching him from the bough to which he was fastened.

To bring him forth from the group, so as to throw the rest between himself and the sentinel's line of sight, was a task not much more difficult; and but little more was necessary to enable our adventurous scout to lead him down the hillside into the recesses of the bay, in the shade of which he could mount him without exposure, and dart off with every probability of easy escape.

But courage and confidence are very apt to produce audacity in the conduct of a man of much experience; and our scout yearned for the fine English saddle and holsters which were carried by the black. Dropping the bridle of his bay, therefore, over a slender hickory shoot, he stole back to the group, and proceeded to strip the black of his appendages. But, whether the animal had some suspicions that all was not right in this nocturnal proceeding, or was indignant at the preference which the scout had given in favor of his companion over himself, it is certain that he resented the liberties taken by the intruder in a manner that threatened to be more fatal to the fugitive than all the pistols of the encampment. He proceeded by kicking and biting to prove his jealousy and dislike, and this so effectually, as to make it a somewhat difficult matter for the scout to effect his extrication from the group, all of whom were more or less restiff, and prepared to retort upon the black the sundry assaults which, in his random fury, he had inflicted upon them.

This led to a commotion which attracted the attention of the sentinel; and his challenge, and evident approach, compelled Bannister to discard his caution and betake himself with all expedition to the steed which he had captured. He darted forward accordingly, and the sharp bang of the pistol followed his appearance on the back of the steed. This, though it awakened only the merriment of the fugitive, aroused the whole encampment. There was no time for contemplation;—none for the expected conference with the landlord. Bannister knew this. He cast an instinctive glance to the northern heavens, as if seeking for their guiding star, then pricking his steed with the point of his knife, dashed away with a hurry-scurry through the woods that defied their intricacies, and seemed to laugh at the vain shouts and clamor of the Black Riders, who were seeking to subdue to order, with the view to pursuit, their now unmanageable horses.

The circumstance that had led to the discovery of Bannister's flight, availed somewhat to diminish the dangers of the chase. Before the refractory steeds could be quieted, and the dragoons on the track of his flight, the tread of his horse's heels was lost entirely to their hearing. They scattered themselves, nevertheless, among the woods, but were soon recalled from a pursuit which promised to be fruitless; while Bannister, drawing up his steed when he no longer heard the clamors of his pursuers, coolly paused for a while to deliberate upon the circumstances of his situation. But a few moments seemed necessary to arrive at a resolution, and, once more tickling his horse's flanks with the point of his knife, he buried himself from sight in the deepest recesses of the forest.

## CHAPTER XXVI.

### SHADOWS AND STRAWS UPON THE SURFACE.

THE excitement at the Middleton barony was succeeded by something of a calm; but not its usual calm. It had now other tenants than those whose quality and sex had maintained its peace along with its purity. The chief of the outlaws, attended closely by his faithful adherent, Watson Gray, was still its inmate; and there was yet another stranger, in the person of a nice, dapper surgeon's assistant, to whom Rawdon had given the wounded man in charge. This young gentleman was named Hillhouse. He was clever enough in his profession. He could take off a leg in the twinkling of an eye; but he was one of that unfortunate class of smart young persons who aim at universal cleverness. There was no object too high for his ambition, and, unhappily, none too low. He philosophized when philosophy was on the tapis, and

"Hear him but reason in divinity,"

you would have fancied the British camp was the very house of God, and the assistant surgeon the very happiest exponent of the designs of Providence. He talked poetry by the canto, and felicitated himself on the equal taste with which he enjoyed Butler and Cowley — the antipodes of English poets. But, perhaps, his happiest achievement was in the threading of a needle; and to see him in this performance was productive of a degree of amusement, if not real pleasure, which could neither be described easily nor well estimated. His adroitness was truly wonderful. Armed with the sharpened thread in one hand, and the needle in the other—his lips working the while with singular indefatigableness—his left foot firmly planted in the foreground, his right thrown back, and poised upon the toe;—and he laughed to scorn the difficulty which the doubtful eye of the needle seemed to offer to his own. His genius, though universal, lay eminently this way. He had the most marvellous nicety of finger in threading needles that ever was possessed by mortal. Unhappily, he was not satisfied with a distinction so notable. He was a universal genius, and aimed at all sorts of distinction. He would discourse of war, and manœuvre armies, so as to confound Hannibal and circumvent Scipio; and, while insisting upon his paramount excellence as a surgeon, was yet perpetually deploring that sacrifice of his better uses and endowments, which the profession required him to make. Convention had done something toward other developments and desires of our subject. He was a gallant, no less than a genius —was ambitious of the reputation of a *roué*, and, according to his own account, had achieved some of the most wonderful conquests among the sex, in spite of the most eminent rivals. His complaisance was prodigious, in respect to the tender gender; and when he considered how hopeless it was, in one man, to attempt to render all happy, he deplored the fate which had made him irresistible, and regretted that but a single life was allowed to execute all the desires even of universal genius. How he pitied the fair, frail creatures who were compelled to hunger hopelessly. He would willingly have had himself cut up in little for their sakes, could the ubiquitous attributes of his mind have availed for the several subdivisions of his body; but, as this could not well be done, he could only sigh for their privations.

Fancy, with such complaisance, the person of the ugliest "Greathead" in existence—a man, with a short neck, head round as a bullet, eyes like goggles, and a nose as sharp as a penknife; a mouth which could hold a pippin, and was constantly on the stretch as if desiring one. Fancy, yet farther, such a person in the house with a woman like Flora Middleton, smirking indulgently upon that damsel, and readily mistaking the cool contempt with which she regarded him, as only a natural expression of that wonder which his presence must naturally inspire in a country-girl—and it will not be difficult to anticipate some of the scenes which took place between them whenever it was the fortune of the gallant to be thrown into company with the maiden.

Mr. Hillhouse was too provident of time in all matters, to suffer any of his talents to remain unemployed, when he could arrange it otherwise. Love-making was regarded as one of these. It was not with him a matter of passion or of sentiment. He had not a single sensibility at work. It was simply as an accomplishment, and as an exercise for his accomplishments, that he condescended to smile upon the fair, and to confer those affections which he otherwise affected to solicit. He himself had no affections—perhaps such a creature never has. He was deficient in that earnestness of character without which the sensibilities are forms rather than substances—the shows of things which only delude, and never satisfy the desires of the mind. He had scarcely seen Flora Middleton before he had planned her conquest. While examining the wounds of Morton, in connection with the head surgeon, he was turning over in his mind, and framing the words of that salutation which he was to address, on the first occasion, to the young lady. It was not many hours after Rawdon's departure, before he commenced his operations. The breakfast-table was the scene. Mrs. Middleton, whom the fatigues and alarms of the night had overcome, was not present; and, looking sad and unhappy, Flora took her seat at the coffee-board.

Mr. Watson Gray and Mr. Hillhouse appeared at the first summons, though the latter did not seem conscious that the room was blessed with any other presence than his own, and that other with whom he condescended to converse. Watson Gray, with sufficient good sense, smiled, took his seat, and said nothing beyond what was required of good breeding. But the surgeon had reached a period in life, when it seemed to him a duty to display himself, and satisfy his companions of his ability to bring out others. Rawdon had said to him, when designating him for the duty of taking care of Morton—"Now, don't make a fool of yourself, Hillhouse;" and Majoribanks, in his hearing, had commented on the counsel, by the remark—"It is almost the only thing that he can not help doing." But neither speech served to restrain a vanity whose ebullitions were habitual; and the young surgeon began to prattle, as soon as the heiress made her appearance. The events of the night, the military movements of the dawn, and the beauty of the morn which succeeded, furnished him with ample topics. He was in hope that the "spirit-stirring drum and ear-piercing fife," and so forth, had not vexed too greatly the slumbers of Miss Middleton;—a wish that the young lady answered with a grave nod, and an assurance which her countenance belied, that she never felt better in all her life. The weather, the never-failing topic, enabled him to dilate copiously from the poets—Milton being the first at hand —with an almost literal description.

"A most lovely morning, Miss Middleton! In this beautiful country, you may be said to realize the truth of Milton's description of another region." Hemming thrice, to relieve himself from an obstruction in the throat which he did not feel, he proceeded, in a sort of chant, to give the beautiful address of Eve to Adam—beginning:—

> "Sweet is the breath of morn, her rising sweet
> With charm of earliest birds," &c., &c.

But nothing could exceed the unction of his look and gesture, when, approaching the conclusion of the passage, he betrayed by his look, tone, and action, the true reason why the selection had been made, and the application which he sought to give to its closing sentence:—

> 'But neither breath of morn, when she ascends
> With charm of earliest birds; nor rising sun,
> On this delightful land; nor herb, tree, flower,
> Glistening with dew; nor fragrance after showers;
> Nor grateful evening mild; nor silent night
> With this her solemn bird; nor walk by moon
> Or glittering starlight, *without thee is sweet*."

Women very soon discern when they have to deal with a fool. At another time, and under other circumstances, Flora might have amused herself with the harmless monster; but she forebore, and quietly replied:—

"In truth, sir, your selection is very appropriate. The description, at this season of the day and year, is very correct, when applied to our Congaree country. One would almost fancy that Milton had been thinking of us. At least, our self-complaisance may well take the liberty of applying his verses as we please. But, sir, do tell me how your patient is."

This was all said with the most indifferent, matter-of-fact manner in the world. The answer to the inquiry was lost in the professional knowledge which enveloped it. A long, scientific jargon ensued, on the subject of wounds in general; then followed an analysis of the several kinds of wounds—gun-shot, rifle, sabre, pike, bayonet, bill, bludgeon—wounds in the head and the hip, the shoulder and the leg, the neck and the abdomen.

"But of all wounds, Miss Middleton, I feel at this moment more than ever convinced that the most fatal are those which are inflicted upon the human heart."

This was followed by a glance of the most inimitable tenderness, while the hand of the speaker rested upon the region, the susceptibilities of which were alleged to be so paramount.

"Your opinion, sir," said the young lady, with becoming gravity, "is confirmed by all that I ever heard on the subject. Indeed, sir, our overseer, who is an excellent judge in such matters, and who was at one time the only butcher in Charleston—prefers shooting a steer through the heart always, in preference to the head. He asserts that while death is certain to follow the hurt in the one region, it is a very frequent circumstance that the hardness of the other renders it impenetrable to the bullet, unless the aim be very good and the distance be very small. But you, sir, ought to be the best judge of the correctness of this opinion."

Watson Gray made considerable effort to suppress the grin which rose in spite of himself to his visage. The scout perceived, in an instant, the latent sarcasm in the reply of the damsel; but the young surgeon was innocent of any unnecessary understanding; and as she kept her countenance with praiseworthy gravity, he was rather led to conclude that her simplicity was of a kind somewhat bordering on fatuity.

"Verily," he thought to himself, "this is a mere rustic; she has seen nothing of the world; lived always in a state of pure simplicity; totally unsophisticated. I shall have but little trouble with her."

With this reflection, he proceeded with great dignity to offer some objections to the opinion of the overseer, to all of which Flora Middleton assented with the air of one who is anxious to get rid of a wearisome person or subject.

But the surgeon was not to be shaken off so easily, and every question which she found it necessary to propose, however simple or little calculated to provoke dilation, only had the effect of bringing about the same results. The same jargon filled her ears—the same inflated style of compliment offended her taste; and, in answer to the third or fourth inquiry as to the condition of his patient, he assured her that "Wounds were either fatal or they were not. Death might follow the prick of a needle, while a man has been known to survive even a puncture of the heart itself;"—here followed another significant glance at the lady;—"but," he continued, with the air of a man who declares the law, "while there is life there is hope.—Hope, as we are told by our little poet of Twickenham, 'hope springs eternal in the human breast;' and the last person, Miss Middleton, whom hope should ever desert, should be the surgeon. So many have been the marvellous cures which the art of man has effected, that he should despair of nothing. Nothing, you know, is impossible with Providence—perhaps, I should say, with art; for many have been its successes, which ignorance has falsely and foolishly attributed to miraculous interposition. Miracles, Miss Middleton, are not common things. I am of opinion, though I would not have you suppose me skeptical or irreligious, that a great many events are represented as miraculous which owe their occurrence to natural and ordinary laws. There was an instance—it came under my own observation in the island of Jamaica——"

"Pardon me, sir, if you please, but if your patient can longer spare your presence, mine can not. I am to understand you, then, as of opinion that Mr. Conway can only survive by what is ordinarily considered a miracle; but which, I am to believe, will be then wholly ascribable to your professional skill?"

"I reckon, Miss Middleton," said Watson Gray, rising from the table as he spoke, " that Mr. Conway stands a good chance of getting over it. He's got some ugly cuts, but he hasn't much fever, and I don't think any of the wounds touch the vital parts. I've seen a good many worse hurts in my time, and though I'm no doctor, yet I think he'll get over it by good nursing and watching."

Mr. Hillhouse was greatly confounded by this interposition. His eyebrows were elevated as Watson Gray went on, and he permitted himself to exhibit just sufficient interest in the interruption as to wheel his chair half round, and take a cool, contemptuous look at the speaker. The latter did not wait for reply or refutation; and the simple directness of what he said was sufficiently conclusive to Flora, who rose also, and — the the gentlemen having finished breakfast — prepared to leave the room. But Mr. Hillhouse was not willing to suffer this movement. He had still more knowledge to display.

"Do not be deceived by this person, Miss Middleton — a very cool person, certainly, not wanting in presumption — a strange person; I should judge him to be the overseer of whom you have spoken."

"No, sir; I only know him as one of the friends of Mr. Conway."

"Ah! a friend of Mr. Conway — a very strange selection. There is nothing about which gentlemen should be so careful as the choice of friends. A friend is a man———"

"Excuse me, sir, — but may I beg your attention, at your earliest leisure, in the chamber of the young woman? Her delirium seems to be increasing."

"It will give me pleasure to obey your requisitions, Miss Middleton; but let me warn you against forming your judgment, upon the subject of Mr. Conway's condition, from the report of this person — this overseer of yours. I doubt not that he is an excellent butcher, Miss Middleton; but, surely it is obvious to you that the art of taking life, and that of saving it, are very different arts. Now, I suspect that he could tell very nearly, as well as myself, what degree of force it would be necessary to use in felling a bullock, but the question how to bring the same bullock to life again———"

"Is surely one that is better answered by yourself, and I should consult you, sir, were it ever necessary, in preference to everybody else."

The surgeon bowed at the compliment, and with undiminished earnestness, and more directness than usual, returned to his subject, if subject he may be said to have who amalgamated all subjects so happily together.

"Mr. Conway, Miss Middleton, is not so bad as he might be, and is a great deal worse, I am disposed to think, than he wishes himself to be. His wounds are not deadly, though he may die of them; yet, though life itself be but a jest, I must consider them serious. This overseer of yours is right in some things; though, I suspect, he only reports my own remarks to Lord Rawdon, made this morning, ere his lordship took his departure. I told his lordship that I considered the case doubtful, as all maladies must be considered; for you know that there is no certainty in life, but death. He has fever, and that is unfavorable; but as he has little fever, that is favorable. In short, if he does not suffer a great change for the worse, I trust that he will get better. Nay, I may admit that I have hopes of it, though no certainties. The surgeon who speaks of certainties, in such matters, is— pardon me, Miss Middleton — little better than a fool."

"I thank you, sir; you have really enlightened me on many subjects. I am very much obliged to you. You must have seen a great deal of the world, sir."

This was said with an air of very great simplicity. It completely deceived the complacent surgeon.

"The world! Miss Middleton, I have sounded it everywhere. I have basked on the banks of the Niger; I have meditated at the foot of the pyramids; have taken my chibouque with a pacha, and eaten sandwiches with the queen of Hungary. I have travelled far, toiled much; spent five years in India, as many in the West Indies, two in South America; and yet, you see me here in South Carolina, still nothing more than second-surgeon to a little army of less than five thousand men, commanded by a general who — but no matter! Lord Rawdon is a good soldier, Miss Middleton — as the world goes — but, burn me! a very poor judge of good associates."

"You must have left your maternal ties at a very early period, to have travelled so far, and seen so much."

"Apron strings" softened into "maternal ties," did not offend the surgeon's sensibilities.

"A mere boy, Miss Middleton; but it is surprising how rapidly a person acquires knowledge, who starts early in pursuit of it. Besides, travelling itself is a delight—a great delight—it would do you good to travel. Perhaps, were you to go abroad for a single year, you would feel less surprised at the extent of my acquisitions."

"Indeed, sir, do you really think so?"

"I do—'pon my honor I do. Your place here is a very fine one. You have, I understand, some ten thousand acres in this estate—'the Old Barony' it's called—slaves in sufficient number to cultivate it, and really everything remarkably attractive and pleasant. I can very well understand how it is that you should not care to leave it even for a season: but if you only knew what a joy travelling is—to go here and go there—see this thing and that—be asked to this fête and that palace—and know that the whole gay world is looking for your presence and depending on your smile; if you only knew this, Miss Middleton, you'd give up your acres and your slaves, your barony and all its oaks; think them all flat, stale, and unprofitable—you'd——"

"Oh, sir, excuse me. You are too eloquent. If I remain longer, I shall be persuaded to go; and I must go in order to remain. Good morning, sir. I trust that you will devote your earliest leisure to the poor young woman."

The surgeon bent and bowed almost to the ground, while his hand was pressed to his lips with the air of exquisite refinement which distinguished that period. The dandy is clearly human. All ages have possessed the creature under one guise or another. The Roman, the Greek, the Egyptian, the Hebrew, all the Asiatics, the English, and the French, have all borne testimony to their existence; and, perhaps, there is no dandy half so ultra in his styles as the Cherokee or the Chickasaw. Nature and art both declare his existence and recognise his pretensions. In this point of view common sense can urge no objections to him.

He clearly has an allotted place in life; and like the wriggling worm that puts on a purple jacket and golden wings, though we may wonder at the seeming waste of so much wealth, we can not deny its distribution, and must suppose that the insect has its uses, however unapparent. The exquisite may stand in the same relation to the human species as the jay or the peacock among the birds. These teach the vanity of their costume while displaying it: as the man of sense learns to avoid the folly, even in degree, which is yet the glory of the fool.

"Charming creature!" exclaimed the dandy, yawning, and throwing himself backward on the cushions of the huge sofa, which stood temptingly contiguous—"Charming creature! She deserves some painstaking. Her person is not fine, but her lands are; her beauties are few, but her slaves are many. She is rather simple, perhaps; but, gad, my soul! he is hard indeed to satisfy whom these fine grounds, excellent mansion, good lands, charming groves, and balmy atmosphere would not reconcile to any sacrifices. We must make it, some day or other, all of us; and though, Augustus Hillhouse, be thou not too nice! Already hast thou suffered many a choice fleshly dainty to slip through thy fingers because of thy fastidious stomach. Beware! Thou art wasting time which is precious. Age will come upon thee! Age! ah!"—with a shiver—"it will need fine mansion, and noble park, and goodly income, to reconcile that to thy philosophy. 'In the days of thy youth,' saith the proverb. I will take counsel of it in season. The damsel's worth some painstaking, and the sacrifice is not without its reward. But such a gown and stomacher as she wears! I must amend all that. There is also an absence of finish in the manner, which too decidedly betrays the rustic. Her voice, too, has a twang—a certain peasant-like sharpness, which grates harshly upon the ear. But these things may be amended!—yes, they may be amended. I must amend them, certainly, before I can commit myself among my friends; for what would Lady Bell, who is a belle no longer, say to such a bodice, such a stomacher, and, above all, to a carriage which shows a degree of vigor so utterly foreign to good breeding. I must teach her languor, and that will be the worst task of all, for it will require exertion. She must learn to lounge with grace, to sigh with a faint-like softness, to open her eyes as if she were about to shut them, and, when she speaks, to let her words slide out through the tips of her lips as if she were striving all she could, short of positive effort, to keep them in. Ah, charming Bell! sweet Lady Charlotte! and thou, dearest of all the dears, fair Moncrieff!—could this barony-girl grow wise in those things in which ye are so excellent, how much lovelier were she than all of ye! Ye are landless, sweet ladies—and therefore ye are loveless. These acres weigh heavily against your charms. Augustus Hillhouse, be not foolish in thy fastidiousness. Take the fruits which the gods bestow upon thee, and quarrel not with the bounty because of the too much red upon the apple. It is a good fruit, and the red may be reconciled, in due season, to a becoming delicacy."

The dandy soliloquized at greater length, but neither his euphuism nor his philosophy finds much favor in our sight. We are not of that class of writers who delight in such detail, and we shall not, accordingly—and this omission may surprise the fashionable reader—furnish the usual inventory of Mr. Hillhouse's dress and wardrobe. Enough that it was ample even for his purposes, and enabled him to provide a change, and a different color, for every day in the month. He had his purple and his violet, his green and his ombre, the one was for the day of his valor, the other for his sentiment, the third for his love-sadness, and the fourth for his feeling of universal melancholy. We shall only say, that his violet was worn at his first interview with Flora Middleton.

While his head ran upon his marriage, a measure which he had now certainly resolved upon, it was also occupied with certain incidental and equally important topics, such as the dress which should be worn on such occasion—for the day of his marriage was the only day he had never before provided for—and the subsequent disposition of the goods and chattels which he was to take possession of with his wife. Stretched at length upon the cushions, with one leg thrown over an arm of the sofa, and the other resting upon the floor, his head raised upon the pillows, which had been drawn from both extremities for this purpose—his eyes half shut in dreamy languor, and his lips gently moving as he whispered over the several heads of topics which engaged his reflection; he was suddenly aroused by hearing the fall of a light footstep behind him. At first he fancied that it might be one of the servants, but a negro is usually a heavy-heeled personage, who makes his importance felt upon the floor, if nowhere else; and when, in the next moment, Mr. Augustus Hillhouse remembered this peculiarity in his nature, he fancied that the intruder could be no other than the fair rustic whose acres he was then disposing of with the most mercantile facility. Nothing could be more natural than that she should very soon find her way back to the spot where it was possible to find him.

Under this impression, he started to his feet with an air of well-practised confusion; and having been at some pains to throw into his countenance an excess of sweetness and sensibility, he turned his eyes, as he fancied, upon the fair intruder, to meet — not the lady of his love, nor one of the gentler sex at all — but a man, and such a man!

Never was creature so wofully confounded as our young gallant. The person who encountered his glance, though but for an instant only, was the very picture of terror — gaunt terror — lean misery, dark and cold ferocity. Clothed in the meanest homespun of the country, and that in tatters, the tall, skeleton form of a man, stood in the doorway, evidently receding from the apartment. In his eyes there was the expression of a vacant anger — something of disappointment and dislike — a look of surprise and dissatisfaction. In his hand, at the moment of his disappearance, Mr. Hillhouse fancied that he saw the sudden shine of steel. But he was so completely confounded by the apparition that he was for a few moments utterly incapable of speech; and when he did speak, the spectre disappeared.

"Who are you, and what do you want?" was the shivering inquiry which he made. A savage grin was the only answer of the stranger, and the next instant the surgeon stood alone.

"The devil, to be sure!" he exclaimed; but, recovering his courage, he darted after his strange visiter. He rushed into the passage-way — out into the porch — ran down the steps, looked out into the court — but in vain. He could see nobody. Even the sentinels, whom he knew to have been placed at the portals, front and rear, were withdrawn; and no object more suspicious than a lame negro met his eye in the whole range of vision that lay within it. He re-entered the house, more than ever satisfied that he had been favored with a visit from a personage whose intimacy implies brimstone and other combustibles; and a sudden resolution to resume his duties, and see at once into the condition of his patients, whom he began to think he had too long neglected, was the result of his supernatural visitation.

The first object of his care was the person of the outlaw—not because of his superior claims, or worse condition, but simply because he felt his nerves too much agitated to encounter the young lady in whose presence it was necessary to practise that nice and deliberate precision of tone and manner, language and address, which form the first great essentials of successful sentiment, in all ages, when dealing with the sex. Regarding Watson Gray as a mere circumstance in a large collection of dependencies—a sort of hanging-peg, or resting-point, a mounting-block, or a shoe-tie in the grand relationships of society—he had no scruple at exhibiting his real emotions in his presence; and he poured forth to the cooler and more rational scout the intelligence of which he was possessed.

Gray regarded the surgeon as a fool, but had no reason to suppose that he was a liar. He saw no reason to doubt that he had seen somebody, and concluded that his alarm had somewhat magnified the terrors of what he saw. But his description of the costume worn by the visiter was so precise and particular, that he well knew that neither the fears nor the follies of the other could have caused his invention of it; and, with graver looks than he himself was aware of, he descended instantly to the lower story.

There he found the sentinels, each at his post, and they swore they had been so from the beginning. This one circumstance led the scout to think more lightly of the surgeon's story; but there was still something in the description which had been given him that he could not dismiss from his consideration. He searched the immediate neighborhood of the premises, but without discovering anything to awaken his suspicions. *He* saw nothing; but a keen watchful eye followed *his* progress, every step which he made, along the avenue.

The father of Mary Clarkson had survived the conflict of the preceding night. It was his spectre which had so fearfully alarmed the contemplative surgeon. He had good reason for his alarm. His sudden movement alone, which enabled the vindictive old man to discern the slight popinjay person of the surgeon, saved him from the sharp edge of the uplifted knife. The *couteau de chasse* of the woodman — an instrument not unlike the modern bowie-knife — had, at one moment, nearly finished the daydreams of Mr. Hillhouse and his life together.

Finding nothing in his search like the object described, Watson Gray was disposed to think that the surgeon had seen one of the soldiers on duty, who had probably found his way into the mansion with the view of employing his eyes or his fingers — for the moral sense of the invading army, officers and soldiers, does not seem to have been very high; but this idea was combated by the fact that Hillhouse had been for many years, himself, a member of the British army, and knew, as well as anybody, the costume of its several commands. The nervous excitement of the surgeon, which was not overcome when Gray returned to the chamber, was another argument against this notion. But a new light broke in upon Watson Gray when he remembered the ancient superstition along the Congaree.

"You've seen the ghost of the cassique," he said, with a conclusive shake of the head; "old Middleton walks, they say. I've heard it a hundred times. He used to wear homespun and a hunting-shirt — though I never heard it was ragged — and the big knife and rifle were never out of his hands. The Congaree Indians used to call him King Big Knife, and, sure enough, he made it work among the red skins whenever they came about his quarters and didn't carry themselves rightly. He was a most famous hunter; and, between the bears and the savages, the knife and rifle had very little rest with him. I reckon it's him you've seen, though it's something strange for a ghost to walk in broad daytime."

The surgeon was not entirely satisfied with this explanation;

not because it seemed very unreasonable, but simply because it clashed with his habitual philosophy.

"Ah, my good friend," he exclaimed patronizingly, "I see you labor under some very vulgar errors. The belief in ghosts is entirely done away with. Ghosts, like continental money, had their value only so long as the people had their credulity. The moment you doubt, the ghosts disappear, and the money is rejected. They found credit only among a simple people and in the early stages of society. As philosophy—divine not crabbed, as dull fools suppose—as philosophy began to shed her beams upon the world"——&c.

Watson Gray had already ceased to listen, and we may as well follow his example. Talking still, however, while working about the wounds of his patient, the surgeon at length awakened another voice; and the faint, but coherent words of the outlaw, summoned the scout to his bedside.

"Where am I?—what does all this mean, Gray?"

But the surgeon interfered, and for five minutes expatiated on the great danger to a patient situated as he was, in using his own, or hearing the voice of any but his professional attendant.

"Nothing, my good sir, can be more injurious to the nervous system, particularly where there is any tendency upward—any mounting of the blood to the brain! I have known numberless instances where the results have been fatal, even of the most trifling conversation. Once in India, a colonel of cavalry, as brave a fellow as ever lived—Monckton—a noble fellow—dressed like a prince—won every woman he looked at, and was happy in never being made to marry any—he suffered from a gunshot wound, got in a desperate charge which he made at the head of his regiment, upon the native troops. The rajah himself fell—and my poor friend Monckton——"

"Pshaw!" feebly exclaimed the outlaw, but with an emphasis and manner sufficiently marked to be offensive.

"Pshaw! pshaw! sir—do you mean 'pshaw!' sir, an epithet of contempt, or——"

The wounded man interrupted him—

"Pray, my good sir, be silent for a moment, while I hear what my friend says. Come hither, Gray."

"I warn you, sir—I wash my hands of the responsibility!" exclaimed the now indignant surgeon. "Pshaw! pshaw!—and to me!"

"Gray, can't you turn that fool fellow from the room?" said Morton, in a tone which was only inaudible to Hillhouse from the feebleness of the speaker. But no such steps were necessary. The indignant surgeon availed himself of the moment to obey the requisition of Miss Middleton, and visit his other patient: and the outlaw and his subordinate were left undisturbed to a long, and, to them, not an uninteresting conference.

This conference had relation to many events and interests which do not affect the progress of this narrative, and do not accordingly demand our attention; but we may add, that no portion of the intelligence which Watson Gray brought his commander was of half the interest, in his mind, as those events which we have previously related, in the occurrences of Brier Park, after the moment of Edward Morton's insensibility.

"That I live at all is almost miraculous," was the remark of the outlaw; "for I had goaded him"—meaning his brother—"almost to desperation, and when my hand failed me I looked for death."

"But why do this?" was the earnest inquiry of Gray; "why, when so much was at stake? I thought you had made it your chief care, and believed it your correct policy, particularly as concerns Miss Flora, to keep him in the dark. Why tell him all—why goad him with this knowledge?"

"So it was my policy, and so I had resolved; but the devil and my own passions drove me to do it; and some other feelings which I could not well account for. Hate, hate, hate! was at the bottom of all, and I suppose I needed blood-letting."

"You have had it—enough of it."

"Ay, but I live in spite of it, Watson Gray, and I feel that I shall still live. I shall not die this bout—not while I am here —here in the same house with *her*, and while all things below are, as you tell me, ripe and favorable. This alone is enough to cure wounds thrice as numerous and thrice as deep as mine. I am here with her, and let me but use these limbs once more, and the victory and the prize are mine. I will wear them, Watson

Gray, with a savage joy which shall find triumph in a thousand feelings which confer anything but joy. She shall know, and he shall know, what it is to have felt with feelings such as mine."

The outlaw sank backward from exhaustion, and Watson Gray found it necessary to enforce the suggestions of the surgeon, and to impose upon the speaker that restraint which his weakness showed to be more than ever necessary. This was a difficult task; the outlaw being impatient to hear particulars, and dilate upon hopes and passions, which filled all the secret avenues of his soul with joy! It was only by warning him of the danger of defeating everything by tasking his powers prematurely, that he was subdued to silence; but his lips still worked with his desire to speak, and while he lay with shut eyes upon his couch, almost fainting with exhaustion, his heart heaved with the exulting images which fancy had already arrayed before his mind, in preparing his contemplated triumph. That triumph included the possession of Flora Middleton, and his escape with her, and other treasures, only less valuable in his own estimation, and of far greater value in that of his confederate. Already he was dreaming of groves in the West Indian islands; of a safe retreat from the snares of enemies; and of the possession of those charms which had equally warmed his mind and his passions. Dreaming, he slept; and Watson Gray availed himself of his repose to snatch a brief hour of oblivion from the same auspicious influence.

## CHAPTER XXVII.

#### GUILT, AND ITS VICTIM.

The course of the surgeon, when he left the chamber of the outlaw, was taken, as we have seen, to the apartment of his other patient. The indignation which he felt at the conduct of Morton, in rejecting, in terms of such contempt, his counsel to silence; expedited his movements, and, muttering while he went, the discomfiture which he felt, he found himself in the presence of Miss Middleton before he had entirely smoothed his ruffled front for such a meeting. But Mr. Hillhouse prided himself on his possession of all those nice requisities which constitute, *par excellence*, the essentials of ladies-man. Among these may be reckoned a countenance which no unruly passions could ever discompose. He started, with an air of studied, theatrical modesty, when, at the entrance of the chamber, he saw the young lady;—passed his kerchief once over his face, and the magic consequences of such a proceeding, were instantly apparent. The wrinkles and frowns had all disappeared, and sweet sentiment and deliberate love alone appeared upon that territory which they had unbecomingly usurped. The surgeon approached trippingly, and in a half whisper to Flora, communicated his apologies.

"I still tremble, Miss Middleton, for I had almost ventured into your presence with an angry visage. The truth is, I am sometimes susceptible of anger. My patient in the opposite apartment proves to be unruly. He has annoyed me. He rejects good counsel, and he who rejects counsel need not take physic. Counsel, Miss Middleton, has been happily designated, the physic of the soul, and should never be rejected——"

"Except, perhaps, when given as physic, sir;—but will you look at this poor young woman. I am afraid you can do but little for her. She grows worse every moment."

"A-hem!—The limit to human art has not yet been found, Miss Middleton. The patient has frequently been rescued from the very fingers of death. My own successes in this respect have been numerous and remarkable. I remember once in Ceylon, sometime in the autumn of 1772, I had a case of this very sort, and a young woman too. She fractured her skull by falling from a window, in an effort to reach her lover. The affair occasioned not a little sensation at the time. The parties were something more than respectable on all sides; but an unconquerable aversion to her lover which her father entertained, threatened to defeat their desires. You need not be told, Miss Middleton, that where a young woman loves, she will do anything to secure the object of her attachment. He was worthy of her. He was an Irishman, his name Macartney—and certainly, for that day, had the most inimitable taste in the arrangement of his cravat, of any man I ever knew. He could make a pendant to it, a sort of *nœud Gordienne*, which I would defy the prettiest fingers in the world to unravel. The knot appeared like a ball, a single globe, from which hung two lappets, being the open ends of the kerchief. Sometimes, with singular ingenuity, he would alter the design so as to leave but one lappet, and then, it might be likened to a comet, with a tail—such a one as I saw at Paris, in 1769. I doubt if you were then quite old enough to have seen that comet, but you may have heard of it. It had a most prodigious tail—fully sixty degrees in length, as computed by the astronomers."

It was with a degree of disgust, almost amounting to loathing, that Flora Middleton listened to the stuff of the voluble exquisite, poured forth all the while that he pursued his examination into the hurts of his patient. It seemed shocking that one could speak at such a moment, on any subject but such as was essential to the successful performance of the task in hand; but that he should enlarge on such wretched follies, with so much suffering before his eyes, seemed to her still more shocking, strange, and unnatural.

It will be remembered that Flora Middleton was a country-girl, to whom the resources and employments of the conventional world of fashion, were almost entirely unknown, except from books; and if she heard anything of such extravagancies in them, they were very likely to be thrown by, as too silly for perusal, and too idle for belief. The plaintive moans and occasional ejaculations of the poor girl offered the only interruption to the garrulity of the surgeon, but did not seem to awaken any feeling. He commented on this insensibility, by a quotation from Shakspeare, which served for the time to divert him entirely from the subject.

"'How use doth breed a habit in a man!' I do believe, Miss Middleton, though I should think just as much of her as before, and feel just as desirous of doing her a service, that I could take off the leg of my grandmother with as much composure and indifference, as perform on the most indifferent stranger. Did you ever have a tooth drawn, Miss Middleton?"

He urged this question with great gravity, but did not wait for the answer.

"A painful operation to the patient, decidedly, and the only surgical operation which I have any reluctance to perform. My objection arose from a very rational circumstance. When in my teens, and a student—a time as you perceive not very remote, Miss Middleton, though my worldly experience has been so extensive and so rapid—I was called upon to extract a tooth from the mouth of a young lady, the daughter of a singing-master in Bath. She was very nervous, and gave me a great deal of trouble to get her to submit. But I had scarcely got my finger into her mouth—being about to use the lancet—when—look what a mark!"—showing his finger—"it will last me to my grave, and, as you see, disfigures terribly the entire member!—She closed her jaw upon me, and—ah! I feel the thrill of horror even now, which seemed to run through my whole system. Nay, by my faith, would you think it—not content with taking hold, she seemed no way disposed to let go again, and it was only by main force that she was persuaded to recollect that my finger had no real or natural connection with her incisors. Young ladies are said to keep possession of their favorites with a tenacity peculiar to themselves, but a mode like this, Miss Middleton, you will readily admit, was neither loving nor ladylike."

As she looked and listened, Flora could scarce forbear the exclamation of "unfeeling fool;" while the reflection which has occurred to every mind which has ever observed and thought, suggested to hers the strong identity which exists between the extremely callous and cold nature, and that in which levity seems a leading characteristic. The extremes inevitably meet. The bear can dance, and the monkey, which is one of the most sportive, if not the most formidable, is one of the most malignant of the wild tribes of the forest. A frivolous people is apt to be a savage people, and the most desperate Indian warriors prefer the looking-glass worn about their necks to any other ornament.

While the surgeon was prating in this fashion, he was extorting groans from the poor girl whose hurts he examined without seeming to be conscious of the pain he gave; and the finger which he presented for examination as that which had so much suffered from the jaws of the lady of Bath was stained with the crimson hues from the fractured skull which he had been feeling. Mr. Hillhouse was considered a good surgeon in the British army; and, it may be, that the very callosity which shocked the sensibilities of Flora Middleton, would not only commend him to the rough soldier, who acquires from his daily practice an habitual scorn of the more becoming humanities, but was, indeed, one cause of his being an excellent operator. His skill, however, promised to avail nothing in behalf of his female patient; and when, at length, after a thousand episodes, Flora obtained from him his final opinion, though it said nothing, it signified much.

The mournful presentiments of the poor girl, expressed to her betrayer but a few days before, promised to be soon realized. Her wounds, mental and bodily, were mortal. Her mind was gone. Her body was sinking fast. The seat of reason was usurped by its worst foe; and delirium raved with unabashed front and unabashed presence, over the abandoned empire of thought. Wild and wretched were the strange and incoherent expressions which fell from her lips. Now she spoke of her childhood, now of her father; and when she spoke of him, her eyes would unclose, and shudderingly steal a hasty glance for a few moments around the chamber—meeting the gaze of Flora

Middleton, they would suddenly turn aside, or fold themselves up again, as if anxious to exclude a painful object from their survey.

But there was one name which, like the keynote in an elaborate strain of artificial music, sounded ever preclusive to the rest; and the keen ear of Flora heard with surprise the frequent iteration, in tones of the most touching tenderness and entreaty, of the name of Edward. Never once did the listener conjecture to whom this name applied. It was the name of the father, perhaps the brother, the dear friend; but never once did she fancy the true relation which made it dear, and fatal as it was dear, to the unhappy victim. Could she have guessed the truth —could she have dreamed, or in any way been led to a prescience of the truth—how would that suffering, but proud heart, have melted at the stern cruelty which its injustice was momently doing to the faithful but absent lover! Her meditations were those of the unsophisticated and pure-souled woman.

"I will not let her suffer," she murmured to herself, while she sad beside the dying creature. "I will not let her suffer, though, poor victim, she little fancies how much suffering her presence brings to me. Her miserable fall, and wretched fortunes, shall not make her hateful in my sight. God keep me from such cruel feelings, and strengthen me against temptation. Let me treat her kindly, and not remember to her detriment that Clarence Conway has been her destroyer. O, Clarence, Clarence! You, of whom I thought such pure and noble thoughts—you, who seemed to me so like a man in excellence—as man was when he spoke unabashed in the presence of the angels—how could you stoop to this baseness, and riot on the poor victim, abusing the fond attachment which proved her only weakness, and which, in the eye of him she loved, should have been her chief security and strength."

Had Flora Middleton lived more in the world, and in the great cities thereof, she might have been less severe in examining the supposed conduct of her lover. Her soliloquy might have been softened, as she reflected upon the numbers among her sex, vicious and artful, who save the betrayer some of his toils, and are caught sometimes in their artifices; but of this class of persons she had no knowledge, and did not even conjecture their existence. She took it for granted that Clarence Conway was the one who was wholly guilty—his victim was only weak through the strength of her attachment. The warmth of her own regards for her lover enabled her to form a correct idea of that overpowering measure which had been the poor girl's destruction; and thinking thus, she had no indulgence for him, whom she regarded as one recklessly, and without qualification, wicked.

But the truth is, even Edward Morton, the real wrong-doer, had not, in this case, deserved entirely this reproach. There was some truth in the sarcasm which he uttered to Mary Clarkson, when he told her that her own vanity had had considerable part in her overthrow. She felt the partial truth of the accusation, and her own reproaches followed on her lips. It would be doing injustice to the outlaw, were we to describe him as indifferent to her situation. There was still something human in his nature—some portion of his heart not utterly ossified by the selfishness which proved its chief characteristic. In the long and earnest conversation which followed, between him and his confidante in his chamber after the exclusion of the surgeon, he had asked and received all the information which could be given on the subject of the events which had made Mary Clarkson a victim to a like misfortune, and in consequence of the same circumstances, with himself. He did not know the fact, nor could Watson Gray inform him, that she received her hurts because of the feeble attempt which she made to come to his relief. But, all the circumstances led to this conviction, and when the outlaw resurveyed the ground over which he had gone, and her unvarying devotedness through the long and perilous period of strife, toil, and danger, which had marked his footsteps;—when he remembered how many had been her sacrifices, how firm had been her faith—the only one true, amid the many false or doubtful, and only secured by purchase;—when the same train of thought reminded him that, for all this devotion, she had received few smiles, and no love, from the very person for whom alone she smiled, and who monopolized, without knowing how to value, all the love of which she was capable;—it was then, possibly for the first time in his life, that the cold and keen reproaches of remorse touched his heart.

"I have done the poor creature wrong—I have not valued her as she deserved. See to her, Gray, for God's sake, and let not that fool of a surgeon, if he can do anything, spare his efforts. If she survives I will make amends to her. I will treat her more kindly; for never has poor creature been more faithful; and I'm inclined to think that she must have been hurt in some idle attempt to come to my succor. You say you found her on the same spot?"

"Very nearly."

"Surely, Clarence Conway could not have drawn weapon upon her!"

"You forget. She was dressed in men's clothes, and in the darkness of the evening."

"Yes, yes—but still a mere boy in appearance, and there never was a brighter moonlight. Nobody would have used deadly weapon upon one whose form was so diminutive and evidently feeble. She was sick, too—she told me so; but I had heard her complain so often, that I gave her no credit for sincerity, and sent her back to watch those d—d plotting scoundrels in the swamp. Would the fiends had them!"

We need not pursue this dialogue farther. The exhaustion of the outlaw left him temporarily oblivious on the subject of the girl; but, towards evening, starting up from a brief, uneasy slumber, his first inquiry was into her condition. When told that her skull was fractured, that she was raging with fever and delirium, the outlaw sank back, shut his eyes, and, though awake, lay in a rigid silence, which showed the still active presence of those better feelings of which it was his misfortune to possess but few, and those too feeble for efficient and beneficial service. How small was their effect, may be judged from the success of the means employed by Watson Gray to divert his mind from the gloomy fit into which he seemed to have fallen. That vicious adherent seized the moment to inform him of the steps he had taken to lay the wrong done her innocence at the door of Clarence Conway, and to convey this impression to Flora Middleton. The exultation of a selfish hope came in to silence remorse, and the outlaw opened his eyes to eulogize the prompt villany of his confederate.

"A good idea that, and it can do poor Mary no harm now; and how looks Flora since she heard it? Have you seen her since?"

"Yes: she looks twice as tall, and ten times as haughty as before."

"Flora Middleton to the life! The Semiramis or Zenobia of the Congaree. As proud as either of those dark, designing dames of antiquity. She fancied that you were pitying her whenever your eyes turned upon her face, and after that her only effort was to make herself seem as insensible and indifferent as if she never had a heart. Ah! Gray, my good fellow, only get me on my legs again before Rawdon is compelled to take to his, and if I do not carry the proud damsel off from all of them, I deserve to lose all future stakes as well as all the profits of the past. Keep that fool fellow of a surgeon from probing me, simply that he may use his instrument and fingers, and let him only do what you think necessary or useful. I can't well believe that such a civet-scented thing as that can possibly be of any use, except to wind silk, or tend upon poodles; and would sooner have *your* doctoring than that of the whole tribe. Get me my limbs again, and the rest is easy."

What was that rest? What were those hopes which gave such a tone of exultation to the voice and language of the wounded man? We need not anticipate. The conjecture is only too easy. What should they be, springing in such a rank soil, and born of such seed as his criminal hands had planted? Dark, deep, and reckless, was the determination of his soul; and wily, in the highest degree, was the confederate to whose aid in particular, its execution was to be intrusted. At this moment it need only be said that, in the mind of the conspirators, nothing appeared to baffle their desires but the condition of their chief. All things seemed easy. The fortune they implored, the fiend they served, the appetite which prompted, and the agents they employed, all subservient, were all in waiting; and he who, of all, was to be most gratified by their services—he alone was unable to make them available. Well might he curse the folly which had brought him to his present state, and denounce the feebleness which delayed the last and crowning achievement on which his hopes and desires were now set. His soul chafed with impatience. He had no resources from thought and contemplation. He could curse, but he could not pray; and curses, as the Arabian proverb truly describes them, are like chickens, that invariably come home to roost. They brought neither peace nor profit to the sick bed of the invalid, and they kept refreshing slumbers from his pillow.

## CHAPTER XXVIII.

#### PHILOSOPHICAL DOUBTS AND INQUIRIES.

The angry feelings which the conduct of the outlaw had produced in the bosom of Mr. Surgeon Hillhouse, had driven, for the time, another affair from his recollection about which he was particularly desirous to speak with Miss Middleton or her grandmother. A ramble in the woods that same morning enabled him to recover his temper and, with it, his recollection; and when the dinner things were removed that day, he fairly conducted the old lady to the sofa, placed himself beside her, and with looks big with the sagacious thought, and busy speculation, he propounded himself as follows in a language somewhat new to him, of sententious inquiry.

"Mrs. Middleton—madam—pray oblige me by letting me know what sort of a looking person was your grandfather?"

"My grandfather, sir—my grandfather!"

"Yes, madam, your grandfather—how did he look—how did he dress—was he tall or short—stout or slender. Did he wear breeches of blue homespun, a tattered hunting shirt of the same color and stuff; and was his *couteau de chasse* as long as my arm?"

"My grandfather, sir! Why, sir, what do you mean?"

"No harm, no offence, believe me, Mrs. Middleton—on the contrary, my question is prompted by grave doubts, and difficulties, and, possibly, dangers! No idle or impertinent curiosity occasions it. Philosophy is seriously interested in your reply."

"My grandfather, sir—why he has been dead these hundred years! I do not think I ever saw him."

"Dead a hundred years! Impossible! Eh! How can that be?" demanded the surgeon in astonishment scarcely less than that which the old lady herself had manifested at the beginning;—"dead a hundred years? Really, Mrs. Middleton—there must be some mistake."

"Indeed, sir—then it is yours, not mine. My grandfather has been dead more than a hundred years. He died in France somewhere in 1680—or '81——"

"Oh he died in France, did he? You are right, madam, there is a mistake, and it is mine. To be sure it was not your grandfather—if he died in France—about whom I wished to know;—it was *Miss* Middleton's grandfather."

"My husband, sir!" said the old lady bridling with dignity, while her keen gray eyes flashed with all the vivacity of girlhood, as she conjectured the utterance of something impertinent from her companion. The surgeon felt his dilemma.

"Your husband, Mrs. Middleton," he stammered—"Can it be? Miss Middleton's grandfather your husband?"

"And why not, sir, when I have the honor to be her grandmother?"

"True, true, most true, madam, but——"

"It does not alter the case very materially, sir, so far as you are interested. Your right is just as great to inquire into the private history of *her* grandfather as of mine. Pray, proceed in your questions, sir, if as you think, so much depends upon it. We are retired country people, it is true, Mr. Millhouse——"

"Hillhouse, madam—Augustus Hillhouse, of his majesty's—"

"Pardon me, sir—Mr. Hillhouse—I was simply about to encourage you to ask your question by assuring you that, though retired and rustic, we are still not utterly insensible, on the banks of the Congaree, to the claims of philosophy. I trust

14*

to see her schools established here before I die,* and may, possibly, have the pleasure of hearing you, yourself, expounding from one or other of her sacred chairs."

The surgeon bowed low at the unexpected compliment without perceiving the smile of irony by which it was accompanied.

"Ah, madam, you do me too much honor. I am but poorly fitted for the high station which you speak of. It is true, I am not indifferently read; I have seen the world—a fair proportion of it at least; and am considered very generally as a man fond of serious and severe investigations in the kindred temples of science and of nature, but——"

"Oh, sir, I have no sort of doubt that you will do well in any of the departments, and if ever we should be so fortunate as to obtain our liberties again, I have no doubt you will be thought of for some such situation."

"Ahem!—ahem! Liberties!—ah!—ahem!"

The termination of the sentence, which intimated a hope of British expulsion, was scarcely palatable to the surgeon.

"But, sir, on the subject of Miss Middleton's grandfather—my husband—the late General Middleton—what would you please to know?"

"Ahem—why, madam, the case presents itself in an aspect of increased difficulty. I had somehow confused it at first, and fancied when I spoke that I was addressing you on the subject of a very ancient relation. The connection being so close——"

"Makes no sort of difference, sir, if your question conveys nothing disrespectful."

The reply of the old lady bewildered the surgeon yet further. He was not sure that something disrespectful might not be conveyed to a very sensitive and jealous mind, in any form of the question, which was to solve his difficulties. In this state of bewilderment, with something of desperation in his air, he proposed another inquiry, seemingly so foreign to the previous topic

* A hope which the venerable lady in question lived to realize. The College of South Carolina, at Columbia, has been long in successful operation, and has the good fortune to have sent forth some of the best scholars and ablest statesmen in the Union. Its increasing prosperity induces the confident assurance that it will long continue a career of so much usefulness and good.—EDITOR.

that Mrs. Middleton began to think him insane as well as silly."

"Mrs. Middleton, do you believe in ghosts?"

"Ghosts, sir!—a very singular question."

"Exactly so, madam, but it is a part of the subject."

"Indeed, sir!"

"Yes, ma'am, and I should be really very grateful if you would say whether you do or do not believe in that supernatural presence—that spectral visitation—that independent embodiment, in shape of limbs, sinews and substance, of the immortal spirit—which is vulgarly entitled an apparition, or ghost? Professionally, madam, as a surgeon, I'm not prepared to look further than the physical organization for the governing powers of the human form. A soul is a something that has eluded hitherto all the search of the anatomist, and the only authority which exists for such an agent, seems to me to be derived from testimonials, more or less authenticated, of the presence and reappearance of those whom we have considered dead, and no longer capable of the uses and purposes, the feelings and the desires, of ordinary life. Now, madam, something of my first inquiry depends upon my last. Pray oblige me, then, by saying whether you do or do not believe in this marvellous anomaly. Do you believe in ghosts or not?"

"Well, sir, to oblige you, though I am at a loss to see the connection between the one question and the other——"

"It's there—there is a connection, believe me."

"Well, sir, under your assurance, or without it, I can have no objection to say that I am very doubtful what to believe on such a subject. So much has been said on both sides—and I have heard so many wonderful stories about such things, from persons of such excellent credit, that——"

"Enough, enough, madam; I see you are not altogether incredulous. Now tell me, madam, did you ever yourself see a ghost?"

"Never, sir."

"Never!—nor any thing, shape, substance, or person, that ever looked like one, or looked like nothing else but one, or that you had reason to suppose was one, or that resembled any departed friend, relative, tie, connection, dependence—in short, did you never see anything that a suspicious mind might not have readily taken for a ghost?"

"Never, sir, to my recollection."

"Well, madam," continued the surgeon, taking courage from his own motion, "on your answer will depend the very important doubt whether I, Augustus Hillhouse, second surgeon in his majesty's 87th regiment of foot, have not been favored by the visitation of the late General Middleton——."

"Sir!" exclaimed the old lady, rising with a most queenly air of dignity and pride.

"Yes, madam, that's it!" replied the surgeon, rising also, and rubbing his hands together earnestly. "Here, while I lay on this very sofa, this very morning, after the breakfast was over, and Miss Middleton had gone—here, alone, I was favored by the sudden presence of one who might have risen from the floor, and, as far as I could see, sunk into it; who might have been, nay, as I have heard, must have been;—but on this head I would have your testimony, and for this reason did I desire to learn from you in what costume it was usually the custom for General Middleton to appear? Oblige me, my dear madam, by a clear and particular description of his dress, his weapons, his height, breadth, general appearance, the length of his nose, and of his hunting-knife——."

"Sir, this freedom—this scandalous freedom!" exclaimed the venerable matron.

"Do not be offended, Mrs. Middleton. I am governed, my dear madam, by no motives but those of the philosopher. I would thank you, then——"

"Sir, I must leave you. You trespass, sir, beyond your privilege. The subject is a sacred one with the widow. Let me hear no more of it."

"But, my dear madam—one question only:—was he a tall person, slender, rather scant of frame—such a person as is vulgarly called raw-boned——"

"No more, Mr. Hillhouse, if you please."

"But his dress, madam—and his nose."

"Good morning, sir."

"His knife—was it long, very long—long as my arm?"

The matron bowed, as she was retiring, with a stern glance of her gray eye, which would have confounded any person but one so thoroughly absorbed in his philosophical follies as to be utterly incapable of observation. He pursued her to the foot of the stairs with a degree of impetuous eagerness, which almost made the old lady fancy that he purposely sought to offend and annoy her—a conjecture which by no means served to lessen the hauteur of her retiring movements.

"But, my dear madam, one word only"—implored the surgeon in an agony of entreaty—"touching his costume; only say whether it was of blue homespun, rather lightish in hue; were his smallclothes rather scantish, and of the same color;—and his hunting frock—was it not a little tattered and torn about the skirts, and on the shoulder?—and——

'She goes, and makes no sign!'"

was the sad quotation from Shakspere, with which he concluded, and which fitly described the inflexible silence in which the matron effected her departure.

"Devilish strange animal is woman! Here now is a question materially affecting the greatest mystery in our spiritual nature; which a word of that old lady might enable me to solve, and she will not speak that word. And why? Clearly, she was quite as anxious for the truth, at the beginning, as I was myself. But the secret is, that her pride stood in the way. Pride is half the time in favor of philosophy. Had her husband, instead of appearing in the ordinary guise of one of the natives—which must be confessed to be a very wretched taste—but put scarlet breeches on his ghost, the old woman would have been willing to acknowledge him. But she was ashamed of a ghost—even though it were her own husband—who should reappear in dingy blue homespun. And she was right. What ghost could hope to find faith, or respect, who paid so little attention to his personal appearance? It seems to me, if I should ever have any desire to 'revisit the glimpses of the moon,' and the favor were afforded me, I should be at quite as much trouble in making up my toilet as I am now; nay, more, for the task would be accompanied by increased difficulty. The complexion of a ghost would require a very nice selection of shades in costume. Whether my violet would not be the most suitable? Really, the question increases in interest. I shall certainly study it carefully. The delicacy of the violet is an argument in its favor, but some deference must be shown to the universal judgment of ages, which represents ghosts as commonly appearing in white. To this, the case of Hamlet's father and General Middleton furnish the only exceptions that I remember. How then should a ghost be habited? How should *I* be habited, appearing as a ghost? The query is one of delicate interest. I must consult with myself, my pocket mirror, and the lovely Flora Middleton!"

This dialogue, and these grave reflections, resulted in the temporary exhaustion of the surgeon. He yawned listlessly, and once more threw himself upon the sofa where he had been favored with his ghostly visitation; but, on this occasion, he took special care that his face should front the entrance. Here he surrendered himself for a while to those dreaming fancies with which the self-complacent are fortunately enabled to recompense themselves for the absence of better company; and passing, with the rapidity of insect nature, from flower to flower, his mind soon lost, in the hues which it borrowed as it went, every trace of that subject to which it had been seemingly devoted with so much earnestness.

Meanwhile Mrs. Middleton joined her grand-daughter in the chamber of poor Mary Clarkson. It needed not the verdict of the surgeon to declare that she must die; and all his professional jargon could not have persuaded the spectator, who gazed upon her pale and wretched features, to believe that she could by any possibility survive. The eternal fiat had gone forth. The messenger of mercy—for such, happily, was the angel of death to her—was on his way. She might sink in a few hours, she might live as many days, but she was evidently dying. But there was a strange life and brightness in her eyes. The vitality of her glance was heightened by delirium into intense spirituality. She keenly surveyed the persons in attendance with a jealous and suspicious glance, the cause of which they could only ascribe to the mind's wandering. Her eyes turned ever from them to the entrance of the apartment; and once, when

Flora Middleton went to place an additional pillow beneath her head, she grasped her hand convulsively, and murmured with the most piteous accents—

"Take him not from me—not yet—not till I am dead, and in the cold, cold grave! Why will you take him from me? I never did you harm!"

Very much shocked, Flora shuddered, but replied—

"Of whom speak you, my poor girl?—what would you have me do?"

"Of whom?—of him! Surely you know?—of Conway! Take him not from me—not—not till I am in the grave! Then—oh then!—it will not need then! No! no!"

The interval of sense was brief, but how painful to the listening maiden!

"Fear nothing!" said Flora, somewhat proudly. "God forbid that I should rob you of any of your rights."

"Oh! but you can not help it!—you can not help it!" cried the sufferer. "I know—I know what it is to love—and to suffer for it! But, will you not let me see him—let me go to him—or bid them bring him here to me! I can not die till I have seen him!"

"That can not be, my poor girl; he is not here. He is gone. I trust that God will enable you to live to see him."

"He is gone! You mean that he is dead! Ha!—can it be that? I did not come in time! I saw them fight! I heard them swear and strike—hard—heavy blows, with sharp steel! Oh, God! that brothers should fight, and seek to destroy each other! I called to them to stop; but I saw their heavy blows; and when I ran to part them—I fell, and such a pain! My poor, poor head! He killed us both—the cruel brother!—he killed us both with his heavy blows."

"My poor girl," said Flora, "do not make yourself miserable with this mistake. Believe what I tell you. Mr. Clarence Conway is in no danger; he escaped. The only sufferer is Mr. Edward Conway, who is hurt. He lies in the opposite chamber."

The words of the speaker were drowned in the shrieks of the sufferer, now, once more, a maniac. Successive screams of a mixed emotion—a something of delight and agony in the utterance—followed the communication of Flora Middleton, and were followed by a desperate effort of the poor girl to rise from the bed and rush from the apartment. It required all the strength of an able-bodied female slave, who watched with her young mistress in the apartment, to keep her in the bed; and the restraint to which she was subjected only served to increase her madness, and render her screams more piercing and intolerable than ever. Her wild, anguished words filled the intervals between each successive scream. But these were no longer coherent. When she became quieted at length, it was only through the exhaustion of all the strength which sustained her during the paroxysm. Strong aromatics and strengthening liquors were employed to restore her to consciousness; and the scientific exquisite from below, startled from his dreaming mood by the summons of the servant, was sufficiently impressed by the painful character of the spectacle he witnessed, to apply himself in earnest to the task of restoring her, without offending the good taste of the ladies by the exercise of his customary garrulity. She was brought back to life, and the keen scrutiny of Flora Middleton discovered, as she fancied, that her senses were also restored.

There was an air of cunning in the occasionally upturned glance of her half-shut eye, which forced this conviction upon the spectator. When Flora changed her position, the eye of the sufferer followed her movements with an expression of curiosity, which is one of the most natural forms of intelligence. She had also become, on a sudden, excessively watchful. Every sound that was heard from without aroused her regards; and, when she saw that she was noticed by those around her, her own glance was suddenly averted from the observer, with an air of natural confusion.

These were signs that warned Flora of the necessity of giving her the most patient and scrupulous attention. It was obvious to all that she could not survive that night. The surgeon, rubbing his hands at nightfall, gave his ultimatum to this effect; and yielded up his charge as hopeless; and the gloomy feelings of Flora Middleton were somewhat modified when she reflected that death could not possibly be a misfortune to one to whom life seemed to have borne only the aspects of unmixed evil. What should she live for? More neglect—more shame—more sorrow!—the blow that forces the victim to the dust, and mocks at his writhings there. Mary Clarkson had surely endured enough of this already. It could not be the prayer of friendship which would desire her to live only for its sad continuance; and to live at all, must be, in the case of that hapless creature, to incur this agonizing penalty. But Flora Middleton could still pray for the victim. Forgiveness might be won for her errors, and, surely, where the penalties of folly and of sin are already so great in life, the mercy of Heaven will not be too rigorously withheld. This was her hope, and it may well be ours.

## CHAPTER XXIX

### THE AVENGER BAFFLED.

The screams of the maddened victim of his lust and selfishness, had reached the ears of Edward Morton in his chamber. They had startled him from slumbers, which no doubt, had their images of terror, such as thronged about the couch of Richard, and sat heavy upon his soul. The piercing agony of those shrieks must have strangely tallied with his dreams, for he started almost erect in his couch, his eyes wild and staring, his hair moist yet erect, his words broken, thick, and incoherent. His attendant, Watson Gray, who had been a faithful watcher beside his couch, ran to him, and pressed him gently back upon the pillows, using such language as he fancied might soothe to quiet his nervous excitation; but, as the shrieks were continued, and seemed to acquire greater volume with each successive utterance, there was still an influence, beyond his power of soothing, to keep the guilty and wounded man in a state of agitation.

"What mean these hideous cries, Gray? was there not some one besides yourself in my chamber before they began? Did they take nobody hence—now, now—but now?"

"No! you have been dreaming only. You are feverish. Be quiet—on your keeping quiet depends everything."

"So it does; but can't you silence those noises? I should know those tones. Can it be—are they Mary's? Is she dying?"

The question was put by the outlaw in low, husky tones, which were scarcely audible. The answer was necessarily uttered in the affirmative, though Gray was reluctant to speak the truth, and would have readily availed himself of a falsehood, had a plausible one that moment suggested itself to his mind.

"They are operating upon her, perhaps?" continued Morton; "that d——d fellow of a surgeon!—he cares not what pain he gives her."

"No, captain, there is no operation necessary. The doctor says it'll be all over with her soon. He's given her hurts the last dressing that she'll ever need."

"Ha! she will then die! She told me of this! I remember; but I did not believe! I would to God she might be saved, Gray! Can nothing still be done? See the surgeon; let him do his best. I'm afraid you've let her suffer."

"No, every thing's been done. Old Mrs. Middleton and Miss Flora have been nursing and watching her the best part of the time themselves."

"And there is then no hope? Poor Mary! Could she be brought up again, I should be more kind to her, Gray. I have been more of a savage to that poor, loving creature, than to any other human being; and I know not why, unless it was that she loved me better than all others. What a strange nature is that of man—mine, at last. How d——nably perverse has my spirit been throughout;—actually, and always, at issue with its own blessing. Ah! that shriek!—shut it out, Gray—close the door —it goes like a sharp, keen arrow to my brain!"

Under the momentary goadings of remorse, the outlaw buried his face in the bed-clothes, and strove to exclude from hearing the piercing utterance of that wo which was born of his wickedness. But, for a time, the effort was in vain. The heart-rending accents pursued him, penetrated the thin barriers which would have excluded them from the ears of the guilty man, and roused him finally to a state of excitement which Watson Gray momentarily dreaded would drive him to a condition of delirium little short of hers. But, suddenly, the cries of terror ceased; so suddenly, that the outlaw started with a shudder at the unexpected and heavy silence.

"It is all over with her. She is dead. Go you and see, Gray. Quickly, go! and tell me. Poor Mary! I could have been more just to her had her claims been less. I can not believe that she is dead. No! no!—not yet; though once I was wretch enough to wish it. Forgive me! God forgive me, for that wish!"

The voice of the outlaw subsided to a whisper. A cold shudder passed through his frame. His eyes were closed with terror. He fancied that the freed spirit of the woman whom he supposed dead, hovered above him, ere it took its final departure. Even the whispering accents which followed from his lips broke forth in spasmodic ejaculations.

"Forgive me, Mary; forgive! forgive! I should have loved you better. I have been a wretch—a cold, selfish, unfeeling wretch! I knew not your worth—your value—and now! Ha! who is there? who?—ah, Gray, is it you? Sit by me; take my hand in yours. Well, she is gone—she sleeps."

Gray had resumed his place by the bedside, while the eyes of the trembling criminal were closed. His approach startled the nervous man with a thrilling confirmation of the partial supernatural fear which had before possessed him.

"She sleeps," said Gray, "but is not dead. Her paroxysm has gone off; and, perhaps, she will only waken when death comes on."

"Ah! what a foolish terror possessed me but now. I fancied that she was beside me!—I could have sworn I heard her faintly whispering in my ears. What a coward this weakness makes me."

"Try to sleep, captain. Remember how much depends upon your soon getting well. We have a great deal to do, you know."

"Ah, true; you are a cool, sensible fellow, Gray. I will try to sleep, but those dreams—those hideous dreams. Keep beside me, Gray—do not leave me."

The slight reference which Gray had made to his worldly schemes and grosser passions, recalled the outlaw to his habitual self. He turned his head upon the pillow, while Gray took one of his hands quietly within his own. Sitting thus beside him, it was not long before he discovered that the outlaw had sunk into a regular slumber; and, releasing his hold, he laid himself down at the foot of the bed, under the influence of a natural exhaustion, which soon brought a deeper sleep upon his senses than that which possessed those of his superior.

Night meanwhile stole onward with noiseless footstep, and a deep silence overspread the whole barony. The sleep of the outlaw was long, deep and refreshing. It indicated a favorable condition of his wounds, such as Watson Gray had predicted. The poor victim in the neighboring chamber seemed to sleep also, but her repose promised no such agreeable results. The lamp of life was flickering with uncertain light. The oil of the vessel was nearly exhausted. Flora Middleton approached her about midnight, and so still was her seeming sleep, so breathlessly deep did her slumbers appear, so composed her features, and so rigid her position, that the maiden was struck with the thought that the last sad change had already taken place. But, as she stooped over the face of the sleeper, her silken ringlets were slightly shaken by the faint breathing from her half-closed lips, which still betrayed the presence of the reluctant and lingering life. She appeared to sleep so sweetly and soundly that Flora determined to snatch a few moments of repose also. She needed such indulgence. She had robbed herself of many hours of accustomed sleep, in watching and waiting upon the wakeful sufferings of her involuntary guest. Calling in the servant whose own slumbers never suffered impediment or interruption in any situation, she resigned the invalid to her care, giving her special instructions to keep a good watch, and to summon her instantly, when any change in the patient was at hand.

Mira, the negro woman to whom this trust was given, was one of the staid family servants such as are to be found in every ancient southern household, who form a necessary part of the establishment, and are, substantially, members, from long use and habit, of the family itself. The children grow up under their watchful eyes, and learn to love them as if they were mothers, or at least grandmothers, maiden aunts, or affectionate antique cousins, who win their affections by bringing bon-bons in their pockets, and join them in all their noisy games. They rebuke the rudeness of the young, follow their steps in their errant progress, warn them of danger, and put them to bed at night. Mira was one of these valuable* retainers, who had watched the childhood of Flora, and received from the latter all the kindness which she certainly deserved.

"Now, Mauma," said Flora, at leaving her, "don't go to sleep. You've slept all the evening, and can surely keep wakeful till I come. Call me the moment the poor girl wakens, or if you see any difference."

Mira promised everything, took her seat beside the couch of the patient, and really set out with a serious determination to keep her eyes open to the last. But when did a negro ever resist that most persuasive, seductive, and persevering of all influences in the South, particularly in the balmy month of June? When did sleep deign to solicit, that he was not only too happy to embrace? Mira soon felt the deep and solemn stillness of the scene. The events of the few days previous had excited her along with the rest; and the exhaustion of her faculties of reflection, which is always a rapid affair in all the individuals of her race, necessarily made her more than ever susceptible to sleep. To do her all justice, however, she made the most strenuous efforts to resist the drowsy influence. She began several grave discussions with herself, but in an under-tone, on the occurrences of the week. She discussed the merits of the sundry prominent persons she had seen—Rawdon and the Conways—not forget- the assistant surgeon, whom she resolved was either a prince or a "*poor buckrah*" in his own country, but which—and a vast interval lay between—she did not undertake to say. But the lamp burned dimly on the hearth—the shadows that flitted upon the walls, in correspondence with its flickering light, increased the gloom—the patient beside her was apparently sunk in the deepest slumber, and it was in vain for the poor negro to contend with the magnetic influence. Her head was gradually bent forward, and, at length, lay upon the bedside. It was not long after this when she slept quite as soundly as if this blessing had never before been vouchsafed her.

When *she* slept, the patient ceased to do so. With that cunning which is said to mark most kinds of delirium, she had feigned the slumbers which she was never more to know. She perceived that she was watched—she knew that she was restrained; and, sane on one subject only, she had employed the little sense that suffering had left her in deceiving her keepers. From the moment when she was told that Edward Morton occupied a neighboring chamber, the only desire which remained to her in life was to see him before she died. For this had she raved in her paroxysm, but they did not comprehend her; and the strong leading desire of her mind had so far brought back her capacities of thought and caution, as to enable her to effect her object. When she saw Flora Middleton leave the chamber, her hopes strengthened; and, when the negro slept beside her, she rose from the couch, stealthily, and with a singular strength, which could only be ascribed to the fever in her system, and the intense desire—a fever in itself—which filled her mind. With a deliberation such as the somnambulist is supposed to exhibit, and with very much the appearance of one, she lifted the little lamp which was burning within the chimney, and treading firmly, but with light footstep, passed out of the apartment into the great passage-way of the mansion, without disturbing the fast-sleeping negro who had been set to watch beside her.

Meanwhile, her miserable and scarcely more sane father, was inhabiting the neighboring woods, and prowling about the premises of Brier Park, as the gaunt wolf hovers for his prey at evening, around the camp of the western squatter. The woods formed a convenient and accustomed shelter, and but little was required to satisfy his wants. He had but one large, leading appetite remaining, and food was only desirable as it might supply the necessary strength for the gratification of that appetite. Animal food did not often pass his lips—ardent spirits never. The stimulus derived from the one desire of his soul was enough for his sustenance. Roots, acorns, and such stray bounty as could be stealthily furnished by the neighboring farmer or his slave, from the cornfield or the potato-patch, had been, since the beginning of the Revolution, the uncertain resource of all the "poor bodies that were out."

As one of these, Clarkson now found it easy to obtain the adequate supply of his creature wants, while in the neighborhood of Brier Park. He soon discovered that he could approach the negro houses, the kitchen, and finally, the mansion itself, without incurring much, if any risk. The soldiers who had been left behind, nominally to protect the ladies, but really as a safeguard to the wounded outlaw, were careless upon their watch. Though stationed judiciously and counselled earnestly by Watson Gray, they saw no cause for apprehension; and conjectured that the scout simply cried "wolf," in order to establish his own importance. He cautioned and threatened them, for he knew the sort of persons he had to deal with; but as soon as his back was turned, they stole away to little nooks in the wood, where, over a log, with a greasy pack of cards, they gambled away their sixpences, and sometimes their garments, with all the recklessness which marks the vulgar nature.

Clarkson soon found out their haunts, watched them as they stole thither, and then traversed the plantation at his leisure. In this manner he had ascertained all the secrets that he deemed it necessary to know. As his whole thought was addressed to the one object, so he neither asked for, nor heard, the information which concerned any other. To know where Edward Conway lay was the only knowledge which he desired; and this information he gained from one of the house servants. He had once penetrated to the door of the outlaw's chamber, but, on this occasion, a timely glimpse of Watson Gray and Mr. Hillhouse, warned him that the hour of vengeance must still further be delayed.

That night, however, of which we have spoken, seemed auspicious to his object. The skies were cloudy, and the moon obscured. A faint gray misty light pervaded the extent of space. The woods looked more gloomy than ever beneath it, and when the sentinels found that the mansion had sunk into its usual evening quiet, they stole away to an outhouse, and were soon swallowed up in the absorbing interests of Jamaica rum and "old sledge." Clarkson looked in upon them as he went forward to the house; but he took no interest in them or their proceedings, when they were once out of his way. He penetrated to the house without interruption, ascended the stairs, and passed with impunity into the very chamber of the outlaw.

The lamp was nearly extinguished in the chimney. A faint light was thrown around the apartment, not sufficient to penetrate the gloom at the remoter ends of it, and it had been particularly placed in such a manner as to prevent it from playing upon the face of the suffering man. In consequence of this arrangement, the greater part of the couch lay entirely in shadow; and while Clarkson was looking about him in doubt which way to proceed, he distinguished the person of Watson Gray, lying almost at his feet upon the floor.

A glance at his face sufficed to show that he was not the man he sought; and, passing around the body of the sleeper, he cautiously approached the bed, and drawing the curtains on one side, was aware, from the deep breathing, and the occasional sigh which reached his ears, that the man for whom he had been so long in pursuit of was lying before him. His heart had long been full of the desire for vengeance, and his knife was ready in his hand. It wanted but sufficient light to show him where to strike with fatal effect, and the blow would have been given. He had but to feel for the breast of his enemy, and the rest was easy. He was about to do so, when the light in the apartment was suddenly increased. He looked up with momentary apprehension. The opposite curtain was drawn aside in the same moment, and he beheld, with terror, what he believed to be the apparition of his long-perished daughter.

Certainly, no spectre could have worn a more pallid or awful countenance—no glance from eyes that had once been mortal, could have shone with more supernatural lustre. The light of delirium and fever was there—and the wild, spiritual gleam, which looks out, in fitful spasms, from the hollow sockets of the dying. The glances of father and daughter met in the same instant, and what a life of mutual wo, and terror, and desolation, did they each convey!

A shriek from both was the result of that unlooked-for encounter. The light dropped from the hands of the dying girl, upon the bed, and was extinguished; the dagger fell harmlessly from his, beside the bosom it was meant to stab. Her hollow voice sounded in his ears, and the words she spoke confirmed all his terrors.

"My father! Oh! my father!" was the exclamation forced from her by the suddenly recovered memory of the painful past: and as he heard it, he darted away, in headlong flight, heedless of the body of Watson Gray, upon which, in his terrors, he trampled, without a consciousness of having done so.

The spectral form of the girl darted after him. He saw her white garments, as he bounded down the stair-flights, and the glimpse lent vigor to his limbs. He heard her voice, faint and feeble, like the moaning whisper of the dying breeze in autumn, imploring him to stay; and it sounded more terribly in his ears than the last trumpet. A painful consciousness of having, by his cruelty, driven the poor girl to the desperate deed of self-destruction, haunted his mind; and her appearance seemed to him that of one armed with all the terrors of the avenger. It will not be thought wonderful by those who are at all conversant with the nature of the human intellect, and with the strange spiritual touches that move it to and fro at will, to state that the effect of her father's presence had suddenly restored his daughter to her senses. At least, she knew that it was her father whom she pursued — she knew that he had spurned her from his presence, and her present consciousness led her to implore his forgiveness and to die. She knew that the hand of death was upon her, but she desired his forgiveness first. The knowledge of her situation gave her the requisite strength for the pursuit, and before her pathway could be traced, she had followed his steps into the neighboring forest.

## CHAPTER XXX.

### THE FATHER AND HIS CHILD.

CLARKSON, with all the terrors of superstitious fright pursuing him, yet with all the instinct of the scout, sought shelter in the woods from all pursuit, whether supernatural or human. He fled with the speed of the hunted deer, and had soon left far behind him the fainting form of his shadowy pursuer. But of this he knew nothing. He looked not once after him, upon leaving the house. Buried in the woods, he was still pressing his way forward, when a voice which, at another time, would have been familiar and friendly in his ears, addressed him, and summoned him to stop. But, under the prevailing apprehension of his heart, he fancied it the same voice of terror which had risen from the grave to rebuke him, and this conviction increased the terror and rapidity of his flight. A footstep as fleet as his own now joined in the pursuit. He heard the quick tread behind, and finally beside him, and, desperate with the feeling that he was overtaken, he turned wildly to confront his pursuer. A hand of flesh and blood was laid upon his shoulder at the same moment, and the voice of our old friend John Bannister reassured him, and reconciled him to delay.

"By Jings!" exclaimed the woodman, "if I didn't know you to have the real grit in you. Jake Clarkson, I would think you was getting to be rather timorsome in your old age. What's the matter, man?—what's flung you so!"

"Ah, John! is that you?"—and the frightened man grappled the hand of the new-comer with fingers that were cold and clammy with the fears that were working in his heart.

"I reckon it is. I suppose you thought by this time, that Lord Rawdon and the Black Riders had made a breakfast upon me, keeping a chip of me, here and there, to stay their marching stomachs upon. But, you see, there's more ways than one of slipping a halter, when a horse can borrow a friend's finger to help his teeth. The acorn ain't planted yet that's to make my swinging tree. I'm here, old man, and out of their clutches, I'm thinking, without losing any of my own hide, and bringing with me a very good sample of theirs. As keen a nag, Jake Clarkson, as ever was taken from the Philistines lies in that 'ere bog —a fifty guinea nag. I've spoiled the Egyptians in my captivity. Come and look at the critter."

"Ah, John, I'm so glad to see you. Stand by me—and look."

"Stand by you, and look! Why, what's to look upon?—what's to hurt you? What's scared you? The woods was never more quiet. I've been all round the barony, and their guard is half drunk and half asleep in an old log cabin between the stables and the negro houses. They can do no hurt, I tell you."

"Not them, John—you don't think I mind them? But, hear you! I've seen *her!*" His voice sunk to a hoarse whisper, and he looked behind him, over the path he came, with undiminished terrors.

"Her? Who? Who's *her?*"

"Mary! Poor Mary! The child I killed!—The poor child!"

"Ha!—She still lives then!"

"No! no!—her ghost. Her sperit! It walks! Oh! John Bannister—'twas a dreadful, dreadful sight. I went to kill Ned Conway. He's lying there, wounded in the house. I've been watching here in the woods, ever since the British went. I went several times into the house but couldn't get a chance at him till to-night. To-night, I got to his room. It was so dark I couldn't see how he lay in the bed; and when I was feeling for him, the curtain drawed up on one side, and then I saw Mary —poor Mary—whiter than the driven snow, all in a sudden blaze of light. Oh! how dreadful white she looked! How awful bright her eyes shone at me. I couldn't stand it; I couldn't look; and when she spoke to me, I felt all over choking. Jist then, it suddenly turned dark, and I run, and when I looked back she was coming after me. She didn't seem to run or walk; she seemed to come with the air; and to fly between the trees——"

"What! you didn't see her after you left the house, did you?"

"Yes! oh yes? She flew after me into the woods."

The woodman struck his head with his palm, as, readily conceiving the true ground for Clarkson's terrors, he thought of the wounded and dying girl in a paroxysm of delirium, flying into the rugged forest at midnight.

"Stay here, stay awhile, Jake, while I go!" said he.

"Don't go—don't leave me!" implored the old man. "It's I that killed her, John, by my cruelty. I driv' her away from the house, and she went mad and drowned herself in the Congaree; and she haunts me for it. She's here near us now, watching for you to go. Don't go, John; don't leave me now If you do, I'll run to the river. I'll drown myself after her."

Bannister found some difficulty in soothing the superstitious terrors of the old man, but he at length succeeded in doing so in sufficient degree to persuade him to remain where he was, in waiting, till he went forward toward the mansion.

"I'll whistle to you the old whistle," said the woodman, "as I'm coming back. But don't you be scared at anything you see. I'm sure there's no ghost that ain't a natoral one. I've never known the story of a ghost yet that it didn't turn out to be a curtain in the wind, a white sheet hung out to dry, or mout be—sich things will scare some people—a large moss-beard hanging down upon a green oak's branches. If a man's to be scared by a ghost, Jake Clarkson, I give him up for a scout, or even for a soldier. He won't do for the woods. There's not an owl in an old tree that ain't his master—there's not a piece of rotten wood shining in the bottom, that ain't a devil ready to run off with him. The squirrel that jumps in the bush, and the lizard that runs upon the dry leaves, is a little sort of 'a coming-to-catch-me,' for sich a person; and, God help him, if a pine-burr should drop on his head when he ain't thinking. If his heart don't jump out of his mouth, quicker than ever a green frog jumped out of a black snake's hollow, then I'm no man to know anything about scouting. No, no! Jake Clarkson, t'wont do for you that's been counted a strong man, who didn't fear the devil nor the tories, to be taking fright at a something that's more like a dream than anything serious. It's nothing but what's nateral that's scared you, I'm thinking, and jist you keep quiet till I go back and see. They can't scare me with their blue lights and burning eyes. My mother was a woman, with the soul of a man, that had the real grit in her. I was only scared once in my life, and then she licked the scare out of me, so complete that that one licking's lasted me agin any scare that ever happened since."

"But my child—my poor child—the child that I killed, John Bannister," said the father in reproachful accents.

"Well, there's something in that, Jake Clarkson, I'm willing to admit. When a man's done a wrong thing, if anything's right to scare him, it's that. But though you was cross, and too cross, as I told you, to poor Mary, yet it's not reasonable to think you killed her; and I'll lay my life on it, if you saw Mary Clarkson to-night, you saw the real Mary, and no make-b'lieve—no ghost! But I'll go and see, and if there's any truth to be got at, trust me to pick it up somewhere along the track. Keep you quiet here, and mind to answer my whistle."

The woodman hurried away, without waiting to answer the inquiries of the unhappy father, whom the words of the former had led to new ideas. The suggestion, thrown out by Bannister, that Mary Clarkson might be yet alive, was intended by the scout to prepare the mind of the former for a probable meeting between himself and his child. He left him consequently in a singular state of impatient agitation, which was far more exhausting to the physical man, than would have been the encounter of a dozen foes in battle; and, with a feebleness which looked like one of the forms of paralysis, and had its effects for a time, the old man sank upon the ground at the foot of a tree, and groaned with the very pain of imbecility.

Bannister, meanwhile, took his way back in the direction of the mansion, and as nearly as possible along the route upon which he supposed his companion to have run. His judgment proved correct in this, as in most particulars. He had barely emerged from the thicker woods, and got upon the edge of the immediate enclosure which circumscribed the area of the household, when his eye was caught by a white heap which lay within thirty yards of the woods. He approached it, and found it to be the object of his search.

The poor girl was stretched upon the ground immovable. The small degree of strength with which the momentary paroxysm had inspired her, had passed away, and she lay supine;— her eyes were opened and watching the woods to which her father had fled. Her hands were stretched outward in the same direction. Death was upon her, but the weight of his hand was not heavy, and his sting did not seem to be felt. A slight moaning sound escaped her lips, but it was rather the utterance of the parting breath than of any sensation of pain which she experienced. John Bannister knelt down beside her. The stout man once more found himself a boy.

"This then," was the thought which filled his brain — "this then, is the sweet little girl whom I once loved so much!"

She knew him. A faint smile covered her features, and almost the last effort of her strength, enabled her to point to the woods, and to exclaim:—

"My father! my father!— There! Bear me to him, John."

The hand fell suddenly, the voice was silent, the lips were closed. A shiver shook the limbs of the strong man.

"Mary! Mary!" he called huskily.

Her eyes unclosed. She was not dead. There was still life, and there might be time to place her in the arms of her father before it was utterly gone. A noise in the direction of the mansion, and the appearance of lights in the avenue, determined the prompt woodman. He wound his arms tenderly about her, raised her to his bosom, laid her head on his shoulder, and as if she had been a mere infant in his grasp, darted forward into the cover of the woods. The alarm had evidently been given at the mansion, he heard the voices of the household, and the sudden clamors of the half-sober and half-sleeping soldiery. But he defied pursuit and search, as, bounding off, in the well-known route, he soon placed his burden at the foot of her father.

"Here, Clarkson, here is your daughter. Here is poor Mary.

She was not drowned. She lives, Jake Clarkson, but she has not long to live. She's going fast. Be quick—look at her, and talk softly!"

Clarkson bounded to his feet, gazed with convulsive tremors upon the pale, silent form before him, then, with the shriek of a most miserable joy, he clasped her in his arms. Her eyes opened upon him. He held her from him that he might the better meet their gaze. She smiled, threw herself forward upon his breast, and was buried within his embrace. In a wild incoherent speech, of mixed tenderness and reproach, he poured forth the emotions of his heart—the pangs of years—the pleasures of the moment—the chiding of his own cruelty, and her misdeeds. But she answered nothing—she heard nothing. Neither praise nor blame could touch or penetrate the dull, cold ear of death. She was, at length, at rest.

"Speak to me, dear Mary. Only tell me that you forgive me all, as John Bannister can tell you I have forgiven you."

"She will never speak again, Jacob. It's all over. She's got rid of the pain, and the trouble, and the vexation of this life; and I reckon she'll have no more in the next; for God knows, jist as well as I, that she's had a great deal more than her share."

"You don't say she's dead?" said Clarkson huskily.

"Well, except for the pain of it, she's been dead a long time, Jacob. But she don't hear you, I reckon, and she don't feel your arms, though you hold her so close to you. Give her to me, Jacob, that I may carry her deeper into the bay. The lights from the house are coming close, and they may find us here."

"Let 'em come!—who cares? They won't want her now she's dead!"

"No; but they may want *us*, Jacob."

"Let them want, and let them seek! We're ready! We'll fight, I reckon!" and his fingers were clutched together convulsively, as if the weapon were still within their grasp.

"Yes, we'll fight," said Bannister, "but not here, and not till we put her out of the way. 'Twon't be right to fight anybody where she is—not in her presence, as I may say."

"True, true," replied the other faintly; "but *I'll* carry her, John."

Bannister did not object, but led the way to the thicket, while the father followed with his burden. There, the woodman drew forth his matchbox and struck a light, and the two sat down to survey the pale spiritual features of one who had certainly held a deep place in the affections of both. It was a curious survey. Their place of retreat was one of those dense sombre masses of the forest where, even in midday, the wholesome daylight never thoroughly came. The demi-obscure alone—

"The little glooming light most like a shade,"

declared the meridian hour; while at midnight the place was dark as Erebus. The broad circumferences of oaks, the lofty stretch of ever-moaning pines, gathered close and solemnly around as if in secret council; while vines and leaves, massed together in the intervals above, effectually roofed in the spot with a dread cathedral vastness and magnificence. The spot had been freely used before by the outlyers, and more than one comfortable bed of dried leaves might be discovered under the oaks.

On one of these the body of the girl was laid. A few paces distant from her feet, in a depression of the earth, John Bannister had gathered his splinters and kindled a little fire, just sufficient to enable them to behold one another, and perhaps make them more than ever feel the deep and gloomy density of the place. The adjuncts of the scene were all calculated to make them feel its sadness. No fitter spot could have been chosen for gloomy thoughts; none which could more completely harmonize with the pallid presence of the dead. The head of the girl rested in the lap of the father. John Bannister sat behind the old man. A sense of delicacy made him reserved. He did not wish to obtrude at such a moment.

Years had elapsed since the father had been persuaded that his child had been lost to him, irrevocably, by death; and this conviction was embittered by the further belief that his own violence had driven her to a desperate end. In that conviction, deep, and keen, and bitter, were the pangs of his soul;—pangs which he could only blunt by the endeavor, hitherto futile, of finding, and inflicting vengeance upon, her betrayer. Dark had been his soul, darker its desires and designs. At length he finds her alive, whom he had fancied he had destroyed. He finds her living, only to see her die. His thoughts may be conjectured, not traced, nor described, as he watched the pale countenance, still beautiful, which lay before him in the immoveable ice of death. He watched her long in silence. Not a word was spoken by himself; and John Bannister felt too sincerely, on his own account, for idle and unnecessary remark. But the stifled nature at length broke its bonds. The heart of the father heaved with the accumulating emotions. Deep groans burst from his lips, and a sudden flood of relieving tears gushed from his eyes. Bannister felt easier as he perceived the change.

"All's for the best," said he, with a plain homespun effort at consolation. "It's best that she's gone, Jake Clarkson; and you see God spared her jest long enough to bring you together that you might exchange pardon. You was a little rough and she was a little rash, and God, he knows, you've both had mighty bad roughing for it ever since. Poor thing, she's gone to heaven, that's clear enough to me. I'm not jub'ous about it. She's been a sinner like the best, but if she wa'n't sorry for it, from the bottom of her heart, then sinner never was sorry. Poor Mary, if she hadn't looked a little too high, she wouldn't ha' fallen so low. She'd ha' been an honest man's wife; but what's the use to talk of that now. It only makes one's eyes water the more."

"It's good, John. It sort o' softens a man!"

"Not too much. A man oughtn't to be too soft about the heart, in a world like this, so full of rascals that need the knockings of a hard and heavy hand. Yet, ef a man ought to feel soft about the heart, jest now, that man's me. It's a sad truth, Jake, I was once jist on the point of axing you and Mary! I was; for I *did* love her, as I ha'n't seen woman to love from that day to this; and but for Edward Conway!——"

"That bloody villain! That thief—that murderer! Ha! ha! But I will have him yet, John Bannister! I was a fool to be frightened away, jist when I had my hand at his throat, and nothing to stop me. There he lay, still and ready for the knife!

Ho! John, jist there! I think I see him now! Stretched out, his eyes shut, his breast open, and nobody looking on——"

"Stop, Jacob Clarkson, God was a-looking on all the time—and Mary Clarkson was a looking on?—and what sent her thar jest at that moment? Who but God! And what did he send her thar for, but to stop you from doing a wrong thing? Look you, Jake Clarkson, you know I don't often stop to think or to feel when fighting's going on. I'm as quick to kill as the quickest dragoon in all Tarleton's brigade. That is, I'm quick to kill when it's the time for killing. But there's a time for all things, and I ain't quick to kill a man that's a-sleeping, and him too, so cut up already, that it's a chance ef he ain't got enough to bury him. I'm a-thinking, Jacob Clarkson, that God has jest given you a good warning, that you must do your killing in fair fight, and not by stealing to a man's bedside when he's sleeping, and he pretty well chopped up already. I reckon you'll be the man to kill Ned Conway yet, ef what he's got don't finish him; and ef it does, you're only to thank God for taking an ugly business off your hands. When I look upon Mary, thar, it puts me out of the idea of killing altogether. I'm sure I wish peace was everywhere. Lord save us from a time like this, when a poor child like that runs into the way of hard blows and bloody we'pons. It makes my heart sort o' wither up within me only to think of it."

But Clarkson was not much impressed by the grave opinions of his companion. He had always respected the straightforward character and manly judgment of the woodman; and there was something very plausible, to the superstitious mind, in the case presented at the outset of the woodman's speech.

"Sure enough! sure enough!" said the old man; "how could she come, jest at the moment I was going to kill him, if God didn't mean that I shouldn't do it jest then! But if he gets well again, John Bannister—"

"Kill him then—I'm cl'ar for that! I'll kill him myself then ef nobody comes before me with a better right. You've got a sort of claim to the preference."

We need not pursue the conference. One question which went to the very heart of John Bannister, and which he evaded, was uttered by the father, as, in passing his hands through the unbound portions of her hair, he felt them clammy with her blood. The revelation of her physical injuries was new to him.

"Oh, God, John Bannister! she bleeds! Her head is hurt. Here! jest here! I didn't mind the bandage before. She didn't die a nateral death. The cruel villain has killed her. He's got tired of her and killed her."

"Oh, no! no! Jacob!" exclaimed the other, with an agitation of voice and manner which betrayed his secret pangs. "No, I reckon not! He's not able to hurt anybody. I reckon —I'm sure—she got hurt by accident. I'll answer for it, the man that struck Mary Clarkson, would have sooner cut his right hand off than ha' done such a thing. 'Twas accident! I'm sure 'twas accident!"—and with these words the poor fellow went aside among the trees and wept like a child as he thought over the cruel haste of his own fierce spirit and too heavy hand.

"God forgive me, for not speaking out the truth, which is a sort of lie-telling after all. But how could I tell Jake Clarkson that 'twas the hand of John Bannister that shed the blood of his child? It's woful enough to feel it."

To bury the dead from his sight became the last duty of the father. John Bannister was for carrying the body to the family vault of the Middleton's and laying it there by dawn of day. But to this Clarkson instantly dissented.

"No," said he; "the Middletons are great people, and the Clarksons are poor and mean. We never mixed with 'em in life, and there's no reason we should mix in death."

"But you don't know Miss Flora, Jacob Clarkson."

"I don't want to know her."

"She's so good. She'd be glad, I'm sure, if we was to put her there. She's been tending poor Mary as if she was her own sister."

"She has, eh? I thank her. I believe she's good as you say, John. But, somebody might come after her, and shut me out of the vault when they please. They wouldn't like me to go there to see Mary when I wish, and wouldn't let 'em put me beside her. No! no! we'll put her in the ground beside the river. I know a place for her already, and there's room for me.

She was born in the Congaree, and she'll sleep sweetly beside it. If you live after me, John, put me there with her. It's a little smooth hill that always looks fresh with grass, as if God smiled upon the spot and a good angel 'lighted there in the night-time. Go, John, and try and find a shovel in the fields somewhere. We've got no coffin, but we'll wrap the child up in pine bark and moss, and she won't feel it any colder. Go, and let me sit down with her by ourselves. It's a long time, you know, since I talked with her, and then I talked cross and harsh. I'll say nothing to vex her now. Go, get the shovel, if you can, and when you come back, we'll take her, and I'll show you where to dig. By that time we'll have day to help us."

Bannister departed without a word, and left the father with his dead. We will not intrude upon his sorrows; but, when the whole history of the humble pair is considered, no sight could be more mournful than to behold the two—there, in that lonely and darksome maze of forest—at midnight—the flickering firelight cast upon the pallid features, almost transparent, of the fair, dead girl, while the father looked on, and talked, and wept, as if his tears could be seen, and his excuses and self-reproaches heard, by the poor child that had loved so warmly, and had been so hardly dealt with by all whom she had ever loved. Conway had ruined her peace and happiness; her father had driven her from her home; and he, who had never wilfully meant, or said, her wrong, had inflicted the fatal blow which had deprived her of life—perhaps, the stroke of mercy and relief to a crushed and wounded spirit such as hers! Truly, there was the hand of a fate in this—that fate that surely follows the sad lapses of the wilful heart! Hers was rather weak than wilful; but weakness is more commonly the cause of vice than wilfulness; and firmness is one of those moral securities, of inappreciable value, without which there is little virtue.

## CHAPTER XXXI.

### AN INTERVIEW BETWEEN THE TWO SCOUTS.

MEANWHILE, the alarm had been given at Brier Park, and the whole house was in commotion. Watson Gray was the first to stumble up, and into consciousness, upon the flight of Mary Clarkson; simply because he had been fortunate enough to feel the full force of the flying footsteps of her father. But several moments had elapsed after her departure, before the discovery of the fact was made, and the pursuit, which was then offered, appears to have taken a wrong direction. Certainly, they did not find the place of her concealment, nor the traces of her flight.

Yet no pains were spared to do so. The circumstances were mysterious and exciting;—to Flora Middleton, particularly so. She reproached herself, though, certainly without justice, for having left the poor girl in the custody of a drowsy servant; and her self-chidings were by no means lessened when the minds of all at the barony appeared to settle down in the belief that, in her delirium, the poor girl had wandered off to the river banks and cast herself into its waters. Thus, a second time, was the innocent Congaree made to bear the reproach of participating in, and promoting, the destruction of the same unhappy life.

In the chamber of the outlaw, the feelings, if less solemn and tender, were surely not less grave and serious. To Watson Gray, the mere death of the poor victim of his confederate, would have been of very small importance. Perhaps, indeed, he would have felt that it was a benefit—a large step gained toward the more perfect freedom of his principal. But there were some circumstances that compelled his apprehensions. Who had been in the chamber? What heavy feet were they that trampled upon him?—and why was that strange and formidable knife resting beside the person of the outlaw?

That somebody, from the apartment of Mary Clarkson, had been in that of Edward Conway, was soon apparent from the discovery of the little lamp which the former had carried, and which had fallen from her hands upon the couch of the latter, in the moment when she saw her father's face. This had been recognised by the servants, and the fact made known in the confusion of the search. But, though Gray felt certain that Mary had been in the room, he felt equally certain that there had been another also. It was possible that, in her delirium, the poor girl may have carried the knife as well as the light, and that she may have meditated the death of her betrayer:—all *that* was natural enough; but Gray felt sure that a heavier foot had trampled upon his neck and breast.

Naturally of a suspicious temper, his fears were confirmed, when, issuing from the house at the first alarm, he found his guards either withdrawn, or straggling toward their posts in almost helpless inebriety. Their condition led him to recall the story of the surgeon. The description which the latter gave of the stranger who had penetrated to the breakfast-room—his garments of blue homespun, and the huge knife which he carried—tended, in considerable degree, to enlighten him on the subject. He called the attention of the surgeon to the knife which had been found on the bed, and the latter, so far confirmed the identity of it with the one which the supposed ghost was seen to carry, as to say that the one was equally large of size with the other; but the former was incomparably more bright. He handled, with exceeding caution, the dark and dingy instrument, and re-delivered it, with fingers that seemed glad to be relieved from the unpleasant contract.

Seeing the surprise of the scout at such seeming apprehension, he began a long discourse about contagion, infection, and the instinctive dread which he had of all cutaneous disorders; to all of which Gray turned a deaf ear, and a wandering eye. The outlaw had been wakened by the unavoidable noise of the search, and had heard with some surprise and interest the circumstances which were detailed to him by Gray.

"How strange!" he exclaimed. "Do you know I had the sweetest sleep, in which I dreamed that Mary and myself were walking over the old rice-dam on the Santee, and I began to feel for her just as I felt then, when I first knew her, and she seemed twice as lovely, and twice as intelligent. How strange!"

Gray had judiciously suppressed some of the circumstances connected with the events of the evening. He had concealed the knife entirely, and forbore stating to him, as well as to everybody else, everything which related to the supposed intrusion of some stranger into the household.

"You have found her, Gray?" said the outlaw, when the former returned from the search.

"No! she is nowhere in the grounds."

"Indeed! could she have wandered to the river?"

"That is what they all think."

"But you?"

"I know not what to think."

"Why should you not think with them?"

"I should, but she did not seem to me to have strength enough for that. The river is a mile off; and she was evidently sinking fast when I saw her this evening."

"Where, then, do you think her?"

"Somewhere at hand. In some outhouse, or some hole or corner—or, possibly, in some ditch, or close nest of bushes, where we can't find her by night."

"Good God! and she has probably perished there—and thus!"

Gray was silent, and the outlaw felt the returning pangs of that remorse which most probably would have remained unfelt, except during the present period of his own inability.

"Poor, poor Mary. I would, Gray, that I could live over some things—some moments—of the past!"

"Do not let it afflict you so much. It can't be helped, and these things are common enough."

Ay, common enough, indeed. Nothing more common than human misery. Nothing more common than the human guilt which causes it. And how coolly do we urge the commonness of both, by way of reconciling our souls to their recurrence!

The philosophy of Watson Gray is, unhappily, of a very common description.

"Yes, yes. But such a catastrophe! You have been looking for her?"

"Yes, for the last two hours."

"But you will go again. You must, Gray."

"With the daylight, I intend to do so."

"That's well. See to her, for God's sake, Gray, and if she lives, let her last moments be easy. If all's over, see her carefully buried . . . It's an ugly business. Would I were free of *that!* I know not any blood that I would sooner wish to wash from my hands than hers."

"That should be the wish of Clarence Conway, not yours," said Gray, taking the literal sense of the outlaw's expression.

"Ah, Gray, the blow, the mere blow, is a small matter. If I were free from the rest, I think nothing more would trouble me. The last drop ran the cup over—but who filled it to the brim? who drugged it with misery? who made the poor wretch drink it, persuading her that it was sweet and pure? Ah, Gray, I fear I have been a bad fellow, and if there were another world hereafter—a world of punishments and rewards!"——

"Your situation would be then changed, perhaps," was the brutal sneer of Gray, "and every privilege which you had in this life would then be given up to her. Perhaps you'd better sleep, captain; sickness and want of sleep are not good helps to a reasonable way of thinking."

"Gray, I suspect you're a worse fellow than myself," responded the outlaw, with a feeble effort at a laugh. "Ten to one, the women have more to complain of at your hands than they ever had at mine."

"I don't know. Perhaps. But I think not. The little I know of them makes me fancy that they're a sort of plaything for grown people. As long as they amuse, well and good, and when they cease to do so, the sooner you get rid of them the better. When I was a young man, I thought differently. That is, I didn't think at all. I had a faith in love. I had a similar faith in sweetmeats and sugar-plums. I liked girls and confectionery; and—perhaps you never knew the fact before—I married one young woman, not very much unlike your Mary Clarkson."

"The devil you did!" exclaimed the outlaw.

"The devil I did marry!" returned the other, gravely. "You speak the very words of truth and soberness. She proved worse than a devil to me. I trusted her like a fool, as I was, and she abused me. She ran off with my best horse, in company with an Indian trader, whom I took into my cabin, fed and physicked. He seized the first opportunity, after he got well, to empty my house, and relieve it of some of its troubles. But I didn't see the matter in its true light. I wasn't thankful. I gave chase, and got my horse back—that was everything, perhaps—just after they had left Augusta."

"And you let the woman go, eh?"

"I left her with him, where I found them; and they liked the spot so well, that I think any curious body that would seek might find them there to this day. I have some reason to believe that she has been more quiet with him than she ever was with me. I don't believe they ever quarrelled, and when she was my wife we were at it constantly."

"You're a famous fellow, Gray!" exclaimed the outlaw, as he listened to a narrative of crime which was only remarkable, perhaps, from the coolness with which the chief actor related it.

"No, captain, not famous. To be famous is about the last thing that I desire; and I'm thinking you don't much care about it. But you'd better sleep now. Take all the rest you can, and don't mind anything you hear. You'll want all your strength and sense, as soon as you can get it, if you wish to get what you aim at."

'No doubt: I'll do as you counsel. But see after the poor girl by daylight."

"Yes, yes! we'll take all the care that's needful," was the response.

To stifle the remorse of his superior, Gray had taken a way of his own, and one that was most successful. The cold sneer is, of all other modes, the most effectual in influencing the mind which does not receive its laws from well-grounded principles. How many good purposes have been parried by a sneer! How many clever minds have faltered in a noble aim by the sarcasm of the witling and the worldling! How difficult is it for the young to withstand the curling lip, and the malignant half-smile of the audacious and the vain! Gray knew his man; and, in his narration, he had probably shown a degree of contumelious indifference to the character of woman, and the ties of love, which he did not altogether feel. It served his turn, and this was all that he desired of any agent at any time. He turned from gazing on the outlaw, with such a smile as showed, however he might be disposed to toil in his behalf, he was still able to perceive, and to despise, what seemed to him to be the weaknesses of the latter.

Leaving the chamber, he descended to the area in front of the dwelling, and drew together, without noise, the file of soldiers that had been left with him by Rawdon. These were now tolerably sobered; and, having taken pains to see that their arms were in good condition,—for it may be said here that the smallest part of Gray's purpose and care was to find the girl whom it was his avowed object to seek,—he led them forth into the adjoining thicket about an hour before the dawn of day.

Of the reputation of Gray as a woodsman we have been already more than once informed, and the suspicions which he entertained were such as to make him address all his capacity to the contemplated search. His little squad were cautioned with respect to every movement; and, divided into three parties of four men each, were sent forward to certain points, with the view to a corresponding advance of all, at the same moment, upon such portions of the woods as seemed most likely to harbor an enemy. Spreading themselves so as to cover the greatest extent of surface, yet not be so remote from each other as to prevent co-operation, they went forward under the circumspect conduct of their leader, with sure steps, and eyes that left no suspicious spot unexamined on their route.

The day was just begun. The sun, rising through the dim vapory haze that usually hangs about him at the beginning of his pathway in early summer, shed a soft, faint beauty upon a gentle headland that jutted out upon the Congaree, and compelled its currents to turn aside from the direct route, making a sweep around it, most like the curve of a crescent. Some thirty steps in the background was a clump of massive trees the principal of which were oak and hickory. They grew around one eminent pine that stood alone of all its species, as it was alone in its height and majesty. At the foot of this tree, and under the cathedral shelter of the oaks, John Bannister was busy in throwing out the earth for the spot chosen by Clarkson for his daughter's grave. The father sat at a little distance in the background, his child's head lying in his lap. The labors of Bannister had been severe, and he would not suffer the old man to assist him. The earth was rigid, and the innumerable roots of the contiguous trees traversed, in every direction, the spot chosen for the grave. Fortunately the stout woodsman had secured an axe as well as a shovel, and the vigor of his arm at length succeeded in the necessary excavation.

To remedy, as far as he might, the want of a coffin, the worthy fellow had stripped the rails from the neighboring fences, and he now proceeded to line, with them, the bottom and sides of the grave. These were in turn lined with pine bark and green moss, and the couch of death was spread with as much care and tenderness, under the cheerless circumstances, as if wealth had brought its best offerings, and art had yielded its most ingenious toils in compliance with the requisitions of worldly vanity.

Bannister was yet in the grave, making these dispositions, when Watson Gray, with his soldiers, advanced upon the party. To old Clarkson the task had been assigned of keeping watch. It was physically impossible that Bannister should do so while deep buried and toiling in the earth. The old man was too much absorbed in contemplating the pale features of his child, and too full of the strife within his heart, to heed the dangers from without; and so cautious had been the approach of Gray and his party, that they were upon the sufferer before he could rise from his feet or make the slightest effort to relieve himself from his burthen.

It was fortunate for Bannister that, being in the grave and stooping at the time, he was below the surface of the earth, and remained unseen at the time when Clarkson was taken. But, hearing strange voices, he immediately conjectured the approach of enemies, and cautiously peering above the grave, beheld at a glance the danger which threatened him. He saw Watson Gray, conspicuous, and standing directly above the person of Clarkson, whose daughter's head still lay in his lap. One of his hands was pressed upon her bosom, as if he felt some apprehension that she would be taken from him. On either hand of Gray he beheld a group of soldiers, and a glance still further, to the right and left, showed that they were so placed as to present themselves on every side between him and the forest. His flight seemed entirely cut off. But the coolness and courage of the woodman did not leave him in the emergency. He had already resolved upon his course, and rising rapidly to the surface, he became visible to his enemies. The voice of Watson Gray was heard at the same instant, calling to him to surrender.

"Good quarter, Supple Jack!—be quiet and take it. You can't get off. You're surrounded."

The tone of exultation in which the rival scout addressed him, made it a point of honor with Bannister to reject his offer, even if he had no reason to suppose that the assurance of safety meant nothing. He well knew, in those days, what the value of such an assurance was; for Tarleton, Rawdon, and Cornwallis, had long since shown themselves singularly reckless of all pledges made to "the poor bodies who were out" in the rebellion of '76.

"Make terms when you've got me, Watson Gray," was the scornful answer of the scout. "The only quarters I ax for is my own, and I'll save them when I've got 'em."

"If you run, I shoot!" cried Gray threateningly. "Look; my men are all around you."

"I reckon then I'll find 'em in the bottom of the Congaree;" was the fearless answer, as the scout leaped for the river bank with the speed of an antelope.

"Shoot!" cried Gray—"Shoot him as he runs! Fire! Fire!"

The volleys rang on every side, but the fugitive remained erect. He had reached the river bank. He seemed unhurt. His enemies pressed forward in pursuit; and the scout clapping his open palms together above his head, plunged boldly into the stream, and disappeared from sight.

Bannister could swim like an otter, and with head under water almost as long. But once he rose to breath, and his enemies, who waited for his re-appearance with muskets cocked, now threw away their fire in the haste with which they strove to take advantage of his rising. When he next became visible, he was on the opposite shore, and bade them defiance. A bitter laugh answered to their shout as he turned away slowly and reluctantly, and disappeared in the distant thickets.

Gray had lost his prey a second time, and he turned, with no good humor, to the prisoner with whom he had been more successful.

"Who are you—what's your name?"

"Jacob Clarkson!"

"Ha! you are then the father of this girl?"

"Yes!" was the sad reply of the old man, as his head sank upon his breast.

"Do you know this knife?" demanded Gray, showing the knife which had been found at the bedside of Morton.

"It is mine."

"Where did you lose, or leave it?"

"I know not. I dropped it somewhere last night."

"Where—at the house of Mrs. Middleton?"

"It may be—I was there!"

"You were in the chamber of Captain Morton!"

"Not that I know on," was the reply.

"Beware! You cannot deceive me. You stood beside his bed. You went there to murder him. Confess the truth:—did you not?"

"No!" cried the old man, starting to his feet. "I did go there to murder a man, but God forbid it. I couldn't, though he was laying there before me. She come between. She made me stop, or I'd ha' killed him in another moment. But it was Edward Conway that I would have killed. I know nothing about Captain Morton."

"Ha! I see it. Hither, Sergeant Bozman. Tie this fellow's hands behind him."

"Hands off!" cried the old man, with a sudden show of fight —"Hands off, I tell you! I must first put her in the ground."

"Give yourself no trouble about that. We'll see it done," said Gray.

"I must see it too," said the old man resolutely.

The resolution he expressed would have been idle enough had Gray been disposed to enforce his wishes; but a few moments' reflection induced him, as no evil consequence could possibly ensue from the indulgence, to yield in this respect to the prisoner.

"The old rascal!" he exclaimed—"let him stay. It's perhaps only natural that he should wish to see it; and as they have got the grave ready, put her in at once."

"Stay!" said the father, as they were about to lift the body. "Stay!—only for a minute!" and while the soldiers, more indulgent perhaps than their leader, gave back at his solicitation, the father sank to the ground beside her, and the tones of his muttered farewell, mingled with his prayer—though the words were undistinguishable—were yet audible to the bystanders.

"Now, I'm ready," said he, rising to his feet. "Lay her down, and you may tie me as soon after as you please."

The burial was shortly over. No other prayer was said. Old Clarkson watched the sullen ceremonial to its completion, and was finally, without struggle or sign of discontent, borne away a prisoner by his inflexible captor.

## CHAPTER XXXII.

### GLIMPSES OF COMING EVENTS.

THE outlaw did not hear of Mary Clarkson's death without some emotion; but the duration of his remorse was short. He soon shook himself free from its annoyances, and in a week more it was forgotten. Of the arrest of old Clarkson, his own previous danger from the hands of the latter, and several other details, connected with his proceedings, Watson Gray did not suffer his principal to know anything. His main object was to get his patient up and on his legs again, foreseeing that a time was approaching, when a sick bed could be no security for either of them in a region to be so shortly winnowed with the sword of an enemy. His scouts occasionally arrived, bringing him reports of the condition of the country: of the prospects of Rawdon's army, and of the several smaller bodies under Greene, Sumter, Marion, and Pickens.

These reports counselled him to make all speed. He did not press the outlaw with the intelligence which he thus obtained, for fear that their tendency might be to increase his anxiety, and discourage rather than promote his cure. To this one object, his own anxious efforts were given, without stint or interruption, and every precaution was taken, and every measure adopted by which the recovery of his patient might be effected. No nurse could have been more devoted, no physician more circumspect, no guardian more watchful. The late attempts of Clarkson had given him a mean opinion of the regulars who had been left to take care of the barony; and to watch *them* was the most irksome, yet necessary duty, which he had undertaken. But he went to his tasks cheerfully, and, with this spirit, a strong man may almost achieve anything.

The tidings which were sometimes permitted to reach the ears of Flora Middleton, were of no inconsiderable interest to that maiden. She heard frequently of Clarence Conway, and always favorably. Now he was harassing the tories on the upper Saluda, and now driving them before him into the meshes of Pickens among the Unacaya mountains. The last tidings in respect to him which reached her ears, were also made known to Watson Gray by one of his runners; and were of more particular importance to both of them than they were then fully aware of. It was reported that a severe fight had taken place between Conway's Blues and the Black Riders. The latter were beguiled into an ambush which Conway had devised, after the ordinary Indian fashion, in the form of a triangle, in which twenty-three of the Black Riders were sabred, and the rest dispersed. Gray did not greatly regret this disaster. He was now anxious to be free of the connection, and, perhaps, he conceived this mode of getting rid of them, to be quite as eligible, and, certainly, as effectual as any other.

"That fellow, Stockton, with his sly second, Darcy, are the only chaps that might trouble us. They suspect us; they know something, perhaps; and if Conway has only cut *them* up, along with the twenty-three, we shall count him as good an ally as the best."

Such was his only reflection as he communicated this news to the outlaw, his principal.

"Ay," replied the latter, "but why was there no lucky bullet to reward the conqueror. That hopeful brother of mine seems to own a charmed life, indeed. I know that he goes into the thick of it always, yet he seldom gets even his whiskers singed. The devil takes care of him surely. He has proper friends in that quarter."

"We needn't care for him, captain, so long as Rawdon lies between us. If you were only up now, and able, we could whip off the lady, and every hair of a negro, and take shipping before they could say Jack Robinson, or guess what we are driving at."

"Ay, if I were only up!" groaned the outlaw writhing upon his couch. "But that 'if' is the all and everything."

"But you are better. You are much stronger. I think this last week has done wonders for you; and, but for the weakness, and the gashes in your face—" The speaker paused without finishing the sentence.

"Very comely, no doubt: they will strike a lady favorably, eh? Do you not think they improve my looks wonderfully?"

There was something of bitterness in the affected indifference with which the outlaw made this comment. The other made no reply, and did not appear to heed the tone of complaint.

"Give me the glass, Gray," continued the outlaw.

He was obeyed; the mirror was put into his hands, and he subjected his visage to a long scrutiny.

"Nothing so shocking, after all. My mouth is something enlarged, but that will improve my musical ability. I shall be better able to sing 'Hail Britannia,' in his majesty's island of Jamaica, or the 'Still vex'd Bermoothes,' to one or other of which places we must make our way. Besides, for the look of the thing, what need I care? I shall be no longer in the market; and my wife is in duty bound to think me comely. Eh, what say you, Gray?"

"Yes, surely; and Miss Middleton don't seem to be one to care much about a body's looks."

"Don't you believe it, Gray. She's a woman like the rest; and they go by looks. Smooth flowing locks, big, bushy whiskers, and a bold, death-defying face will do much among a regiment of women. I've known many a sensible woman—sensible I mean for the sex—seek a fool simply because he was an ass so monstrous as to be unapproachable by any other, and was, therefore, the fashion. The ugliness is by no means an objection, provided it be of a terrible sort. I don't know but that success at first is as likely to attend the hideous as the handsome; that is, if it be coupled with a good wit and a rare audacity."

"The notion is encouraging, certainly; and I reckon there's something in it—though I never thought of it before."

"There is! It is a truth founded upon a first experience of the woman heart. Beauty and the Beast is a frequent alliance."

"I reckon that was the secret of the snake getting the better of Mother Eve in the garden."

"Yes: the snake was as bold and subtle as he was ugly. The

boldness and subtleness, reconciled the woman to the beast; and, once reconciled, to behold without loathing, she soon discovered a beauty in his very ugliness. If not handsome, therefore, be hideous; if you wish to succeed with woman:—the more hideous (the wit and audacity not being wanting) the more likely to be successful. The game were quite sure if, to the wit and boldness, you could add some social distinctions—wealth or nobility for example. A title, itself, is a thing of very great beauty. Now were I a lord or baronet—a count or marquis—you might slash my cheeks with half a score more of such gashes as these, and they would, in no degree, affect my fortune with the fair. In that is my hope. I must buy a title as soon as I have my prize, and then all objections will disappear. Still, I could have wished that that d—d spiteful brother of mine had subjected me to no such necessity. He might have slashed hip or thigh, and gratified himself quite as much in those quarters."

"Let us carry out our project, and you have your revenge!"

"Ay, and there's consolation in that for worse hurts than these. But hear you nothing yet from below? What from Pete? If the boats fail us at the proper time, we shall be in an ugly fix."

"They will not fail us. Everything now depends on you. If you can stir when the time comes——"

"Stir—I can stir now. I mean to try my limbs before the week's out, for, as the fair Flora forbears to come and see me, I shall certainly make an effort to go and see her. Has the poison touched, think you? Does she feel it—does she believe it?"

The outlaw referred to the slander which Gray had insinuated against Clarence Conway.

"No doubt. She's so proud that there's no telling where it hurts her, and she'll never tell herself; but I know from the flashing of her eye, after I said what I did about Colonel Conway and Mary Clarkson, that she believed and felt it. Besides, captain, I must tell you, that she's asked after you more kindly and more frequently of late. She always asks."

"Ha! that's a good sign; well?"

"I said you were more unhappy than sick. That you'd got

over the body hurts, I had no doubt. But then, I told her what an awful thing to fight with one's brother, and how much you felt *that!*"

"Ha! Well, and then?"

"She sighed, but said nothing more, and soon after went out of the room."

"Good seed, well planted. I shall cultivate the plant carefully. I fancy I can manage that."

"Psho!—Here's the surgeon," said Gray, interrupting him with a whisper, as Mr. Hillhouse appeared at the entrance.

The surgeon had forgotten, or forgiven, the slight to which his patient had previously subjected him. He was not a person to remember any circumstance which might be likely to disparage him in his own esteem. Besides, his head was now running upon a project which made him disposed to smile upon all mankind. We will allow him to explain his own fancies.

"Mr. Conway, good morning. I trust you feel better. Nay, I see you do. Your eyes show it, and your color is warming;—a sign that your blood is beginning to circulate equally through your system. Suffer me to examine your pulse."

"I feel better, sir, stronger. I trust to get fairly out of my lair in a week. I shall make a desperate attempt to do so."

"You *are* better, sir; but do nothing rashly. A week may produce great results. There are but seven days in a week, Mr. Conway—but a poor seven days—yet how many events—how many fates—how many deeds of good and evil, lie in that space of time. Ah! I have reason to say this from the bottom of my heart. A week here, sir, at this barony, has changed the whole aspect of my life." A sigh followed this speech.

"Indeed! And how so, pray!"

"You see in me, Mr. Conway, a man who has lived a great deal in a short space of time. In the language of the ancient poet—Ovid, it is—my life is to be told by events, and not by lingering years. It is a book crowded with events. I have passed through all the vicissitudes of a long life in Europe, India, and America. I have ate and drank, marched and fought—played the man of pleasure and the man of business—stood in my friend's grave, and often at the edge of my own;—saved life, taken life; and practised, suffered, and enjoyed, all things, and thoughts, and performances, which are usually only to be known to various men in various situations. But, sir, one humbling accident—the trying event, which usually occurs to every other man at an early period of his life, has hitherto, by the special favor of a benign providence, been withheld from mine!"

"Ah, sir, and what may that be?" demanded the outlaw.

"I have never loved, sir—till now. Never known the pang, and the prostration—the hope and the fear—the doubt and the desire—till the fates cast me upon the banks of the Congaree! Melancholy conviction! that he who has survived the charms of Europe and India—who has passed through the temptations of the noble and the beautiful, the wealthy and the vain, of those beguiling regions—should here be overtaken and overcome by the enemy in the wild woods of America."

"Indeed! It is indeed a most dreadful catastrophe! Gray, hand the doctor a chair, a glass of water, and if you have any Jamaica——"

"No, no!—I thank you, no!—I will take the chair only."

"And pray, sir," said the outlaw with a mock interest in the subject—"when did you suffer from the first attack, and who do you suspect of bewitching you?"

"Suspect of bewitching me!—a good phrase that!—I like it. My suspicions, sir, as well as yours, should naturally be strong that I am the victim of a sort of witchcraft; for, how else should a man fall so suddenly and strangely in a strange land, who has stood unshaken by such affections, through such a life as mine?"

"Very true! a very natural reflection, sir. But you have not said who you suspect of this cruel business."

"Ah, sir, who but the fair damsel of this very house. What woman is there like unto her in all the land?"

"Ha! It is possible!"

"Possible!—why not possible?" demanded the surgeon. "Is she not young, and fair, and rich in goods and chattels, and who so likely to practise sorcery?"

"True, true!—but doctor, are you aware that you are not

the only victim? She has practised with perhaps greater success on others."

"Indeed! Tell me, I pray you, sir!"

"Nay, I can only speak from hearsay. My friend here, Mr. Gray, can tell you more on the subject. The story goes—but I must refer you to him. Gray, take a ramble with Mr. Hillhouse, and see if you can not match his witchcraft case with one or more, much worse, if possible, than his own, and springing from the same fruitful source of mischief. Let him see that he does not lack for sympathy."

Gray took the hint, and the surgeon readily accepted the invitation to a walk, in which the former continued to give to his companion a very succinct account of the duel between the brothers, and the engagement supposed to be existing between Clarence and Flora. The artful confederate of the outlaw, taking it for granted that a person so supremely vain and silly as the surgeon, might be made to believe anything, and could scarcely keep secret that which he heard, arranged his materials in such a way as to make it appear that the fight between the brothers arose in consequence of the cruel treatment which Mary Clarkson had received at the hands of the younger. A purely magnanimous motive led the elder brother into the difficulty.

"Now, Mr. Conway, your patient, as soon as he heard that Colonel Conway was courting Miss Middleton, pursued him, only to reproach him for his breach of promise to the poor creature. The proud stomach of Colonel Conway couldn't bear that, and he drew upon Mr. Conway and wounded him in the face before he could put himself in preparation. The poor girl who had been following the colonel, everywhere, in boy's clothes, ran between them, and got her death, there's no telling by whose hands. And so the case stands, at present. Mr. Conway, your patient, of course wouldn't speak against his brother; and I s'pose, the marriage will go on between him and Miss Flora, unless—— she may have changed her mind since you've come to the barony."

"Ah! ha!" said the surgeon. "You've enlightened me very much, Mr. Watson Gray. I'm greatly your debtor. You are a man of sense. I thank you, sir—I thank you very much. Suppose we return to the mansion. I am anxious to change these garments."

"Change them, sir! What, your dress?"

The blunt mind of Gray couldn't perceive the association of ideas taking place in the brain of his companion.

"Yes, I wish to put on a dove-colored suit. The dress which I now wear, does not suit the day, the circumstances, nor my present feelings."

"What, sir?" demanded Gray in feigned astonishment. "Have you got a change for every day in the week? I have but *one* change in all."

The surgeon turned upon the speaker with a look which plainly said:—

"Impertinent fellow, to venture upon such an offensive comparison."

He contented himself, however, with remarking:—

"The wants of men, my good friend, differ according to their moral natures, the moods, and changes of mind by which they are governed. I have no doubt that two suits will be ample enough for *your* purposes; but for me, I have always striven to make my costume correspond with the particular feeling which affects me. My feelings are classed under different heads and orders, which have their subdivisions in turn, according to the degree, quality and strength of my several sensibilities. Of the first orders, there are two—pleasure and pain; under these heads come cheerfulness and sadness; these in turn have their degrees and qualities—under the first is hope, under the second, fear—then there are doubts and desires which follow these; and after all, I have omitted many still nicer divisions which I doubt if you could well appreciate. I have not spoken of love and hate—nor indeed, of any of the more positive and emphatic passions—but, for all of which I have been long provided with a suitable color and costume."

"You don't mean to say that you've got a change suitable for every one of these?" said the woodman with some astonishment.

"You inquire, Mr. Gray, with the tone of one who will not

be likely to believe any assurance. Oblige me by witnessing for yourself. I had arranged to examine my wardrobe this very noon, as a sort of mental occupation, with which I relieve the tedium of repose, and bad weather, and unpleasant anticipations. Do me the favor to assist me in this examination. We may probably gather from it some useful lessons, and I will endeavor to explain, what is at present very imperfectly understood, the singular propriety of my principles. You shall be able, when you have heard my explanation, to know, from the dress I wear, what particular condition I am in that day. A man's costume, if properly classed, is a sort of pulse for his temper. This morning, when I rose, under the influence of one set of moods, I put on a meditation costume. I am in a brown dress you see. That shows that, when I put it on, I was in what is vulgarly called a 'brown study.' Circumstances, the ground of which you can not, perhaps, conjecture, prompt me to go back and change it for one of a dove color. You may perhaps comprehend the meaning of this hereafter.

"I reckon it's something about love, that dove color," said Gray bluntly. "Dove and love always go together."

"Ah, you are quick. You are naturally an intelligent person, I suspect. You will comprehend sooner than I expected. But come and see — come and see."

"This fool will do us excellent service," said the outlaw, when, at his return, Watson Gray recounted the events of the interview.

"He will go to Flora Middleton in his dove-colored small-clothes, and find some way of letting her know what a scamp Clarence Conway is, and what a martyr I have been to the cause of innocence betrayed. You did not let him guess that I had a hankering after Flora myself?"

"Surely not: I just let him know enough of the truth to lie about. A fool can do an immense deal of mischief with the tail-end of a truth."

"Which is always slippery," said the outlaw. "Well, mischief can do us no harm. In this case, it is our good — it works for us. Let him kill Clarence Conway off in her esteem, and *he*, certainly, is not the thing to be afraid of. But did you really count his breeches?"

"No, God help me! I shook myself free from him as soon as I could. I'd as soon pry among the petticoats of my grandmothers. But he had an enormous quantity. I reckon he's used up all his pay, ever since he began, in this sort of childishness."

The conjectures of the outlaw, as respects the course of the exquisite, were soon realised. But a few days had elapsed when he availed himself of an opportunity to pursue Flora as he saw her taking her way through the grounds in the direction of the river. His toilet, however, was not completed when he caught a glimpse of her person through the window; and the task of completing it—always one of considerable pains and duration—enabled her to get considerably the start of him. She had passed the sentinels, who were sauntering at their stations, and had reached the lonely vault where her ancestors reposed. The solemn shadows of the wood by which it was encircled pleased her fancy; and the united murmurs of the pine-tops and the waters of the Congaree, as they hurried on at a little distance below, beguiled her thoughts into the sweet abodes of youthful meditation.

Flora Middleton was, as we have endeavored to show, a maiden of deeper character and firmer qualities than usually distinguish her age; perhaps, indeed, these characteristics are not often possessed in equal degree among her sex. Firmness of character usually implies a large share of cheerfulness and elasticity; and these also were attributes of her mind. Her life, so far, had been free from much trial. She had seldom been doomed to suffering. Now, for almost the first time, the shadows of the heart gathered around her, making her feet to falter, and bringing the tears into her eyes. The supposed infidelity of Clarence Conway had touched her deeply—more deeply than even she had at first apprehended. When she first heard the accusation against him, and saw the wretched condition of the poor girl whom she believed to be destroyed by his profligacy, she said, in the fervor of virtuous indignation which prevailed in her mind:—

"I will shake him off for ever, and forget that I ever knew him!"

But the resolution was more easily taken than kept. Each

subsequent hour had increased the difficulties of such a resolution; and, in the seeming death of her hopes alone, she discovered how entirely her heart had found its life in their preservation. When she believed the object of her attachment to be worthless—then, and not till then, did she feel how miserable its loss would make her heart. Perhaps, but for the very firmness of character of which we have spoken, she would neither have made nor maintained such a resolution. How many are the dependent hearts among her sex, who doubt, mistrust, fear, falter—and yet, accept!—who dare not reject the unworthy, because they can not forbear to love.

Flora Middleton felt the pain of the sacrifice the more deeply in consequence of the conviction, which her principles forced upon her, that it must yet be made. Could she have faltered with her pride and her principles, she would not have found the pain so keen. But she was resolute.

"No! no!" she murmured to herself, as all the arguments of love were arrayed before her by the affections—"No! no! though it kill me to say the words, yet I will say them. Clarence Conway, we are sundered—separated for ever! I might have borne much, and witnessed much, and feared much, but not this. This crime is too much for the most devoted love to bear."

She was suddenly startled from her meditations by a slight whistle at a little distance. This was followed by a voice.

"Hist!" was the gentle summons that demanded her attention from the thicket on the river-banks, as she turned in the direction of the grounds. Her first feminine instinct prompted her to fly; but the masculine resolution of her mind emboldened her, and she advanced toward the spot whence the summons proceeded. As she approached, a head, and then the shoulders of a man, were elevated to the surface, as if from the bed of the river; and a closer approximation proved the stranger to be an old acquaintance.

"John Bannister!" exclaimed the maiden.

"Yes, Miss Flora, the very man—what's left of him."

"'What's left of him,' John Bannister? Why, what's the matter? are you hurt?"

16*

"No, no, Miss Flora—I say 'what's left of me,' only because, you see, I don't feel as ef I am altogether a parfect man, when I have to dodge and shirk about, not able to find my friends, and always in a sort of scatteration of limbs, for fear that my enemies will find me. I am pretty well to do in health at this present, thanks be to God for all his marcies; though, when you saw me last, I reckon you thought I was in a bad fix. But I give 'em the slip handsomely, and used their own legs in coming off."

"How was it, Bannister?... But come up. You must be standing rather uncomfortably there."

"Pretty well-off, thank ye. There's a dug-out under me, and as I've only a word or two to say, I needn't git up any higher to say it."

"Well, as you please; but how did you make your escape from the British, John?"

"Ah, that's a long story, Miss Flora, and there's no needcessity for telling it, any how. Some other time, when the war's over, and every man can be brave a bit, without danger, I'll let you know the sarcumstances. But jest now, what I come for is to give you warning. You've got a sly rascal as ever lived in your house, at this present, that never yet was in any one place so long without doing mischief—one Watson Gray——"

"Why, he's attending on Mr. Conway."

"It's a pair on 'em, I tell you. That Watson Gray's after mischief, and it's a mischief that has you in it. But don't be scared. I want to let you know that there's one friend always at your sarvice, and nigh enough to have a hand in any business that consarns his friends. If anything happens, do you see, jest you hang a slip of white stuff—any old rag of a dress or handkerchief—on this bluff here, jest where you see me standing, and I'll see it before you've gone fur, or I'm no scout fit for the Congaree. Ef there's danger to you, there's help too; and, so far as the help of a good rifle and a strong arm can go—and I may say, Miss Flora, without familiarity, a good friend—dang my buttons ef you sha'n't have it."

"But, John, from what quarter is this danger to come? What is it? how will it come?"

"Ah, that's the danger. You might as well ax in what shape Satan will come next. But the d—'s in your house, that's enough. Be careful, when he flies, he don't carry off much more than he brought in. Maybe you'll see a man, to-morrow or the next day, coming to Watson Gray's. He's about my heft, but jest with one half the number of arms. He's a stout chap, poor fellow, to be cut short in that way. Now, you can trust him. Ef he says to you 'Come,' do you come. Ef he says 'Stay,' then do you stay; for he's honest, and though he seems to be working for Watson Gray, he's working handsomely agin him. You can trust him. He's *our* man. I convarted him to a good onderstanding of the truth of liberty; but I had to make every turn of it clear to him before he'd believe. We had two good argyments to try the case; but I throw'd him the last time, and he's been sensible to the truth ever sence. 'Twas him that helped me out of the British clutches t'other day. But we won't talk of that. Only you jest believe him, and hang out the white flag, here under the bluff, ef ever you need a friend's sarvice."

"You confound and confuse me only, John Bannister, by what you have said. I believe that you mean me well, and that you think there is some danger; and I am willing to trust you. But I don't like this half-confidence. Speak out plainly. What am I to fear? I am a woman, it's true, but I am not a coward. I think I can hear the very worst, and think about it with tolerable courage afterward; nay, assist somewhat, perhaps, in your deliberations."

"Lord love you, Miss Flora, ef I was to tell you the little, small, sneaking signs, that makes a scout know when he's on trail of an inimy, you'd mout-be only laugh. You wouldn't believe, and you couldn't onderstand. No, no! jest you keep quiet and watch for the smoke. As soon as you see the smoke, you'll know there's a fire onder it; which is as much as to say, jest when you see anything onderhand going on—scouts running this way, and scouts running that, and Watson Gray at the bottom of all and busy—then you may know brimstone's going to burn, and maybe gunpowder. Keep a sharp eye on that same Watson Gray. Suspicion him afore all. He's a cunning sarpent that knows how to hide under a green bush, and look like the yallow flow'r that b'longs to it."

"You said something about Mr. Conway—Mr. Edward Conway, John?"

He's another sarpent. But——"

The head of the scout sank below the bank. He had disappeared, as it were, in the bottom of the river; and while Flora Middleton trembled from apprehension, lest he had sunk into the stream, she was relieved by the accents of a voice at some little distance behind her, as of one approaching from the house. She turned to encounter Mr. Surgeon Hillhouse, *now*, in his dove-colored small-clothes.

## CHAPTER XXXIII.

### THE RETURN OF THE BLACK RIDERS.

The reader is already familiar with the business of the surgeon, and has probably conjectured the sort of answer which he received from the heiress of Middleton Barony. His dove-colored garments, and rose-color address, availed him little; though, it may be added, such was the fortunate self-complaisance of the suitor, that, when he retired from the field, he was still in considerable doubt of the nature of the answer which he had received. It was still a question in his mind whether he had been refused or not.

According to his usual modes of thinking, his doubts were reasonable enough. He had taken more than ordinary pains to perfect himself in the form of application which he intended to use. His fine sayings had been conned with great circumspection, and got by rote with the persevering diligence of a schoolboy or a parrot. He had prepared himself to say a hundred handsome phrases. The colors of the rainbow, and the various odors of the flowers, had been made to mingle in a delicate adaptation to his particular parts of speech, in all the best graces of that Euphuism of which, among his own *clique*, he had been usually recognised as the perfect master. He knew that Lady Belle would have turned up her eyes to heaven, in new-born ecstasies, had he but spoken his pretty speeches to her; and those of Lady Grace would have been filled with tears of a similar delight. How could he bring himself to believe that they had been thrown away on the unpractised auditories of the maid of Congaree?

The more he asked himself this question, the more difficult became his belief, and by the time that he reached his chamber, he was convinced that, at the most, he had only suffered an evasion—such an evasion as dandies are apt to practise upon their tailors, when they avoid, without refusing, payment—such an evasion as a cunning damsel might practise upon her lover, lest a too sudden concession might cheapen the value of her charms. So consoling was this new conviction, that he determined, in discarding his dove-colored small-clothes, not to put on his "Nightshade,"—so he called his "Despondency" or "Disappointment-dress;" but to select a dark orange-tinted garment —his "Pleasant-sadness"—as more certainly expressive of mingled hope and doubt, than any other color. The serious examination which took place in his mind, and of his wardrobe, before his choice was determined, served, beneficially, to sustain his sensibilities under the shock which they had necessarily suffered. That evening he was pleasingly pensive, and his eloquence was agreeably enlivened by an occasional and long-drawn sigh.

Flora Middleton did not suffer this "Mosca" to afflict her thoughts. Naturally of a serious and earnest character, she had other sources of disquietude which effectually banished so light an object from her contemplation; and nothing could so completely have mystified the surgeon, as the calm, unmoved, and utterly unaffected manner with which she made the usual inquiries at the evening table.

"Does your coffee suit you, Mr. Hillhouse? Is it sweet enough?"

"Would all things were equally so, Miss Middleton. We might dispense with the sweet in the coffee, could we escape from the bitter of life."

"I should think, sir, that you had not been compelled to drink much of it; or you have swallowed the draught with wonderful resignation."

"Alas!—have I not!" and he shook his smooth, sleek locks mournfully, from side to side, as if nobody had ever known such a long continued case of heart ache as his own. But Flora did not laugh. She was in no mood for it; and though the frequent *niaiseries* of the surgeon might have provoked her unbounded merriment at another time, her heart was too full of her own doubts and difficulties not to deprive her, most effectually, of any such disposition now.

The next day she was somewhat startled at the sudden arrival of a man at the barony, whom she instantly recognised as the person meant by John Bannister when he spoke to her the day before. His frame was large and muscular, like that of Bannister, but he was deficient in one of his arms. She fancied, too, that he watched her with a good deal of interest, as he passed her on the staircase, making his way to the apartment of the invalid, and his attendant, Gray. It was evident that Bannister had some intimate knowledge of what was going on among her inmates, and this was another reason why her own anxieties should increase, as she remembered the warnings to watchfulness which the worthy scout had given her. She was well disposed to confide in him. Strange to say, though she knew him chiefly as the friend of Clarence Conway, and had every present reason to believe in the faithlessness and unworthiness of the latter, her confidence in, and esteem for, John Bannister, remained entirely unimpaired. The wonder was that Conway should have so entirely secured the affections of such a creature. This wonder struck Flora Middleton, but she had heard of such instances, and it does not seem unnatural that there should be still some one, or more, who, in the general belief in our unworthiness, should still doubt and linger on, and love to the very last. We are all unwilling to be disappointed in our friends, not because they are so, but because it is our judgment which has made them so. Bewildered, and with a heavy heart, that seemed ominous of approaching evil, Flora retired to her chamber with an aching head, while our old acquaintance, Isaac Muggs, the landlord, was kept in busy consultation with the outlaw and his confidant.

We pass over all such portions of the conference as do not promise to assist us in our narrative; and the reader may fancy for himself the long ejaculations, which the landlord uttered, at finding his old associate and captain reduced to his present condition;—ejaculations, which were increased in length and lugubriousness, in due proportion with the treachery which Muggs meditated, and of which he had already been guilty.

"Enough, enough of your sorrow, good Isaac," said the outlaw with some impatience: "these regrets and sorrows will do for a time when we have more leisure, and as little need of them. Give me good news in as few words as possible. Your good wishes I can readily understand without your speaking them."

Muggs professed his readiness to answer, and Watson Gray conducted the inquiry; Morton, assisting only at moments, when moved by a particular anxiety upon some particular point.

"Did you meet Brydone before you separated from Rawdon's army?"

"Yes: he joined us at Ninety-Six."

"He told you the plan."

"Yes."

"You are willing? You've got the boats?"

"I can get them."

"When—in what time?"

"Well, in four days, I reckon, if need be."

"Are you sure?"

"I reckon, I may say so. I'm pretty sartin."

Here Morton turned upon the couch, and half raised himself from it.

"Look you, Muggs, you speak with only half a heart. You seem scared at something. What's the matter with you, man? are you not willing?"

"Yes, cap'in, I'm willing enough. Why shouldn't I be willing? I'll do all that you ax me."

"That is, you'll get the boats in readiness, here, at the landing, within four days; but, are you willing to fly yourself? You are not fool enough to fancy that the rebels will let you remain here when the army's gone, to enjoy what you've despoiled them of."

"No great deal, cap'in, I reckon."

"Ay, but there is Muggs! You cannot deceive me, though you may the rest. I know your gains, and a word of mine would send them flying much more rapidly than they were ever brought together. Do not provoke me, man, to speak that word."

"Well, cap'in, I dont want to provoke you. Don't I tell you that I'll do all you wish."

"Ay, but you seem d——d lukewarm about it, Muggs; and you have not said whether you are willing to join our fortunes or not. Now, you join us, heart and soul, body and substance, one and all, or we cut loose from you at once. You are in our power, Muggs, and we can destroy you at a moment's warning. But it's neither our policy nor wish to do so. You can help us materially, and we are willing to help you in return. Bounty lands await you in the West Indies. You will live with old friends and neighbors, and with your guineas——"

"Mighty few of them, I reckon, cap'in," said Muggs.

"Few or many, you can only save them by flight. Are you ready? Beware how you answer! Beware! You must go with us entirely, or not at all."

An acute observer might have seen, while the outlaw was speaking, an expression of sullenness, if not resistance, in the face of the landlord, which did not argue the utmost deference for the speaker, and seemed to threaten an outbreak of defiance. But if Muggs felt any such mood, he adopted the wiser policy of suppressing it for the present.

"'Swounds, cap'in," he exclaimed, with more earnestness than he had before shown in the interview—"You talk as if you was jub'ous of me,—as if I worn't your best friend from the beginning. I'm willing to go with you, I'm sure, wherever you think it safest; but you're mistaken if you think I've got so much to lose, and so much to carry away. Mighty little it would be, if the rebels did find every guinea and shilling in my keeping."

"Pshaw, Muggs, you cannot blind me with that nonsense. Be your guineas few or many, it is enough that you know where to carry them, and how to keep them in safety. And now, what of Rawdon? Where did you leave him?"

"At Ninety-Six."

"He had beaten Greene?"

"Run him off from the siege only."

"Well: what next. Does Rawdon leave a garrison at Ninety-Six?"

"I reckon not. There was some talk that he means to sarve it as he sarved Camden. Burn the town and tear up the stockade."

"As I thought. That's, certainly, his proper policy. Well! was the troop still with Rawdon?"

"No: they were gone after Conway, somewhere above upon the Ennoree."

"May they find him, and batter out each other's brains at the meeting," was the pious and fraternal wish of the outlaw.

"And now, Muggs," he continued, "the sooner you take your departure the better. Get your boats ready, yourself and guineas, and be at the landing here, at midnight, four days hence."

"So soon!" said Gray. "Do you think, captain, you'll be able by that time?"

"Ay! able for anything. I must be able. This flight of Rawdon will render mine necessary, with as little delay as possible."

"But he has not fled yet?"

"Pooh! pooh! A retreat in his condition, is only another word for a flight. But if he does not yet fly, he will have to do so, before very long. He is preparing for it now, and I have for some time past been aware of the approaching necessity. He must not descend the country before I do, that is certain; and if I can descend the Santee in boats, I can endure a wagon the rest of the way, to the head of Cooper river. The rest is easy. The important object is to secure faithful boatmen; and with you, Muggs, and a few others, upon whom I can rely, I have no doubts, and no apprehensions."

The landlord was dismissed upon his secret mission. Watson Gray conducted him to the banks of the river, where lay the identical boat in which our friend John Bannister had approached the shore in seeking the interview with Flora Middleton. It was huddled up in the green sedge and bushes at the edge of the river swamp, and thus concealed from the eyes of the passing spectator. Before parting, Gray gave his final instructions to the landlord, in which he contemplated every matter essential to the journey, and, perhaps, conducted the affair with less offence to the feelings of the latter than had been the case on the part of the outlaw. Scarcely had Watson Gray gone from sight, before Bannister emerged from the swamp thicket and joined the other.

"He's a cute chap, that same Watson Gray, as ever beat about a thicket without getting into the paws of a black bear at rutting season. I'm a thinking ef the man was decent honest, I'd sooner have him in a troop of mine, than any man I knows on. He's a raal keener for a sarch. I'd reckon now, Isaac Muggs, from the way he slobber'd you over in talking, that he was a meaning to swallow you when all was done. It's the way with the big snakes, when the mouthful is a leetle big at the beginning."

"I reckon that's his meaning, Supple Jack,—I'm jub'ous that's what both he and the cap'in are a conjuring."

"And I am thinking, Muggs, that he was a trying to ease off something that he said to you before, which went agin the grain, and made the teeth grit."

"'Twan't him that said it — 'twas the cap'in."

"A pair on 'em — both sarpents, — mou't-be, different kinds of sarpent; but the bite of a rattle or a viper, is, after all, the bite of a sarpent; and it don't matter much which a man dies of, when both can kill. But what made the captain graze agin your feelings?"

"Why, he's a trying to make a scare of me about staying here, when he's gone. He says there's no safety for me among the rebels."

"I reckon, Isaac Muggs, there's an easy answer for all that. You've jest got to p'int to me, and say, 'That 'ere man convarted me by strong argyment,' and I reckon nobody'll be so bold as to touch you after that."

"He threatened me too;—and I to be the first to advise him to make long tracks from the troop!"

"I'm mighty sorry you ever gin him such advice, Isaac," said Bannister, rebukingly.

"Yes: but though he made b'lieve that he was angry, and all that, now, to-night, he tells me how he's been getting ready a long time for a start."

"I b'lieve him! Indeed, I knows as much! Well, I'm willing that he should get away, Isaac Muggs, without any hurt to hair or hide. For, though he desarves hanging and quartering as much as ever man desarved it, yet he's come of the same blood, half way, with Clarence Conway; and for his sake, I'm willing to let Ned Conway get clear of the hanging. I shouldn't be so mighty anxious to help him out of the way of a bullet, for that's the business of a soldier, to die by shot or steel, and it don't disgrace him, though it's hurtful to his feelings. I'd help to find the boat for him myself, and send him on his way, ef he was content to git off with his own hide in safety. But when he's after his villany to the last—when I know that he wants to carry off another Congaree gal, and, this time, agin her will——"

"I'm a-thinking, Supple, that you're clean mistaken in that. Neither him nor Gray said a word about it."

"Not to *you*, Isaac. They'd ha' been but small sodgers if they had. No! no! They know'd that twa'n't the way to get their business done, to make it more difficult. They were rather jub'ous of you, you say yourself, though all they pretended to want of you was, jest to carry off the cap'in. Would it ha' made it any easier to tell you that they wanted you to help to carry off the young woman from her friends and family; and, as I'm thinking, to stop also in their way down and clean the plantation of his father's widow of all it's niggers? No! no! Isaac! They know how to play the game better than that. They tell you they play for high and low, only; but watch them well, and they'll make their Jack too, and try mighty hard to count up game! But, the game's in our hands now, Isaac: at least, I'm a-thinking so. As for you and your guineas—I don't ax you how many you've got—but jest you do as I tell you, and

I'll answer for their safety. We'll get the boats and the hands between us, and we'll have 'em all ready when the time comes, and if the gal is to be whipped off, it won't make it less pleasant to us to have the handling of her. Do you cross the river now, and be sure and put the boat high up in the creek. I'll keep on this side a leetle longer. I have a leetle matter of business here."

"You're mighty ventersome, Supple."

"It's a sort o' natur', Isaac. I always was so. A leetle dance on the very edge of the dangerous place, is a sort of strong drink to me, and makes my blood warm and agreeable. I'll jest scout about the woods here and see who's waking and who's sleeping; and who's a-tween sleeping and waking like myself."

The first attentions of Jack Bannister were paid to the sleeping. He watched the progress of his comrade, until his little barge had disappeared from sight in the distance, then made his way with the intensity of a natural affection, to the lonely spot where his hands had dug the grave for Mary Clarkson, and where her body had been laid. Here he paused a few moments in silent meditation, then proceeded to the dense thicket to which, on the night when she fled from the barony, he bore her inanimate person.

When he reached the spot, he kindled his light, and drew from a hollow tree a hatchet and rude saw which had been formed from an old sabre, the teeth of which had been made by hacking it upon some harder edge than its own. He then produced from another place of concealment sundry pieces of timber, upon which he had already spent some labor, and to which his labor was again addressed. Gradually, a long, slender, and not ungracefully wrought shaft of white wood appeared beneath his hands, into which he morticed the arms of a cross, with a degree of neatness, and symmetry, which would have done no discredit to the toils of a better artist, under the more certain guidance of the daylight. This little memento, he was evidently preparing, in silence and seclusion, and with that solemnity which belongs to the pure and earnest affection, for the lonely grave which he had just visited. With a fond toil, which withheld no care, and spared no effort, he now proceeded—his more heavy task being finished—to a portion of his work which, perhaps, was the most fatiguing of all the labors of love which he had imposed upon himself. This was to cut into the wood the simple initials of the poor girl for whom the memorial was intended. Our worthy woodman was no architect, and the rude Gothic letters which his knife dug into the wood, may perhaps have awakened, subsequently, the frequent smile of the irreverent traveller. He possibly anticipated the criticisms of the forward schoolboy, as he murmured, while sweating over his rude labors—

"It's a precious small chance for l'arning that Jack Bannister ever got upon the Congaree; but it's the best that I can do for poor Mary, and I'd ha' been willing to give her the best of me from the beginning. But twa'n't ordered so by Providence, and there's no use for further talk about it. If I hadn't used a man's we'pon upon her, I'd be a-mighty deal more easy now, but God knows, 'twasn't meant for her—'twasn't any how from the heart—and 'twas nateral that a man should strike, hard and quick, when he finds another jumping out upon him from the bush. Who'd ha' thought to find a gal in man's clothes, jest then too, in the thick of the fighting? But the Lord's over all, and he does it for the best. That sorrow's done with, or ought to be done with; and the sensible person ought to be satisfied to look out and prepare only for them that's yet to come. This board is a sort of line between them old times and the coming ones; and these two letters shall say to Jack Bannister, nothing more than—'Look for'a'd, Jack; there's no use in looking back!' Yet everybody can make 'em out, though they may read quite another lesson. They'll laugh, may be at such printing. It's bad enough, sartin; but it's the best I could do. There's a mighty ugly lean about that 'M.,' jest as if it was a tumbling for'a'd upon the 'C.'—yet I thought I had got the two running pretty even together. Well, there's no helping it now. It must stand till the time comes when I can pay the stonecutter to do a good one."

From his horn, he filled with powder the lines which he had cut in the wood, and then ignited it. The blackened traces made the simple inscription sufficiently distinct, and the good fellow, shouldering his rude monument, bore it to the grave, and drove it down at the head of the inmate.

He had not well finished this work, before he fancied that he heard foreign sounds mingling suddenly with the murmurs of the Congaree, as it plied its incessant way below. He listened, and the murmurs deepened. He went forward, cautiously, through the wood, and it was not long before he discerned the advance of a body of men, all well mounted, whom, upon a nearer approach, he discerned to be the Black Riders.

John Bannister was not a man to be alarmed easily; but he retreated, and stole into the cover of a bay, the thicket of which he knew was not penetrable by cavalry. Here he crouched in silence, and the formidable band of outlaws slowly wound along in silence, through the forest, and on the very edge of the thicket in which he lay concealed.

A new care filled his bosom, as he beheld their progress in the direction of the barony. He had no means of contending with such a force, and where was Clarence Conway? Feeling for his commander, and sympathizing with his affections, the first thought of Bannister had reference to the new dangers which beset the path of Flora Middleton. He was surprised, however, to perceive that the banditti came to a halt but a little distance from him. They alighted, the words of command were passed along in whispers, and in ten minutes they prepared to bivouac.

## CHAPTER XXXIV.

### MESHES.

"Well, it's mighty strange, I'm thinking, that they don't go for'a'd. They're as cautious and scary, now, as ef the whole of Sumter's rigiment was at the Park. They're after some new mischief that's more in want of a night covering than any they've ever done before. Well, we'll see! There's Watson Gray with his corporal's guard at the house; and here's the Black Riders here; and if the two git together, it's precious little that John Bannister can do, with the help of Isaac Muggs, and he with one hand only. Ef I could work poor Jake Clarkson out of their fingers, he'd make a third, and no small help he'd give us in a straight for'a'd, up and down fight. But, I'm jub'ous he stands a bad chance in the grip of Watson Gray. Ef I could git round now to the barony, and show reason to Miss Flora to slip off to the river, I wouldn't wait for Ned Conway to stir; but I'd hide her away in the Congaree, where the swamp-fox himself couldn't find her. But then there's no hope of that. There's a strange way of thinking among young women that's never had the blessing of a husband, as ef it wouldn't be so decent and dilicate to trust a single man under such sarcumstances; which is mighty foolish! But something must be done, and John Bannister must be in the way of doing it. Lord love us!—ef he would only send Clarence now, with fifty of his troop, among these bloody black refugees!"

The course of John Bannister's thoughts may be traced in the above soliloquy. The good fellow felt the difficulties of his own position; though, it is clear, that apprehension for himself was the last subject in his mind; the only one which awakened no anxiety, and called forth little consideration. To rescue Flora Middleton was his sole object. He knew the desires of Edward Conway for that maiden, and naturally concluded that the arrival of his troop would give him the power to accomplish his wishes, even by violence, if necessary. It was therefore a reasonable occasion for surprise and conjecture, when he found the outlaws taking their halt and supper on the skirts of the barony, and in profound silence and secrecy. That they should keep aloof from their captain, when nothing lay in the way to prevent or retard their reunion with him, was naturally calculated to mystify the scout. He little knew the character and extent of those malign influences, which prevailed among that wild and savage body, unfavorable to their ancient leader.

It was with increasing concern and interest that Bannister, in following and watching the movements of the outlaws, found them about to throw a line of sentinels between the grounds of the barony and the river landing. This measure denoted certain suspicions which they entertained, as he fancied, of the practices in which he had been recently engaged; and it became necessary that he should find means to apprise his comrade, Muggs, on the other side of the Congaree, of the danger that awaited any undue exposure of his person in his future crossings to and fro.

"A long swim!" muttered the faithful scout, with a slight shiver, as he surveyed the river; "and rather a cold swim, too, at midnight; but I'll have to do it. If I don't, they'll riddle poor Isaac's belly with bullets, when he's thinking of nothing worse to put in it than his breakfast. But I must dodge about the house first and see what's a-going on in that quarter. It seems mighty strange that they shouldn't have made themselves known to their captain. What's to be afeard of? But rogues is always a myster'ous and jub'ous sort of things. A rascal never goes straight to his business. If he has to shake hands with you he does it with a sort of twist, and a twirl, and sometimes a squint, that looks every which way but the right one. Now, it's reasonable that a good scout should shy off, and dodge, and make himself as squat and small, under a bush, as he naterally can, and as a big body will let him. But when the game's a straight-for'a'd one—when there's no dangers nor no inimy, and only one's own affairs to see after—it's a sign of a rogue all over that he shirks. It shows that he shirks from the love of the thing, and not because it's a needcessity."

John Bannister did not suffer his moral philosophy to keep him inactive. He was one of those who philosophize yet go forward — a race of which the world has comparatively few. In obedience to his determination, as expressed above, he stole through the ways which had been sufficiently traversed by his feet to be familiar, which led him, without detection, to the grounds immediately about the mansion. At the front door of the dwelling, which was closed, he saw one sentinel on duty. But he yawned, emphatically and loud, more than once while the scout watched him; and by his listless movements seemed evidently weary enough of his post to leave it to itself at the first seasonable summons. The most perfect military subordination was not preserved by him as he paced to and fro along the court. He sang, and whistled, and soliloquized; and, not unfrequently, relieved the dull measured step of the sentinel by the indulgence of such a gavotte as a beef-eating British soldier of the "prince's own" might be supposed capable of displaying in that period of buckram movement.

"He'd hop higher and dance a mighty sight better," murmured John Bannister, as he beheld the "signior of the night" in this grave exercise, "ef he was only on the 'liberty' side of the question. He gits a shilling a day, and a full belly; but he ain't got the light heart after all. Give me a supper of acorns, b'iled or unb'iled, in the Santee swamp, before all his hot bread; if so be, the cause I'm a-fighting for can't give me a better heart to dance than that. Lord! he can no more shake a leg with the Congaree Blues than he can sight a rifle!"

Contenting himself with this comparison, and the brief survey which had induced it, he turned away, and, traversing the settlement, came to the out-house in which, once before, he had seen the guard busy in their gaming practices. A light glimmering through the log chinks apprized him of the presence there of an occupant; and, approaching cautiously, and peeping through an aperture in the rear of the mud structure, he was struck with the sight of an object, to him, of very painful interest. This was Jake Clarkson, very securely fastened with ropes, which confined both his hands and feet.

The old man leaned, rather than sat, against the wall of one section of the building. A dull composure, which seemed that of a mortal apathy, overspread the poor fellow's countenance. His eyes were half closed, his mouth drawn down, yet open, and the listlessness of death, if not its entire unconsciousness, prevailed in the expression of all his features.

Four of the British soldiers were present in the apartment; two of them stretched at length upon the floor, seemingly asleep, and the other two, busy to themselves, playing languidly at their favorite game, which they relieved by a dialogue carried on sufficiently loud to enable Bannister to learn its purport. From this he gathered enough to know that the improvement of Edward Conway was such as to promise them a change, for which they pined, from the dull monotonous recurrence of the same unexciting duties, to the adventures of the march, and all those circumstances of perpetual transition, which compensate the rover for all the privations which he must necessarily undergo in leaving his early homestead.

But the eyes and thoughts of Bannister were fixed on the prisoner only. The pressure of surrounding foes only made him the more anxious to gather together and secure his friends; and thinking of poor Mary was also calculated to make him eagerly desirous to recover her father. This desire grew more keen and irresistible the more he watched and reflected, and it was with some difficulty that he restrained his lips from the impetuous assertion of his determination to release him from his bonds or perish. This resolve, though not expressed aloud, was still the occasion of a brief soliloquy.

"Dang my buttons, ef I don't try it! If there's time it can be done, and there's no harm in trying. A rifle in Jake's hands is a something that acts as well as speaks; and if so be, we're to have trouble, a bullet from a twisted bore is a mighty good argyment in clearing the track for the truth. It's a sort of axe-stroke, leading the way for the grubbing-hoe."

Ten minutes after, and Jake Clarkson was roused from his stupor by the slight prick of a sharp instrument from behind him. The nervous sensibility of the old man had been pretty well blunted by time, trial, and misfortune; and he neither started nor showed the slighest symptom of excitement. But his eyes grew brighter, his mind was brought back to the world in which his body lingered still, and a lively apprehension was awakened within him, lest the gambling soldiers should see, or hear, the hand that he now felt was busy in the effort to extricate him from his bonds. He did not dare to stir or look; but he was already conscious that the *couteau de chasse* of the woodman, fastened to a long stick, had been thrust through the crevices of the logs, and was busily plied in sawing asunder the cords that fastened his arms. These had been tied behind the prisoner, and he prudently kept them in that position, even though, in a few moments after, he felt that their ligatures had yielded to the knife.

The workman ceased from without. His task, so far as it could be effected by him, seemed to be ended; but the feet of the prisoner were still secured. The friendly assistant seemed to have disappeared. A full half hour elapsed and Jake heard nothing. The soldiers still kept at their game, and the prisoner, exhausted with the excitement of his new hope, leaned once more against the wall.

In doing so he again felt the sharp prick of the knife-point. Cautiously, but with nerves that trembled for the first time, he availed himself of one of his freed hands to possess himself of the instrument; which now, separated from the handle, had been left by the scout for the farther benefit of the prisoner. He clutched it with strange delight. The momentary impulse almost moved him to spring to his feet, and bound upon the guard with the most murderous determination. But the prudence of his friend's course from without, was not wasted upon him, and he contented himself with quietly securing the knife behind him, placing his hands in the same position in which his cords had previously secured them, and, with new hopes in his bosom, preparing to wait the proper moment when he might safely proceed to finish the work of his emancipation.

Satisfied that he had done all that he could, at this time, for the rescue of Clarkson, the scout took his way back to the river, the banks of which he ascended a few hundred yards, and then, without reluctance, committed himself to the stream. Half-way across, the rocks afforded him a momentary resting-place, from which he surveyed, with a mournful satisfaction, the white cross which his hands, but a little while before, had reared upon the grave of Mary Clarkson. It stood conspicuous in sight for several miles along the river.

The still hours of the night were speeding on; and the murmur of the river began to be coupled with the sudden notes of birds, along its banks, anticipating the approach of the morning. A sense of weariness for the first time began to oppress the limbs of the woodman, and it needed a strong and resolute mental effort to prevent him from yielding to sleep upon the slippery black rock which gave him a temporary resting-place in the bosom of the stream. Plunging off anew, he reached the opposite banks, fatigued but not dispirited. Here, he soon transferred the duties of the watch to his comrade. To the landlord he briefly communicated the events of the evening, and bestowed upon him the necessary advice for caution.

Meanwhile, a spirit equally anxious and busy, pervaded the breasts of some few in the encampment of the Black Riders. The watches had been set, the guards duly placed, and the sentinels, being made to form a complete cordon around the barony, Lieutenant Stockton, acting as captain, went aside, in consultation with his apt coadjutor, Ensign Darcy. The tone and language of the former were now much more elevated, more confident and exulting, than usual. The realization of his desires was at hand. He had met the approbation of Lord Rawdon, in the conduct which he had displayed in the management of his troop during the late march, and nothing seemed wanting to his wishes but that his immediate superior should be no longer in his way. To supersede him, however, was not easy, since the personal grounds of hostility which Stockton felt could not be expressed to their mutual superior; and these were such as to lead the former to desire something beyond the mere command of the troop which he had in charge.

It was necessary not merely to degrade but to destroy his principal. The humiliating secret which Edward Morton possessed, to his detriment, was equally an occasion for his hate and fear; and all his arts had been exercised to find some pretext for putting out of his way a person whose continued life threatened him with constant and humiliating exposure. Circumstances had co-operated with the desires of the conspirators. The secret of Edward Morton had been betrayed. It was known that he desired to escape from the troop;—that he was planning a secret flight to the city;—that he had already sent off considerable treasure; and, that he awaited nothing but a partial recovery of his strength, and the arrival of certain boats which had been pledged to him by the landlord, Muggs, to put his project in execution.

In thus proceeding, he had violated the laws of the confederacy—the fearful oath which bound the outlaws together—an oath taken in blood; and the violation of which incurred all the penalties of blood. No wonder that Stockton exulted. His proceedings were now all legitimate. His hate had a justifiable sanction, according to the tenets of his victim, equally with himself. It was the law of the troop. It was now indeed his duty to prosecute to the death the traitor who would surrender all of them to destruction; and the only remaining security left to Morton was the rigid trial to which his band was sworn. The bloody doom which his treachery incurred, was to be inflicted only after the fullest proofs that it was justly merited. In this lay his only chance of safety, and this chance rested upon a slender foundation. One of his special and most trusted agents had been bought over by the machinations of Darcy, and had betrayed him. He had involved another of the band in his developments, and this other had confessed. Two witnesses concurring against him and the proof was held to be conclusive; and of these two witnesses Stockton was now secure.

But other considerations were involved in the deliberations of the parties. Edward Morton they knew to be a desperate man. Watson Gray was a man to be feared as well as hated. These were in possession of a strong brick dwelling, with probably a dozen musketeers under arms, and commanded by Rawdon to obey them in every particular.

It was no part of the policy of Stockton, to come to blows under such circumstances. Some artifice was necessary to effect his objects. To get the soldiers out of the way, to baffle Gray, and secure possession of Edward Morton, was the design which they had resolved upon, and this required considerable management, and excessive caution in their approach. Besides, one of their witnesses was absent on a scout, and to declare their purpose, until he was present to maintain it by his oath, would have been premature and imprudent. It was also their object to capture the landlord, Muggs, whose proposed agency in securing the boats for the flight of Edward Morton was known to the conspirators through the individual who had first betrayed his employer to his enemies. Hence the watch which had been set upon the river-landing, and which had compelled Bannister to swim the stream that night.

These matters formed the subjects of deliberation between the two conspirators. Their successes, so far, made them sanguine of the future; and the rich rewards which it promised them, made them equally joyful. The treasures of their captain were to be equally divided between themselves, and we find them accordingly quite as busy in counting, as in securing their chickens.

"Pete Flagg has charge of the negroes, over two hundred already, and there are those from the place of his stepmother, which he planned to take off with him in these boats of Muggs. I know where to go for his guineas—ay, to lay my hands upon the vault; but we must get the memorandum acknowledgment which I reckon he has about him, from John Wagner, who keeps his money. There must be three thousand guineas at the least."

"We share equally," said Stockton, with eager eyes. "That of course is understood."

"Yes: but there should be a private paper between us," said Darcy.

"What need? we know each other."

"Ay, but the best friends can not be too cautious. I have drawn out a little memorandum which we can both sign to-morrow."

"Agreed; I'm willing. But no witnesses, Darcy—that would ruin all."

"Yes—that's the d—l. Let the troop once know what we

count upon—and our chance would be as bad, or even worse than his. We should hang with him!"

"Him we have! Him we have! I would Brydone were here. I long for the moment to wind up our long account of hate. It will be the sweetest moment of my life when I command them to drag him to the tree."

"Be patient—don't let your hate risk our gains. We can get nothing by working rashly. These eight or ten soldiers that he has here would make desperate fight. That scoundrel, Gray, must have suspected us when he asked Rawdon for them."

"Well, well—he'll have his turn also."

"I doubt we'll have to fix him along with the captain. He's a bird out of the same nest."

"I shall be willing. I have no love for him."

"Did you tell Brydone when to meet you here?"

"Yes!—that's all arranged!"

"By that time we ought to have possession of the captain."

"Ay, then or never. We must have him and all things in readiness by the time Brydone comes. Are you sure of the men? Is there none doubtful?"

"None. There's a few milk-hearted fellows only, but they're of the scary sort. They'll offer no opposition when they find so many against them."

"Be sure of them, also, if you can. I'd even give something to make all sure. There must be no bungling at the last moment. If there is, and he has any chance to talk, he is so d—d artful of tongue, that he'd work courage into the most cowardly heart. I fear him still."

"I do not. I know *them*, and I know *him*," replied the subordinate. "His day is done. He hasn't the same power over them that he had of old, and the late profits have enlightened them considerably on the subject of your better management."

"Yes, those guineas were good arguments, I think."

"Famous. But the better is to be shown. His treachery is the best. Let them but know conclusively that his purpose is to give them up, break the law, and leave them—perhaps, betray them into Sumter's clutches—and there will be but one voice among them, and that will be, 'Death to the traitor!'"

"So be it. To-morrow night we have him, and with the rise of another sun he dies."

"Yes, if Brydone comes in time for the trial."

"Brydone or not, Darcy—he dies."

## CHAPTER XXXV.

### BAGATELLE BEFORE BUSINESS.

This will suffice to show the policy of the confederates. Their plans of treachery were nearly complete, and they were weaving them with the silent industry and circumspection of the spider, who already sees and has chosen his victim.

Little did Edward Morton fancy, at this moment, the web that environed and the dangers which threatened him. He himself was busy in his own plans of similar treachery. His wounds were healing fast, his strength returning, and with his strength came back the old passions of evil which had heretofore inflamed his heart to its own debasement. The mournful fate of the poor Mary Clarkson had already passed from his thought, and almost from his memory; and, if remembered at all, it was only in connection with the new feeling of freedom which he felt in her absence. Her death he now regarded as a sort of Providential interference, by which he was relieved of a burden at the auspicious moment when it must have become more burdensome than ever.

Circumstances seemed to favor him on every hand; and the influence of mind upon matter was never more favorably shown than in the improvement of his health and strength, under the agreeable sensations which he experienced from a review of all the promising results which seemed to await only his recovery. In a few days his bark, richly freighted, was to bear him away to a region of security and peace, in which, free from all harassing dangers which had so long attended his progress, he was to enjoy the fruit of his toils, and taste the luxuries of a fresh and long-desired delight. He would shake himself free from his old connections—a wish long since entertained; he would fly with the woman whom he loved, from the foes whom he feared and hated—to the peace for which he had yearned, and to that affluence which a mercerary appetite for gain had already accumulated in abundance.

No wonder, then, that, revelling in these convictions, he laughed and sang at intervals, as Watson Gray and himself discussed their mutual plans and glowing expectations. The skies never seemed to look down more propitiously bright than upon their joint wishes and performances; and even Watson Gray, habitually stern and composed in his bearing and demeanor, condescended to join in his principal's merriment, and to minister to his mirthful mood, by a relation of such of the particulars of the surgeon's wooing as had come to his knowledge.

We have seen the share which Gray had in promoting the objects of Hillhouse. He knew, of course, that Flora Middleton would scorn such a suitor. He had already beheld the indifference—to call the feeling by its most innocent epithet—with which she regarded him; and he, as well as the outlaw, knew enough of human, or rather woman nature, to be sure that the result of his application would be at once amusing and unsuccessful. Gray recounted, for the benefit of his superior, the preparatory toils which Hillhouse had undergone at his toilet—partly in his presence—in determining upon the colors of his suit, the style and pattern of his dress, and the manner, audacious or subdued, in which he should make his first approaches. In choosing his costume, he seemed disposed to realise the pictorial satire with which the ancient artists used to describe the self-perplexity of the Englishman in putting on his clothes:—

"I am an Englishman, and naked I stand here,
Musing in my mind what garment I shall wear;
Now I shall wear this, and now I shall wear that,
And now I shall wear—I can not tell what."

The reader is aware that the dove-colored suit was triumphant; but he does not so well know the peculiar air which marked the carriage of the suitor. Watson Gray had seen him depart, and had beheld him on his return. We know, that by the time Hillhouse got back to the house, he had fairly convinced himself that the unqualified rejection of Flora Middleton had been, in reality, nothing more than that ordinary mode of evasion among the sex, of the uses of which none of them are wholly ignorant, and with which they simply mean to heighten the value of their subsequent concessions.

Thus assured, his countenance wore nothing of discomfiture in its expression. Nay, so perfectly triumphant did it seem, that Gray, who could not altogether believe that the world possessed any instance of such thoroughly self-blinding vanity, began to tremble lest Flora, with that weakness of the sex which makes them miracles of caprice upon occasion, had, in her unhappy moments, been over-persuaded and had yielded. Staggered for an instant by this apprehension, he was left but a little while in doubt. When Hillhouse gave the tenor of her answer, Gray laughed outright, and hurried away to share the pleasure with his superior. The surgeon followed him to the chamber of the outlaw, as soon as he had succeeded in adopting the symbol of a fitting sentiment for the new change which he contemplated in his garments; and, without intending any such favor, he delighted the invalid by a candid revelation of the events which had just taken place, and which he deemed to be so favorable to his desires.

"May you always be so fortunate!" was the generous wish of the outlaw, as the surgeon concluded his narrative.

"Thank you. You are too good. I doubt not I shall be. But, in truth, is it not wonderful that a country girl — a mere rustic, as she is — should be able to practise those arts which belong only to fashionable life?"

"An instinct — an instinct, my dear sir."

"Well, 'pon my affections, I think so."

"They're all alike, Mr. Hillhouse — high and low, rich and poor, city-bred and country-bred — they all know how to baffle the ardent, and stimulate by baffling."

"It will somewhat reconcile me to the event," said the surgeon. "I had my apprehensions about the poor girl's bearing in good society. I should have felt the awkwardness of bringing into the upper circles the unsophisticated damsel of the woods, such as she seemed to be at first; but now——"

"The instinct of the sex will usually supply the want of training—it will save you every annoyance; but, even were it otherwise, Mr. Hillhouse, how charming would it have been to have shown her in the fine world as the beautiful savage from the Congaree!"

"Gad, yes! I never thought of that."

"An aboriginal princess."

"Like Powkerhorontas! Ay, I have heard of that princess. She was a Virginian princess. My old friend, Sir Marmaduke Mincing, told me all her history—how she had fought her father, and rescued the captain—what was his name?—But no matter—lt was something very low and vulgar. She married him; and Sir Marmaduke, who had seen her, said she had really a very human countenance, and was quite like a woman; but"—lifting his hands in horror—"her feet? They were monstrous. They were four feet, rather than two. Ha, ha! four feet! Do you take me with you, Captain Conway? Four feet rather than two!"

"Ha! ha! ha!" roared Gray; and Conway also echoed the laughter of the surgeon, but it was rather at himself than his wit.

"But the feet of your princess here, Miss Middleton, are really very good, and rather small feet, Mr. Hillhouse. They will occasion no fright!"

"Ah, true, quite respectable as feet—quite respectable! She will do; and your idea, sir, that she would be so *distingué*, appearing in the character of *la belle sauvage*, reconciles all objections wonderfully. I think much better of the young creature than before. I do, really."

"No doubt you should; but Mr. Hillhouse—not to interrupt the pleasantness of your dreams—let me remark that war and love do not enjoy the same camping ground long, as they do not often employ the same weapons. The one is very apt to scare away the other. You, sir, have little time to lose. Are you aware that Lord Rawdon is in full retreat?"

'Retreat—from what?"

"The enemy—the rebels. He has been compelled to evacuate Ninety-Six."

"Evacuate! what an unpleasant word!"

"You'll find it so, unless you proceed in your attack with increased vigor. You will soon be compelled to evacuate Brier Park, leaving *la belle sauvage* to the care of other savages not so beautiful, and possibly something more dangerous."

"You discompose my nerves, Captain Conway. May I learn if all this be true—be certain?"

"Too true: ask Mr. Gray. He brings me the intelligence. He has just received it."

"Sure as a gun," said Gray.

"And with quite as startling a report," continued the outlaw. "What you do will need to be done quickly. You must press the siege."

"Night and day," added Watson Gray.

"You can't stop for regular approaches," continued Morton. "Remember you have nothing but field-works to contend with——"

"And, for——" added the surgeon, rubbing his hands with a gentle eagerness.

"Sap and storm at the same moment, Mr. Hillhouse. You must go through and over the works both; or expect to raise the siege very shortly. I doubt if you have three days left you. Lord Rawdon will be on his way for the Eutaw before that time."

"My dear friend! you rejoice while you alarm me. I will not suffer any delay. But haste is so vulgar."

"Except in flight."

"Ah! even there; one can not dispose his garments well, and the face is flushed, and the manner is flurried. But there are cases of necessity——"

"Imperative necessity!"

"Yes; when we have to dispense with ordinary rules of conduct."

"All active movements are of this sort, whether they contemplate flight or assault. Your affair combines both. You must make your attack shortly, for *your* retreat must soon follow that of his lordship."

"True, most true!"

"And how honorable is it to carry off a prisoner even in flight!"

"It softens the necessity—it takes the shame from defeat."

"It redeems it," said the outlaw; "and such a prisoner, too! Ah! Mr. Hillhouse, you are certainly a man to be envied."

"My dear captain, you do most certainly flatter me. But I was born under a fortunate star. I have been thus fortunate always, and particularly among the sex. Remind me to relate to you some curious successes which I have had. But not now. I must leave you now. Forgive me that I am thus abrupt. But I go in obedience to your counsel. I go to prepare for the war. By the way, those metaphors of yours were well carried on. I shall endeavor to recall them at the first leisure; those, in which you spoke of the prosecution of my present purpose, by sap and storm, and so forth. I suspect, captain, that you, too, have been rather a fortunate person, in your own experience, among the women. But, *your* field has not been a difficult one. Women are very accessible in America, though I certainly do not agree with my old friend, but present enemy, the Marquis de Chastellux,* who says that a Frenchman may do anything with the women of your country."

"Does he say that?—the scoundrel!" exclaimed the outlaw, with a burst of provincial indignation.

"Now," continued the surgeon, "had he said Englishman for Frenchman, there would have been some reason in it; though it isn't every Englishman, either, of whom such a thing might be said."

The outlaw and his comrade both looked serious. The reply of the former was made with some effort at composure, and the "wreathed smile" upon his lips was the result of some struggle with his sterner passions.

"No, sir; the instances are not frequent, I suspect. But the

---

* For what the Marquis does say, see his "Travels in North America," New York edition, p. 260. The sample of complaisance is very French and amusing.

opinion may naturally be entertained in its full extent by one who has been, and is destined to be, so uniformly successful everywhere."

"Thank you, captain—you are too flattering. But I confess —I *have* had my successes—I have, Heaven knows!"—with an air of profound humility, as he bowed himself out of the apartment.—"Heaven knows, I have had successes which might well turn the heads of wiser men than myself."

"The ape!—the monstrous ape!" exclaimed Morton, "was there ever such an ape!"

"A long-eared ass!" muttered his more rude companion; "a long-eared ass, if ever there was one! If Miss Flora don't pull his ears, it won't be because she don't see 'em."

"No! It's devilish strange that such a fellow should preserve his follies amidst all his changes, and while pursuing a life which, more than any other, would be likely to lop off the affectations and conceits of boyhood."

"Well, I reckon," said Gray, "he's just like a great many others, who know they can't pass for wise men, and are determined to pass anyhow. A fool would rather you'd see him as a fool than not see him at all."

"Egad!" exclaimed Morton, with all the enthusiasm of a new idea, "Egad! I think I'll see this fellow at his follies. I'll make an effort, Gray, to get down stairs this very afternoon."

"Don't think of such a thing," said Gray.

"Ay, but I will! I feel strong enough for it, and a change of objects will do me good. I long to feast my eyes, also, upon the charms of the fair Flora. Zounds! had it been Clarence Conway, who lay sick and wounded in her dwelling, what a difference! She'd have deigned him a glance before this! She'd have sat beside his bed, and her hand would have been in his, and she would have played with his hair, and her long locks would have floated upon his cheek! Damnation! that fortune should thus smile upon one, and blast the other always! Thus has it been from our cradle. By heavens, Gray, I tell you, *that* man—boy and man—ay, when he was but a brat of an infant —a squeaking, squalling, unconscious brat of an infant—this jilting Jezebel, called Fortune, showered her gold and jewels, about him even then, and has clung to him ever since, with a constancy hardly ever known to any of her sex. All around seemed to toil in his behalf, everything tended to his benefit; ay, even when I toiled in his despite, I have been compelled to curse the vain labor which redounded only to his good! and I—"

"You've had your good fortune, too, captain!" said Gray, condolingly.

"Have I!" cried the other, dashing the mirror, upon which he had looked at that moment, into fragments at his feet; "have I, indeed? I must read it in these gashes, then! I must feel it in this feebleness; in these wounds which fetter my activity now, when safety, life, success, everything, depends upon my strength and freedom! No, no! Gray; my good fortune is yet to come!"

"Don't distrust Fortune, captain. I'm thinking she's been your friend quite as much as his. She's helped him in some things, perhaps; but how is he any the better for them? As for Miss Flora doing for him what she wouldn't do for you, that's all in my eye. I reckon that she looks on him now a little blacker than she ever looked, or ever will look, on you. Well, what next? After all his fortunate gettings, where is he? And after all your misfortunes, where are you? Why, he's just on the brink of losing everything, and you are just that nigh to getting all that he loses, and perhaps a great deal more."

"Would it were now!—would I were sure. But, Gray, I have my fears, my doubts. Past experience teaches me that good fortune is never more doubtful, than when it wears the sweetest and most promising countenance. We have to depend upon others. That is always the great drawback to a man's chances. Should that fellow, Muggs, now fail us with his boats."

"Don't you fear. He will not fail."

"And Flora! God! could I be sure of that!"

"And what's to hinder? The one answers for the other."

"Ay, not much to hinder, if we use violence. Main force may carry her off, and shall, unless she yields readily; but I tell you, Gray, I'd give half that I'm worth—half of all my spoils—but to be spared this one necessity."

"What, captain, you're not getting mealy-mouthed in the business. Your conscience ain't troubling you, sure?"

"No! It's not that I have any scruples; but I would enjoy the blessing of a willing prize, Gray! That, that is everything!"

"Lord knows," rejoined the other with a yawn, "you had a willing prize enough in Mary Clarkson."

"Speak not of her, Gray," said the other in half-faltering accents—"not now! not now!"

"She was a willing prize, and one you were willing enough to get rid of. Give me the prize that *don't* consent in a hurry—that gives me some trouble to overcome. I wouldn't give a shilling for a wagon-load of that fruit that drops into the mouth the moment it opens for it."

"Nor I. Nor is that what I mean, Gray; I mean only that I should like to forbear absolute violence. I do not object to the opposition or the difficulty, if I could *win*, by my own wit, wisdom, attractions—win through her sympathies, and not by strife. And I must still try for this. I will see Flora this very evening. I will get down to the supper-table. I am strong enough for it; and I will see for myself how she manages this silly witling. The truth is, Gray, I'm not altogether satisfied that she will feel that scorn for the fellow that we feel. *We* judge of a man according to his own manliness; but this is not the mode of judging among women. They look at the streamers of the ship, and her gaudy paint; while men look to see if her timbers are good; if she follows the helm, if she is taut, and trim, and steady upon the wave. I believe that where it depends upon a woman's heart—where her affections are firmly enlisted—she will be true to the death, and in spite of death; but, when the matter is referable only to the judgment, I lose all confidence in her. She is then to be watched narrowly, and guided cautiously, and kept from the breakers, among which she otherwise would be sure to run. Now, Flora Middleton is a woman whose mind will take a large share in her affections. She'll hardly suffer her feelings to get entirely beyond the control of her judgment; and it may be advisable that I should assist, at her next conference with this gudgeon, in order to help him somewhat in the exposure of his more ridiculous qualities."

"It don't need, captain. I reckon she's seen 'em all for herself, long before this. You'd better not go down. Better keep all your strength for the time when you'll need it all."

"What! man! Do you think I could fail *then?* Impossible! No! no! Gray. You're getting quite too timid to be a safe counsellor, and I'm resolved to have a glance at Flora Middleton this evening, though I die for it. I think the sight of her will give me new strength and spirit. Besides, man, it is time that I should try my experiment upon her. If you are right—if she believes that Clarence Conway has been doing those evil deeds which I need not acknowledge, and has dismissed him for ever from her regards—then this is the very time to urge my claims and be successful. Personally, there is very little difference to the eye between us; unless these d——d scars! Ha! didn't you let her know that they were got fighting with Clarence in defence of injured innocence, and all that! If so, they will not seem so very uncomely. There is yet another circumstance, Gray: I flatter myself that the contrast between myself and her present suitor, the surgeon, even in his dove-colored breeches, will hardly be against me. Is not that something—are not all these things something? If I can *persuade* her, we diminish some of our labor, and several of our difficulties; and that must be tried *first*. I must play the lover as well as I can, before I play the conqueror. I must *woo* my bride, before I resort to the last mode of winning her."

"You'd better keep your bed two days longer."

"Pshaw! get me some proper clothes. I wish I had the pick of the surgeon's wardrobe, for, of a truth, Gray, I have but little choice of my own. I suspect my small clothes are of all colors, with the blood and dust of that last brush; but, no matter about the stains here and there; if you can only get me tolerably trim. I should rather be as unlike my popinjay rival as possible, on such an occasion."

The outlaw kept his resolution, in spite of all the exhortations of his comrade; and that evening, surprised the family, and the surgeon, Hillhouse, not the least, by his sudden entry into the *salle à manger*.

## CHAPTER XXXVI.

### A VISION.

Edward Morton, could he have always kept his blood in abeyance, would have made a first-rate politician. He had superior cunning, but he had, at the same time, too much earnestness. He yielded himself quite too much up to his subject. He could not tamper and trifle with it. His impetuosity defeated his caution; and, in every respect in which he failed, he could reproach himself only as the true cause of his failure. The stuff which he had expressed in conversation with Watson Gray, about the influence of fortune, did not deceive himself. He knew better, whenever he permitted himself to think gravely, and speak honestly; but men get into a habit of deceiving themselves while seeking to deceive others; and fortune has always been compelled to bear the whining reproaches of mankind whenever their own wits go a-blundering. Pride makes them unwilling to admit the fault to be in themselves, and fortune is a good-natured damsel, who seldom resents the imputations cast upon her. They clamor accordingly, and without fear, at her expense; and grow familiar with the language of unprofitable and unintended declamation. It scarcely needs that we should remark how unfrequently they make acknowledgments of her bounty. When successful, it is their own excellent art, audacious courage, admirable skill, and manly accomplishment, that achieve the conquest; and the smile which denotes their satisfaction with all the world, betrays first the gratifying conviction that they themselves are good against all the world.

Edward Morton was by no means ignorant of his own defect of character. He knew his impetuosity of blood, and he feared it. It was necessary to guard particularly against *that*, in all his intercourse with Flora Middleton. Of this he had previous experience. He knew her acuteness of intellect. The very simplicity of her own character, and the directness and almost masculine frankness of her temper, made it somewhat difficult to elude her analysis. Besides, she already suspected him. This he knew. He had every reason to suppose, in addition, that the late close intercourse between herself and Clarence Conway, however brief, had enabled the latter to afford her some information of the true state of their mutual feelings and interests.

But, in due proportion with the small amount of knowledge which he possessed, was the reasonable apprehension which he entertained of the extent of what she knew. She might know much or little. He had every reason to fancy that she knew *all;* and his chief hope lay in the fruitful falsehoods which his wily coadjutor had taken occasion to plant within her mind. If these falsehoods had taken root—if they flourished—perhaps the difficulty would not be great to make her doubt all the assertions of his brother.

"If she believes him this villain—well! She will believe more. She will believe that he has slandered me—nothing can be more natural—and if one task be well performed, it will not be hard to effect the other. But I must be wary. She is as keen-eyed as a hungry eagle—looks far and deep. One hasty word—one incautious look—and her sharp wit detects the error, and all must be begun anew. I must be cool now, or never. With everything at stake, I must school my blood into subjection, if, indeed, I have not already lost enough to make the pains-taking unnecessary."

Such were his thoughts, and such the hopes, upon which he founded his new purposes of deception. The surprise of all parties was great, and openly expressed, as he suddenly entered the supper-room. But the outlaw saw with pleasure that the surprise of the ladies did not seem coupled with any coldness or dissatisfaction. It has not been necessary for us to say, before, that Mrs. Middleton had visited the invalid in his chamber. She had done all the duties of hospitality and humanity. He had accordingly no cause of complaint. He could have no reason to expect the like attendance from the *young* lady; and the gentle courtesy of the latter would have convinced one even more suspicious than Morton, that she had no hostile feeling whatsoever at work against him.

The inquiries of both were kind and considerate. He was requested to occupy the sofa entirely, and to place himself at ease upon it; a permission which had the effect of transferring the reluctant person of the surgeon to a contiguous chair. The deportment of this person had been productive of far more surprise to the ladies, than the appearance of the outlaw. Flora Middleton had informed her grandmother of the suit which she had rejected; and it was, therefore, greatly to the wonder of the one, and the consternation of the other, that they were compelled to witness, in his deportment, the language of confident assurance;—of a success and exultation, in tone and manner, as unequivocal as ever betrayed themselves in the action of a triumphant lover. His smirkings were not to be mistaken; and the old lady looked to the young one, and the young one returned the glance with equal vexation and bewilderment.

The arrival of Morton had the effect of bringing some relief to the females of the party, and possibly to diminish, in some degree, the impertinent self-complaisance of the surgeon. For this, the ladies were grateful to the outlaw; and hence, perhaps, the greater benignity of the reception which they bestowed upon the latter. But still there was quite enough of pleased impudence manifest in the visage of Hillhouse, even after the coming of Morton; and when the first courtesies which followed his entrance were fairly ended, he took occasion to say something on the subject to this happy person.

"Really, Mr. Hillhouse, I am surprised at the unusual degree of happiness which your countenance exhibits this evening. What is it makes you so peculiarly happy. Have you good news from the army? Is his lordship about to relieve you. Do you think of Charleston and the next Meschianza?"

The surgeon simpered, smiled anew, and looked with most provoking *empressement* at Flora Middleton. Before he could frame the intricate and exquisite reply which he was meditating, that young lady availed herself of the occasion, to prove, as well she might, that she was no willing party to the peculiar happiness which his countenance expressed.

"I thank you for that question, Mr. Conway—I was about to make the same inquiry; for, really, I never saw a gentleman put on so suddenly the appearance of so much joy. I fancied that Mr. Hillhouse must have had a fairy gift, as, you know, happens to us all *in childhood;* and then again, I doubted, for there are reasons against such a notion. But, in truth, I knew not what to think, unless it be that it is surely no earthly joy which has produced, or could produce, so complete an expression of delight in the human face. I declare, Mr. Hillhouse, I should be glad for mamma's sake—if for the sake of no one else—that you would let us know what it is that makes you so supremely happy. There's nothing pleases old people so much, you know, as the innocent pleasures of young ones."

"Ah, Miss Flora, do *you* then ask? It is, indeed, no earthly joy which has made me happy."

"You are then really happy?" said Conway.

"Really, and in truth, I may say so. A dream——"

"What! and is it a dream only? Well, I thought as much," exclaimed Flora.

"Nay, Miss Middleton, life itself, for that matter, is a sort of dream. But, in ordinary speech, mine is not a dream. I have had a vision——"

"A vision!" exclaimed Conway.

"A vision, sir!" said the old lady, putting on her spectacles, and looking around the room.

"A vision! Do you see it now, Mr. Hillhouse? Where? What was it like?" The demand of Flora was made with all the girlish eagerness of one who really believed in the prophetic faculty of the present seer.

"Yes, what was it like, Mr. Hillhouse?" asked the outlaw, "I am very curious to hear! a vision!"

"Like!" exclaimed the surgeon, "like! like an opening of heaven upon me. A sudden revelation of delight, a cloud of glory; and the shape within was that of—a woman!"

"Dear me!—only a woman!" exclaimed Morton, affectedly.

"Only a woman, sir!" cried the surgeon, with an air of profoundest gallantry; "and what lovelier object can one see in this visible creation—upon the earth or in the sky——"

"Or the waters under the earth."

"Nay, I'm not so deep in the world, Mr. Conway," said the surgeon; "but when you ejaculate in wonder, sir, because my vision of unspeakable delight takes the shape of a young and beautiful woman——"

"What's the color of her eyes—and hair, Mr. Hillhouse?" was the interruption of Conway. "Give us now a just description, that we may judge for ourselves what sort of taste you have in matters of beauty."

Hillhouse looked to Flora Middleton with an expression which said, as plainly as a look could say—"Behold with me! The vision is again before us!"

Flora Middleton rose from her chair. She seemed to anticipate the words; and the scorn and vexation which overspread her features, became evident to all persons in the room, except, perhaps, the single obtuse individual who had provoked them. She was about to leave the apartment, when the sudden and hurried words of Edward Morton arrested her, with a new occasion of wonder, more legitimate than that which the surgeon entertained.

"By heavens, Mr. Hillhouse, I too have a vision, and one far less lovely, I think, than yours. Pray, look to that door, if you please. There was a strange visage at it but a moment ago. Look! look!—a man, not a woman; and one not from heaven, I should think, though it may be——"

Before the surgeon could reach the door, or Morton could finish the sentence, a dark figure entered the room, confronted the party, and taking from his face a black mask, with which it was covered displayed to the anxious gaze of the outlaw his own late lieutenant, and always bitter enemy, Captain Stockton. The latter had heard what Morton said, and concluded his speech, perhaps, in the most fitting manner.

"From hell, you would say, would you! and you are right, sir. I came from hell, and I am come for *you*. You are prepared for travel, I trust!"

The behavior of Morton was equally fearless and dignified. He had a game to play in the eyes of Flora, and a difficult part to act in more eyes than hers. His agitation had not been concealed, at the first sudden exhibition which Stockton had made of his hostile visage at the entrance; but, when the person of the intruder was no longer doubtful, his firmness came back to him; and no person, on the verge of the precipice, could have looked down with more indifference than he, upon its awful abysses. He raised himself with composure from the sofa, and directing the eyes of Stockton to the ladies, calmly remarked—

"Whatever you may be, and whatever your purpose, as a man, remember where you are, and be civil to the ladies."

He was answered by a grin, and yell of mingled exultation and malice.

"Ay! ay! I will remember. Don't suppose I shall ever forget them, or yourself, or even that pink-looking gentleman in the corner, who smells so sweetly, and looks so frightened. Ha! ha! Did you ever know the devil to forget any of his flock. Ladies, you know me, or you should. You will know me soon enough. I am old Nick, himself, you may be sure of that, though I go by several names. My most innocent one is perhaps the most familiar to you. I am the captain of the Black Riders. *Do you deny that?*" he demanded, at the close, turning full upon Edward Morton.

It did not need that the latter should answer this inquiry, for the alarm which this bold annunciation produced, prevented his words from being heard by any ears but those of the intruder.

"You may be the devil himself, for anything I know or care."

"Indeed! you are bold. But we shall see. You will find me a worse person to deal with, perhaps. You are my prisoner: remember that."

"I know not that!" exclaimed Morton, rising with evident pain from the sofa, upon which he had sunk but a minute before, and looking the defiance which he had no means to enforce. His attitude was, however, threatening;. and drawing a pistol from his belt, the intruding outlaw levelled it full at the head of his superior. The eye of Morton did not shrink. His gaze was undaunted. Not a muscle of his face was discomposed. At that instant Watson Gray suddenly entered the apartment, strode between them, and confronted Stockton with a weapon like his own. At the same time he thrust another into the hands of Morton.

"There are two to play at this game, Stockton," was the cool remark of Gray. "Ladies, leave the room, if you please. We need no witnesses: and you, sir, unless you can kill as well as cure, you may as well follow the ladies."

This was addressed to the surgeon.

"I have no weapon," was his answer.

"Pshaw! look to the fireplace. A brave man never wants a weapon."

Hillhouse possessed himself of the poker with sufficient resolution; but he evidently looked with great dissatisfaction upon the prospect before him, of soiling his dove-colored suit in an unexpected *melée*. Meanwhile the ladies had disappeared, and the only social influence which might have prevented bloodshed was necessarily removed in their departure.

## CHAPTER XXXVII.

### A PARLEY.

"What does all this mean, Stockton?" demanded Gray.

"What you see. The meaning's plain enough, Watson Gray," was the insolent reply.

"Ay, I see well enough that you are disposed to murder your superior; but on what pretence? How will you answer to Lord Rawdon for this insubordination—this mutiny? for it is no less. Captain Morton has the commission of Sir Henry Clinton. He is your commander."

"Yes, but he is the property of the troop, also."

"Well, what then—suppose we allow that?'

"That is enough. He is a traitor to them."

"Ha!—a traitor!"

"Yes! a base, dishonest traitor."

"How? in what way is he a traitor?"

"He is sworn to be true to them."

"Well—if to be mangled in their battles is to be true to them, he certainly has been true a long time."

"Mangled in *their* battles!" quoth the other, with a sneer. "Mangled in his own. Had he been fighting their battles, with less regard to his own, he would have escaped his mangling. 'Tell that to the marines.' We know better. We know that he is a traitor to his comrades. He has sold them for a price, and has abandoned them to their enemies. His life is forfeit by his own laws."

"This is a mere fetch, Stockton. There is no ground for such pretence. You are the enemy of Captain Morton. We all know that of old. You are contriving it against him to destroy him. Beware! You know me quite as well as I know you. I tell you, that if you go one inch on either hand from the right, your neck stretches on the gallows in the sight of all Charleston!"

"Pshaw! Watson Gray. You don't hope to frighten me at this time of day with your big words. I know what I'm about. Captain Morton is a traitor to the troop, and we'll prove it. He is false to his oath, and will be made to answer all its penalties."

"That's well enough; but what gives you the right, till the thing's proved, to lift pistol to his head?"

"The thing's proved already."

"What! without a trial?"

"We've two witnesses against him."

"Where are they? *We'll* hear them—not you. You are a little too fast."

"You shall hear them both. You shall hear *me* too. I am now the captain of the troop. They have made me so by their free voices. *He* is nothing, now, but one of us—a common soldier, under suspicion, and waiting for his sentence."

"Look you, Stockton: I'm better used to acting than talking. I know you of old, and I see you're bent to kill your captain, whether or no. You're hungering to step into his shoes: but the moment you pull trigger on him, that moment I pull trigger on you. There's two to one. Take your chance now for life; for I'm getting angry."

"Two to one, indeed! Look at the windows, man, and you'll see *twenty* to one," was the triumphant response of Stockton.

Gray looked as he was bidden, so did the surgeon Hillhouse, but Morton kept his eyes fixed upon those of his lieutenant.

"Well, do you see? are you satisfied? There is no chance for you," said the latter.

"I see only what I expected to see," was the answer of Gray. "I did not look to see you venture here without good backing. I knew you too well for that. These twenty men are enough to eat us up. But, before you can get help from them, we'll make mince-meat of you. You are a fool if you think otherwise."

Stockton looked upon his destined victim with equal rage and disappointment.

"What! you refuse, then, to surrender him to me?"

"We do."

"Well, we shall see what we can do with a few more pistols," replied the ruffian, and with these words he prepared to leave the room. But Gray placed himself between him and the entrance.

"Stay," said he—"not so fast. You've got into the cane-brake with the bear. You must ask permission when you want to leave it."

"What! do you mean to keep me?"

"Yes; you shall be a hostage for the rest. We must have terms between us, Richard Stockton, before we let you off."

"What terms?" demanded the other, angrily.

"Where's our guard?"

"Fastened up in the loghouse, where they're all drunk."

"They must be released; and you must answer to Lord Rawdon for making his soldiers drunk and incapable, while on duty at a British military post."

"Who says I made them drunk?"

"I say so."

"You can not prove it."

"You shall see. If I can prove that one of your troopers did it, it will be necessary for you to show that you did not employ that trooper in doing it."

"Watson Gray, I will have satisfaction out of you for this."

"All in good time, Stockton. You don't suppose that I'm likely to dodge from a difficulty with you or any man? But it's useless for you to ride your high horse across my path. By the Eternal, man, I'll tilt you into the ditch in the twinkle of a mosquito!"

"You talk boldly; but let me tell you that you're not altogether safe from this charge against Morton. You're suspected of treason to the troop, as well as he."

"Tsha, tsha, tsha! Catch old birds with chaff! Look you, Stockton: don't you suppose you can carry this matter as you please, either by scare or shot. We're up to you any how. Now, look you: if you think that either Captain Morton or myself wants to escape from trial, you're mistaken. But we'll have a fair trial, or none at all."

"Well, won't we give him a fair trial?"

"No: not if you begin it with the pistol."

"I only want to make him a prisoner."

"Well, you sha'n't have your wishes in that—not while I can stand ready with such a muzzle as this close upon yours. Now, hear me. Give orders to Ensign Darcy, whose little eyes I see dancing at that glass there, and who's at the bottom of all your mischief—give him orders to let our men loose from the loghouse, and send them here; and, in the mean time, let him draw his own men off from the house. When that's done, we'll come to terms about the trial."

"Agreed," said the other, and he made a new movement as if to take his departure, but the wily Gray was still on the alert.

"No! no!—my good fellow!—You must stay as a hostage, lieutenant, 'till the matter's all arranged. You can speak to Darcy from where you stand—through the pane as well as if your arm was round his neck."

The vexation of Stockton may be imagined. He strove vainly to suppress it. He was compelled to submit. Darcy was summoned, and would have entered, with his men following, but Watson Gray's prompt accents warned him, that, if he came not alone, he would bring down on the head of his confederate the bullets of himself and Morton. Sharing the chagrin of his superior, Darcy, accordingly, made his appearance alone, and received his instructions.

When he had drawn off his followers, and disappeared himself, Gray persuaded Morton to retire to his chamber with the assistance of the surgeon. This measure had, perhaps, become absolutely necessary to the former. The efforts which he had made to sustain himself, as well in the interview with the ladies, as in that unexpected one which followed it;—and the excitement which the latter necessarily occasioned, had nearly exhausted him. Nothing but the moral stimulus derived from his mind—its hate, scorn, defiance—sustained him so far from fainting on the spot; and this support did not maintain him much longer. He did faint when he reached his own apartment.

"And now, Stockton," said Gray, when they were alone together—"what's all this d—d nonsense stuff about Captain Morton's treachery and mine? Out with it, man, that we may know the game."

"No nonsense stuff, I assure you. The proof is strong enough against him, and brushes your skirts also."

"Proof indeed. You see, I don't stop to let you know, lieutenant, that I look upon you as a man that will contrive, wherever you can, against the captain. I know that you hate him—you can't deny it,—though it's the strangest thing to me why you should hate a man who has never given you any cause for hate, and has always treated you well and kindly."

"Indeed! Do you really think so!" exclaimed the other bitterly. "Well, I shall understand, that, to knock a man over with the butt of your pistol, and send him afterward under guard to prison, with a recommendation for the halbirds, is a way to treat well and kindly."

"Pshaw! Is that all?"

"All! ay, and enough too!"

"My good fellow, you ought to be grateful that he didn't set you a swinging from the first tree. I heard of that affair, and was sorry for it; but you deserved all you got, and something more. He might have hung you without trial, or shot you down where you stood. You were in absolute mutiny."

"We'll say no more about that, Watson Gray. He's had his chance, and I'll have mine. So far from it's being nonsense stuff which is against him, the proof of his treachery is clear as noonday."

"Well, prove it, and he must stand his fate. All he asks, and all that I ask, is a fair trial. But what is the sort of treachery that he's been doing?"

"Making arrangements to fly and leave the troop in the lurch. Getting boats to carry off the plate and negroes from Middleton barony and other places, without letting the troop come to a share. You can't deny that's death by our laws—rope and bullet!"

"Granted: but, again, I ask you, where's the proof?"

"Brydone!—Ha! you start, do you? You didn't expect that?"

"Start!—a man may well start at hearing of such a falsehood from the lips of a fellow like Brydone, who was always counted one of the truest fellows we ever had."

"Yes; you didn't think *he'd* desert you, eh?"

"Desert!—Look you, Stockton, I don't believe that Brydone ever said such a word. Did you hear him yourself?"

"Yes—I did."

"Where is he? Bring him before me."

"Time enough. He's not here with us at present. But he'll be here sooner than you wish."

"Ah!"—and the scout paused, while his brow gathered into deep, dark folds which indicated the pressure of accumulating thoughts. He suddenly recovered his composure, and turning, with a quiet smile upon his more blunt companion, he proceeded:—

"Stockton, I see your game. I need not tell you that I am now convinced that you have no such proof, and that Brydone never told you anything hurtful to the captain. If so, didn't you know that he was to have a fair trial?—Why didn't you bring your only witness? and did not you also know, that, by the laws, no one could be found guilty but by two witnesses? Now, you only speak of one——"

"Ay, ay! but there's another, Watson Gray. Don't suppose

I got so far ahead of common sense in this business as to stumble in that matter. No! no! I hate Ned Morton too much—too thoroughly and bitterly—to leave my desire for revenge to a doubtful chance. The whole matter was cut and dry before we came down from 'Ninety-Six.' We have two witnesses of his guilt."

"Well, who's the other?" asked Gray with seeming indifference.

"Isaac Muggs!"

"What Isaac, the one-armed! But you don't call him a man, surely—he's only part of a man!"

"You don't mean to stand for such an argument as that?" demanded Stockton gravely.

"Oh, no!" responded the other with a laugh. "Let him go for what he's worth. But——"—here his indifference of manner seemed to increase, as, yawning, he inquired—

"But when are these witnesses to be here? When may we confront them?"

"Sooner than you wish," was the reply. "We look for Brydone to-morrow, by the dawn; and as for Isaac Muggs, we expect to catch him very soon after, if not before. We hope to be in readiness along the river banks, to see whether he brings up the boats which are fit to carry such a valuable cargo, as you've got ready here to put in them."

"Ah!—so you've got the Congaree under guard, have you?" demanded the other with the same seeming indifference of manner.

"It will be somewhat difficult for him to find *you* without first finding *us*," replied Stockton with a chuckling sort of triumph.

"So much for Isaac, then. I suppose he brings Brydone along with him?" was the carelessly expressed inquiry of Gray.

"No! no! He will be more certain to arrive, and comes more willingly. Rawdon despatched him below with a letter to Colonel Stewart, at Fairlawn, and he will be here too soon for your liking. He comes by the road. Do not think we ventured upon this business without preparation. We made nice calculations and timed everything to the proper moment. Brydone sleeps to-night at Martin's tavern, so we may expect him here by sunrise. We'll be ready, at all events, for the trial by twelve o'clock to-morrow. At least we can take his testimony and wait for Muggs. But I calculate on both before that time."

Watson Gray seemed for a moment lost in thought. His dark bushy brows were bent down almost to the concealment of his eyes.

"It seems to worry you!" said Stockton with a sneer.

"Worry me! No! no! Stockton, you're only worrying yourself. I was thinking of a very different matter," replied the other with a good-natured smile.

"Well, do you say that you'll be ready for the trial then?"

"We're ready *now;* ready always for fair play. But you must draw off your troop."

"Very well. I have no objection to that, for I can draw 'em on again at a moment's warning. If you don't keep faith you'll sweat for it. I'm agreed to anything that don't prevent the trial. Where shall it be—here?"

"Here! Oh, no! To have your sixty men rushing upon us at close muzzle-quarters! No, no! We'll have it in the woods, near the river, where my half-score of muskets may be covered by the trees, and be something of a match for your troop. Besides, the women, you know!"

"Well, I'm willing. There's a clayey bluff just above, facing the river-bend. There's something of an opening, and I reckon it's a sort of graveyard. I see a new grave there and a cross upon it. Let the trial be there."

"A new grave and a cross upon it!" mused the other. "That must be Mary Clarkson's grave; but the cross! Ah! perhaps Miss Flora had that done. She's a good girl! Well, I'm agreed. Let it be there—just at the turning of the sun at noon."

"Keep your word, Gray, and the worst enemy of Ned Morton——"

"Yourself!"

"The same! His worst enemy can ask nothing more. If we don't convict him——"

"You'll swallow the Congaree!"

"You may laugh now, but I doubt if you will to-morrow;

and I know that Ned Morton will be in no humor to laugh, unless he does so because he likes dancing in air much better than most people."

"Well, well, Stockton; we shall soon see enough. To-morrow's never a day far off, and here comes Darcy to relieve you. But as for your hanging Ned Morton, why, man, your own troop will hardly suffer it."

"Ha! will they not? Is that your hope?" said Stockton, with an exulting sneer.

"Perhaps!" replied the the other, with a smile.

The entrance of Darcy arrested the conference.


## CHAPTER XXXVIII.

### A WITNESS SILENCED.

THE business of the two had reached its close before the return of Darcy with the British guard which he had released. Some other matters were adjusted between them, and Lieutenant Stockton was at length permitted to depart, while Watson Gray, at the same moment, received from Darcy the still half drunken soldiery. It may be supposed that neither Stockton nor Darcy was altogether so well satisfied with the result of their expedition. The game was fairly in their hands; but the precipitation of Stockton, arising from a too great feeling of security, and a desire to exult over his threatened victim, led to that exposure of his own person of which Watson Gray so readily availed himself. The reproaches of the subordinate were not spared.

"But it comes to the same thing," said Stockton. "He is still ours. He is pledged to appear at the trial."

"Ay, but suppose he does not come?"

"Then the delay follows, and no worse evil. We have men enough, surely, to pull the old house about his ears."

"With the loss of half of them! A dear bargain," replied the dissatisfied lieutenant.

"Not so bad either. We can starve them out in three days. But there's no fear that Gray will not keep his word. They will come to the trial. They flatter themselves that we shall see nothing of Isaac Muggs, whom they've sent away, and I told them of no other witness than Brydone. I said nothing of that skulk, Joe Tanner. He and Brydone are enough, and knowing the absence of Muggs, they'll come boldly on the ground, and walk headlong into the trap we've set for them."

"It's well you've had that caution, Stockton; for, of a truth, you have so far played your cards most rashly. We've got desperate men to deal with, and that Watson Gray has got more sense in one little finger than you carry in your whole body."

"That's not so civil, Mr. Darcy."

"No! but it's true; and when you're trifling with the game of both of us, it's necessary to jerk you up suddenly with a sharp truth now and then, by way of a curb to your paces. There's another matter that your proceeding has spoiled, Stockton."

"What was that?"

"The gutting of the house."

"Oh! that follows, of course.

"A bird in the hand, you know. They may have time now to hide away the valuables."

"It will be a close hole that our boys can't creep into. Where they've gone we can follow. But there's no doubt, Darcy, that I've given up one chance which befriended us. It's only putting off for to-morrow what might have been done to-day. Our appetite will be only so much the keener for the delay. Did you see Miss Middleton?"

"Ay—did I not!" replied Darcy. "Look you, Stockton, I stipulate for *her*. You must not think to swallow all—rank, revenge, riches—and still yearn for beauty. She must go to my share of the booty."

"Yours! Pooh, Darcy! what should give you an amorous tooth? Don't think of it, my good fellow. I've set my mind upon her. It's a part of my revenge. She's the game that's turned Ned Morton's head—it was to disgrace him before her that made me blunder—and unless I show him that she, too, is at my mercy, my triumph will be only half complete."

Darcy muttered something about the "lion's share," and his muttering reminded Stockton that he was too valuable an assistant to be trifled with.

"Pshaw!" he exclaimed, "let us not squabble about a woman. I don't care a shilling about her. But she's common stock, you know. It must be according to the will of the troop."

We forbear listening to other heads of their private arrangements. They proceeded to rejoin their men and to see about the disposition of their sentinels, in secrecy, along the banks of the river, wherever they thought it probable that a boat could effect a landing. They did not bestow a very close watch along the land side, or in the immediate neighborhood of the house, for they well knew that Morton could not escape, in his present condition of feebleness, by any but a water conveyance. He was their chief object, and they regarded his fate as now unavoidable.

The safety of the landlord, Muggs, it has been already seen, was secured by the persevering and sleepless efforts of his new comrade, John Bannister. When the latter had swam the river, and joined him on the other side, the two laid themselves quietly down to sleep in a place of security, having resolved to get up at an early hour, before dawn, and, urging their boat up stream with united paddles, keep on the same side of the river until they could, without detection, cross to that on which the enemy lay. Their aim was to reach a point above the usual landing places of the barony, and out of the reach, accordingly, of the line of sentinels, each of which John Bannister had beheld when he was placed.

The worthy scout was resolved to do all that he might, at any risk, for the safety of Flora, and for her rescue from the ruthless villains by whom her house was surrounded. He did not conjecture the state of affairs between the former captain of the Black Riders and his troop; and did not fancy that there was any cause of apprehension for the fate of Edward Conway, though such a conviction would have given him but little uneasiness.

At the appointed hour he awakened his companion, struck a light, reloaded his rifle, the flint of which he carefully examined; and, having put himself and Muggs in as good condition for a conflict as possible, he shoved his canoe up the stream.

The work was hard, but they achieved it. They plied their paddles vigorously, until they were enabled, with the help of the current, to round the jutting headland where slept the remains of Mary Clarkson. They had scarcely pulled into shore when they were startled by the sudden rising of a human figure from the earth, out of the bosom of which, and almost at their feet, he seemed to emerge. Bannister pushed back from the shore, but the friendly voice of Jake Clarkson reassured him. He had effected his escape, in the general drunkenness of the soldiery, though how that had been brought about, he could tell but little. Those who had drugged their cups, had evidently confounded him with the rest, for they furnished him with a portion of the potent beverage also. Of this he drank nothing, and the consequence of his sobriety was his successful effort at escape. In the darkness, he had been enabled to feel his way to the spot where his daughter slept.

He could give no further explanation; nor did Bannister annoy him on the subject. He was content with the acquisition of a stout fellow, whose aim was deadly, and who had contrived to secure his rifle from loss in all his several mischances. This he still carried upon his arm, and Bannister contented himself with instructing him to get it in readiness.

"See to the flint and priming, daddy Jake, for the time's a-coming when I wouldn't have you miss fire for the best pole-boat on the Congaree."

If there was toil among these honest fellows, and among the outlaws in the neighborhood of whose camp they were hovering, there was toil and anxiety also in the dwelling, to which, though with different feelings, the eyes of both these parties were directed. Sleepless and prayerful were the hours which the fair ladies of the mansion passed after that wild and fearful interruption which they experienced in the progress of the evening meal. But, in the chamber of Edward Morton, a more stern and immovable sentiment of apprehension prevailed to increase the gloom of his midnight watch, and to darken the aspects of the two who sat there in solemn conference.

Watson Gray, though he naturally strove to infuse a feeling of confidence into the mind of his superior, could not, nevertheless, entirely divest his thoughts of the sombre tinge which they necessarily took from his feelings, in considering the events which the coming day was to bring forth. There was something excessively humbling to a man like Edward Morton, in the idea of ever being tried for treachery by those whom he had so often led; — and to be placed for judgment before one whom he so heartily despised as Stockton, was no small part of the annoyance. The assurances which Watson Gray gave him did not touch this part of his disquietude. The simple assurance of his ultimate release could not materially lessen the pang which he felt at what he conceived to be the disgrace of such a situation.

"Life or death, Gray," he said, "is after all a trifling matter. I have the one here," touching the hilt of a dirk which he had just placed within his bosom, "or here," and his fingers rested on the handle of the pistol which lay beside him on the bed.

"Either of these will secure me from the indignity which this base scoundrel would delight to fasten upon me; and, as for life, I believe I love it no more than any other soldier who knows the condition of the game he plays and the value of the stake he lays down. But, to be hauled up and called to answer to such a scamp, for such a crime, is, really, a most shocking necessity. Can't we mend the matter no way? Can't we tamper with some of the men? There are a few whom you could manage. There's Butts, both the Maybins, Joe Sutton, Peters, and half a dozen more that were always devoted to me, though, perhaps, among the more timid of the herd. If you could manage these; if you could persuade them to join us *here*, with your bull-head British allies, we should be able to make fight, and finish the copartnership in that manlier way. By Heaven, I'm stirred up with the notion! You must try it! I shall be strong enough for anything when the time comes; and I feel, that in actual conflict with that villain Stockton, I could not help but hew him to pieces. Bring us to this point, Gray!

Work, work, man, if you love me! If your wits sleep, wake them. Now or never! Let them save me from this d—nable situation and bitter shame."

The confederate shook his head despondingly.

"No doubt if we could get at these fellows, or any half dozen in the troop, they might be bought over or persuaded in some way to desert to us; but do you not see that the difficulty is in getting at them? Were I to venture among them, I should be served just as I served Stockton to-night. I should be hampered hand and foot, with no such chance of making terms of escape as he had. No, captain, I see no way to avoid the trial. You must make up your mind to *that*. But I don't see that you will have anything more to apprehend. Muggs is out of the way, and won't be back in three days. He's safe. One witness is not enough, and as for Brydone—"

"D—n him! D—n him! The double-dyed traitor! And he was paid so well too!"

"That was the mistake, I'm thinking. He got too much for that last business. He considered it the last job that you'd ever give him, and he immediately cast about for a new employer. He's got him, but I do not think he'll keep him long."

"May they cut each other's throats!" was the devout prayer of the outlaw, to which Gray responded with a deliberate

"Amen!"

What was further said between the two that night, was of the same temper and concerned the same business. Their hopes and fears, plans and purposes, so far as Watson Gray deemed it essential that his principal should know them, underwent, as it was natural they should, a prolonged examination. But Gray felt that the outlaw would need all his strength for whatever events might follow, and determined, therefore, upon leaving him to repose. Besides, he had some schemes working in his mind, which he did not declare to his principal, and which it was necessary that he should discuss entirely to himself.

He had already taken care that his score of men, by this time quite sobered, should be strictly cautioned on the subject of their watch for the night, and so placed, within the dwelling, as to baffle any attempt at surprise or assault from without. The soldiers did not now need much exhortation to vigilance. They had already had some taste of the fruits of misbehavior, as in their beastly incapability of resentment, the outlaws had amused themselves with a rough pastime at their expense, in which cuffs and kicks were the most gentle courtesies to which the victims were subjected.

Having exhorted them, with every possible counsel and argument, Gray summoned the surgeon, Hillhouse, to a brief conference, and assigned to him certain duties of the watch also. Though a frivolous, foolish person, he was temperate, and the chief object of Gray was to keep the soldiers from any excess during an absence which, it seems, he meditated, but which he did not declare to them, or to his associate, Morton. It was only necessary to intimate to Mr. Hillhouse what havoc the Black Riders would make if they could once lay hands upon his variegated wardrobe, to secure all the future vigilance of that gentleman.

All matters being arranged to his satisfaction, Gray stole forth at midnight from the mansion, none knowing and none suspecting his departure; and, with the practised arts of a veteran scout, he contrived to take from the stables the fleetest horse which they contained. Him he led, as quietly as he could, into the woods which lay to the west, and remote equally from the encampment and sentinels of the Black Riders. Their watch was maintained with strictness, but only on the river side; and, uninterrupted, Gray soon succeeded in placing himself in full cover of the forests, and out of the neighborhood of the enemy's sentinels. He kept within the cover of the woods only so long as sufficed for safety; then, hurrying into the main road, he pursued his way down the country, at a rapid canter.

The object of Watson Gray, in part, may be conjectured, by a recurrence to that portion of the dialogue which he had with Stockton, in which the latter accounted for the absence of Brydone, the most important witness whom he could array against the fidelity of Captain Morton. He determined to go forth, meet Brydone, and bribe, or dissuade him from his meditated treachery. He had, if the reader will remember, wormed out of the less acute and subtle Stockton, the cause of Brydone's absence; the route which he would take, and the probable time of his arrival in the morning. To keep him back from the approaching trial he believed to be more important than he allowed to appear to Morton. He knew that their enemies would not be able to secure the testimony of Muggs, the landlord, within the allotted time, even if they succeeded, finally, in securing his person;—and he did not doubt that Stockton was prepared with some other witness, of whom he said nothing, in order the more effectually to delude the defendant into the field. This was, indeed, the case, as we have already seen from the conference between Stockton and his more subtle confederate, Darcy.

"At all events," soliloquized the scout, "at all events, it will be the safe policy to keep Brydone out of the way. I must send him on another journey. He sleeps at Martin's tavern. Let me see;—Martin's is but fourteen miles. He can ride that at a dog-trot in three hours. He will probably start at daylight, and calculate to take his breakfast at the barony. That is Stockton's calculation. I must baffle him. Brydone must put off eating that breakfast."

Watson Gray did not continue his horse at the same pace at which he started. He drew up, after the first five miles, and suffered him to trot and walk alternately. He had not gone more than seven, when day broke upon the forests, and the keen eyes of the scout were then set to their best uses, as he surveyed the road upon which he travelled. By the time the sun rose he had gone quite as far as he intended. It was not a part of his policy to be seen at Martin's tavern; or seen at all, by any one, who might reveal the fact hereafter that he had gone upon the same road over which Brydone was expected.

No man was better able to foresee, and provide against all contingencies, than Watson Gray. His every step was the result of a close calculation of its probable effects for good and evil. He quietly turned into the woods, when he had reached a thicket which promised him sufficient concealment for his purposes. Here he re-examined his pistols, which were loaded, each, with a brace of bullets. He stirred the priming with his finger, rasped the flints slightly with the horn handle of his knife, and adjusted the weapons in his belt for convenient use.

He did not dismount from his saddle, but took care to place himself in such a position, on the upper edge of the thicket, as to remain unseen from below; while, at the same time, the path was so unobstructed from above as to permit him to emerge suddenly, without obstruction from the undergrowth, at any moment, into the main track.

In this position he was compelled to wait something longer than he had expected. But Watson Gray, in the way of business, was as patient as the grave. He was never troubled with that fidgety peevishness which afflicts small people, and puts them into a fever, unless the winds rise from the right quarter at the very moment when they are desired to blow. He could wait, not only without complaint or querulousness; but he prepared himself to *wait*, just as certainly as to *perform*. To suffer and to endure, he had sufficient common sense philosophy to perceive, was equally the allotment of life.

His patience was sufficiently tested on the present occasion. He waited fully two hours, and with no greater sign of discontent, than could be conjectured from his occasionally transferring his right and then his left leg from the stirrup to the pommel of his saddle, simply to rest the members, as they happened to be more or less stiffened by the want of exercise. All the while, his eyes keenly pierced the thicket below him, and his ears pricked up, like his steed's, which he also cautiously watched, with the habitual readiness of a practised woodman. At length the tedium of his situation was relieved. The tramp of a horse was heard at a small distance, and as the traveller came up to the thicket, Watson Gray quietly rode out beside him.

"Ha! Watson Gray!" exclaimed the new-comer, who was the person expected.

"The same, Joe Brydone," was the answer of Gray, in tones which were gentle, quiet, and evidently intended to soothe the alarm of the other; an alarm which was clearly conveyed in his faltering accents, and in the sudden movement of his bridle hand, by which his steed was made to swerve away to the opposite side of the road.

If his object was flight, it did not promise to be successful, for the powerful and fleet animal bestrode by Gray left him no hope to escape by running from his unwelcome companion. This he soon perceived; and, encouraged perhaps by the friendly accent of Gray's voice, was content to keep along with him at the same pace which he was pursuing when they encountered. But his looks betrayed his disquiet. He had all the misgivings of the conscious traitor, apprehensive for his treasonable secret. On this head Gray did not leave him very long in doubt.

"I've been looking for you, Brydone."

"Ah! why—what's the matter?"

"Nay, nothing much, I reckon, only—you're expected at the barony."

"I know:—I'm on my way there now."

'Ned Morton expects you!"

"Who: the captain?" with some surprise.

"Yes! a base charge is made against him by that scoundrel Stockton, and he wants you to disprove it."

"What's that?" demanded the other.

"Why, neither more nor less, than that the captain has been making preparations to desert the troop, in violation of his oath."

"Well, but Gray, that's the truth, you know," said Brydone with more confidence.

"How! I know!—I know nothing about it."

"Why, yes you do. Didn't you send me yourself to Isaac Muggs, and tell me what to say and do?"

"Brydone, you're foolish. If I sent you, didn't I pay you for going; and isn't it a part of our business that you should keep the secret if you keep the money? You got paid for going, and got paid for keeping the secret; and now we expect you to go up and prove this fellow Stockton to be a liar and an ass."

"I can't do it, Gray," said the other, doggedly.

"And why not? There are more guineas to be got where the last came from."

"I don't know that," was the reply.

"But you shall see. I promise you twenty guineas, if you will swear to the truth, as I tell it to you, on this trial."

"I can't, Gray. I've told the truth already to Captain Stockton, and to more than him."

"But you were under a mistake, Brydone, my good fellow. Don't be foolish now. You will only be making a lasting enemy of Captain Morton, who has always been your friend, and who will never forget your treachery, if you appear in this business against him."

"His enmity won't count for much when they've tried him, Gray. He must swing."

"But mine will count for something. Would you be making an enemy of me, also? If you go forward and swear against him, you swear against me too."

"I can't help it — it's the truth."

"But where's the necessity of telling the truth at this time of day? What's the use of beginning a new business so late in life? You've told Stockton, it seems; go forward then, and downface him that you never told him a word on the subject, and I will be your security for twenty guineas."

"I can't; — I told Lieutenant Darcy also, and several others."

"Ah! that's bad — that's very bad. My dear Brydone, that's unfortunate for all of us."

"I don't see how it's unfortunate for more than him," said Brydone, with recovered coolness.

"Why yes, it's a loss to you; a loss of money, and, perhaps, something as valuable. But there's yet a way by which you may mend it, and prevent the loss. You shall have the twenty guineas, if you'll just take the back track down the country, and be gone for five days. I don't care where you go, or what you do in the meantime, so that you don't come within twenty miles of the barony."

"I can't think of it," said the other obstinately.

Watson Gray regarded him earnestly, for a few moments, before he continued.

"How a fellow of good sense will sometimes trifle with his good fortune, and risk everything on a blind chance. Joe Brydone, what's got into you, that you can't see the road that's safest and most profitable?"

"Perhaps I do," replied the other with a grin of the coolest self-complaisance.

He was answered by a smile of Gray, one of that sinister

kind which an observing man would shudder to behold in the countenance of a dark and determined one.

"Brydone," he said, "let me give you some counsel—the last, perhaps, I shall ever give you. You're in the way of danger if you go up to the barony. There will be hot fighting there to-day. Captain Morton's friends won't stand by and see him swing, to please a cowardly scamp like Stockton. You can save yourself all risk, and a good share of money besides, by taking the twenty guineas, and riding down the road."

"Ah, ha! Watson Gray!—but where then would be my share at the gutting of the barony?"

"The share of a fool, perhaps, whose fingers are made use of to take the nuts from the fire."

"No more fool than yourself, Watson Gray; and let me tell you to look to yourself as well as the captain. There's more halters than one in preparation."

"Ah, do you say so?" replied Gray, coolly, as the other jerked up the bridle of his horse and prepared to ride forward.

"Yes! and I warn you that *you* had better take the road *down* the country, rather than me. Your chance isn't so much better than that of Ned Morton, that you can stand by and see him hoisted, without running a narrow chance of getting your neck into the noose. Now, take my word, for what I'm telling you—you've given me what you call good advice; I'll give you some in return. Do just what you wanted me to do. Turn your horse's head and ride down the country, and don't trust yourself within a day's ride of the barony. By hard pushing, you'll get to Martin's in time for breakfast, while I'll ride for'a'd and take mine at the barony."

"You are very considerate, Joe—very. But I don't despair of convincing you by the sight of the twenty guineas. Gold is so lovely a metal, that a handful of it persuades where all human argument will fail; and I think, that by giving you a sufficient share of it to carry, you will stop long enough, before you go on with this cruel business. You certainly can't find any pleasure in seeing your old friends hung; and when it's to your interest, too, that they should escape, it must be the worst sort of madness in you to go forward."

"You may put it up. I won't look. I'll tell you what, Watson Gray — I know very well what's locked up in Middleton barony. I should be a pretty fool to take twenty guineas, when I can get two hundred."

Meantime, under the pretence of taking the money from his bosom, Gray had taken a pistol from his belt. This he held in readiness, and within a couple of feet from the head of Brydone. The latter had pushed his horse a little in the advance, while Gray had naturally kept his steed in while extricating the pistol.

"Be persuaded, Brydone," continued Gray, with all the gentleness of one who was simply bent to conciliate; "only cast your eyes round upon this metal, and you will be convinced. It is a sight which usually proves very convincing."

But the fellow doggedly refused to turn his head, which he continued to shake negatively.

"No, no!" he answered; "it can't convince me, Watson Gray. You needn't to pull out your purse and waste your words. Put up your money. I should be a blasted fool to give up my chance at Middleton barony, and Ned Morton's share, for so poor a sum as twenty guineas."

"Fool!" exclaimed Gray, "then die in your folly! Take lead, since gold won't suit you:" and, with the words, he pulled trigger, and drove a brace of bullets through the skull of his wilful companion. Brydone tumbled from his horse without a groan.

"I would have saved the ass if he would have let me," said Gray, dismounting leisurely; and, fastening his own and the horse of the murdered man in the thicket, he proceeded to lift the carcass upon his shoulder. He carried it into the deepest part of the woods, a hundred yards or more from the roadside, and, having first emptied the pockets, cast it down into the channel of a little creek, the watery ooze of which did not suffice to cover it. The face was downward, but the back of his head, mangled and shattered by the bullets, remained upward and visible through the water. From the garments of Brydone he gleaned an amount in gold almost as great as that which he had tendered him; and, with characteristic philosophy, he thus soliloquized while he counted it over and transferred it to his own pockets.

"A clear loss of forty guineas to the foolish fellow. This is all the work of avarice. Now, if his heart hadn't been set upon gutting the barony, he'd have seen the reason of everything I said to him. He'd have seen that it was a short matter of life and death between us. Him or me! Me or him! Turn it which way you will, like '96,'* it's still the same. I don't like to use bullets when other arguments will do: but 'twas meant to be so. There was a fate in the matter—as there is pretty much in all matters. He *wasn't* to listen to arguments this time, and I *was* to shoot him. He was a good runner—and that's as much as could be said of him—but a most conceited fool. . . . Well, our reckoning's over. He's got his pay and discharge, and Stockton's lost his witness. I was fearful I'd have to shoot him, when I set out. The foolish fellow! He wouldn't have believed it if I had *told* him. With such a person, feeling is the only sort of believing: a bullet's the only thing to convince a hard head. He's got it, and no more can be said."

## CHAPTER XXXIX.

### A SEQUEL TO AN EVIL DEED.

The probable and ultimate task which Watson Gray had assigned to himself for performance, on quitting the barony that morning, was fairly over; but the murderer, by that sanguinary execution, did not entirely conclude the bloody work which he had thus unscrupulously begun. He was one of those professional monsters, whose brag it is that they make a clean finish of the job, and leave behind them no telltale and unneces-

---

* The two numbers which compose the name of the old state district of Ninety-Six, expressing the same quantity when viewed on either side, suggested to one of the members of the legislature a grave argument for continuing the name, when a change was contemplated, and effected, for that section of country. A better argument for its preservation was to be found in the distinguished share which it had in the Revolutionary struggle.

sary chips which they might readily put out of sight. He had no scruples in pocketing the money which he had taken from the garments of Brydone; but he knew that the horse of the murdered man could be identified; and accordingly, though with much more reluctance than he had manifested in the case of his master, he decreed to the animal the same fate. He brought him to the spot where he had thrown the body, and despatched him in like manner, by putting a brace of bullets through his head. Then, with all the coolness of the veteran ruffian, he reloaded his weapons where he stood, and, having done so, returned quietly to the spot where his own steed had been fastened.

But the "fate" about which Watson Gray had soliloquized, after the usual fashion of the ruffian, was disposed to be particularly busy that day and in that neighborhood. The gratuitous killing of the horse, though designed to increase the securities of the murderer, helped really to diminish them. The report of his last pistol had awakened other echoes than such as were altogether desirable; and he, who had so lately sent his fellow-creature to his sudden and fearful account, was soon aroused to the necessity of seeking measures for his own life and safety.

He had left the plain which he had made memorable by his evil deed, not more than half a mile behind him, when he was startled by the mellow note of a bugle in his rear. A faint answer was returned from above, and he now began to fear that his path was beset by cavalry. Could it be that Stockton had got some intimation of his departure from the barony, and, suspecting his object, had set off in pursuit? This was the more obvious interpretation of the sounds which alarmed him. This was the most natural suspicion of his mind.

He stopped his horse for a few seconds on the edge of the road, and partly in the cover of the wood, undetermined whether to dismount and take the bushes, or boldly dash forward and trust to the fleetness of his steed. But for the difficulty of hiding the animal, the former would have been the best policy. He chose a middle course and rode off to the left, into the forest, at as easy a pace as was possible. But he had not gone a hundred yards before he espied the imperfect outlines of three horsemen in a group, on the very line he was pursuing. They were at some distance, and did not, probably, perceive him where he stood. Drawing up his reins, he quietly turned about, and endeavored to cross the road in order to bury himself in the woods opposite; but, in crossing, he saw and was seen by at least twenty other horsemen.

The brief glimpse which was afforded him of these men showed him that they were none of Stockton's, but did not lessen, in any degree, his cause of apprehension, or the necessity of his flight. The pale-yellow crescent which gleamed upon their caps of .felt or fur, and their blue uniforms, apprized him that they were the favorite troopers of Clarence Conway; and the wild shout which they set up at seeing him, too plainly told the eagerness with which they were resolved to dash upon their prey. Gnashing his teeth in the bitterness of his disappointment, he growled in loud soliloquy, as he drove the spurs into his charger's sides, and sent him headlong through the woods.

"Hell's curses on such luck. Here, when all was as it should be, to have him cross the track. It will be too late to get back to the captain!"

At this time, the apprehensions of Watson Gray seemed entirely given to his superior. The idea of his own escape being doubtful, did not once seem to cross his mind. He looked up to the sun, which was now speeding rapidly onward to his meridian summits, and muttered,——

"Eight good miles yet, and how many twists and turns beside, the d—l only knows! Would to Heaven that Stockton would only come into the woods now. There could be no more pretty or profitable game for us, than to see his rascals, and these, knocking out each other's brains. Where the deuce did Conway spring from? He's after Stockton, that's clear; but what brought him below? Not a solitary scoundrel of a runner in all last week, to tell us anything—no wonder that we knock our skulls against the pine trees."

Such were his murmurings as he galloped forward. The pursuit was begun with great spirit, from several quarters at the same time; betraying a fact which Gray had not before expected, and which now began to awaken his apprehensions for his own safety. He was evidently environed by his foes. There had been an effort made to surround him. This, he quickly conjectured to have been in consequence of the alarm which he himself had given, by the use of firearms, in his late performances.

"So much for firing that last pistol. It was not needful. What did I care if they did find the horse afterward. Nobody could trouble me with the matter. But it's too late for wisdom. I must do the best. I don't think they've closed me in quite."

But they had. The very first pistol-shot had been reported to Conway by one of his scouts, and the troop had been scattered instantly, with orders to take a wide circuit, and contract to a common centre, around the spot whence the alarm had arisen. The second shot quickened their movements, and their object was facilitated by the delay to which Gray was subjected in the removal of the body of Brydone, and in the search which he afterward made of the pockets of his victim. He soon saw the fruits of his error—of that which is scarcely an error in a sagacious scout—that Indian caution which secures and smooths everything behind him, even to the obliteration of his own footsteps.

He had ridden but a few hundred yards farther, when he discovered that the foe was still in front of him. Two of the "Congaree Blues," well mounted and armed, were planted directly in his track, and within twenty paces of each other. Both were stationary, and seemed quietly awaiting his approach.

A desperate fight, or a passive surrender was only to be avoided by a *ruse de guerre*. The chances of the two former seemed equally dubious. Watson Gray was a man of brawn, of great activity and muscle. He would not have thought it a doubtful chance, by any means, to have grappled with either of the foes before him. He would have laughed, perhaps, at the absurdity of any apprehensions which might be entertained in his behalf, in such a conflict. But with the two, the case was somewhat different. The one would be able to delay him sufficiently long to permit the other to shoot, or cut him down, at leisure, and without hazard. Surrender was an expedient scarcely more promising. The Black Riders had long since been out of the pale of mercy along the Congaree; and the appeal for quarter, on the part of one wearing their uniform, would have been answered by short shrift and sure cord.

But there was a *ruse* which he might practise, and to which he now addressed all his energies. He lessened the rapidity of his motion, after satisfying himself by a glance behind him, that he was considerably in advance of the rear pursuit. He was now sufficiently nigh to those in front to hear their voices. They charged him to surrender as he approached; and, with a motion studiously intended for them to see, he returned the pistol to his belt, which before he had kept ready in his hand. This was a pacific sign, and his reply to the challenge confirmed its apparent signification.

"Good terms—good quarter—and I'll surrender," was his reply.

"Ay, ay!—you shall have terms enough," was the answer; and the young dragoon laughed aloud at the seeming anxiety with which the fugitive appeared to insist upon the terms of safety. Gray muttered between his teeth——

"He means good rope; but he shall laugh t'other side of his mouth, the rascal!"

Maintaining an appearance studiously pacific, and giving an occasional glance behind him, as if prompted by terror, Gray took especial care to carry his horse to the right hand of the farthest trooper, who was placed on the right of his comrade, and, as we have said, some twenty paces from him. By this movement he contrived to throw out one of the troopers altogether, the other being between Watson Gray and his comrade. Approaching this one he began drawing up his steed, but when almost up, and when the dragoon looked momentarily to see him dismount, he dashed the spurs suddenly into the animal's sides, gave him free rein, and adding to his impetus by the wildest halloo of which his lungs were capable, he sent the powerful steed, with irresistible impulse, full against the opposing horse and horseman. The sword of the trooper descended, but it was only while himself and horse were tumbling to the ground. A moment more, and Watson Gray went over his fallen opponent with a bound as free as if the interruption had been such only as a rush offers to the passage of the west wind.

But a new prospect of strife opened before his path almost the instant after. One and another of Conway's troop appeared at almost every interval in the forest. The pursuing party were pressing forward with wild shouts of rage and encouragement from behind, and a darker feeling, and far more solemn conviction of evil, now filled the mind of the outlaw.

"A life's only a life, after all. It's what we all have to pay one day or another. I don't think I shortened Joe Brydone's very much, and if the time's come to shorten mine, I reckon it wouldn't be very far off any how. As for the captain, he don't know, and he'll be blaming me, but I've done the best for him. It's only on his account I'm in this hobble. I could easily have managed Stockton on my own. Well, neither of us knows who's to be first; but the game looks as if 'twas nearly up for me. It won't be the rope though, I reckon. No! no! I'm pretty safe on that score."

The dark impressions of his mind found their utterance, in this form, in the few brief moments that elapsed after the discovery of his new enemies. They did not seem disposed to await his coming forward, as had been the case with the dragoon whom he had foiled and overthrown. They were advancing briskly upon him from every side. He would willingly have awaited them without any movement, but for the rapidly sounding hoofs in the rear. These drove him forward; and he derived a new stimulus of daring, as he discovered among the advancing horsemen the person of Clarence Conway himself.

Watson Gray had imbibed from his leader some portion of the hate which the latter entertained, to a degree so mortal, for his more honorable and fortunate brother. Not that he was a man to entertain much malice. But he had learned to sympathize so much with his confederate in crime, that he gradually shared his hates and prejudices, even though he lacked the same fiery passions which would have provoked their origination in himself. The sight of Clarence Conway aroused in him something more than the mere desire of escape. Of escape, indeed, he did not now think so much. But the desire to drag down with him into the embrace of death an object of so much anxiety and hate, and frequent vexation, was itself a delight; and the thought begat a hope in his mind, which left him comparatively indifferent to all the dangers which might have threatened himself. He saw Conway approaching, but he did not now wait for his coming. To remain, indeed, was to subject him to the necessity of throwing away his resources of death and of defence, upon the less worthy antagonists who were closing up from behind. Accordingly, drawing both pistols from his belt, he dropped the reins of his horse upon his neck, and gave him the spur.

"Beware!" cried Conway to the troopers around him, as he saw this action—"the man is desperate."

He himself did not seem to value the caution which he expressed to others. He dashed forward to encounter the desperate man, his broadsword waving above his head, and forming, in their sight, the crescent emblem of his followers. With loud cries they pressed forward after his footsteps; but the splendid charger which Conway bestrode, allowed them no chance of interposition. The resolute demeanor, and reckless advance of Conway, probably saved his life. It drew the precipitate fire of Watson Gray, and probably disordered his aim. The bullet shattered the epaulette upon Conway's shoulder, and grazed the flesh, but scarcely to inflict a wound. Before he could use the second, a henchman of Conway's, a mere boy, rode up, and shivered the hand which grasped it by a shot, almost sent at hazard, from a single and small pistol which he carried. In another moment the sweeping sabre of Conway descended upon the neck of the outlaw, cutting through the frail resistance of coat and collar, and almost severing the head from the shoulders. The eyes rolled wildly for an instant—the lips gasped, and slightly murmured, and then the insensible frame fell heavily to the earth, already stiffened in the silent embrace of death. The space of time had been fearfully short between his own fate, and that which the murderer had inflicted upon Brydone. His reflections upon that person, may justify us in giving those which fell from the lips of Clarence Conway, as the victim was identified.

"Watson Gray!" said he, "a bad fellow, but a great scout. Next to John Bannister, there was not one like him on the

Congaree. But he was a wretch—a bad, bloody wretch;—he's gone to a dreadful and terrible account. Cover him up, men, as soon as you have searched him. Lieutenant Monk, attend to this man's burial, and join me below. We must see what he has been about there. You say two pistol shots were heard?"

"Two, sir, about ten minutes apart."

"Such a man as Watson Gray, never uses firearms without good cause—we must search and see."

Dividing his little force, Conway gave the order to "trot," and the troop was soon under quick motion, going over the ground which they so recently traversed. The search was keen, and, as we may suppose, successful. The body of Brydone and that of his horse were found, but, as he was unknown, it excited little interest. That he was a Black Rider, and an enemy, was obvious from his dress; and the only subject of marvel was, why Watson Gray should murder one of his own fraternity. It was midday before Clarence Conway took up the line of march for Middleton barony, and this mental inquiry was one for which he could find no plausible solution until some time after he had arrived there. Let us not anticipate his arrival.

## CHAPTER XL.

#### BUCKLING ON ARMOR.

It may readily be supposed that the disappearance of Watson Gray caused some uneasiness in the mind of his principal; but when, hour after hour elapsed, yet brought neither sign nor word which could account for his absence, or remedy its evil consequences, the uneasiness of the outlaw naturally and proportionally increased. The fearful hour was speeding onward to its crisis, as it seemed, with more than the wonted rapidity of time. The aspect of events looked black and threatening. Wounded and feeble, wanting in that agent who, in his own prostration, was the eye, and the wing, and the arm, of his resolves, Edward Morton could not shake off the gathering clouds of apprehension which hung heavy about his soul. He had risen at the first blushing of the day, and, with the assistance of a servant, contrived to put on his garments. The sword which he was scarcely able to wield—certainly, with no efficiency—was buckled to his side;—but his chief reliance, in the event of a last struggle, lay in his pistols, of which an extra pair had been provided by Watson Gray, the moment he discovered the probable danger of his superior.

As the day advanced, and Gray did not appear, the outlaw felt it necessary to make those preparations, the chief duty of which now promised to devolve upon him; and with some difficulty, descending to the lower story of the house, he proceeded to drill his men in anticipation of the worst. He had already resolved not to go further, unless Gray made his appearance in season and counselled the measure. He had, from the first, been opposed to the trial; though he could not but acknowledge that the arrangement had been most favorable, at the time, which his confederate could hope to make. He was now more thoroughly confirmed than ever in his determination to keep his defences, and convert the mansion house into a stronghold, which he would surrender only with his life.

The surgeon, Hillhouse, was present, with a double share of resolution, to second his resolve. The picture which Watson Gray had judiciously presented to his mind, the night before, of the sacking of his various wardrobe, by the sable mutineers, had been a subject of sleepless meditation to him the whole night, and had imbued him with a bitter disposition, to kill and destroy, all such savage levellers of taste and fortune as should cross his path or come within shooting distance from the windows. His person was decorated with more than usual care and fastidiousness that morning. He wore a rich crimson trunk, that shone like flame even in the darkened apartments. This was tapered off with stockings of the softest lilac; and the golden buckles which glittered upon his shoes, also served to bring "a strange brightness to the shady place." His coat, worn for the first time since he had reached the barony, was of the rich uniform of the British Guards. Altogether, Surgeon Hillhouse in his present equipments, made a most imposing figure. His person was not bad, though his face was monstrous ugly; and he possessed a leg which was symmetry itself. He measured at annual periods, the knee, the calf, and the ankle, and by a comparison with every other handsome leg in the army, he had been able to satisfy himself that his was the perfect standard. It did not lessen the military effect of his appearance, though somewhat incongruous with his display in other respects, that he wore a common belt of sable strapped about his waist, in which were stuck half a dozen pistols of all sizes. He had a taste in this weapon, and had accumulated a moderate assortment, most of which were richly wrought and inlaid with bits of embossed plate, of gold and silver; carvings and decorations which took the shapes of bird, beast, and flower, according to the caprice or fancy of their owner; or, it may be, the artist himself. The more serious and stern outlaw met this display with a look of scorn which he did not seek to suppress, but which the fortunate self-complaisance of the other did not suffer him to see.

"You don't seem, Mr. Hillhouse," he observed, as they met, "to anticipate much trouble or danger in this morning's work."

"Ah sir! and why do you think so?" demanded the other with some curiosity.

"Your garments seem better adapted for the ball-room and the dance, than for a field of blood and battle. You may be shot, and scalped, or hung, sir, in the course of the morning."

"True, sir, and for that reason, I have dressed myself in this fashion. The idea of this extreme danger, alone, sir, prompted me to this display. For this reason I made my toilet with extreme care. I consumed, in my ablutions, an entire section of my famous Chinese soap. You perceive, sir, in the language of the divine Shakspere"—stroking his chin complacently as he spoke—"'I have reaped the stubble field also—my chin was never smoother; and, in the conviction, sir, that I might be called upon this day, to make my last public appearance, I have been at special pains to prepare my person to the best advantage, for the inspection of the fortunate persons who will make the final disposition of it. To die with dignity, and to appear after death with grace, has been the reflection which has occupied my mind this morning, as I made my toilet. My meditations were necessarily of a melancholy complexion. If these rogues are to inherit my wardrobe, let me make as much use of it as I can. I may probably secure this suit to myself by dying in it like a man."

The outlaw scarcely heard these forcible reasons—certainly he did not listen to them. He was already busy in disposing, to the best advantage, of his half score of muskets. The house was one of comparatively great strength. It was of brick, built for service, and had been more than once defended against the assaults of the Congarees. With an adequate force it might have been held against any assailants, unless they brought artillery. But the little squad of Edward Morton was wretchedly inadequate to its defence, even against the small force of Stockton. It required all of his skill, courage, and ingenuity, to make it tolerably secure. He now more than ever felt the absence of Watson Gray. The readiness of resource which that wily ruffian possessed, would, no doubt, have been productive of very important assistance. Even if the garrison could hold out against assault, they could not hope to do so against famine. The provisions of the plantation were already at the mercy of the Black Riders.

The outlaw surveyed his prospects with sufficient misgivings. They were deplorable and discouraging enough. But he never once thought of faltering. His soul felt nothing but defiance. His words breathed nothing but confidence and strength. He laughed—he even laughed with scorn—when Hillhouse said something of a capitulation and terms.

"Terms, sir! ay, we'll give and take terms—such terms as lie at the point of these bayonets, and can be understood from the muzzle of gun and pistol. Terms, indeed! Why do you talk of terms, sir, when we can beat and slay the whole gang of them in twenty minutes! Let them approach and give us a mark at all, and what chance can they have, with their pistols only, against these muskets? Really, Mr. Hillhouse, for a gentleman of high rank in his majesty's army, I am surprised that you should hold such language. If you dread the result, sir— you are at liberty to leave the house this very moment. Go, sir, to a place of safety, if you can find it; or make your own terms with our enemies, as you or they please. Try it, and you'll find that your fine clothes will be one of the best arguments for hanging you to the first tree;—the Black Riders have long since learned that the finest bird is to be first plucked. We shall remain where we are, and probably inherit your wardrobe after all."

The surgeon was abashed and confounded for the moment. He had not often been compelled to listen to such language; nor did the outlaw intend it so much for the ears of the person whom he addressed as for those who listened around him. He knew the value of big words and bluster, in a time of doubt and danger, to the uninformed and vulgar mind. He felt that nothing could be hoped for, at the hands of his small party, if any of them were suffered to flinch or falter. *He* knew the importance of all that he himself said; but the surgeon did not once suspect it. He recovered from his astonishment, and, after a brief delay, his wounded pride found utterance.

"Really, sir—Mr. Conway—your language is exceedingly objectionable. I shall be constrained to notice it, sir; and to look for redress at your hands at the earliest opportunity."

"Any time, sir—now—when you please—only don't afflict me with your apprehensions. If you can not see, what is clear enough to the blindest mule that ever ploughed up a plain field, that these scoundrels stand no sort of chance against us, in open assault—no words of mine, or of any man, can make you wiser. Like Rugely, you would surrender, I suppose, at the enforcement of a pine log."

A hearty laugh of the soldiers attested the inspiring influences which they had imbibed from the confident bearing and words of Morton, and their familiarity with an anecdote which, but a little time before, had provoked much mirth in both parties at the expense of a provincial officer, in the British army, served to increase their confidence.* It may be supposed that this

---

* Colonel Rugely had command of a British stockade near Camden, which was garrisoned by an hundred men. It was summoned by Colonel William Washington. "Washington was without artillery; but a pine log, which was ingeniously hewn and arranged so as to resemble a field-piece, enforced, to the

burst of merriment did not diminish the anger of Hillhouse; but he contented himself with saying that he should "bide his time."

"You are right, sir, in this respect," said Morton, "we have neither of us any time for private squabbles. Do your duty manfully to-day, Mr. Hillhouse, and if we survive it, I shall be ready to apologise to you to-morrow, or give you whatever satisfaction will please you best. But now to work. These shutters must be closed in and secured."

The lower story was completely closed up by this proceeding. The shutters, of solid oak, were fastened within, and, ascending to the upper story, Morton disposed his men in the different apartments, with strict warning to preserve the closest watch from the windows, at every point of approach. Having completed his disposition of the defences, he requested an interview with the ladies of the house, which was readily granted. The outlaw and surgeon were accordingly ushered into an antechamber in which, amidst the stir and bustle of the events going on below, the ladies had taken refuge. The gentlemen were received with kindness. At such moments—moments of sudden peril and unexpected alarm—the human ties assert their superiority, over the forms of society and the peculiar habits of education, through the medium of our fears; and even the suspicions which the ladies might have had, touching the character of Edward Morton—whom they knew only as Edward Conway—and the contempt which they felt for the fopperies of Hillhouse, gave way entirely before the pressing and mutual necessities which prevailed to the probable danger of the whole.

But, in truth, the appearance of the outlaw, at that moment of his own superior peril, was well calculated to command the admiration even of those who loved him not. Man never looks so noble as when he contends calmly with the obvious danger—when, aware of all its worst characteristics, he yet goes forth to the encounter, with a stern deliberate purpose, which sustains

commander of the post, the propriety of surrendering, at the first summons of the American colonel. This harmless piece of timber, elevated a few feet from the earth, was invested by the apprehension of the garrison with such formidable power, that they were exceedingly glad to find a prompt acceptance of their submission."—*History of South Carolina*, p. 187.

him unshrinking to the last, and suffers him, at no moment, to seem palsied, weak, or indecisive. Edward Morton wore the aspect of this firmness, in the presence of the ladies. They knew that he was the destined victim whom the Black Riders professed to seek, and seek only;—they knew not exactly why—but their conjecture, naturally enough, in the absence of more certain reasons—assumed it to be in consequence of his Americanism.

Whatever might be the cause, to be the foe of the Black Riders was, in all likelihood, to be the friend of virtue and the right; and as he stood before them, erect for the first time after weeks of painful sickness and prostration—more erect than ever—with a demeanor that did not presume in consequence of his situation—nor challenge, by doubtful looks and tremulous tones, that sympathy which might well be asked for, but never by, "the brave man struggling with the storms of fate;"—he insensibly rose in the estimation of both, as his person seemed to rise nobly and commandingly in their sight.

His voice was gentle and mournful—in this, perhaps, he did not forbear the exercise of some of his habitual hypocrisy. He did not forget for a moment that the keen glances of Flora Middleton were upon him; and like most men of the world, he never forgot that policy which casts about it those seeds which, as they ripen into fruit—whatever the degree of probability—the same hand may gather which has sown.

"Ladies, I am sorry to tell you that my presence has brought danger to your house."

The venerable lady replied, promptly:—

"I trust, Mr. Conway, that, with the assistance of your followers, you will be able to keep the danger from it."

"Alas, madam, I must not disguise from you the truth: we are as one to ten only; we may slay many of the assailants, but if they are led by ordinary courage, they may eat through these walls in our spite. I have one hope—that Watson Gray, who left the house last night, will return in season, with a sufficient force to baffle them in their attempts. All that can be done now will be to keep off the moment of danger—to parry for a while, and protract as long as we can, the storm which will come at last."

"Mr. Conway, I would not disparage your judgment or your valor; but the late General Middleton, when scarcely at your years, beat off three hundred Congarees from the very threshold of this dwelling."

The outlaw modestly replied, with a bow of the head:—

"We will do what we can do, Mrs. Middleton; but we have a poor squad of ten men in all, not including Mr. Hillhouse and myself. I have no doubt Mr. Hillhouse will do his duty as becomes him——"

"As becomes a gentleman fighting in the presence of the fairest lady——"

Morton continued his speech in season to interrupt some stiltish common-place of the surgeon, which could only have been disgusting to the ladies.

"As for myself, you know my condition. I can die—I need not, I trust, say that, no man could feel it hard to do so, under such circumstances as prevail over us at present—but I have little strength to make my death expensive to our enemies. There is one thing, Mrs. Middleton, that I have deferred speaking to the last."

He hesitated, and his eyes were fixed sadly for a moment upon the face of Flora, then, as he met her glance, they were instantly averted.

"What is that, sir?" demanded the old lady.

"It is this, madam: there is one proceeding by which it is yet possible to avert from your dwelling the strife which will shortly threaten it."

"In God's name, sir, let it be resorted to——"

"If it be right—if it be proper, only, mother," cried Flora, earnestly, putting her hand upon the wrist of her grandmother.

",Certainly—surely, my child," was the reply. "Peace and safety are to be purchased only by just conduct. Speak, Mr. Conway, what is the alternative?"

"Professedly, madam, these ruffians seek me alone, of all this household. I am the sole object of their hate—the victim whom they have singled out for their special vengeance. Were I in their hands——"

"Surely, Mr. Conway, you would not think so meanly of my

mother and myself," was the hasty interruption of Flora Middleton, "as to fancy that we could be pleased at your giving up any security, however partial, such as our house affords you, because of the possible annoyance to which we might be subjected on account of this banditti. I trust that you will be able to defend the house, and I hope that you will do so to the last."

The outlaw seemed to catch fire at the manner of the generous girl. Her own flashing eyes were full of a flame to impart enthusiasm to the dullest spirit; and he exclaimed, with a more genuine feeling of zeal than was usual with him:—

"And, by heavens, I will! You have stifled the only doubts which I had of the propriety of making your house my castle. I need not say to you that the hostility of these scoundrels to me is, perhaps, little more than a pretence. Even were I given up to them, and in their hands, they would probably sack your dwelling. They are just now, I suspect, released from nearly all restraint and subjection, and about to fly the country. Lord Rawdon has gone, or is on his way below, by another route, with all his forces; and the men of Sumter, Lee, and Marion, are pressing at the heels of his lordship. Perhaps I speak with literal accuracy when I say that your safety depends on mine. If I fail to make good the house against these Black Riders—you already know their character—I tremble for you! Your safety shall be no less in my thoughts, during this conflict, than my own; and I repeat, once more, my readiness to die before outrage and violence shall cross your threshold."

"We thank you, sir—from the bottom of our hearts, we thank you, Mr. Conway——"

Morton bowed, as he interrupted the strain of feminine acknowledgment:—

"Let me now beg you to seek the garret; there you will be in tolerable safety. If we do not again meet, do me the justice to believe that I spared neither limb nor life in your behalf. I may fall, but I will not falter."

"God be with you, Mr. Conway!" was the ejaculation of both ladies. A blush tinged the cheek of the outlaw—a tremulous emotion passed through his veins. When, before, had the pure of the purer sex uttered such an invocation in his behalf?

"Can it be an omen of ill,"—such was his reflection—"that it is spoken, as it would seem, in the last moment of my career?"

"I thank you, Mrs. Middleton; I thank you"—to Flora, but he did not speak her name. The direction of his eye indicated the person to whom he spoke. His look and air were not unadroit. He still remembered his policy; and Flora Middleton fancied, as she turned away, that she had not often seen a nobler-looking personage. The contrast between himself and Mr. Hillhouse, perhaps, helped to strengthen this impression. A grave monkey is, of all objects, the most lugubrious, and the plain statements of the outlaw had suddenly made the surgeon very grave. He really did not imagine that things were in so deplorable a condition. Thinking over them rendered him forgetful of his fine sayings, and the attempt which he made to throw some pathos into his parting address to the ladies, was ridiculous without being easy, and elaborate and strained without being free or graceful. When they had gone, Mr. Hillhouse found a more ready tongue, and once more began to intimate the propriety of terms and a flag of truce.

In India, once, an affair of the Sepoys—very much like the present—a sort of mutiny and insurrection—"

"No more of this nonsense," said Morton, with the old habit of command which belonged to the captain of the fierce banditti by which he was now threatened. "It's time, Mr. Hillhouse, to be a man, if you ever hope to be like one. Do you hear that trumpet, sir? It is a summons—it opens the business. You talk of terms and overtures—how do you like the idea of making them from the balcony of yonder porch? What! it does not please you? Yet it must be done. Musketeers, to the windows! Cover the approach to the porch, and shoot as I bid—see that no man comes within pistol-shot. I, myself, will parley with these scoundrels.

The door of the great passage-way which divided the dwelling centrally was thrown open, and the outlaw presented himself in the balcony to the eyes of the Black Riders, who had assembled, some thirty or forty in number, in detached groups, about fifty yards from the building. A yell of ferocious exultation hailed his appearance from below, and attested the excited feelings of malicious hate with which they had been wrought upon to regard their ancient leader.

## CHAPTER XLI.

#### THE SIEGE AND STORM.

A SMILE of mixed bitterness and derision passed over the lips of the outlaw, as he hearkened to the rude but mighty uproar.

"Dogs!" he muttered, "there was a time when I would have made you crouch beneath the lash to your proper attitude!—and I may do so yet. I am not wholly powerless even now!"

As they shouted, an involuntary movement was made by several among them. They rushed toward him, as if their purpose had been to approach him with determined violence. Several of them were dismounted, and these, waving their pistols aloft, were evidently disposed to bring themselves within the necessary distance which should permit of the certain use of their weapon. But Morton, in the intervals of their clamor, suffered them to hear his brief, stern command to the musketeers, whom they might behold at the windows, to be in readiness and watchful.

"Shoot down the first scoundrel that advances with arms. Take good aim and spare none, unless I bid ye."

This order produced a pause in their career. Some incertitude seemed to prevail among them, and, at length, Morton distinguished, beneath a tree in the distance, the persons of Stockton, Darcy, and two others, who were evidently busy in the work of consultation. He himself quietly took his seat upon one of the benches in the balcony, and patiently waited the result of this deliberation. His pistols, broad-mouthed and long, of the heaviest calibre, were ready in his hand and belt, and all well loaded with a brace of balls.

Meanwhile, his resolute appearance, placid manner, and the indifference which his position displayed, were all provocative of increased clamors and commotion among the crowd. They were evidently lashing themselves into fury, as does the bull when he desires the conflict for which he is not yet sufficiently blinded and maddened. Cries of various kinds, but all intended to stimulate their hostility to him, were studiously repeated by the emissaries of his successor. Not the least influential were those which dilated upon the spoils to be gathered from the contemplated sack of the barony — an argument which had most probably been more potent than any other in seducing them away from their fealty to the insubordinate desires of Stockton.

Morton watched all these exhibitions without apprehension, though not without anxiety; and when he turned, and gave a glance to his few followers within the house — drilled men, stubborn and inflexible, who could easier die, under the command to do so, than obey the impulse to flight without hearing the "retreat" sounded, but who had no other resources of mind and character beyond the dogged resolution taught by their military life — his heart misgave him. He felt what he himself might do in command of the Black Riders against such defenders as he then possessed; and he did not deceive himself as to the probable result. One hope yet remained. It was that Watson Gray was somewhere busy in his behalf. His eyes often stretched beyond the park, in the direction of the high road, in the vain hope to see his confederate, with some hastily-gathered recruits, marching to his rescue. At that very moment Gray was quivering in the few brief agonies of death, which he endured under the sabre of Clarence Conway.

The deliberations of Stockton and his confederates were soon at an end, and with them the doubts of the outlaw. Stockton himself made his appearance in the foreground, bearing a white handkerchief fastened to a sapling. His offensive weapons he ostentatiously spread out upon the earth, at some distance from the mansion, when he came fairly into sight. His course, which was intended to inspire confidence in himself among his followers, had been dictated by Darcy.

"They must see that you're as bold as Ned Morton. He comes out in full front, and you must do no less. You must go to meet him. It will look well among the men."

There were some misgivings in Stockton's mind as to the probable risk which he incurred; nor was Darcy himself entirely without them. Morton they knew to be desperate; and if he could conjecture their intentions toward him, they could very well understand how gladly he would avail himself of the appearance of Stockton to extinguish the feud in his blood. The idea, in fact, crossed the mind of Morton himself.

"That scoundrel!"—he muttered as Stockton approached him—" is the cause of all. Were he out of the way—and a single shot does it!—but, no! no!—he has put down his arms; and then there's that base scoundrel Darcy in the background. Were I to shoot Stockton, he would bring out another of these blood-hounds to fill his place. I should gain nothing by it. Patience! Patience! I must bide my time, and wait for the turn of the die."

Meanwhile, Stockton advanced, waving aloft his symbol of peace. Morton rose at his approach, and went forward to the railing of the balcony.

"Well,"—he demanded—"for what purpose does Lieutenant Stockton come?"

"Captain Stockton, if you please. He comes to know if you are ready to deliver yourself up for trial by the troop, as was agreed upon by Watson Gray yesterday."

"Let Watson Gray answer for himself, Captain or Lieutenant Stockton. He will probably be upon your backs with Coffin's cavalry in twenty minutes. For me, sirrah—hear the only answer I make. I bid you defiance; and warn you now to get to your covert with all expedition. You shall have five minutes to return to your confederates; if you linger after that time—ay, or any of your crew—you shall die like dogs. Away!"

The retort of Stockton was that of unmeasured abuse. A volume of oaths and execrations burst from his lips; but Morton resuming his seat, cried to the musketeers—

"Attention—make ready—take aim!"

Enough was effected, without making necessary the final

command, to "fire." Stockton took to his heels, in most undignified retreat; and, stumbling before he quite regained the shelter of the wood, fell, head foremost, and was stretched at full length along the earth, to the merriment of some and the vexation of others among his comrades.

The fury of the conspirator was increased by this event; and he proceeded, with due diligence, to commence the leaguer. His corps were suddenly commanded to disappear from the open ground; and when Edward Morton saw them again, they were in detached parties, preserving cover as well as they could, along the edges of the park, the avenue, a small thicket of sassafras and cedar that lay along the northern skirts of the mansion-house, and such of the outhouses and domestic offices, as could bring them near enough to act upon the defenders without exposure of themselves.

The body thus distributed was formidably numerous when compared with that of Morton. His estimate made them little less than sixty men. Immediately in front, though beyond the sure reach of musketry, Stockton, himself, prepared to take his stand, surrounded by some half dozen of his troop; and among these, to the increased annoyance of Morton, he saw one who unslung a rifle from his shoulder. At this sight he at once withdrew from the balcony, secured the door, and commanded his musketeers to sink from sight, and avoid unnecessary exposure. The warning was just in season. In the very instant while he spoke the glass was shattered above his own head, and the sharp, clear sound which accompanied the event attested the peculiar utterance of the rifle.

"A little too much powder, or a young hand," said Morton coolly. "Give me your musket, one of you?"

He took his place at the window, detached the bayonet from the muzzle of the gun, and handed it back to the soldier.

"But for the steel"—meaning the bayonet—"the smooth bore would be a child's plaything against that rifle. But I have made a musket tell at a hundred yards, and may again. We must muzzle that rifle if we can."

The gun was scarcely lifted to the eyes of the speaker before its dull, heavy, roar was heard, awakening all the echoes of the surrounding woods. The men rushed to the window, and as the smoke lifted, they perceived that the party of Stockton was dispersed, while one man stood, leaning, as if in an attitude of suffering, against a tree. The rifle, however, appeared in another hand at some little distance off. Morton shook his head with dissatisfaction, as he recollected that while there were fifty men in the ranks of the enemy, to whom the rifle was a familiar weapon, to disarm one, or a dozen, was to do little or nothing for his own and for the safety of his party. In a few moments after, sudden cries and a discharge of firearms from the opposite quarter of the building betrayed the beginning of the strife where Mr. Hillhouse commanded.

"Keep as well covered as you can, men; but watch well that they do not close in with you. You are but twelve feet above them, and at that distance a pistol is quite as dangerous as a musket. I leave you for an instant only, to look at the rear."

There, he found Hillhouse, doing his duty as bravely as if he had no fine uniform at hazard.

"You take a needless risk," said Morton, as he beheld him flashing one of his pretty, but trifling weapons, at the invaders, and exposing, the while, his entire person to their aim. "There will be time enough for that when they are pressing through the breach."

"They are at it now," said the other, with a momentary forgetfulness of all his circuitous phraseologies. "They've got ladders, and are trying to mount."

"Indeed!" cried the outlaw, drawing his sabre from the sheath, and pushing Hillhouse aside, with a seeming forgetfulness of his own wounds and infirmities. He approached the window, and saw the truth of the surgeon's representations. A squad of the Black Riders had, indeed, pressed forward to the wall sufficiently nigh to plant against it, the rack, which they had taken from the stables; and which furnished them a solid and sufficient ladder to carry up two men abreast. Hillhouse, in his haste had suffered the four musketeers who had been allowed him, for the defence of the rear, to fire simultaneously, and, in the interval required by them to reload their pieces, the ladder had been planted, and half a dozen sable forms were already darting upward, upon its rungs.

"Reload, instantly!" Morton cried to the musketeers. "Keep your small pistols for close conflict, Mr. Hillhouse—they are fit for nothing better."

The now cool, observing outlaw, receded a moment from the window, while a blaze of pistol-shot from without, shivered the glass. He awaited this discharge, only, to advance, and with better aim, to level a brace of pistols at the same moment, among his foes, just when the ladder was most darkened, and trembling, with their forms.

Of the foremost assailants, when the broad muzzles met their glance, one dashed resolutely forward up the ladder, but received the bullet through his brain and tumbled headlong backward; while the other, with less audacity, endeavoring to retreat, was forced onward by those behind him. He had the alternative only, of throwing himself over, which he did at the risk of a broken neck; and the bullets of the remaining pistol, which Morton had drawn from his belt, were expended upon the rest of the scaling party, by whom they were utterly unexpected.

This discharge had the effect of clearing the ladder for an instant; and Morton, commanding two of the musketeers, who had now reloaded, to keep the enemy at a distance, by a close watch from an adjoining window, endeavored, with the aid of the remaining two, to draw the ladder up, and into the window against which it rested. But the weight of the massive frame was infinitely beyond their strength; and the outlaw contented himself with cutting away the rungs, which formed its steps, with his sabre, as far as his arm could reach. He had not finished this labor ere he was summoned to the front. There, the enemy had also succeeded in drawing the fire of the musketeers; and then, closing in, had effected a permanent lodgment beneath the porch below.

This was a disaster. Under the porch they were most effectually sheltered from any assault from above, and could remain entirely out of sight, unless they themselves determined otherwise. How many of them had succeeded in obtaining this cover, could not be said by the soldiers. Their conjecture, however, represented it at ten at least — a force fully equal to that which was engaged in the defence.

The brow of Morton grew darker as he discovered this circumstance. The net of the fates was evidently closing around him fast; and, for a moment, he gazed anxiously over the distant stretch of the road, in the fond hope to see Watson Gray riding in to his succor. But he turned away in hopelessness at last. His despondency did not, however, lead to any relaxation of his courage, or of that desperate determination, which he entertained, to make the fight as terrible to his foes as their hostility threatened to be terrible to him. A momentary cessation of the strife appeared to have taken place. The outlaws, who were beneath the balcony, remained perfectly quiescent.

"They can do nothing there, unless we let them. Now, men, do you keep your arms ready. Throw away no shot at the cracking of a pistol. What should it matter to you if the fools snap their puppies all day at a distance of fifty yards. Let no more of them join these below the porch, if you can help it — let none of these get away if bullets can stop their flight; but do not all of you fire at once. Keep one half of your muskets always in reserve for the worst."

While giving these instructions, Morton was prepared in getting his own weapons in readiness. The strife once begun, with the loss of men to the assailants, could not, he well knew, come to an indefinite or sudden conclusion. There was to be more of it, and his chief apprehensions now arose from the party which had found lodgment under the portico below. To the lower story he despatched one of his soldiers, whom he instructed to remain quiet, in the under passages of the house, in order to make an early report of any movements which might take place in that quarter.

He had scarcely adopted this precaution before the clamors of battle were again renewed in the part where Hillhouse was stationed. Twenty shots were fired on both sides, without intermission, in as many seconds, and, in the midst of all, a deep groan and the fall of a heavy body in the adjoining room, struck cold to the heart of Morton. He could ill afford to lose any one of his small array. He hurried to the scene of operations, and found that one of the soldiers had fallen. He still lived, but the wound was in his bosom; and a hurried inspection showed it to be from the fatal rifle. The ragged orifice, wrought by the peculiar revolutions of the deadly twist, was large enough to have received a small fowl egg. The dying man looked up to the outlaw, as if to ask if there was any hope. So Morton understood the appealing inquiry in his eyes, and he answered it with soldierly frankness.

"Make your peace with God, my good fellow; it's all over with you. You'll be dead in five minutes."

The man groaned once, shivered fearfully, then turned upon his face. His arms were once stretched out—his fingers endeavored to grasp the floor, then relaxed, then stiffened, and he lay unconscious of the rest. He was dead. Morton stepped over his body and took a hurried glance at the window.

"We have shot three of them," said Hillhouse.

"Would it were thirty! But all will not do. Are you loaded, men, and ready?"

"Yes!" was the answer of all.

"Then keep ready, but keep out of sight. Wait till they mount the ladder, expend no more shot, but rely on the push of the bayonet. There are four of you, and they have but the one ladder. The rifle can not be used while they are on it, and at no other time need you show yourselves."

Such were the hurried directions of the outlaw, which were interrupted by the renewal of the conflict. Once more they were upon the ladder, but, this time, the clamors arose also in front. The attack was simultaneous in both quarters.

"Oh, for twenty muskets, but twenty,"—cried the now thoroughly aroused Morton, as he made his way once more to the little squad which he had left in front—" and dearly should they pay for this audacity! Nay, if I only had my own strength!" he murmured, as he leaned, half fainting, against the door lintel in the passage.

A new assault from another quarter, aroused him to the consciousness of his increasing dangers, and stimulated him anew with the strength to meet it. The thunders of an axe were heard against the lower door of the entrance, and from the portico where the party had previously found a lodgment.

"This was what I feared! The trial, the danger, is here at last! But the game is one at which both of us may do mischief. I must be there to meet them. Heaven send that Stockton may be the first to find entrance!"

The soldier now appeared from below giving him the information, which he no longer needed, of the dangers that threatened from that quarter. The cheering reply of Morton sent him down again.

"Ay, ay, back to your post! You shall have help enough before they get in — before you need it."

From the upper part of the house he drew all the soldiers with the exception of three. One of these kept his place in the front, the other two in the rear, where the attempt had been made to force an entrance by means of the ladder. These stations were left under the direction of the surgeon. The greater danger was now below. He considered the efforts of those above to be feints simply.

"Mr. Hillhouse, you have only to be wary. Your two bayonets, with your own pistols, will keep down all your enemies. But, should you apprehend otherwise, draw the musket from the front of the house to your assistance. There is perhaps less likelihood of assault from that quarter. Below the struggle must be made hand to hand. The passage is narrow, and six stout men may be able to keep it against twenty. Farewell, sir — be firm — I may never see you again."

The surgeon had some tender philosophy, gleaned from his usual vocabulary of common-places, to spend, even at such a moment, and Morton left him speaking it.

He hurried down stairs with the six soldiers, whom he stationed in the passage-way, but a little in the back-ground, in order that they should not only escape any hurt from the flying fragments of the open door as it should be hewn asunder, but that a sufficient number of the banditti might be allowed to penetrate and crowd the opening. Meanwhile the strokes of the axe continued with little interval. The door was one of those ancient, solid structures of oak, doubled and plated with ribs which, in our day, might almost be employed for beams and rafters. It had been constructed with some reference to a siege from foes who used no artillery; and its strength, though it did not baffle, yet breathed not a few of the assailants, before it yielded to the final application of the axe. As the splinters flew around them, Morton wiped the heavy and clammy dews from his forehead. Cold chills were upon him, and yet he felt that there was a burning fever in his brain. The excitement was too great;—the transition from the bed of wounds and sickness, he felt, must work the most fatal effects even if he survived the struggle. But the solemn conviction had at length reached his soul that he was not to survive. The awful truth had touched his innate mind, that, in a few hours, he must be a portion of the vast, the infinite, the strange eternity.

"Surely! I shall not find it hard!" was the audible speech which this conviction forced from him. He started at the sound of his own voice. Thought was painful and torturing. The pause which had been allowed him, left him only to agony; and he longed for the coming on of the strife, and the reckless conflict, to relieve him by their terrible excitements, from thoughts and feelings still more terrible.

This relief, dreadful as it threatened to be, was now at hand. The massive bolts which secured the frame-work of the door were yielding. Some of the panels were driven in—and the soldiers were preparing to lunge away, through the openings, at the hearts of the assailants. But this, Morton positively forbid. In a whisper, he commanded them to keep silent and in the background. Their muskets were levelled, under his direction, rather under breast height, and presented at the entrance; and, in this position, he awaited, with a stillness like that which precedes the storm, for that moment when he might command all his bolts to be discharged with the unerring certainty of fate.

Moments now bore with them the awful weight of hours; the impatient murmurs deepened from without; the strokes of the axe became redoubled; and the groaning timbers, yielding at every stroke, were already a wreck. Another blow, and the work was done! Yet, ere the dreadful certainty yawned upon them—ere the chasm was quite complete—a wild chorus of yells above stairs—the rush of hurrying footsteps—the shrieks and the shot—announced to the gloomy outlaw, below, the occurrence of some new disaster. His defences were driven in above!

A troop of the outlaws had, in fact already effected their entrance. They had literally clambered up the slender columns of the portico in front—the sentinel placed in that quarter having been just before withdrawn to the rear by Hillhouse, who deemed that he would be more useful there, and under his command. This, with a vanity natural to such a person, he desired to make as respectable as possible. Lifting one of the sashes, without being heard in the din which prevailed below, they had found their way silently into the apartment. Stealing cautiously along the passage, they had come upon the surgeon, while himself and little squad were most busy with the assailants from without. The skirmish between them had been short. The first notice that Hillhouse had of his danger, was from the pistol-shot by which he was stricken down. His men turned to meet their new enemies, and in the brief interval that ensued, other foes dashed up the ladder, through the window, into the apartment, and put the finishing stroke to the conflict there.

Hillhouse was not so much hurt as not to be conscious, before sinking into insensibility, that the outlaws were already stripping him of his gorgeous apparel. His scarlet coat had already passed into the hands of a new owner.

Meanwhile the work was going on below. Morton, when he heard the uproar above, readily divined the extent of his misfortune. But he was not suffered to muse upon it long. His own trial was at hand. The door was finally driven from all its fastenings, there was no longer any obstruction, and the living tide poured in, as Morton fancied they would, in tumultuous masses. Then came the awful order from his lips to "fire!" It was obeyed by the first file of three men, kneeling; the remaining three followed the example a moment after; and yells of anguish ensued, and mingled with the first wild shouts of triumph of the assailants!

It was a moment of mixed pain and terror! Perhaps, if they could have recoiled, they would have done so. But this was now a physical impossibility. The crowd in the rear pressed forward and wedged their comrades who were in the foreground;

while the bayonet plied busily among them. But what could be done, in that way, by six men in a hand to hand conflict with six times their number. The strife was dreadful, but short. Man after man of the outlaws, was spiked upon the dripping steel; but the mass, unable to retreat, were driven forward, mad and foaming, under the feeling of desperation which now filled their hearts. They had now ceased to think or fear, and rushed like the wild bull upon the ready bayonets. The soldiers went down under the sheer pressure of their crowding bodies. The Black Riders darted among and over them, searching each heart separately with their knives; and the only strife which now remained was from the unavoidable conflict among themselves of their jostling and conflicting forms. The hoarse accents of Stockton were now heard, pre-eminent above the uproar, giving his final orders.

"Take Ned Morton alive, my merry fellows. He owes a life to the cord and timber. Save him for it if you can."

Morton had reserved himself for this moment.

"Ye have tracked the tiger to his den!" he muttered, in the shadow of the stairway, where he had taken his position, partly concealed in the obscurity of the passage. The crisis of his fate was at hand. The party from above were now heard hurrying downward, to mingle in the *melée* below; and he levelled his pistols among the crowd in the direction of Stockton's voice, and fired — and not without effect. He was now too deliberate to throw away his bullets. One of them passed through the fleshy part of the shoulder of his inveterate enemy, who was in the advance; while the other prostrated in death one of his most forward followers.

Stockton screamed with mingled pain and fury, and with sabre lifted, darted upon his foe. Feebly shouting his hate and defiance, Morton also lifted his sword, which he had leaned on the steps beside him for greater convenience, and advanced gallantly to meet the ruffian. They met, and the whole remaining strength of Morton, treasured up for this very crisis, was thrown into his arm. But the tasks through which he had already gone had exhausted him. The limb fell nerveless by his side, and ere the blow of Stockton descended, he had sunk down in utter insensibility at the feet of his opponent.

The conflict was ended. The pledge made to the ladies of the mansion had been fully redeemed by its defenders. Not one of them remained unhurt; and the greater number were already stiffened in the unrelaxing grasp of death. The outlaws had paid dearly for their victory. No less than sixteen of the assailants had been slain; and the arts of Stockton, which had originally won them over to his designs, and made them hostile to their ancient leader, now derived additional support from the sanguinary feeling which had been induced by the bloody struggle in their minds. They were now reconciled to that decree which determined that Morton should be their victim. They needed no more persuasion to resolve that he should die upon the gallows.

The first impulse of Stockton, as he straddled the inanimate body of the man whom he so much feared and hated, was to spurn it with his foot—the next to make his fate certain by a free use of his sword upon it; but the cold malignity of his character prevailed to prolong the life and the trial of his enemy. The utter impotence of Morton to do further harm, suggested to Stockton the forbearance which he would not otherwise have displayed. It was with some pains only, and a show of resolution such as Morton had usually employed to hold them in subjection, that he was enabled to keep back his followers, who, in their blind rage, were pressing forward with the same murderous purpose which he had temporarily arrested in his own bosom. With a more decided malignity of mood, he gave a new direction to their bloody impulses.

"Away!" he cried, "get a hurdle, or something that will take him out without much shaking! He has life enough in him yet for the gallows!"

A shout seconded with approbation the dark suggestion, and the crowd rushed away to procure the necessary conveyance. A door, torn from an outhouse, answered this purpose; and the still breathing, but motionless form of Edward Morton, was lifted upon it. Unhappily, he wakened to consciousness in a few moments after leaving the threshold of the dwelling. The purer atmosphere without revived him; and his eyes opened to encounter the biting scorn, and the insulting triumph, of the wretches he had so lately ruled. His ears were filled with the gross mockeries of those whom his bloody resistance had stimulated to new hate and a deeper ferocity of temper.

A bitter pang went keenly through his heart; but he had still a hope. He had kept one hope in reserve for some such occasion. Long before, when he first commenced that dark career of crime, the cruel fruits of which he was about to reap, he had provided himself with a dagger—a small, stout, but short instrument—which he hid within his bosom. This instrument he devoted to the one particular purpose of taking his own life. He had decreed that it should be sacred—not to employ language illegitimately—to the one work of suicide only. But once, indeed, he had almost violated his resolve. The same instrument he had proffered to poor Mary Clarkson, in a mood, and at a moment of mockery, scarcely less bitter than had fallen to his own lot. The remembrance of the circumstance touched him at this instant, and humbled, in some degree, the exulting feeling which was rising in his breast, at the recollection of his resource. But he did exult, nevertheless. He felt that the dagger was still about him, hidden within the folds of his vest; and, with this knowledge, he was better able to meet the vindictive glance of his foe, who walked beside the litter on which the outlaws were bearing him to the wood.

"Bring him to the Park!" commanded Stockton. "He will hang there more conspicuously, as a warning for other traitors."

"No! No!—not there!" said Darcy, interposing, "the ladies can see him from the house."

"Well, and a very good sight it is, too!" replied the other, brutally; "they've seen him often enough dancing on the earth, I fancy; it may be an agreeable change to behold him dancing in air awhile."

A few serious words, however, whispered in his ears by Darcy, prevailed with Stockton to effect a change in his brutal resolution; and the cavalcade took its way in the direction of the woods where the encampment of the Black Riders for the night had been made. It was intended that there the crowning scene of hate and punishment should take place.

## CHAPTER XLII.

#### HATE BAFFLED BY JUSTICE.

MEANWHILE, what had been the condition of mind of the ladies in the dwelling? They had heard the greater part of the bloody struggle going on below — the shots, the shouts, the groans and shrieks, and all the infernal clamors of that strife of moral feelings and physical passions, in which man, alone, of all the animals, is permitted to indulge. The rending of bolt and bar had also been audible, and they readily conjectured all the rest. They finally knew that the barriers were forced; and when the first rush of the strife was over, and the silence of death prevailed for the first time below, then did they feel assured that death himself was there, surrounded by all his melancholy trophies.

How terrible was then that silence! For the first time during the whole period of their suspense, did Flora Middleton yield herself up to prayer. Before, she could not kneel. While the storm raged below, her soul seemed to be in it; she could not divert it to that calmer, holier contemplation, which invests the purpose with purity, and lifts the eye of the worshipping spirit to the serene courts of Heaven. Her father's spirit was then her own, and she felt all its stimulating strength. She felt that she too could strike, should there be occasion; and when, at one moment, the clamor seemed to be approaching, her eye kindled with keener fire, as it looked round the dim attic in which they had sought refuge, as if in search of some weapon which might defend it.

"It's all over!" at length she exclaimed, when the silence had continued the space of half an hour. "They have left the house, mother."

"Do not trust to go out yet, my child," was the answer of the grandmother. "I fear some trick, some danger;—for why should they leave us undisturbed, so long."

"Hark! mother!—there is a noise below."

"Yes; I think so! I hear it!"

"A footstep!—I should know that footstep! A voice! It is—it must be the voice of Clarence Conway."

The keen sense of the interested heart had not deceived the maiden. Clarence Conway was, indeed, within the dwelling. With limbs that trembled, and a heart that shuddered as he advanced, the young commander trod the avenues of the dwelling which bore such bloody proofs, at every footstep, of the fearful conflict which we have faintly endeavored to describe. The victims were all unknown to him, and their uniforms, those equally of the British and the banditti, did not awaken in him any sympathy in their behalf. On the contrary, it would seem that enemies alone had fallen, and the inference was natural enough that they had fallen by the hands of those who were friends to the country.

But how should the patriots have assailed the enemy in the dwelling which, hitherto, among all the Americans, had been considered sacred? Even though it had been made their place of retreat and refuge, such, he would have preferred it to remain, sooner than its peaceful and pure sanctuary should have been dishonored by such unholy tokens. But the more serious concern which troubled him, arose from his apprehensions for Flora and her grandmother. He hurried through the several chambers, calling on their names. Well might his voice thicken with a husky horror, as he heard the responses only of the deserted apartments, in so many mocking echoes. At length, when he was most miserable, and when, in his further search in the upper chambers, he dreaded lest he should happen on their mangled remains, his ear recognised, or he fancied, an answer in those tones which were then doubly dear to his senses.

"Flora, dear Flora!" he cried aloud, but with a rapidity of utterance which almost made his syllables incoherent, lest he should somehow lose the repetition of the sweet assurance which he had so faintly heard before. The door of the attic was thrown open in the next instant, and the voice of the maiden summoned him to her presence.

He clasped her in his arms with a fervor which could not be put aside; which no mere looks of reserve could discourage or repulse; nay, under circumstances of relief to the maiden which wrought in her mind a momentary forgetfulness of his supposed perfidy.

"Thank God, you are safe!" was his fervent ejaculation; "but tell me, dear Flora, what means the horrible carnage which has taken place below?"

"Oh, Clarence—your brother! Is he not there—is he not among the slain?"

"No! he is not among them—what of him? I see none among the slain but British and sworn enemies."

"Then they have made him prisoner—the Black Riders—they made the assault upon the house because he was in it; their avowed purpose being to execute death upon him as a rebel."

A sad smile passed over the lips of Clarence, as he heard these words, and his head was shaken with a mournful doubt.

"He has nothing to fear *from them*, Flora!" he replied, "but where are they? How long is it since this dreadful affair took place."

"Scarce an hour. The horrible strife I seem to hear now. To my senses it is scarcely ended."

"Enough! I must believe you then. I must fall upon these bloodhounds if I can. Farewell, dear Flora—farewell, for a little while."

"But your brother—remember, Colonel Conway, that he *is* your brother!"

"Colonel Conway!" exclaimed the young soldier, with a surprise that was greatly increased as he beheld the looks of the speaker, now suddenly cold and frozen.

"There is something wrong, Flora, I perceive; and it all comes from that same brother, whose relationship you are so anxious to have me remember. Would to God that he had remembered it. But I will save him if I can. You may be right—he may be in danger. Those bloody wretches would not make much difference between friend and foe, in their love of strife and plunder. But meet me not with such looks when I return."

"Fly, if you would save him. I tremble, Colonel Conway, lest you should be too late!"

"Colonel Conway, again! Flora Middleton, you have again listened to the voice of the slanderer. There must be an explanation of this, dear Flora."

"There shall be, but fly now, if you would be of service— if you would lessen the difficulties of that explanation."

"Be it so! I leave you, Flora, but will leave a few trusty men to rid your dwelling of these bloody tokens. Meanwhile, spare yourself the sight; keep your present place of retreat, till you hear my voice. Farewell."

"Farewell!"—the word was uttered by Flora with emphatic fervor. From her heart she wished *him*, of all others, to fare well! She looked with a longing, lingering gaze after his noble form, so erect, so commanding, so distinguished in all its movements, by the governing strength of a high and fearless soul within.

"Can such a presence conceal such baseness!" she murmured, as she returned to the attic. "Can it be, dear mother?" was the apparently unmeaning expression which fell involuntarily from her lips, as she buried her face in bitter anguish in the bosom of the maternal lady.

Clarence Conway immediately set his troop in motion. He detached his more trusty scouts in advance. At the moment of leaving the house, he had no sort of intelligence which could designate the position of the Black Riders, or even assure him of their near neighborhood. Not an individual was to be seen around the dwelling. The slaves of the plantation, at the first approach of the conflict, took flight to the swamp-thickets; and in these they would remain until long after the storm had overblown.

Conway moved forward therefore with the greatest caution. He might be entering an ambuscade, and certainly had reason to apprehend one, in consequence of the sudden flight of the banditti from the mansion-house before they had sacked it. The idea that Edward Conway had anything really to fear from those whom he too well knew to be his confederates, was something of an absurdity, which he found little difficulty in dismissing from his mind. He rejoiced, at the first moment of receiving the intelligence, that his brother lived—that he had survived the fiercer conflict which had taken place between them.

But, an instant after, and he almost regretted that such was the case. It was his duty to pursue him as a public enemy, and one of a cast so atrocious that, he well knew, if taken, his life would probably be required by the hands of the summary avenger. The stern justice which in those days required blood for blood, had long since selected the fierce chief of the Black Riders as a conspicuous victim for the gallows; and Clarence Conway, as a means to avoid this cruel possibility, issued the sanguinary orders to his troop to show no quarter. The tenderest form of justice called for their extermination in the shortest possible manner.

This resolve was made and the command given, after he had been advised by the scouts that the enemy were collected in force upon an open ground on the river bluff, a short mile and a half above. The scouts reported that a good deal of confusion appeared among them, but they could not approach sufficiently nigh to ascertain its particular occasion; having returned, in obedience to orders, as soon as they had traced out the enemy's place of retreat. They also conveyed to Conway the further intelligence that they might have gone much nearer with impunity—that the foe, so far from forming an ambush, had not, in fact, taken the usual precautions against attack—had not thrown out any sentinels, and might be surprised with little difficulty.

Upon hearing this, Clarence Conway gave orders for a division of his force into three equal parties; one of which was despatched to make a circuit, and gain a point above them on the river; a second was ordered to traverse the river banks from below; while he, himself, leading on the third division, was to burst suddenly upon them from the forest—the nearest point from which the attack could be made.

These orders had scarcely been given, before the sound of a rifle was heard, in the direction of the spot where the outlaws were assembled, and this was followed by a confused clamor, as of many voices. This hurried the movement. What was the meaning of that shot? Did it indicate alarm among the enemy? Were they apprized of his approach? Clarence Conway, in all his conjectures, made no sort of approach to the real nature of that one rifle-shot, and yet it was of some importance to him and to his feelings. It rendered a portion of his task less irksome, and far less difficult.

Silently, he led the way for his division — not a bugle sounded — scarce a word was spoken, and the parties separated on their several courses, with no more noise than was unavoidable, from the regular and heavy tread of their horses' feet. It was fortunate for them, perhaps, that the banditti which they sought were only too busy in their own purposes to be heedful of their foes until it was too late. But let us not anticipate.

The Black Riders had borne their victim, with slow steps, upon his litter, to the spot which had been chosen for his last involuntary act of expiation. Their advance was preceded by that of our old friend, the watchful scout, John Bannister. Anxious, to the last degree, for the safety of the ladies of the barony, he had tracked the steps of the outlaws to the assault upon the dwelling — following as closely upon their heels as could be justified by a prudential regard to his own safety. He had beheld so much of the conflict as could be comprehended by one who was compelled to maintain his watch from a distant covert in the woods. The cause of the fight, and the parties to it, were equally inscrutable to him; and this, too, added not a little to the anxiety which filled his mind. This anxiety grew to agony when he discovered that the defences of the dwelling were broken down, and the house in the possession of the banditti. The fate of Flora Middleton was in their hands, and he was impotent to serve or save her. His anguish was truly indescribable, as it was nearly insupportable.

But he was suddenly aroused from its indulgence, when he beheld the crowd, as, leaving the house, it advanced through the grounds to the very spot in the woods in which he had made his hiding-place. It became necessary to decamp; and as he sped back to the place where he had left his canoe in the custody of the landlord and Jacob Clarkson, he was somewhat surprised to find that they continued to follow in his footsteps. Somewhat wondering at this, and at their brief delay in the dwelling which they had entered after so obstinate a conflict, he ordered Muggs to put himself, Clarkson and the canoe, into close cover, while he, advancing somewhat upon the higher grounds before them, could, from a place of concealment, observe the movements of the enemy, and prescribe the farther conduct of his own attendants.

He had not long to wait. The Black Riders brought their prisoner to the very spot where the body of Mary Clarkson lay buried. The fainting form of the outlaw chief was leaned against the head-board which the devoted Bannister had raised to her memory; and, as the anguish following the transfer of his body to the ground from the door on which it had been borne, caused Morton to open his eyes, and restored him to consciousness, the letters "M. C." met his first glance; but their import remained unconjectured. He had not much time allowed him for conjectures of any kind. His implacable foe, Stockton, stood before him with looks of hate and triumph which the prostrate man found it difficult to endure, but utterly impossible to avoid.

"It is all over with you, Ned Morton," said the other. "Will you beg for your life—will you supplicate me for mercy?"

A smile of scorn passed over the lips of the outlaw.

"My life is not in your hands," he replied; "and, if it were, it should be thrice forfeit before I should acknowledge your power and ask your mercy. I bid you defiance to the last. I look upon you without fear, though with unsuppressed loathing, as I quit the world; and, in this way, do I baffle all your malice."

As he spoke these words, he drew the little stiletto suddenly from his bosom, and plunged it desperately, and with an effort of all his strength, full at his own heart. But the blow was baffled. The hand of Darcy, who had placed himself behind Morton without his knowledge, was extended at the moment, and grasped the arm which impelled the weapon.

"Not so fast!" cried Stockton, as he wrested the dagger from his hand, and flung it from him, "there's no cheating the halter. It's a destiny!"

The baffled outlaw writhed himself about, and looking round upon Darcy, with a bitter smile, exclaimed—

"May your last friend fail you, as mine has done, at the last moment!"

A faintness then came over him, his eyes closed, and he sank back exhausted upon the little hillock which covered Mary Clarkson. Little did he at that moment conjecture on whose bosom his body temporarily found repose.

"Up with him at once," cried Stockton; "or he will cheat the gallows at last."

An active brigand then ran up the trunk of a slender water oak that stood nighest to the spot. The rope was flung to him and fastened; and two of the banditti, stooping down, raised the fainting outlaw upon their shoulders, while the noose was to be adjusted. As his form was elevated above the level of the rest, the crowd shouted with ferocious exultation. This brought back to the eyes of their destined victim, a portion of their former fire. He recovered a momentary strength. He looked round upon them with scorn. He felt his situation, and all the shame, and all the agony—but his glances were full of life and defiance, and his cheeks were utterly unblenching. The moment of danger, and even of disgrace, was not one to fill his fierce soul with apprehension.

"He'll die game!" muttered John Bannister, who, at length, as he recognised the features of Edward Conway, began to conjecture the truth, and to comprehend the circumstances which were lately so inscrutable.

"He'll die game; he's got some of the good blood of the Conways in him, after all. But it's a mortal pity he should die so, for the family's sake. It's a good name, and he's the blood-kin of Clarence."

The scout lifted his rifle, as he thus soliloquized. The evident desire to interpose, and save the victim from one fate by the substitution of another, was strong and anxious in his mind.

"But, no!"—he said, after he had drawn his sight upon the pale brow of the outlaw.—"If it's to be done at all, Jake Clarkson's the man to do it. He's got a sort of right to Ned Conway's life. Jake! Jake!"

He called up the desolate old man, who, on the lower ground by the river, had not seen these proceedings.

"Jake!" he said—"is your rifle loaded?'

"Yes!"

"Then look, man!—there's your enemy—there's Ned Conway—it's him that they're a-lifting up among them there. I 'spose they want to do him some partic'lar kind of honor, but it's jest over poor Mary's grave!"

The words were electric! The old man grasped and raised his weapon. He saw not the purpose of the crowd, nor did he pause to ask what was the sort of honor which they were disposed to confer upon the outlaw. He saw *him!—his* face only! *That* he knew, and that was enough. A moment elapsed— but one!—and the report of the rifle rang sharply along the river banks. In the same moment the men who were lifting Edward Morton to the tree, dropped the body to the ground. The work of death was already done! Their efforts were no longer necessary, as their design was unavailing. The bullet had penetrated the forehead of the outlaw, and his blood streamed from the orifice upon the still fresh mould which covered the victim of his passions. The Black Riders turned to the quarter whence the shot had come, but the boat of John Bannister, bearing himself and his associates, was already at some distance from the shore.

## CHAPTER XLIII.

### CONCLUSION.

THE rage of Stockton at being thus defrauded of his prey at last, though violent, was of no effect. He discharged his own pistol at the boat which contained the fugitives; an idle act, which was followed by a like discharge from some twenty of his followers. They might as well have aimed their bullets at the moon. John Bannister answered them with a shout — which, to their consternation, found an echo from twenty voices in the woods behind them. They turned to confront an unexpected enemy. Clarence Conway was already upon them. His little band, in advance of the other two divisions, began the fray as soon as it had reached within striking distance; and the sudden effect of the surprise compensated well for the inadequacy of the assailing party. The broadsword was doing fearful execution among the scattered banditti, before Stockton well knew in what direction to turn to meet his enemy.

But the power which he had thus so lately gained, was too sweet, and had called for too much toil and danger, to be yielded without a violent struggle; and, if mere brute courage could have availed for his safety, the outlaw might still have escaped the consequences of his indiscretion. He rallied his men with promptness, enforced their courage by the exhibition of his own; and his numbers, being still superior to the small force which had followed Conway through the woods, the effect of his first onslaught was measurably neutralized, and the issue of the conflict soon grew doubtful.

But it did not long remain so. The division from below soon struck in, and the outlaws gave way. They broke at length, and endeavored to find safety by flying up the banks of the river; but here they were met by a third division of Conway's squadron, and their retreat entirely cut off. Hemmed in on every side, assured that no quarter would be given them, they asked for none, but fought and died upon the ground to which they had been forced.

It was the fortune of Stockton to fall under the sabre of Clarence Conway; while Darcy, leaping into the river, perished beneath a blow from the clubbed rifle of John Bannister, whose boat, a moment after touched the shore.

Nothing could exceed the rapturous expressions of his wild whoop of joy at this unlooked-for meeting. Meeting with his friend and leader, in a moment of such complete victory, amply atoned to him for all the trials, risks and anxieties, to which he had been exposed, from the night of their separation. Not one of the Black Riders escaped the conflict. The greater number fell beneath the swords of their conquerors; but some few, in their desperation, leapt into the Congaree, which finally engulfed them all. Clarence Conway, after the close of the conflict, devoted a few painful moments to the examination of the bloody field. But John Bannister threw himself between his commander and one of the victims of the day. The eye of Clarence, searchingly fell on that of his follower; and he at once divined the meaning of the interruption.

"It's here then, that *he* lies, John? How did he die?"

"Yes, Clarence, there he is;—a rifle bullet kept off a worse *eending*. He died like a brave man, though it mou't be he didn't live like a good one. Leave the rest to me, Clarence. I'll see that he's put decently out of sight. But you'd better push up and see Miss Flora, and the old lady. I reckon they've had a mighty scary time of it."

"I thank you, John. I will look but once on the son of my father, and leave the rest to you."

"It's a ragged hole that a rifle bullet works in a white forehead, Clarence, and you'll hardly know it; said the scout as he reluctantly gave way before the approach of his superior. Clarence Conway gazed in silence for a space upon the inanimate and bloody form before him; a big tear gathered slowly in his eyes; but he brushed away the intruder with a hasty hand, while he turned once more to meet his followers who were slowly gathering in the back ground. He felt, even at that moment, a cheering sensation, as he knew that his brother had fallen by another hand than his. That pang, at least, was spared him; and for the rest, the cause of sorrow was comparatively slight.

"He could have lived," he murmured as he turned away from the bloody spectacle—"He could have lived only as a dishonored and a suspected man. His path would have been stained with crime, and dogged by enemies. It is better that it is thus! May God have mercy on his soul!"

Our story is on the threshold of conclusion. We have little more to say. Flora Middleton and her lover were soon reconciled, and the misunderstanding between them easily and promptly explained. Jacob Clarkson and John Bannister were living and sufficient witnesses to save Clarence Conway the necessity of answering for himself, and of denouncing his late kinsman. Between unsophisticated and sensible people, such as we have sought to make our lovers appear, there could be no possibility of a protracted session of doubts, misgivings, shynesses and suspicions, which a frank heart and a generous spirit, could not breathe under for a day, but which an ingenious novelist could protract through a term of years, and half a dozen volumes. In the course of a brief year following these events, the British were beaten from the country, and Clarence and Flora united in the holy bonds of matrimony. The last was an event which nobody ever supposed was regretted by either. John Bannister lived with them at the barony, from the time of their marriage, through the pleasant seasons of a protracted life. Many of our readers may remember to have seen the white-headed old man who, in his latter days, exchanged his *soubriquet* of Supple Jack, for one more dignified, though, possibly, less popular among the other sex. He was called "Bachelor Bannister," toward the closing years of his life, and, when in the presence of the ladies, did not quarrel with the designation. His long stories about the Revolution, of his own feats and those of Clarence Conway, were remembered and repeated by him, with little variation, to the last. In this he differed considerably from ordinary chroniclers of the old school, simply, perhaps, because his stories were originally more truthful, and his memory, in spite of his years, which were "frosty yet kindly," was singularly tenacious to the end. Our narrative has been compiled from particulars chiefly gained, though at second-hand, from this veracious source.

John Bannister lived long enough to see the eldest son of Clarence Conway almost as good a marksman with the rifle, and as supple a forester, as he himself had been in his better days; and his dying moments were consoled, by the affectionate offices of those, whom, with a paternal wisdom, he had chosen for his friends from the beginning. It may be stated, *en passant*, that our exquisite, Mr. Surgeon Hillhouse, neither lost his life nor his wardrobe in the conflict at Middleton Barony. He survived his wounds and saved his luggage. His self-esteem was also preserved, strange to say, in spite of all his failures with the sex. He was one whom Providence had wondrously blessed in this particular. Of self-esteem he had quite as many garments, if not more, than were allotted to his person. He certainly had a full and fresh suit for every day in the year.

THE END.

From the S. Lewis engraving, Plate VIII of the Atlas accompanying John Marshall's *The Life of George Washington* (1807).

# EXPLANATORY NOTES

by

Edwin T. Arnold

These notes are intended to identify persons, places, events, quotations and obscure or archaic words and terms in the text of *The Scout*. Special emphasis has been placed upon the Revolutionary War history in this novel, including, when possible, the identification of Simms' sources and his departures from them.

Dedication: "Colonel William Drayton": A descendant of William Henry Drayton, the Revolutionary leader, Colonel Drayton (1776-1846) was a prominent jurist and a leader of the anti-nullification faction in South Carolina.

7.1 "the period when our story opens": Early May 1781.

7.9-10 "The south, wholly abandoned": In his *South-Carolina in the Revolutionary War* (1853), Simms held that the southern army was composed almost entirely of troops from the states of Virginia, Maryland, North and South Carolina and Georgia: "We find no proof, any where, that New England ever supplied the States, *south of the Potomac*, with any troops, except when the army was under immediate control of the commander-in-chief, as at the seige of Yorktown. The eastern troops,—by which we mean those of New England—*never came farther south, during the whole war, than this point* . . ." (pp. 24-25).

7.19-21 "Florida . . . realm of refuge": David Ramsay, in *The History of South Carolina: 1670-1808* (1809), maintained that "many of the disheartened royalists abandoned their plantations, and went either to the province of Florida, or among the indians. In both cases they were tools in the hands of the british and ready to co-operate with them against their countrymen who favored revolutionary measures" (I, 216).

8.9-32 "Gates, the successful commander at Saratoga": General Horatio Gates (c.1728-1806) was in command of the Northern Continental Army when he met the British army under General John Burgoyne at Saratoga, New York, in the fall of 1777. Although he failed to obtain an unconditional surrender from the British and in spite of accusations concerning his lack of military skill, his victory there was sufficiently impressive to allow him to challenge Washington, unsuccessfully, as supreme commander of the American forces. On 13 June 1780, Gates was directed by Congress, against Washington's wishes, to take control of the southern armies. When Gates assumed command on 27 July, the military situation in the South was considered almost hopeless. With the surrender of Charleston in May, the British had gained control of almost the entire state of South Carolina. The army Gates inherited was exhausted, with little food or equipment, and was largely untrained. According to most sources, Gates brought with him 1400 Continental troops, consisting of divisions from Maryland and Delaware under the former command of Baron DeKalb, but more than half of Gates' army was made up of unprepared militia.

Despite the poor state of his army, Gates was confident of success against the British. He mistakenly believed that he commanded a force of 7000 men when in truth it was less than half that number. However, Simms is mistaken in stating that the American regulars were outnumbered three to one, for the British troops numbered only some 2300 men. Because of poor planning and against the advice of other officers, Gates allowed himself to be forced into a premature encounter with the enemy led by Lord Charles Cornwallis at Camden. This first battle of Camden took place on 16 August 1780, and the result was a disaster for the Americans. Gates vainly tried to rally his troops, but soon he too left the field and by night was in Charlotte, North Carolina, approximately seventy miles away. American losses were placed at 2000 killed, wounded or captured. All American artillery and most supplies were seized by the British. Simms presents a detailed account of this battle and the events leading to it in *The Partisan*.

On 5 October 1780, the United States Congress ordered an inquiry into Gates' actions at Camden, and Gates also demanded a trial in order to exonerate himself. However, this trial never took place, and in 1782 Congress repealed its first resolve, thereby officially relieving Gates of charges of negligence in the debacle.

8.33-9.34 "General Greene succeeded to the command": General Washington chose Nathanael Greene (1742-1786) to replace Gates on 14 October 1780. But between that time and 2 December 1780, when he officially relieved Gates of command at Charlotte, Greene had to re-establish supplies of food, medicines, horses and artillery for the impoverished army he was to lead, an army which numbered about 2000 Continentals and militia. One of Greene's first moves as commander was to secure the co-operation of such partisan leaders as Marion, Sumter and Pickens, whom Gates had ignored. As Simms notes, it became Greene's initial policy to avoid any direct conflict with the superior forces of the British until he could build up his own. Instead, he relied heavily on guerrilla warfare, harassing the British with small attacks and then retreating before the larger forces could gather.

9.36-38 "North Carolina . . . began to feel the shame": At the Battle of Camden, only one regiment of the North Carolina militia stood and fought; the rest fled in panic. When Greene took command, he noted that North Carolina, beset by political infighting, had "not a man on foot" (William Johnson, *Sketches of the Life and Correspondence of Nathanael Greene* [1822], I, 351). The North Carolina Legislature finally dispatched its state militia to Greene under the command of General William Smallwood of the Continental Army.

9.38-10.3 "Virginia": Virginia sent the legion under Colonel Henry Lee, a company of some three hundred men. Colonel John Greene also brought another four hundred recruits. In his *Life of Greene* Simms states that 1000 more men had been raised in Virginia but could not be sent to Greene because of lack of sufficient clothing (p. 124).

10.18 "Lord Cornwallis": Lord Charles Cornwallis (1738-1805) succeeded Sir Henry Clinton as commander of the British troops in the southern states after the surrender of Charleston. He was left 4000 men with which to keep the apparently defeated colony of South Carolina in control and to carry forth the conquest of North Carolina and Virginia.

10.26-29 "King's Mountain": On 7 October 1780, the loyalist troops of Patrick Ferguson (1744-1780), a major in the 71st Highlanders, were attacked and defeated by a small army of backwoodsmen under the nominal command of Colonel William Campbell (1745-1781). The battle became a massacre and Ferguson's body is said to have been butchered by the victorious Americans. This defeat caused Cornwallis to abandon his proposed invasion of North Carolina and Virginia and was therefore a devastating setback for the British.

10.29-31 "Tarleton . . . at the Cowpens": The Battle of Cowpens occurred near the North Carolina border in present day Cherokee County on 17 January 1781. Brigadier General Daniel Morgan (1736-1802) of the Continental Army, with a force of 940 men, was attacked by Lieutenant Colonel Banastre Tarleton (1754-1833), one of the most feared British leaders in the South. Tarleton's soldiers numbered 1100, but Morgan, with the Broad River at his back cutting off any possibility of retreat, nevertheless managed to outmaneuver the British commander and take the victory. British losses were placed at 784 killed, wounded or captured; Americans lost twelve killed and sixty wounded. This battle resulted in the destruction of the 71st, one of the best British regiments, and effectively ended Tarleton's military career in the state.

10.31-35 "Marion . . . and Sumter": Francis Marion (c.1732-1795) and Thomas Sumter (1734-1832) were primarily responsible for the guerrilla warfare carried on against the British in South Carolina. Marion, the "Swamp Fox," used the swamps of eastern South Carolina as his place of refuge. He would emerge to attack the enemy and then retire into the wilderness to the utter bafflement of the British. Sumter led several bands of partisan cavalry and so successfully dogged the British that Lord Rawdon offered five hundred guineas for his betrayal. Together, Marion and Sumter effectively prevented any firm British control of the state during Greene's absence.

11.6-10 "forced . . . from the field": Following the Battle of Cowpens, Cornwallis pursued Greene across North Carolina to the Virginia line, but failed to catch him. Cornwallis then retired to Hillsboro, North Carolina, in order to build up his own forces. He also hoped that by threatening the seat of the South Carolina government, which was then situated in Hillsboro, he could draw Greene back into the state for fight. On 15 March 1781, Greene and Cornwallis met in the vicinity of Guilford Court-House, near Greensboro. The American troops abandoned the field and lost valuable artillery in the process. Cornwallis was awarded the victory, but it was a costly one for the British leader. He actually lost more men than Greene, and, following the battle, found his troops too weak to withstand another attack by the American forces. Thus Greene was able to force the British to retreat into Virginia, leaving the Americans free passage back into South Carolina. Once in Virginia, Cornwallis' path eventually led to Yorktown, where he surrendered to Washington in October 1781.

11.12-13 "Lord Rawdon": When Cornwallis left the state to pursue Greene into North Carolina, he gave Lord Francis Rawdon (1754-1826) command of the British troops in the interior of the state, outside the vicinity of Charleston. Rawdon was only twenty-seven at the time, but quickly proved himself to be a capable leader. When Greene returned to South Carolina following Cornwallis's retreat into Virginia, Rawdon was stationed at Camden with nine hundred of his best men. Camden was one of the most important of the British strongholds, and it was to this outpost that Greene directed his troops.

11.20-27 "Hobkirk's Hill": The Battle of Hobkirk's Hill was fought on 25 April 1781. Greene had camped outside the city of Camden, approximately three miles from Rawdon's forces, on 19 April. He was expecting reinforcements from Virginia and from Sumter and was confident of victory. However, these troops did not arrive. The armies were therefore nearly equal in strength and, as Simms notes, both sides lost almost the same number of men in the battle. Rawdon proved himself an able commander by first attacking the American troops, catching them somewhat by surprise, then by outflanking them and thus causing great confusion. At the height of the battle, Lieutenant Colonel John Gunby of the 1st Maryland ordered his men, who were attacking, to hold their line in order to regroup. The order was misunderstood as a call for retreat, and an important opportunity for victory was lost. Although Gunby was able to rally his men, Greene blamed him for the defeat and called him before a court of inquiry, which acquitted him of all charges except an error of judgment. As with Cornwallis's victory at

EXPLANATORY NOTES 479

Guilford, Rawdon's success was in name only, for soon thereafter he was forced to abandon Camden to the Americans.

12.3-4 "Cornwallis . . . 'surrounded by timid friends and inveterate foes'": Simms may have derived his phrasing here from a March 1781 letter of Cornwallis to Lord George Germaine, in which he complained: "Our situation for the former few days had been amongst timid friends, and adjoining inveterate rebels . . ." (*Correspondence of Charles, First Marquis Cornwallis* [1859], I, 519). Simms' source for this letter is not known.

13.9-12 "one moment operating on the Savannah": Simms is illustrating geographically the wide range of territory plundered by these terrorists. The Savannah forms the border between South Carolina and Georgia on the west, while the Pee Dee flows through the northeastern part of the state. The Blue Ridge Mountains are located on the northern border between South and North Carolina, and the metropolis— Charleston—is on the coast.

13.13-18 "little bands": Following the fall of Charleston in May 1780, there was a virtual absence of both civil and military authority in South Carolina. The British were unwilling and the Americans unable to control the gangs that roamed the state. Ramsay, in *The History of South Carolina: 1670-1808*, described the situation and concluded, "Rapine, outrage, and murder became so common as to interrupt the free intercourse between one place and another. That security and protection which individuals expect by entering into civil society, ceased almost totally" (I, 448). The only protection for the outlying settlers was thus found in such small groups as Simms describes, groups which themselves sometimes exacted bloody revenge for the wrongs done them. At the time of Greene's return in the spring of 1781, Governor Rutledge was able to re-establish some form of order through the appointment of magistrates in all sections recovered from the British. This, however, was only a temporary peace, and with the movement of the American armies toward Charleston in the summer of 1781, the outlaws returned for a last, bloody reign.

13.19 "The district of country called 'Ninety-Six'": In 1781 the district of Ninety Six was considered the western frontier of South Carolina. In 1785, the district was divided into the counties of Edgefield, Abbeville, Newberry, Laurens, Union and Spartanburg. The British fort and town of Ninety Six were located about six miles east of the Saluda River in what is now Greenwood County.

13.22 "fifteen hundred widows and orphans": Ramsay, in his *History: 1670-1808*, places this number at fourteen hundred (I, 452).

13.26-27 "that hour is . . . the darkest": "It is always darkest just before the day dawneth." Thomas Fuller, *Pisgah Sight*.

13.33 "Wateree": The Wateree flows southeast through central South Carolina. It joins the Congaree below Columbia to form the Santee River.

15.2-6 "Spenser": Edmund Spenser, *The Faerie Queene*, Book II, Canto VI, 5.3-4.

19.35 "buckram restraints": Buckram was a type of coarse cloth or linen stiffened with paste or gum. The word was synonymous with "stiffness" or "starchiness."

20.5 "small yellow crescent": An ensignia worn by the partisan faction. Since there were few uniforms to be had, such signs were one of the few ways to identify the loyalties of a stranger. The loyalists often wore pine sprigs in their hats.

20.19 "Santee hills beyond": The High Hills of the Santee rise in the southern part of Sumter County, a little above Jack's Creek, and run to within five miles of the east bank of the Wateree River.

21.26-28 "Greene's drawed off from Camden": Following the Battle of Hobkirk's Hill, Greene withdrew to Gum Swamp, about five miles from the battle site. On 3 May, he led his men across the Wateree River, to the west of Camden, in order to intercept Watson and to prevent supplies from reaching the city from that part of the state.

21.28-31 "Marion . . . Lee": Before the Battle of Hobkirk's Hill, around 6 April, Colonel Henry "Light-Horse Harry" Lee (1756-1818) had led his troops south and united with Marion near the Santee River. As Greene prepared for battle with Rawdon, Marion and Lee laid siege to one of the most important of the British posts, Fort Watson, located at Wright's Bluff on the Santee, northeast of Orangeburg. The siege lasted from 15 April until the 23rd, two days before the battle at Camden. On the 23rd, Lieutenant McKay, the fort's commander, surrendered. Watson's fall broke Rawdon's communications with Charleston. After the surrender, Marion and Lee crossed the Santee and moved on Fort Motte, which they reached on 8 May. Located on the Congaree near its junction with the Wateree, Motte was the principal depot for convoys from Charleston to Camden. The fort, which consisted of a large house surrounded by field works, was fired by burning arrows and surrendered on 12 May.

21.31-34 "Our gin'ral, Sumter . . . Catawba . . . Taylor . . . Granby": The Catawba is the principal stream which flows into the Wateree River above Camden. Following the battle at Camden, there would have been many "stragglers" in the area. General Thomas Sumter led bands of local cavalry paid only by the plunder they could gather. These bands often operated as separate units from Greene's main army, and during

EXPLANATORY NOTES 481

the winter of 1781 they had been harassing the British forts in the middle section of the state. Sumter had started the siege of Fort Granby, which was located about three miles below the junction of the Broad and the Saluda rivers and one-half mile below the present city of Columbia, on 19 February 1781. The fort was defended by some three hundred men under the command of Major Andrew Maxwell, a loyalist from Maryland who had a reputation for being more interested in profits than in victories. At the beginning of May, Sumter left the siege in the hands of Colonel Thomas Taylor of the South Carolina militia while he attacked the British at Orangeburg. After Sumter's departure, Lee and his men arrived at Granby and, much to the dismay of both Taylor and Sumter, negotiated a surrender with Maxwell on very generous terms to the British. The fort capitulated on 15 May 1781, with no losses on either side.

21.35 "Butler": Captain William Butler (1759-1821) was a captain in the South Carolina Rangers under Pickens. His father and brother were both murdered by a band of marauders led by William "Bloody Bill" Cunningham. Butler surprised and dispersed this gang in late May 1782. That he should be looking for Edward Conway and the Black Riders is appropriate, as he seems to have carried out a personal vendetta against such outlaws, and against Cunningham in particular.

22.3-4 "above the Congaree": The Ninety Six District, which was then the frontiers of the colony, was located west and north of the Congaree River, which is formed by the confluence of the Broad and Saluda rivers at Columbia.

23.16-20 "fall of Charleston . . . list of prisoners . . . parole . . . British regiments to the West Indies": On 12 May 1780, General Benjamin Lincoln surrendered Charleston to Sir Henry Clinton. On 1 June, Clinton offered a system of pardons and paroles to those who would agree to support the Crown or to consider themselves prisoners. However, on 3 June, all of these paroles were declared void, and their holders were required either to fight for the British or to be considered as rebels and therefore liable to punishment. Clinton, in an effort at appeasement, had offered to send those who would side with the British as soldiers to the West Indies so that they would not be forced to fight against their countrymen. General William Moultrie was offered command of a British regiment there, but refused to accept. Over five hundred did agree to this offer, however. Many of the prominent civilian leaders in Charleston and elsewhere who refused their support were eventually taken prisoner; some, like the group sent to St. Augustine, Florida, were exiled. Simms explored this problem in greater detail in *The Partisan* and *Katharine Walton*.

25.13 "Butler's men": Butler's Company of Volunteers was recruited largely from the Edgefield-Ninety Six region of South Carolina.

# EXPLANATORY NOTES

25.23 "Pickins' men": General Andrew Pickens (1739-1817) was a leader of the South Carolina State Troops. He owned a plantation in the Ninety Six District and had dealt the British loyalists an early defeat at the Battle of Kettle Creek in Georgia on 14 February 1779. After the surrender of Charleston he was placed on parole by the British and, considering himself bound by his oath, refused to fight for the partisans. However, when his plantation was plundered and burned by marauders under Major James Dunlap, Pickens felt himself released from his pledge and resumed the battle. Greene had ordered Pickens to operate between Ninety Six and Augusta to prevent movement of supplies or troops between the two posts.

28.12-16 "the West Injies": Ramsay reported that during the British occupation of Charleston some 25,000 slaves were taken from South Carolina, although later historians have suggested that this figure is inflated (*History: 1670-1808*, I, 475). However, when the British evacuated the city in December 1782, they did take 5333 Negroes with them.

31.3-4 "a lady of Barbadoes": Barbados is a British island in the West Indies. Thus Edward Conway is not "American born" as is his brother Clarence, whose mother is "a young lady of the Congaree."

31.11-15 "Clarence . . . was finally adopted": Edward, as first born son, should have inherited the property of his father. However, as Clarence was legally adopted by his mother's parents, he superseded Edward as heir.

44.31-33 "excesses and violence": Ramsay writes, "To reimburse their losses, and to gratify revenge, they [the 'exasperated whigs'], in their turn, began to plunder and to murder" (*History: 1670-1808*, I, 448). Clarence Conway is naturally apologetic for the whigs' actions, but Edward is correct in pointing out that both sides were guilty of great violence, whatever their reasons. See note 55.23-26.

45.15 "Black Riders": Although Simms seems to have invented this particular band of outlaws, he was drawing on his knowledge of actual gangs which terrorized the country during the war. Men such as "Bloody Bill" Cunningham, Colonel James Dunlap, David Fanning and "Bloody Bill" Bates are still remembered in the legends and traditions of South Carolina. Edward Conway is given the characteristics of several of these bandits. Simms in no way exaggerates the fear that these men caused among the people, nor the horror of their deeds. See, for example, Joseph Johnson, *Traditions and Reminiscences of the American Revolution* (1851), pp. 396-402.

46.22 "Esau": In Genesis, the brother of Jacob. Esau is characterized by his hirsuteness.

# EXPLANATORY NOTES

47.13-16 "I've hearn . . . sculps of dead persons": The practice of wearing disguises was not an uncommon one among these bands. Some were known to carry the insignias of both loyalists and rebel groups, using whichever was appropriate in order to gain the confidence of the party they intended to plunder. Most of these men belonged to no party and were thus known as "outliers." Johnson records Bloody Bill Bates' leading of such a band, composed of Cherokees and loyalists disguised as Indians, who massacred the inhabitants of Gowan's Fort on the Pacolet River and those at Mills' Station in North Carolina in November 1781.

49.26-28 "Watson's on the road": Colonel John Watson Tadwell Watson, for whom Fort Watson was named, had in March 1781 led an expedition to find and defeat Marion. Following four encounters in three weeks with the Swamp Fox, Watson hastily retreated to the British post at Georgetown. After the Battle of Hobkirk's Hill, Watson and five hundred men marched toward Camden to reinforce Rawdon. Despite the efforts of Sumter and Lee, they arrived at Camden on 7 May. Because Bannister and Conway are on the east side of the river between Rawdon at Camden and Watson at Georgetown on the coast, they are directly within the British line of march.

49.29-30 "call in his people from Ninety-Six and Augusta": The forts at Camden and Ninety Six in South Carolina and Augusta in Georgia were the three most important frontier posts held by the British. That Rawdon was considering the evacuation of these posts indicated the extremity of his situation.

51.4 "on the same road, toward the Wateree": This is probably the road shown in Mills' *Atlas* (1825) running north through the Sumter District from Nelson's Ferry through Manchester, Statesboro and on toward Camden. This road parallels the Wateree and passes through the Santee Hills.

52.10 "'imminent deadly breach'": *Othello*, I, iii.

54.26 "Cantey's": Although there is no record of a Muggs' Tavern, a Cantey's Tavern was situated on the north side of Jack's Creek in the Sumter District, about ten miles northeast of Fort Watson.

55.23-26 "Nothing . . . has secured them . . . but the foolish violence": In the early days of the Revolution, 1775-1776, when the whigs were largely in control, the Revolutionary committees, led by Arthur Middleton and William Henry Drayton, attempted to persuade the inhabitants of South Carolina to swear their support for the rebel movement. In *The History of South Carolina* (1860), Simms records that Middleton "moved to attach estates in case of the flight of the owners, and to *excommunicate* from all social privileges all persons who should

484   EXPLANATORY NOTES

refuse to sign the association" (p. 187). Tar and feathering was one method used to encourage people to sign. Simms deals with this practice in *Joscelyn* and *Mellichampe*.

55.28 "Cape Fear to St. Catharine's": Cape Fear is located on the coast of North Carolina, just above the South Carolina border. St. Catharine's is on the coast of Georgia, below South Carolina.

55.36-37 "some great family on the Congaree": Although Simms may have had a specific family in mind, the Conways are probably largely fictional. There is no record of a Conway plantation on the Congaree at this time. However, since the brothers' father married into a prominent Congaree family, the plantation could have been under his wife's family's name. Nevertheless, no specific source for this plantation has been found.

59.8-9 "Bill Cunningham can do, and he's twice as spry as ever": "Bloody Bill" Cunningham (c.1756-1787) was one of the most notorious leaders of terrorists in the back country of South Carolina. Cunningham first led his marauding parties into this area in 1778, but his most fearful ravages occurred in the summer and fall of 1781, when he plundered his way through Laurens and Edgefield counties, in the Ninety Six District, with a band of over three hundred men. During this period he was held responsible for the brutal deaths of some thirty-five people. His gang was finally dispersed by William Butler. See note 21.35. After the war, Cunningham fled to Florida and finally to England. Simms' great interest in Cunningham is evidenced by the five lengthy articles he wrote for *The Southern Literary Messenger* in review of the biographical appendices on the Cunninghams which appeared in the 1845 edition of Curwen's *Journal and Letters*. Two of the five articles were devoted exclusively to William Cunningham. However, despite Simms' apparently extensive knowledge of his subject, in *The Scout* he places Cunningham in the Congaree region at too early a date. Cunningham did not begin his final raids until after the evacuation of Ninety Six, when the American armies were mostly absent from this section of the state.

59.23-24 "very beginning of the season": The summer of 1781, when the marauding began in earnest.

63.5 "country born": The argument between Muggs and Darcy illustrates the unique characteristics of a civil war which the Revolution showed in the South. When Muggs calls it a "family quarrel," he is expressing the opinion of most historians.

63.28-29 "Irishmen . . . Yagers . . . Scotchmen . . . Jarmans": By this point in the war, the British were using large numbers of foreign or untrained soldiers. Yagers refers to soldiers of the Austrian infantry, known for their shooting skill; Jarmans are Germans.

64.4-6 "Rawdon's going to vackyate . . . he'll make Camden sich a blaze": Rawdon abandoned Camden on 10 May 1781, but not before burning a large part of it. He then moved south of the Santee River and on towards Charleston.

64.12 "Sumter rides the road now from Ninety-Six to Augusta": In the first few weeks of May, Sumter was leading the attack against the British post at Orangeburg. It is unlikely that he would have been in the Ninety Six District as Muggs says. See note 21.31-34.

68.28-29 "Watson's sentinels": Clarence Conway is referring to Colonel John Watson, who had joined forces with Rawdon, not Fort Watson, which had already fallen to the Americans. See note 21.28-31.

73.4-7 "the old Dutchman—the brick-burner": Robert Mills describes this section of the Sumter District as being a "fine body of brick mould land" (*Statistics of South Carolina* [1826], p. 751). By Dutchman, Edward presumably means German, according to the terminology of the day. Dutch Fork, for example, located between the Saluda and Broad rivers, was well known for the large number of German loyalists living there.

75.15 "Dukes's": Mills' *Atlas* records Duke's Mills located on the Gin Branch of Rice Creek in the northern tip of Richland County. It was situated near a road leading to Camden.

91.3 "continental copper": Refers to the currency issued by the Continental Congress during the war. Its value fluctuated greatly and suffered tremendous depreciation in the latter days of the war and afterwards. Ramsay states that by 1780, paper currency had depreciated 8114%. This state gave rise to the phrase "not worth a continental."

91.5 "Governor Rutledge of South Carolina": John Rutledge (1739-1800). Elected governor in 1779, Rutledge was forced to flee to North Carolina after the British invasion. There he worked for the relief of the state. He returned to South Carolina in 1781 and began re-establishing civil government. See note 13.13-18.

97.25-27 "For every drop . . . heart of every prisoner": The practice of executing prisoners in retaliation for the enemy's execution of their captured became a fairly common one. On 26 August 1781, following the execution of Isaac Hayne, Nathanael Greene issued a proclamation in which he stated that it was his intention "to make reprisals for all such inhuman insults, as often as they shall take place." He indicated that he would punish the regular British officers captured in battle, and not loyalist militia leaders. He concluded, "I cannot but lament the necessity I am under of having recourse to measures so extremely wounding to the sentiments of humanity, and so contrary to the liberal principles upon which I wish to conduct the war" (Gibbes, *Documentary History* [1853], III, 116). Francis Marion, who was known as one of the kindest of military leaders, sent a letter to Colonel Nesbit Balfour in which he explained the practice he would follow: "Lord Rawdon and Colonel Watson have hanged three of my brigade for supposed crimes, which will make as many of your men in my hands suffer" (McCrady, *History of South Carolina in the Revolution, 1780-1783* [1902], II, 152).

99.9 "shirt of Nessus": In Greek mythology, Nessus was the centaur who was killed by Hercules while attempting to carry off the hero's wife. Before dying, Nessus gave Hercules a poisonous shirt which eventually killed Hercules in turn.

109.6 "Iago": Villain in Shakespeare's *Othello* who is known for his cunning and ability to manipulate others.

109.30-110.5 "The wrongs . . . were about to be redressed": The revenge exacted against these marauders was severe. Cunningham barely escaped—on a fast horse—from William Butler and was forced to leave the country. Others, like Dunlap and Bates, were murdered after being captured and imprisoned. See note 467.38-468.2.

118.2 "bearding the lion in his den": Sir Walter Scott, *Marmion*, VI, xiv.

126.30 "college in England": It was a common practice, especially in Charleston, for wealthy families of English ancestry to send their sons to England for their education. Many of the Revolutionary leaders, such as Drayton and Middleton, were educated there.

127.16-17 "John Stuart, the Indian agent": Stuart (c. 1709-1779) was British Superintendent of Indian Affairs for the Southern Department. In 1775 he was accused of encouraging the Indians to fight against the rebels and was forced to flee to Florida. The degree of Stuart's guilt has lately come into question. See introduction to *Joscelyn: Centennial Edition* (1975) for a more detailed discussion of Stuart.

132.2 "Maham": Colonel Hezekiah Maham (1739-1789) of the South Carolina State Dragoons was best known for the invention or perfection of the "Maham towers," large log structures topped by a protected platform on which small cannon could be mounted and fired down into a besieged fort.

EXPLANATORY NOTES 487

139.3-4 "He'll ride a horse to death": Tradition has it that Bill Cunningham, when pursued by Butler and his men, so wore out his horse "Ringtail" in escaping to Charleston that it died of exhaustion after reaching the city. Cunningham is said to have wept at its death and to have had the bells in Charleston toll in its memory. Simms disputes and ridicules this story in his 1846 articles on Cunningham in *The Southern Literary Messenger*.

139.37-38 "block up Boston harbor": Boston Harbor was closed on 1 June 1774, for a variety of reasons, among them the "Boston Tea Party," the whig destruction of tea in protest against the Tea Act of 1773.

143.13-15 "the prince of Wales . . . at Hanging Rock": On 6 August 1780, Sumter and Major William Richardson Davie, with a party of eight hundred partisans, defeated five hundred loyalists and British soldiers at Hanging Rock in Lancaster County. The Prince of Wales' regiment, known as the Loyal American Volunteers, defended Hanging Rock and was nearly annihilated by the partisans.

143.16 "the Dutch Hessians": Mercenary soldiers hired out by a number of foreign principalities, most notably that of Hesse-Cassel, ruled by Frederick II.

143.28-29 "I would ha' gathered you": Matthew 23:37.

148.14 "General Oglethorpe's Highland regiment": General James Edward Oglethorpe (1696-1785), founder of the colony of Georgia, brought a regiment of seven hundred men in 1738 for the defense of the colony against the Spanish in Florida.

149.22 "the three contiguous rivers": probably the Congaree, Wateree and Santee.

151.27 "Jack Sheppard": A novel by William Harrison Ainsworth (1805-1882). Published in 1840, it was the story of a roguish highwayman.

151.28 "Cruikshankses": George Cruikshank (1792-1878) was a British artist and caricaturist who illustrated the works of Dickens and Ainsworth, among others.

151.29-30 "'Quiz,' 'Phiz,' 'Biz,' 'Tiz'": "Quiz" was the pseudonym for Edward Caswall (1814-1878), an English author. "Phiz" was Halbot Knight Browne (1815-1882), an English caricaturist. There is no record of a "Biz" or "Tiz."

153.2-3 "Olin Massey . . . ": Although men with the last names of Massey, Jones and Burns are listed as having fought for South Carolina during the Revolution, there are no records of any men by these particular names in Sumter's group.

153.9 "Wassamasaw country": A low-lying region of land northwest of Charleston, to the east of the Santee, noted for the prevalence of malaria.

153.37-38 "'at one fell swoop'": *Macbeth*, IV, iii.

154.32-33 "Charlestown in the great siege": The Siege of Charleston lasted from February to May of 1780. The British forces were led by Sir Henry Clinton; the city was under the defense of General Benjamin Lincoln. Despite Lincoln's efforts, Charleston remained extremely vulnerable to attack, exposed as it was to water on three sides. The people of the city begged Lincoln to surrender, which he did on 12 May.

157.33-34 "Sumter . . . Orangeburg": Sumter left the Siege of Granby and attacked the British at Orangeburg. The British surrendered on 11 May 1781. See note 21.31-34.

157.35-36 "Greene . . . to 'siege Cruger": Greene moved toward Ninety Six on 17 May 1781. He arrived before the fort on 22 May. Colonel John Harris Cruger (1738-1807) was loyalist commander of DeLancey's 1st Battalion. He had replaced Colonel Nesbit Balfour as commander at Ninety Six in August 1780.

162.6-7 "Columbia . . . was not in existence": The city of Columbia was chartered in 1783 and was made capital of the state because of its central location.

162.12-17 "Granby . . . surrendered": The fort was surrendered on 15 May 1781. See note 21.31-34.

162.24-28 "Lord Rawdon . . . Nelson's ferry": Rawdon left Camden on 10 May. See note 64.4-6. Fort Motte, located on the Congaree near its junction with the Wateree, fell on 12 May to the forces of Lee and Marion. Nelson's Ferry, on the Santee, was evacuated on 14 May. The British destroyed their fortifications and supplies before withdrawing.

163.7 "advancing to the Saluda": The Saluda flows from the up country of South Carolina southeast, passing near Ninety Six, until it joins the Broad to form the Congaree at Columbia.

163.11-12 "the high banks of the river": At the confluence of the Broad and Saluda, there were falls of thirty-four feet. Edward and his troops are above the falls, apparently in the V formed by the two rivers, as Edward can see the point of juncture.

166.25-27 "Death is . . . a very good thing for one . . . so very miserable in life as yourself": On one of his raids, Major James Dunlap is reported to have carried off a young girl named Mary McRae. Refusing his amorous advances, she was kept a prisoner by Dunlap, and according to tradition, died of a broken heart. Dunlap was later shot, though not killed, by her fiancé, a Captain Gillespie of the Fairforest region. It is possible that Simms had this story in mind in his tale of Mary Clarkson and Edward Conway.

173.33-34 "proud baronial privileges of Carolina": There was, in the early days of settlement in South Carolina, a legal aristocracy created by the Crown. Its nobility were divided into landgraves, cassiques and barons, and each was given a landed estate of 48, 24 or 12 thousand acres, according to his title. The titles were to be hereditary. General Middleton, the founder of Brier Park, is later referred to as "the venerable cassique of Congaree" although Brier Park contains only 10,000 acres.

174.23 "Brier Park": Although the Middleton family owned some of the most beautiful estates in South Carolina, there is no record of a Middleton plantation such as Simms describes located on the Congaree. Nevertheless, such plantations did exist in this area. Probably the most famous was "Richland," the plantation of Colonel Thomas Taylor. This plantation was located on the site of the present Columbia and, according to tradition, gave its name to Richland County.

174.36-37 "old General Middleton, the patriarch of the Congaree country": The Middletons were one of the most prominent families in the history of South Carolina. In using the name, Simms was probably paying tribute to the family as a whole rather than one specific branch of it. However, as we learn from other passages in the novel, Flora's grandfather, the founder of Brier Park, was noted as an Indian fighter. In 1760, Colonel Thomas Middleton commanded the South Carolina troops against the Cherokees in one of the last major campaigns of the Indian wars. Marion, Pickens, Moultrie, Isaac Huger, Henry Laurens and others served under him in this campaign. He died in 1766, survived by one son, William, who died in 1768. Another possible source for General Middleton is Captain John Fairchild, who acquired land in the vicinity of Columbia, on the north side of the Congaree, as early as 1743. He was well known as a surveyor and Indian fighter.

184.3-4 "Balfour . . . Stuart": Colonel Nesbit Balfour (1743-1823) had been commander at Ninety Six before Cruger, but was, in 1781, commandant of the British garrison in Charleston. Balfour is a major character in Simms' novel *Katharine Walton*. Colonel Alexander Stuart, sometimes spelled Stewart (c.1741-1794), succeeded Rawdon as commander of British troops outside of Charleston. He led the British forces at Eutaw Springs in September 1781. See note 273.30-35.

197.36-37 "the Alexandrine method . . . knots of the moral Gordius": When Alexander the Great was faced with an intricate knot, of which the oracle had said that whoever could loosen it should rule Asia, he solved the problem by severing the knot with his sword.

202.3-4 "'Amaryllis in the shade . . . Næera's hair'": Milton, *Lycidas*, ll. 67-69.

202.21 "Rawdon . . . to relief of 'Ninety-Six'": Rawdon's march from Charleston to Ninety Six actually ran farther south than Simms has it here. They were at no time during the march so near the Columbia region.

202.27 "Coffin": Captain John Coffin (1756-1838) of the New York Loyal Volunteers led a cavalry of loyalists. He accompanied Rawdon to Ninety Six, and was considered one of the finest of the loyalist soldiers.

202.29 "we can annoy Rawdon": Greene, on hearing of Rawdon's approach, ordered Sumter to impede the enemies' progress through constant harassment.

206.5 "'The Congaree Blues'": There is no record of a unit with this name serving under Pickens. Many regiments were called the Blues after blue was adopted as the official Continental Army uniform color in 1779, but most soldiers, especially in the militia, wore no uniforms at all, fighting instead in their work or hunting clothes.

212.6 "a day for every dog": *Hamlet*, V, i.

223.31 "'Let the dead bury their dead'": Matthew 8:22.

225.23-27 "the main body . . . consisting chiefly of the Irish regiments": The British reinforcements which made up most of Rawdon's force were newly arrived from Ireland on 3 June. On 7 June, Rawdon left the city with these troops for the relief of Ninety Six. The siege had begun on 22 May.

233.22 "the truth will out": *The Merchant of Venice*, II, ii.

236.31-32 "Lee's legions . . . in the neighborhood": Lee and his troops may have been moving toward Augusta where they arrived on 23 May to aid Pickens and Elijah Clarke in the siege of the forts there. Thomas Browne surrendered the garrison on 5 June 1781.

238.11-12 "two thousand men or more": Rawdon's force numbered just at 2000 men.

243.7-9 "Lord Rawdon . . . one of the sternest leaders": Rawdon's reputation was that of a good, but harsh soldier. Simms' description of him is fair.

EXPLANATORY NOTES 491

250.11-14 "These rascally horse of Lee ... in the shape of intelligence": It was one of the ironies of this battle that it could have been so easily avoided. Rawdon sent messages from Camden and from Charleston for Cruger to abandon the fort and retire to Augusta. However, Lee and Pickens so well prevented communications with the fort that Cruger was unaware of Rawdon's wishes and prepared his best for the defense. Thus a needless and bloody siege occurred.

250.23 "Major Banks": No record of a Major Banks has been found. This is possibly a misprint for Marjoribanks (see note 262.36).

251.17-19 "Colonel Cruger's black charger": According to Johnson's *Traditions* (p. 303), Cruger's horse was stolen by one of Francis Marion's scouts. However, this theft occurred near Ninety Six, not at the forks of the Congaree. Marion gave the horse to James Simons.

253.12-15 "Such fluctuations": Simms' depiction of the rate of desertion is accurate. Following the Siege of Ninety Six, the entire four regiments of volunteers under Sumter deserted in one day. Marion also had constant trouble with his men. On 9 May 1781, Greene wrote Marion concerning this problem: "I am sorry the Militia are deserting because there is not greater support. If they were influenced by proper principles, and were impressed with a love of liberty and a dread of slavery, they would not shrink at difficulties. If we had a force sufficient to recover the country, their aid would not be wanted, and they cannot be well acquainted with their true interest to desert us, because they conceive our force unequal to the reduction of the country without their assistance" (Gibbes, *Documentary History*, III, 67-68).

259.24 "serene sky of May": This is a mistake on Simms' part, as the Irish reinforcements did not land in Charleston until the 2nd of June, and did not begin their march toward Ninety Six until the 7th.

261.12 "'perilous stuff'": *Macbeth*, V, iii.

262.36 "Majoribanks": Major John Marjoribanks of the 19th Regiment. He was always respected by his American enemies, and was known as "the foe to oppression, and guardian of the unfortunate" (Garden, *Anecdotes of the American Revolution* [1822], p. 71). He was a hero at Eutaw Springs, where he was wounded. He died on 22 October 1781, on the march back to Charleston following this battle. See Simms' account of Marjoribanks in *Eutaw*.

271.10 "Camden massacres": Following the first battle of Camden, Lord Cornwallis had ordered the commanders of the various forts to hang all men who had first fought with the British and had later taken up arms with the rebel forces. Several of the prisoners taken in the Battle of Camden and later at Fishing Creek (18 August 1780) were hanged as rebels, apparently without proper trial.

273.30-35 "the Eutaws": The Battle of Eutaw Springs took place on 8 September 1781. It was the last major battle of the Revolution in South Carolina, but again ended in a victory for neither side. Both the Americans and British were plagued by heat and disease, but the British, unused to the climate, suffered the most. As Simms notes, approximately fifty British soldiers died from heat and fatigue during the march from Ninety Six after the siege.

275.10-15 "He had, in concert with Colonel Butler . . . Cunningham": Butler's rout of Cunningham did not take place until May 1782. See notes 21.35 and 139.3-4.

275.22 "General Pickens . . . against the Cherokee": Soon after the evacuation of Ninety Six in the summer of 1781, Indians and a group of loyalists began a series of raids in the back country. Pickens led a troop of 394 men against them and over a period of fourteen days burned thirteen villages and killed nearly forty Indians.

276.21-285.2 "The post of Ninety-Six": Simms' description of the Siege of Ninety Six is taken largely from William Johnson's *Sketches of the Life and Correspondence of Nathanael Greene* (1822).

276.26 "Prince George": Fort Prince George was located near the Cherokee Indian village of Keowee on the Keowee River in the northwestern corner of the state.

276.31-32 "the fierce domestic strife first began": On 19-21 November 1775, a party of whigs under Major Andrew Williamson was besieged by loyalists under Patrick Cunningham near Ninety Six. The few men lost on both sides were the first men killed in battle in the Revolution in South Carolina. A truce was eventually proposed, but proved to be only temporary, and on 22 December 1775, the two sides again clashed at Great Cane Brake. Although the loyalists were defeated in this battle, the section around Ninety Six became a loyalist stronghold. See *Joscelyn* for a fictional account of this sequence of events.

278.6-8 "six hundred men . . . halters around their necks": Cruger's force numbered 550 men, and was composed entirely of Americans. They feared death as traitors if captured.

278.9-10 "Greene commenced the siege under very inauspicious circumstances": Greene began the siege on 22 May 1781, with a force of 1100 men. However, Cruger had had time to prepare for the attack. Greene was doubtful of success on first seeing the defenses Cruger had erected. Nevertheless, the attack was directed against the Star Battery, the best protected part of the defense. The Americans began digging a mine on the first night, about seventy yards from the Star Battery, but were attacked and lost several men. Greene then moved his lines back to a safer distance and entrenched his army for attack. The first parallel

EXPLANATORY NOTES 493

was begun immediately. The siege lasted from 22 May until 18 June 1781, when Rawdon relieved the fort and Greene was forced to retreat without victory.

278.26-27 "the enemy summoned to surrender": The second parallel was completed on 3 June. The summons to surrender was signed by Otho Williams, Greene's adjutant general, rather than by Greene himself. Cruger considered this an insult, and thus the siege was prolonged.

278.30 "'Maham towers'": Invented by Colonel Hezekiah Maham, these towers were first used at the siege of Fort Watson. Simms apparently repeated this error from Johnson. See note 132.2.

280.4-6 "The arrival of Conway announced the approach of Rawdon": According to McCrady, Greene learned sometime around 10 June 1781 that the British reinforcements had landed in Charleston (*History*, II, 287-290). On the 14th it was reported that Rawdon was near Orangeburg and heading to Ninety Six. However, Conway did not arrive in camp until the 17th. Although the exact date when Cruger learned of Rawdon's approach is not known, it was probably earlier than the 17th, as Simms has it.

280.30 "Such is the story told by tradition": Local tradition gives the woman's name as Kate Fowler, who was in love with a Captain Reagan, one of Cruger's officers. When the British marched to Charleston, she is said to have gone with them. She was abandoned by Reagan and returned to Ninety Six where she died. According to most sources the message was delivered by a horseman who rode through the American line into the fort.

281.27-28 "Kosciuzko": Tadeusz Andrzej Bonawentura Kosciuzko (1746-1817), Polish patriot who served under Greene throughout the war. As chief engineer, he was criticized by Lee for directing the siege against the Star Fort and not against Fort Holmes, which protected Ninety Six's water supply.

282.8-13 "Lee . . . Benson": Henry "Light-Horse Harry" Lee and his men had arrived at Ninety Six on 8 June, following the fall of Augusta on 5 June. Lieutenant Colonel Richard Campbell of the 4th Virginia Regiment was killed at Eutaw Springs on 8 September 1781. Captain Robert H. Kirkwood (1730-1791) of the 1st Delaware commanded one of the finest companies in the Continental Army and was thus called after Diomed, the Greek hero of the Trojan Wars. Lieutenant Colonel John Eager Howard (1752-1827) was an officer in the 2nd Maryland and was later wounded at Eutaw Springs. Captain Michael Rudolph (c.1754-1795) of Lee's legion had received Browne's surrender at Augusta and would lead the assault against the stockade, Fort Holmes. Captain George Armstrong of the 1st Maryland was the only American officer killed at Ninety Six; he died on 18 June, during the last attack.

Captain Perry Benson of the 1st Maryland was wounded in the same attack.

282.32-35 "He brings with him three fresh regiments from Ireland": The Irish regiments were the 3rd, the 19th, and the 30th. The "regiment of Boze" refers to the Hessian regiment of von Bose which had fought at Guilford under Major Du Buy. The six hundred loyalists were members of the South Carolina Regiment of Royalists, converted into cavalry and commanded by Captain John Coffin. McCrady (*History*, II, 291, 306-307) indicates that the 30th Regiment did not accompany Rawdon to Ninety Six but later joined him at Orangeburg. Rawdon's troops numbered 2000, not 3000 men as Greene says here.

283.3 "Harrison": A Major Harrison was in command of a large body of loyalist cavalry which marauded much as did Cunningham's forces. In fact, this Harrison was killed by Captain Daniel Conyers at Wiboo Swamp in March 1781.

283.4 "Washington": Lieutenant Colonel William Washington (1752-1810) of the 3rd Continental Dragoons was near Granby at this time. One of Greene's most valuable soldiers, he was wounded and captured at Eutaw.

283.15 "Lieutenants Seldon and Duval": Lieutenant Samuel Seldon of the 1st Virginia and Lieutenant Isaac Duval of the 1st Maryland led the assault on the Star Battery, the most dangerous action of the entire siege. They and their men were caught in the ditch surrounding the Battery and almost annihilated; two-thirds of them were killed. Seldon survived the attack but his right arm was shattered and had to be amputated. Duval also survived, but was later killed at Eutaw Springs.

284.25-26 "There were mistakes enough in this siege": Greene's main error seems to have been in directing the attack against the Star Battery, and Simms centers his description on this aspect of the siege. The ditch around the Star was eight to nine feet deep. The parapet was eleven to twelve feet high, and with the sandbags Cruger had added, the defense walls often reached fifteen feet. The hooks and ropes used by Duval and Seldon's men were not long enough to be effective. The crossfire made possible by the construction of the Battery should have further discouraged any such attempt.

284.38 "The greater part of their men were killed or wounded": In all, Greene lost 185 men killed or wounded; Cruger had twenty-seven killed and fifty-eight wounded. The two-thirds that Simms mentions refers to the men lost in the attack on the Star Battery.

285.5 "the retreat": To escape the advancing troops of Rawdon, Greene's army moved northeast on 19 June 1781, over the Saluda and on beyond the Bush River into what is now Newberry County.

EXPLANATORY NOTES 495

295.25 "Butler and Cowley": Samuel Butler (1612-1680) was the author of *Hudibras*, a satiric attack on the Puritans. Abraham Cowley (1618-1667) was primarily a writer of love poetry.

296.11 "to confound Hannibal and circumvent Scipio": Hannibal (247-183 B.C.) was the Carthaginian general who invaded Italy in the Second Punic War by crossing the Alps. He was finally defeated by the Roman general Scipio Africanus (237-183 B.C.).

298.7 "'spirit-stirring drum and ear-piercing fife'": *Othello*, III, iii.

298.20-21, 27-33 "Sweet is the Breath . . . *thee is sweet*'": John Milton, *Paradise Lost*, IV, 641-642, 650-656. Line 652 reads, "On this delightful land, nor herb, fruit, and flow'r."

300.19 "'while there is life there is hope'": John Gay, *Fables*, XXVII, *The Sick Man and the Angel*, I, 49.

300.20-21 "'hope springs eternal in the human breast'": Alexander Pope, *An Essay on Man*, Epistle I, 95. Pope's home was at Twickenham.

314.9 "'How use doth breed a habit in a man'": *The Two Gentlemen of Verona*, V, iv.

314.24 "Bath": A fashionable resort town in southwest England.

319.8 "Semiramis or Zenobia": Semiramis was an Assyrian queen who, according to myth, built Babylon after the death of her husband, King Ninus. Zenobia was the Queen of Palmyra who challenged the Roman Empire in her attempt to conquer eastern Europe in 271 A.D.

320.6-7 "curses . . . come home to roost": Robert Southey, motto to *The Curse of Kehama*.

322.34-35 "The College of South Carolina": The South Carolina College, now the University of South Carolina, was established by the State Legislature in December 1801, and went into operation in 1804.

324.7-8 "his majesty's 87th regiment of foot": The 87th Regiment was raised in England in July 1779. It was sent to the Leeward Islands in January 1780, then returned to England and disbanded in 1783.

325.16 "'She goes, and makes no sign!'": *2 Henry VI*, III, iii.

325.35 "'revisit the glimpses of the moon'": *Hamlet*, I, iv.

326.7 "Hamlet's father": The ghost of Hamlet's father appears fully armed and helmeted. *Hamlet*, I, iii.

329.16 "Richard": In Shakespeare's *Richard III*, V, iii, Richard is visited by the ghosts of those for whose deaths he is responsible. This is the night before he takes the field against Richmond. Simms draws several parallels between Edward and Richard throughout the novel, especially after Edward is disfigured.

333.34 "'*poor buckrah*'": A *buckra* or *buckrah* is the Gullah word for white man.

336.3 "'old sledge'": A card game known in England during the 17th century as All Fours. This game and a similar one called Seven-up were very popular in the United States until replaced by poker.

344.13 "Erebus": The place of darkness between Earth and Hades.

356.16 "Good quarter": A promise of safe surrender. At the Battle of the Waxhaws, 29 May 1780, Americans under Colonel Abraham Buford were surprised and defeated by the English under Lieutenant Colonel Banastre Tarleton. When they sued for quarter, they were butchered by the British. From the massacre came the term "Tarleton's Quarter," which meant no mercy would be shown to any.

361.14 "'Still vex'd Bermoothes'": *The Tempest*, I, ii. "Bermoothes" refers to the Bermudas, a place of safety for Edward Conway.

373.27 "'Mosca'": The shrewd, parasitic servant to Volpone in the play of that name by Ben Jonson.

376.17-18 "Bounty lands await you in the West Indies": It was British policy to offer lands as rewards to Americans willing to fight on the British side. However, it was also an American practice, and a valuable one, since Congress and the states had no authority to draft soldiers. Washington, in 1776, had recommended to Congress that recruits be offered at least 100 or 150 acres of land, a suit of clothes and a blanket for enlisting.

377.13-14 "somewhere above upon the Ennoree": The Enoree flows southeastward through the upper western part of the state and joins the Broad above Richland County.

377.33 "the head of Cooper river": The head of the Cooper is near Monck's Corner in the southeastern section of the state. At the time of the Revolution the river was navigable thirty-four miles inland from Charleston and offered Conway a good means of escape.

379.19-21 "he wants to carry off another Congaree gal, and, this time, agin her will": See note 166.25-27.

EXPLANATORY NOTES 497

395.12-18 "Powkerhorontas": Pocahontas (c.1595-1617). An Indian princess, daughter of Powhatan, she supposedly saved the life of Captain John Smith in 1608. She later married John Rolfe, not John Smith, and in 1616 went to England, where she died.

396.26 "Lord Rawdon will be on his way for the Eutaw": Rawdon was forced by ill health to leave for England soon after the evacuation of Ninety Six. The command was taken by Colonel Alexander Stuart, who led the British at Eutaw Springs.

397.22-24 "the Marquis de Chastellux": Francois Jean de Chastellux (1734-1788) wrote *Travels in North America in the Years 1780, 1781, and 1782* (1787). He served in the French army in America and favored the American cause.

404.32 "Meschianza": An elaborate party consisting of a series of entertainments. One of the most famous was that put on by John André and Oliver DeLancey for Sir William Howe on his departure as Commander-in-Chief of the British Army in May 1778.

408.23 "Sir Henry Clinton": Clinton (c. 1738-1795) was Commander-in-Chief of the British Army in America. He led the siege on Charleston and after its surrender he returned to New York, leaving the British forces in the South under the command of Cornwallis. Confident of having brought the South under submission, Clinton also took a large number of British soldiers with him and thus left Cornwallis without sufficient strength to fight effectively against the partisans. In May 1781, Clinton resigned his command and returned to England.

410.26 "Richard Stockton": On page 183 Stockton's first name is given as Harry.

414.34-35 "Colonel Stewart, at Fairlawn": Fairlawn was a British stronghold, located just below Monck's Corner on the Cooper River.

415.1 "Martin's Tavern": There was a Martin's Tavern located near Ferguson's Swamp. It served as headquarters for Greene immediately following the Battle of Eutaw Springs in September 1781.

429.29-31 "the legislature . . . when a change was contemplated": On 8 March 1787, the General Assembly officially changed the name of the town of Ninety Six to Cambridge. Cambridge remained the capital of the district which was still known as Ninety Six.

438.32 "'I have reaped the stubble field also'": 1 *Henry IV*, I, iii.

440.27-28 "Rugely . . . at the enforcement of a pine log": Colonel Rowland Rugely was a loyalist whose estate was known as Rugely's

Fort. Washington surrounded the fort on 4 December 1780. The details of Simms' footnote are accurate.

444.18-19 "Lord Rawdon . . . is on his way below": Leaving Ninety Six, the British marched by way of Fort Granby to Orangeburg and then to Charleston. *The Forayers* and *Eutaw* follow this retreat.

445.23 "Sepoys": Indian natives who served as British soldiers.

446. "THE SIEGE AND STORM": While there is no record of such a large mutiny among any of the loyalist gangs of marauders, leaders did have to deal with small insurrections from time to time. According to Siebert's *Loyalists in East Florida* (1929), David Fanning had to put down a small uprising on the part of his men, but it did not equal the scope of the one Simms describes here.

467.38-468.2 "Jake Clarkson's . . . got a sort of right to Ned Conway's life": Several of the bandit leaders were eventually killed by men who had personal vendettas to settle. Although Cunningham escaped from Butler, Dunlap was shot and wounded by Gillespie, the betrothed of Mary McRae (see note 166.25-27), and was later murdered after having been captured by the Americans. Bloody Bill Bates was shot and killed while in jail by a man named Motley, whose family Bates had massacred at Gowan's Fort. Similarly, after the surrender of Fort Grierson in Augusta, the commander of that fort, Colonel James Grierson, was killed for revenge by his whig captors.

472.3 "'frosty yet kindly'": *As You Like It*, II, iii.

CPSIA information can be obtained
at www.ICGtesting.com
Printed in the USA
FFOW02n1646201114
8916FF